As We Already Are

Amata Rose

PublishAmerica
Baltimore

PublishAmerica has allowed this work to remain exactly as the author intended, verbatim, without editorial input.

ISBN: 978-1-4489-5584-8
PUBLISHED BY PUBLISHAMERICA, LLLP
www.publishamerica.com
Baltimore

Printed in the United States of America

For Alexa, Pam, and Sarah
Sisters in Soul and Dance

ACKNOWLEDGMENTS

Many thanks to John McManigle for his careful and considerate feedback and editing. John, you are truly my white knight.

Thanks also to my very close friend Dani Zahoran for sorting through my monstrous first draft and giving me the fantastic suggestions that shaped up this manuscript. Chica, thanks also for the late-night conversations that brought these people to life and that gave me the encouragement to keep going.

I am also grateful to Mary Lou and James Michael Talamo, who helped answer the many awkward medical questions I needed to have answered for the more technical aspects surrounding Chloe and Carmen's births.

Thanks to professors Charlotte Holmes and Gregg Rogers, and James Matthew and Mary Lou Talamo for their help in perfecting my query letter.

Finally, thanks to Megan Kittisopikul for helping me unlock my wireless capabilities so I could send my final manuscript to PublishAmerica. I don't know what I would have done in the middle of South Dakota without you, Megan!

—A.R.

As We Already Are

PART ONE

Carrie pulled the windbreaker closer around her, the midnight color striking against her auburn hair. A light drizzle chilled the air as she looked out at the graveyard behind her house. The flat, plain-like grass, patched in greens and dead browns, contrasted the steel gray of the sky, the cracked white of the tombstones, the lusty green of the pines lining the horizon. Her mother and father had not found out about the graveyard until the house had been built and the fence of evergreens between their property and the graveyard had been torn down—but even after the discovery, her parents had insisted on remaining. Corman, in particular, had no tolerance for superstition of any kind. Christine had used the letters on the tombstones to teach Carrie how to read, and the birth and death dates to teach her addition and subtraction. Carrie had wandered the forlorn paths of the graveyard too many times to be afraid; the site had been a place of comfort and calm during her turbulent adolescent years.

But now she stood on the cement patio outside her house, her back against the cold brick wall, her windbreaker pulled close, her eyes scanning the distance as the old-fashioned church bells chimed the hour. A large droplet of chilled rain exploded on her cheek, and she brushed it away. The sliding door opened behind her, releasing a warm puff of air and the aroma of hot spiced cider and gingerbread cookies. Carrie turned and smiled as the lanky adolescent boy stepped outside and quickly shut the door behind him. Chris had shot up like a reed; he was almost as tall as she was. She wouldn't have recognized him if she hadn't known he was her brother.

"What are you doing out here?" he asked her. "It's freezing."

She ruffled his hair. "Just thinking."

"Are you going back to Penn State tomorrow?"

She nodded.

He leaned against the sliding glass door, his cheeks bitten by the cold of early August, his carrot mop of hair blazing against the hunter green of his jacket. "You weren't here for very long."

She tucked a wayward curl of hair behind her ear. "Chris—"

"It's okay. I understand."

She paused. "I'm sorry we didn't have a chance to talk more."

He shrugged.

"We have some time now," she continued. "So what's going on in your life?" When he was quiet, she smiled. "I'm sorry to pull a Carly, but I have to know. Are you interested in anyone right now?"

"No," he said. "I pretty much hate people right now."

"I felt like that when I was your age," she said.

The cornflower blue eyes trained on hers were too old for their years. "Really?"

She looked out at the graveyard. "When I was fourteen, I was disgusted with the human race. Hating, as Wordsworth would say, what man has made of man." She paused, shivered in the cold, but kept a smile on her face. "And I believed that I didn't belong in this world. I remember not really knowing where I belonged. Just knowing—or thinking—that it wasn't here."

He was silent for a moment, then he looked at her furtively. "Carrie, don't think I'm psycho or anything, but sometimes I want to kill myself."

"Sometimes we all do," she said, and paused. "But things *will* get better if you stick them out. And you'll become more comfortable with who you are."

"Life seems so monotonous," he said.

She glanced at him. "There are wildcards. People you meet and things that happen which you could never expect, and which will make you glad you stuck around." She put one arm around him, gave him a brief hug.

AS WE ALREADY ARE

"You know, what, Chris? I, for one, would be terribly sad if you weren't here. So would Mom. And it would matter to all the people you wouldn't meet, who you would have impacted in some way."

"What about the people Dad would have met?" Chris said. "We needed him. I needed him. And he's not here, is he? But we're all going on with our lives. So if you take one person out of the equation, what difference does it really make?"

"Dad didn't have the choice," she said, her eyes on the sky. "You do."

"I'll never forgive the man who shot him," Chris said.

"He was in the military." She looked at him levelly. "He knew the risks."

"I know." He paused, and when he spoke again, his voice cracked in a way she knew wasn't because his voice was changing. "But I still don't understand why he had to die…"

She hesitated, watching his expression, then said. "I'm going inside. Do you want to come?"

He shook his head. "I think I'll stay out a little longer."

She put her hands back in her jacket pockets, shivered. "Well, don't stay out too long. It's cold."

"Okay," he said, and looked out over the graveyard. "Are you coming to Aunt Julie's with us?"

"Definitely. I'll come get you when it's time to leave."

He nodded. She went inside and then glanced out the glass door at his tall, hunched profile. Though two years had passed since their father's death, they had somehow never addressed the topic. She knew she would have to talk to Chris more, but she sensed that then was not the time.

Chris's words echoed in Carrie's mind as she went into the dark living room and snapped on the lights.

"Oh, I'm sorry," she said, then paused. "Calder, are you awake?"

He was not. Since he was sleeping without a shirt she could see that he had lost most of the muscular toning he had worked for in high school. Like Carly, he had inherited dark hair from Christine; his hair had grown longer, and tangled around his face in disheveled waves. Carrie dimmed the lights, then maneuvered to the candle cabinet. A candle from the top of the pyramid fell, knocking several candles in a downhill avalanche. Calder grunted and turned over in his sleep, but did not wake. Bracing the remaining candles in place with one hand, Carrie attempted to withdraw the candle she wanted from its place. The lights flared one degree higher, and Carrie turned to see her fifteen-year-old sister hovering over Calder, one hand resting on the hips of her low-slung jeans and the other tossing a brightly-colored hackey sack up and down.

"What are you doing, Carly?" she whispered, closing the cabinet's door behind her.

Carly turned and smiled at her. She put a finger to her lips, then threw the hackey sack at Calder's chest hard enough to leave an angry imprint. His eyes flew open, revealing the trademark cornflower blue inherited by all of the Crenshaw children except for Carrie.

"Wake up, you lazy ass," Carly said.

He groaned. "Go away."

Carly picked up the empty bottle on the ground beside him, then tossed it at him. "You should know better than to leave this stuff where Mom can find it. She's going to be mad at you."

"She's already mad at me," he mumbled, remaining motionless as Carly slipped the empty Corona bottle under his pillow. "I'm twenty-two. I'm allowed to drink."

"Get up and come on," Carly said. "I'm not peeling all the carrots myself."

He mumbled.

"Calder, we gotta be at Aunt Julie's at four and Mom's freaking out cuz she needs help."

"Let Carrie help her."

Carrie had not been aware that he knew of her presence. "Hi, Calder."

He grunted, not opening his eyes.

Carly punched him on the shoulder. "Chris is right. You have turned into a good-for-nothing waste of life."

"I don't care what Chris thinks of me," he said, but Carrie noticed a certain stiffness in his movements as he turned away from Carly and buried his face again in the pillow. "When Chris is twenty-two, he'll think about things differently."

Carly picked up the hackey-sack, tossed it half-heartedly at Calder, and turned to Carrie. "Come on. You can help me."

"It's good to see you, too," she said, following Carly into the kitchen, noticing her sister's changed form—her broadened shoulders, her curved hips. Time had happened, not just to her, but to Calder, to Chris, to Carly. As she watched Carly's light, spritely step, she wondered how much had changed.

"So do you have a boyfriend now?" she asked as she lined up beside Carly and accepted the carrot she was handed.

"Shh." Carly turned and scanned the kitchen. "Is Mom here?"

"No. She went out to get gas."

"So long as you don't tell her."

"Everything you say to me is kept in strictest confidence," Carrie said, scraping at the stubborn dirt on the carrot's skin, reminding herself that the young woman standing beside her was her little sister—whose hair she had tucked back when Carly was crying over a fight with their father, whose hot tears had soaked her shirt the night before she left for college, whose trembling voice had told her not to go. Carrie blinked and worked harder at getting the scum off the carrot. "I always want you to feel like you can talk to me about anything…"

Carly shrugged. "I like someone, but you know the rule. No suitors until sixteen."

"I've been working on Mom about that for you."

"You'll never get her to budge, not even by a day. You know how she won't change any of the rules, now that Dad's gone and she can't conference with him."

Carly wrinkled her nose and threw a carrot that was more than half rotted through into the garbage can between them. "Besides, Mom doesn't trust me."

"Regarding what?"

"In general."

Carrie fished the carrot out of the garbage, rinsed it off, cut off the bad part, and began peeling it. "You've always had a good head on your shoulders. Especially about boys and relationships. As soon as I can get her to see that, you'll be able to do whatever you want."

"I'll probably turn sixteen before then," Carly retorted. "How's Damien?"

The question jolted her. "What all did I tell you about him?"

"Only that he was an artist." Carly looked at her. "What kind of art does he do?"

She flushed. "He hasn't shown me his work yet. He promised, and we made plans...and then he disappeared for the summer."

"That's weird. You should ask him about it when you both get back."

"I intend to," she said, knowing she was on dangerous ground with Carly looking at her so expectantly. She tried to change the subject. "Why don't you tell me about the guy you like."

Carly decapitated a carrot. "His name is Cesar Wilde."

"If you married him," Carrie said, trying to sound serious, "you could keep the C tradition alive."

"Not funny." Carly chopped the carrot into uniform circles. "If I have a son, I'm naming him Anthony, and if I have a daughter I'm naming her Elena. None of this stupid insistence on naming children only with the third letter of the alphabet."

Carrie remembered the time after Chris had been born when a fifth child had been expected, to be named Carl or Candy depending on the gender. For as much as Christine had cried, Carrie thought she was also relieved by the miscarriage; she had been forty-five at the time and had confided to Carrie years later that she was too old to be raising children from the start again.

"Carlotta." Carly said. "Who names an innocent little baby something like Carlotta?"

"The name works for you," Carrie said.

"I don't look like a Carlotta."

"But you look like a Carly." She paused. "When you were little you loved the name Carlotta. You insisted that everyone call you by it, even though you couldn't pronounce it. But tell me more about Cesar."

"He's the star offensive player on the basketball team. I've seen him doing drills, and I saw him at JoAnne's party the other night and we talked for awhile and he seemed to enjoy talking to me. But he hasn't called me or anything."

"Have you thought about asking him out?"

Carly frowned. "That's not how I do things. I always wait for the guy to make the first move."

"Sometimes you have to go after what you want."

Carly shrugged. "It's not like he's the center of my life. And like I said, I don't really need a boyfriend right now. But you're twenty. You better get moving."

"I'm not going to comment on that," Carrie said. "But it's good to see you so confident and beautiful. I'm proud of you."

Carly shrugged, looked into the sink for another carrot and found with utmost joy that there were no more. She put down her peeler, rinsed her hands, and stretched. "Thanks for the help."

"Where are the plastic bags for these?" Carrie nodded at the shredded pile of orange in the sink before her. "I know they'll clog the disposal."

"Let Calder get them. Let him get his hands dirty in a good way, for once." The mischievous gleam returned to her eyes. "I'll go wake him up."

Carrie moved into the laundry room, where she found the plastic bags stashed in the exact same spot where they had always been. She went back into the kitchen and cleaned the shreddings herself. She saw Carly leave the kitchen with a bowl of water, and she knew when she heard Calder start shouting that Carly had successfully accomplished her ruse.

"Would you kids come on?" Christine yelled as Carrie came into the garage carrying a brown saran-wrapped salad bowl on top of a cake box. "We don't have any time for dilly-dallying!"

Carrie saw her siblings in the driveway playing basketball—Carly and Chris laughing as Calder missed a shot and swore. Christine saw Carrie juggling the plates and moved forward to help her.

"Here, honey, let me take those." Christine put the food in the car, packing the bowl and cake box between the other food she had prepared.

The basketball flew into the garage.

"Sorry!" Calder yelled.

Christine sighed. "Thank you, Carrie, for being so mature."

15

Carrie watched her reposition the food to create a pathway into the van. "Sometimes I feel like I'm thirty-five."

"Oh, honey," Christine said, shifting a bag of Doritos. She turned. "Carly! Calder! Chris! The sooner we leave the sooner you get to see your cousins!"

There was a clatter as Calder threw the basketball into the toy bin on one side of the garage, then the muffled sound of whispering and giggling as he and Carly approached the car.

"Chris!" Christine called, then turned. "Carrie, would you go get your other brother? I left something inside."

Carrie went outside and saw Chris crouched near the ground.

"Isn't it a little cold to be playing basketball?" she asked him.

"Never," Chris said. "Carrie, look what I found."

She bent down. "What?"

He was staring intently at a patch of grass sprouting through the pavement. "The grass. It's shaped like a dog."

She tilted her head. "Where do you see that?"

"Come on!" Carly shouted from the garage. "You have a whole hour to talk on the way there!"

"There," Chris said, pointing, standing. "That's its head."

She looked at the grass as he walked to the garage.

"Carrie!" Christine called.

She wouldn't have seen the dog shape if Chris hadn't pointed it out. She turned and headed into the garage.

"I call shotgun, both ways," Calder said as he slid into the front seat.

Carrie climbed into the back seat beside Chris, who smiled at her. She tapped him on the shoulder. He unplugged the earphones of his iPod and looked at her.

"Do you remember when we used to sing songs during these rides?" she asked. "When we'd sing Disney songs, and you'd sing the guys' parts and I'd sing the girls'?"

"And Calder and Carly would tell us to shut up? Yeah. That was fun."

She paused. "So do you want to go bowling next time I come home? You'd have to teach me because I don't remember how to bowl, but is that something you'd like to do?"

"When do you think you'll come home next?"

She paused. "Maybe over winter break."

Chris searched her expression, then flashed her a thumbs' up sign. Before she could say anything else he plugged his earphones back in, closed his eyes and leaned his head back. Carrie remembered he got carsick easily. She did as well, but she couldn't help looking out the window at the familiar scenery passing by her in a blur of shapes and colors.

Climbing out of the van an hour later, she was greeted with the tingle of fiery pins and needles creeping up her legs. She stared at the familiar house, a sprawling Tudor that looked more like a resort lodge amidst the ample yard and towering trees. When she was younger, Carrie had envied her cousin Justine for the fabulous clothes and jewelry that fit her model-shaped figure perfectly; when she got older, she envied the summer trips to the Bahamas, Egypt, Rome, Greece. When she got older still, she realized that the love between Corman and Christine was worth far more than the trips or the money. Carrie had grown up an outcast, but in a family that was otherwise knit tightly together—without the verbal abuse, without the threats of divorce and the frequent occurrences of siblings running away.

She heard Jericho, the purebred collie Justine had gotten from the local pound, barking loudly. She looked out to see him running around frantically in the enclosure where Justine kept him, wagging his scruffy tail and yapping, half-strangling himself on his chain. Carrie loved Jericho. He was a wild, tangled thing, his spirit untamed though he had been abandoned by his previous owners. He represented every good quality of the Julie-Giles side of the Crenshaw family—toughness, strength, hardiness—without the self-destructive sadness that plagued the Crenshaws. Though as she watched Jericho straining against his chains, his yapping hoarse and strangled as his choke collar tightened around his neck, Carrie thought maybe the destructive, pain-loving bug had bitten him, too. She slid open the van's door and started to walk over to Jericho.

"Carrie!" Christine yelled. "I need help unloading the car."

"Just leave something in the back for me!" she called over her shoulder.

She continued walking over to the enclosure, shivering at the nip in the late December air. The dog popped up into the air when he saw her coming.

"Jericho, sit," she said.

He sat down obediently, his long, matted tail thumping the hard, cold ground beneath him. She bent and ran her fingers through his fur, grimacing as they came back black with dirt.

"Justine doesn't take very good care of you, does she?" she asked, as he thumped his tail. "But she loves you."

Justine's animals—the dog, the two rabbits, the three cats, the score of fish, the iguana, the set of parakeets—were largely left to fend for themselves. The cats had a sly, intelligent look in their slitted eyes, their coats sleek from rodent protein. The rabbits lived in the little garden to the side of the house during the summer, free to munch on the wild vegetables, though they hopped around in a corner of the three-car garage during the colder months. The animals weren't neglected so much as they were allowed to live wild—free. Carrie gave Jericho a final pat; he had not lost the gleam in his eyes or the prance in his step. She knew Justine loved her animals and lived for them—she just didn't know how to take care of them, like she didn't know how to take care of herself.

Carrie walked back to the van and found that everything had been taken inside. She sighed and walked up to the house, opened the door, and stepped into the warmth of the kitchen in time to see Christine hug Julie.

"The Cs are here," Christine said. "Scattered already, but all here."

"The Js welcome you." Julie smiled, a tired smile. Carrie stood in the background. Julie, Giles, Jonathan, Justine, Jordan, Joshua...all Js except for Julie's husband, which Justine made up for by nicknaming herself Gem. Carrie understood how it was hard for Julie's and Giles' secretaries to keep them straight, but she had grown up seeing her cousins every holiday and frequently in between; they had come to seem like her immediate family. She no longer thought about Calder without thinking of Jonathan, of Carly without considering Jordan, Chris and Joshua...herself and Justine. They were always grouped in pairs, the four Crenshaws of one clan and the four Crenshaws of the other, since the members of each pair were within one year of each other. Each pair also had striking similarities. The gene pools for the families were close; Christine and Julie were sisters, and Corman and Giles had been brothers.

Meanwhile, Julie had spied her.

"Carrie, please take off your shoes while you're in the house. It's these carpets. I just can't keep them clean."

Carrie slipped out of her shoes, then walked over to give Julie a hug. "Do you need any help?"

"No, dear. We're going to eat in awhile. Make yourself comfortable. It's so good to have you here." Julie paused. "Even if you are only here for a week. Out of the whole summer."

Carrie smiled tensely, then went to where she saw her grandmother and grandfather sitting together at the living room table. Her grandmother was reading the Christmas cards that Julie had lined up along the table.

"Hi, Grandma," she said.

"Hello," she replied, then looked up and smiled. "Carrie, you're home!"

"I am. Hi, Grandpa."

"Carrie." He pressed her hand warmly. "Carrie, you're beautiful." He turned to her grandmother. "Isn't she beautiful?"

"She's always been beautiful."

"But never this beautiful," he said, staring at her. "You look so happy."

"Thank you," she said, her cheeks flushed. Guilt hit her as her grandfather beamed at her, his eyes filled with pride. She thought about Damien and the feelings he inspired in her, and she didn't feel beautiful. The honest, open admiration in her grandparents' eyes cut through her, and she looked down. But if she had done something wrong, why wouldn't they be able to see it? Why would they think she looked more beautiful than she had before?

After her grandfather had gone into the den to watch the football game blaring from the sixteen-inch screen, she listened to her grandmother relive her years as a high school teacher. Carrie listened, and then she talked about the volunteering she was doing at the local high school and about how she was looking forward to student teaching though she might be graduating a semester late.

"And how is waitressing going?" her grandmother asked, patting her hand.

"My coworkers are much nicer now. And I'm considered a senior server, since so many others have left."

"As long as you're happy," she said. "Remember, Carrie, that's all that really matters. I'm so happy to see that you have your life under control. Not like Justine."

"What's going on with Justine? Christine started telling me, but—"

"Oh, honey," she said, lowering her voice. "She's just so stressed out about school. She's such a perfectionist about everything, and while I know how important grades are to you children, she doesn't need to stress like she does." She squeezed Carrie's hand. "My prayer to the Good Lord is that you children are happy. Just happy. I keep telling Justine she should drop out of all those sciences and teach history. She loves history, and teaching is such a rewarding profession, but she thinks that because everyone in this family is a doctor she has to become one. I know she loves animals and wants to take care of them, but I can't see Justine being a vet."

"Justine has to find her own way," Carrie said. "No matter how much you want her to teach, Grandma, if it's not what she wants…"

There was a subtle shift of movement in the corner as Justine slipped into the room, as lithe as one of her fierce cats. Carrie fought to keep her face neutral as she stared at her cousin. Justine was by far the prettiest girl Carrie had ever seen, with the kind of beauty that had inspired love poems, worshippers, and a series of stalkers over the years. Her chestnut colored hair fell to her waist in thick, rolling waves; her almond shaped eyes were hazel-brown and fringed by long, dark lashes. Justine was slim and tall, with an extremely feminine form and an air of elegance and vulnerability. But Justine's face had taken on a lean, hungry look, and there were purplish, bruise-like shadows under her eyes. Even from the distance, Carrie could see that Justine's eyes glittered too brightly, and that her cousin trembled slightly as she walked into the room.

"Hello, Gem," Carrie said.

"Carrie." Justine gave her a quick hug. "I've been thinking about you so much lately."

"I've been thinking about you, too." Justine was never far from Carrie's thoughts, as they had always been paired together by their families. "How have you been? How is your first year at Grove City going?"

Justine smiled again, a smile identical to Julie's tired, worn grimace. "I'm not doing so well."

"Justine, come talk to us," their grandmother said from behind them. "I was just telling Carrie about what a wonderful profession teaching is, and how wonderful you would be as a history teacher."

Justine shrank away. "I'm not teaching. I refuse to be a part of the system that crushes children's souls and makes them sacrifice themselves and their freedom. For grades. Stupid, pointless things that mean nothing."

"It's different when you're on the other side of the desk," their grandmother said. "And if Carrie can overlook her high school experience, why can't you?"

"Carrie will be a wonderful teacher," Justine said, meeting Carrie's eyes. "Because she's going to change things. But I can't teach."

"Why not?" their grandmother asked.

"High school destroyed me," Justine said, and she stepped away from them both. "Don't ask me to return to the thing that killed me."

Justine left and Carrie looked at her grandmother, who was staring down at the tablecloth.

"I just want her to be happy," she said. "Why can't she just do what makes her happy?"

Carrie saw the pain deepening in her grandmother's eyes. She didn't have the heart to say life wasn't that simple—but her grandmother knew.

"I'm going to talk to that girl," her grandmother mumbled. She pushed herself to her feet and walked with dignity into the kitchen.

Jonathan—the eldest of her cousins—entered the dining room carrying a full plate. He sat down beside her.

"Hi, Carrie," he said, picking up his fork and placing it a centimeter away from his nose, his tired eyes scrutinizing it. "This fork is dirty. Do you see this splotch?"

21

"Here, take mine," she said, pushing her unused utensil towards him. "It's clean."

"No, I'll just use mine," he said, wiping the fork's blade on his green polo shirt. "This one is mine, and you've used your fork."

"I just touched it."

"There, it's fine now." He looked at his fork again critically before plunging it into the potatoes in the center of his plate. "Don't you have any potatoes? They're the best."

"Maybe next time around." She watched their grandmother leave the room, then speared a spinach leaf out of her salad and thought about how far Jonathan had come in battling his OCD. When she was younger, his neurotic behavior had frightened her. But she was older; she had needed to break down herself to appreciate how hard it was to get back up. She was proud of him; he had decided to fight by devoting his life to becoming a psychiatrist so he could help other people who were going through what he was experiencing.

"How's Pacifica?" she asked, knowing he had chosen to go to graduate school there for his clinical license and an additional degree in Abnormal Psychology.

"I'm not going to complain. I knew that the practicum was largely based on psychological subjects which don't interest me, but I make the time to read about what does interest me. I just need the piece of paper from Pacifica so that the world will recognize that I am aptly qualified to legally counsel people."

She did not ask how in depth he had gone into his self-directed research; part of his therapy with the one psychiatrist who had made a major difference in his life had been to have him read voraciously—to distract him, to intrigue him, to tire his brain so it wouldn't torment him.

"What are you doing now?"

"I'm working with drug and alcohol abusers right now," he said, fiddling with his fork, wiping the blade clean on his napkin. "Some suicide attempters. I'm a facilitator of group therapy and general group counseling. No individual work right now and not really the kinds of problems I want to deal with, but I'm getting the necessary experience and I don't want to discredit that."

22

She paused. "Do you ever get depressed working with your clients? Listening to all those people talk about addiction and wanting to kill themselves?"

"You have to learn to understand the patient's problem without taking in their negativity and the chaos governing their lives. The only dangerous part about psychiatry occurs when psychiatrists become like Icarus—when they fly too close to the sun. The trick is learning how to get close to the fire without getting burned." He paused. "Though it helps that I've never had the problems my patients have."

She speared her baked beans. "I'm proud of you, Jonathan. You're an inspiration to me."

"Thank you, but I wouldn't go that far, Carrie." He paused. "You seem to be doing pretty well yourself. How is Penn State treating you?"

"I have a lot on my mind."

"About anything in particular?"

She thought for a moment. "A guy," she said, as Justine came in from the kitchen and sat down—probably having fled from their grandmother.

Justine smiled encouragingly. "Tell us more, Carrie."

"He's different than any one I've ever met before," she said. "He has no respect for conventions at all, and he lives his life with this reckless *joie de vivre*..." She paused. "But I don't think he's wild, in the traditional sense. I met him in the last couple months before summer, and then...he just disappeared."

Justine listened with wide, nonjudgmental eyes. "How did you meet him?"

She hesitated. "He threw a rock through my window."

"What?" Jonathan said.

She fell silent. Calder came in, sat down, and looked at her seriously for once. Carrie looked around the circle of attentive, caring faces; she valued the times when she was alone with her cousins.

"I'm sensing a lot of red flags there," Jonathan said, when she had remained silent. "From a psychological standpoint."

"If he is wild, are you sure you aren't trying to save him?" Calder asked. "That's what I did with Janice. I didn't see the red flags because I wanted to change her."

She shook her head. "I don't want to change him. I like him for who he is."

Justine nodded. "It's the curse of the Crenshaw women. We're always attracted to terrible men."

"He's not terrible," Carrie said.

"Or it could be the result of what I will call the strange attraction theory," Jonathan said, as if she hadn't heard him. "You could be attracted to him, Carrie, because he's so different from everything you've been exposed to—especially coming from this family. The key is how to get close to the fire without getting burned. In your interactions with this young man, Carrie, just don't be Icarus."

She wished she hadn't mentioned Damien. "Thanks for the advice. I'm going to go get some more food."

Justine followed her into the kitchen. "Carrie, don't listen to Jonathan and all his talk of the strange attraction theory. I think it's romantic that you've met someone. If he makes you happy, you should go for it."

"Thanks, Gem," she said, feeling the bond between her and Justine. She watched

Justine take a brownie from the pile their Aunt Carol had made. She supposed that her extremely health-conscious aunt would let Justine eat anything she wanted, as long as she ate; Carrie had seen Justine's dinner, which had consisted of a couple of spinach leaves, a sole potato chunk, and a roll. "How's Grove City?"

"You can see it's not going well," Justine said. "Everyone at Grove City is very kind to me, but at the end of the day I go back to my room and I'm alone with the silence. Being by myself is terrifying. I can't control my thoughts and I—"

"That seems to be a recurring theme in our family," Carrie said. "You'd think we'd have figured out how to deal with it by now."

Justine looked at her. "I don't understand why we all have to fight so very hard."

"It's better that way."

"Maybe you're right." Justine paused, then looked down. "At least there's one good thing about coming from this family."

"What's that?"

"We won't be afraid to die." Justine looked out the window into the darkness of evening. "After this life, when the struggle is finally over, there will be only peace and rest. And our family deserves that."

Carrie forced a smile. "My life is all I have. I don't want to die."

Justine looked at her, and Carrie returned her stare.

Carrie walked to the van dazed, looking up at the black velvet sky and the diamond stars that winked at her. She had gone from being the black sheep of the family to a source of positive energy—Julie's words—in a space of two years.

Christine touched her shoulder, gently. "Carrie, would you mind driving? I'm getting a migraine and Calder drank too much of the wine."

Carrie silently took the keys from Christine as the rest of her family piled into the van. She had never before realized how hard the gatherings must be for her mother, to be amidst the boisterous pairs and to not have Corman there beside her.

"Are you okay?" Carrie asked, lowering the radio's volume.

"I'm just tired, honey. The roads are slippery, so please be careful. If you feel uncomfortable at any time, pull over and let me know. I just want to rest for awhile."

"I'll wake you when we get home." She glanced at Christine, saw her eyes were already closed.

Carly and Calder were asleep twenty minutes into the drive; twenty-five minutes later, Chris was also asleep, the pensive line usually creasing his forehead smoothed out. Christine never opened her eyes and Carrie thought she was asleep until she swerved to miss a deer three miles from their house, and temporarily lost control of the car.

"Careful," Christine said, her eyes still closed. "Are you getting tired, Carrie? Do you want me to drive?"

"We're almost home. Ten minutes or so." Her eyelids felt filled with cement. She opened her window slightly, letting a slither of crisp air into the car to keep herself awake until she pulled into the garage and parked the car. Christine roused herself.

"Should we let them sleep in the car?" she asked Carrie.

"You're the nurse." Carrie glanced at Calder, who had assumed a yogic-looking position that would have had him howling in pain had he been awake; at Carly, who was drooling onto Calder's shoulder; at Chris, who was curled into the fetal position. "Is it good for them to sleep in shapes like that?"

"They'll probably get sore," Christine said, then raised her voice. "Kids, up."

Carrie dropped the keys into Christine's outstretched hand and got out of the car as the groans of her roused siblings started. She stood in the driveway, looking up at the sky.

"How come Carrie isn't helping us?" Carly whined.

"Your sister has done enough," Christine said. "Don't complain, Carly."

Carrie looked at the stars and inhaled deeply. She heard her family members troop inside, the screen door opening, closing, opening. Christine came to stand beside her. They were both silent for a moment.

"Thank you for all your help today, Carrie."

Carrie nodded, glad for the company. "Are you feeling better?"

"I just need to get some sleep." She sighed. "God, it's a beautiful night."

Carrie nodded again.

"I'll leave the front door open for you," Christine said. "Remember to lock it before you go to bed." She paused. "I wish you could have come home for longer. We miss having you here."

She nodded.

"Don't stay up too late, honey."

She felt the tremor that passed through her as the garage door grated closed, felt the emptiness that took Christine's place. She felt crazy, confused, strangely content. She let her mind alternate between peaceful blanks and rampant thoughts. At some point she went inside, and the silence of the night entombed her in dreamless unconsciousness.

She left with Christine early the next morning, driving back to university in the midst of an imminent storm. As she drove, Carrie saw Damien in her mind: his dark disheveled hair, his flashing eyes, his long simian feet which were always dirty from going barefoot outdoors. She was aware of how forbidden the rising heat in her body felt.

She had met him in March, when the air carried the smell of melting snow and damp earth and new life. She allowed herself to remember their first encounter—the memory blazed most vividly in her mind. She had gone to confront him the evening he broke her window; he had stopped the work he had been doing, apologized, and offered her a chair.

She had refused. *What the hell did you think you were doing?*

Trying to get your attention.

She had been too stunned to respond.

Don't worry, he had said, and smiled. *I already bought a replacement pane. I can fix your window tonight, if you'd like.*

She could only look at him—the wide slope of his cheekbones and the flush of health that made his bronzed skin glow, the shock of black hair that fell over the wide sweeps of his dark eyebrows and into his equally intense dark eyes. He had been wearing jeans and a plain white T-shirt, and the music from his computer had played softly in the background.

He had fixed her window, then they had talked.

She remembered what they had talked about—work and life and how they were both doing—but none of that seemed important. What she remembered in painful detail was his white T-shirt and how his lean body had slouched in his chair. There had been something hanging in the air between them, something flowing between his sloping form and her tense body perched in the chair and the white computer with its soft music. She had thought for the longest time about what it was. She had tried to place the quality of the energy, and she had tried to understand why when she thought of Damien she always kept coming back to that moment.

She looked out her window at the storm. The wind splattered bullets of rain against her window pane, blearing her vision, and the torrents of rain on the roof of the car drummed the melody of a graveyard band. She wanted to be closer to the power of the storm, to the rain and the streak lightning and the howling wind. Wanted it to live inside her, to make her wild, to inundate her with its magic...

That was how she had wanted to be with Damien—closer to him than his own thoughts. And when she looked at the storm and realized it was the same feeling, the connection clicked into place.

In that first moment with Damien there had been magic, a feeling that had inundated all of the hours she had spent with him since that first encounter. Every night they had talked for hours outside on his porch; then, at the beginning of summer, he had left the university town without telling her where he was going. She had worked extra hours to save up for the upcoming school year, hoping each day he would come back. But with his continued absence, she had finally given into Christine's repeated demands that she come home.

Though she had only been gone for a week she was glad to be going back to her apartment, to wait for him to return. Her heart beat faster. She had not seen him in two months; she wondered if over the summer he had changed.

"I wish you could have stayed home longer," Christine said, breaking into her wayward thoughts. "But you must be glad to be getting back."

Carrie glanced at her and was surprised to see that Christine was smiling slightly.

"You put on a very brave face when you come home," Christine continued. "But I know that home isn't a good place for you, Carrie. As much as I hate to admit it, I know that you need to be in a college town. Surrounded by other young people and opportunities."

"I'm glad you understand," Carrie said, wondering if Christine wanted her to refute the statements she was making. "Sometimes I feel like I hurt you because I come home so infrequently."

The smile left Christine's face; her lips became a tight line. "I just wish you would spend some more time around people your own age."

"It's harder to find a niche than you might think."

"You haven't found anyone special, Carrie?"

How to answer that? she thought. Christine sensed her hesitation; she waited, and let Carrie determine how much to tell her.

"I've gotten pretty close to my neighbor," Carrie said, at last.

"Oh? Maybe I can meet him, after I drop you off."

She tried to keep her tone even and light. "I don't know if he's come back for the summer, yet."

Christine paused. "Is he a Christian?"

"No." Carrie could not smother the ironic smile that sprang to her lips. "But I like him for who he is."

"As long as you're happy," Christine said, and paused. "You're too close to the center of the road. Come closer to my side."

"I know how to drive. There's no one behind me." She caught the edge in her voice and paused. "I really appreciate that you don't mind driving up to Penn State with me."

"It's nice to have a chance to talk," Christine said.

"It's still a long drive."

"Maybe some day we'll be able to afford a car for you." She paused. "Though I really would miss this time to talk with you, Carrie."

She made herself say the words. "I don't know why. When I've hurt you like I have."

Christine sighed. "I'm your mother. I'll love you no matter what. We've been through this before."

"Only vaguely." Carrie paused. "Why is that the pattern in this family? Why do issues first get talked about years after they happen?"

Christine's tightly regulated face did not betray any emotion. "Acceptance is always the first step, Carrie. And that can take time."

"Our family seems to take everything to the extreme."

Christine smiled. "You can't choose the family you're cursed with, kiddo."

"I didn't mean to sound like that," Carrie amended. "It's just that I don't understand why we get hit harder by almost everything."

"But we also get back up," Christine said softly. "Crenshaws can only stay down for so long, and then we move on."

Carrie's eyes fell to the golden band on Christine's finger. "Do you ever think of getting married again?"

"No." Christine's face set like marble. "I loved your father very much. I know you and he disagreed, but he always tried to do what was best for you. He was devoted to me and to you kids, one-hundred percent." She paused. "Do you and Damien do things besides visit?"

The suddenness of the question startled her. "Damien and I are just friends. You know I don't have time, that I want to be serious about my writing."

"You've always been serious about your writing," Christine said.

She was surprised that Christine sided with Damien. "I know what you want for me. What you and Carly want for me."

"What is that, Carrie?"

She kept her voice neutral. "You want me to get married and start a family so you can be a grandmother and she can be an aunt."

"I just want you to be happy."

"I am happy." Carrie knew that further discussion would lead to a fiery debate, and she was tired of arguing.

Christine glanced at her, then looked out her window.

A light drizzle fell from the swollen sky as Carrie pulled into the parking lot behind her rented room. She got out of the car quickly, her eyes scanning the front of the adjacent house. Too late, she realized that the gesture was not lost on Christine.

"I'm going to use your restroom before I drive back," Christine said quietly.

Carrie nodded. "I'll wait for you here."

She kept her eyes on the slate sky and tucked her hands into the pockets of her windbreaker as her mother disappeared into her house. Then, she heard him say her name.

She turned abruptly as the side entrance door to his house closed shut. She felt time stop. She took one step towards him. She barely heard the door open to her house open behind her.

But his dark eyes flicked by her. She became aware of Christine, standing close behind her, and cleared her throat.

"Christine," she said. "This is Damien."

"It's nice to meet you," Damien said.

Christine smiled. "I've heard so much about you."

His laughing eyes flickered past Christine to Carrie. "Carrie and I became very good friends last summer."

She realized for the first time what he was wearing—an easy excuse. "I don't want to make you late."

His eyes flicked over her face; like lightning he caught onto the train of her thoughts. "Unfortunately, I am off to work." He smiled at Christine. "Excuse me for being so rude as to run off."

Christine shook her head. "It was nice to meet you."

"It was very nice to meet you," he replied, then he turned the slightest bit, so that the angle of sunlight cut deep circles of shadow under his eyes. "I'll talk to you later, Carrie. I promise."

She tried not to let the rampant emotions running through her show on her face as he walked away, but she knew Christine understood.

"I love you, Carrie," Christine said.

She nodded and returned the hug Christine gave her, then walked to the car. Her thoughts followed Damien down the street. Already wondering when she would have a chance to be alone with him again, she waved as she watched Christine pull out of the driveway, and then she went inside to wait.

Sam's town felt empty when he went home—like he had walked in on a staging of his autobiography while the cast and crew were on a coffee break. The town's sites had not changed, but something essential had always been missing for him after Claudia was gone. Being home felt like going somewhere he no longer belonged.

His father was on a business trip, and he hated to leave his mother alone. But he was ready to go back to university. He was waiting for his mother to come home from bridge with the neighborhood ladies so he could say goodbye, and then he would take off.

His mother pulled into the driveway around 10:30 that night. Sam heard the old Volkswagen clunk into the garage from where he lay in his room, staring up at the bare ceiling, listening to the silence. He left his room when he heard the door unlatch, then watched his mother stumble in.

"Hey, Ma," he said, realizing she was drunk. "Do you need any help?"

"No, no…"

He moved to help her. "How was bridge with the ladies?"

"Oh, you know." She hiccoughed, leaning on his arm. "We're just a bunch of old gooses, abandoned by our husbands, trying to pass the time…"

"Did they let you drive home like this?"

She crossed her arms in front of her chest. "Don't take that tone with me, young man. Your mother still has everything under control."

"I get worried about you when you get like this."

She moved away. "I'm a little tired, is all."

He knew better than to ask her about his father's business trip or when he would be getting back. "Did you eat anything yet?"

"No."

"Why don't I make you something?" he said, searching for an excuse. "And while I'm cooking you can go lie down."

"That sounds wonderful, Sammy," she said. "Thank you. I might have one of my headaches coming on."

"Go lie down," he said, gently.

"What are you making?"

"It's a surprise."

"I'll be in the living room, on the sofa."

"Okay, Ma."

"Sammy, make some of whatever it is for Claudia, too. For whenever she gets back from the studio."

He swallowed, his eyes filling with tears. "I will. Go lie down."

She left and he stood in the kitchen, unable to move, concentrating on his breathing. So she had popped some of her anti-depressant pills as well as drinking with the neighborhood ladies. When she combined the two, she forgot, and he was forced to remember. About Claudia—that she was gone. That she had killed herself.

He understood how his mother could forget when her mind got foggy: Claudia had spent most of her time away from the house. He had frequently heard her come in through her window at two o'clock in the morning; he waited for the grating sound before he let himself fall asleep. Most nights she would come into his room and ask if he were awake. Then, sometimes she would talk to him. He had grumbled at the time, but he had never minded the night visits that woke him because he adored her.

They had all known that Claudia wanted to be a singer; she always explained her night excursions to their parents by saying that she was working on her CD at her friend's house—that she needed a room where she could practice melody and pitch in absolute silence. Only Sam knew where she really went, because one night when she stopped into his room, he had asked how recording had gone—and she had looked at him from behind her dark eyeliner and spoken quietly.

I didn't record tonight, Sammy. I was with Luke.

He could still remember that night—still saw her seated on the edge of his bed, her hands folded on her black velvet skirt, the moonlight filtering through the blinds and painting tiger stripes of light and shadow across her face.

Is that where you go at night?

Sometimes. Not every night. She had kissed the top of his head, had bent down and knelt beside him, putting her cool cheek against his warm one.

Don't worry, Sammy. He's a good guy. An artist. He helps me with my music. Pause. *Don't tell Mom and Dad.*

I won't.

Goodnight, kiddo. Her fingers had rustled through his hair once and then she had gone, silently as a shadow. She had been seventeen at the time, with less than two years to live. Had he known, he would have told her to give herself more time for her dream to come true, to let her life play out. But she had always done what she wanted; she would not have been persuaded by her younger brother.

He decided to drive back the next morning. He went over to the living room and saw his mother sprawled out on the sofa with her mouth open, snoring. He covered her with a blanket and turned down the light, then went back to the kitchen. He locked both of the doors and turned off the kitchen lights, then went to his room and lay down on his bed. Fully dressed, he stared at the ceiling in the dark as the passing headlights of a car sent shadow figures dancing around the walls of his room.

That evening when Carrie saw the light in Damien's window burning brightly, she built up her courage and forced herself to climb the stairs to his third story apartment. She knocked. The door opened.

"Carrie," he said, but he sounded surprised.

"Hi," she said, not giving herself a moment's hesitation to back down. There was no need for further greeting; she felt like he had never left. "Are you ready to go?"

His dark eyes flashed over her. "What do you mean?"

"You said last summer that you would show me your studio. We never got around to it."

"I said I would show you my studio?"

She paused, sensing his confusion. "Don't you remember?"

"I remember everything," he said immediately. "Especially talking until the sun came up."

She smiled. "I've never enjoyed sunrises so much."

"Neither have I," he said. "Probably since I'd never seen any before I met you."

She felt again the strange affinity—the sense of connection and understanding that flowed between them.

"Did you go home over the summer?" he asked.

"For a week." She felt something slipping away and tried to recapture it. "Show me your art?"

He hesitated. "I'd rather not."

She smiled. "I'm not giving you the option."

He stood and looked at her, brooding, in a moment that revealed he did take life more seriously than he claimed. Then he laughed, and the illusion was gone.

"Come along, then," he said, striding forward.

Damien DeMatteo. She heard his name playing like soft music through her mind as she hurried to keep up with him.

He led her to the Visual Arts building on campus and his studio space—an artist's haven flooded with natural sunlight. She stepped by him into the center of the high-ceilinged room after he unlocked the door. Rows of painted canvases lined the walls. Light danced masterfully over sylvan lakes and wooded glades, and pristine portraits smiled softly in a way that felt too living and real.

"Well," he said from behind her. "What do you think?"

Though his talent was obvious, she found herself disengaged. Still, she wanted to leave a good impression. "They're beautiful."

"I'm glad you like them. They're almost technically flawless." He came to stand beside her. "I'm very proud of—"

But something felt very wrong all of a sudden, and she turned to look at him. "Stop it."

He paused. "Don't you know it's rude to interrupt?"

"It's rude to lie."

"Lie?"

"You're not proud of these paintings," she said, unaware of the basis founding her words. "Not that you shouldn't be, but..."

He watched her silently.

"You don't care about these paintings," she repeated, feeling the blood rush to her face.

"Every artist cares about his work," he said softly. He went by her to a portrait of a young woman sitting in front of a window, her chin propped up on her hand. He held the portrait at arm's length. "I won money for this one, Carrie. The judges said this young woman was the embodiment of the heart—longing, sadness, regret." His lips curled. "You know, this young woman reminds me of you. Except that there's something essential in you that is lacking in her. Whatever that thing is— don't let it die."

She looked at the woman's expression and felt chilled.

"You want to know the truth?" He paused. "You're right, Carrie. I hate this painting. There's no spark, no spirit, no life."

"The painting is perfectly respectable," she countered.

"Perfectly respectable." He shook his head. "They're all perfectly respectable. That's why I hate them all."

She looked at him, startled, as he started to walk away from her. "Where are you going?"

"I was surprised when you mentioned my studio," he said, stepping in front of a locked cabinet at the other end of the room. "Surprised that I really had mentioned it to you and surprised that you remembered. But now I realize I had a hypothesis about you last summer when I met you. I want to test it today. Come here."

She crossed the room to stand beside him as he opened the cabinet. Without looking at her, he handed out the canvases. Canvases with slashes of color, violent and savage and undefinable shapes that unleashed the fury of hell inside of her heart.

"Do you like these better?" he asked softly. "These depraved and ugly and utterly inhuman—"

"Stop," she said, distracted by the art. "They're not. These are the only things in this room worth a damn."

"That doesn't say much for you or me," he said.

The other paintings were still in the periphery of her vision—the canvases with the reflective light, the peaceful skies and landscapes—but her attention remained on the darker canvases. The more she stared, the more she expected to see the paintings move, for whatever was living underneath the paint to crawl out.

"You should show these," she whispered. "These Others."

He laughed. "I've never shown these to anyone but you, and I'll never show them to anyone else."

"Damien, I'm being serious."

"Yes, I know you are," he said, and paused. "You like them?"

"They're real," she said, stepping closer to the paintings. "I can't believe this is inside you."

Suddenly his hands were on her shoulders, jerking her back. He turned her to face him, and she thought the intensity of his look would kill her.

"I shouldn't have shown you," he said. "But I thought it would—"

"You're hurting me," she said.

He paused. She looked directly back at him, not moving, and his lips curled.

"Good," he said, at the same time he let her go.

She watched as he collected the Others and locked them in the cabinet. He turned off the lights and walked ahead of her without speaking or turning back; the sun's brightness did not seem to dispel the mantle of darkness that had come to hang over him. She paused when they reached the intersection between their adjacent houses, uncomfortable with his silence.

"Thank you for showing me your studio," she said. "I enjoyed seeing your art."

"You can be honest." He stopped and turned back. "Be blunt, like you were before. You know I'll understand if you don't want to see me after this."

"What?" she said, confused. "Of course I want to see you. I'd stop by tonight, but I have to work."

His dark eyes studied her face. "Tomorrow night?"

"I'd love to," she said.

His dark eyes studied her face, and then his expression went blank. For an instant only, and then the blankness was replaced by the flash of his eyes and the charismatic confidence in his smile.

"I'll be around," he said, starting towards the side door of the house. "Stop by any time."

That night, in between waiting on her tables, she covered twenty napkins with her neat black cursive—another story inspired by him. At the end of the night she left those twenty napkins outside the door of his room.

Coming back from a night run the first weekend back to university, Carrie looked at her house and felt her heart sink. She should have expected the drunken laughter, the loud music—but she had hoped her housemates had changed over the summer. She looked over at Damien's window; his light was on. She changed direction and climbed the stairs to his room. He opened the door on her first knock.

"I want to talk to you," she said. There was no need for greeting.

"Now?" His dark eyes burned at her with the same dangerous intensity that made her feel like live wires were laced around her heart.

"I know it's late," she said. "If now's a bad time—"

"Now is a perfect time," he said. His eyes traveled down the long waves of auburn hair trailing down her back, then he looked directly into her hazel green eyes. "What did you have in mind, Carrie?"

She wanted, suddenly, to twine her fingers through his hair, to pull his body to hers and feel the beating of his heart overpowering her own pulse. She wanted to melt into him, to be closer to him than his own thoughts.

Do it, she told herself. *Ask him.*

"Do you want to..." she started, then, "why are you looking at me like that?"

He smiled. "You're blushing."

It's Damien. She made herself look at him. *Just ask him, and he'll meet you halfway...*

He stood in the doorway, his eyes lit with that pulsating energy, his wolfish features relaxed and blank—waiting.

"Do you want to go for a walk with me?" she asked.

A moment's surprise flickered over his face, then his lips twitched in amusement.

"Ten thirty on a Saturday night in a college town," he said. "And you want to go for a walk."

"Yes. And I want you to come with me."

There was a pause, and then he said, "Look at me, Carrie."

Raising her eyes to meet his was like pushing against a steel barricade. He was watching her with a peculiar mix of curious and cutting calculation—the way he always looked at her when he thought she wasn't watching him.

"What made you decide we should go for a walk tonight?" he asked, his features smoothing out when he saw he had her attention.

No, she wouldn't tell him. "I found a marvelous tree."

"A tree," he repeated.

She nodded. "I want to show you."

He ran his hand through his dark hair and stared at her. There was something predatory in his stance, and for a moment she felt deeply unsettled—certain that she would not be safe alone with him. Her heart trilled pleasantly. *But it's Damien,* she reminded herself. She came back to the thought of the unexpected attraction that seemed to link them, the intuitive knowledge that she could take the risks she was afraid to take with him because he would meet her halfway...

Suddenly his attention snapped away from her face, diverted to the window in the wall of the third story hallway. The strong lines of his jaw clenched, then he turned from her.

"Let me get my shoes," he said. "I'd love to go for a walk with you tonight."

Alarm bells in her mind. "You never wear shoes."

He turned back to her, smiled. "You're right. Never if I have to. I just wanted to make sure you were paying attention. Let's go."

There had been something in his eyes, she thought. *In that brief moment when he turned away...something that hadn't been there when he turned back.* But she didn't have long to think about the change, because within seconds she was outside with him walking beside her. Walking away from their houses, and ahead lay a walk under the stars and the kind of experience she had wanted, so desperately, for so long. The chance to be alone with him again.

Absorbed in her thoughts, she didn't notice that he glanced at her house, then trained his eyes on her face with that unique and searching look that would have disappeared in a moment had she been aware enough to see it. She was conscious only of the heat of his body beside her as they walked.

"You know," he said, breaking the silence between them. "You really shouldn't run by yourself at night."

"It's perfectly safe."

"I wouldn't want anything to happen to you," he said. "Aren't you afraid something might happen?"

She glanced at him. The streetlights cut shadows across his face as he looked down at the sidewalk. He was scowling slightly.

"I don't think you should talk," she said.

His scowl deepened. "You said you wanted to talk."

"You know what I mean."

"No," he said, and his voice was oddly quiet.

She reached out and linked her fingers through his. The touch of his skin sent heat racing up her arm. "Yes, you do."

"No." He withdrew his hand from hers as if he had been scorched. "I'm not sure I do."

"The silence was beautiful." She tucked her hands into the pockets of her jeans and pretended that she wasn't hurt. *There was no reason she should be.*

"Maybe I'm afraid of silence," he joked.

"You're not afraid of anything," she mumbled. "That's what I really meant. You shouldn't tell me to be afraid that something might happen when you."

Then she felt his hand on her wrist, slowly pulling her hand out of her pocket. His fingers laced through hers.

"Carrie," he said, and still she felt the wonderful warmth of his hand. "Don't admire me for that."

"But I do," she insisted, feeling the soft breeze that blew by them caressing away the heat from her burning face. "You aren't afraid of anything or anyone."

"I have nothing to lose," he said. "Hasn't anyone told you that you should avoid the man who has nothing to lose?"

Her fingers tightened around his in response. "I think it should be my choice."

"You don't know anything about me."

"You're wrong," she said. "I know everything I need to know about you." She paused. "I trust you."

"You haven't known me for very long," he said. There was an edge in his voice.

"It doesn't matter," she said. "I don't trust people easily, if ever. But I trust you."

"That's not very logical," he said. "Considering I got your attention by throwing a rock through your window." He paused. "I am sorry about that—"

"You've already apologized," she said absent-mindedly.

He dropped her hand. "I'm usually smoother in my approach to the ladies."

Ladies? she wondered. She glanced over at him and realized for the first time that something about him seemed—different.

"I'm surprised I didn't scare a girl like you away," he finished.

Her confusion remained. "What do you mean, a girl like me?"

"You're so innocent, Carrie," he said. "You must have trusted me from the moment you saw me."

"I did." She stopped and faced him. They had walked by the final streetlight, and in the murky darkness he looked dangerous.

He smiled, and it was the wrong reaction. "Must you always be so serious about everything, sweetheart?"

Chills crept up her spine. *This is Damien,* she reminded herself. He was the same person who had walked into her backyard at four in the morning on those summer nights to keep her company around the fires she built...

He was the same person who had created the series of paintings that had unlocked a hidden part of herself....

He was the same Damien DeMatteo who was her friend and kindred spirit, whose very existence in her life had promised to open new worlds to her, who filled her with hope and gratitude and spirit...

But now his presence was speaking to a different part of her—a savage, animal side that no one else had ever dared to acknowledge existed.

He didn't need to touch her to make her feel like her body was on fire; his nearness was enough. She took a step back and realized that he had not moved—that the very power in his eyes had given her the impression that he had come closer to her. The tone of his voice called her like the tide, pulling her to him.

"Freedom from fear is absolute freedom," he said. "You're right about that, Carrie. But until you let down the walls, you'll never be free. I could help you—"

"You are helping me," she said. She forced herself not to back away from him—to look him directly in the eyes. "That's why I'm so grateful that you're my friend."

"Your friend." He looked at her, hard. She felt every hope she had ever had about him crash out of her body, leaving her feeling frighteningly empty.

"I know that's not what you're thinking," he said finally. "So I won't make you lie to me by asking if that's what you really—"

"I never lie," she interrupted.

"That's what you said last summer."

"That hasn't changed," she said. "I still don't believe in lying."

"But you believe in acting against your heart."

"No."

"You could have fooled me." He paused. "Unless you don't feel it."

"I don't know what you mean."

He stepped closer to her. He brushed her hair away from her face, then curled his hand around the back of her neck and traced a path down her shoulder. His eyes never left hers.

"That," he said.

"Oh." Her cheeks were flaming.

He made her look at him. His eyes were dark with moonlight, and his hands on either side of her face made her giddy.

"Did you know, Carrie," he continued. "That the highest point of an endothermic reaction is when the substance is the most unstable?"

"No, I didn't," she said.

"I mean," he said. "That sometimes it's better to have the ground shaking under your feet. Security is the only true illusion."

"I agree with you," she said, feeling weak.

His lips curled, and he let her go. "Never mind, Carrie."

"Do you want to talk more about—" she started.

"No."

She didn't move. "Are you angry with me?"

"You wouldn't care if I was." He paused. "It must be nice to be so strong all the time."

She looked at him. She didn't feel strong.

He paused. "Is this your tree?"

She looked over and instantly felt calmed. The tree's massive limbs towered over them, its canopy of leaves a gently rustling music in the wind. She stepped up to the tree and wrapped her arms around the ancient trunk and instantly felt all of the tension and anxiety drain out of her body. She pressed her lips against the rough bark, then stepped back to find Damien watching her.

"I guess that tree's luckier than I'm going to be tonight," he said.

She turned quickly back to the tree. "I don't know what it is."

"It's a beautiful tree," he said.

"I just wanted to show you." She started walking down the sidewalk, embarrassed, then realized that he wasn't following her. She turned. He was standing and staring at the tree, his back towards her. She wondered why all her thoughts were swept away like footprints in the sand, except for that sole image of him.

He turned and walked back to her. "Thank you."

Though she walked beside him, she felt as if he were enveloped in a cocoon of solitude. She hesitated to break into his reverie, but when they reached the intersection between their houses, she touched his arm long enough to get his attention.

"Thank you for going for a walk with me," she said.

He looked at her strangely, as if her words had brought him back from somewhere far away. He glanced by her, to her house.

"Are you going to be okay tonight?" he asked.

"They'll leave me alone."

"They had better." He paused. "Did they tell you they were throwing a party?"

"They don't talk to me."

He frowned. "Why are you living with them again?"

She shrugged, not wanting to continue the conversation. "Same reasons as last year."

"Still, not many single females would live with all guys."

"I didn't know you knew I lived with all guys."

He looked at her sharply. "Every guy on this block knows you live with all guys."

"I needed a place to stay." She didn't understand why he was searching her. "I didn't have a choice."

"Neither did they."

"No." She bit her lip. "They aren't very happy about it either."

He looked at her for a long time. She saw judgment in his eyes, and she was crushed by the weight of her own failure. Then, he said, "Fuck them, Carrie."

She laughed, suddenly, at the irony of his words. "I most definitely will not."

She realized, halfway through her sentence, that all traces of humor had left his face. He disappeared into his house and let the door slam behind him. She watched him, almost went after him, then turned and went into her house. She made her way through the crowds of people crammed into the hallways and climbed the stairs to her room. She closed her door, exhaled, dropped to her knees to greet her guinea pig, then stood and walked to her window.

The light in his room was on, and she saw him standing in front of his window looking towards her room. He raised one hand; she waved back. *Goodnight.* The light in his room went out.

Even with the noise from downstairs and outside her room, she heard the screech of the side entrance door of his house opening. Her heart soared as she waited on edge, and then she saw him walk by her house. Panic kicked in, and she did not know why. She felt compelled to send a prayer after him—but it had been years since she had prayed.

Her door opened, diverting her thoughts from her obsessed musings. She turned around quickly, then relaxed when she saw who had entered her room. He was the only one of her housemates' friends whom she recognized; he was the only person who had ever been kind to her.

Confusion clouded his usually cheerful blue eyes, and he hesitated in her doorway. "Sorry," he said. "I was looking for the bathroom."

"First door on your left," she said.

"I thought this was…thanks." He mumbled his response and closed her door quickly.

She sat in thought for a moment. She had spoken to Sam only once; he had only had time to ask her name, and she time to respond, before her housemates had herded him away from her. He had called over his shoulder that it was nice to have met her, and for some reason those words had affected her more than they should have.

Idle musings—but perhaps better than some.

When she woke at eight o'clock the next morning, she noticed first the sunlight streaming into her room through her open window and the dust mites flickering like fireflies in the golden beams. Then she noticed the piece of paper that had been slipped under her door.

Rubbing the sleep from her eyes, she picked up the paper and recognized the formulas from having had honors physics in highschool. Her brow creased in confusion, then she flipped the note over.

Dearest Carrie, the note said. *Three cats chase a mouse. The mouse runs and cowers in the corner. The cats surround the mouse and it squeaks. It runs and the cats chase it with no avail. Yours, Sam.*

She knew Sam was an English major; he would never have taken a college level physics class. Someone else had to know about the riddle, then. Was his note a joke? Or some plot to get her to move out of the house for next year? She threw the note on her desk and left her room.

The last revelers had passed out an hour ago, and the house was quiet.

She avoided the empty bottles on the staircase and the scattered Red Dixie cups and made her way into the kitchen. Pancakes. Even though she burned the first batch—her thoughts kept getting away from her— she was proud of herself for making the effort to take care of herself.

Two quick raps on the side door broke through her thoughts. Carrie decided the second batch of pancakes were already burned and crossed out of the kitchen. Her heart thumped unevenly when she saw her visitor. She forced herself to open the door calmly.

"Good morning, Damien," she said.

"Smells good in here," he said.

"Would you like to come in?" she asked without thinking.

"I would love to."

As he stepped by her, she remembered the state of the house. She walked into the kitchen after him and went directly to the stove. As long as she had something to concentrate on—not burning the next batch of pancakes, for example—she would be fine.

"Carrie?" His deep voice resounded with disbelief. "What the hell happened to your house?"

She turned, pretended disinterest. "Oh, that. How should I know?"

He looked back at her, his dark eyes kindling. "Your housemates?"

When she didn't answer, he said angrily, "I can't believe you let them get away with this."

"It's not my place to tell other people how to live," she said. "And it's not my place to clean up after them either."

"Then I'll clean up."

"No, you won't." She flipped a pancake in her haste to do anything besides look at Damien. The batter, still uncooked, dripped onto the skillet. "They'll clean up when they wake up. They always do."

She turned in astonishment when she heard the first of the bottles shatter on the ground, turned in time to see Damien sweep the remaining bottles off the counter. His eyes burned at the glass slivers on the ground, and she shied away from the look he fixed on her before she realized the anger was not directed at her.

"Now you have to let me clean," he said. "Because *I* made the mess."

She shrugged, a mask of indifference she was far from feeling. "You can make your own choices in life, same as them. I won't stop you from cleaning if you want to."

"Not going to try to change me," he said. "I wonder if you knew…"

"Knew what?"

"Knew how dangerous to you I really am."

She caught his playful smile and threw the spatula at him. He was leaning against the counter, but his reflexes were lightning quick; he caught the spatula and in the next moment he was beside her.

"You know something, Carrie?" he asked, his voice low. "Being this close to you is like feeling the heat of a chemical reaction going off in my heart."

"That was the worst simile I've ever heard." She blushed and put out her hand for the spatula.

"You're going to burn those," he said.

She took the spatula from him. "Thank you for looking out for the well-being of the pancakes."

"I certainly don't want to eat burned pancakes, and life is all about what I want. Remember that about me." He paused, then put his hand on her wrist as she reached toward the skillet. "No, try it like this."

She watched a he flipped the pancake using only the skillet, then shook her head. "I'd drop the pancake on the ground if I tried that. And given the state of the ground…"

"Try it," he insisted. "All you have to lose is one slightly burned pancake."

There was an unfamiliar gravity in his voice. She took the skillet from him, then successfully flipped the pancake.

"See," he said. "You sell yourself short. Always."

"Do you want some breakfast?" she asked.

"Now we just have to get you to take some bigger risks." He laughed when she looked at him pointedly. "I understand, Carrie. You don't want to talk about these things. Well, I'm going to make you talk about them. Because I sense that no one else will. Everyone else puts you on a pedestal, don't they? But I realize that you're human. That you have thoughts, and hopes…"

Suddenly his hand was on her forehead, then trailing along her cheek and caressing her lips. Down her neck to her heart…

46

"...and needs," he finished.

"Don't." She took his hand in hers, moved it away. Her voice was unsteady.

He stepped away, his eyes locked on hers. "I'm sorry."

She paused. "I liked the speech. Just not—"

"The speech." His back faced her, and she couldn't read his expression. "Never mind the speech. Why don't we eat in your living room...no, I see your living room is in an equally deplorable state."

"We can go in my room." She took two plates out of the cupboard above the stove, then looked at the pile of pancakes she had made. "I'm sorry that most of them are burned. I've been distracted."

He was beside her, once again. "Don't ever apologize to me. I would be honored to eat your pancakes, madame."

"They're burned," she repeated.

"You really don't know much about college guys, do you, Carrie? We eat anything. Trust me, the pancakes are fine."

Reluctantly, she put two pancakes on his plate.

"More," he said, gravely.

She couldn't help it; she smiled.

"Thank you," he said, after she had added two more pancakes. "Now we may proceed."

The words held an appealing ring for her; they struck her intuition as something important that she should remember. But it was so hard to think clearly when he was beside her...

"Can I sit on your bed?" he asked as they walked up the stairs to her room. "That would make this meal even better. Then I could tell people you made me breakfast in bed."

She stopped in front of her door without saying anything.

"All right, Carrie," he agreed from behind her. "I understand the feminist in you is rebelling."

"It's not that," she said, and opened her door.

"Hello, munchkin," he said, as soon as he saw the tan furry ball of her guinea pig streak across the floor. Then he looked up. "Carrie, where's your bed?"

"I got rid of it," she said.

Her guinea pig came over to her as she kicked off her black boots. She scooped him up and held him against her shoulder, amused by the tawny ridges of his hair that stuck up in random places. She loved the little animal fiercely.

"Why?" he asked.

She hesitated. "There's a saying that living close to the ground helps you think more clearly and be more aware of your environment."

"I don't think that saying was meant to be taken literally. Besides, you're on the second floor." He paused. "What's the real reason for getting rid of your bed?"

"I just didn't want it anymore, okay?"

"No," he said, sitting cross-legged on the floor. "I won't accept that answer."

A flash of annoyance. "Any other person would realize I don't want to—"

"Precisely," he said. "But you wouldn't have invited any other person to come eat burnt pancakes with you in your room on a spontaneous Sunday morning, so there must be some reason why I'm here. And I want to know why you got rid of your bed."

She hesitated. "I was sleeping too much."

"Carrie. You never sleep. We both know that."

She looked up to find him analyzing her; she let him look. She had told him the truth. But half the truth was a lie, and she had promised herself she would never lie to him.

"And because..." She paused, feeling like she was treading on dangerous ground but not being able to stop her next words. "And because it felt empty."

"Empty?" he prompted.

But she could not tell him any more. She could not tell him that as she lay in her bed every night she was plagued by the certainty that he should have been there beside her, holding her in his arms...that the feeling of loneliness and emptiness and her desire to be with him had confused and tormented her so much that she had done the only thing she could to get rid of that feeling...

She smiled, aware that his eyes were flying like lightning over her face. "I really prefer to sleep on the floor."

"These pancakes are delicious," he said. "You should try them."

She tried to ignore the sinking feeling that she had disappointed him. Obligingly she took a bite of her forgotten food, but she was not hungry. She put the plate on the floor in front of her, then petted her guinea pig when he came over to munch.

"Where did you go last night?" she asked.

"We all have our secrets," he said. "For example, the real reason you got rid of your bed. Hypothetically, Carrie, if you addressed whatever that real reason was, would you sleep in a bed again?"

"I suppose so," she said. "But I don't know why you're so concerned about my bed."

"Remember that life is all about what I want."

"You want me to have a bed?"

"For reasons of my own," he said.

"What reasons?" She was conscious that her face was burning.

His lips curled. "So you can get a good night's sleep."

She glanced at him, and his smile grew.

"Come now, Carrie," he said. "If you're going to talk your way around what's on your mind, then so can I." He stood, stretched. "Thanks for breakfast."

He had eaten every last crumb of the pancakes—hers, too—without her realizing it. She stood abruptly as he picked up the plates. She didn't want him to go. She followed him out of her room, down the stairs.

"Thanks for coming over," she said, then stopped by the side entrance door. "Why exactly did you come over?"

"To see you," he said. "I never have any reason other than that, do I, sweetheart?"

She looked at him for a long time, wondering why his words had affected her in a negative way. "This visit felt different."

"What do you mean?"

"I don't know." She shrugged. "But I feel like you came for a very specific reason this time."

"Maybe I came to make sure you were okay," he said. "Last night after I let you return to the drunken carousel of your housemates and their friends, I couldn't get you off my mind no matter where I went."

"You are such a liar." She wanted to believe his words though she knew she shouldn't, though they made her feel shaky inside.

He laughed. "Thanks again for breakfast, Carrie. I'll see you around."

She watched him go and realized she had let him leave without answering any of her questions—which, she realized, he would never have accepted from her. She washed their dishes, ignoring the rest of the mess that surrounded her, then went back to her room where Colby was whooping in indignation because Damien had eaten his pancakes. She remembered the first time Damien had entered her room and realized she let Colby run around loose; some emotion had flickered over his face—surprise? disgust?—replaced by amusement, replaced by a question—and she had told him the truth. She let Colby run around because it hurt her to see the spirit of any animal tamed, though she kept Colby's cage because sometimes he liked to be in the secure place.

She had felt silly explaining this to Damien; she had known him for less than a week at the time. She had stumbled around trying to explain, and she had quoted Maya Angelou and rambled that the caged bird could sing.

Yes, he had said, leaning back in her desk chair and fixing the full intensity of his dark eyes on her. *I suppose you're living proof of that.*

And her fascination with him had begun.

The front door to the apartment complex banged open, jarring Sam out of his thoughts. He looked up.

"Still a pig pen, I see," Damien remarked as he strode into the kitchen.

Sam shrugged. "Would it feel like a home, if it wasn't? Come on in, before the pizza gets cold."

Damien walked into the apartment and sat down across from Sam. He glanced down the hallway. "It sounds like someone died."

Sam shook his head. "I don't mind."

"I don't know why she listens to music like that," he said. "Does she still keep to herself?"

Sam nodded. "She certainly doesn't care for any of us." He paused. "And I don't know why you keep visiting, because she clearly doesn't care about you, either."

"I visit because I enjoy your company," he retorted.

Sam glanced at him; though he did not respect him, Sam admired Damien's charisma and ability to find humor in every situation.

"I'm over her indifference." Damien grabbed a slice of pizza from the box on the table between them. "So tell me about your girl."

The question seemed to snap Sam out of his trance. "She's not my girl."

"Yet. Is she seeing someone else right now?"

"Not that I know of."

"That could work for or against us." He paused. "You're not being very helpful, Sammy. You have to give me more details. I already wrote that note for you, and you haven't even told me her name."

"Her name is Carrie," Sam said. "Carrie Crenshaw."

For a moment, Damien sat very still. Then, he smiled. "I wouldn't put it past you to fall for a girl whose name has that kind of alliteration."

"I met her in my fiction writing class," Sam said. "She's an amazing writer and an amazing person, but she has no confidence whatsoever because she's living with these jerks who won't even talk to her."

"Then why is she living there?"

He shrugged. "I think there was something about the house that she didn't want to leave. But she must have gotten over it."

"What do you mean?"

"She's moving out by the end of the week."

"What are you doing, stalking her?"

Sam shook his head. "My friends told me I could move in with them because she's leaving, so I'll probably do that. Since this place is crazy." He paused. "Maybe Carrie should move in here. She and Tessa would probably get along great, and then I'd know where to find her."

Damien looked at him. "She's not interested in you?"

"Carrie? Or Tessa?"

"Carrie."

"I don't think she's interested in anyone, except her characters." He paused. "I need to get a hobby, stop thinking about her so much. What do you do in your free time? I know you sure as hell don't study."

"I get high." He leaned back, put his feet on the table. "Off of life, mind you."

Sam shook his head. "Maybe we could come up with a hobby together."

"No time." He lit a cigarette. "So, do you think Tessa is going to keep hiding from me forever?"

"I don't know that she's hiding from you. She just works, all the time."

"Don't I know it," he said, drily. "It wouldn't hurt her to loosen up."

"Or for you to settle down." Sam looked at him disapprovingly. "She's going to smell that, you know."

"And hate me for it?" Damien took the cigarette from his mouth, looked at it. "She already hates everything I do, so I might as well enjoy myself." He arched his eyebrows. "But for your sake, Sammy, and since I am your guest, I'll put it out."

Sam winced as he extinguished the cigarette on the wooden table near his seat. "I can't believe you're related."

He shrugged. "Different mothers."

"She kept her mother's name?"

Damien exhaled smoke. "Of course she did. Our father was a cad." He stood, stretched. "That's why I kept his name—as a reminder that it doesn't pay to be virtuous in this world. But I'm going to knock on her door. I don't wait this long for any one."

"Why don't you give me directions to your place," Sam said. "And if she wants to see you, she'll know where to find you."

"Nope. I don't want you to know where I live."

Sam looked at him keenly. "What's wrong with your place?"

"Nothing." His eyes sparked. "But you and I aren't the best of friends, Sam."

"At least you're honest."

He laughed. "No one's ever called me that before."

Sam's smile hitched. He watched Damien walk down the dark hallway to Tessa's room, and in that moment, he could not have said which one he liked least.

"Hello, beautiful," Damien called out to her, as she walked by his house on the way to her own.

Carrie squinted against the sun to see him—his wild back hair, his untamed features, the lazy slope of his profile lit gently by his porch lights. She quickly buttoned the thick fabric of her waitressing uniform; she had not expected to see him—or anyone—on her walk back to the apartment at 2 AM, and she had left her blouse open against the summer night's heat. She changed her direction and started up his sidewalk.

"Did you just get off work?" he asked, coming to meet her halfway. She nodded.

"It's late," he said.

"I'm glad you're still up." She drank in his features and wondered why, beside him, she felt infected with energy. "And that you're here."

"I decided to wait up for you," he said. "See if you wanted to go looking for any more trees."

She sighed in exasperation. "I'm going to go home and make some dinner, then go to bed."

"Really? So you don't have time to sit down, put up your feet, have a beer and a chat with your friendly neighbor?"

"You know I don't drink."

He paused. "How about the rest of it?"

In response, she followed him up the porch steps and over to the mismatched folding chairs. She collapsed into one, and before she had a chance to say anything else, he bent down and took hold of her shoe. She sat up.

"Relax," he said.

She felt a shiver jolt up her leg and run through her spine. He took off her shoes slowly, then gently propped her legs up on the railing in front of them.

"So where are you planning on living?" he asked her.

She looked at him, confused. "Next door to you."

"Your housemates mentioned you were moving out." He lit a cigarette. "I wanted to ask you why."

"I'm not moving." She stared at the glowing butt of his cigarette. "I didn't know you smoked."

"Maybe your housemates are planning on kicking you out," he suggested.

"They wouldn't..." she started, then paused.

"You know they would," he finished.

She became aware of something more important than what he was telling her, and glanced over at him. "Are you okay?"

He glanced at her and leaned back in his chair. "Never better. Why do you ask?"

"You're smoking. And you haven't shown me any new art in awhile."

"I'm done with art."

"What?" she asked, deeply disturbed. "Why?"

"Tell you what. I'll paint you a picture. Will that get you to stop asking all these stupid questions?"

She coughed. He snubbed the cigarette on the arm rest of his chair, then stuck the cigarette behind his ear.

"Why don't we talk about something else," he said. "Like how your housemates are planning on kicking you out—"

"I'm not moving," she repeated. "So we don't have to talk about it."

"Fine." He glanced at her. "Why don't you tell me something interesting that happened to you today?"

"Nothing."

"That's depressing," he remarked. "Did anything interesting happen yesterday?"

She started to reply, then paused. "Someone slipped a riddle under my door."

"Who?"

She shrugged. "One of my housemates' friends."

"What did it say?"

"I don't remember exactly—"

"Go get it."

She unpropped her legs from the railing and tucked her feet under her; she glanced at him.

"Well, you kept it, didn't you?" he asked.

She responded with an equally hostile tone. "Of course I kept it. It intrigued me. I didn't know exactly what he was trying to imply, but I have a generally good idea and I'm not exactly ecstatic about it."

"Maybe you misinterpreted the riddle," he said. "I'd give you my

54

feedback, but there's no way I can know what to say if you don't go get the damn note."

She stared at him. He had never spoken to her like that before; she felt half inclined to refuse his implicit request. She wanted his opinion on the note, however; she had wanted to hear his thoughts from the first moment she saw the riddle, but she had not wanted to give him the impression that a note from another guy held any meaning for her.

When she left her house again and walked up the sidewalk to his porch, she realized he was watching her every move. She handed him the note silently, then sat back down in the chair beside him. He unfolded the note, glanced over the contents.

"Love, Sam." He handed the note back to her. "Sounds like someone has a crush."

"It doesn't mean anything," she reassured him. "He was drunk when he wrote this. In fact, I'm relatively sure that my housemates put him up to it."

"What makes you think that?"

She flipped the paper over. "Sam is an English major. He wouldn't have scrap paper like this. But Dan would."

"Dan's the one in the basement?"

She nodded. "He's the engineer. He'd have an extra physics worksheet lying around."

"So might other people."

"What do you think it means?" she demanded.

"They see you as a mouse and themselves as cats," he said. "Isn't that all that matters?"

"I'm not a mouse." Her eyes flashed. "And I don't 'cower in the corner.' I'm not afraid of them."

"Then why do you stay locked in your room all the time?" he asked.

"I have things to do."

"Like study?"

She bristled at his tone. "I don't study."

He leaned back in his chair. "We both know you make top notch grades, Carrie. Even though you take eight courses a semester."

She decided to ignore his tone. "I'm in my room because I'm writing."

"About me?"

"Yes."

"Really?"

"You know you're my Muse," she said dismissively. "But my door is never locked. You know that." She waited for a sarcastic remark, but he did not give her one.

"If you want to know what the riddle means so badly," Damien said. "Then maybe you should ask Sam."

"I'm not going to see Sam," she said. "And I don't know why you're making this note into such a big deal."

"I'm not the one trying to psycho-analyze the ramblings of a drunken fool."

"You asked to see the note," she said. "I wouldn't have cared to discuss it, if you hadn't—"

"If you hadn't cared about the note, you wouldn't have kept it," he challenged her.

Silently, she stood and walked away from him.

"Don't leave me like this," he sang out from behind her. "I don't want you to be mad at me."

"I'm not mad at you," she responded. "I'm hungry. Goodnight."

She heard him chuckle, but did not permit herself to look back at him. Once inside the house she realized she was too tired to eat, and she passed out on the futon in the living room without changing out of her waitressing uniform.

She dropped a note on his desk when she walked in. Sam looked at the paper—plain, white, folded once. He tried to catch her eye, but she had already taken her seat and was reading silently.

Carrie. That was the red-head's name. A week earlier, her green eyes sparkling, she had said that writing was magic and that the weight of words should be taken seriously. He wondered about her, for more reasons than one.

Almost everything he knew about her he had learned from his friends. She built fires. She had a guinea pig and a fish. She decorated her room with so many plants that it looked like a rainforest. She burned incense and listened, alternatively, to Pink Floyd and Tchaikovsky.

They had been in the same fiction writing class for over a month, and this was the first sign she had given that she was aware of his existence. Should he read the note then—or when he got back to his apartment? He looked at her again, furtively, and saw her hazel green eyes directly on him, a compelling force in her stare. He opened the note.

Hey kitty kat. Wait for me after class.

That stupid note he had written her—it hadn't even been his idea. He glanced at her quickly, but she had locked eyes with their creative writing professor—a lanky graduate student with wavy chestnut hair who always wore an olive green tweed coat. All the other women in the class had a crush on him, but Sam could not tell with Carrie, because she was different.

She stayed after class; he had to wait for her in the hall. His hands were sweating, and he stuffed them into his pockets and leaned against the white plaster wall as he stood and thought about her.

"I thought you'd left," she said.

He looked up, startled, and saw her standing beside him. "You worried you had missed me, eh?"

"No," she said. "I knew if I didn't catch you now I would see you some other time. But I'm glad you waited, so I could see you alone."

He shrugged, to mask the thrill he felt "What did you talk about with Ridinger anyway?"

"We talked about my writing."

"What about your writing?" he prompted.

"About how I can improve." She paused. "Where are you going anyway?"

"Now? Or in life?"

Her eyes measured him. "I'm going back to the house."

"I could walk you home," he offered. "I need to see Dan, anyway."

They walked for a moment in silence, and then she looked at him.

"Sam. I need to talk to you about something." She paused. "I heard you're thinking about moving into the house."

"This week," he said. "And I don't want us to be strangers, Carrie. I want to get to know you. Maybe we could exchange what we write for feedback." He saw her looking at him strangely, and stumbled over his next words. "When I found out that there was an open room in your house—"

"That room would be mine." There was no friendly smile; her eyes bore into his. "I don't appreciate that you're trying to kick me out of my own house."

"Back up," he said. "They told me you didn't want to live there any more."

"I have no intention of leaving that house until I graduate," she said.

"I had no idea you wanted to keep living there," he said. "I'm certainly not going to kick you out. And I don't think they can, either." He felt her relax beside him, and he risked a glance at her. "That said, can I ask *why* you want to keep living there?"

"You can always ask me anything you want," she said. "And I'll answer you as honestly as I am able."

"That's a somewhat odd statement to make," he said, but when she looked at him he was the one who felt odd. He felt the back of his neck burning and the flush creeping up his ears as it always did when he was embarrassed. He asked quickly, "Well, what's your answer?"

She looked away from him. "It's cheap. Close to campus."

"You could find a different apartment that's cheap and close to campus—"

"I could. But I don't want to."

"You're clearly not telling me something," he said. "But I'm not going to push you—"

"Thank you."

He paused. "They might be my friends, but don't lump me in the same category as them. I don't want you to get the wrong impression of me."

She smiled, and the spontaneous gesture transformed her. "My first impression of you was made a long time ago."

His stride became constricted. "But this is the first time we've talked."

"No," she said. "Not really."

He searched her face, but her eyes were trained on the blue sky. He looked away quickly. "I had hoped you wanted to talk to me about something else. Besides me kicking you out of the house."

"I did," she said. "Your riddle. I appreciated the creativity, but I don't like what you were trying to tell me."

They had reached the white block of a house where she lived—the Marshmallow, he called it. He felt the flush creeping up his neck. "What do you think I was trying to say?"

"Come on, Sam," she said, opening the door. "Three cats and a mouse?"

"You missed the point." Bluntness, he figured, would work best. "The point of the note was just to get your attention. Carrie, I'd really like to get lunch with you sometime."

She jerked; he had never seen her so startled. He wished they weren't still standing outside of her house where her housemates could seem them, but he sensed he was lucky to have gotten her to agree to be alone with him, and he wanted to push his luck. If her housemates saw and asked about it, he could make up a coincidence or scheme, or he could flat out lie.

He looked over and saw her watching him alertly. He grinned at her.

"Come on, Carrie," he said. "If you really think I'm asking you for some ulterior motive, shouldn't you jump at the chance to observe me and try to figure out what it is? That's what we do as writers, isn't it?"

"I have plenty to write about already, thank you."

He frowned. "That's not a very good attitude to have as an author. You should always be on the look out for interesting people and experiences."

"And you, I suppose, are one of those," she said.

"I'll surprise you, Carrie. I promise you that."

"I'm intrigued," she said. "All right, Sam. When?"

When. If he could only answer that question, then he would have a whole block of uninterrupted time with her, in some place away from the drama of the university.

"Tomorrow," he said finally. "We can meet at my place, unless that makes you uncomfortable."

A shadow crossed her face, and he thought she seemed uncertain. "It'll be cheaper if I make lunch," he continued.

She paused, looking not at him but at the large oak tree that stood near the house, shadowing the Marshmallow with its encompassing canopy of leaves. "Where do you live?"

He gave her detailed directions to his house.

"It will be nice to talk to someone," she said tentatively. "As a friend. I want us to be very clear about that."

He could be patient. "You've got it. Why don't you bring your writing? Something like the last piece you turned in."

"Daddy's Girl?" she asked.

He nodded. "Your first story was good. But even with all the action from the sex and drugs, it felt like there was something missing."

She laughed. "Experience." Then she looked at him, as if maybe she had said too much.

"The scenes were realistic enough," he said, knowing he would analyze her response later. "I meant that your first writing sounded like mine does when I'm writing something I don't really care about."

"It's strange you should notice that," she said. "Sam, I can't figure out why I wrote those other stories. I don't *like* those stories. But when I sat down to write that's what started to come out."

He didn't like the dark, brooding look that had come into her eyes and tried to divert her attention. "In 'Daddy's Girl,' the relationships are still complicated, but you captured something real. Something pure, as if from a key essence of your own heart."

"I want to write about family relationships," she said. "Eventually. It's insightful of you to realize that there's a difference. In the writing."

He tried to move past her, into the house, but she remained in front of the door.

"What?" he asked.

"I want us to be very clear about one more thing, Sam." She looked at him directly. "I'm not a mouse."

"Carrie, forget I ever—"

"I don't play games with people," she said. "And I don't like it when people play games with me."

"We're clear on that," he said.

"Good." She relaxed, then paused. "I'm sorry if that came out sounding hostile."

"It's okay. You have to look out for yourself."

She opened the screen door and held it open for him, then followed him inside. She started up the stairs to her room—to play Mozart or Metallica—but he called out to her.

"Remember to bring your writing tomorrow," he reminded.

"I will." She stopped on the landing and looked down at him. "Just so you know, Sam, I'm a vegetarian."

"No problem," he said.

He heard her door close. Something different this time—Led Zeppelin. He smiled. He liked her already.

"I called Seven Springs," Sam said, as Damien idled into the kitchen. "A guy said there isn't that much snow, but that the skiing should be good enough."

"It'll give us a challenge. Right, Sammy?"

Sam looked at the orange Gander Mountain parka Damien handed him. "You want me to wear this?"

Damien raised his eyebrows. "It will look good on you. Do it for all the snowbunnies we're going to run into on the slopes."

"No woman would give me a second glance if I'm dressed in that," he said.

"Maybe not. But no woman would miss you the first time around." He smiled, then shrugged. "We'll take it with us. You don't have to wear it, but it'll be there in case you change your mind. It doesn't hurt to be prepared, Boy Scout Style."

"You were in the Boy Scouts?"

"I was an Eagle Scout." Damien paused. "Until I realized the bloody bastards don't let chicks in."

Sam realized how much the temperature had dropped when they walked outside. He put on the parka and tried to see his reflection in the grimy windows of the forest green Mitsubishi.

"Jesus Christ," he said. "I look like I just got out of a mental hospital."

"You know what they say, though. Crazy guys do it best. Might end up working for you, Sam."

Sam unzipped the jacket and threw it into the backseat as he climbed into the car. "That really wasn't that funny."

"You know I don't mean half the things I say." Damien slapped the dashboard as the car stalled the first time he tried to start it. "Piece of shit."

The engine started and Damien glanced at Sam as he pulled out of the driveway. "You don't seem to appreciate my derogatory jokes. You must have a girl on your mind." He caught Sam's curt nod and looked at the steering wheel. He paused. "Carrie?"

Sam nodded. "I'm enchanted by her."

Damien glanced at him. "Always dangerous. You don't think she's playing games with you?"

"She wouldn't. She told me she believes in honesty."

"Then maybe you shouldn't."

"If you had met her, you'd understand." He paused. "I've been in her room, and she has honesty listed as one of her key virtues on a piece of paper in her room."

"You're kidding me."

"Keep your eyes on the road."

"Nothing's coming. We're all alone out here."

Sam checked his own mirror, though he knew Damien was right. "She's like that Emily Dickinson poem. 303."

"What, did she have that plastered on her wall, too?"

"You don't know her."

"Your descriptions aren't exactly helping. 'She's like that Emily Dickinson poem. 303.'"

He paused. "I'm an English major. I can't help it."

"Yes, you can. Just say she's difficult to describe." He paused. "Or tell me what that means."

"She selects her own society and then closes herself off. That's what I was trying to say." Sam paused. *Why was he talking about a girl like Carrie to a guy like Damien?* "Do you know what you're doing after graduation?"

"I'll figure it out. Things always fall into place." He smirked. "More or less in pieces, in my case, but what really matters anyway?"

Sam glanced at him. "You don't mean that."

"I do." He paused, then continued. "This girl you're talking about, Sam. If she has any kind of focus or direction, then she's lucky. But doesn't that kind of devotion turn you off?"

"No. I admire her for it."

Damien smiled. "So what are you going to do next?

Sam glanced at him. "I'll probably apply to graduate school and go in for my—"

"No. I meant with Carrie. Clearly, my little note scheme wasn't enough." Damien paused. "How did that go over with her, by the way?"

Sam didn't look at him. "She liked it. She said no one had ever tried to communicate with her by using riddles before."

"But you didn't follow up." His voice was low. "I give you a way to catch her attention, then you don't follow up."

"I don't understand why you seem to care. I would think your philosophy would dictate going after some other girl who would be more likely to—"

"We're talking about you, not me." He shrugged. "Different rules."

"I'm not so sure I agree with your rules."

"You shouldn't. You'd never be able to keep up with them."

Sam pressed his forehead against the cool pane of the window and watched the blur of scenery as it passed them by. "The riddle scheme wasn't a total failure. I'm having lunch with her tomorrow."

Damien paused. "Let me know how it goes."

"I will," Sam promised.

She was twenty minutes late getting to Sam's apartment. She rang the doorbell and waited as the accumulated flakes of snow melted into water droplet jewels on her hat, her coat, her hair. The snow was unexpected, but she had come to accept the bizarre weather in State College. She rang the bell again, then tried the doorknob.

"Hello?" She cracked open the door. "Sam?"

"Come in, Carrie," he called. "I'm in the kitchen."

She closed the door and headed towards where she had heard his voice, passing a glass table with a half-eaten pizza on it, discarded socks on the sofa, and a few unwashed plates scattered on the floor. She followed the smoke to the kitchen. Sam was pulling a char-blackened mess out of the oven. He looked up as she entered.

"Hey," he said. "I'm having a bit of a problem here. Fire extinguisher."

"Where?"

"There."

She followed the direction of his head nod and hefted the extinguisher off its hook. "How do I.—"

"Just pull up and…not on me!"

"Sam, I'm so sorry." She propped the extinguisher up against the wall. "I've never used one of these before…"

"At least the fire's out." His face was blank as he scooped the wayward foam off his body and dropped it onto the smoking remains from the oven. "There. Problem solved."

She removed her coat and offered it to him, but he shook his head.

"I have a towel in my room," he said. "I don't mean to be inhospitable, but I'm going to get cleaned up."

She paused. "Thank you for not being angry."

He looked at her oddly. "No problem. Make yourself at home."

He tossed the blackened pan into the sink and left the kitchen without looking at her. Carrie crossed the kitchen and propped open the window. She heard the distinct rattle of a shower curtain being drawn, then the sound of running water. She glanced at the black and white clock suspended from the wall; she should have at least five minutes.

She moved out of the kitchen and quickly found his room; the door was wide open, the soggy pile of his discarded clothes on the floor. The walls were bare except for a bulletin board on the side farthest away from his window, which contained a single photograph. She walked over to the bulletin board and saw a much younger Sam, a gawky adolescent with a cloud of light brown hair billowing up from his youthful face, not tanned deeply enough to hide a spattering of freckles. The photo-Sam's mouth was open in a grin that revealed two very prominent gaps in his smile, and his eyes were slightly out of focus. A young woman had her arm draped protectively around Sam's sunburned shoulders, and was staring directly at the photographer with fierce intensity. The girl's lips were set in a tight scowl, her presence dark against the bright blue sky and grainy sand of the beach background. The girl's eyes—cold gray hazel—were darkened by eyeliner, and shoved through one eyebrow and earlobe were spiked pieces of metal. The oversized black bathing suit she wore hung on her slight frame and revealed prominent collar bones and pale, flawless skin. Carrie noted one last detail of the young woman—a small black crescent moon tattooed over the arched eyebrow with the earring—and then she heard the shower's water turn off. She went back to the kitchen, pausing as she heard the door to his room close quietly, then scraped the hunk of charred food out of the pan and into the garbage. She had the pan cleaned and dried when Sam came in.

"I want to apologize..." he started, then noted the cleaned plate. "You didn't have to do that."

She shrugged. "What were you making?"

"For you," He hesitated. "Eggplant Parmesan."

"Then I'm glad it burned. You shouldn't have gone to the trouble. I would have been happy with peanut and jelly."

"Good," he said. "I have that."

She watched as he pulled out the jars and the bread. "Can I do anything to help you?"

"No, I'm all right now."

She paused. "I'm sorry I'm late. I got lost."

He shrugged. "If you had been on time, you probably would have saved our lunch. And while I'm sure it would have been better than the standard peanut butter and jelly, we would have missed out on all this fun."

Carrie glanced at him. He met her eyes and held them, but she did not look away.

"Carrie, I'm actually a decent cook," he said. "I got distracted. But before it slips my mind, I want to apologize for the state of the apartment."

"I don't care," she said. "The clutter makes your apartment seem much more representative of your world."

"*I* don't live in filth." He cut the two sandwiches down the middle and separated them onto two plates. "I told my roommates to clean up their sh...their stuff, but—"

"I really don't mind. I would have told you, if I did." She followed him into the living-room and noticed that he had picked up the socks, discarded the pizza box, and straightened the pillows on the second-hand sofa. "Thank you for lunch."

He sat down and handed her a plate. He kept his eyes on his sandwich.

"I'm glad we're finally going to have a chance to talk. Get the mystery cleared up."

"Mystery?"

"Not every girl would agree to live with three random guys."

"What do you mean?"

He looked at her face and decided she really was that innocent. She grew uncomfortable with his sustained silence.

"I should get to class," she said, standing abruptly.

He put down his plate. "You just got here."

"I have to go," she said. "I shouldn't be here."

"Carrie—"

But she was already walking towards his front door, her step brisk. He followed her and was surprised by the fire burning in her eyes when she turned to him.

"I'm sorry, Sam," she said. "But I have to go. Thanks for lunch."

"You didn't eat anything," he said.

Suddenly she stopped her frantic pace and gave him her full attention. "The invitation was more than enough. I really appreciate it."

"You're not making a lot of sense."

"I'm sorry," she said. "I can't explain."

"Maybe some other time," he said. "I still want to talk to you."

She looked confused, then nodded.

He made a last attempt to detain her. "Did you bring me a story?"

She reached into her coat pocket and handed him a slightly crumpled packet of papers. She hesitated. "Do you have one for me?"

"I do. Here." He went into the kitchen, then handed her the copy he had put on the counter for easy access. He glanced over what she had given him. "Why are there teeth marks on this?"

"Colby," she said. "My guinea pig. He eats everything."

He smiled, caught a smile from her in return and decided to try one more time to have a conversation with her. "Before you go, Carrie, will you answer something for me?"

"Yes," she said immediately.

"Enlighten me as to the occasion when I made my first impression on you."

"Last year," she said. "Darren threw that party with all of his friends, and you were making fake ids."

Remembrance flashed through his mind. "You heard me ask if anyone had scissors, and you brought us yours."

"Yes," she said. "And you asked me to marry you."

"I did?" His embarrassment was not alleviated by the amusement he saw flashing in her eyes. "I must have been drunk. I mean, I guess I remember that, too."

"That was a long time ago, Sam."

"It was," he said. "Funny that we both remember it so clearly."

"I remember because you were the first person in that house to be kind to me." She paused. "I appreciated it. A lot."

He felt his pulse quickening. "Carrie, can I see you again?"

"I'll see you in class, Sam."

"I want to see you outside of class."

"Sam." She paused, her hand on the doorknob. "I told you, before I came here…"

"A guy has to try," he said. "And I'm going to keep trying, Carrie."

"You're wasting your time," she said.

"Unless there's another guy involved, I'm not wasting my time."

She looked at him, and opened the door. "Thanks for having me over."

"Any time." He closed the door behind her and then went to the window and watched as she trekked down the snow-flecked sidewalk, her shoulders hunched against the cold, her blue beanie perched on her head in marked contrast to the hair falling down her back like flame.

"Lucky bastard," he muttered. "Whoever he is."

He turned away from the window and went back to his room, where he picked up his soggy clothes and tossed them carelessly into the laundry basket.

She left the downtown area and walked quickly towards the Sackett building on campus, fully intending on going to her American Literature class. But she was already ten minutes late—and when she passed the sprawling building with its rows of glass windows and formidable upstanding pillars, she knew she would never be able to go in. The urge to write had hit her suddenly—an urge she had never been able to deny.

She swerved away from Sackett, her pace increasing. Already her mind was taking her farther and farther away from Penn State and her mundane life. For the first time in a long time, she wasn't searching for Damien; his voice, as she passed his house, startled her.

"Where are you off to in such a hurry?" he asked her.

She stopped in the sunlight and blinked at him. His features blurred in her mind, blending into his face—and then her vision cleared. Only the glare of the sun. "Home."

"Aren't you supposed to be in class?"

"Aren't you?" she shot back.

He stood up and came down the porch steps. The way his eyes raked over her sent blood rushing to her face. Slowly he circled her, cutting the circle closer on his second rotation. Finally she turned to face him and saw a wolfish grin of amusement light his face.

"Where are you coming from?" he asked.

She noticed he had another cigarette behind his ear. "Sam's."

In retrospect, she wished she would have said she was coming from class and spared herself the violent reaction his expression underwent. Still, she was distracted; her mind wanted her to hurry, hurry, before her characters and their dialogues slipped away from her.

"I finished your painting," Damien said, sounding a million miles away. "But I have to be at work in half an hour. Can you come over tonight?"

There was something thrilling in the deep, low tone of his voice. She hesitated. "I can come over after work. If that's not too late."

He smiled. "I'll wait up for you. I won't keep you any longer now, since I know the only reason you skip class is to write."

In the past few moments, under the intensity of his undivided attention, she had forgotten about her writing. But that didn't matter; she always wrote about him. He was smiling because he knew, because she let him read almost everything she wrote—on the restaurant's napkins in between her tables, on the back of her university notes, on anything she could find when the inspiration found her. Once, a poem on the inside of her hand. He had kissed her palm when she finished reading it to him, and her hand still burned with the memory of his lips pressed to her skin...

She looked up and met his gaze. The air hung charged between them. "I'll see you tonight," she promised.

Her heart was still racing as she went to her house, and she would not permit herself to fully realize the direction of her thoughts. She cranked out words into her notebook, ending with a mess of jumbled sentences and phrases that revealed the true turmoil of her emotions.

Her heart sank as she wheeled her grime-streaked bike into her house. The restaurant had been understaffed, and she had ended up staying for four extra hours to help close. She had every intention of going to see Damien—but it was much too late. Still, she would not break her promise to him. She climbed the stairs to his apartment and pushed open his door without knocking.

He was sitting at his desk, his head lowered over his hands. She thought for a moment he might have passed out, but then he looked up.

"Carrie," he said, and a flash of emotion lit his dark eyes.

"I'm sorry," she said. "I didn't mean to stand you up. I got home from work late and I—"

"It doesn't matter." He straightened. "You're here now."

He stood and walked towards her. The heat of his eyes was unbearable, and when he wound a strand of her cinnamon colored hair around his finger, she felt her entire body gravitate towards him. The spark was there, and she knew that tonight could be different.

To divert him, she pushed the book she had brought against his chest, then felt the bolt that went through her when he put his hand over hers. "I want you to read this."

He looked directly at her, and his hand tightened around hers. "Read what?"

"Where the yellow bookmark is," she said, struggling to maintain a steady tone.

"I want you to read 'The Dialogue Between the Priest and the Dying Man'."

He cocked an eyebrow. "You're reading the Marquis de Sade?"

She looked away. "I wanted to find the most subversive voice I could, and test my convictions against—"

"Better to test them with real life experience, Carrie." He ran his fingers lightly up her side. She tried to step away. He did not let her. His arm twined around her waist and he drew her close. She put a hand on his chest; her hand vibrated with the crazy beating of his heart. He covered her hand with his and brought her palm to his lips. His kiss was soft and hot against her skin.

She felt her face flushing. "Damien—"

"I thought you said you trusted me," he said.

"I do."

She was powerless to move away. "But I don't want to use you like this."

He paused, for a second too long. "What if I want to be used?"

She shook her head. "No."

He didn't let her go. "We've had some good times together, haven't we, Carrie?"

She had to force herself to speak, to say the words, to seek the truth and give him a chance to refute what she had heard...

"I heard you've had a lot of fun with a lot of girls," she said.

His eyes, calculating, flashed over her face. "That's the cause of your resistance, then. Not that you don't want to use me, but that you don't want to be like those other women..."

She did not hear him; she was struggling to keep her voice steady. "What I heard. I don't want to believe it. I *can't* believe it. Not about you."

"You can't be that naive." He crossed the room, then studied her from the distance of the faded chair by his window. "Does it surprise you that I've been with other women?"

"No."

"But you look hurt, nonetheless."

She tried hard to keep her composure, but she felt her face crumbling. "It doesn't matter. I still want to be with you."

"I guess that since I'm your Muse you have to keep in contact with me." His voice mocked her. "How's the novel coming, darling?"

"You don't understand." She realized how close she was coming to finally telling him that she loved him and that she wanted to stop talking and thinking and let him take her in his arms and hold her for a while. If only she hadn't learned...

"Carrie?" He stood abruptly. "Damn it, don't cry."

She moved away from him and sat down on the edge of his bed, turning her face away until she was sure she could remain composed. Her eyes fell on the ladder he had made from discarded coils of rope. He had let her use the rope ladder once to descend to the second floor roof; he had held the rope ladder steady as she climbed out his window. He had cheered her on because he knew she was afraid of heights, and then he had come down and stood beside her, and they had looked at the stars...

She glanced up and realized she had not needed to worry about being able to look him in the eye. He was staring down at a sheet of sketch paper in his hand, an odd look on his face. The emptiness in his eyes scared her.

"What's wrong?" she whispered, terrified.

"Your painting, madame," he said, tonelessly.

He turned the painting around. She felt instantly unsteady. She knew this power had been inside him—this beauty, this sensitivity to channel whatever had gone into the painting. Essence, his essence, stared at her in the glowing fireflies weaving in and out of the mist, in the silver brocade of the full moon caressing the dark pines with its magical light, in the opaque figure of a howling wolf beside a tall, dark evergreen tree.

She was not aware that she was moving towards him, called by what she saw in the painting, by that fierce attraction she felt for him—but suddenly, she was near him, closer to him than she had ever been before, and she was reminded that there were no walls anymore.

"Do you want to know why I painted it for you?" he asked.

She kept her eyes on the painting, but felt the tension between them that was always there. She shook her head.

"The painting reminded me of the time we went for a walk that one night," he continued. "When you were so excited to show me that tree."

"I enjoyed our talk that night."

"Our talk." He laughed.

"Why are you laughing?"

"I'm just agreeing with you, that I enjoyed our talk," he said, and paused. "Do you like the painting?"

Finally, she raised her eyes to meet his—and something inside her recoiled.

"I asked you a question," he said.

Coldness crept into her consciousness, and the awareness that something was very wrong. "I love it."

She heard the click of his lighter, like some far away, distant thing. His eyes, dark and dangerous, held her fascinated—but then she smelled the smoke, and her eyes flew to the bottom corner of the painting, where the acrylic had started curling in black streaks, eaten by the fire. She lunged for the painting. He caught her around the waist, restrained her, held the painting away from her. She struggled against him, but he was strong; his grip on her was tight and unrelenting, crushing her to him.

She watched as the flames licked at the canvas, until nothing was left but a curling mess of black ashes and a thick stream of acrid gray smoke. He dropped the remains of the painting, and the ashes floated to the floor as the flickering flame died. She went slack, and as soon as he let her go, she backed away from him.

"You bastard," she said, and her voice trembled.

When he smiled, she felt the blackness of hatred coil through her as powerfully as the feelings of love and hope had moments before. Her hands clenched into fists by her sides, and her breath came in shallow, ragged bursts. She felt tears building up in her eyes, but she would never let him see her cry. She trained her attention on the ashes littering the ground. "How could you?"

"It's really quite simple," he said. "You wanted the painting from me. I wanted something from you. We can't always get what we want."

"What?" A moment's confusion cut through her anger. "What do you want from me?"

"One night," he said.

"Don't touch me." Still she felt powerless to move away from him as his hand cupped her cheek.

His eyes glinted with triumph. "The pedestal comes crashing down, and you find you're just like everyone else."

She slapped him. She listened to the echo of the ugly sound, felt the stinging sensation of the force on the palm of her hand. His arm tightened around her for the slightest moment and she felt herself respond, and then he let her go. And laughed.

"You might not believe me, Carrie," he said, his eyes dancing. "But you're making a mistake in trying to remain virtuous. Because you're acting against what you want to make that choice. And nothing good ever comes from that."

She said nothing, but moved towards the door. His eyes followed her.

"Come back when you decide to stop fighting what you feel. Not before then." His voice held an undercurrent of something that deeply unsettled her. "But I like seeing you like this. So utterly human."

Anger, disgust, uncertainty coursed through her, and she turned to him in a rage.

Suddenly the smile died on his lips. He tucked the cigarette behind his ear and stood, a new light in his eyes. She stood, frozen, as he started towards her, then turned with him as he walked around her in a wide circle.

"Stand still," he ordered, and took another turn around her when she obeyed. He came to a stop directly in front of her and tilted her face up. His eyes traced the lines of her features. His touch was rough, his proximity unromantic; his attention to her was the appraisal of an artist's eye.

"You'll have to sit for me sometime," he said finally. "You're beautiful."

She blinked back the tears that came into her eyes with the recognition of the Damien she knew. "Paint me now."

"I can't paint you now." He let her go. "Not when you're so goddam sad."

"I don't know why you're acting like this. Like two different people." Her jaw set. "But I still care about you."

He turned to face her, and anger flared in his dark eyes. "Get out of here, Carrie."

The darkness of his look frightened her. She felt like she was suffocating, choking on the stale air in his room. She stumbled away from him, dazed by her conflicting emotions, knowing only that she had to get away from him, had to get out of his room...

But she did not want to be in her room, where she would be able to see his window, because the desire to be with him was still there—

unrelenting, irrational, devastating. She felt the vestiges of his warm touch on her skin like a Sahara wind, whispering heat into her heart. She went to her living room, but the futon was hard, the living room drafty and cool, and she could not sleep. Feeling half mad, wondering why friendship no longer seemed to satisfy him, she fell off the futon and raced out of her house. She ran down Park Avenue to the Blue Course golf course, relishing the strength in her body, the coolness of the night, the darkness of the woods away from the streetlights.

On the unlit bike trail she slowed, determined to walk until her head cleared. A full moon hung in the dark sky, and around her the tall, lonely trees seemed cognizant of her emotion. She felt a comfort, a presence, on the lonely path she followed, but once filled with the quiet serenity, she turned out of the golf course and walked back home.

The light in his room was off.

Sam pulled his windbreaker tightly around him as he walked outside and watched his breath streaming out in front of him like the mists on a Scottish moor. He missed Scotland, though he had only been there for a semester. He had picked up the habit of going for long walks by himself at night—a habit he had carried back with him. When his heart rebelled against his mind, when being young and ignorant became a liability rather than a liberation and he could not sleep—he walked. He walked for miles, with only the stars in the sky to keep him company, and hoped that in exhausting himself physically he could gain some mental serenity.

He had seen a drop of dried blood on the sink in their bathroom. He had searched for an instrument, for a bloody tissue in the garbage can which he could attribute to an unintended nose bleed—but there was nothing. She had removed whatever she had used to do the cutting, if she had cut herself.

He hadn't talked to Tessa in two weeks, and could tell that she still lived in his house only because he occasionally heard the recordings of Gregorian chants coming from her room, saw candles flickering in her window, glimpsed her briefly in the halls as she went to her room from class or the shower. He liked seeing her out of the shower the most, because then—with the dark eye-makeup she wore washed away, her face rosy from the steam of hot water—he was reminded that she was human. At other times he was not so sure. He tried to talk to her on the rare occasions he saw her, but her answers to his inquiries were always brief and to the point; he had gotten the distinct impression that she preferred to keep to herself.

He realized he shouldn't be worried about her. Tessa Beaumont radiated, if anything, a sense of austere self-sufficiency. But he did worry, because Tessa reminded him of Claudia. Claudia had been interested in the things Tessa liked, and Claudia had seemed fine, too. He hadn't seen the warning signs with Claudia, and then one day, when he was fourteen, he had come home and found her dead. He didn't want to make the same mistake with Tessa, if Tessa was in any kind of similar danger...

He had gone through her room once, when she had been in the shower—to reassure himself that she would not end up like Claudia. The search had greatly comforted him; though the candles and pentacles were there, Tessa had filled her room with flowers and plants and painted on the wall in elegant black letters, *Life is beautiful.* He had left on seeing the wall; he had only wanted to make sure she was okay. She had never found out about his excursion into her private sphere.

He realized, afterwards, that there was very little resemblance between Tessa and Claudia—that maybe his propensity to protect Tessa resulted rather because she reminded him of Carrie, due to their similar living conditions—except that, compared to Carrie, Tessa seemed even less human. She made no attempt to get to know any of them—even though they were all half in love with her, to the best of Sam's knowledge—nor did she seem aware of the cool attitudes of his housemates towards her, after they realized her complete lack of interest in them.

Sam turned away from College Avenue and wandered north, passing the tall spire of Old Main and the lantern lit walks, noting the relative deadness of the campus at 3:00 AM. He passed the streetlights and headed towards the darkness at the North end of campus, near the golf course. He craved nature, not the solitude of empty streets.

Beside him on the glistening street, a sleek black Buick roared by, spraying him with gray sludge. He turned in that direction in irritation, and from the corner of his eye, he saw a flash of auburn disappearing into the darkness of the woods.

Carrie? He wouldn't put it past her, but running that late by herself wasn't safe. His brow furrowed, but there was nothing he could do. She hadn't seen him—and she had been running fast. He turned onto Park Avenue, hoping that she might double back and see him.

He wished he hadn't burned the Eggplant Parmesan. That was the next item on his mental list to consider as he continued his ambling, solitary journey.

Carrie was sitting on the porch when Sam walked up to the Marshmallow in the early morning. Her hands were stretched out over a small fire burning in the middle of the sidewalk.

"Carrie?"

"Good morning, Sam," she said.

He stared at her. "Did they lock you out last night?"

She looked at him reproachfully. "They didn't do it on purpose, Sam. I left the house to go for a walk, and when I came back the door was locked. There was no way they could have known I had forgotten my keys."

He didn't tell her that it was common knowledge that she never carried her keys, because she never locked her doors. "How long have you been out here?"

"Since three," she said, not looking at him.

"Jesus Christ, Carrie," he said. "Why didn't you wake one of them up?"

"I didn't mind being out here." She paused. "Do you have a key?"

"Dan gave me a key, since he knew I would be coming over so early…"

"Can you let me in?"

He started. "Sure."

He moved by her awkwardly as she stood and stamped out the flames of the fire. As she passed him he felt the cold radiating from her body. He followed her inside.

"I'm glad you're an early riser," she said, putting on a kettle for tea.

He stared at her. "Promise me that the next time you get locked out, you'll wake someone up."

She turned and looked at him for a moment. "No," she said. "The next time I get locked out, I'll break in. Last night, I just wanted to build a fire."

She turned the stove to the number four; he knew it was the number four because if they turned the burners any higher initially the smoke detector would go off.

"Why do you build fires?" he asked.

"I was a camp counselor for awhile," she said, going to the cupboard for a mug. "I learned so I could teach the kids, and I guess I got addicted. Oh, I forgot about the ashes."

He saw her go back into the hallway, heard the screen door slam shut and the metallic scraping of the shovel on the cement sidewalk outside the white block house. She came back a minute later, her cheeks freshly rosy from the biting cold of the winter air. She shook her head. "Snow in November."

"You could have caught pneumonia," he started.

She shrugged. "If I hadn't had a match to get the fire going, I could always have gone next door. I have a friend who would have let me stay there if I asked."

"So why didn't you ask her?"

Carrie looked up, and he knew she wasn't going to answer his question. "Would you like a cup of tea, Sam?"

"I'll pass," he said, wracking his mind to see if his friends had told him anything about whoever lived next door. "I'm going to wake Dan."

"Good luck," she said. She moved back to the stove, turned the dial up to eight. Her silence implied that she was waiting for him to leave.

"Carrie." He paused. "I won't tell them about the fire."

She turned. "I don't care if you do."

"I mean, I won't let them know that they successfully locked you out."

She looked at him, hard. "Cats and mice, Sam?"

He was confused. "What?"

"Never mind." She paused. "Thanks for letting me in."

"Any time," he said. "I'll see you in class."

She went up the steps to do whatever work she hadn't gotten through the night before, as if nothing out of the ordinary had happened at all.

Christine wanted her to come home.

That one question—*When are you coming home?*—upset Carrie more than everything else going on in her life. The thought of going home, of going back, still made her profoundly uneasy, though she did not doubt her mother's sincerity in wanting to see her.

She returned the letter to its envelope with shaking fingers, looked out her window, and saw the room in the house across from hers was dark. What a show she would have to put on, if she went home. Christine would never approve of the way she lived: skipping classes to work on her writing, waitressing instead of studying, attaching herself to a drug-abusing artistic genius. Being dysfunctional had never proved an obstacle to the Crenshaws' solidarity in accepting their own back to *where they belong,* as Christine wrote—but would they accept Damien? Carrie remembered her cousins' reactions to the little she had told them about him; they would never accept him if they knew all that she had learned. She didn't want to be questioned about him—not when everything had become so confused in her own mind.

Nor had she answered Damien's casual questions about why she never went home; any response would have revealed the paranoia, the neurotics, the intensity, the drive for achievement, the unhappiness in general, the dark pasts and hidden secrets of the Crenshaw clans. How could she possibly introduce Damien to the essence of her family and expect him to accept it? To have him accept her?

Because she still wanted him to accept her, despite the changed dynamic between them, despite what she had learned about him. And for their story to continue playing out, she needed to be near him. Even if he hurt her. Shaking, she hid Christine's letter in the bottom drawer of her desk.

She knew she would not be going home until winter break. But winter break was closer than she cared to realize, and she wondered if there were enough time left to make sense of the change in Damien before she left.

Sam startled her. He could tell by the way Tessa jerked when he came into the kitchen and said her name, by the way she spattered droplets of cream colored batter onto the counter. He was not surprised by her reaction: it was four-thirty in the morning, and she was dressed in a black taffeta slip that did not cover much of her pale skin.

"I didn't know you were awake," Tessa said as she walked to the table and picked up a black lace cover up. His eyes followed her as she pulled the folds of the garment tightly across her body.

"I just got home," he said. No marks that he could see, not on the wrists or the arms.

"From work?" She knotted the belt around her waist.

"Yeah." He leaned against the counter. "What are you making?"

"Sugar cookies."

"At 4:30 in the morning?"

"Would you like some?"

"Thanks, but I'm going to bed." He paused. "You never sleep, do you?"

She shrugged. "I'm not tired."

He listened to the long, deliberate scraping strokes she made with the spoon against the side of the bowl. "Just for the record, Tessa, I am trying to be nice to you."

"Thank you, Sam."

His comment had not even meant enough to get her to stop stirring the batter. "I just don't want you lumping all of us together. I know Ryan and Claude haven't been the most friendly people in the world, but you do stay in your room all the time—"

"I hadn't thought about it."

"You mean you haven't even noticed how they avoid you?"

She looked at him, finally, with her strange eyes—eyes like translucent blue glass. "I can't desecrate my free time by worrying over trifles, Sam."

He felt the gaze of her pale blue eyes like a weight; he wanted to go to his room and he wanted to take her with him. He crossed himself quickly, without thinking.

"Why did you do that?" she asked him sharply.

"For my sinful thoughts, because you look beautiful." There was no point in lying to her; Sam felt like she could read his mind. "Do you think less of me for thinking so?"

She smiled, the first smile he had ever gotten from her. She turned her back on him. "I respect you more for your self-awareness. Goodnight, Sam."

He paused. "The batter shouldn't be watery like that. You need to add some more flour."

"How much?"

He moved next to her, surprised by her openness to his suggestion.

"Try half a cup to a cup," he said, trying not to mind when she moved rigidly to the side. "My mom and I used to…well, you wouldn't care about that. Good night."

"Good night," she said. "Thank you for your help."

He started to leave, and then a thought flashed through his mind and he turned back. "Tessa, it's not a big deal or anything, but when you're done taking a shower would you mind not pulling the curtain closed?" He paused. "I always think someone's behind the curtain and forgot to lock the door, and I wouldn't want to walk in on you."

"That's very polite of you," she said. "But that's not why you asked. You're afraid of something."

He felt himself go cold. "You say that as if you knew for a fact—"

"I do know." She stopped stirring. "I don't know exactly what…but that is none of my business." She turned away. "I'll remember about the shower curtain, Sam."

"Thank you," he said. "By the way, Tessa, I'm going to be going home soon for winter break. You should pretty much have the place to yourself."

He heard the scraping of the spoon stop for a brief moment, then start again. She said nothing. He left her in the kitchen scraping away at the bowl.

He did not bother to turn on the light as he stripped out of his clothes and stumbled over to bed; he was exhausted and wanted to pass out. Though he could not see the photograph of Claudia on his bulletin board he knew it was there, immortalizing them both, immortalizing the moment, and he wondered again why she had killed herself, and why he had to have been the one to find her.

Carrie kept her eyes focused narrowly on the road in front of her as she approached her house, willing herself not to look at Damien's window. She had left in the middle of her nineteenth century literature exam because she felt the compulsion to write—not because she had wanted to see him. But his silhouette was there, dark against the white walls of his room, and she found herself distracted. She hurried into the white block of a house and went directly to the kitchen. She was relieved to find no one was there.

She dropped her backpack on the floor and left her coat and gloves on the counter. She would write later; she had to calm and focus herself first. Forcing herself to sing in rebellion against everything she was feeling, she assembled the ingredients she would need. The basement stairs creaked and the door opened, and suddenly Sam was standing before her.

The song died on her lips, and a fierce blush blazed across her cheeks. "Hi, Sam. I didn't know anyone was here."

"Just Dan and me." He smiled at her. "I heard you singing and I thought I'd come up and say hello. You have a beautiful voice, you know."

"Thank you," she said.

"What are you making?"

"Brownies."

He hesitated. "Are you okay?"

She glanced at him sharply. "I'm fine."

"It's just that my sister used to bake when she was upset," he said, suddenly. "She was such a smart girl, and she never let on she was unhappy. But one night when I was younger, I couldn't sleep and she was up cooking and I could tell that something wasn't right, and from then on I could always make the connection."

Carrie waited until she was sure he had finished speaking. "Is she the reason you like to cook?"

"I hadn't thought about it," he said.

She looked down. "You can help me, if you'd like."

"Only if you take the blame if they burn. I don't want another mark on my permanent record."

She laughed, relinquishing the boxed mix. "Would you mind reading what I'm supposed to combine?"

"Sure." He put his elbows on the counter, leaning down for support.

"Sam, don't..." she started, but he already felt the counter moving downward, already saw the open container of flour sliding off and upending itself on the floor.

"I'm sorry," he said.

"It's not your fault." She stooped to pick up the container of flour. "This house is falling apart. I should have warned you."

"Is there some way that we can save most of the flour?" he asked.

"Why try?" She shrugged, then a mischievous gleam entered her eyes. The next moment the flour container was empty, the remaining contents spilled over his head.

"You didn't," he said, wiping the powder from his face as she sat on the floor in front of him, hands covering her mouth and her wide eyes announcing that she couldn't believe she just had. He grabbed an egg.

"Don't..." she started.

"Retribution!" he hollered, and the egg sailed through the air and exploded against her shoulder.

"Ow," she said.

Instant regret. "Did I hurt you?"

She stood and turned her back on him. He stayed where he was. "I'm sorry, Carrie."

She turned back to him. She had three eggs cradled against her chest; her other hand tossed an egg up and down. Up and down.

"You wouldn't," he said.

She smiled. "All's fair in love and war."

"Then throw the eggs," he said. "But not clichés, Carrie. Not—"

The three eggs soared at him like missiles. He threw up his arms to shield himself, grinning as the eggs exploded against his body. He stood to chase after her, then saw that she had stopped smiling.

"Hi, Dan," she said.

Sam's six foot two, blond hair and blue-eyed friend stood on the threshold of the kitchen, his mouth half open.

"What the hell is going on here?"

"Good question," she said. She turned. "What were we doing, Sam?"

"Making brownies," he said.

She moved back to the bowl, calmly flicking egg off her shoulder. "Don't worry. I'll clean everything up."

Dan continued to stare at her as she tore open the brownie package and poured the contents into the bowl.

"Are you coming back downstairs, Sam?" he finally asked.

"I should get cleaned up first."

Dan stared at them; then they were alone again together. Sam glanced at her, but her back was to him.

"I'm going to take a shower," he said. "I'll be back to help you clean up."

"I don't mind." Her voice was unreadable.

He did not look at her as he left, already knowing her eyes were still glowing with laughter. He didn't trust himself to say anything to her just then.

"Carrie!"

His voice, somehow clear over the angry claps of thunder, cut straight to her heart. She opened her eyes, blinked back the stinging streams of water flowing down her face. The rain blurred her vision, but she saw the outline of his profile backlit by the light of his apartment room. Her heart leapt, but she closed her eyes and tried to shut him out of her thoughts.

"What the hell do you think you're doing?" he yelled.

She turned her face up to the rain and did not answer him.

The sound of a screen door opening and closing. She kept her eyes closed, wanting to sense if she could feel him as he came towards her— but the air around her remained empty and cold. She opened her eyes and saw him standing under the overhang of the porch, rain dripping like melted crystal all around him.

"Come out of the rain," he called.

"I don't want to," she said, trying to seem nonchalant when his presence was hurting her. "You come out here."

Without waiting to see his reaction she closed her eyes and tuned into the sound of the rain and the feel of the clothes sticking clammily to her skin. Her heart was pounding.

"Carrie," he said again, this time right beside her.

"Isn't it beautiful?" she asked, not looking at him. "The wind and the thunder and the rain, but most of all the lightning."

"Why is the lightning your favorite?"

She looked up at the sky as streak lightning broke over their heads and threaded its way through the dense, blue-gray cloud. "Because it makes me afraid that I'm going to die."

"That makes perfect sense, Carrie."

"It does," she said, ignoring his sarcasm.

"I'm starting to understand you." He paused. "From now on when you refer to something as beautiful, I'll know to be prepared for something painful, violent, or morbid."

"The lightning makes me realize how much I don't want to die," she said softly. "It makes me realize how grateful I am to be alive."

When he was silent she opened her eyes and looked at him. The storm had blown a tornado through her thoughts and they were all out of order; she couldn't understand why he was looking at her like that.

He brushed a wet strand of hair away from her face. "Will you come inside?"

He had asked her the same question moments before—but it was different now. The events of the past weeks—the repeated innuendos, the burned canvas, the dark flash of his eyes and his anger—broke through the sudden thrill of her emotions but disappeared with the next flash of lighting. The storm was magic; everything except the pounding of her heart seemed trivial in its midst.

The look he fixed on her was ravenous with impatience. The force of his naked desire filled her with a sense of power and confidence. She felt the storm at her back and drew strength from its unleashed fury; she felt not herself, but a wild and untamable thing.

She did not move away when he stepped closer and put his arms around her. She did not respond at all as he pulled her closer to him, so close that she had to look up at him to maintain eye contact, to see the passion burning in his eyes.

"You're beautiful," he said.

"So you think I'm violent and morbid and ugly…" she started.

His arms tightened around her. "Carrie."

His passion would suffocate her. She looked into his eyes and suddenly she was terrified, terrified of the thought of leaving the shelter of the rain for the room at the end of the third story hallway, the cheap white-washed apartment where he wanted to be alone with her.

She thought of them there, behind the closed door, and heard the undeniable command that she leave him immediately, that she remain away from the forbidden ground and the wild dance of his eyes…

"I'm going to stay right here," she said.

His arms remained locked around her waist. "It's safer inside."

"You know it's not," she argued. "It just seems safer."

He stiffened. "You're going to stand here in the rain. You're crazy."

"You're standing in the rain," she challenged. "If that makes me crazy, then that also makes—"

"The only reason I came out into the rain was to come and get you," he said. He dropped his arms from around her but remained dangerously close. "If you're not coming back with me, then I'm going back inside."

"I do want to talk to you." She could not ignore the coldness that had crept into her heart. "We could go for a walk."

"No."

She looked at him hopefully. "You're already wet."

The look he fixed on her was murderous. "I can't believe you," he said slowly. "To be in the midst of something so powerful and not to be moved an inch." He broke off abruptly, turned away from her. "Enjoy your walk, Carrie."

As she watched him leave her, as she heard the screen door close behind him, she felt deeply shaken—as if he had been the reason for the sudden surge of happiness and power within her and not the storm, and that when he had left he took with him the chance for some great opportunity. She turned her back on his house and walked onto the sidewalk, beside the street that ran with water like a dark river, but with each step she lost confidence. She wanted to be with him, in that cheap white-washed room at the end of the third story hallway.

The power of the storm now struck her with more fear than beauty, and as she walked back to the white block house she became increasingly sure that she would be struck by the lightning. Even then the adventure would have been worth it, to have been—for one moment—swept up in the heady power and beauty of that moment when she had felt that wild and untamed thing inside her.

She went inside as the last traces of the storm rolled by overhead, but realized that in that moment all she felt was wet and cold.

Inexplicable.

She looked out her window at the dark, gaping emptiness of his window. She turned her attention uneasily back to the open notebook in front of her, stared at the ink that had crawled across the pages like black blood.

The words were always about him.

She had not seen him in three weeks.

She had fought herself successfully every night to keep from going to him, and she could not fight any longer.

Don't act against your intuition, she pleaded with herself, even as she realized she was steeling herself to see him that night, no matter what—because she had to see him before she left. She was sure nothing good would come from willingly putting herself into that center of dead energy she felt—but she could not accept not understanding why the dynamic between them had become so dangerous.

Late, too late for her to be going to his apartment, but she went anyway. She struggled against the inner rebellion and wave of panic she felt as she climbed the steps to his apartment. Her jaw set in resolution; she would never be afraid of confronting him. Not when she loved him. She knocked, and when he opened the door she knew she had made a mistake.

His hair had grown and tangled around features slashed with shadows from the hallway light. His eyes, red, skittered over her face, giving her the distinct impression that he did not see her.

"What the fuck do you want?" he snarled.

She stood on the threshold of his room, trembling, too shocked not to respond.

"I wanted to see you," she said. "I'm sorry, I'll come back if this is a bad—"

"I don't want you to come back," he said. "Haven't I made that clear to you by now?"

She stared at him. He was shaking with rage; she could see it radiating off of him in the tenseness of his neck and shoulders. "What's…what's wrong?"

"You're not supposed to be here."

She felt like she was confronting a savage animal; she barely found the courage to stand her ground. "Damien."

He turned and stared at her. Neither one of them knew what to do with that locked gaze, but he made the first move.

"I'm going to ask you nicely." He exhaled. "To get the fuck out of this house right now."

She bit her lip. "Aren't you a *hero*."

"Carrie." For a moment he spoke in the tone of voice she recognized, and she lifted her tear-filled eyes to him. The anger and hatred that burned in his eyes destroyed any scrap of confidence she felt, and she backed away from him. She kept backing away from him, and she was glad when he didn't follow her.

"I just wanted to say goodbye," she said. "I won't bother you anymore."

She saw him pause, but before he could say anything, she turned and fled.

Carrie stared at her reflection in the mirror, then quickly lowered her eyes. Her hands trembled as she turned on the tap water, and when she reached for the toothbrush it fell out of her hands and clattered into the sink. She flinched: the noise sounded like the report of a gun, the water that bled into the drain like the crashing of waves over a cliff…

If she hadn't fallen in love with him, there wouldn't have been a problem. If she hadn't remained in love with him, there definitely wouldn't have been a problem. But there was a problem.

She had to get out of the house. She had to get away from him.

The night's cool air cut through her winter jacket, and the slush on the street soaked through her brown canvas shoes, freezing her toes. She stopped on the sidewalk as a car zinged by on College Avenue, then turned away from the streetlights and walked down the connecting alley. She was not ready to go home to confront her unfinished homework or her writer's log, and she had enough on her mind to justify letting herself walk until she uncluttered her thoughts.

She stopped two shops down from the main street, in front of a sign above a narrow shop that she must have passed by dozens of times without noticing. The moon reflected on a sign which portrayed the design of a hand with an Egyptian-looking eyeball in the palm. She stared through the dark windows, the vapor from her breath frosting the glass in front of her as she read the displayed information.

??Palm Reading Special $15??
Below which, was written in elegant script:
Tarot Spreads. Crystal Gazing. Incense and more.

She looked up at the sign as snowflakes rained down around her like silver glitter; she was standing in front of Madame Sally K's, the local fortune-telling shop. Carrie peered into the windows again, then jerked as the door to the shop opened. A young woman, bundled in a thick gray scarf and a white ski jacket lined with faux fur, stepped out and closed the door behind her.

"Hey, Carrie." The young woman smiled and lowered her hood; her hair shone like finely spun gold. "I don't think you recognize me, but we work together at the restaurant. I just started my training."

"How long ago did you start?" Her voice sounded odd, disjointed, and Carrie cleared her throat.

"Two weeks. I've only worked with you once, though. I'm Tessa."

Carrie shook her hand, glanced at the store. "Do you work here?"

"I help out," Tessa said. "Mainly just with Tarot, because I'm fascinated by the cards. By the archetypes, and the truths they represent."

"You believe in this stuff?"

"Not the fortune telling aspect of it," Tessa said. "But I've found the Tarot to be a powerful tool for self-discovery, when used correctly." She paused. "The shop will be open tomorrow, from eight to ten, if you wanted to get a reading."

"I'm just passing by," Carrie said. "I just got off work, and I needed to clear my head."

"That place can be a zoo," Tessa agreed. "But I heard you talking to one of the cooks the other night. It sounded like you were having a really good conversation."

"With Sam?" She nodded. "Conversations like those keep me sane. They give me something to live for."

"I would really like to talk to you at some point." Tessa paused. "Do you have time to get a cup of coffee?"

"Now?"

She shrugged. "Why not?"

Carrie paused. "I have some time."

Tessa smiled as they started walking. "So tell me more about Sam."

"There's nothing to tell, Tessa."

"I don't believe you," she said. "I've heard him ask you out at least three times."

Carrie felt herself blushing slightly and was glad the darkness would not reveal her sudden emotion to Tessa.

"He's not serious."

Tessa kept her tone light. "He sounded pretty serious to me."

"He knows I'll refuse." She did not understand the sudden affinity she felt for Tessa. "That's why he asks me."

"You should accept his offer. Make it a joke on him, if it's a joke at all. You have to leave yourself open to people who come your way. Sam is a good guy." Tessa paused. "I know. You should ask him out for coffee."

"I don't want to give him the wrong idea."

Tessa shook her head. "I mean the next time he asks you out drinking, ask him out for coffee. Give him an alternative and see what he does."

"I'll think about it," she said. "Can we talk about something else?"

"Sure," she said immediately. "Let's get inside, though. It's freezing out here."

Carrie looked up in alarm at the neon lights of the Diner; time had passed more quickly than she had realized. She followed Tessa inside, then trailed after the waitress to a red vinyl-covered booth in the Diner.

After they ordered, Tessa added a cream to her coffee and studied the swirling pattern of the milk. Carrie watched her intently.

"Let's talk about the animus," Tessa said.

"What?"

"The ideal male essence, traditionally representative of all your strengths as well as all the strengths you wish to have. The male's equivalent is the anima—the idealization of woman, as presented in so much of the poetry we read. What I think is interesting is that the animus is the embodiment of a soul, while the anima is an embodiment of the spirit. Is there a difference, I wonder, between the two?"

Carrie smiled. "You don't lose any time getting to the heart of a discussion, do you?"

"Can't afford to. People who like to discuss things are few and far between." She added another cream to her coffee. "I have to make the most of every encounter with a kindred spirit that I can."

She felt refreshed and decided not to waste any time either. "You learned about these concepts from studying the Tarot?"

"They came up in a book I was reading."

"How did you get involved with this?"

Tessa took a sip of her coffee, smiled, removed the straw and put it on the napkin in front of her. "Religion never resonated with me. I wanted more knowledge, so I turned to the occult." She sighed. "Carrie, don't look at me like that. 'Occult' doesn't refer to dark magic or evil energy. 'Occult' simply means hidden knowledge. The field has gained a negative connotation because it's forbidden knowledge. The knowledge that got Adam and Eve kicked out of the Garden. Damning knowledge."

"You want that?"

"I want truth," Tessa said, looking at her levelly. "So do you."

"You assume."

"Maybe," Tessa replied, her voice soft. "But I believe it's okay to take chances every once in awhile. You know, I'm not supposed to have caffeine. No mind-altering substances of any kind, but my head hurts so badly." She took another sip of her coffee, then switched to the tall glass of water beside it. "I'm just being honest, Carrie. I think you're different. I think you have a very strong intuition, or else very strong forces acting on you right now in life. I've learned to trust my instincts." She paused again. "So what's your story?"

"My story?" Carrie paused. "I've written my life into so many different ones."

"You're a writer?" Tessa's blue eyes searched her face. "Do you have a Muse? Someone who inspires you?"

"I do. But it's complicated."

Tessa sipped the last of the water out of the glass. Her eyes, moonlike, never wavered from Carrie's face.

"His name is Damien," she said finally.

The change in Tessa's expression was instantaneous. She inhaled so sharply that Carrie looked at her, concerned.

"Do not go back to that house," Tessa said, in a voice that chilled her.

Carrie glanced at her. "I haven't even told you anything about him, and already your intuition is strong enough to tell me to stay away?"

Tessa's eyes shifted. "I'm sorry for not listening."

"That's not the point, Tessa. I don't care about apologies. I'm trying not to go back to his house." She paused. "But if he came to me, I don't know if I'd be able to turn him away again. And I don't like knowing that the distance between us is less a conscious decision on my part, and more a result of disinterest on his."

"If the end result—your moving on—is the same, why does it matter?"

"I want a clean break. I want to know that at some point in the future, I won't think about him. And until *I'm* the one who consciously makes that decision, I don't know how I'll be able to be sure."

"You are making a conscious decision, Carrie. You're taking a stance every time you stop yourself from going to him. Direct your action, and the Universe will conspire to help you. If you make the effort to...what?"

"When you say 'The Universe,' what do you mean?"

"I don't believe in God. So I use those words as a substitute."

Carrie paused. "You were saying something about directing action."

"If you make the effort to seek out inspiration elsewhere, you'll find it," Tessa continued. "Something will happen. As you let him drop out of your life, other people will become more important to you, other influences will become more meaningful."

As Tessa broke eye contact, Carrie was left feeling disoriented. She forced herself to take a sip of the strong coffee in front of her and felt grounded once more.

Carrie paused. "I'd like to talk to you more, but I have to get home."

"I should go, too," Tessa said, standing.

Carrie followed Tessa out into the night, welcoming the biting cold that reawakened her to reality. Tessa inhaled deeply, then turned to Carrie.

"Thank you for agreeing to come with me. I enjoyed talking with you." She smiled. "I'll see you at work."

"Stay warm," Carrie called as she walked away, across the street and back towards her house. The restaurant, her schoolwork, even her thoughts of the past hours, seemed very far away.

"It's the liberal hot spot," Tessa told her, stamping her boots on the black mats inside the bookstore café. "It's the coolest place in this entire town. You can get any book you want here."

The inside of the store was brightly lit, with colorful paper cranes and glittering plastic snowflakes hanging suspended from the ceiling. The soft rhythm of bongo drums beat in the corner where three African Americans with beards and dreadlocks were pounding away, their eyes closed, lost in the world of their music. Carrie scanned the crowd, noting an elderly man in the corner whose head had sunken onto his chest in sleep; a pink-haired young woman and a handsome, athletic looking male in a corner locked in an intense conversation; a woman with dark sunglasses and long, steel-gray hair pulled back in a ponytail bobbing her head in time to the music, a cane resting against the side of her table and a Golden Retriever in a black harness panting at her feet.

"Esoterica, philosophy, how-to-garden books," Tessa said. "It's all here, and if they don't have what you want, they can special order it, just like any mainstream book store. Let's get our coffee, then we can go into the stacks where it's quieter."

The stacks were past the lights and music of the café. Carrie glanced around the jam-packed shelves as Tessa led the way to the back of the store, a coffee in her hand.

"This place seems completely removed from the rest of the store," she said.

Tessa nodded. "You can lose track of time back here. This place is a mind trip."

"Do you write here?"

"I'm not a serious writer. I have other outlets for my creative energy."

"What do you do?"

"Belly dance," Tessa said. "And if you've never tried it, I'm going to teach you. I've never found another activity that gives females so much confidence and self-respect. Dancing helps sharpen my intuition, too. When I'm done dancing for an hour by myself I feel so much stronger. So much more put together."

"How did you get interested in belly dance?" she asked casually.

Tessa paused for so long that Carrie was afraid she wasn't going to answer. "Growing up, I needed something to do to get away from my house. Something to make me feel confident. Belly dance seemed like a good choice. I followed the flash of intuition." She smiled. "I'm glad I did. My dance instructor became one of my best friends, and she helped me get settled into the Burrough Street Youth Haven."

"You ran away?"

"When I was fifteen."

Carrie paused. "If it's too personal..."

Tessa shrugged. "My dad used to beat me and my mom. My brother was usually too high to stop him. It got to a point where I couldn't take it anymore." She waved away the words that Carrie was starting to say. "I've been on my own for awhile, and belly dance made life bearable before then. By the way, my Belly Dance One class starts in two weeks. Sessions aren't that expensive, but if you don't have the money I'll teach you for free, since you're my friend." She paused. "What is your family like, Carrie?"

"Large and dysfunctional."

Tessa shook her head. "Every family is dysfunctional nowadays."

Carrie looked at her quickly. "I don't want to give you the wrong idea. I love my family."

"Must be nice." She paused. "So tell me more about Sam."

"Sam?" Carrie looked at her blankly. "Tessa, I don't want to get caught up in another infatuation."

"What *do* you want?" Tessa asked.

To let myself love, she started to say, but bit back the words. She shook her head. "I don't know."

"What we have to understand right now is that we have to be honest with each other." Tessa paused. "Regardless of how you act, you should never deny what you feel, Carrie."

Carrie felt the weight of Tessa's attention on her; she was suddenly sure that Tessa knew exactly what she was thinking and blushed. She glanced away from her. "I asked Sam out for coffee."

For a moment, Tessa was silent, and Carrie sensed she was disappointed. "And?"

"He looked at me like I was crazy," Carrie said. "And all of the other cooks laughed."

Tessa smiled. "What did you say to him?"

"I told him I would love to go out for a cup of coffee and an intellectual discussion." She paused. "No one took me seriously, least of all Sam."

"But you asked him and he heard you. And now you've demonstrated to the Universe that you're willing to open yourself up to new possibilities. Everything will get easier from this point on."

"But those possibilities right now seem…terrifying." Carrie paused. "And Tessa, trying to see other people right now feels dishonest."

Tessa's eyes bore into her. "What do you mean?"

"I want…" Carrie paused, and could not bring herself to say the words.

"You said you didn't know what you wanted," Tessa challenged her quietly. "Were you telling me the truth?"

"No." Still, she would not be able to tell Tessa what was truly on her mind. "Don't you ever worry about making a mistake by being too open?"

"I live my life as I think is right." Tessa paused. 'If that's not enough in the end, then fuck that."

Carrie smiled. "I've never heard you swear before."

"It's a shock, isn't it?" Tessa paused, and then her eyes lit up. "Carrie, there's a Hafla next Sunday."

"A what?"

"A belly dance and pot-luck combo. You should come. You'll meet a lot of interesting people, and they often showcase the different kinds of belly dance, like Tribal, Egyptian, Cabaret..."

"I'd like to come." She paused. "How much does it cost?"

"It's free. Just bring some food to share." Tessa glanced at her face. "What reservations do you have?"

She hesitated. "Wasn't belly dancing created to seduce men?"

"NO, way off the mark. The original bellydancers would perform for the women in the harems, not the sheiks. Belly dance is all about the feminine. Think about it: in almost every other form of dance, the guy leads. But in belly dance there's usually one woman up on the stage, showing the passion of her spirit."

"You speak about it with such intensity."

"You should see me when I'm dancing. Then you would understand. It's one of the most important parts of my life."

"If I'm not working, I would love to go."

Tessa grinned. "Fabulous. I'll plan on having you come with me. In the meantime, try to get off work." She rummaged through the handbag she had brought and pulled out a black leather-bound book. "Here. I want you to read this paragraph and tell me what you think."

Carrie flipped the weathered pages until she came to a faded plum ribbon. "This paragraph, right here? What should I focus on while I'm reading?"

"General overall impression," Tessa said. "Let me know what you think."

Carrie glanced at her, then began reading.

As Carrie sat in her room, her back against the wall and Tessa's book propped open on her knees, she realized that every word she read contradicted her previous conceptions about what Tarot was—but also raised a weight in her chest, as if she were partaking in a forbidden pagan ritual. Yet she couldn't put the book down; she had been reading for over two hours before she looked at the clock and realized the time. She reluctantly put the book on her desk, then stared at the pile of unfinished university work.

Lately she hadn't been able to force herself through the work. Classes and professors came and passed like fragments of dreams. The intensity of her present completely absorbed her thoughts—the increasing complexity of her work relationships, her new friendship with Tessa, and her thoughts of Damien, *haunting her*...but Tessa had told her to focus her thoughts away from him, and she would try.

Carrie opened her textbook on W.B. Yeats and skimmed "The Song of the Wandering Aengus," before she stopped. She frowned at the glossy cover of the ninth edition of Yeats's Poetry, Drama, and Prose. She should have been more interested, given the obsession Yeats had for a woman named Maud Gonne that too closely resembled her present obsession, but she still could not make herself read and understand the poems. She glanced at the stack of books on her desk that had cost her over five hundred dollars—more than two months of waitressing money—but none of them contained anything that could help her. When she glanced down she saw that her hand had closed around the black leather covering of the book Tessa had lent her, and she was not surprised when she continued reading.

The sweat rolled down his forehead and into his eyes as he squinted at the line of tickets in front of him. Behind him, the saute grills sizzled with chicken fajitas; Sam added a sprinkling of cheese to the Chicken Parmesan he had just finished, pushed the plate through the counter to the waiting waitress, turned back to the fajitas, and took them off the grill. He had gone from dishwasher-to-be-waiter to saute chef in a matter of three weeks, after the management found out he could cook when he had 'accidentally' made himself a meal at the end of a long shift. As a cook he could flirt with the waitresses and make them smile when they came in flustered, and he made a steady seven dollars an hour doing what he loved.

"Minute and a half, Carrie," he said, looking up.

"Okay, Sam."

"That'll give us time to chat," he added.

She looked startled; she had already started going back to the expediting area to tray up someone else's food. He was glad that the saute area was at the extreme end of the kitchen and that they were alone.

"I took an Introduction to Art class my freshman year, and one of the things we learned about was tonal balance: the harmony between light and dark." He could see she was interested; he continued. "My professor drew a simple triangle on a piece of white charcoal paper. 'Nothing has meaning,' she said, 'without context. This is just a line, a shape, not a light or a dark.'" He took the fajitas off the grill, passed them to the waitress who came for them, then turned back to Carrie.

"Continue," she said. "Light and dark."

"Then she drew these harsh black streaks around the outline of the triangle. She said, 'Now you have a light inside the dark.'" He paused. "I see the light in your stories, but I also see a lot of darkness."

"That's so very insightful of you Sam," she said. "Conflict is a key element of literature. How's that Fettuccine Alfredo coming along?"

"Thirty seconds." He paused. "What's inspiring the darkness in your writing?"

She grabbed the plate as he pushed it through the window towards her. "I wouldn't read into my stories too much, Sam."

"I don't believe you."

"Drop it, Sam."

He paused. "I'm just glad there's a whole counter between us. You look like you're ready to throw something at me."

"I just might."

He smiled. "So you're okay?"

"I'm fine." She looked at him like he was crazy.

"Thank you for asking. Now, can I ask you something?"

"Shoot."

"Has Dan told you about anything going on in his life right now?"

"No," Sam said, startled. "But I don't really see him—or any of your housemates—that much any more. We're all busy. Conflicting schedules."

"Oh," she said, bending down to slide the tray onto her shoulder. "Why?"

"He's been quiet lately."

"I thought you said they never speak to you."

"They don't," she said, impatiently. "But I can still notice when they're acting differently."

"Dan's a pretty stable guy," Sam said. "I wouldn't worry about him. If something's going on, he'll be able to handle it."

"I know I shouldn't care. But I still worry about them." She paused. "Is that wrong?"

He shook his head. "Stupid, but not wrong." He paused, then swallowed. "Carrie. How about that cup of coffee?"

She looked at him blankly, and then she left the kitchen. She came back holding a porcelain coffee cup. She pushed it to him through the window of the counter.

"I'm so sorry I forgot about it," she said. "I've been running around like my head was chopped off. You take one sugar, right?"

She didn't understand when he burst out laughing; the cooks often asked the waitresses for drinks, and the waitresses as often forgot to get them. He lowered his face as he sliced corned beef, his visor hiding everything except for his lingering grin.

He pushed the coffee back at her. "Wake up, honey. I think you need this more than I do."

"Don't call me honey," she said, staring at the white porcelain mug he had pushed back. "Is something wrong with the coffee?"

"I never asked you for a cup of coffee," he said.

Her brow creased. "I thought I heard you…."

He could not remember ever seeing her so bewildered. "I did ask you for coffee, but I meant to ask if you would like to go out for a cup of coffee. We could talk. Have an intellectual discussion."

"You want to go out for coffee. With me. To talk."

He nodded.

"When?"

He realized he had never expected her to accept. All he had to say was one word, in response to that *when*, and he could not.

"Sam?" she prompted.

"Tonight?" He opened his mouth and found that knowledge of the English language had not deserted him. "How about after we get off work?"

"When do you get off?"

"Around seven."

She flipped open her wait pad, scribbled some digits on a loose sheaf of paper and passed it to him. "Here's my number. Don't call before nine. I'll be writing, and I don't want—"

"To be disturbed. I understand. I won't call before nine."

She looked at him oddly.

He looked back. "I'll call at exactly nine o'clock."

She paused. "You seem kind of surprised."

"Yeah." He paused. "I'm kind of surprised."

"Why? I've wanted to talk to you forever. Just not in the contexts you kept offering."

"Get out of here," he said.

"I'll see you tonight." She walked out of the kitchen, shaking her head.

He watched as she left the kitchen, her long auburn hair pulled back in a simple ponytail that trailed in waves down to her waist. She was naturally beautiful, unlike the other waitresses with their finely applied makeup and glittering silver and gold bangles. Maybe that was why she responded to sincerity—because there was such a lack of it around her. He would talk to her about her writing; he sensed a genuine conversation would go a long way with her.

When her phone rang at nine o'clock, Carrie did not understand the excitement she felt. For a moment she thought of Damien and felt guilty, then she reminded herself that she and Sam were not going on a date; they were going out to talk. That was what she *wanted*.

"Hello?" she said, hoping he was calling her to cancel.

"Carrie? It's Sam. How's the writing going? Are you done?"

"Yes." She didn't tell him she hadn't been writing—that she had not been able to concentrate.

"Where do you want me to meet you? At your house?"

She hesitated, and then realized that her hands were sweating and the phone's static sounded too loudly in her ears. The feeling of forbiddenness grew stronger, and she swallowed. "If you have other plans I won't be offended."

There was a long pause. "You're not thinking about bailing, are you?"

"Maybe," she admitted.

"I'm not going to let you bail on me, Carrie. You gave me your word." He paused. "I know the perfect place, but it's too far away to walk. I'll come pick you up. I'll be there in fifteen minutes."

"I don't know."

"You can tell me what you're worried about when I get there in fifteen minutes. Dress casually."

He hung up. A wave of panic coursed through her. But she remembered the *joie de vivre* that let Sam face life with a daring, reckless attitude—an attitude she admired but lacked, which she had also noticed in a *certain other person*. She wondered if she could learn that perspective from Sam.

She realized then that Sam could be very good for her.

He arrived at her house fifteen minutes after he called her, a feat Carrie found amazing considering the roads were rivers of congealed slush and ice. She saw his battered car pull into the driveway and went to meet him before he got out. He unrolled the car window as she approached.

"I would have come in and gotten you." He paused. "You look beautiful. Will you be angry with me for telling you that?"

She was glad that he couldn't see her blushing in the darkness. "Sam, I don't think we should drive out of State College. The roads are—"

"The roads are fine," he said.

She hesitated, then crossed to the passenger side of the car and got in.

"Relax," he said, as he pulled back onto the road.

"I am relaxed."

"Look at how you're sitting."

She unclasped her hands and slouched against the seat. He motioned to the car's radio tuner.

"You can change the channel if you want."

"I like this."

His hands tightened around the steering wheel. "Right. I forgot that you liked hard rock."

She sat silently and he glanced at her. "Do you even want to be here, Carrie?"

Unknowingly she had clasped her hands in her lap again; she made herself unclench them. "I wouldn't be here if I didn't want to be."

"What's on your mind? Be honest."

She glanced at him. "You want honesty?"

"I do."

"Good." She glanced out the window.

"So?"

She glanced down at her hands. "I'm nervous."

"What?" He didn't know if he had heard her correctly.

"I don't have a lot of one-on-one interaction with people," she said. "If you want to convince me that I don't have fun, go ahead and use that statement against me."

He wasn't going to try. "Do you like being alone?"

"I've never really thought about it." She paused. "I don't mind it."

"Not many people can say that."

She looked at him, then stared out the windshield at the dark sky in front of them until the car hydroplaned.

"I have it under control," he said, inwardly cursing the weather and wondering if she hadn't been right, that maybe they would have been better off walking somewhere in State College. But he had wanted to take her out.

"I wasn't reacting to your driving," she said. "It's my phone."

"Who is it?" he faltered.

"My mom." She seemed surprised.

"Go ahead," he said. "I don't mind."

She flipped open the cover and pressed the phone to her ear. "Hello?"

Sam was respectfully quiet, hoping to catch snatches of the conversation.

Carrie was silent for a long time, and when he glanced at her he saw her face had become paler than usual. He pulled over to the side of the road.

Carrie didn't seem to notice. As she listened, her eyes widened. Her brow creased and a frown formed on her lips. "Oh my god."

"What?" he implored. "Carrie, what is it?"

She made no indication that she had heard him. "Of course I'll come home. I'll come home tonight. No, my classes are finished." Pause. "I want to be there. No, stay with Justine. I'll find a ride home."

"What?" he asked again. Already he had put the car in reverse to take them back. "What happened?"

Carrie turned to him, as if seeing him for the first time. "My cousin. My cousin is very sick. My mother thinks she might die."

Sam stumbled for words. "When someone you love is sick, it's easy to exaggerate. She probably isn't that—."

"My mother is a nurse."

He had nothing to say. He had never seen her so pale, and he did not know what he would do if she started crying. But she did not cry. He saw the muscles in her jaw clench into hard lines, saw her cinnamon-brown eyebrows draw together, saw the resolution in her eyes.

"Where's the Greyhound station here? I need to get home."

"You can't take a Greyhound."

"I have to get home tonight."

He shook his head. "Greyhounds take forever, and unless you live in a major city then you'll have to walk to your destination. And buses are expensive."

"I have money from waitressing." She stood. "I don't mind walking from wherever the Greyhound station drops me off. I need to get on the next bus."

"Let me take you."

"I can't let you do that," she said, so shocked that she dismissed his offer instantly. "But I would appreciate it if you could tell me where the closest Greyhound station is."

"Atherton Street," he said, exasperated. "But if your cousin is really sick, you should let me take you home. We could leave tonight."

She stared at him. "It's two and a half hours to my home town. And I'm staying all weekend."

"I'll have someone cover my shifts," Sam said. "And I'll drive you."

"I'll find a way to get there myself."

"I can get you there faster."

"I don't want you to feel obligated."

"I don't. And you won't be obligated to do anything for me in return."

She paused. He gave her time to think. Finally, she said slowly, "How much are the tickets?"

He wanted to kick something. "Carrie."

"You don't know my family, Sam."

"I know you. That's enough."

She shook her head. He looked at her, frustrated.

"What are your obligations?"

"What?"

"If you love your cousin and want to be with her as quickly as you can be—a direct course home, instead of a round about loop with any number of delays—then you'll let me take you home and you'll drop this crazy Greyhound idea."

"That's not fair." Her eyes, void of tears, were full of anxiety.

"It's rational," he said. "But I'll let you pay for gas, if that makes you feel more comfortable. And if you want me to bring you back up to State College, I'll need a place to stay. But I can always sleep in my car if you'd prefer."

She relented, barely. "Don't be ridiculous."

"I realize this is very serious. You look as white as a sheet right now." He realized she was considering his offer. He started speaking authoritatively, as if the matter had already been decided. "I'll drop you off at your house. Give me half an hour to run some errands, then I'll come pick you up and we can go."

"Half an hour?" she asked uncertainly.

"Half an hour," he repeated. "Then I'll get you home as fast as I can."

She hesitated. "Why are you doing this?"

He shrugged. "I'm a nice guy."

"You are. But no one is that nice."

"Just trust me, Carrie. I'm doing this because I want to." He paused, glancing at the Marshmallow as it came into sight. "I'm true to my word."

"Thank you," she said.

"Off you go," he started, but she had already opened the car door. He watched as dashed off in the direction of her house, her soaked sneakers slapping against the slick sidewalks.

A warning roll of thunder growled overhead. He had a lot to accomplish in the half hour. All for a girl. How Damien would laugh at him.

At eight-thirty PM, Tessa left her room and started walking towards downtown State College. She was not afraid. Living at the Burrough Street Youth haven had taught her how to look out for herself.

She locked the Movement Art's studio door after she entered, then moved into the bathroom and changed out of her street clothes and into her practice costume. The harem pants and bra streamlined the muscles of her body as she moved. The silver coins and beads attached jingled as she walked back into the studio.

She pushed the play button on the CD player in the studio's corner, knowing that the dancing would center her again. She closed her eyes and began to warm up. Her motions felt stunted and her legs cramped, but she forced herself through the familiar routine, knowing her wayward thoughts would come under control as she practiced. But her body refused to move in time with the beat. Tessa opened her eyes and stood frozen in the center of the dance studio, staring at the three identical images of herself reflected back from the studio's mirrors. Very slowly, without moving her head, she scanned the area outside the studio. She exhaled. She knew she was safe, that no one was there; it was twenty-eight degrees outside and it was dark.

She had felt that way—weak, vulnerable, paranoid—too many times when she was by herself to let her feelings prevent her from doing something she loved. Tessa closed her eyes and let herself go, and as her body relaxed she felt the resistance she had originally felt slip away. The intensity of the beat made her dizzy. When the CD stopped she opened her eyes, and the studio came sharply back into view. Tessa looked down, surprised to see the floor littered with the metallic coins from her costume. She had not realized how passionate her dancing had been.

Time had gotten away from her again; it was already fifteen past ten. She hurried across the studio to the bathroom, where she dried off and dressed quickly. She packed her outfit, still slightly damp, and shut off the lights to the studio. She scanned the alley, then turned to lock the studio door. She didn't see the person slouching in the archway until she glanced up and saw his figure reflected in the glass. As she started to scream, a hand covered her mouth.

"I saw you dancing," the man slurred. "You looked real good."

Carrie slammed open the door to her house, oblivious to the frantic slapping of her wet shoes against the stairs leading to her room or the protesting creak of the old railing she used to propel herself forcefully up the flight of stairs. Dave was on the landing, but as she barreled up the stairs he took one look at her and stepped back into his room.

She did not have time to explain to him; she did not care to take the time to explain to him. She flung open the door to her room and sidestepped her guinea pig as he dashed past her. She tripped over a shoe she had left in the middle of the floor and crashed into her dresser; the pile of dirty dishes she had stacked became unbalanced, crashed to the floor, and splintered inches from the startled guinea pig.

"Christ!" she screamed in alarm, but Colby was already running under her bed, unhurt, squealing in excitement or terror. She gingerly pushed the shards of broken glass out of her way, then knelt and peered under the bed.

"Come here," she demanded. "I don't have time to clean this up and you can't get glass in your feet. I can't let you run around."

Two bright eyes stared back at her. Colby did not move.

"Colby," she said, slapping her fist into the carpeted floor. "Colby, I don't have time for this."

She held up her hand, saw a shard of glass jutting out of it and a small pool of blood forming on her palm. Wincing slightly, she extricated the shard from her hand, then closed her eyes. She had to get Colby out of harm's way, and then she had to pack. Carrie opened her eyes and scooped as much of the glass she could find into a pile. She walked over to the wire cage and tapped it.

"Colby," she said.

A questioning sound came from under the bed. She tapped the cage again, trying to control her emotions and panic. Colby bounded out, whooping, and scampered to the cage. She watched anxiously as he hopped into his cage, but relaxed when she saw him sniffing around for a treat before attacking his water bottle. She closed the wire door quickly to keep him away from the mess, then stopped and stared.

"Damn," she said. "I didn't even think about you."

She had twenty minutes. She could think while she packed. She kicked the remaining shards of broken plates and cups out of her way, and hurried to the storage closet near the end of the hallway. The black travel suitcase she had brought to college should be stacked in the very back, buried behind her housemates' accumulated junk.

I don't want to alarm you, Carrie, but Justine is very ill.

She swore loudly and started throwing the junk out of the way, unaware of the thumping crashes she was making,

Aunt Julie had to go to Grove City and get her

only knowing that she had to calm herself down and that she couldn't let herself cry.

She's home. She's resting, but she's very ill and she might not make it.

I'll come right home.

"Fuck," she said. "Fuck. Where is it?"

On the other side of the hallway, Dave's door closed very audibly. She continued looking for the black suitcase as his stereo blasted to life. Her eyes scanned the musty interior of the empty closet and then she turned, saw the mess she had made, and started throwing everything back into the closet.

"Carrie, what are you doing?" Dan's voice drifted to her from the hallway. "I can hear this racket from downstairs in my room, and my lightbulb keeps shaking and..."

For once he sounded respectful, but in her haste she did not notice. She wheeled around. "Have you seen my black suitcase, Dan?"

"Your suitcase?"

"My suitcase!" she shrieked, then took a deep breath when she saw the

106

shock on his face. "There was a suitcase in here. A black suitcase. *My* suitcase."

"I know what you're talking about," he said. "I didn't know it was yours. Monica and I are going to Italy over spring break and I took it. I didn't think you'd mind."

"I need the suitcase. Now."

"Okay," he said. "Okay, let me get it."

By the way he took the stairs three at a time, she could tell he was frightened of her. She continued shoving the junk back into the closet, then slammed the door to keep the junk from tumbling back out. When she turned, Dan was standing on the landing, the suitcase in his hand.

"What the fuck is wrong?" he said, glancing from the frenzied expression on her face to Dave's closed door, through which Sublime was playing at an ear-shattering decibel. Carrie grabbed the suitcase from his hand and dashed into her room, slamming the door behind her.

"You're all crazy!" Dan yelled in the hallway.

She crossed her room to the dresser and grabbed a change of clothes, underwear, bra, socks—into the suitcase. She opened her door, ran into the bathroom, grabbed a toothbrush and toothpaste, ran back to her room and flung them into the case. She dumped her school books on top of everything, grabbed an assortment of notebooks and threw them in. That was everything, except Colby. She glanced at him as he munched happily on his food, and thought darkly for a moment of adding him to the conglomeration in the suitcase and leaving the zipper partly open so he could breathe...but she would never. She knew Sam would let her bring her animals home in his car if she asked—but she couldn't ask him. She thought fleetingly of the Greyhound, but Sam was right about everything. He had offered her a way home, she had accepted, and she wasn't going to back down if he didn't. She needed to get home. She picked up her phone, dialed.

"Carrie?" Tessa, on the other line, sounded odd to her—shaky. "I was just thinking about calling you."

"Tessa." She couldn't speak quickly enough. "I have to go home. My cousin is sick. She might die."

Tessa was silent for a moment. "What can I do, Carrie? Anything?"

"Colby," she said. "Can you watch Colby? And feed my fish Coleridge? For three days?"

"I'll stop by every day. Or do you mind if I crash at your place for the weekend? It's kind of a long walk."

"Of course. *Thank you.*" Carrie paused. "I'm a mess right now. My room is a mess. I knocked over plates and they broke and Colby's shavings are everywhere and I don't know if I'll have time to clean before my ride leaves."

"I won't mind." She paused. "You have a ride home?"

"Sam's taking me."

"Sam from work?"

"Yes. I don't know why—"

"We'll talk later," Tessa said. "Do what you need to do. I'll be over later tonight."

"I'll leave my keys outside, under the bush, so you can get in."

"Thanks. Carrie, I'm going to let you go. Don't worry about your little guys. I'll take care of them."

"Thanks. Tessa, I appreciate this so much."

"Bye, Carrie." Tessa hung up.

Carrie looked back at her room, then dialed Tessa's number again. "Tessa, I'm really sorry I'm going to miss your performance. I know you'll do an amazing job. Good luck at the Hafla."

"Thanks, Carrie." A note of warmth entered Tessa's voice. "Call me if you need anything else."

"I will." Carrie ended the call, realized she was shivering. She slipped out of her wet clothes and tossed the soggy pile into her laundry basket, then scrambled into clean, dry clothes and looked at the clock. Sam wouldn't arrive for another ten minutes, if he arrived on time. Carrie raced out of her room again and went to the hallway closet, swearing as the imprisoned conglomeration of junk and stored materials spilled out into the hall. She grabbed the broom, dustpan, and vacuum cleaner and sprang back to her room, knowing she had just enough time to rearrange her room and regain her composure. She did not want Sam to see her acting as crazy as she felt.

She went back into the hallway and pulled out the last remaining trash bag in the box. She gathered as much broken glass as she could, then bolted down the stairs. Outside the coldness of the air cut her; the unrelenting darkness burned her. She went to the end of the driveway and dropped the bag into one of the metal trash cans. And then she saw the side door to the adjacent house open abruptly.

"Carrie."

She jerked. His appearance, the direct confrontation, surprised her so much that for a moment she stood there, silent.

His voice was grim. "I need to talk to you."

She looked at him—her heart pounding, her head throbbing—*over two weeks of nothing*—and she said nothing.

He paused. "I don't want to play mind games with you—"

"You've made it very clear how you feel about me," she said. "You don't matter to me any more."

"That's what I thought." He shifted. "I thought you were only using me for those novels you want to write so badly. As a muse I'm important to you, but other than that—"

She brushed by him. "I can't talk to you about this now. I have to go."

"Go where?" he asked.

She didn't answer him. She raced back inside to finish packing and wait for Sam.

When he got back to his apartment, frozen, Sam was surprised to find the kitchen light on. He walked into the room cautiously and started. For a moment he thought the young woman hunched over the table was a ghost; then, he realized Tessa was reading a book. She turned red-rimmed eyes on him as he came in.

"Hi, Sam," she said.

Her voice was steady, but something about her seemed fundamentally changed. He found he did not know what to say.

"What happened?" he asked finally, thinking the question was ridiculous because it was *Tessa*. But the words had been torn from him, and he felt a sudden flash of concern when she didn't smile casually at the question.

She drew in a deep breath. "Sam, I…"

More than a stab of concern now. "What?"

She looked down at the table and clenched her pale hands together. "I...I got attacked."

Her tears had made her crystal blue eyes larger, her pale face even whiter. She looked like a fairy princess from a story book, and he knew that if he looked at her long

enough he risked becoming enchanted.

"Are you okay?" he said, the words rushing, rushing. "Did you call the police?"

"He didn't hurt me." She managed a smile. "I knocked him out, then I called the police. He's much worse off than I am. When he wakes up, he's going to be in jail."

"So you're just shaken up." Relief—greater than he would have thought possible. "Do you want to talk about—"

She bit her lip. "No. I know you have to go get Carrie."

A shock of surprise. He had, somehow, forgotten about Carrie. "Tessa, this is serious. I need to know that you're okay—"

"Thank you," she whispered, and suddenly her arms were around him.

He could feel the silky smoothness of her hair against his cheek, the wild smell of her shampoo. His arms tightened around her.

"You're the only one in this house who has ever shown me any kindness," she said. "And some night I will thank you for it, in a different way than I must do so tonight." She let go of him, stepped back. "Thank you, Sam. I'm okay. Please go to Carrie. She needs you."

She slipped out of the kitchen before he had a chance to respond. He stood looking at the doorway she had left, then checked his watch helplessly. There was no time. No time to think. He looked down the hallway to Tessa's room, torn, but he heard her music start playing and he heard the echos of her command to him. He turned and left the apartment, hoping Carrie wouldn't be angry that he would be late.

He got back in his car and drove to her house and stood in the rain on the stoop outside. He rang the bell, then almost fell when she opened the door and flung her arms around him.

"Hey," he said.

110

"Thank you," she mumbled into his shirt. "Sam, thank you…"

He patted her on the back, distracted, then stepped away. "Is that all you're taking?"

She nodded. She hadn't needed the suitcase after all. Everything had fit into a shoulder bag she had gotten for five dollars at Old Navy. He glanced at her window, directly above them.

"And your hamster? Will he be okay?"

"Tessa's taking care of him." Carrie headed towards Sam's car. "But thanks for asking about him. Sam…"

"Yes," he said, realizing somehow from Carrie's words that Tessa really was, somehow, fine. "We can leave now."

Carrie halted by the passenger side of the car, glancing at the storm clouds up above them. "Did you have the time to do everything you needed to do?"

"Go on." He motioned at the car's door. "It's open, and you're getting wet."

She hesitated, then opened the door and got in. He turned on the windshield wipers—changeable State College weather—then glanced at her as she buckled her seatbelt. He had hoped there would not be an awkward silence between them, but he had expected it.

"This all seems so drastic," she said as she looked out the rain-bleared window.

"I can't argue with that," Sam said, in what he hoped was an agreeable tone. "But I don't mind."

"But my mother." She glanced at him. "My mother wouldn't have called me, wouldn't have told me it was serious if it hadn't been."

Sam flicked the windshield wipers to a higher speed. "This is your cousin we're talking about, right? Not a brother or sister?"

"My family is close." She was tapping her fingers against the seat of the door; he wondered if she knew she was doing it. "I see my aunt's family about as much as I see my own. And Justine and I…we've always been close. It's a strange kind of closeness." Mercifully she stopped tapping the car door and clenched her hands in her lap instead. "I don't mean sleep-over and confiding crushes close. Justine and my sister Carly have always been closer on that level. But Justine and I have a lot of the same issues, in different forms."

He shifted to the passing lane even though the road in front of him was empty except for a tiny red car off in the distance. "Tell me about this family of yours."

When she spoke he wasn't sure that she had heard him because he didn't immediately make the connection between her words and his question. "Where do you live, Sam?"

"I live in Westchester."

"Westchester? That's two hours away from where I live."

"Do I make a left here?"

Her eyes flicked up to the green and white road sign. "Stay straight until the next exit. I had no idea you lived so far away. You can stay in my older brother's room. He goes to school eight hours away so he won't be home, but I'm sure he wouldn't mind."

"Thank you. I'll take you up on your offer." He paused. "You know, you don't have to justify yourself in wanting to go home, even if Justine isn't as badly off as your mom may think."

"I know," she said, her hands clasped in her lap.

"I'm glad I'm going to meet your family," he said.

"My family is one of my greatest blessings," Carrie said. She was back to tapping again. "But there are a lot of..."

"What?" he prompted, when she hesitated.

"There are a lot of problems in my family," she said. "A lot of mental afflictions."

"Like what?"

She glanced at him, surprised. "You want to know?"

"I might as well know what I'm getting myself into," he quipped, not liking how serious she had become again. "But if you don't want to tell me, I can always make my own diagnoses."

"I'll tell you, if you want to know. My family might not be too happy about that if they knew. But," she turned to him, "we can't help what's in our genes, and I'm proud of how far my family has come."

He could tell her how beautiful she looked when that passionate light came into her eyes and her jaw clenched in resolve, but he knew it would make her uncomfortable. "Go ahead and hit me. I'm ready."

Her defenses came down. "Paranoia, neuroses, chronic and severe depression. Anger management problems. Passive-aggressiveness. OCD. Alcoholism. Alzheimers." She paused. "Insanity?"

He laughed. "Yet you seem okay."

He had meant it as a joke, and her silence startled him into realizing that no one had ever told her before.

"Carrie? You're okay," he repeated.

"I have my whole life to pay forward, for some of the things I've done," she said. "But I know I'm lucky. Sometimes, when I go home and I see.... when I see everything, I realize what's in my genes and I…I can't ever have children, Sam. I could never procreate knowing that I might pass any of this down to them. What if a son of mine would spend half his time looking down at his hands looking for blood that isn't there or worrying that something he said had started the war in Iraq, or a daughter of mine would lose her mind and waste away slowly…"

So that's why you want to be alone, he thought, and said, "Do you think yours is the only family that has problems? I could hit you with just as long a list of genetic illnesses in my family. All these things you listed don't seem too bad to me."

"But you can't know how my family members suffer."

"And neither can you. You didn't get the brunt end of it." He paused. "Some of those illnesses are controllable, like alcoholism. And Alzheimers doesn't hit until you're older and have had a chance to live." He took his eyes from the road, just long enough to look at her. "I'm not trying to make the struggles of your family any less valiant, but not having children because you're afraid of poison in your genes…that seems drastic to me. There are a lot worse things out there. Like cancer, or albinism, or what's that disease called, where people can't go out in the sunlight? Whatever it is, that. Diseases that shorten your life or eat away at your body…" He paused. "To me, mental diseases seem to be more under our control. You can treat cancer with surgery or radiation therapy, but as an individual you can't will the tumor away. Unless you're a self-actualized medicine man or something."

"Are you saying that people with mental diseases have them because of a lack of will?"

"No," he said. "But I'm saying that, with mental diseases, at least you can put up a good fight. If you're depressed, for example, you can train yourself to think differently so you can improve your perspective. I'm not saying that overcoming mental obstacles isn't a challenge…"

"I understand what you're saying, Sam. I don't know if I agree with you or not."

"At least there's not suicide in your family," he said. "But my family has that one covered."

She paused. "Sometimes I worry about my little brother, Chris. I can't get him to talk to me, and I don't know how he can keep everything bottled up inside. He's such a good kid, but he's different, and life hasn't been easy for him."

"How old is he?"

"Fourteen."

"That's a tough age. Not that my experience was that ordinary…" He broke off. "But maybe I should be grateful. I spent so much time in therapy trying to come to terms with losing Claudia that everything else—puberty, hormones, making the cut with grades or getting a date for the dances—didn't seem to matter at all. The usual adolescent dilemmas seemed trivial."

Sam began tapping his fingers against the steering wheel. After a moment, she looked at him.

"What are you doing?" she asked.

"Creating a symphony," he said, alternating the beat of his fingers. "You're the bass and I'm the melody."

She glanced at her hand, suddenly realized her fingers had started drumming monotonous staccatos. She stopped hastily. "I'm sorry. That must have been driving you crazy. Have I been doing that the whole time?"

He nodded. "Almost the whole time."

"I didn't even realize."

"We sounded good together," he said. "We were making music." He turned off the radio. "Try it again. No, a little faster." He added an impromptu rhythm. "See?"

Incredibly, she smiled.

Sam stopped tapping. "Just remember we're all fucked up in this world. Humans have been fucked up for centuries, but somehow they've survived. Somehow we will, too."

"Such an optimistic thought."

He shrugged. "Turn or straight?"

She glanced at the road. "Turn. This is the exit. From here, get onto 22." She paused. "I don't know how you can see to drive through all this rain."

"Symbolism," he said.

"What?"

"Never mind."

She looked out her own rain-bleared window. "So how do you feel about my family, after what I've told you?"

"I want to meet them," he said.

Sam had to keep waking her up; she drifted off to sleep five times by his count. He would have been content to let her sleep peacefully beside him, but she had told him to keep her awake.

"Carrie," he said gently, as he watched her eyelids start to close once again. "When was the last time you slept?"

"Last night," she said, sitting up.

"How long?"

"Two hours."

"I mean, when was the last time you really slept? Six hours or more." He paused. "You look exhausted."

"I've been having trouble sleeping." She smiled. "I guess you passed your insomnia on to me."

"Sorry." Unlike her, he was wired. "I could pull over and let you sleep for an hour or so. I brought a book; I could read."

She shook her head and leaned back drowsily as the lights of a shopping plaza appeared on their right.

"I don't want to sleep," she repeated. "But I wouldn't mind stopping for something to eat. Are you hungry?"

"We could stop," he said. "I am hungry, and we still have an hour and a half to go."

"Can we go to Wendy's? Maybe if I have some food in my body, I'll be able to stay awake."

"Wendy's sounds great." He pulled into the parking lot, parked the car and handed her a ten dollar bill. "Get me a bacon cheeseburger, will you? I want to stretch for awhile."

She took the money without comment and went into the restaurant. He leaned against the car and watched the random traffic. The rain had stopped; the sky was too dark to be seven o'clock. He could already see faint traces of the moon in the sky. The air was still crisp and cool, but he wasn't uncomfortable in his blazer and jeans.

"Here."

He took the paper bag she handed him. "That was quick."

She shrugged. "Ten minutes."

"Ten minutes?" He had zoned out.

"Are you still okay to drive, Sam?"

"I'm fine." He saw her looking at him with concern and felt irritated. "I'm a little tired, but I'm fine."

"I could drive if you want to."

"I said I'm fine." He paused. "Let's just sit down and eat."

She looked at the darkening sky. "Do you want to go inside? It looks like it might start raining again."

He paused, hesitant to tell her he wanted the silence of the parking lot—that the very thought of entering the bright, noisy restaurant disheartened him. She waited for him to answer, then glanced at him quickly.

"It's a beautiful night," she said. "Can we eat out here?"

"Here?" He could not keep the relief out of his voice. "It's raining."

"Drizzling."

"Fine by me." He started to unwrap the aluminum foil from the burger, then paused when he saw she was looking at him. "What, Carrie?"

"Can we eat on the roof of your car?"

He burst out laughing; maybe he was more tired than he knew. He would take a nap, first thing, whenever they got to where they were going...if he could.

"Why was that funny?" she asked.

116

"What would possess you to have an idea like that? But here, I'll help you up."

She looked at him. He held his hand out to her.

"I'll give you a lift so you don't get mud all over the side of my car. Use the space above the tire as a foothold."

Tentatively, she put her bag on top of the roof and took his hand. Seconds later he was sitting beside her.

"This isn't bad," he admitted.

Beside him, she smiled and opened her bag. They ate in silence, watching the cars go by and letting the rain fall on them.

"You should know one more thing," Carrie said, finally. "About my family."

"What's that?"

"My sister Carly. Stay away from her."

He raised his eyebrows. "Why's that?"

"Because if she sees you around me, I'll never hear the end of it, and neither will you. She'll have a wedding dress picked out for me by the end of the night."

"Sisters do that, don't they?" He smiled. "Claudia would always ask me if I was interested in anyone, when she was still alive."

"I'm sorry," she said.

"Not as sorry as I'll be," he said, "if you keep censoring everything you say around me, because you're afraid of offending me or hurting my feelings."

She glanced down at her hands.

He paused. "Carrie, I like that you speak your mind, and that when you speak it's because you actually have something meaningful to say. So when you're around me, say what you think."

"I'll keep that in mind." She slid off the car. "How was your sandwich?"

He sat looking down at her, feeling the coldness that had replaced the warmth of where she had been sitting beside him. He forced a smile.

"Soggy." He paused. "But I feel better now. How about you? Do you feel re-energized?"

"I don't think I'll fall asleep on you again."

Sam looked up at the sky. He felt tired and he felt old. He wished the stars were out. He didn't want to make a wish on the moon, the sickle-shaped moon glaring down at him like an evil eye. Besides, what wish did he have? What he wanted—really wanted—was out of his reach, and there was nothing he could do about it. He slid off the car's roof, knowing Carrie was waiting for him inside the car.

Carrie's room was crammed full of books and music. Tessa smiled when she saw her own belly dance CD and Tarot book. She slipped *Baladi Plus* into Carrie's CD player and looked around the room again. Carrie had created her own poet's corner, a shrine to the writers she admired: their portraits, some inspirational quotes. A dark blue wall hanging of a Celtic knot blazed across one of the walls, beside another hanging of a wolf stalking through a forest. A blanket had been flung over the room's side window. Tessa gently pulled back one corner and saw the house beside Carrie's. She let the blanket fall back into place. Colby started whooping in his cage, and Tessa scooted her overnight bag out of the way so she could drop down on her knees, reach through the cage's bars and scratch his head.

"We'll get you out of there soon," she promised.

Fifteen minutes later she had cleaned Carrie's room and released Colby from his cage. Colby sniffed her fingers, then darted around the room. Tessa unpacked, then decided to meditate. She sat in a lotus position and controlled her breathing. She became aware of how the light from Damien's room filtered into Carrie's, even through the blanket. But Carrie shouldn't have to block out the sunshine, so she could block him out. Tessa would talk to her. Or maybe she would talk to him. She exhaled, raised her arms to temple pose. She had three days. In three days, so much could happen. For now she would meditate and quiet her thoughts. She already knew what her next move needed to be.

"Hello, Damien," Tessa said.

He turned. His dark eyes showed surprised. "Who let you in?"

"You left your door unlocked, brother dear."

He turned away from her. "Just tell me bluntly what you want, and you'll get it. No reason to act any differently around me."

"I'm not the one acting," she said. "And so you have no

misconceptions about my intentions regarding this visit, be assured that I come strictly as a matter of business. I'll be out of your presence as soon as I possibly can be."

"Excuse me," he said, in a mockingly courteous manner. "I'm glad to know you feel comfortable enough around me to come to my apartment, uninvited, and then insult me to my face..."

She sighed. "Do you insist on drawing this out?"

He leaned against the wall. "What do you want, Tessa?"

"I want to talk to you about Carrie."

"No."

She looked at him levelly. "She's my friend."

"I didn't think she had any friends."

"I want you to stay away from her."

He cupped his hand around a cigarette, lit it. "Carrie's a woman, just like any other woman. She's not getting any special treatment from."

"She's *not* like any other woman," Tessa said. "She's not a liar. You shouldn't have called her one, and you shouldn't have treated her the way you did."

He turned at the tone of her voice. His smile was cold. "You know why I did."

She blinked. "Is it true, then?"

He turned away from her, tossed the remainder of his cigarette out the window. "How the hell should I know? No one ever explained women to me, and Carrie isn't like any one I've ever..." He broke off. His dark eyes accused her.

"Watching someone while they sleep." Tessa shook her head. "That *is* perverted."

"I don't..." he began.

"You told her you watched her while she was sleeping," Tessa said, her eyes glinting. "She always thought you meant from across the street. She doesn't know you've been here with her, before. Night after night."

"You're crazy."

"I feel your presence in her room. How many times have you slipped into her room, without her knowing, and stood and watched her sleep?"

"I wouldn't be able to get into her house..." he started.

"They leave their door unlocked. I know that, as well as you do." She kept her cool eyes on him. "Don't lie to a psychic."

"Then don't ask me these stupid questions," he muttered.

She paused. "Did you know that your name is very similar to the Greek word *daemon*? The Greeks believed that daemons were their guiding spirits, their guardian angels. But the word daemon is one letter away from another word. Demon. Don't you find that ironic, that your name is so similar to both words?

"No," he said. "Our father actually knew what he was doing when he named me after the Devil. He taught me the lesson right then that you're only free when you have nothing to lose. He signed my contract for Hell at my birth. It's probably the only decent thing he ever did in his life."

"Do you honestly believe that?"

"I have no regrets. How many people can say that?"

She frowned. "I think the way you live your life is absolutely vulgar."

"And I think that is your opinion," he said. "I understand that meditating, clear thought, and self-control are important to you. But I've chosen a different way to make my own meaning."

Their eyes locked. Tessa held his gaze for a long while before she spoke, deliberately.

"I don't know how much of your perspective is what you believe, and how much of it is a cry for help," she said. "How much of it is that you want to teach Carrie to take risks, and how much of it is that you want to drag her down with you."

"This conversation is closed, Tessa."

She smarted. "You can't..."

"Tessa." His voice was cold. "I told you I didn't want to talk about Carrie."

Tessa stood. "Thank you for your time."

He smiled, dangerous. "When the hell are you going to learn to give up on conventional politesse? Tell me I'm an asshole and be—"

"I shall never stoop to your level," she said. "Have a good night."

She heard him laugh as she left his apartment, and she understood why Carrie was in love with him. She realized the danger of that continued attraction and turned on the landing.

"Damien."

She had caught him in the midst of a reverie; he looked up, without the full force of his charismatic indifference.

"Just so you know," Tessa said. "I'll be staying in Carrie's room this weekend, in case you intended on watching her. She asked me to take care of her animals."

"That's good. You'll take better care of them than I would." He paused. "Where is Carrie this weekend?"

She looked at him, pointedly. "With Sam."

"Really."

She nodded.

His dark eyes flashed as he smiled at her. "Your insinuations are unnecessary," he said. "I already know that Carrie hates me. You don't have to worry about a thing."

She turned and left his apartment. The flash in his eyes had told her that she had more to worry about than even he knew.

"Is this it?" Sam asked, glancing out the window. Even though darkness had long since fallen, he could see the house towered two stories tall and sprawled out across the property.

"Turn here," she said.

"You have a lawn," he said, pulling into the brick driveway. "You didn't tell me you lived in a mansion, Carrie."

"It's not a mansion," she said.

The house was the size of at least two of his houses combined. He looked down and was welcomed by a picturesque straw mat painted with tiny pink flowers and purple block letters; he looked up and was greeted by a fabric angel hanging from the center of the door, grasping a large red felt heart between its plump arms. She was already halfway up the porch steps before she realized he had stopped following her. She turned.

"Sam, are you coming?"

"I can't believe you live here."

"I don't. Anymore."

He paused. "You're sure it's okay if I stay here?"

"We talked about this in the car. It's fine." She paused.

"Christine…Mom…will be delighted to have you here."

"But she doesn't know me."

"My mother loves all our friends. She might be surprised, but…." She seemed to be trying to convince herself as well as him. "So maybe she'll be really surprised. Sometimes my family isn't very open to people outside our group. But you're my friend, and you'll be accepted as such."

He glanced at the house again. He would not admit to her that he was intimidated. "Are they all asleep?" he asked, stalling.

"Carly and Chris will be in bed." Carrie reached into her jacket pocket and pulled out a key. "Christine will be up since I told her I was coming home tonight. But she has to be at the hospital at five tomorrow, so you probably won't see much of her tonight."

So they would be alone together. "Maybe I should find somewhere else to stay."

"No," she said, knocking gently.

Carly opened the door. She smiled when she saw Carrie, and then her eyes slid past her and centered on Sam. She smirked.

"*Hello*, handsome," she said, putting her hands on her hips. "Who are you?"

"Carly, this is Sam. He's the friend who brought me home."

"Hi, Carly," Sam said. "It's nice to meet you."

"Nice to meet *you*." Carly eyed Sam, then turned to Carrie. "You brought a *boy* home?"

"It's nice to see you, too," she said. "Why are you still up?"

Carly shrugged. "How long are you staying home?"

"Till Sunday."

"Is *he* staying with us?"

Carrie looked at her directly. "Sam's going to stay with us for a couple of days. I don't want any comments from you."

Carly grinned.

"I mean it," Carrie said. "Don't annoy him."

Carly shook her head. "I'm going to bed."

"Carly."

Carly paused. "What."

"I missed you." Carrie hugged her. "I'm home for two days. We'll catch up."

Carly patted her awkwardly on the back. "Will Sam be joining us?"

"That's enough from you."

Carly smiled. "So you know, Mom's up waiting for you in the study." She paused, then looked mischievously at Sam. "I wish I could see her reaction, when she sees *him*."

"Carly."

"I'm going." She started up the stairs.

"She's cute," Sam said, after Carly had disappeared.

"She's something else." Carrie turned to him. "I'll introduce you to Christine, then I'll let you get settled in Calder's room."

Sam followed her through the house, noting everything from the candles on the table to the cheery wallpaper to the grade reports hung up on the refrigerator. Carrie led him down a short hallway and knocked. One of the most dignified looking women Sam had ever seen opened the door. On seeing Carrie, the woman's tired face lit up, and she threw her arms around Carrie and pulled her into a tight hug.

"Carrie, I'm so glad you could come home."

"How is Justine?" Carrie blurted out. "I'm so worried."

"She's doing better. We'll talk more tomorrow." Christine stepped away. "Now it's late and you must be tired." She paused. "Who is this charming man?"

Carrie turned, surprised by the tone of her mother's voice. "This is Sam. He drove me here." She paused. "He can stay in Calder's room for the weekend, can't he?"

"Of course." She extended a hand. "Welcome to our home, Sam. Thank you for bringing Carrie back to us."

He nodded. Christine turned to Carrie. "Have you shown him Calder's room?"

"Not yet. I wanted to make sure—"

"I can show him," a voice piped up from behind them.

"Carly." Christine's voice, soft and soothing a moment before, became stern. "Young lady, what are you doing awake? You have to be up early tomorrow."

"I'll show Sam where Calder's room is," Carly repeated, "then I'll go to bed. And you and Carrie can talk, or whatever."

"It was nice to meet you, Sam," Christine said. "I look forward to talking to you more tomorrow."

Sam nodded again, then followed Carly out of the study. Christine watched them, then turned her attention to Carrie. Their eyes locked; Carrie shifted.

"You look busy," Carrie said. "I don't want to keep you up."

"Close the door, Carrie. I have some time to talk to my eldest daughter, especially since I haven't seen her for two months." She smiled as Carrie closed the door and sat down. "You should have seen how excited Carly was when she heard you were coming home. She insisted on staying up until you got here."

"I never would have known it."

Christine paused. "Carly's a difficult young woman to understand. She has a good heart, but sometimes I worry about her. The friends she keeps…if you could see what they wear, how they act…."

"Carly has her head on straight."

"But I worry, since I'm not around as much as I could be—"

"You can only do so much," Carrie said. "Besides, girls who are Carly's age want their independence."

"But what girls who are Carly's age need are mothers." Christine paused. "Will you go see Justine tomorrow?"

"I'd like to. Will you tell me what…so I know before…."

"She stopped eating because of the depression," Christine said. "She fainted in her biology lab when she was staying after hours to do extra work. Thankfully, her lab partner was there to take care of her, and then she reported Justine to the university health services." She paused. "Justine is giving up slowly, and until she makes the decision to fight herself, there isn't anything we can do."

"You said she was sick?"

"She's very sick. We'll talk more, after you've seen her." Christine smiled gently. "Will you be staying with Carly in your old room?"

"Where else would I sleep?"

Christine looked at her closely. "Sam is a good person, Carrie?"

"He is," she said, understanding. "And we're just friends."

"Have you known him long?"

"He knows my housemates." She shrugged. "I had class with him, and he offered to drive me here and I…"

"I trust you. You're an adult, Carrie. I'm proud of the person you've become." She stood. "I'll see you in the morning. I'm glad to have you home."

Carrie hesitated. "Goodnight."

Christine gave her a hug. "Don't stay up too late."

"I won't. I'm going to check on Sam, then write for awhile." She paused. "Thank you for letting him stay."

Her clear blue eyes measured Carrie. "You didn't give me much of a choice, did you?"

"I didn't."

"Carly will never let you live this down, you know."

Carrie glanced up, saw the twinkle in Christine's eyes. Christine squeezed her shoulder.

"I trust your judgment," she said, catching and holding Carrie's attention. "Sam is welcome here."

Carrie nodded, then lowered her head as the door closed softly and she was left alone in the study. After Corman had been killed, Christine had taken over the space. She had replaced the black leather sofa with an antique wooden desk and chair and the leather bound books on military tactics and maneuvers with her thick medical textbooks, replaced the navy drapes with rose-peach ones. The room had gone from one of dark precision to one of comforting welcome. Carrie paused for a moment, basking in the peace she felt in the room, grateful that Christine was finally treating her like a woman. But standing next to Christine, Carrie felt very young, and the memories came back in flashes: five years old, and Christine holding back her hair as she vomited into the toilet; fourteen years old, and Christine hand-washing the panties stained with blood and explaining to Carrie about the changes that were taking place in her body; seventeen years old, and the expression on Christine's face when Calder came home drunk for the first time and called Christine a bitch; two weeks later, when Christine drove to the county correctional center to pay the bail Calder had gotten for a DUI and then chauffeured him to his community service. How could Christine ever consider her a woman?

125

The gap between them was huge; Carrie did not know how she could ever measure up, how she could ever become as strong as her mother was. She blotted the tears from her eyes and climbed the steps to Calder's room.

"You're lucky," Sam said, when she opened the door.

"I know," she said. "Carly didn't bother you, did she?"

Sitting on the edge of Calder's bed, he looked stunned and lost. "No, she didn't bother me."

Carrie paused. "I'm going to go see Justine tomorrow."

"Do you want me to come with you?"

"Yes."

He didn't look at her. "Do you want to sit down for a moment?"

She moved into Calder's room and sat down by Sam on the edge of the bed. "Thank you for bringing me home, Sam. I really need to be here right now."

If he had looked at her, she might have kissed him. But he sat on the bed, shoulders hunched, and nodded absently before he turned to her.

"I can already tell there's something special here, Carrie. I don't want you to try to censor or hide any of it." He looked down at his hands. "Being here must bring back a lot of memories."

"I don't remember that much. I've repressed most of my high school years. I just wanted to get away. I don't want to talk about it."

"Too hard?"

"No. Just part of the past." She returned his stare. "I don't know why I trust you so much all of a sudden, but I do. Maybe I'm too tired, or maybe it's too late."

He glanced at her face, then took her hand. "Everyone here loves you."

She removed her hand from his, and by the way she was holding her head so that her hair shielded the side of her face, he could tell she was crying.

"Goodnight," she said. "I'll see you tomorrow."

He stood. "Carrie…"

The door opened. Carrie stepped back, and he saw the expression on her face change abruptly.

"I'm not interrupting, am I?" Carly strode into the room in a pink pajama top with matching bottoms with monkeys on them. She sat down next to Sam and winked, then looked at Carrie.

"What do you want, Carly?" Carrie asked.

Carly shrugged. "I just wanted to make sure you were behaving yourself."

Sam laughed. Carly glanced furtively at him, then looked at Carrie. "Honestly, what's wrong with him?"

Carrie looked at Sam for help. "Sam...."

"I want to hear this," he said, softly. "Well, what's wrong with me?"

Carrie scowled at him before she turned to Carly. "Carly, talk to Calder or Chris if you want to be an aunt."

"Calder is an idiot," Carly said. "And Chris is too gloomy and, besides, too young. The average man gets married at age twenty-seven, and Chris is only fourteen. I can't wait that long." She looked critically at Sam. "How old are you?"

"Twenty-three," he said.

Carly looked at Carrie. "And Calder is way too whacked up for anyone to fall in love with him. So it has to be you."

Carrie paused. "I believe you have to be up early for swim practice tomorrow."

"That's why I'm here. I wanted to see if you were both going to keep yelling at each other all night, because I can't sleep and I need to be up early."

"We weren't yelling," Sam said.

"You were," Carly said. "Geez, Carrie, you finally find a nice guy and now all you can do is scream at him."

"I was not screaming," Carrie said, looking at Sam. He shrugged.

"Anyway," Carly said. "Are you sleeping in our room tonight?"

"Where else would I...." She broke off. "Goodnight, Carly."

"Don't make any noise when you come in. Though I probably won't be able to sleep anyway." Carly turned to Sam. "She says all these weird things in her sleep."

"How would you know?" Carrie asked, unable to stop the faint blush from creeping up into her cheeks. "I haven't even been home for you to know that."

"I know." Carly looked at her, then got off the bed and moved to the door, where she paused and then smiled over her shoulder. "Goodnight, Sam."

"Goodnight, Carly," he said.

Carly closed the door behind her. Sam turned to Carrie.

"So what kind of things do you say in your sleep?"

"Goodnight," she said, moving towards the door. "I'm leaving to see Justine at two o'clock tomorrow afternoon, if you care to come."

She closed the door softly behind her. Sam stood and went to the one window that overlooked the rain-slicked street below. He watched the rain fall. At some point he heard the front door close, then he saw her walking away from the house. He turned from the window; he didn't like the idea of watching her when she couldn't see him. He moved to the black duffle bag he had brought and pulled out his Norton Anthology of English Literature and his writing notebook. He had to get his work done over the weekend but he also wanted to get to know her family members; he already sensed a strong ally in Carly. The clock said one AM and he was actually tired—maybe even tired enough, for once, to get some real sleep. The reading could wait.

He lay down on the floor because sleeping in strange beds had always bothered him. He stared up at the ceiling; he would stay awake until Carrie got back safely from wherever she was. He would have gone with her had she asked him, but going after her in the middle of the night might have startled her.

Without hearing her come back or turning off the lights, Sam fell asleep.

She could tell Sam was still awake when she returned from her walk because the light in Calder's room was burning brightly. Sam had told her about his insomnia, and he must feel strange to be at her house, alone in her scapegoat brother's messy room. Carrie went inside and locked the door behind her; Christine was worried about break-ins, though the neighborhood was safer than where Carrie lived in State College…

She stopped and stood in the shadows, alert, listening. There was another light on in the house, the soft glow visible through the arch in the living room. She had no ready means of defending herself—but Damien had taught her that everything could be a weapon. He had shown her, one night, how to make her hands into stiff blades to deliver maximum pain to an attacker. She held her hands ready as she made her way towards the living room, knowing she also had the element of surprise—which was a weapon itself.

She peered inside the entrance of the living room. Her heart skittered; for a moment she thought the white clad figure reclined on the sofa was a ghost.

"Chris? What are you doing up?"

He had been reading; her voice startled him and the book fell to the floor. His face was almost as white as the plain T-shirt he was wearing over his boxers, but he smiled shakily when he saw her.

"Hi, Carrie." He bent down to retrieve the book. "Mom said you were coming home."

She walked slowly over to him. If she asked him outright he would deny that anything was wrong. "What are you reading?"

"Gulliver's Travels."

"For school?"

"Yeah." A shadow flickered across his face. "Carrie."

"What's wrong?" she asked instantly.

He paused and swallowed, his Adam's Apple bobbing, and then the words burst forth from him. "There's a man in Calder's room. I didn't want to wake up Mom so I came to get you, but your door was locked. I didn't know what to do so I came down here because the phone is here and I could call the police if he woke up and tried to hurt anyone…"

She laughed. She knew she shouldn't—he looked pale and scared and worried—but she could not help herself.

"You're going to wake up Carly and Mom," he said, the worry easing out of his face. "What's so funny?"

She continued to smile. "That's Sam, the friend who brought me home. He's going to stay the weekend because he lives far away."

"Oh," Chris said, his cheeks crimson. "Well, how was I supposed to know? I got up to go to the bathroom and I saw the light on under Calder's door and I thought that maybe he had come home."

"And when you opened the door you found a stranger there." She looked at him with amusement and respect.

"I wanted to be able to call the police if I had to." The crimson in his cheeks turned scarlet. "No one told me."

"You're very heroic," she said. "But I promise you that Sam won't hurt anyone." She glanced at the clock and was startled to see how late it was. "You should probably get to bed, to run your best tomorrow. I'd like to come see you compete, if you wouldn't mind."

"If you want." He shrugged. "But I don't know how well I'm going to run since..." His eyes slid to the clock, then down at the book laying upside down in his hands.

"Nerves keeping you up?" she asked. "Mine would sometimes, when I had a big race the next day and was worried about the competition."

"It's not that," he said. "It was just...Sam. Now that I know everyone is safe, I can go to bed."

"Chris, one second."

He turned.

"What was Sam doing when you went into Calder's room?"

"He was lying on the floor, sleeping." He looked up at the ceiling, which he had done for as long as she could remember when he was trying to think or recall something from far back in his memory. "And he was snoring."

She was delighted. "Thank you. You get a golden star for everything. I'm proud of you."

"I know," he said. "You tell me all the time in the letters you send me."

"So you get the letters?" she asked. "I never knew if you did, because you never write back. Do you like it when I send you letters, or are they annoying?"

"I like them," he said. "I like getting mail."

"Then I'll keep writing to you."

He paused. "Where were you just now?"

"I was out walking. I needed some time to think."

"Were you thinking about Justine?"

She nodded.

He glared at the blank walls. "She stopped eating."

"I heard." She forced herself to smile as she realized how pale and nervous Chris looked.

Gulliver's Travels went sailing across the room and smacked into the wall, sending the picture Christine had hung—*family is about being there for each other, in times of joy as well as sadness*—slanting dangerously to the right. Chris turned his smoldering blue eyes on her, his face haggard. "She's not even trying. She's letting herself be depressed and letting herself die and she's not even fighting it and if she would only try…" He took a deep breath, his thin shoulders heaving.

She kept her face blank as she stood and went over to the wall and righted the picture. "You can't let what's happening to Justine eat away at you, Chris. You're always going to run into people who are destroying themselves. You're fourteen now and a young man, and I'm not going to hide the truth from you."

"I'm fifteen," he said. "Fifteen."

She looked at him, surprised, and understood why Christine said the time passed too quickly, that she should treasure her time because it was all she had and it would be gone before she knew it.

"Fifteen," she corrected. "Sorry."

"That's okay," he said. "You have more important things on your mind than how old I am."

"That's not true," she said.

He shook his head. "What were you saying?"

She paused. "You're old enough to realize that, in general, people make bad choices. You can sympathize, you can try to help, but don't let their problems get to you. You're not responsible for other people."

He stared at her; she could see the shock and surprise in his eyes. Replaying the words she had spoken, she realized how harsh they had sounded, and that he was only fourteen…fifteen.

"Don't apologize," he said, reading her face. "Don't apologize when you're right."

She looked at him sadly. *He was so strong.* "What time do you have to get up?"

"Six."

"You better do some power sleeping, then."

He hesitated. "Will you drive me to my race tomorrow?"

"Don't you want to ride up with your team?"

"I would rather go with you. Then we can go see Justine afterwards."

The bus rides—being away from everyone in her family and around people her own age—had always been her favorite part of being on the track and cross country teams, but she did not question him. She nodded.

"I'm just running the four by eight," he said. "Because I hurt my ankle, and Coach doesn't want me straining it. The semi-finals are next weekend and he wants me to do my best there. But it's the first event after the preliminaries."

"I know."

"We can leave right after that, since I'm not going to run anything else."

Cheering for her teammates had also been a favorite part of her running experience, but she nodded again. "Are you sure you don't want anyone else to come see you run?"

"Yes," he said, then paused. "I don't want them to be proud of me. Only you can come, because you understand."

The tears sprang into her eyes and she blinked rapidly. "I think Sam would like to come."

"He looked really tired. You should let him sleep."

She wondered what was bothering Chris so much that he wanted to talk to her for the two and a half hour drive to Erie, where Christine had said his meet was taking place.

"All right," she said. "If I'm asleep when we need to leave, wake me up. I'll be right here."

"Why?"

"Carly locked me out of our room." She shrugged. "Why? Who knows. She's Carly."

Chris nodded. "I'll write a note for Mom letting her know you're taking me so that she doesn't have to drive back from the hospital to take me to meet the team bus at the high school. I'm sorry to ask and I know it's a hassle…"

"I'm glad you asked me. I can't wait to spend some time with you."

"Thank you," he said. "Thanks. I'm really glad you came home."

She forced herself to smile, to make her voice take on the joking tone she always used with him. "Get to bed, Chris!"

Anything to get him out of the room because she couldn't keep the tears checked any longer. They were flowing freely down her face soon after he left, and of all people, she couldn't let Chris see her cry.

Carrie leaned against the cold steel railing at the bottom of the stadium's stands, a white Styrofoam cup of steaming coffee clutched in one gloved hand. Chris was going through his warmups near the jumping pit, removed from his teammates and from the other runners preparing for the race. His face seemed set in stone, his every motion full of intensity and fierce concentration. From the distance she could see his eyes were closed; not once did he look up from his stretching to look at the competitors. He had entered "The Zone"; he was focused inward, preparing himself mentally as well as physically. He would not hear the buzzing conversation of the crowd of shivering parents in the stands or the excited and anxious chatter of the other runners on the field. He would not smell the greasy hot dogs sizzling or the thick, rich coffee brewing in the concession stand area nearby.

He would see nothing because his eyes were closed, cutting out the distractions; he would hear nothing until the announced *final call, Boy's 800 Meter Run,* and then he would open his eyes and move to the starting line without seeing any of the other runners. From the time the gun went off and the smoke still lingered in the chill air to the moment he crossed the finish line, his breath ragged from exertion and his muscles screaming with pain, he would race against himself as much as he would race against the other runners around him.

The microphone speaker's voice announced the *last call* for the Boy's 800 Meter Run, and Carrie unclenched her hands from the railing and went to sit in the front row of the stands so she could be in the front row, cheering him on. She knew how badly he wanted to run, how badly he wanted to win, especially since he wasn't supposed to be running the straight eight-hundred meter race that day at all.

She watched the runners line up, then looked to where Chris's coach stood in a bulky blue and white windbreaker and sweatpants, whistle and clipboard in hand. He was a round, florid man who—Christine said—pushed his runners too hard and took their running too seriously. Chris's opinion differed; he wanted a serious coach to help him achieve excellence. Carrie saw in the tenseness of the coach's face that he was as nervous as she was as he watched Chris move to the starting line. They both knew that Chris should not be running the race because of his ankle.

Chris had made the decision to run the 800 meter after his team floundered in the 4 x 800 meter relay; the second runner had been hung over from a party the night before and had jogged his part. By the time Chris had been handed the baton, the team had been so far behind that the coach had told Chris to run his race as slow distance to test out his ankle. Their team came in second to last. Chris had gone off to be by himself; she had found him a half an hour later, when he asked if she was willing to wait around for him so that he could run the straight eight-hundred-meter since he had convinced the coach to let him take the place of his hungover teammate. Carrie had thought about confronting the coach until Chris told her he had threatened to quit if the coach refused to let him run. Chris was one of the best runners on the team, and he was usually quiet and non-confrontational. The coach had agreed to let Chris run. If Carrie had been Coach Wiand, faced with Chris's fierce intensity and quiet conviction, she would have made the same decision.

The starter raised his arms, and the runners hunched into ready positions. Six bodies tensed, six pairs of ears strained for the report of the gun. She did not breathe. Suddenly, the starter relaxed. One of the boys had forgotten to tie his shoe; he bent down to tie it, then looked up at the starter, who raised his arms a second time....

"Carrie!"

She turned to look over her shoulder, and in that moment the gun went off and she missed the start. She turned back to the race, her eyes scanning the track.

"Go, Chris!" she yelled, glad to see he had gotten off to a good start, that he had come out from the line strong and had established his position in the first lane after rounding the corner of the first hundred meter stretch. Then, she turned. "Hey, Sam."

He jogged down the row of bleachers to meet her, his gray sweat pants and navy blue hoodie reflecting Chris's team colors. She kept her eyes on the track, not knowing what to say to him; in the stretch of the morning with her fatigue and anxiety about Chris, she had forgotten about Sam. But Sam was an adult; he could take care of himself and she was not responsible for entertaining him.

"Where is he?" Sam asked, glancing at her stony face and then following her gaze to the track.

She pointed. "Second runner in the front of the pack. He's coming around the three-hundred meter mark right now."

She broke into a cheer, her voice lost among the noise in the stadium of screaming parents and teammates.

"How long is this race?" Sam asked her, when the runners had passed and the noise in the stadium had quieted.

"He has four-hundred meters to go. One lap."

"I understand the metric system."

She turned to him. "I didn't know if you were familiar with it."

He did not say anything.

She felt a pang of guilt. "I guess it would be stupid to ask if you drove all the way up here."

"You ditched me." He kept his eyes on her in the hope she would look at him. "What was I supposed to do but follow you?"

Her brow furrowed and her eyes darkened momentarily. She stood abruptly, and he knew nothing he had said had the power to so suddenly drain her face of color.

"Something's wrong," she said. She shot out of the bleachers, down the steps, and around the asphalt pavement that ringed the red track. Sam turned his eyes to the track and saw that the tall, lanky young man she had pointed out as her brother had fallen back to fourth place and was limping severely as he ran. His shoulders dipped savagely as he stumbled along the track, the jaggedness of the movement exaggerated because the kid was still trying to run fast as hell. Sam watched him fall, then saw him continue his hop along the track, putting next to no weight on his left leg at all. A streak of navy blue and white hurtled across the field and Sam realized the tall, stout man must be the coach, because he was heading in a beeline towards the loping figure—though Carrie was already there. Sam could see her hanging onto the fence surrounding the track, screaming. If Chris heard her he did not show it; he continued his staggering hop around the track, his head level and facing forward as another runner smoothly passed him.

Now Sam could see the coach hunched over into what looked like a wrestler's ready position, his hands on his knees, his florid face red as he started yelling, trying to get his runner's attention. If Sam had not witnessed the wrenching gait, he would have thought they were yelling encouragement or inspiring words; the thin, muscled arms pumped faster, propelling Chris forward at a quicker hop. But Sam knew something was wrong and so did the people around him; while some people continued cheering for their runners, many stopped and exchanged glances and questions, and Sam saw concerned confusion on many faces that turned to watch the unknown runner continue his bizarre hop around the track. Chris had one hundred and fifty meters to go, and though the other runners were locked in an intense battle on the final hundred meter stretch, most of the spectators' eyes were back at the 650 meter mark.

Sam stood. He jogged down the steps and around the asphalt ring to the beginning of the three-hundred meter mark. He saw Carrie and the coach continue to yell at Chris to stop, and he knew they were wasting their time. The kid's face was haggard and drained of color under its heavy sheen of perspiration, but his arms continued to scissor forward and back. Sam could hear him breathing heavily as he rounded the corner, and Sam found himself cheering, encouraging him onward.

Chris opened his eyes. They were cold blue and glittering feverishly, and focused with deadly intensity on the stretch of track before him. He put his full weight on the leg causing the limp, and he ran. Sam yelled for him, drawn in by the intensity on the straining face, following the figure to the end of the last stretch.

Chris finished the race a minute after the last runner. He crossed the finish line, collapsed, and was shuttled away in an ambulance, his face an embalmed white. He never said a word.

Sam followed the ambulance and made Carrie go with him, because he could see she was shaking too hard to drive.

"Carrie."

"What." She paused. "I'm sorry, Sam. I didn't mean to snap."

He saw her wince; Chris had snapped one of the tendons in his leg as well as fracturing his ankle. Sam stepped away from the white hospital door where he was looking through the small rectangular window and came to sit in the stiff-backed chair beside her. He had always hated hospitals: the white walls, the sterilized smell in the corridors, the lowered voices of patients and doctors conversing. He had been in an emergency room only once before.

"He'll be okay," Sam said, struggling with his thoughts. "He won't be able to run for awhile, but he'll be able to walk without crutches in a couple of months."

"He wanted to win that race, Sam. That's why I'm worried. I know that with time he'll be all right physically, but he really wanted to win that race."

"I could tell," Sam said. "I saw his face. But it took a hell of a lot of strength for him just to finish. Doesn't he know that?"

"That won't be enough. Not for a Crenshaw."

They both looked up as the hospital door swung open. Chris limped out on a pair of wooden crutches, followed by an ER nurse dressed in light blue scrubs. He didn't look at either of them, and kept his burning eyes lowered. A light scarlet colored his cheeks.

"Here he is," the blue-clad nurse announced cheerfully. "He'll be good as new in no time. Miss Crenshaw, will you come with me for a moment…"

"Of course." Carrie stood. "Chris, why don't you keep Sam company for a minute while I go talk with the nurse."

Chris nodded in acknowledgment but kept his head lowered as he moved himself over to the seat she had vacated. Sam patted the cushion of the seat to welcome him, but Chris sat down without glancing at him, and after he had stacked the crutches against the wall, sat with his hands clenched in his lap.

"Miss Crenshaw?"

Carrie watched Chris anxiously for a moment, then met Sam's eyes. He smiled at her and she looked away. "I'm ready."

"This will only take a minute," the nurse said, talking to Chris in a honied voice. "You were a very good boy."

"He's fifteen years old," Carrie said, evenly. "You shouldn't talk to him like he's a child."

The nurse smiled and motioned for Carrie to follow her.

"Carrie, wait," Sam said. "Do you have enough to cover—."

"Yes," Carrie said, and Chris relaxed. "I'll be back in a minute."

She followed the nurse, the white door cutting them off from sight. Sam sat in awkward silence beside Chris. He had never had problems interacting with kids or adolescents before, but for once he was at a loss for words.

"Thanks for leaving me the note this morning," he said, finally, "to let me know where you and Carrie were."

Chris nodded in acknowledgment.

He paused. "Carrie didn't tell you to leave it, did she?"

Chris shook his head.

"That was considerate of you, you know."

Chris shrugged.

"So how did you know to leave me a note?" Sam asked, wishing Chris would make eye contact with him. Chris shrugged, and there was silence.

Sam looked at the white wall in front of him. "Why do you suppose they don't have a clock here? Do you think it's so that people don't know how long they've been waiting?"

"It's the emergency ward," Chris said. "No one here has to wait very long."

"Guess not." Sam stretched and slouched, trying to look relaxed and comfortable. Beside him Chris sat ramrod straight, his eyes shifting from his hands to the crutches leaning against the wall. Self-consciously, Sam straightened his posture.

"You put up a good fight today," he said.

Chris stiffened. "I lost."

"Is that what matters?"

"I had to win today."

"That's not what I asked you."

"You wouldn't understand." Chris's voice was bitter, but Sam could tell he was trying to be polite.

"Maybe not." Sam shrugged. "But I still want to know what matters most, when you run a race. Do you really think that winning is everything?"

"Winning was everything today."

"Carrie told me on the way here that you weren't supposed to run that race." When Chris didn't respond, Sam added in a low voice, "Running like you did makes me think you must have been running for something. For something or someone."

Chris shifted. "Did Carrie tell you?"

"About what?"

The gravity with which Chris was looking at him made his boyish face older than its years. "About our cousin Justine."

Sam exhaled slowly. "Yeah. She did."

"I was running for her." Chris's eyes darkened. "And I...."

"You finished. You fought and you finished."

Chris looked away. "It doesn't matter."

"It does." Sam paused. "I can't think of a more symbolic ending to your race."

"Are you an English major like Carrie?"

"I am." Sam met Chris's eyes. "Sorry, bud, but we're trained to see symbolism in everything."

"Do you write, too?"

"I do." He paused. "Not like your sister does, though. She's a very talented, and a very dedicated, writer."

Chris's cheeks flushed with pride. He shifted in his chair and moved his eyes from the crutches to the blank spot on the wall where Sam had been staring a moment before. "Why is the race's end symbolic? Because no matter how much I wanted to win, I couldn't beat the odds?"

"That's not what I had in mind." Sam let the silence grow heavier, hoping that Chris was would not let pride keep him from asking for what he wanted.

"Why is it symbolic?" Chris asked again.

"You did what you wanted to do, and you didn't give up. You don't think that's an appropriate way to end a race?"

"I thought you were going to say something more profound."

"Sorry to disappoint. But Carrie told me that, more than success, your family valued the fight."

Chris turned to him. "What did Carrie tell you about our family?"

"Not much," Sam admitted. "She doesn't talk much about herself."

Chris continued to look at him, hesitant. Sam returned his attention to the white hospital doors.

"I wonder what's taking so long," he said. "Usually hospital procedures are quick. They give you a couple of forms and you sign and go along your way."

"It would be the forms," Chris said. "Carrie won't sign anything until she's read every word. It's something Dad told us to do, before we put our names in agreement on a contract."

"Do you get along with your dad?"

"He's dead," Chris said.

"I'm sorry." Sam took a penny out of the pocket of his jeans, then began flipping it over and under the fingers of his right hand, the copper flashing in the hospital lights in the hallway. He did it automatically, hating to have his hands idle and having made a habit of the trick to keep him occupied when sitting through hours of university lectures.

"I heard you yelling for me," Chris said, after a pause. "When I came to the seven hundred meter mark."

"You seemed pretty intent on running. I didn't know if you'd hear me or not."

"I heard you," Chris repeated. "You were the only one telling me to go." He paused. "Can you show me how to do that?"

Sam paused, then continued moving the penny when he saw Chris watching the coin's movement. "This?"

Chris nodded.

"It's not as hard as it looks," Sam said. "You just have to learn the trick and then practice."

He held the penny out to Chris and Chris started to reach for the coin, and then the white hospital doors opened. Chris stood abruptly, forgetting about his leg, and winced as he fell back into the chair. The penny fell from Sam's fingers to the cold, plain floor.

140

"Everything okay?" Sam asked, as he bent down to look for the penny.

"Fine," Carrie said. She picked up the penny and handed it to Sam. She took the crutches leaning against the wall and handed them to Chris. "There were just some forms to fill out and—"

"Can we go see Justine?" Chris asked.

Carrie glanced at him. "We should get you home."

"You promised."

"By the time we get back to Greensburg, Chris, visiting hours will be over."

He looked away. "Did you call Mom?"

"I've tried calling home, but she's not answering her phone. She's probably working." She paused. "We'll go see Justine tomorrow."

"You're going back to Penn State tomorrow."

"You can go tomorrow afternoon," Sam interrupted, looking at Carrie. "I can leave as late as seven."

She paused. "I work at five."

Sam shrugged. "We'll leave around two then. You'll have plenty of time to pay your cousin a visit before then." He broke off because Carrie and Chris had locked eyes in a silent dialogue; for the moment, he felt invisible.

"I want you to come," Chris said finally, turning to Sam. "When Carrie and I go to visit Justine, I want you to come."

He saw surprise flash across Carrie's face. Rather than responding, he pulled the penny out of his pocket and handed it to Chris.

"Keep it for good luck," he said.

Chris turned his face away.

"I'll teach you the trick some time this weekend." Sam continued to hold out the coin. "Take the penny, so you can practice."

After a moment Chris reached out and took the penny. As Carrie sent Sam a questioning glance, Chris put the penny in his pocket and nodded.

"Where's Chris?"

Carrie looked up from where she was reading in the living room to find Christine standing in the doorway, her white nurse's jacket half on and half-off, exposing her teal green scrubs.

"He's sleeping," Carrie said. "He was tired after his race and his hospital experience and disappointed that we couldn't visit Justine until tomorrow." She closed her book. "You look exhausted."

Christine nodded, placing the jacket on top of the sofa. "Would you mind? Five minutes?"

Carrie shook her head, and began kneading the tenseness out of her mother's shoulders.

"Is Chris alright? What did the nurse say?"

"Simple fracture," Carrie said. "And a torn tendon. I wrote down the information and stuck the note on the refrigerator."

"Thank you, Carrie."

"What happened at work today? I tried calling you but no one answered."

"Emergency baby," Christine mumbled. "Born with a caul obstructing his breathing. One thing after another. I couldn't leave the doctor's side. But I came home as soon as I got your message." Christine winced as Carrie kneaded out a knot in her right shoulder. "Did Chris seem okay?"

"Chris seemed fine."

"I'm so glad he's talking to you."

"He hasn't seen me for awhile."

"He doesn't talk to me much, any more."

"He's got a good head on his shoulders, just like Carly does."

"I know," Christine said, sighing. "But I worry. Times have changed so much from when I was growing up. I'm an old woman now." She smiled, and then the smile sagged. "I know they have to face the same pressures, but drugs weren't so easily accessible and sex before marriage wasn't so openly accepted. And I worry that Chris doesn't have a male role model." She paused. "Except your brother, who I'm glad he doesn't imitate."

"He has his coach," Carrie interjected. "He seems to admire him."

"Don't speak to me of that man." Christine pushed herself up from the chair. "You don't see Chris the night before a race, when he's so nervous that he's going to let his team down, or every day when he comes home from practice and looks exhausted but then goes out to run on his own because that man says the team relies on him. That kind of pressure and stress is not healthy for a child of Chris's age."

"You can't protect him from the world forever."

"That's why I pray for you all. Every night." She paused. "Are you going back to the university with Sam tomorrow?"

"We're going to leave after I visit Justine. We'll probably drop Chris off here and then take off."

"And we've barely had time to talk. You'll just have to come home again sometime soon." She paused when Carrie remained quiet. "Sam seems like a nice person, though I haven't seen much of him. Is he in Calder's room?"

"He's out walking."

"You didn't want to go with him?"

"I wanted to wait until you got home. I thought you would want to know about Chris."

Christine smiled. "Thank you, Carrie. So how is everything up at school?"

"Fine."

"How's Damien?"

She kept her tone neutral. "I don't really see him anymore."

"Keep the old friends while you make new ones," Christine suggested.

"It can't be like that," Carrie said, looking around the empty living room. "I'm not interested in being friends without benefits."

Christine frowned. "I think the term is 'friends with benefits,' Carrie. At least, Carly tells me that's the rage today…and I've told her I better not catch her in any such kind of relationship. Good for you, honey."

"Maybe it was a Freudian slip." Carrie paused. "Maybe I'm misconstruing the situation. Maybe I'm the one who wants more, and I'm not comfortable with that."

"Carrie?"

Carrie shook her head. "He probably doesn't even think about me anymore. I haven't seen him in over a month."

"That doesn't mean he's forgotten you."

"It's better if I don't see him."

Christine paused. "If he were the one, would you let yourself fall in love with him?"

Carrie bristled. "I don't buy all this talk about 'the one.' I don't think I'd ever be happy with one person."

"Why do you think that?"

"I'm not going to be the same person five years from now—or at least I hope I'm not. So even if I found someone now, maybe then he wouldn't be right for me later, or I wouldn't be right for him."

"You change together."

"If you're with someone, you have limitations on how much you can change. And I wouldn't like that."

"That's not necessarily true, Carrie. Having another person love you, and loving another person, doesn't mean your personal growth has to stop." Christine adjusted some of the overflowing papers on her desk. "Instead of thinking of a romantic partner as an obstacle in your way, think of that person as a witness to the many different phases you will go through. Loving someone else can show you quite a bit about yourself." She paused. "I've been your mother for twenty years, and my love for you never stopped you from growing, changing, going in directions I never could have dreamed of."

"Being in a romantic relationship is different. It would be too easy to compromise myself."

"The right person wouldn't let you. If you meet someone who loves you, he won't let you sacrifice yourself for him."

"Love?" She paused. "Who loves anyone these days? All men want is sex."

Christine raised an eyebrow. "Do you think it was any different when I was your age, Carrie? You just have to stay true to yourself."

"Ideally," Carrie said after a pause. "I think I'd prefer three. Three lovers."

"*Three*," Christine said.

"I'm not saying that will happen. But right now I want someone who doesn't want any long-term commitment, but who wouldn't accept a one-night stand either. He'd be someone to have fun with, someone to help me get over all the awkwardness." She glanced at Christine, but continued. "The second man would be my soulmate, in the traditional sense—someone I would really love and someone who would love me in return. We'd help each other and support each other and learn to live with and accept each other. Then, when I was really starting to know I loved him, he would disappear. He would leave me or he'd die or something would happen."

Christine sighed. "Why?"

"Because then I'd be back on my own again." Carrie paused. "I never want someone to mean so much to me that having him gone would destroy me. That would be the final lesson of the second man; I would need to learn how to live on my own again."

"And the third person?"

Carrie could tell she was trying to be patient and nonjudgmental. "The third man would be someone in a similar situation, maybe someone who had lost his wife and had been so in love with her that he would want to remember what being with her had been like. We'd be companions; we'd grow old together. We'd share our lives together and we'd be happy, but we'd both know that if there's another life after this one, we'd go back to our previous lovers, to our soulmates." She paused. "So, ideally, three."

Christine sat quietly for a moment. "Can't they all be the same person, Carrie?"

"No."

"Why?"

"The relationships involved are too different to exist in one person."

"But you said people change. What if you met someone who had the same ideas as you?"

"I probably wouldn't recognize him."

Christine paused. "We'll have to continue this conversation in the morning, Carrie. Just make sure you're making smart life choices and taking care of yourself. Your partner can make life beautiful, or he can make your life a living hell. If you need proof of that look at our family. Love is not something to take lightly."

"I know," Carrie said, and paused. "I didn't even mean to tell you any of this."

"Mothers have a way of finding out," Christine said. "And I like talking with you. I'm not promising that I'll agree with what you say, but I will respect that you are an adult now and in charge of your own life. You've always accepted the consequences of your actions. I ask only that you remember that when you're presented with a situation and have to make a decision, your choice makes a change. Never forget who you are or what you're worth. I just want you to be happy. I love you."

Carrie lowered her head to keep Christine from seeing the tears in her eyes. "I love you, too."

"I'll see you in the morning, honey."

"Goodnight," Carrie said. "Can you wake me up before you leave for work tomorrow?"

Christine nodded, and Carrie left. She went up the stairs and let herself silently into the room she shared with Carly. She heard Sam stumbling up the steps in the dark, and then she fell asleep.

Sam woke up late Sunday morning—around noon—and the house was empty except for Carly, who was sitting in the Crenshaw living room painting her toenails pink and poring over a biology book the size of a medical text. He was glad he had fallen asleep fully dressed.

"Hey, kiddo," he said. "Doing homework?"

She looked up and smiled, the nail polish collected at the end of the brush hovering dangerously above the cream-colored carpet. "Hi, Sam. Yeah."

"How's it going?"

She stuck her tongue out at the book. "I don't understand any of it. Mom usually helps me but she's working today, so I'm trying to make sense of *something* so that when she comes home tonight we can go over everything else."

"So you cram," he said. "I do, too."

"I'm not cramming," Carly said. "I've been studying for this test for two weeks but nothing makes sense, and Mr. Colmer just added this unit on parasites on Thursday and he thinks we should know it well enough for tomorrow's test. Like, I can only study so hard."

"I could try to help you," he said. "But I haven't had biology for—."

"It's okay. I'll wait for Mom to get home. She's the only one who can explain things to me so I understand them. With everyone else, I'm hopeless." She paused. "I got up early and made pancakes for everyone. There are some left on the stove if you're hungry. Oh, never mind." She pushed aside her book and stood, walking on her heels out of the room. "I'll make you breakfast Carly-style."

He followed her into the kitchen and watched as she pulled out a plate. She plopped two thick pancakes on it.

"Maybe not so much," he said, as she started to slather the pancakes with whipped cream.

"You'll like it. I promise." She added another circle of whipped cream onto the growing mound, then picked up a metal container which she started shaking over the top of the conglomeration. She reached for another metal container, flecking the creamy mound with specks of brown.

"Confectioner's sugar," he said. "And?"

She stared at him. "Huh?"

"The white stuff is confectioner's sugar, isn't it?"

"No. It's powdered sugar. It's not." She snorted. "I don't know what you just said."

"I bet they're the same thing."

She handed him the container; he sprinkled some of the white powder on his hand, tasted it, nodded.

"What's a confectioner?" she asked.

"A confectioner is like a cook," he said, taking the fork and the plate she handed him as he sat down. "Thanks."

As she went into the living room, he eyed the mess in front of him. He wasn't hungry; he was frustrated. He wanted to know where Carrie was and why she kept abandoning him, but he'd clean his plate for the kid's sake. Carly came back into the kitchen, toting her textbook, and sat down across from him at the other end of the table.

"Aren't you going to eat?" she asked.

He ended up with more whipped cream than pancake as he stuck the first forkful in his mouth. His eyes widened.

"Wow," he said. "Carly. This is really good."

"Don't speak with your mouth full," she responded, looking down at her book. She flipped a page. "I told you."

"I mean, these are good enough to sell at the restaurant where I work," he said, attacking the pancakes with his fork. "That was really nice of you to get up early and make breakfast for your family."

"I do it all the time, but Mom and Chris usually don't let me make my special for them." She paused. "What do you do at the restaurant?"

"I cook."

"I've never heard of guys cooking before," she said. "My dad would never cook, even if it was to turn on the oven to cook something Mom had already made. Like when Mom was running late at the hospital or picking one of us from school or whatever. We'd always have to wait till she got home before we could eat. But then I learned how to use the stove, so I could turn the oven on so dinner was ready when Mom got home. Chris tried to help once, but Dad flipped out and said Chris should be doing something else, like training for running or something, so Chris never did it again. Or he'd do it in secret, so Dad wouldn't see."

"Well, I cook," Sam said. He wondered why Carrie had said Carly kept to herself; the girl seemed dying to talk to someone.

"Are you any good or do you burn stuff?"

"I'm good." He paused. "I'll have to cook you dinner sometime, because I can see you don't believe me."

Her eyes sparked. "So you're coming back?"

"I hope so." He paused. "Carly, do you know where everyone is?"

"Yeah," she said. "I was just waiting for you to ask. Mom's at work and Carrie and Chris are at the hospital visiting my cousin."

A flash of anger shot through him. "Do you know what time Carrie left?"

"I was asleep."

"How far away is the hospital?"

"You should probably just stay here." She began to apply a second coat of polish to her nails. "By the time you get to the hospital, they'll probably be back." She paused. "She said you wanted to leave around two. We could play a game or something if you're bored."

"That's okay," he said. "I have some work I can do. I'll wait for her to get back."

Carly paused. "I thought you'd be angrier."

"I'm not angry."

"You should be," Carly said. "Carrie's been ditching you all weekend. You should be a lot angrier."

"I don't think it would be appropriate if I went raging around the house, do you?" he asked. "Carrie was pretty straightforward with me. She needed to come home. She needed a ride."

"Carrie's never straightforward about anything." Carly paused. "Which is really funny, because she tries so hard to be."

He felt like they were talking in circles. His patience was fraying and he felt like hitting something. Though he kept his face blank, Carly picked up on his mood.

"It's okay to show her you're angry, Sam."

"I thought men weren't supposed to show any emotion."

"Media construction," she said.

He stared at her. "Media construction?"

Carly nodded. "True reality is deformed by societal norms and media construction. That's why it's so hard to find anything real. If you show emotion around Carrie she'll probably like it. Because it's real."

"Really."

"I have to study," Carly said. "Or I'm going to fail. Then my GPA will come down and I might not get into the college I want, and then I'll fail in life. At least that's what Calder says."

He could not tell if she was being serious or sarcastic. "I wouldn't worry too much about failing."

"I was kidding." She paused. "You should talk to Carrie when she gets back. And I hope you come here again, Sam. I like you."

She breezed out of the room. He smiled, his anger abating, then went over to the window and stared outside. The sky remained a swollen, bruised blue, but the weather had mellowed. At least he wouldn't have to worry about snow on the drive back to the university, and he wouldn't have to worry about her driving back from the hospital and skidding off the road.

"Thanks again for breakfast, Carly!" he shouted.

She peeked her head around the corner. "You're welcome."

"Everything was delicious," Sam said, in a softer tone. "Good luck studying."

"Yeah," she said, leaving him alone at the counter.

An hour and a half later Sam heard a car door slam, and his anger and frustration rekindled. He grabbed his backpack and started down the steps. He had planned to head her off, but when the front door opened, Chris walked in.

"Bye," he said, his voice choked. Sam started to reply but Chris plowed up the stairs, carrying his crutches, without looking at him. He turned to see Carrie walk in, her eyes troubled. She looked from Sam to his bag, and her shoulders sagged.

"Are you ready to leave?" she asked.

The sight of her tired, haggard face and the sign of dejection in her lowered shoulders did not assuage his anger. He wanted to shake her, to hit her, yet he never would; he would give her the opportunity to explain her actions to him before he jumped to conclusions.

"How did everything go?" he asked.

She shrugged. "Is Carly here? I told her I'd drive her to her friend's house so they could study."

"I took Carly to her friend's house," Sam said. "An hour ago, when you and Chris weren't back. I owed her one, since she made me breakfast."

Carrie smiled. "Pancakes a la Carly?"

"Something like that."

"Thank you, Sam."

He inhaled, then stepped away from her. "Is Chris alright?"

"Chris is mad at Justine," she said. "And he's mad at me. But he'll be fine."

"Why is he—"

"Sam." She sighed. "I don't want to talk now. I'm sorry if I'm blowing you off, but—"

"We have to get back to the university."

"Is it that late already?" Carrie paused. "We went to see my mother after we visited, and Chris won't want me to say goodbye, so I guess we can leave now."

"Unless Chris isn't going to be all right here by himself."

"Chris is fifteen," she said, glancing at him. "Let me get my stuff and then we can leave."

He waited in the front hallway as she walked slowly up the stairs. He remembered the anticipation he had felt when entering her house and wondering whether or not he would make a good impression on her family. But Chris and Carly had accepted him, Christine seemed too tired and busy to care and Carrie—Carrie had made it clear, multiple times, that they were friends—if that. He watched her come back down the steps.

"Did you say goodbye to Chris?"

"I did." She nodded. "He's a good kid. He gave me a hug even though he's mad as hell at me."

"Why is he mad at you, of all people?"

"He wanted you to come see Justine," she said. "He's mad that we left without you."

"I'm a little angry about that myself."

She looked away. "Chris said he wanted to see you. Do you have a few minutes to talk to him?"

"Sure," Sam said, pushing his anger to the back of his mind. "I'll be right back."

He found Chris's room easily because it was the only one with a closed door. He knocked gently. "Hey, Chris? It's Sam. Carrie said you wanted to see me."

The door opened. Chris hobbled back into the room and sat on his bed, then propped his crutches against the wall. Sam caught the penny Chris tossed to him.

"Can you show me the trick?"

Sam sat down next to him, demonstrated, then handed the penny to Chris. Without saying a word, Chris started the penny's dance across his fingers. Sam smiled.

"You're a quick learner."

The penny's dance stopped. "Thanks."

"No problem." Sam stood, stretched. "I bet that makes it hard for you when you don't get something right away, though." He paused. "We're going to get going, but it was nice to meet you."

"Thank you for bringing Carrie home."

Sam did not say what was on his mind. He nodded at the penny in Chris's hands. "Keep practicing, so you don't forget, and—"

"Sam. Carrie appreciates your friendship. She just doesn't know how to interact with men. She hated our dad, and…" He paused. "She just has a lot of barriers. But maybe I'm betraying her trust, to tell you."

Sam shook his head. "I already knew. I mean, she had to trust me to let me stay here, right?" He was unsettled by how old Chris's eyes looked. "Sometimes you just have to wait for people to come around."

"Do you think Justine will come around?"

Sam paused. "I can't know that, Chris."

Chris was silent, then he spoke. "Thank you for your honesty."

"Take care of yourself. That's all you can do, Chris."

"I think I'm going to practice this trick now." Chris glanced down at the penny.

Sam nodded. "I'll close the door on my way out."

He went back down the stairs, saw Carrie waiting anxiously for him at the bottom.

"Let's go," he said.

She followed him out of the house, then went to the passenger side of his car and yanked on the handle.

"Easy," he said. "It's not an automatic. I have to unlock it for you."

She stood waiting. He unlocked the door, feeling how she tensed as he came near her. He crossed to the driver's side and saw that she had reached across the seats and unlocked the door for him. He got in the car.

"Thanks," he said.

"You're welcome," she said, staring straight ahead.

He started the car. "I'm not driving for almost three hours in silence," he said, pushing a dog-eared black case towards her. "Pick something."

She flipped through the case as he backed out of her driveway. "I've always wished I had more knowledge about music in general."

"You can borrow as many of them as you want. Or I'll burn you a copy if you find something you like. Or I can make you a sampler."

"That's the kind of thing a friend would do."

"I'm your friend, aren't I?" His hands clenched the steering wheel. "I drove for three hours so you could see your family. How can you doubt my intentions?"

"I still don't know what your intentions are," she said.

"Why have you been such a bitch this weekend?"

She looked at him, clearly startled. "I'm not being a bitch. I don't know what—"

"You have been a bitch," he said. "This entire weekend you've either ditched me or you've avoided me. And while Chris and Carly are great people to hang around with…"

"I think you forgot the purpose of my visit home, Sam," she said. "I came home to see my family, and I came home to see my cousin who is sick. Dying."

"Don't use your cousin as a reason for avoiding me."

"What?"

He paused. "I'm sorry that Justine is living through hell right now, but I'm not sorry that Justine might die. People act like death is a big tragedy, but I've never bought it. Death sets you free. That's what I believe, and even if it's harsh, I'm not going to lie about it to you."

She stared at him fixedly, then shifted her gaze out the window and remained silent for long enough to make him wonder if he had overstepped his boundaries.

"It's not harsh," she said, finally. "It's what I think, too. Sam?"

"What?"

"If you hadn't said something, I don't think I would have. I don't talk about death like that to other people."

"It makes you wonder, doesn't it?" he said. "Or it makes me wonder, at least, how many people feel exactly like we do and don't say anything because that opinion counters the status quo. Your sister called it media construction." He paused. "I apologize for being such an asshole."

"What are you talking about? I told you I feel the same—"

"I mean using Justine as an example." He paused. "How was the visit?"

Carrie looked out the window. "Justine is trying to kill herself. She won't do anything blatant, because she believes suicide will damn you to Hell and she doesn't want to do anything that goes against the Bible. But she sleeps as much as she can now, with the hope that every time she falls asleep she won't wake up. That's what she said, while Chris was standing right there." She paused. "It pisses me off, Sam."

"Of course it does," he said. "Especially if she said that in front of Chris."

"He's fifteen," Carrie snapped. "He's fifteen, a vital fact that both Justine and Calder don't seem to realize. I'm sorry that their worlds are falling apart, but a fifteen year old is *not* the person to confess their depression or debauchery to. And Chris will listen, no matter what they say, because Chris is like that. They're the adults. They should be able to control themselves."

"What are you suggesting they do? Lie to him?"

"They need to get help," she said.

"I thought you said Justine was seeing a psychiatrist."

"She is."

"That's a step."

"We're taking Route 22 first." Carrie turned away from him, her brow furrowed and her lips pressed into a scowl.

He paused. "Why have you avoided me this weekend?"

She was silent. Sam pulled off to the side of the road with a jerk and stalled the car, and kept a frown on his face as she looked at him questioningly.

"Carrie, I can accept you avoiding me," he said. "But not lying to me."

She stared at him. "I haven't lied to you."

"You lied. You told me we would go see your brother run and that you wanted me to come with you to see Justine. You told me you wanted to introduce me to your family and everything that your family was."

"I'm not discussing this with you right now."

"We're not discussing," he shouted. "I'm yelling at you and you're sitting there and not saying anything!"

She unbuckled her seatbelt. "Let me out right here, Sam. I'll walk, I'll hitchhike, but I won't let you yell at me."

He reached over her, pushed down the lock on her door, and kept his hand over it. "You're not walking. Don't be ridiculous."

She tried to pry his hand off the lock. He clamped his hand over hers. She glared at him.

"Get control of yourself," she said.

His hand tightened on hers.

She sighed. "You're right. I have been a bitch. Because I know you like me, and I don't want to lead you on."

"Why is it so important to you to not lead guys on? Most girls do it all the time. Guys do it to girls, too. It's a mutual thing."

"I don't agree with playing mind games."

He gripped the steering wheel with both hands. "Forget that I brought it up. Forget about it all. When we get back to the university I won't bother you again."

"I don't want that, Sam," she said. "I like you. I'd be very sad if I never saw you again."

He paused. "Are you going to keep acting like a bitch?"

She nodded.

"Sucks to be me, then," he said.

"You'll get over me." She paused. "If I keep acting like this."

"Why do you think that?"

"I'll never give you what you want."

"I've known from the start that you won't ever be my girlfriend. That reason doesn't help me at all."

She looked at him. "Your girlfriend."

He looked down. He was ashamed that he had lost control around her. "Thanks for letting me stay with you."

"I'm sorry I wasn't a better hostess." She said the words mechanically, but her voice was soft. "I really am sorry, Sam."

He silently started the car; it had stalled. The engine revved and went dead. He tried again, to no effect. He slumped against the driver's seat, hands gripping the steering wheel.

"This is awkward," he said.

"Awkward moments reveal character."

He tried to start the engine again, and the car roared to life. She looked out the window listlessly, a sad, perplexed look on her drawn face.

"I don't wonder why you wanted to hitchhike," he said. "I haven't been the best company."

"You've been great," she said. "Thanks for everything, Sam."

He pulled back onto the highway, unwilling to let the awkward silence

155

continue though he believed her, that awkwardness did reveal character, and that at the moment he was struggling to bring out the better side of his.

"Do you like the music?" he asked.

"It's not how I thought Pink Floyd would sound," she said. "I always thought they were hard rock or metal, and they aren't, at all."

"No, they're not," he agreed. "Do you want to listen to something else?"

"Yes," she said. "If you don't mind, I'd like to listen to the CD I found before the Objectivist lecture. I haven't had a chance to listen to it yet." She paused. "I wanted to wait until we could listen to it together."

Her words mollified his anger slightly. "Do you have it with you?"

She unzipped her duffel bag, shifted the contents, then handed him the CD. He inserted the CD into the player, then put the Pink Floyd CD back into its case and back into the storage compartment between them without taking his eyes from the road.

"How can you do so many things at the same time you're driving?" she asked.

"I go on a lot of trips by myself. I'm used to it."

She looked at the dashboard. "I hope it works. Sometimes they don't, and sometimes they skip."

The music that issued forth from the car's speakers surprised them both; powerful rhythms of pulsating beats, a symphony of screaming instruments that reminded him of a throbbing headache.

"Classical?" he asked.

"Beethoven."

"I didn't think anyone listened to classical music anymore. That's exaggerating, but—"

"He was a tormented individual," she said. "Can't you hear it in his music? Listen."

He stopped speaking and listened, and while he had never particularly liked classical music, he felt the chords and harmonics resonating inside his body.

"It's powerful," he said.

"It's perfect," she said. "He's my favorite classical composer."

He hesitated. "Carrie."

She turned to him.

"Chris." His hands tightened on the steering wheel. "Chris isn't into drugs or anything, is he?"

She stared. "Don't be ridiculous. My family doesn't mess around with things like that."

"Right." There had been a faint smell in Chris's room that he had thought he recognized, but he was sleep deprived and could easily have been mistaken. He focused on the music: the strident notes of various instrumentals tumbling over each other in a chaotic way that somehow melded into harmony. He had not known that such power, such passion, could be expressed wordlessly, but he agreed with her: the music was perfect.

He parked in front of her house, then got out of the car so he could walk her to the door. He saw her glance at the house next door, then turn her face away almost immediately. He glanced up in time to see the black silhouette leaning out the window move.

"Carrie, watch out," Sam said suddenly, and pulled her closer to him. Seconds later, a beer bottle exploded on the sidewalk where she had been standing moments before. She stared at the shattered glass and heard Sam yelling beside her. Then she heard the voice she had been longing—and afraid—to hear.

"Carrie! You slut!"

She glanced up at his window, saw him hanging half out of it. His drunken words were unmercifully coherent.

"You liar!" he yelled. "You're a fucking whore, just like the rest of—"

Rage boiled through her. She bent down, picked up the neck of the broken bottle and hurled it up the three stories. The glass exploded below his window and forced him to duck back into his room.

"Coward!" she exclaimed, triumphant. "Damn you, Damien!"

A hand on her shoulder reawakened her to Sam's presence. She turned towards him, saw the confusion and anger on his face.

"*Damien?*" he asked.

She shook his hand off and kicked the snow. "Small world."

"Go inside," he said, after a pause. "He picked the wrong night to fuck with you."

"Leave him alone." She started towards the side entrance of Damien's house.

"Carrie," Sam said sharply. "The Elizabethans—or the Victorians—believed that the light of a full moon made a person crazy."

She paused, as if shocked by an invisible fence. Past the light in Damien's room, a full moon hung in the dark velvet sky. She turned back to Sam.

His face was grim. "They believed that a person under the influence of the moon could not be held responsible for his or her actions."

Sam's words upset her. She stood and stared at him, She remembered Tessa's words

please don't go over to that house again

and her promise to herself, that her decision to leave him behind fringed on never going back to him.

"Carrie?" Sam stood watching her. His face had become a mask. "You're bleeding."

She looked down, saw the crimson staining the ivory of her gloves and the jagged tear in the fabric.

"The bottle must have cut you," he said. "When you—"

She turned to her house, dismissing her hand. He continued to stare at her. "Carrie? I *know* Damien. I've never seen him act like that before."

"It doesn't matter," she said.

"Yes, it does matter. I—"

"Go home, Sam," she said, her voice uncharacteristically grim.

He stared at her, incredulously—but a hardness had come into her features. He felt as if he had disappeared. She did not speak another word to him; she walked briskly into her house. The screen door slammed behind her.

The light in the highest window of the house next door was still on. Sam checked himself from going over and finding his way to that room. Carrie would be furious with him if he interfered, and Sam did not want to speak to Damien then. He glanced at the roads and realized they were much worse; he wouldn't be able to drive home for the night. He would have to walk.

As was his custom, he thought as he walked. He thought about Carrie—and so he had to think about Damien.

Damien had listened to him rave about Carrie Crenshaw and had never mentioned that he lived next door to her. Never mentioned there was something going on between them. Sam felt a flash of anger, a sudden realization why Damien had never wanted to meet at his house. But Damien had also helped him come up with creative ideas for catching Carrie's interest. The conflicting actions didn't make sense.

He did not feel the cold as he walked. His face had gone numb after five minutes of exposure to the outside chill, and his thoughts carried him far away. In the aftermath of what had happened that night, Sam knew he would rather lose Damien's friendship than let him hurt Carrie.

Images flashed through her mind in rapid succession: Chris, his face contorted with pain, the muscles jumping in his arms as they scissored back and forth; Justine, her skeletal features surrounded by a cloud of billowing, lackluster hair; Damien, his words slurred and angry, cutting her heart like the broken bottle had jagged into her skin. Fire burned in her heart and her hands clenched; she left her room.

She paused when she stood in front of Damien's house.

Her eyes swept over the bright orange recycling bin's contents, saw nothing but empty cans and water bottles—nothing of any weight, nothing she would be able to get up to the third story, and she didn't want to take any chances. Her aim wasn't good, and if she hit a window on the second floor by accident, the neighbors would call the police.

She crossed the distance between their houses, found his recycling bin and the cans and bottles inside it. An empty bottle of Corona clutched in her hand, she retreated to her porch. Away from State College, it had all seemed so out of whack—her desire, her obsession, the extremity of her constraint. But her absence from him had made her desire that much stronger. And she was angry. Angrier than she had ever been before, for what he had said to her, in front of Sam...

The bottle left her hand, splintered against the brick wall near his window. The house remained silent. Carrie bit her lower lip, tasting blood, and waited. All she wanted was for him to come out to her.

But he did not. She waited five minutes, shaking, and then she crossed over to his porch again and grabbed another bottle. This one shattered against his window. This time his silhouette appeared threateningly, to disappear a moment later.

Suddenly she was afraid. She turned and walked back to her house, went up the stairs, into her room. She felt mad, pursued inwardly by a wild beast she had to escape or let loose.

The white walls of her room called out to her. Instinctively she grabbed her paints and clambered onto her desk. She had squirted a first uneven streak of color onto the plastic palette when she heard the downstairs door open. Jerking, she almost dropped the palette. Her hand shook as she smeared two pale streaks onto the wall. Her door opened.

"What the hell do you think you're doing?" he growled. "Throwing bottles at my window and then—"

She felt his challenge, felt the anger inside her rise up to meet it. She turned to him, wild. Like a shock their eyes connected. She staggered under the intensity of his gaze, but she did not back away from him.

"Sam?" he said, prowling towards her, his hands clenched into fists. He stopped inches from her, the nearness of his body overpowering, then gripped her by her arms and forced her to look at him. "Sam?"

Looking up at him, she realized he was completely sober.

He bent towards her. She could not stop him; she did not want to. His lips bit into hers; his grip was painful. She felt the echo of his heartbeat inside her own, and her thoughts spun out of control. His kiss was like acid, burning through her veins and combusting her nerves into channels of running fire. She closed her eyes. Her breath escaped as he pushed her against the wall, then climbed up onto her chair to get a better grip on her.

She kept her eyes closed when he gave her a chance to breathe. She could not look at him.

"What were you painting, Carrie?" he asked, his voice soft and dangerous.

His hands were on the wall, on either side of her face, and she could feel his strong legs enveloping hers on the desk, locking her in place. In her mind she saw the pathetic streaks of color, felt the stronger color creeping into her cheeks.

"A butterfly," she trembled.

His soft laugh made her open her eyes. His attention was on the wall behind her, and slowly he let her go and lowered himself off her desk.

"Keep going," he said. "Don't let me disturb you."

She slammed the palette onto her desk. She crossed the room, cutting off his exit. Surprise—something more—flickered through his dark eyes. Angry energy lit her movement as she walked towards him, pushing him back into her room. His lips curled, and he turned his back on her. He walked calmly to her desk and picked up her palette, leaving her speechless with confusion.

"Look," he said. "Like this."

She watched as he dabbed a point of green onto the smears she had painted. With several flicks of the brush, he added threads of veins into the splotch. Then he turned to her, and she felt the heat of his smoldering eyes. They made her feel faint.

"Are you watching?" he asked.

She nodded. She watched as he dipped the brush into the slate-blue mix and added a series of delicate lines that turned the ugly smears into a delicately contoured wing. He gestured at the blue and jade butterfly he had painted on the wall.

She hesitated. "Will you show me again, from the start?"

"What's your favorite color?" he asked.

She answered without pause. "Orange."

He looked away from the wall long enough to pick out the bottle of acrylic orange paint and three different tones of red. Before her eyes a delicate, fluttering form took shape, its appearance like a tiny flame, a tiny spirit of hope on her white walls.

"I want you to try it," he said, stepping back.

She took the brush from him with trembling fingers and made a series of thick, wobbly lines inside the wing. He shook his head and smudged away the awkward marks with his finger.

"Try again," he said. "Get closer to the wall. Forget I'm here."

She climbed onto her desk and tried her best to ignore him as she focused on the wall. She was far too conscious of having him near her—of his smell, of his warmth, of the dizziness he made her feel...

"Breathe," he said.

She exhaled, but her hand shook as she moved the brush closer to the wall. Then his hand was on hers, guiding her, and the lines she drew were delicate.

"Much better," he said, his voice disappointingly professional. "Try it on your own."

She shook her head. "I'd rather watch you."

He took the brush from her, his eyes lingering on her face. "Carrie."

His hand, under her chin, forced her to look at him. But she could not have looked away from him had she tried. She felt as if nothing existed in the world except for him and the paint and the bare white walls.

"The day I showed you the Others," he said. "That day you accepted the darkest side of me, Carrie. You can't imagine how that affected me."

It was not what she had expected him to say. He let her go and she backed away, stumbled into her bed, and sat down.

"Go to sleep," he said, turning around. "I promise I'll behave."

She looked at the broad outline of his shoulders, the sweeping motion of his hand as he blended color and created tone. "I'm not tired."

"You must be exhausted." He turned and looked at her. "You never sleep."

She took a deep breath. She did not want to risk speaking—but she had to tell him. "I want...I want to be with you. When you're like this. I don't want to—"

"Carrie." He took one step towards her, and then he jerked—as if something had pulled him back. He stood looking at her, a mere distance of feet separating them. She waited for him to come to a decision; she sensed that her longing and hope was written clearly in her expression. His eyes lit with emotion and he exhaled—a long, ragged sound.

"Damien." She saw he was shaking and started to move towards him. "Are you—"

"I'm going through withdrawal," he said, turning his back on her.

162

"Leave me alone, Carrie. It'll pass in a moment. It'll help if I can distract myself."

She looked at him, concerned, but he was already dipping the brush into the paint, already scanning the empty space left on her wall.

"You shouldn't be around me right now," he said.

"Please don't go."

He hesitated, but he didn't turn to look at her. "I suppose I can behave. As long as I don't see you—"

"I'll be invisible," she whispered. "I trust you. Good night."

He tensed. "Goodnight."

She lay down on her bed and pulled the covers tightly around her. She closed her eyes. She was not sure whether he was aware of her existence anymore, but she was happy. She didn't know when he finished painting; she drifted off long before then.

At some point he must have turned off the lights and left. She dimly remembered hearing his footsteps and something like butterfly wings brushing against her cheek right before she fell asleep. But that might have been part of a dream she could not remember.

He had gone some time in the night, and he had left a living mosaic of acrylic butterflies, tiny ruby-throated hummingbirds, and creeping, gnarled vines on her previously white wall. She fell out of bed and crawled to the mural; she could almost feel the delicate flutter of the butterflies' painted flight, the manic quiver of the hummingbirds' wings. The black eyes of the multi-colored birds sparkled with avian intelligence.

With one hand pressed against her cheek, Carrie stepped back to the center of her room. She could not remember anything about the night before except telling him to paint, trusting him as she fell asleep and he worked. She reached for her boots and slipped them onto her feet. She ran her fingers through her long auburn hair, and though she had fallen asleep in her clothes she did not change.

She stepped outside and felt the crisp bite of the winter air lace by her. The snow, a pristine and sparkling white, reflected the light of the early morning sun as if filled with shattered prisms. She took a deep breath and felt the cold cut a burning pathway to her lungs; the sudden pain echoed in her heartbeat and made her suddenly aware of how happy she was—of how beautiful life could be. She started towards his house, and stopped.

Even with the glare of the sun, she could see that his blinds were drawn. Through the half skewed slats she could see the wall of his room, blank and bare—a peek into the world where she wanted to belong. Something about the angle of the blinds—something in the constricted pounding of her heart—countered the nascent hope and love blooming inside her. Something in the undercut of the wind warned her away, alerted her that something was wrong.

She shivered. The night before remained in the forefront of her mind, a golden and beautiful memory that somehow seemed out of place with the events of the past week. She knew, as she stood ankle deep in the shimmering snow and looked up towards his room, that she would never be able to face him. Not after a night like last night, when she realized what he could be.

If she went to him and he presented that other face to her, she knew that the betrayal would destroy her. Perhaps she had survived his mood swings because she believed, somewhere in her heart, that she deserved the treatment—that the feelings he inspired in her, different from anything she had ever felt before, justified the devastating confusion and anxiety that his changing behavior evoked. But last night—in a moment of clarity, of revelation, of magic similar to that which she had felt on their first encounter—she had sensed that he loved her. If he loved her, and treated her that way—or really if he truly loved her at all…

The thought of having him return the love she felt for him unhinged her completely.

She would never be able to face him.

The wind whipped her hair away from her face as she walked down Park Avenue, on her way to class, her heart sounding a call she could not answer.

Sam was still fuming when he reached his apartment. His hands shook as he fumbled with his key. The door slammed open and for one moment he had a thought—*Tessa*—he didn't want to wake her. But the kitchen light was on...and there she was, sipping tea at the kitchen table.

"Hello, Sam," she said, looking up.

He paused, his anger temporarily suspended. "What are you doing up?"

She shrugged. "I sensed you would need to talk to me. What happened?"

"I took Carrie home tonight," he said, not hesitating though he didn't know if he should speak. "I drove her home, and the guy next door—"

"Damien." Her expression did not change.

"You knew?"

Tessa paused. "You had no idea that she's in love with him?"

"How could I have?" Sam asked. "You haven't said anything, and he's been encouraging me to go after her myself."

"That, at least, was half decent of him."

Sam stopped ranting and stared at her. Tessa's cold blue eyes had that mesmerizing effect on him.

"I didn't want to make a big deal out of their attraction," she said. "I've been trying to steer her away from him, and I think he has, too." She paused. "Which would be a first, for him. Usually if he wants someone, he doesn't care about the mess he leaves behind."

Sam swallowed. "So you think—"

Her gaze was cool. "I don't think my brother is capable of love. But it sounds like Carrie is the closest he's ever come."

"Tessa." He didn't know how far to push the conversation. "He threw a bottle at her. She could have gotten hurt."

"If he had wanted to hurt her, he wouldn't have missed." She paused. "I would let Carrie fight her own battles. Just be a good friend to her. Like you've been to me."

"Like I've..." he started, but broke off mid-sentence as Tessa stood up.

"Go for a walk, Sam," she said, going to the sink and rinsing out her tea cup. "You'll feel better."

He was exhausted, stressed out from university work and work at the restaurant, but he knew lying in his bed was pointless; he would toss and turn as the pale moonlight bled into his room, and he would not be able to sleep. "Do you want to come with me?"

She hesitated, then shook her head. "You have a lot to think about."

His eyes lingered on her for a moment, then he turned and went out of the house.

As he walked he remembered what else was bothering him—what was making him confront the fact that they were graduating in May—in less than four months—and that life existed outside of college and was going to begin a whole hell of a lot sooner than Sam was ready for it to start.

Dan was considering getting engaged. What was bothering him, why Carrie had said he was acting differently, was because Monica had asked him to marry her. *Bullshit*, Sam had said when asked for advice. *Make her wait until you're ready, until you ask her. Girls are so quick to want rings on their fingers.*

Two and a half years.

Two and a half years are nothing compared to the decades you'll have to spend with her if you marry her.

Dan had looked at him and clammed up.

The snow seemed inordinately beautiful on nights when he couldn't sleep. Sam stopped and stared at the traffic lights marking the intersection. Maybe it was the combination of contrasts, the white on the black. Looking at the stars had the same effect on him.

Despite his reaction to Dan's situation their brief confrontation had stayed with Sam. Resolution, like heated steel, burned in his heart as he walked and thought and decided that he would try even harder to get Carrie to fall in love with him.

"Do you like art?" Sam asked Carrie the next day, as she was cleaning up after her shift.

She paused, then tucked her cleaning rag into her belt. "Depends on what kind."

"Someone told me there was this exhibit I should go see." He paused. "It might be fun to go together."

"When?" she asked.

"I don't know, and I don't know where yet, but—."

166

"You let me know the details," she said. "I'd love to go see some art with you."

It seemed to Carrie that every time she agreed to see Sam it rained: a steady, unrelenting downpour, complemented by billowing gray clouds and the threatening roll of thunder.

Her window was open, letting in a cool breeze and the sounds of the growling thunder and pattering rain. She had agreed to have Sam pick her up within the half hour and had been looking forward to his visit until she had gotten Chris's letter. Carrie sat in her room, the letter in her hand, savoring the uneven script. With every moment that passed, she prayed that Sam would not arrive, because if Sam arrived before she was finished reading then she would feel rushed. She did not want to feel rushed. The letter was the first Chris had written to her in six months; the last one had been a scribbled thank you note for a birthday present she had sent him through the mail.

The letter itself was a page and a half of large, loopy letters because he had tried to write in cursive and he was terrible at writing in script. She had read his letter three times already—Christine was working too much and he was worried about her, his leg was doing better and he was working twice as hard to build upper body strength while he recovered, he never saw Carly because she was studying all the time and she was thinking about quitting the swim team because she had bashed her legs twice on the diving board and besides she had too much work to do anyway.

Carrie read closely, trying to read in between the carefully written lines. She had already thought of taking the letter somewhere else so she wouldn't be there when Sam arrived, and the lack of guilt she felt when she thought of canceling on him proved to her what she had already known—that she should never commit herself to anyone, or anything, except her writing. She needed the freedom to change plans on a moment's notice. Even as she skimmed the rest of Chris's letter, her mind was focused on the postscript.

P.S. How's your writing coming?

She wanted to go to one of the empty classrooms in the Sackett building on campus, where it was quiet and there were no distractions:

only the classroom with its empty blackboard and rows and rows of empty desks and chairs. She went to her closet and pulled out her blue windbreaker; she had to leave quickly if she was going to leave, because Sam would be there at any moment. He would be angry, but she had no obligations to him. She had said she would go with him, but what was that promise compared to the drive inside of her? She did not believe in breaking promises, but the drive was not always so strong, and Sam and the art gallery could wait.

She crossed her room hastily, slipping into the windbreaker as she went. She opened her desk drawer and grabbed a handful of pens, then dropped them into her canvas bag along with her notebook. She started towards the door but might as well have walked into a wall because of how forcefully her mind chided her. The art gallery would *not* wait; she could not possibly expect Sam to go with her on a later date if she stood him up, and she could not go by herself because she did not have a car. Her heart panged painfully and she stood, torn, before realizing that her moment of hesitation had cost her the choice. She heard the downstairs door open; she heard Sam's footsteps approaching the stairs; she retreated into her room. She thought of closing the door and locking it, of turning off the lights and going to hide in her closet.

"Hide in my closet," she said. She forced herself to stay exactly where she was.

"What was that?" Sam asked, coming into her room.

"Hey, there," she said, forcing a smile.

He looked at her quizzically, taking in the tote bag and the windbreaker wrapped around her. "I see you're ready to go."

She crossed the room and dropped her bag on her desk.

"Weren't you going to take it with you?" he asked.

She said nothing.

"What, were you on your way somewhere else when I cut you off?" he said, smiling. Then, he stared at her. "You were going to ditch me again."

"I wasn't."

"You were."

"I…wasn't sure." She waited for him to explode.

"Come on," he said, finally. "Let's go. I don't have time to figure you out if the gallery closes at eight."

As she followed Sam to his car, she thought about the silence that he was making no attempt to break, and she realized she had hurt him.

"Sam," she said, and didn't know where to go from there.

"Why don't you pick something for us to listen to," he said.

She reached between them and picked up his black CD case, then extracted the scratched disk and handed it to him. He turned the volume to half-blast: too loud for conversation. He kept his eyes on the road. She looked out the window.

Sam thawed towards her ten minutes into the drive and started telling her about the exhibit. The gallery was located in an old house forty-five minutes away from the university campus; the retired art critic, Eugene R. Whittaker, had bought land in rural Pennsylvania and turned an abandoned barn on his property into an art gallery that showcased bizarre art by upcoming artists. Sam had searched the local library for more information, but found only that Whittaker had taught tenth grade at an all boys' prep school in Massachusetts before he moved to Pennsylvania and wrote a series of art critiques that had gained him fame. The site said only that the new artwork would be on public display until March twenty-third at sundown; on all other days the gallery would be open until eight. It was then six o'clock.

"Sam."

Her voice startled him. "What is it, Carrie?"

"Are you sure we're going the right way? I know you said this place was out in the country, but we've been driving for almost an hour." She paused. "I feel like we should have been there by now."

He glanced at the clock: 6:50 PM. She looked out the window again. The familiar scenery had changed to rolling green hills and fields of wheat glistening dully in the gathering dusk. How much else had she missed, zoning out like she had?

"I don't know," she said. "I got the directions from Mapquest. They should be accurate. Wait."

He stepped on the brake; she put a hand on the side of the car to steady herself.

"What about that road?" she asked. "Why don't you turn there?"

He glanced in the direction she had indicated. "I didn't even see that. It's hidden by the trees."

She took the directions from where he had taped them to the dashboard. "I noticed these directions indicated a sharp turn and a hidden driveway. I've never seen directions like that on Mapquest. You've been going straight for this last stretch, haven't you? On this road?"

"Yes," he said. "Were you asleep?"

"I was somewhere else." She handed him the map.

He took the turn, wincing slightly as a low-hanging branch scraped across the hood of his car. "It's getting dark."

"We'll be there soon," she promised. "I'm sure we can convince Eugene Whittaker to keep the gallery open a little longer. Collectors love showing off their stuff."

"Will we even be able to see anything?"

She paused. "I'm sure there will be lights if the barn has been remodeled into a gallery."

He sighed. "Just keep your eyes open for anything that even remotely resembles civilization."

She looked at the road in front of them and realized she was afraid to ask him why he was doing this for her. He caught her looking at him and turned to face her.

"Watch the road," he said.

"I am." She touched his arm with one hand. "There. Look right. Is that it?"

He saw a conglomeration of shadows resembling the hulk of a house and a sagging silo—barely visible in the sinking sun's light.

"We'll find out." He turned sharp right and guided the car towards the house. "Seems like you were wrong about the lights, if this is the right place."

There were no signs, no lights except for a glimmer burning in a window of the barn's loft. Sam parked the car and killed the engine. Neither of them moved. After a moment, he turned to her.

"Do you want to get out?" he asked. "Or do you want to go home?"

She felt strange, like her reality was silly putty stretched out of shape. Her eyes focused on the silver sliver of the half moon in the sky. Sometime in the past hour the rain had stopped.

"Let's get out," she said.

"Should be interesting." He paused. "I got a hint that the artwork would be dark. That's all."

"Then this artist picked the right place to showcase it." She opened her door. "Let's go check it out before it gets completely dark. If this isn't the right place, I don't want to be here."

He nodded. The temperature had dropped, and she was glad she had brought her windbreaker. She heard the crunching of gravel, and then Sam was standing beside her.

"Should we go to the barn? Or try the house first?"

"I don't think anyone is home," she said, her eyes settling on the dark house. She pulled her jacket more tightly around her. "Did any of those articles you read explain why he left that school in Maine?"

"Massachusetts," he said. "I'm glad it wasn't Maine. My family has a house up there we use for the summer, and I don't like to think that whoever owns this place might have been running around while we were..." He broke off. "No. The articles didn't say anything. Let's go to the barn."

She stayed close to his side. Together they began walking towards the barn, its single light guiding their way. She was grateful they were surrounded by open farmland on all sides; there was nothing anyone could hide behind.

"I feel like I'm in a horror movie," she whispered.

He turned on her suddenly and growled. She shrieked.

"Don't do that," she said, giggling.

He grinned at her, then swaggered towards the barn. The double doors were closed; he grabbed one by the handle and pulled. It did not open.

"Reach into my backpack, will you?" he asked. "There should be a flashlight in there somewhere."

"Good idea." She rummaged through the pack and pulled out the hard plastic cylinder. She clicked on the light and handed it to him.

"Always be prepared." He gripped the handle of the barn door again. "Here we go."

He yanked. The door groaned.

"It's locked from the inside," he said. "There's probably a wooden plank you have to move. When I open this door as much as I can, I want you to put your hand through and push up, then grab onto the other door handle and pull. My grandfather used to have a barn like this when I was little. I loved going there. Then Gramps died from lung cancer, and his estate got sold." He paused. "No more barn adventures."

"I'm sorry for your loss," she said.

"You ready?" he asked.

"Maybe we shouldn't."

He shrugged. "Your call. We're here. I don't see what we have to lose."

"Our lives?"

He laughed. "We'll look and leave. No harm done."

"All right."

"One, two…. three." He yanked the door open. "Up and over."

She felt the plank slide to the side before meeting resistance. "I think that's it."

"Pull," he grunted.

She grasped the other handle and pulled the door open. Inside the barn something was moving; they could both hear it.

"Shit," Sam said.

She ducked as something hurtled towards her, then burst out laughing when Sam jumped away from her.

"What the fuck was that?" he asked, standing with his back against the barn wall. "Jesus, Carrie, why are you laughing?"

She took the flashlight from him. "Barn owl. That's all."

"Is that what it was?" He stared out into the night. "How can you tell it was a barn owl? Because it was in a barn?"

She shook her head. "I got a glance at its face when you were jumping around, shining your light everywhere. Barn owls have really large eyes but just a sliver of a beak, like this." She tried to demonstrate with her mouth.

"How does that go again?" he asked, amused.

"I'm not doing it again so you can make fun of me." She stepped into the barn, flashlight in hand, and froze. He couldn't understand her paralysis because he was still outside the barn, in the warm air and the soft moonlight. The flashlight dropped from her hand.

"Carrie?" He moved noiselessly into the barn and she stepped close to him, her fingers intertwining with his. The flashlight lay on the ground, casting its light through the clean hay scattered there.

"There's someone in here," she whispered.

"What?" His warm hand still clamped around her cold one, he bent to pick up the flashlight and stood. "Hello?"

He saw the body. He jerked beside her, then let the light play around the barn's interior. There were more of them, six more—but they were life-sized portraits of women.

"We're here," Sam said, softly, beside her. He let go of her hand, went silently up to the first portrait and let the beam shine across it. "Hey, Carrie, look at this."

She went to stand beside him, her fear temporarily forgotten. The first portrait she had seen was easily six feet high—a girl on an antique porch swing, her head thrown back, her long blond hair spilling over the swing. She was not naked, but she was not clothed—her body was sensual but undetailed, as if someone had wrapped a sheet of peach silk around her. All the portraits were like that—lithe, beautiful young women, their bodies blank, the expression concentrated in their eyes and their faces. She moved beside Sam, staring at the portraits in turn.

"These are amazing," Sam said, sweeping the beam back and forth.

How many girls had modeled these positions for him, given him these smiles? She swallowed, fighting the tears that welled up in her eyes.

"Who did you say was the artist?" she asked him, hope not even lifting mangled wings to counter the intuition of the man who had portraited the women.

The beam of his flashlight stayed steady as he turned to her. His words carried weight, and she wondered if he was lying to her.

"The articles didn't say."

Her voice was guarded. "Why did you want to come here with me?"

"I knew you liked art," he said, too casually.

She paused. "I want to go home, Sam. It's late and I'm scared and I want to go home."

"I feel like we're trespassing, anyway." A note of relief escaped into his words. "But we've got to close up the barn first. All right?"

She nodded, not letting him see her face. They closed the barn in silence. The house remained dark as they got back into the car, the only light the single bulb in the loft of the barn. Sam started the engine. They did not talk until he had backed away from the house and down the hidden road, until they were back on the marked road to the college.

"Powerful, if you want my opinion," he said. "That's all I can say. You?"

"I didn't like them."

"Those girls." He didn't seem to have heard her. "The way he captured their emotion, the life in their eyes, the pure joy and ecstasy…"

"The artist has talent." She shivered. "But I thought the women looked inhuman. Cold and empty. The way their bodies weren't filled in…."

Sam paused. "I thought the exhibit was worth the drive, even if we only stayed for a minute…" He glanced at her, a dark suspicion in his mind. "Carrie."

"What?"

He paused. "Do you know who created those paintings?"

She kept her attention deliberately focused out the window, though the scenery was far too shadowed for her to see anything. "I'm sure you can find out more about him on the website, if you want to see more of his work or get in contact with him."

"That's not what I asked."

"I don't understand why you're so interested."

"I don't understand why you're so defensive." He glanced at her, then looked away. "Silly notion of mine. Forget it."

"What?" she asked reluctantly.

"It's just that…" He glanced in the rearview mirror, though they were alone on the road. "Those women. They all looked like you."

"Like me?"

"Like you."

"Don't be ridiculous."

"The faces," he said. "Something about the faces was the same, and they reminded me of you. But you don't even know the guy, so forget I said anything."

She was quiet, looking out the window. He was about to speak again when she looked at him and smiled. "Thanks for driving, Sam."

"Sure."

She turned her head and looked out the window. "Do you mind letting me out here? I want to walk the rest of the way home."

Sam was grateful for the unvoiced agreement not to discuss the night's excursion further. "Will you be okay to walk home alone this late?"

She laughed, put her hand on the car's door handle. Obediently he pulled to the side of the road. She gave him a smile, then got out of the car.

You don't know that he's an artist, do you?

His hands clenched around the steering wheel. He had stumbled upon an unwanted revelation and did not want to make his epiphany any clearer to Carrie than it should have already been.

As she walked towards her house, she heard the scrape of a snow shovel, and then saw someone dressed in a bulky blue ski jacket in front of her house. She stopped, her hands in her pockets to protect them from the cold. When the snow-shoveler looked up, she froze.

So did he. Then, Damien propped the snow shovel against the side of her house and stood looking at her.

"I thought you were asleep," he said.

She could not make herself say his name. "Why are you shoveling snow this late? I'll do it tomorrow when I get up, before I go to class."

"I knew you would," he said. "Why don't they ever take a turn?"

"You mean my housemates?" She shrugged. "I get up before anyone else does. I don't mind doing it. But thank you for shoveling. That was very kind of you."

He kept his eyes on her. "Where have you been?"

She shivered. "Your art exhibit."

"What were you doing there?"

"Sam asked me to go."

"Sam." His voice was indifferent. "Did you have a good time?"

Something was wrong with his eyes—they seemed oddly empty to her.

"No," she said.

"Why not?" His voice held a smirk.

She stepped by him, keeping her step brisk so he wouldn't know that she wanted him to reach out and stop her—to not let her by him. "Thanks again for shoveling."

175

She didn't wait for his response. The screen door clacked behind her as she stepped into the warmth of the house. She paused on the landing leading to her room, her hand on the doorknob. She forced herself to think about new people, about new experiences...

But when she did, she felt hollow. She added a handful of alfalfa to her guinea pig's cage and watched as Colby munched happily. She latched Colby's door shut, then turned off her lights and fell into bed. She looked up at her ceiling; she was exhausted, without having accomplished anything productive that day. But homework and writing would have to wait. She needed time to think.

Outside she could hear the steady scrape of the snow shovel against the sidewalk, a metallic lullaby.

She was not surprised that she could not sleep. She waited until she heard the side door of his house open, and then she got up. She did not look back as she walked away from his house. She raised her eyes and looked at the stars and regardless of what she was trying to make herself feel, her jealousy, her anger, her sadness slipped away. A silent stillness like steel settled within her—cold, strong, wordless, but there. She continued walking down the street, past the single light of the street lamp that marked the entrance to the park. She walked until the hardness of concrete gave way to the gravel of the bike trail—hedged by woods, engulfed in darkness. She continued walking, knowing that the park and the trail would be deserted at the late hour.

A soft breeze rustled up, moving the leaves of the trees in breathing whispers. Her spirit hungered for the sheltering woods and the dark mosaic of leaf-tree silhouettes, and she stepped off the path. She stooped and took off her shoes, then her socks. She wanted to feel the grass, spiked with chilled dew from the rain, beneath her feet. She left the clump of her belongings and moved on, staying close to the path.

The path serpentined around a mountain of rocks and a cluster of silent trees. She broke away from the path and headed towards the woods. Silver moonlight drenched the plain-like land, and she cast a furtive look at the hills, at the path, at the moon, one last time before she pulled her shirt over her head. Confident that she was the only person there, she peeled off her pants and stepped out of her underwear. Then she unclipped the wire hooks of her bra and let the garment fall away from her. The wind nipped at her bare skin, but she was not cold. She edged closer to the woods.

Her nakedness was a distant reality of which she had to keep reminding herself. The humming noise of the kitchen, the waitresses's shouts, customers and professors talking, people's eyes and expectations—those things she had left behind on stepping into the woods. The gently moving trees, the silver moonlight, the wet grass beneath her feet and the cool air around her were the only realities. She sat down, clasped her hands around her legs, and put her head on her knees. The air wrapped around her like friendly arms, and she felt the serenity of the moonlight and the whisper of the trees. She raised her head and looked at the moon. Her hair, let loose, warmed her back and emphasized her exposure. Yet she felt safe, and, beneath the stars, she felt beautiful.

Thoughts of Damien assailed her suddenly, and like a thunderclap, like the breaking sound of glass with the first stone he had thrown at her window to get her attention, her emotions awakened. She unwrapped her arms from her legs and stared up at the sky defiantly. The emotion she felt overwhelmed her. There were no words, no thoughts—only the anger, anxiety, frustration, awe, gratitude, awareness of the beautiful night.

She stood, finding as she started walking again that she was not quite stable. Her body felt awkward, huge, not her own. She forced herself to walk slowly, her feet screaming in protest as feeling came back and splinters of twigs and small stones gouged into the soles of her bare feet. The feeling of serenity, of peace and companionship with the night, faded as she walked.

She found her clothes in the pile where she had left them and dressed as deliberately as she could. She started walking again, veering closer to the path. She found her socks and shoes and put them on again; she did not know why she had to act with external calm, only that she did. Upon leaving the woods, she welcomed the inanimate houses, the thin red face of a stop sign, the street lamps like artificial fireflies. The night seemed alive to her, like it could speak if only she could understand. She realized she should feel crazy, but she did not. She felt awake. Open. Alive.

The day's events had faded; only the moments under the moonlight seemed starkly real to her. When she got back into her house and climbed the stairs to her room, she looked at the clock and saw it was exactly thirteen minutes after three. She did not know when she had gotten back or how long she had spent talking to Damien, so she could not determine how long she had been in the woods.

Her fevered eyes fell on the mural, and suddenly she hated the delicate mosaic of butterflies and hummingbirds, of thorns and vines...

She heard echos of their conversation. The gentle hum of his voice, the warmth of his body, the whisper of his words...

It was a spontaneous decision.

She descended the creaky steps to the basement and reached for a can of paint sitting above the washer. She loosed the can, then walked up the basement stairs and started towards her room.

She wrenched her desk away from the wall and shoved it to the center of the room. She pried the lid off the can. She wanted the mural gone. She slashed an opaque streak of white across the masterpiece.

Her effort to destroy the mural steadily zapped the murderous energy out of her; by the time she covered the last tiny hummingbird she was trembling. She laid the brush down on her desk and turned away like a zombie. She fell into her bed; after only a moment she was asleep.

Sam did not keep his distance from her. He spoke to her on her first day back to the restaurant.

"Do you mind if we talk for awhile?" he asked.

She shook her head. "I only have two tables."

"I meant after work. Can I walk you home?"

She paused, then she nodded. Her shift seemed to last longer than usual, though she ended up waiting for him as he finished closing down the kitchen and then joined her in the back alley.

"Carrie, I want to know what's going on," he said, after a long, tense silence.

"Nothing, Sam." She hunched her shoulders against the cold. "What do you say we just let it all go?"

"If that's what you want." He paused. "Just let me say I'm sorry I lost my temper. I inherited it from my dad, and I'm always annoyed when I can't control it."

"If you're angry, at least you're showing something real." She paused. "But I don't think you lost your temper. By the way, I like the fictional story you wrote based on our trip to the art gallery."

He frowned. "What do you think of the romantic subplot?"

"The romance could be there," she said carefully. "It's not uncommon for two people to suddenly realize they're madly in love with each other, without any real change or warning." She looked away from him. "Did you mean to make Carla seem like such a cold-hearted bitch?"

He threw a cleaning rag at her; she laughed and dodged the attack easily.

"I'm going to miss working with you," she said.

Tessa was in the kitchen, cleaning. She looked up and asked the question on Sam's mind. "Are you quitting, Carrie?"

Carrie surveyed the few remaining tickets. "I want more time to write."

Sam looked away from her, but Tessa threw down the rag she was using to clean the desert counter. Carrie brushed by her into the front dining section.

Tessa followed her. "What's bothering you?"

Carrie shrugged. "Nothing."

"Why are you quitting?"

"I don't like staying in one place for too long."

"You should keep working here." Tessa hesitated. "You can't beat the money. And I know that you don't mind the hours, since they keep you away from your house on weekends."

Carrie turned to Tessa. "Did something happen last weekend when you were at my house?"

"I talked to Damien."

"What?"

Tessa glanced at her. "I told him to stay away from you."

Carrie's face was pale marble. "I don't want you looking out for me, Tessa."

"Someone needs to." Tessa watched their manager walk by, then turned back to Carrie. "You don't realize how dangerous Damien is. He feels like he has nothing to lose, and the man who feels he has—"

"Complete and utter liberation," Carrie mumbled.

Tessa paused. "You shouldn't listen to anything he has to say. He's never serious about anything he says."

Carrie looked at her oddly. "Do you know him somehow?"

"Just the vibe I get from him." Tessa looked away. "But at least he thinks you hate him."

A stab of panic. "But I don't."

"Not at all?"

Carrie sighed. "Hate and love can be so similar."

"Carrie, don't tell me you think you love him."

"You told me to never deny what I feel." She paused. "I can't deny that I want him, Tessa. I see the red flags, but he's the one I want."

"Think about how much he hurt you," Tessa said quietly.

Carrie shook her head. "I can't forgive the way he treated me, but I can't blame him for being what he is. And I'm sure that I want him."

"Carrie."

"I know he cares about me," she said. "Because of little things that should seem insignificant—but weren't."

"Like what?" Tessa asked tiredly.

"Like using orange in his paintings because he knows it's my favorite color."

"Carrie." Tessa's voice turned harsh; she had to stop Carrie's rambling before she stumbled any closer to the truth. "Why hasn't he come after you, then? If he cares about you so deeply, then why does he go chasing after other girls? Or..." Her eyes burned darkly. "Why haven't you gone after him more aggressively, if he's so important to you?"

"I'm not going to throw myself at his feet." She paused, defiant. "As to the other women, he's not a guy who could ever be tamed. He'll never belong to anyone, and he'll never be content with anyone. And I wouldn't want him to be, because then he wouldn't be Damien."

Tessa watched another waitress walk by and lowered her voice. "Do you want my advice, Carrie? One way or another, try to get some closure on this. You don't want to leave so much unfinished, or you'll end up a ghost for the first part of your next life."

Carrie laughed.

Tessa turned to her. "It's not funny, Carrie. Ghosts are doomed to wander aimlessly around the world—empty, alone—until they can resolve their issues keeping them from rest."

"And what the hell do you think I'm doing now?" Carrie asked her.

Tessa said nothing.

"So maybe you'll understand why the prospect doesn't frighten me." Carrie glowered. "I simply don't care."

Tessa glanced at her. "Let's have a girl's night after we close. We'll make popcorn, watch a movie…"

"No, thank you. I want to be alone."

"Rethink the two weeks notice, Carrie. Please."

Carrie turned in the direction that would take her home. "I don't think so, Tessa."

Tessa watched her walk into the kitchen, a sudden apprehension weighing her down.

If Carrie could have picked one night to avoid Damien, it would have been that night. But when she turned onto Park Avenue she saw him standing in the middle of his lawn, his back to her, his arms crossed behind his back, his feet spread shoulder-width apart—staring at her house. For one brief minute she felt an intense urge to turn and flee down the street, then double back and take the back entrance to her house so that he would not see her. Something prompted her forward; she swallowed and moved with halting steps until she stood in front of her house.

"Damien? What are you doing?"

He turned at the sound of her voice and smiled when he saw her.

"Go to your house," he said, flinging his arm out towards the dark building. "Go."

She felt as if she were in a dream. The words came and went before she had a chance to realize what she was saying. "I want to talk to you."

"Why?" he asked.

"Because I haven't seen you and I miss you."

"All right," he said, softly.

She went to stand beside him. "How are you doing?"

"I'm waiting," he said. "Waiting for the firing squad."

She stared at him.

He nodded. "They're going to come out of your house and shoot me. Any time now." He bent down and picked up an empty beer can by his feet. He tapped it on the pavement three times, then stood and faced her house again, putting his hands behind his back and spreading his feet again.

"Now they'll come," he said.

She tried to keep her voice steady. "No one's going to come out of my house. Everyone's asleep and I just got off work." She paused. "I'm going to go inside and make dinner. I haven't eaten all day."

"That's a good idea," he said. "Go inside and make yourself something good. Then go to sleep. You never sleep."

"That's what you should do," she said. "Go to your room and sleep off whatever you smoked."

"No point." He paused. "Soon I'll be dead."

She paused. "Do you want to die?"

"I'm not afraid to die."

She paused again, not knowing why her inner defenses towards him had suddenly come crashing down. "Why do you think I hate you?"

"You never let me near you," he answered.

She paused. "You've never even asked me out on a date."

He laughed. "Would you like that? A date with yours truly?"

She did not answer him. He hummed a tune under his breath.

"I've never asked a girl out on a date before," he said.

"Then how—"

"Why you should hate me," he interrupted, in a moment of coherence. "I have yelled at you, and I have made you cry." He went back to looking at her house. "I had to. I can't tell you why. But I'm sorry."

She stood beside him, speechless. He recommenced swaying side to side. Suddenly, it was very important for her to get through to him. She slipped her hand into his and was relieved when his fingers tightened around hers.

"Come inside with me," she said. "I'll tuck you in."

"Will you stay?"

She shook her head.

"All right," he said, the haze slipping back into his eyes. "But don't try anything now. I'm not in my right mind."

He started towards his house and she followed him. In his room she barely had time to pull back his covers before he fell into bed fully dressed. Silently, she stooped and kissed him on the forehead.

"Goodnight," she said.

"Carrie," he said. "I…"

She bent down to hear what he had started to say, but his eyes closed and the words died on his lips. She moved back to the entrance of his room. She stood looking at him sleeping peacefully, then she turned off the lights, closed his door, and left. Her steps on the stairs were heavy, but her mind was empty. She was completely numb.

She could not trust Damien. She would have to shut down her feelings, live without hope or expectation that she would ever be able to follow her heart's trajectory.

She wondered if she could even live that way.

She had woken bleary eyed, her head throbbing. She could not remember what she had been dreaming, only that the dream had terrified her. She shuddered, realizing how cold she was all of a sudden. She had zoned out; she was in the kitchen again without any remembrance of how she had gotten there.

"Your food is up." Sam was watching her, concerned.

She blinked, looked at the ticket line and saw the white ticket with her name at the top. She forced a smile on her face. "Thanks, Sam."

"Do you want to come over after work?" he asked, seeing through her.

She paused, then nodded.

After they closed the restaurant he walked beside her, trying to match her brisk pace. Her skin was porcelain white in the moonlight, her cold hazel eyes staring directly at the ill-lit street in front of them. They passed the Cinema Seven on their left, its parking lot deserted.

"We could probably get in," he suggested, knowing she liked to wander and explore. "No one would be there. We could explore."

She shook her head. "Let's keep walking."

They kept walking. Carrie did not want to talk, and he gave up trying to make conversation after a few futile attempts. He led her to the apartment complex; she followed him silently.

"Why are you quitting?" he asked her, opening the door.

She had forgotten to talk to her manager at the end of her shift. *So be it.* She shrugged and followed him inside.

"It's quiet here," she said, stomping her boots on the mat outside his door.

"My housemates are at a party, and Tessa is doing some kind of nature ritual tonight. She said she couldn't start it until after midnight." He paused. "Do you want some hot chocolate?"

She took off her gloves. "Sure."

"It'll just take a moment," he said, sudden heat coursing through him. "Make yourself comfortable."

She moved into the living room and sat down on his couch. He came back five minutes later and handed her a steaming mug of cocoa, then set his mug on the table in front of them and sat down at the opposite end of the sofa. He wasn't sure he trusted his interpretation of her passivity.

He clasped his hands in his lap. "Carrie, I know how you feel about me."

"How do I feel?" She set her mug on the table and looked at him.

He moved across the sofa towards her, slipped an arm around her shoulders. She did not move, and he dropped his arm to encircle her waist. She closed her eyes and dropped her head onto his shoulder. Having her in his arms should have made him happy, but he felt nothing. She seemed, if anything, very, very tired. He removed his arm from around her waist, put his hands firmly on her shoulders and shook her gently. She opened her eyes, looked at him.

"You're not even thinking about me, are you?" he asked.

She stared at him and said nothing.

"Get out," he said suddenly, moving away from her. He put his head between his hands and massaged his temples. "Just go."

She stood. He saw, in alarm, that she had not even taken off her coat. She left without a word. He picked up the two untouched mugs of hot chocolate and took them over to the sink, where he watched the syrupy liquid disappear.

"Shit," he said. He left the mugs in the sink and raced across the apartment. He flung open the door. She was not in the hallway.

"Carrie!" he yelled. Without his shoes, without his jacket, leaving his door open, he raced down the three flights of steps and out into the street, his eyes scanning the emptiness in front of him. He called her again and was answered by silence. He walked around the building, walked for ten minutes in the direction she would have gone, but she had disappeared. He walked back to his apartment, his head down, wondering what kind of an asshole he had to be to kick a girl out onto the roads in the middle of the night to walk upwards of two miles by herself. He said a quick prayer that she would be all right, then went into his room to confront another sleepless night.

Carrie did not mind walking alone. She relished the silence, the time to think, the dark and calming night.

She wanted to scream, to shatter the serene stillness of the night. Instead, she hummed as she continued walking. She was off track again. How far she didn't know. All her vain thoughts about Damien, all her curiosity and self-imposed restraint, had come to nothing but wasted time. Had she focused her energy—as Tessa would say—into something she truly wanted, where would she be? Not spying on his empty window through half drawn blinds. Who would she be, if she had never met him? The thought sent a shiver down her spine. But she had learned from him; he had tested her, and she had stuck to her convictions. She would not get the chance to thank him, but he did not have to know.

Somehow she knew she would not see Damien—the Damien she loved then—again. She wondered if her heart would ever forgive her.

Sam was sitting on the sofa when Tessa returned to the apartment. She took one look at him sitting with his head between his hands and closed the door softly behind her. He did not look up. She went and sat down by him.

"What's wrong, Sam?"

He turned, surprised by the gentleness in her voice. The cold had bitten her cheeks rosy, and her blue eyes danced. He looked away quickly, reminded of the attraction he felt for her.

Her eyes scanned his face. "Is this about Carrie?"

He found he did not want to conceal anything from her. "She came over tonight."

Tessa waited.

"I'll spare you the details." He found himself looking directly into her eyes. "Not that there were any."

"She didn't want you to push things." Tessa paused. "And you didn't, because you're a decent guy."

"More than that." He looked at his hands. "I always thought that, if it came down to that kind of moment between us, I would feel like fireworks were about to go off. But I didn't feel much of anything at all. I felt less than I'm feeling right now, sitting next to you."

"Do you mean that, Sam?"

He glanced at her, saw her eyes held an open invitation. He blinked. Her gaze did not waver.

"All you have to do is ask," she said quietly.

He stared at her. He realized he wasn't prepared to realize what he was feeling.

"I know you've liked me for a long time," she continued. "I've been waiting for you to realize what your encounter with Carrie showed you tonight."

She held out her hand. He felt the warmth of her flesh, felt something inside him break loose.

Tessa stood. "My room is this way. I don't think you've ever been in there before."

He followed her. She closed her door softly behind her and turned out the lights.

Carrie found out Sam and Tessa were dating a week later. She went for a walk by herself that night and realized she would have a hard time finding someone like her, who would choose to be alone. She walked aimlessly, already knowing she had nothing to fear from the night.

The book Tessa had lent her on the Tarot was sitting on her desk at home; she would read some, and then she would go to bed. She breathed in deeply. The air was leaden with moisture, refreshingly warm with the promise of summer heat. She was not ready to let such a beautiful night slip by unappreciated, but beauty, like that night's beauty, was meant to be shared. She went inside.

Tessa had not expected the gentleness, the candle-light dinners he cooked himself, the red rose he slipped into her purse after she had worked an eleven hour shift at the restaurant that had left her close to tears. She was surprised by how quickly she opened up to Sam, by how emotional she got when they made love. One time she had cried and told him how much his kindness meant to her, how much she appreciated him, and he had kissed her and told her to be quiet, and she had fallen asleep, feeling warm and safe in his arms.

Tessa stood on the porch in front of the white block house, waiting. After a moment, Carrie opened the door and smiled. "Come inside. You have so much to tell me."

At the kitchen table, Tessa looked down at the mug of tea in her hands. "It's not really as spontaneous as it seems. I've liked him for a long time, Carrie."

"I never would have known. You kept trying to encourage *me* to go out with him."

"I didn't want to fall in love." She looked into her empty tea cup, stirred the tea leaves. "People like me don't do very well in relationships."

"Why do you say that?"

Tessa's eyes were troubled. "I love my independence, and I'm largely unwilling to share my life with anyone. And I don't like men in general. But I trust Sam, and so far, I've enjoyed his company."

Carrie paused. "Sam would never hurt you, never cheat on you."

"He knows I'd leave him if he did." Tessa smiled, and Carrie was glad to hear the strength in her friend's voice. "Carrie, do you understand what I'm saying? I didn't want to fall in love, but with Sam I feel like I didn't really have a choice."

"You're allowed to love."

"I don't want to hurt him."

Carrie glanced at her quickly. "Don't worry about what might happen down the road. Enjoy where you are." She paused. "I've never seen you so happy."

Tessa bit her lip. "I can't believe I'm graduating so soon. I'll miss you. Promise you'll keep in touch."

"I will." She could not look at Tessa. "Are you leaving tomorrow?"

Tessa nodded. "We'll stop by your house before we go, if you won't mind."

Carrie gave her a hug. "I'll see you tomorrow."

Tessa nodded, and after she had left, Carrie realized they had both been crying.

Her housemates had left for the summer without saying goodbye. Carrie did not care; she would not see them again.

She had not talked to Damien. The light still burned in his window, but he kept his blinds down and no longer inhabited the outside porch on sunny days. They would still be attending the same college the next fall, but she was moving to a different house and she saw no reason to go back and visit him—like she saw no reason to say goodbye.

Her hunger for solitude and peace consumed her. Despite her increasing reclusiveness, she was content. Over the summer she would write, work, and visit her family. The following year she would graduate.

She was ready to move on. She wanted to leave State College behind her. She would become a teacher; she would remain a writer. She was excited that the future would hold challenges and obstacles for her of a different kind; the struggles that came with college no longer interested her. She had taken her stance, and she had not veered in action. If she was alone, at least she was good company, strong in herself. Or was she really weaker for the semester's struggles?

She heard a crash on the window beside her; for one moment, she was wildly hopeful. In that moment she realized that no issue, no part of her heart, was as closed off as it seemed.

She went to her window, the blue fabric of her nightgown slipping off her shoulder as she looked down into her front yard. She felt a dash of disappointment: Sam. She drew back from the window, put on a terry-cloth robe to cover the nightgown, and walked down the steps and out her front door. Sam stood in the space between the two large trees on the edge of the property, his silhouette backlit by the lamps lining the street.

"Hello, Carrie," he said, when she came out. "I'm leaving. I just wanted to say goodbye."

She smiled at Sam, grateful. "You're not staying for graduation?"

"No." His eyes flicked over her, then he looked up at the sky, the stars, and stretched. "I'm not sitting through a three hour ceremony so I can watch thousands of strangers graduate alongside me, all so I can get handed a blank piece of paper. My parents can't make it, and that would be the only reason I'd go through with it."

"Congratulations anyway." She stepped up to him and gave him a hug. He embraced her warmly, but as she stepped back she realized there was something missing from his touch that she had hoped would be there.

"Thanks."

"Are you going home?"

"I finished with finals today," he said. "And though it's late I want to get home. Tessa is in the car if you want to say goodbye." He paused. "Do you mind if I use your bathroom before we leave? Long drive."

"You know where it is."

"Thanks."

As he went inside, she walked to where he had parked behind her house. Tessa unrolled the window as she approached.

"You look beautiful," Carrie said. "What's Sam doing to you?"

Tessa blushed. "Did you say goodbye? Sam was so adamant about saying goodbye to you before we left."

"Are you staying with him this summer?"

"Visiting." Tessa frowned suddenly. "Carrie, I'm sorry I didn't get to see you much today."

"I'm glad you stopped by," Carrie said.

"I know you still mean a lot to him." She smiled. "It would have hurt him, if he couldn't have said goodbye to you. And I couldn't leave without seeing you. You're the only true friend I've ever really had."

Carrie hugged her through the window and felt the tears come into her eyes. She heard the door to her house close, and straightened to see Sam walking towards them. She plastered a smile on her face; he smiled back at her.

"Goodbye, Carrie," he said.

"Goodbye," she said. "Have a safe drive home."

Carrie stood in front of her house, arms crossed in front of her robe, and waved when Sam honked twice—short staccatos in the stillness of the night. She watched until his car pulled away and disappeared down the road, and then she turned and went inside. She would have been fine either way, but she was glad that they had said goodbye.

PART TWO

Tessa Beaumont-Sampson pulled the fine-toothed comb through her short blond hair, making it lay like thick gold plates against her face. She was twenty-six years old. She searched the face of her reflection and noticed that her face had gotten fuller and that the look in her china blue eyes had softened.

The room farthest east in the house she had claimed for her meditation room. She rose each morning with the sun, and the Rose Room received the most natural sunlight. She loved the Rose Room; she loved everything about the gray stone house that looked like a cottage from a children's story. They had replaced the black asphalt driveway with white cobblestones, Sam had installed a wooden swing out in front, and she had placed statues of fairies and laughing children around the walkway. And she had planted flowers, hundreds of flowers—roses and rhododendrons and daffodils. In summer, the full bloom of the plants and flowers hid her house behind the wild and unrestrained life.

She always thought of the house as hers; although Sam had allowed all of her additions, he had not approved of any of them. Her favorite addition was a wind chime she had found at a junk shop on one of her solitary drives and bought for a dollar-fifty. She had hung the chime outside of the Rose Room; from there, she could see the first glowing rays of dawn filter through the glass bodies of the tiny doves. When a slight breeze blew, the silver orb at the base of the chime set the birds soaring.

The gentle clinking of the silver chimes sounded like soft singing. Tessa would listen, and she would smile.

A cup of stale black coffee sat on her desk besides piles of paper. The sight of the color-coded papers made Tessa nauseous and she looked away, not ready to face the accumulation of Pennsylvania standards, curriculum requirements, lesson plans, and her reflections on her teaching for the past four years. She had never had any problems with her students or the school, but she still felt edgy and nervous before the first day. She enjoyed her students, and being at the school gave her a reason to be away from Sam and Kindra. Sometimes when she was at the school, or in the Rose Room, she was able to forget that they existed.

She picked up the mug and went into the kitchen, where she dumped the day-old coffee into the sink. There was little in the world that could make her happier than sitting at her desk in the Rose Room with a steaming mug of freshly brewed coffee, looking out a sunny window at the bursting flowers she had planted. She went outside and lit a cigarette to calm her nerves, then looked up at the still dark sky and listened to the delicate chiming of her glass birds in the distance. She would have to be at the school in an hour, and she wanted to go through her plans one more time—to make sure she was ready. She closed her eyes and felt how tired she was and how glad she was for the rigid doorframe behind her, giving her support. The bittersweet fragrance of her flowers drifted to her on the breeze. She smelled the bitter nip of late August—a hint of decay—as the chimes continued their whispered melody. Tessa opened her eyes and moved inside to finish her preparation.

The day went well, despite her lack of sleep. She found the students attentive and polite—and bored with her already. She went home to her fairy house substantially less worried, and she decided to take herself out to dinner at a restaurant—Sandy O'Hara's—that she had wanted to try for some time. She wrote a note to Sam, telling him where she was going and asking him to pick up Kindra from daycare, and then she drove towards Pleasant Gap.

She parked in the almost empty parking lot by the sign lettered in Irish Green and walked to the front entrance. She opened the door and moved into a darkened lobby, where another tan and green sign announced that she should wait patiently to be seated. Mirrors, surrounded by Celtic knot borders, reflected her image from all sides.

A young woman dressed in a long black skirt and an emerald green top emerged from the shadows. "Miss?"

"One." Tessa followed the young woman into the main dining area.

"A waitress will be with you in a moment," the hostess said, and faded back into the shadows before Tessa had a chance to thank her.

Tessa forgot about the menu in front of her as she looked around. Tealight candles in silver holders flickered on each mahogany table, and orb lights, like full moons, hung from silver chains above her head. Emerald green hangings embossed with Celtic patterns in silver brocade covered three of the walls; the east wall had been painted.

Tessa left her purse and her pack of cigarettes on the table and wandered over to examine the mural. A single Celtic cross stood out against a golden dawn sky, and in the foreground of grass and clover, leprechauns and goblins frolicked and struggled with each other. The artist had painted good-natured expressions on the rosy faces of the leprechauns but had made no attempt to disguise the ugliness of the hobgoblins; they stared back at her, red eyes impish and glowing, their faces like toughened leather.

The seamless harmony of the savage with the beautiful stunned her. She traced one of the hobgoblin's sneers, almost expecting to feel the pointed tips of the protruding teeth.

"Miss? Are you ready to order? Or if you need more time, I can come back."

Tessa turned and saw a waitress standing by her table. The smile, the direct gaze of her eyes, were unmistakable.

"Carrie?" she said, alarmed.

The waitress stared at her blankly.

"Tessa," Tessa reminded her. "Tessa Beaumont. We went to college together."

Recognition flew across her face, as swift and sharp as a bullet.

"Tess," Carrie said. "I didn't recognize you."

"I've gotten fatter," she explained. "But you look great. Really great."

A single streak of white highlighted the left side of Carrie's hair, still the color of autumn leaves. But her eyes—the same dusky green—now held an edge. Something hard, unrelenting, cold.

"How have you been?" Tessa stammered.

Carrie smiled, and in a gesture that countered the coldness Tessa saw in the jagged lines of her face, gave her a hug.

"It's so good to see you," she whispered.

Tessa's eyes swept over the empty tables around her. "Do you have a moment to talk?"

Carrie shook her head. "I shouldn't. I need this job, Tessa. My writing hasn't taken off like I had hoped it would."

They walked back to Tessa's table. "So you're writing? And waitressing?"

Carrie smiled. "I prefer to call it chasing a dream."

Tessa smiled back at her. "I lost touch with you after I graduated. But I've thought of you often. What have you been doing, all this time?"

"What do you want to know?"

"Anything you'd care to tell me."

"I went to the Peace Corps after graduating, to the Dominican Republic." She broke off, smiled. "Now, I waitress. I pay my bills. I write to keep myself sane. Where has life ended up leading you?"

"I'm a teacher at Greensburg Salem High School."

"Greensburg? That's my hometown."

"Really? I've taught there for the past four years."

"You look happy," she said. "I'm glad. I'm so glad, Tessa."

Tessa blinked back the tears that started up in her eyes at the loneliness she heard in Carrie's voice; Carrie would not want her pity. She folded her menu closed, handed it to Carrie.

"I'll have something vegetarian," she said. "Then come talk. I've missed you."

Carrie walked away and came back a moment later, and after looking around the restaurant, slid into the seat opposite Tessa.

"Fuck my manager," she said, in a tone of voice that reminded Tessa

strongly of their college days. "But even if we aren't busy, I can only sit for a minute."

Tessa nodded. "I'll call you. We can have lunch and—"

"I don't have a phone."

"Oh. Then how can I get in touch with you?"

Carrie hesitated, then pulled a piece of paper out of her waitpad. Tessa noted that the paper was the receipt of a previous customer's bill; Carrie had always saved them, used them, recycled them, back when they had worked together.

"Call that number," she said. "You won't get a voicemail. There will be a beep, and then you'll have to talk fast."

"Whose number is it?"

"His name is Stephen, but don't use his name in your message. And mention my name, so he knows why you're calling. Let me go check on your food, Tessa."

She disappeared, and Tessa tucked the paper carefully into the folder she had brought with her—the folder that contained her students' first freewriting essays that she planned to read through while eating. Carrie came back carrying a tray full of steaming food.

"Eggplant Parmesan," she said. "My favorite vegetarian item on the menu by far. I hope you like it."

"Thank you. It looks amazing."

"Can I get you anything else right now?"

"I have a question, Carrie. About that mural." She paused. "What do you think of it?"

"It's savage. A perfect mix of light and dark." Carrie frowned. "I come to work every day to see that painting."

"Who painted it?"

"The mural is signed, Tessa, in the lower left-hand corner." She turned away. "Enjoy your meal."

Tessa told herself that the sky in the mural could not possibly have darkened, that the hobgoblins' eyes and the leprechauns' gold were the same shades they had been before—that paintings could not change.

She would have to remember to check for the artist's name before she left. She placed the linen napkin across her lap and looked at the only

other customers—a young couple holding hands across the table and frowning down at their food. She spread her students' papers out in front of her and started to skim; she would read over them again at home, when she could devote her full attention to them; then, she wanted a general idea. Reaching the end of the stack, she paused and counted twenty-four papers; she was supposed to have twenty-five. Unbelievably, she could not remember which student had been absent. Her eyes flicked back to the mural, then shifted to the couple as Carrie came over and asked them if everything was okay.

The man loudly condemned the food while his girlfriend smirked. Tessa's eyes narrowed as Carrie stood there. The Carrie she had known would not have apologized and neither did the Carrie before her; Carrie told the man quite a bit, all politely, but none of it was an apology. Tessa put her napkin on her cleaned plate and her silverware in her empty glass, as they had done when waitressing together. Moments later, Carrie came by with a check and smiled when she saw the dishes.

"Thanks, Tessa. You didn't have to do that." She did not meet Tessa's inquiring eyes. "I can take that whenever you're ready."

Tessa looked at the bill and put forty dollars on the table. She stood and walked over to the mural. She stooped and found the signature, then stared at the spiky script. Hidden in a bed of clover, the signature read:

Damien DeMatteo

She had forgotten. She turned and saw Carrie walking towards her. The coldness had returned to her eyes.

"Did you need change?" Carrie asked quietly.

Tessa noticed the two twenty dollar bills were clenched in Carrie's hands. "Keep it. If you think it's too much, you can take me out to lunch, sometime when you're not working."

"Thanks," Carrie said. "I'd like to see you for lunch."

Tessa nodded and Carrie walked away to ask the man if he wanted a refill. Tessa left the restaurant, after nodding distractedly to the farewell of the smiling hostess. She slipped into her car and turned the windshield wipers to the highest setting. She was not able to rid herself of the image of the mural with its striking clash of green and gold; of the signature, its

letters spiky but distinguishable; of what those letters meant to the closest friend she had ever had.

Carrie's eyes, when they had met Tessa's, had been haunted. The expression on Carrie's face had shown that the mural was a constant reminder of an unfinished story, and Tessa realized that Carrie had never gotten the closure she needed.

Tessa called the number Carrie had given her as soon as she got back to her fairy house, but the machine cut her off mid-sentence. She called again, but could not get through; the machine on the other line announced her number had been blocked, then gave way to the disconnected dial tone. Disconcerted, she went to a pay phone and dialed; she got through and dropped Carrie's name, though she did not have time for much else. Her call was not returned.

Her mystery student showed up late on the fourth day of class: a tall, lanky young man with thoughtful blue eyes who listed his interests as martial arts and reading science fiction. The name Christopher Crenshaw had meant little to her until she saw him, when she realized he was Carrie's brother. The hair—the dusky autumn auburn—the curve of the nose, the high cheekbones, and the broad forehead were almost identical. Tessa made him introduce himself, an activity which revealed that he was already well-known and well-respected among his peers—as she had expected. She had queried her students about his continued absence, and few students had seemed willing to incriminate him. Only Miranda Baxter, a young Latino with dark hair she pinned in place with a fresh flower, had explained quietly that Chris rarely came to class because he was so intelligent, and that he had won so many awards for the school through enrichment program contests that most teachers let him alone.

Tessa was not one of those teachers. She kept Chris after class and questioned his behavior, then found with his absence of the next two days that he could not be coerced. Chris would not be defiant or insolent in class, but he would do what he wanted. She discovered that Chris had formed a close alliance with Ralph Palmer, the head of the honors committee and the instructor of the Advanced Chemistry class. Palmer— though he had only taught at the school for a few years—was subordinate only to the Principal and Vice Principal. None of the education classes she had crammed into her senior year schedule at Penn State had indicated that such a new teacher could have risen so quickly in the school's hierarchy; but Palmer had come to the small suburban highschool with mysterious credentials, and he had played his cards right. He vouched for Chris's absences, and his reasons were not something she could override as a new teacher. If he dictated that Chris's absences were justified, then she had to make her classes so interesting that Chris would attend of his own volition. He would be her challenge of the year.

She called Carrie—or rather, she called Stephen—and left another message. By this time, she had his system down. Her message consisted of: *Carrie. Chris.* As she had thought might happen, she received a message from Carrie shortly after leaving the two word message.

"Will you meet me?" Carrie asked softly, as soon as Tessa picked up her phone.

Tessa confirmed a location—it would be a much needed drive for her—and she hung up. She looked at the unit plan she had been working on, then grabbed her keys and headed out the door.

As Tessa turned off the engine, she was aware of the extra pounds she had gained and how different the years must have made her look—while time had only deepened Carrie's austere beauty. Carrie was standing in front of the house, waiting for her.

"Nice place," Tessa said, her eyes sweeping the high reaching Victorian facade, the well-maintained concrete sidewalk, the mailbox shaped like a lighthouse and the gold-plated numerals of the house's address.

"Stephen lives here," Carrie said, shivering in the cold. "We have to walk to get to my place, but you can park here."

Tessa parked and came to stand beside her. "I hear water."

"There's a stream in the back. I'll show you."

Tessa smiled at Carrie. "Lead the way."

A white picket fence, linked in the middle by an iron gate, separated the house's neatly manicured lawn from the woods that bordered the property. Carrie unlatched the gate to let Tessa through, then relatched the gate and turned to the woods. Her step was sure as turned into the copse of evergreens.

"Carrie?" Tessa said, hurrying to keep up with her. "Who is Stephen?"

"Stephen Whittaker."

"But who is he?"

"He's a mystery writer. And my landlord."

Tessa did not know whether to press on or to let the matter drop, but Carrie continued speaking without further prompting. "How did you meet?"

"There was an art collector who died a few years ago," she said. "His name was Eugene Whittaker. He specialized in collecting experimental art, and prided himself particularly on discovering new artists. He bought the collected works of someone I knew, once…"

Tessa let the silence of the evergreens envelope them before gently interjecting. "Damien?"

Her face lost its color, and her eyes became sad. "It was Damien," she said. "I told you he was a genius, when he applies himself. Which, even now, is sporadically. I've followed his work as best as I can, but…" She shook her head. "But it's been a long time since I knew him. I don't even know where he is, now."

They continued walking down the path cut into the evergreens until they came to a gray brick building with a tin roof—what looked like a dilapidated shed to Tessa. Carrie opened the door and gestured at Tessa to follow her. Tessa had to duck to get inside, and then she looked around her in surprise.

"You live here?"

"I do." Carrie went to the corner of the one-room building and lit a single taper candle sitting on an old table. "One moment, Tessa. I didn't want to leave the candles burning unattended."

She picked up the taper and started moving around the room, lighting candles until the small space brightened. The light from the candles splintered against shards of broken glass that Carrie had hung from the ceiling, sending twinkling reflections of color along the walls. A cot sat in the other corner, covered in a worn red, blue, and orange patch quilt. The cement floor was covered partly by a tattered rug made of various colored threads. Carrie moved across the room and opened one of the windows—barely large enough for a cat to slip through. Tessa noticed there were also chimes hung from the ceiling that emitted silvery tinkling sounds in the slight breeze.

"It's beautiful," Tessa said.

"I like it."

"But how do you manage?"

"I work most days, so I eat in the restaurant. I bathe in the stream, since it's only a little ways from here." She smiled. "It's amazing what you can do without."

Tessa stared at her. "But why do you choose to live this way?"

She shrugged. "This is what I wanted. A room of my own, in the middle of natural beauty, with no distractions. So I can work."

Tessa noticed a notebook laying open on the table. "Don't you get lonely?"

"I see people at the restaurant."

"That's all you need?"

Carrie was silent for a moment. "All I need to do is stay sane."

"What about love?" Tessa said. "Or do you and Stephen—"

"Stephen is my landlord."

"I didn't mean to imply." Tessa paused, flustered. "When you said you were his muse, I assumed."

"You should know me better," she said blandly.

"I thought your life had turned into a bad fairy tale, Carrie."

Carrie shook her head. "Stephen's as much of a recluse as I am. He claims that knowing I'm back here is enough for him, and all I need from him is continued permission to live here."

Tessa paused. "Why candles?"

Carrie looked at the flickering candles dripping wax down onto the shelves built into the walls. "They seem more natural than electric light. They add feeling, like a presence, to this place. The atmosphere helps me write."

"This is unreal." Tessa kept her eyes fixed on the flickering flames. "How did this happen?"

"I was getting to that."

Tessa sat down in the single chair by the table and looked at Carrie. She waited for Carrie to begin speaking.

"Eugene Whittaker collected Damien's work," Carrie said. The candlelight threw flickers of shadow across her face. "He displayed his art in an old abandoned barn he had turned into a studio for his collections. The art collection contained portraits of young women. I went to see it, with Sam, and he was the one who pointed out that all of the girls looked like me." Carrie looked away, her eyes settling on another candle. "I didn't believe him. But apparently other people saw what Sam saw. Stephen was one of those people."

"Sam, who worked with us?" Tessa interrupted.

Carrie nodded. "I haven't seen him, not since we graduated. I saw in the paper, though, a few years back…"

"We got married," Tessa said, not looking at her. "But I didn't mean to interrupt you."

"Tessa—"

"Please continue."

Carrie glanced at her, but continued. "Though Stephen is a novelist, he followed his father's forays into art. He saw the gallery and, like Sam, theorized that there was one woman behind the various portraits. Then, years later, he saw me working at the diner."

"And he remembered?"

"You don't forget Damien's work. It gets inside your head. It stays with you." She paused. "Stephen asked me to marry him as soon as I came up to the table, saying my face had haunted him since he had seen the gallery. Tessa, you know I don't attract attention like that."

"That's what you think, Carrie."

She shook her head. "Stephen is an exception. But when I refused his offer, he said he would give me anything I wanted. I was living in a shithole at the time, so I asked if he knew anywhere I could stay. I didn't believe he would let me stay here until we drew up my lease and a contract, until he let me build this house. I trusted him only enough to make this happen, and then only after he had come to Sandy O'Hara's dozens of times and I had found out who he was. I had to be sure, before I moved here, that his proximity would not present complications. It hasn't. Everything you see I've bought for myself."

Tessa glanced around the room at the brick walls, the faded blankets, the candles, the glass. The chimes tinkled; from the open window, she could hear the whisper of the stream somewhere in the thick of the evergreens.

"Are you happy?" she asked.

"I'm accomplishing what I need to accomplish. That's all that matters."

"How can you tell if you're accomplishing what you need to?"

"It's getting cold," Carrie said. She got up and shut the window. "That's better. What I wanted to talk to you about—"

"Don't change the subject, Carrie."

"…was Chris. What did you want to tell me about Chris?"

"Carrie."

"Tessa, what about Chris? Is he sick? Is he hurt?"

"Chris is my student," Tessa said, to reassure her. "I thought you might want to know."

"He's a senior now, isn't he?" Carrie reached above her head, twisted the strand the glass was hanging from, and let go. The shard spun, sending rainbow slivers racing along the walls. "I haven't seen any of them in so long."

"He's well-liked," Tessa said. "And he's a rebel in his own way. You would be proud of him."

She smiled. "I've always been proud of him."

Tessa paused. "He doesn't come to class much, but he has the system on his side. This teacher, Ralph Palmer—"

"Ralph Palmer?"

Tessa nodded. "He's very involved with the school, and so Laura— our principal—gives him more leniency and privileges than I think, personally, she should. I can't even say anything about Chris's absences because he brings legitimate excuses, but, Carrie, it's just not right. There *can't* be that many enrichment programs. For all I know, Chris goes to Mr. Palmer's room and they *talk*."

"Have you talked to Laura?"

Tessa sighed. "What could I say? Chris makes up all his work and gets straight As, and, like I said, this Mr. Palmer must have charmed Laura because she's aware of the situation and she permits it." She broke off.

"Chris would probably benefit from seeing you. Why don't you come back with me for a couple of days? You can stay at my house, and you could talk to him."

"I haven't seen him in four years, Tessa. Not since I graduated. He won't want to see me."

"You're wrong. He does want to see you." Tessa routed through her purse, then extracted a folded sheet of notebook paper which she handed to Carrie. "This is his first freewrite. I let my students write about anything they wanted. Chris wrote that, and turned it in voluntarily."

Carrie glanced at the paper too briefly to read the contents. "He didn't write much. How do you grade this?"

"Read it. Out loud."

Carrie moved the paper closer to a candle and read. *"I want to know why the ones I love leave me. They're taken from me by death, by a change in the wind...they leave with no warning and no explanation. Got any answers to that, teacher?"* Her eyes scanned the script again, then she handed the paper to Tessa. "He sounds insolent."

"He sounds angry," Tessa said. "I wish I could get through to him, but I don't know how. I don't even know if I can, since he doesn't come to class...."

"What did you write back to him?" she asked.

"I haven't seen him since," Tessa said. "He comes to less than fifty-percent of my classes."

Carrie smiled.

Tessa looked around the room again. "Why didn't you ever use your teaching degree? You were always so excited to tell me about your tutoring, and—"

"I love children," Carrie said. "I love teaching. But I hate school. I hate the system. I hate how school gives students a false impression of what's important in life."

"Carrie," Tessa said, gently. "When you teach, you close the door. No one knows what goes on in your classroom besides you and your students. There's very little the school does to monitor your teaching, once the door is closed."

"Until they put cameras in the classrooms," she said, bitterly. "The

System hasn't caught onto that possibility yet. Right now it's doing the best it can to suppress teachers' spirits with its standardized tests."

"Is this all you want?" Tessa looked around. "A shed in the woods, a half-filled notebook of ideas, a job where you cater to people who treat you like their servant?"

"It's enough."

"It's not enough. You can't live like this, Carrie. You can't waste your talents like this."

"I never asked for my talents," she said softly, as if she were thinking of something else.

"But you've got them. And they're gifts which you're wasting. You could be shaping young lives, Carrie, making a difference—"

"I don't want that kind of power."

Tessa blinked. "It's not about power."

"Everything is about power."

Tessa paused. "I can't believe you would settle for this."

"I chose this. I didn't settle."

"Didn't you?" Her ice blue eyes were unrelenting. "I refuse to believe that this is all you want. I refuse to believe that you put up with sixteen years of school to do something, to be someone, you could have been after you turned eighteen. You're afraid of something, Carrie."

"No, Tessa. I'm not."

Tessa folded her hands in her lap. "Come back with me. Come observe my classroom. High school might not be what you remember it to be. You have nothing to lose."

Carrie was silent, drumming her fingers against the cover of her notebook. "Not right now. Come back in a week and let me know if the school will let me observe you."

"Thank you," Tessa said. "I'll meet you here in a week, same time. I'll tell Chris you say hello."

"Don't," Carrie said. "It'll be better for both of us if he forgets that I exist."

"Someday you'll explain this to me," Tessa said. "For now, I'm not going to push my luck." She snapped the cover of her purse closed and stood. "Think about what I've said."

"Thank you for coming, Tessa."

"I'll talk to you soon," she said.

Carrie stood. "Let me walk you back."

"I'll be fine."

"You're sure?"

Tessa nodded and let herself out the door, latching it closed behind her. She stared up the path, surprised by how quickly dusk had fallen, by how much darker the overreaching canopies of the trees made the wooded area. She glanced back, once, and through the windows of the little hut, she saw Carrie's candles flickering brightly.

Mrs. Fanny Caruthers had given birth prematurely and was on sabbatical. Tessa returned a week later with the news that the school had a tenth grade English long term sub position open.

"You have to apply," Tessa said. "You're more than qualified. The fact that you graduated from the College of Education and got an English degree as well, with honors..."

Carrie's eyes were on the glinting shards of glass, the tapered candles. "Tessa."

"It's only a part time position, but it's such a good opportunity for building experience, in case you want to continue teaching after—"

"I can't teach."

Tessa stared at her, dumbfounded. "Why not?"

"I've told you. I dedicated sixteen years of my life to organized education, and that's enough. Waitressing might not seem ideal to you, but at least I have freedom."

"Working whenever you're told, taking shit all the time from people like that couple you served when I was there? Is that what you call freedom?"

"I never have to do anything I don't want to."

"Carrie, waitressing must tire you out, with the long shifts and crazy hours."

"And teaching doesn't tire you? It's about the compromise involved." She paused. "Do you think I could grade papers? Do you think I could stand in front of a bunch of adolescents every day, knowing that not one of them cares what I'm talking about so long as they get As on their report cards? It would be a waste of my time."

"You don't mean that."

"I do."

"You majored in what you're criticizing."

"I'm not surprised. My life has been one contradiction after another."

Tessa sighed. "You know that any job requires give and take."

"That's how people die before their time, Tessa. They give a little, and before they know it they've compromised everything."

"That's extreme," Tessa said.

"The more extremely you live life, the more you get out of it." Carrie walked over to the window and stood looking out. "I'm not afraid. I know I could teach if I wanted to."

"You want to," Tessa accused her. "You want to and you should. You're intelligent and creative, and you could have a large influence on so many children who need someone to look up to and…"

"If I wanted to teach, I would," she repeated.

Tessa stood. "You've been given a gift that is also a *passion*. I know how much you want to teach. You just have to trust yourself enough to be a shaping influence on someone else. You aren't supposed to be a recluse."

"You can't know that."

"I can. I do." Tessa paused. "I did a reading on you, before I came, because, honestly, Carrie, I can never tell how you're going to react to anything. I know you don't believe in the cards, but…why are you smiling?"

She shook her head slightly. "I'm glad you did the reading, Tessa."

"But—"

"It was probably the first time you picked up your Tarot deck in a long time." Carrie's voice dropped. "When was the last time you danced?"

"I don't see where you're going with this."

"You do." Carrie looked directly at her. "What I'm saying is that educators are surrounded by convention, by repression, by a judgment so fixed and consistent that even the strongest get worn down. The System will find what defines you and will then proceed, directly or indirectly, to destroy that. You get no support for being an individual in the school system, from your staff or from your students. With the new importance on college and getting jobs, students don't care about knowledge. They'll take a teacher who will give them an easy A any day over a teacher who will blow their minds and give them a B for their efforts. And knowledge is too important to me to degrade it like that."

"You're being a coward," Tessa said. "By staying away from something you think might tempt you to betray yourself, you're already betraying yourself. You're saying you don't trust yourself enough to be tested. That's more of a compromise, in my mind, than trying and failing."

"Nicely said." Carrie paused. "But my answer remains the same."

"Maybe I got sucked in," Tessa said. "But for the first time in my life I'm happy."

"You sacrificed the two things that were most precious to you," Carrie said. "Your belly dancing, and your solitude."

Tessa shook her head. "I didn't sacrifice. I changed. I moved on in my life. I found something which became important to me, and I believe in my teaching. If you're still the same person you were in college, then you've stagnated."

"Not if I knew what I wanted then."

Tessa frowned. "What have you missed because you've been so focused on achieving one thing in life?"

"What I've gained is being able to face myself at the end of the day, knowing how much I let go so that I could go after something I want."

"You're stagnant," Tessa said. "Your asceticism and self-containment have led you into a false sense of security. If you don't change you won't evolve, and if you don't evolve, you'll die. There is an equal risk of suicide in stagnation as there is in compromise." She paused. "Take this job. It's only part-time. You'll have time to do whatever else you want to do, and when it's over, it's done. You're not obligated to teach for any longer."

"How long?" she asked, after a considerable pause.

"Till the end of June. Not even a year." Tessa stared at her. "We need people like you."

Carrie turned to face her. "I'll never go somewhere based on that belief. Too self-righteous."

"Whatever you believe, you are needed," Tessa said. "The school knows they need someone. They don't know how much the students need someone like you. You're good at shaking other people up, Carrie. Shake things up a bit for yourself. I'll put in a good word for you."

"No."

"You won't do it?"

"You are not to put in a good word for me. I'll apply, and I'll get the job. But I don't want your name linked to mine, and after a few months, neither will you."

"Well." Tessa smiled, stood. "I'm glad that's settled. You're making the right choice, Carrie. You know that, don't you? If you ever need help with lesson plans or anything..."

Carrie stood by the door and held it open. "I'll see you soon, Tessa."

Tessa paused, between the candlelight and the night. "You'll see, Carrie, how much this job will come to mean to you."

"Goodnight, Tessa."

"Goodnight, Carrie."

The door closed softly behind her. As Tessa walked away, she wondered why she felt like she had betrayed Carrie.

"Meet Miss Crenshaw, while you're here," said Laura Knockridge, Principal of Greensburg Salem High, as Tessa walked into her office later that week. "She'll be teaching tenth grade English temporarily for us."

Tessa asked Carrie about the interview later, as she sipped coffee at a Starbucks and Carrie looked around the café listlessly.

"She asked why I had waitressed," Carrie said. "But they needed someone, and I have my college degree and my good record."

"Do you really feel like you're compromising?"

"I'm doing this for now." She paused. "How's Chris?"

"I wouldn't know," Tessa retorted. "I barely ever see him. How are your other family members?"

"They're doing well," Carrie said. "They're pulling through. Calder has a job on Wall Street. He still drinks pretty heavily and he might not be as happy as he could be. But he's making money, so he's doing what he wants. Carly is going into her junior year at Saint Mary's, certain that she wants to teach elementary school kids. My mother joined a ladies book club at the library. I get my information from her." Carrie paused. "If nothing else comes out of this teaching experience, I'm glad that this job has given me the opportunity to reconnect with my family. It's been too long."

Tessa hesitated. "Sometimes you lose me, Carrie. Even in college you loved your family, but you wanted a certain distance."

"I know. That hasn't changed."

"Still?"

"I've realized I don't have to cut my family out of my life in order to live on my terms." Carrie paused. "But I was still afraid of coming back, even though my mother never asks questions."

"But how did she respond?"

"She accepted the renewed correspondence instantly, as if she had expected it, like all these years gone by without a word had never existed. I can't fathom my mother, Tessa. Her selflessness, her kindness, her ability to forgive, her love…"

"She sounds like an admirable woman."

"She is," Carrie said. "But I wouldn't want to be her."

Tessa knew that Carrie had seen Chris in the halls of the school, and that he had ignored her. Carrie still asked about him, and when Tessa did not weave news of him into their conversations, she felt Carrie's eyes on her, searching. Chris did not come to class most days, but Tessa told Carrie all she could.

Carrie went to fundraisers and helped with PTA meetings. She played the game, or *kept the small rules so she could break the big ones,* as she paraphrased from Orwell's 1984, a book she had introduced into the tenth grade curriculum. Tessa had not lost her sixth sense; as she had predicted, Carrie was bringing change to the school, and Carrie's students were thawing her. Carrie started to sit in on Tessa's classes during one of her prep periods, she started reading books about teaching, and she asked Tessa how she could improve her lessons.

"I feel like they're afraid to challenge my authority," she told Tessa. "They think I'm a genius."

Tessa hesitated to tell her that so did the teachers—that most had come to regard the new long term substitute teacher as foreboding, austere, and extremely intelligent. Most of the other teachers had not reached out to Carrie like they had to Tessa, but Carrie did not notice. She ate lunch every day by herself in her classroom, and she spent her other prep period in the same classroom—writing. She was writing again, though she would not tell Tessa what the newest novel was about. To the best of Tessa's knowledge, however, Carrie was not disliked; she simply intimidated.

Tessa would have said something had Carrie given her a moment's pause, but they were in a coffee shop and Carrie was in the midst of one of her frequent rants.

"It doesn't matter if I know the material," Carrie said. "*They* need to know the material. I want them to grasp the knowledge that these poems, these works of literature, can offer. I want them to understand, and it's important that they realize why they need to understand."

Then came the day when Tessa listened to the message that Carrie had left on her phone, telling her she needed help, giving Tessa directions to get to the apartment building where she was staying. Tessa dropped off the latest bunch of student papers at her fairy house and then drove, getting lost only once because the turnoff to the apartment building was sharp. Carrie had not included her apartment number in the message, and Tessa had no way to find out because Carrie still did not have a phone; she had used the school's to leave the message. As Tessa pulled around the corner looking for a place to park, she spied Carrie slamming a faded basketball against a rusted backboard with apparent anger. Tessa killed the motor. She got out of the car. Though she doubted anyone would steal the car, she locked her doors.

"Carrie, what are you doing?"

Carrie threw the basketball at her. Tessa barely had time to put up her hands in defense before the ball slammed into her with stinging force.

Carrie watched as the ball dribbled away down the court. "You were supposed to catch it."

"Well, I…" Tessa started, then waited as Carrie jogged back from retrieving the ball. "What's wrong?"

"Come inside," she said. "I need your advice."

Tessa followed her, silently rejoicing when she saw that the outside of the building belied the adequacy of the interior. The halls were brightly lit and clean. Carrie's room, though plain, was well-ventilated and carpeted, and she had a mattress instead of a cot. Carrie nodded at a fold out chair she had propped up in the corner.

"Sit down."

Tessa sat.

"I did something I wasn't supposed to do today," Carrie said, pacing. "I was on my way out of the school late and was worried about getting to work on time. I was by the north entrance of the school and one of the student restrooms was right there, so I thought that since it was after hours, it wouldn't be a problem if I used it."

"That's understandable—"

"I walked into the bathroom and there was a girl." Carrie paused, but Tessa doubted it was for effect. "She had a protractor, and she was *cutting* herself with it."

"Would she talk to you?"

"She started crying as soon as she saw me and answered everything I asked her."

"In that case, refer her to the guidance counselors."

Carrie slammed her fist on the table. "It's not just this one girl and her personal history, Tessa. There is an entire culture of insecurity among our female students. I have, at most, two young women who have any shred of self-esteem. We have to help these girls. We have to help them become strong and independent. Don't you see what I'm saying?"

"I see," Tessa said, after a moment's pause. "But not everyone can save the world. The world couldn't continue if everyone were like you. The world exists because people are willing to compromise and be insecure."

"So you think we should let these young women flounder and kill themselves?"

Tessa had never seen Carrie so hysterical. "Having girls hurt themselves is completely different. You did the right thing in getting this girl the help she needs and in wanting to help prevent others from—"

"I know I'm right," Carrie said. "I don't need the encouragement. The only thing I need is your help."

"I'll help in any way I can,' Tessa said. "But I don't know what you want me to do."

"I want to address the larger problem," Carrie said. "These girls. They live for their friends, their boyfriends, sometimes their families, but they do very little for themselves. They see themselves as a means to an end. I want to give them something that will make them feel intensely alive, beautiful, powerful…something they can do by themselves, for themselves."

"You want to empower them," Tessa said. "How?"

"I want to start a belly dance club."

Tessa almost laughed. "Carrie, starting a belly dance club is not going to solve this problem."

"It will help." Her voice was firm. "Don't you remember how it feels to be in a room of women with different stories, experiences, shapes and sizes and ages, who come together and recognize each other as equals? To be in that space, out of the male eye, away from society's expectations? And then how it feels, after learning even the simplest movement, to close your eyes and abandon yourself to the music? Don't you remember, Tessa?"

"I haven't danced in a long time."

Carrie inhaled. She propped open the window to let in the soft night air. She undid her bandanna, shook out her hair, lay the bandanna on the counter beside her.

"Carrie?" Tessa said, unnerved by the silence. "I just don't know if I can start the club."

"I didn't ask you to start a club. I wanted to know if you think the idea for the club will be approved, because I can't always judge how other people will react."

"What do you want me to say?"

"Tell me honestly what you think."

"I don't want to discourage you. And I don't want to give you false hope."

Carrie turned. "If you tell me it will work, I'll have the knowledge of your belief and faith, and that will help me if I'm unsure or if I run into problems. If you tell me it won't work, then I'll do everything in my power to prove you wrong."

"When did you become such an optimist?"

"Would you call that optimism?" she asked.

"Can I have some time to think about it?"

"No."

Tessa stared at her. "If I'm unsure I'm going to say no and then you'll lose the support you might have had."

"And if I let you delay your decision, I'll lose time. Go with your gut instinct and save yourself the worry and deliberation."

Tessa obeyed. "I don't think the idea will be approved. That's my honest opinion."

Carrie blinked. "Why?"

"Do you understand how outsiders see belly dance?" Tessa asked. "Parents, the school board, administrators, will never approve of a belly dance club. Someone is bound to see it as subversive."

"You can help me explain that the dance isn't like that."

"I'm sorry, Carrie. I can't help you."

"Why?"

"I take my students on trips," Tessa started. "I have them participate annually in all kinds of programs that the board would not approve for other teachers, solely because I have a good reputation and I'm responsible. If I lose that, I'm putting all of my students at a disadvantage. This isn't just about me, Carrie."

"You were given a gift."

"Don't start with that."

"You were given a gift," Carrie repeated. "We have to take our life experiences and lessons and use them to help others get through this life and enjoy it. I'm not above using the same line you used to persuade me to take this job."

"Don't make this into something it's not. I said no."

"Fine," Carrie said, pacing like a caged bear. "I shouldn't tell you this. It breaks the rules of student-teacher confidentiality. But the girl I referred was one of your students."

"One of *my* students?"

"Miranda Baxter."

Tessa could not speak. Carrie's words brought to mind the image of the tall, slim twelfth-grader, her sleek hair held back by a colorful flower, her smile beaming warmth and self-assurance.

"I have now betrayed a student's confidence," Carrie said. "Something I promised myself I would never do."

Tessa unglued her lips. "I'll help you."

"I knew you would." Carrie smiled. "Goodnight, Tessa."

Tessa found herself outside without knowing how she had gotten there, confronting the empty basketball court and the crumbling facade of the apartment complex. She looked up, and there were no stars.

The founding of Carrie's club formed a schism amongst faculty members, but after the club's official approval by Principal Laura Knockridge, not even the most vehement attacks on the club's scandalous nature could uproot the club's existence. Tessa smiled tightly as she heard other teachers' barbed words in the faculty room. She sipped her coffee and remained silent. The response to the club had been huge; already Carrie had started weekly meetings after school showing videos, teaching improvisation, and letting the students talk to each other about life. She also made them read; Tessa had seen the pink tell-tale cover of the required readers in the hands of many of her female students: the origin of bellydance, photos of costumes, descriptions of the different styles, and, tucked into the very back, a sample CD of belly dance music the girls could use to practice. Tessa had seen the pink cover peeking out from behind Miranda's textbook during her class, and she had demanded that Miranda relinquish the packet. Tessa returned the reader to Miranda the next day—after she had read through the contents.

Tessa confronted Carrie on meeting her in the female faculty restroom. "I want to talk to you."

Carrie turned off the faucet, began to air-dry her hands. "About the club?"

"About the club." Tessa paused. "I've seen the packets. You're doing a fabulous job, you know."

"Thank you."

"How did you get Laura's approval? And a substantial budget?"

"Laura didn't give me a budget."

"Then how…"

"Laura gave me permission," Carrie said. "The rest I can handle on my own."

"You're paying out of pocket?"

"How can I afford it," Carrie said. "Say it, Tessa, if that's what you mean to say. A temp's salary and tip money doesn't add up to much."

"Then you did it," Tessa said, after a pause. "You sold your first book."

"I did. But that's not paying the bills. The girls help. I copied the packets, but they each gave me a dollar for the CDs, and they each take a turn bringing in food each week for when we've finished practicing."

"That's fabulous, Carrie." Tessa paused. "Why didn't you tell me when you found out you were going to be published?"

"It didn't seem important."

"Didn't seem important?"

"This is only the first step. I have much more work to do."

"But this is your dream, Carrie, coming true! How exciting! We should go out and celebrate."

Carrie looked at her levelly. "When you act with such exaggerated enthusiasm, I can tell you're not excited at all."

"That's ridiculous." Tessa swallowed. "You're my friend."

"We've drifted apart."

"You're cold, Carrie."

"I've been told that before, Tessa."

"I could never live like you do."

"You don't have to."

The bathroom door opened. Tessa turned quickly and started washing her hands, though she had washed them moments before, as Carrie drifted out into the hallway.

One night Tessa stayed later at the school than usual grading papers, and as she passed the classroom where she knew Carrie held practice, she heard the rhythms she had loved so much, and she felt the urge to move to the beat she could barely hear. She forced herself to walk faster. That time in her life had passed, and she was in no position to reawaken her old passions. She had not danced in years, but when she heard the news that

Laura was on the verge of disbanding the club, she found herself on the way to the principal's office.

"An interesting subject for you to bring up," Laura said, after Tessa announced she had heard rumors about the belly dance club. "I was under the impression that this club meant very little to you. And rumors, I know, don't interest you at all. I've always liked that about you, Tessa. You know your business, and stay out of other people's."

Tessa smiled. "Anything that involves my students is important to me."

"Carrie is just too new." Laura sighed. "The storm of protests I have had from the community…"

"What if I took over the club?"

"You want to take over the club?"

Tessa hesitated, then nodded.

"Your reputation and record at this school are flawless," Laura mused. "You are recognized as a teacher of merit, and undoubtedly some of the protests would stop if you became involved with the club. But why would you want to take that risk, Tessa?"

"Like I said, I'm interested in the well-being of my students. This club seems to have raised the confidence of our girls, and I think that's an important development."

"I have no problem with your involvement in the club," Laura said, after a pause. She sighed. "You know our students are my top priority. My instincts tell me that this club will be good for our girls. If you're willing to take responsibility for the club, and if you can get Carrie to transfer her duties as the club's sponsor over to you, then I see no reason why the club can't continue." Laura paused."I don't like being in the middle of faculty disputes. But I will step in if the club—under whoever's leadership— oversteps its bounds. Understood?"

"Understood," Tessa said, smiling and standing. "Thank you once again, Laura, for your time and consideration."

Laura nodded and shuffled the papers in front of her.

"One more question for you, Laura."

Laura looked over her rectangular glasses to where Tessa was standing by the door. "Yes?"

"What kind of cookies do you like? I volunteered to bring dessert for the PTA meeting tomorrow night, and I'm at my wits end trying to decide what I should make."

"Old-fashioned chocolate-chips are my favorite," Laura said, peering at the papers in front of her. "I'll see you at the meeting, Tessa."

Tessa nodded and left, knowing that Laura's eyes were following her as she walked away.

The girls offered repeatedly to help Carrie put the room back in order after they danced, but letting them help would mean cutting down the time they used to dance, to talk, to support each other. And with their help, she would have had to leave the school earlier—the school that had started to feel like a refuge. The thought made her uneasy; she made herself repeat the motto she had learned to live by: that she could leave it all behind, that she could start again somewhere else with the same vigor and energy. She watched the girls gain confidence, opening up to her and to others. These girls meant something to her; she had worked for them, she had fought for the club...

Their smiles, on the way out, relieved her. She had brought in modern music from Lebanon for a challenging change of pace, and she was glad that none of her dance students seemed frustrated. She crossed the room and unplugged the CD player from the classroom's single outlet. She heard the scrape of a desk's metal leg and turned to see Chris adjusting a desk, his thin but broad shoulders supporting an overweight backpack jammed with books.

"Hi," he said.

She went to the teacher's desk where her newsboy bag—full of organized papers to be graded and her copy of the tenth grade English textbook—lay waiting. She had not talked to Chris since the time she had first encountered him in the hall, when he had turned away. She picked up her belongings and smiled at him.

"Hello, Chris. It's good to see you."

"Yeah," he said.

Keeping a professional tone with him was not as hard as she would have thought. She did not know him any better than any of her students—yet he was her brother, and the space between them was filled with tension.

"Can I help you with something?" she asked.

"Look," he said, after a long silence. "I didn't come here to apologize for not making an effort to see you while you've been here—"

"I understand why you don't want to see me, Chris."

He paused. "But that's not what I came here to talk to you about."

She kept her voice controlled. "Why did you come here?"

"I'm getting there, okay? But it's not.... it's not easy for me to say." He paused. "Can I get a lift home with you? I missed the activity bus."

"Of course," she said, a second too late to seem natural. "Let me just get my things and—"

"Carrie."

"Yes?"

He paused. "I'm not talking to you right now just because I missed the bus. It's only four miles, and I could walk..."

"The thought never crossed my mind."

He looked at her, skeptically. "I missed the bus on purpose."

"I can give you a ride, Chris."

"I wanted to talk to you about..." He fell silent.

She gathered the remainder of her belongings. "We can talk in the car. Do you have all your stuff, or do you need to go to the locker room?"

"I'm ready," he said. "I just don't know where you parked."

"I'll show you." Toting the packed newsboy, she led him around the back of the building to the beat up red Cavalier she had scrounged up at a used car dealership.

"Sweet ride," he said.

"It was cheap, but it runs." She unlocked the doors. "Congratulations, by the way. Christine told me your team came in first place at last week's cross country invitational and that you got a personal record."

"Yeah." He sat down in the passenger's seat and closed the door. "Thanks."

"Do you mind if we swing by the library?" she asked, knowing the short drive to the house would not be long enough for him to tell her whatever he needed to tell her. "I want to pick up some audio material for my Monday's class. The library closes at six and they aren't open on the weekends."

"I don't mind."

They drove to the library in silence. She invented something for herself to check out while he wandered aimlessly through the stacks, and when they went back to the car he started talking immediately.

"What I wanted to talk to you about is Miranda," he said in a voice that was purely business, "I just wanted to say thank you."

"I need a little more information before I can give you a proper response to that."

He paused. "Don't tell Mom, but Miranda and I have been dating for the past year and a half, and for most of that time she's been hurting herself. I know I should have told someone, but she told me to let her handle it. And I felt like I couldn't tell anyone then, because she lets me deal with my issues on my own." He paused. "But now she's stopped, and she's happy again and she said it was because of you when I asked her, because you didn't judge her and because you let her talk to you. So thanks."

She kept her eyes on the road. "Miranda was willing to help herself after someone gave her the initial push. You probably helped her, too, by being there for her, and by not giving up on her."

"Maybe."

She paused. "I don't know if you know how much a strong guy can help pull a girl through hard times, or how much a weak one can hurt her—"

"I haven't been strong for her," he interrupted. "She was strong when I met her and I loved that, and then she broke down and started hurting herself and I couldn't respect her after that." He paused. "There was even a time when I was going to break up with her."

Carrie remained silent until she was sure he had finished speaking. "People who hurt themselves need help, not judgment."

He glanced at her. "I didn't know what to do. I really didn't."

"Sometimes being there is enough," Carrie said. "Sometimes, it's not. For Miranda, it was."

"You can't know that's true."

"You can't know that it's not." She paused. "Have you thought about how you would act differently, if a similar situation comes up again? Or if Miranda runs into trouble again? That's where you should direct your focus, Chris—forward. Not back. Not to guilt, or regret, or apology." She glanced at the mile-marker. "We're almost home. Do you want to stop and talk about this some more?"

"I told you more than I intended to."

"Home you go, then."

He settled back into the seat, stiffly. She accepted his coolness; trust was slow and difficult to rebuild. She pulled into the driveway of her childhood house and waited as he unbuckled his seatbelt.

"Thanks," he said, as he opened the door. "For the ride and stuff."

She nodded, then pulled out of the driveway. Chris continued straight for the house, and when he did not turn back to wave, she understood.

Carrie sat alone in her room, her eyes tracing the path of an ant as it skittered up the wall. A slight knock rapped through the quiet. She roused herself and crossed the room, pausing to prepare herself before she opened the door.

"Hello, Tessa," she said, relaxing.

"Hello, Carrie. Beautiful evening, isn't it? Do you mind if I come in? I have some exciting news."

"I don't mind."

"Whatever is that?" Tessa asked, her eyes trailing to the object Carrie had left propped near the door.

"It's a metal chair leg."

"Why is it there?"

"In case I open the door some night and someone is there who shouldn't be."

"Why wouldn't you look through the peep hole?"

"I don't have one."

"A chair leg, Carrie?"

She shrugged. "The metal was weak enough for me to twist off the leg, which is heavy enough to brain someone without inflicting death."

"Is crime prevalent in this area?"

"Moderately."

"If you're afraid, I'll give you money to get a stronger lock, or—"

"I never said I was afraid."

"But you have a chair leg by your door."

"The chair leg is a precaution."

"A strong lock would be a better precaution."

"This is hardly what you came here to talk to me about. Have a seat, Tessa." She paused. "Will you take some tea?"

"Thank you," Tessa said, seating herself on the bed. "But I'd rather not."

Carrie stopped heading towards the kitchen and looked at Tessa expectantly. Tessa could not stand the direct stare; she pushed on to business.

"I've come to talk to you about your belly dance club."

"I thought you wanted to talk to me about something serious."

Tessa stared at her. "But the club is serious. We all know how much time and effort you've put into—"

"Who is 'we'?"

"You must know about the controversy the club has caused," Tessa said. "The whole community is in an uproar. You were at the last PTA meeting."

Carrie smiled. "Excellent cookies, by the way."

Tessa hesitated. "Thank you, but—"

"I suppose you talked to Laura about the club."

"I know you didn't want me to step in," Tessa began, "but the truth of the matter is that Laura was going to ask you to revoke your sponsorship of the club. Parents have complained about the readings you give the girls and the nature of the club itself. You know how some people are." She shrugged. "Anything alternative to accepted conventions—"

"They view as satanic," Carrie said.

Tessa grimaced. "The parents are only looking out for the best interests of their daughters."

Carrie paused. "So you're taking over the club."

"I never said—"

"I know that's the only way Laura would have let the club survive," she said softly. "I have no doubt that you'll do a fabulous job."

Tessa frowned. "Don't you want to stay involved with it at all?"

Carrie turned to face Tessa. "I'm tired of the club."

"Excuse me?" Tessa said.

"I never stay in one place, working on one thing, for too long."

"Do you intend to wander from thing to thing, place to place, for your entire life?

Carrie paused. "My writing is the only exception."

"What about when you grow old and don't have energy to keep making new beginnings? You'll be left nowhere and with no one."

"I suppose I'll have you looking over my shoulder," Carrie said. "You don't seem to think I'm capable of living life on my own."

"How can you be sarcastic? When I've taken—"

"What exactly have you taken?" Carrie looked at her. "Don't you see that you've given? Given me back my time, which I value more than anything else."

"You're impossible," Tessa said, standing.

"Don't be angry, Tessa. You've gotten what you wanted."

"I don't understand how this got so blown out of proportion," Tessa said. "I feel like I—"

"The girls just learned Figure 8 hips," Carrie said. "I told them we'd learn head slides and chest slides on Wednesday, but you can teach them anything you want. And don't forget your purse. It looks expensive."

Tessa snatched her purse from its place beside the bed. "I'll see you on Monday, Carrie. It was good to talk."

"Goodnight, Tessa."

"Goodnight," she said, curtly.

Carrie heard the door close, and for one moment she put her head down on her hands and listened to the stillness in the apartment. Then she sat up and continued following the progress of the tiny ant along the wide, blank wall.

Tessa wondered how she could gain the girls' trust. They loved the community and the atmosphere that Carrie had created; they had not warmed to her as she had hoped. Tessa was impressed by how much they had learned, but she felt they were holding back. She caught Carrie in the faculty lounge filling up the coffee mug she brought with her every day.

"Can I talk to you before you go back to prepping for class?"

Carrie smiled. "You know how I spend my prep periods, Tessa."

"It's about the club."

Carrie turned. "How is the club going?"

Tessa hesitated. "They talk about you. All the time."

"I'm sure you're doing a wonderful job."

Tessa paused. "I've seen them coming to visit you during homeroom period."

"They trust me and they're comfortable with me, so they're going to come to me. I'm sure you'll gain their confidence with some more time."

"Would you really mind stopping by? For just one practice? The club is taking up more of my time than I thought and I—"

"When is your next practice?"

"Friday at four."

"I'll stop by."

Tessa smiled. "Carrie, I really appreciate this."

"I'm just going to observe."

"You can do whatever you like. I'm just glad you're coming. Now, I really must let you go back to your writing, as I have a fabulous lecture for my fourth period today. We're starting the Romantics, and Byron is up to bat." She smiled. "If you stick around you'll get some of the fun classes, instead of these basic level classes where the kids are just trying to get through."

"I like my classes," Carrie said. "I like the challenge, and the students are meeting my standards. We're studying the transcendentalists, and they really seem to be enjoying—"

"That's the bell for next period! Maybe we can get dinner after Friday's class?"

She paused. "I'll be working."

"Oh." Tessa smiled. "Maybe I'll stop by for a cup of coffee or something, if the diner isn't too busy."

Carrie smiled at her, and Tessa turned away before Carrie could see her frown.

Tessa arrived late to the club meeting on Friday, having met some of the other teachers in the hall and getting pulled into a discussion on an upcoming assembly. She rushed to the classroom, prepared to apologize, but the girls did not even notice her as she entered; they were clustered around Carrie. Tessa saw the light in the girls' faces, heard their enthusiasm as they chattered to one another.

"Girls," she said, and they turned to her. "This was supposed to be the surprise I promised you, but since I'm late, I see you've already found out. We have a very special guest today."

Miranda Baxter glanced at Carrie and started a round of applause. Tessa glanced at Carrie and saw a half-smile quivering on her lips.

"I apologize for being late," Tessa said. "We should get started. Girls, take out your mats so we can begin with warmups. Miss Crenshaw, please join us."

Carrie started to protest, but Miranda handed her a mat. Tessa ran through the warm up and taught the girls *mayas* and *toxemes*—and she felt the extra energy and happiness in the room. As Tessa began the cool down, Carrie stopped her.

"The girls told me you've never danced for them," she said in a low voice.

Tessa glanced at the girls. They had all moved to the back of the classroom and were sitting on their knees.

"I promised them you would," Carrie continued.

Tessa started to protest, but Carrie moved to the CD player in the corner.

"Mrs. Beaumont?" she said. "Are you up for it?"

Tessa had not performed since her college days—but Carrie's direct stare forced her to look at the expectant girls.

"I haven't prepared anything," she stammered.

"Just dance," Carrie said. "Like you used to."

Tessa felt herself move to the center of the room.

"Ready?" Carrie asked.

Tessa nodded. As the music filled the room, Tessa recognized the song. She glanced at Carrie, frozen. Carrie looked back at her, but she did not pause the music. And Tessa danced. She had not forgotten the choreography; her arms flowed in serpentine motion, her undulations overtopped her shimmies. She finished the dance and heard the thick silence in the classroom. Then Carrie started to clap, and the girls joined. When the applause died down, Carrie turned her attention to the girls.

"I want you girls to work your hardest for Mrs. Beaumont," she said. "Give her your full support, your trust, and your thanks for her teaching. And for her performance. It took more courage for her to perform today than she knows." She paused. "*Namaste*, Tess."

A chorus of *Namastes* rang through the room. Tessa smiled and nodded; a tear slipped out of her eye. "Girls, you'll be late," she said, her voice trembling as Carrie came to stand beside her. "Miss Crenshaw and I will clean up."

Miranda glanced at them, standing side by side. "I could help."

"Thank you," Carrie said, because Tessa could not speak. "But we'll be fine."

Miranda shifted her backpack. "Thank you for coming, Miss Crenshaw. We're all really glad to see you again."

Carrie smiled and nodded at her, then turned to Tessa after the girls had left.

"That was my song," Tessa said. "The one I prepared for the hafla you missed—"

"You were fabulous. Then, and now."

Tessa smiled shakily. "How did you know?"

"I bought the DVD," Carrie said. "The one they were selling after the performances. I felt terrible that I had missed the hafla, especially because I knew how excited you had been to show me your routine. Tessa, why haven't you danced for the girls before?"

"I've been afraid to."

"But the more passionate you are about dancing, the more passionate they'll become about learning. I've found that true of any kind of teaching."

"They were passionate because you were here," Tessa said. "Didn't you see how happy they were? Can't you come back?"

"I'm not as good of a dancer as you are."

"It doesn't matter. I've never seen their energy so high. They want you here."

Carrie paused. "I miss them."

Tessa watched as Carrie moved the desks back into position. "You made me face something today. Something I've been afraid of, for a long time."

"I know."

"I'm going to pay you back, Carrie."

Her voice was low. "I don't have anything to face."

"Carrie, look at me."

Carrie adjusted a desk, then looked at her reluctantly. Tessa held her gaze. "You don't have to go through life alone," Tessa said.

Carrie picked up the bag she had brought with her, then went to the CD player. She opened the player and removed the CD. She went to Tessa and handed the CD to her.

"I want you to keep this," she said. "I have to get to work."

"We have practice again on Wednesday. Come back." When Carrie hesitated, Tessa searched her face. "I'll stop by the diner. Later, when you're not busy."

Carrie nodded and left. Tessa stood for a moment, looking out the window, the CD pressed against her chest and the bright yellow of the school's activity bus in her peripheral vision.

Carrie was sitting at the desk in her classroom, grading papers, when she heard a knock on her door. She looked up.

"Good morning, Carrie." Laura Knockridge's full face was flushed above the line of thick pearls around her neck.

"Good morning."

Laura smiled. "I just wanted to let you know that I'm going to have one of our faculty members observe your next class. Regulation protocol."

"I understand."

"He's one of our best," she said. "Ralph Palmer."

Carrie paused, then smiled. "Please tell Mr. Palmer that he is more than welcome to come observe any time."

After Laura left, Carrie found she could not concentrate. She stopped editing and waited for the five minutes before her next class to elapse. She smiled and welcomed her students, and as she was about to begin her lesson, she heard a knock on her door. She turned.

"Good morning, Miss Crenshaw. Did Principal Knockridge tell you I was coming?"

Her eyes connected with his, and she paused a moment too long before she nodded. "Good morning, Mr. Palmer. Yes, she did. Please take a seat in the back."

"Thank you." He smiled at her, his dark eyes dancing. She turned abruptly and went to straighten her handouts for the day.

"Hey, Mr. P!" a student piped up. "What are you doing here?"

Carrie turned and saw that Ralph Palmer had taken a seat and was looking disapprovingly at the student who had spoken. She walked to the front of the classroom. She was shaking.

"We're going to get started." Her voice, however, was steady. "We're going to move from Emerson to one of his close friends. Henry David Thoreau. Who can read the quote on the board for me?"

A student volunteered and stumbled through the words, but gave her the time she needed to compose herself. She thanked the student for reading, then turned and surveyed her class.

"I went to the woods because I wished to live deliberately," she repeated. "To front only the essential facts of life, and see if I could not learn what it had to teach, and not, when I came to die, discover that I had not lived." She paused. "Today, we're going to begin reading Walden."

And she forgot he was there until the end of the class, when he came directly up to her after her students had left.

"I'm impressed," he said. "You're having tenth graders read Walden?"

"They can handle Thoreau," she said, not looking at him. "They need to be challenged." She looked up, her eyes narrowed. "It's nice to finally meet you. I've heard so much about you."

"I assure you, the rumors are all true," he said, smiling. "But let me be sincere for a moment, Miss Crenshaw. I'm glad to have you on the team."

"I'm glad to be here." She did not let her focus waver from his face, aware that he had not looked away from her once. She shook the offered hand; the touch of his skin still sent lightning racing through her body. His eyes darkened, and he dropped her hand quickly. She smiled until he had left, and then there was her next class to keep her calm. But as she drove to the restaurant after the school's dismissal bell, she was consumed by a violent spasm of shaking.

The diner was not crowded, and he spotted her immediately. He wondered what she had done with her life, how she had ended up at Greensburg Salem, why she was waitressing at Dee's Diner on a Friday night. He did not request her section, but he ended up there anyway. As he sat down and spread the menu in front of him, he saw her approach his table.

"Hello, Carrie," he said, as soon as she was standing before him.

"Hello," she said. "*Mr. Palmer.*"

Her moss green eyes looked directly into his dark ones, but he could not be sure she recognized him. "I'd like an iced tea and a cheeseburger. American cheese, rare. And can I have an ash tray?"

She took the menu he handed her. "Actually, there's no smoking allowed in the restaurant."

"What a shame. Don't you think that's a shame?"

"Honestly, I don't." She paused. "I'll be back with your drink in a moment."

He settled into his seat and spread the newspaper he had brought in front of him, then looked up when she came back with his iced tea. "Thanks, sweetheart."

Her eyes flashed at him. "My name is Carrie."

He arched an eyebrow. "Or Miss Crenshaw, if I prefer?"

"If you prefer."

He paused. "Could I have some ketchup? For when the burger comes?"

She nodded, then came back a moment later and set a red plastic bottle in front of him. "Anything else?"

"Yes. An answer, to a question." He paused. "Carrie, what are you doing here?"

She looked back at him, steadily. "I could ask the same question about you."

"I'm just a paying customer."

"Then I'm just a waitress." She looked at him levelly. "Why the name change?"

"I wanted a new start."

Her eyes sparked. "You think a new name will change who you are?"

"Four years helped," he said. "So did the new job, the new haircut, the new outlook…though I never said I wanted to change *who* I was. Just some of the choices I made."

"Congratulations." She started to move away.

"Carrie." She turned; her face had become like marble. He paused. "I recognized you, as soon as I saw you in the halls. But I'm surprised you recognize me."

"My god," she whispered. "How could I not recognize you?"

He stared at her, but she turned abruptly and disappeared into the kitchen. When she came back carrying his food, he did not look at her.

"Tessa doesn't even realize I'm her own brother," he said. "And we've been working at the school together for over three years. But we were never close."

"You don't want her to know?"

He shook his head.

"Then I won't tell her."

He paused. "I'll take my check, whenever you're ready."

She put a slip of paper down on the table beside him. He scribbled on the receipt, then handed it back to her. Her eyes widened when she saw the tip amount.

"It's yours," he said. "Keep it."

She started to protest, but at that moment the door to the restaurant opened, and Tessa walked in and spied them.

"Hello, Ralph," she said, flouncing over and frowning.

"Mrs. Beaumont. I'd offer you a seat, but I was just leaving."

"Oh, well," she said. "I actually came here to see Carrie." She turned. "I told you I would stop by. Carrie, have you met Ralph?"

"We've been recently acquainted," she said, guardedly, her eyes on him.

"Oh, that's right." The confusion cleared from Tessa's blue eyes. "Laura said he turned in a glowing evaluation of your class."

"I was just explaining to Miss Crenshaw that I'm head of the Outdoors Club." His eyes remained locked on Carrie's face. "And that I need a co-sponsor. I thought she might be interested, considering Chris is one of our wilderness leaders."

Suddenly, both their attentions were on him.

"Since you brought up the subject," Tessa said, her voice cool. "Could you please explain to me why you write him so many passes to miss my classes?"

"He's a brilliant student," Ralph said. "You should be proud of him."

"I am," she said. "I'd like to see more of him, however."

"I'm sorry if I have caused you any inconvenience, Mrs. Beaumont." He stood. "But Chris has a Gifted IEP, and I've been put in charge of his enrichment program. Most of his other teachers are aware of this, but since you're relatively new to the school, I see how you could have remained uninformed."

"I'll talk to you in a minute," Tessa said to Carrie. "I think I have to be officially seated in your section."

Carrie started bussing the table as Tessa walked away. He watched her. She straightened, the dirty plate and glass in her hands, and met his gaze.

"I want to talk to you about my brother," she said, unaware that Tessa was staring at them from the host podium.

But he was aware of Tessa's attention, and he did not care for it. "The Outdoors Club offer is still open. Think about it." He paused. "Come find me and I'll talk to you. Goodnight."

She did not answer him, and he felt her watching him as he left. He had expected the coldness, considering she recognized him, but at least he had her attention.

He was not aware of her until he walked out of the AP Chemistry's storage closet, drying his hands on his work shirt. He stopped when he saw her; he had not expected her to come to him so soon.

"Carrie," he said, closing the storage closet's door behind him. "How good to see you. Please come in."

She stepped into the room, her head held high. "I didn't know if you'd be here, since it's after hours."

He smiled. "I've learned a trick to teaching. If I stay till five and do my work and planning for the next day, I can go home and forget about teaching. Did you just get out from instructing your little belly dancers?"

"I help with the club now. I no longer instruct it."

"I'm surprised you'd admit that to me."

"Why?"

"You would seem more influential, more powerful, if you had retained your leadership."

"I'm not interested in power."

"All strong women are interested in power."

Her eyes burned. "Not that kind of power."

"What kind of power?"

"Power based on appearance," she said, "and not based on truth. I'm aware of your position in this school."

"Is that so," he said, returning her gaze. "If you're familiar with my position in this school, then you should know that I'm..." he broke off, smiled at her. "What did you want to talk to me about?"

"You said you needed a co-sponsor." Her voice was steel. "For your club."

"So you want to be near your brother. Here's a hint, Carrie. It's not a smart idea to look at someone like that when you're asking for something." He sat down at the cluttered desk in the front of the room, trying to hide a smile as her eyes continued to bore into him. "Do you have any outdoors experience? Backpacking, hiking, rock climbing, canoeing, kayaking?"

"I'll learn."

He looked at her. "How do you propose to do that?"

"You'll teach me."

He raised his eyebrows. "What makes you believe I'd be willing to teach you?"

"You're a teacher," she said. "And you need a co-sponsor."

"You don't seem particularly qualified." He paused. "I could use your help, but I'm looking for a co-sponsor who can also act as a guide. For each trip we take, especially the weekend trips and those over spring and winter breaks, there always need to be at least two guides in case something should happen. I've hired guides in the past for our day trips, but having a co-sponsor who could double as a guide has always been my true incentive in wanting a co-sponsor at all."

"Some help would be better than none."

He smiled indifferently. "I wouldn't say that. I've been doing fine on my own since I started the club three years ago. But, since you brought it up, I'll tell you the same thing I tell my students. If you're willing to learn, I'm willing to help you."

"I've always wanted to learn." She paused. "And if I'm not able to handle it, you'll let me know."

"No," he said. "If you feel you're not able to handle it, then *you* let *me* know. Otherwise, I'll push you until you get it right. I don't give up on people."

"Thank you." She paused, ignoring the bait in his last words. "When...how should I begin?"

"Our club meets Tuesday afternoons at four," he said. "Will that be a problem for you?"

She shook her head.

"I'll ask you to be here by three-thirty so we can go over the day's agenda," he said. "Our next meeting is tomorrow, but you can start coming next week if you'd prefer."

"I'll come tomorrow," she said, turning to go.

"Carrie."

She turned sharply when she heard the way he said her name. She remained silent.

"If you haven't been on many outdoor trips, you might not know this," he said. "But things happen. Weather gets bad unpredictably. People get hurt. I don't want to scare you, because the actual number of serious incidences is minuscule. The injuries usually amount to a few blistered feet, a few scrapes and bruises. I'm telling you because the hardest part of being my co-sponsor is not going to be learning how to handle injuries, to use the gear, to tie the knots, to know the changing weather patterns and corresponding safety precautions." He paused. "You're going to have to trust me. When something happens, we're going to have to work together to get our young adults out of danger's way and to keep them calm. There has to be constant, open communication between us. If I tell you to do something, you're going to have to do it without questioning me. Can you do that?"

"I can," she said, and paused. "In context."

"I just wanted to check." He measured her with his eyes, and she did

232

not look away. "I'm glad that won't be a problem for you."

"I'll see you tomorrow," she said, turning quickly and exiting the classroom.

He watched her go, then looked at the mess of papers on the desk in front of him. Within seconds he had them arranged in stacks, neat, as he liked them. There was a knot in his chest, and he wondered if, given their past history, he had just made a mistake.

"That's wonderful, Carrie," Tessa said, glancing at her. "Isn't it wonderful?"

They were alone, straightening up after Friday's practice.

"Yes."

"This is perfect for you. You've always loved the outdoors, and you never had time in college to join the Outing Club because you were always working. But you don't look happy."

"You should have seen his face when I showed up at the meeting on Tuesday."

Tessa's brow furrowed. "I'm sure Ralph's glad to have you. He's been looking for a co-sponsor for awhile now. It takes a lot of time to organize trips, and no one wants to put in—"

"I'm not talking about Ralph. I'm talking about Chris."

"Oh." Her brow smoothed, then furrowed again. "What were you saying about his face?"

"He's never looked at me like that," Carrie said. "Completely blank, like he didn't want me to see anything he was thinking or feeling. I don't want to ruin his senior year for him, and if he doesn't want me to be a part of the club, he would never tell me."

"Don't you realize that if you don't help out with the club, Chris will probably have fewer chances to go on trips?"

"What do you mean?"

"Haven't you been listening at the meetings? The school's budget has been cut again. That means clubs get less funding. There's more than one reason Ralph has been looking for a co-sponsor who can double as a guide. If he has to pay guides, he has to cut back the number of trips."

"He didn't tell me that," Carrie said. "I wondered why he accepted me so quickly, despite my lack of experience."

Tessa bit back what she had been on the point of saying and smiled. "I'm sure Chris won't mind having you there, and I'm sure you'll do a great job with the club."

"I have so much to learn."

"That's good. It's always good to be a beginner at something. It gives you something to work for, and keeps your sense of wonder alive."

"As long as I keep our students alive," she retorted. "That's what's beautiful and scary about nature. You have no control." She hesitated. "Sometimes I wish…"

"Sometimes you wish…" Tessa prompted her, then turned and saw Ralph Palmer standing in the doorway. She started. "Ralph, you startled me."

"I see," he said. "I apologize for interrupting, ladies. Has Chris been coming to class, Mrs. Beaumont?"

"More frequently," she said, cooly.

"I'm glad." He paused. "Carrie, may I speak to you for a moment?"

Tessa's eyes slid between them. He kept his eyes on Carrie. It was one of the only times Tessa had seen Carrie look unsure, but the moment passed quickly. Carrie glanced at her, then nodded and followed Ralph out of the classroom.

"What are you doing this weekend?" he asked.

"I'm grading research papers," she said. "And I have to work."

"I'd like to meet with you to go over my expectations for the club. If you have any ideas or suggestions then we could go over them as well." He paused. "I could meet you at the diner during one of your shifts after the rush hour has passed, if that's the only time that will work for you."

"That might be best," she said. "If you wouldn't mind."

He looked at her; he was not smiling. "When do you work?"

"Tonight," she said. "Tomorrow night, and Sunday morning."

He glanced at the classroom. "I'll let you go back to your meeting, but I'll see you soon."

Carrie backed into the classroom, never letting her eyes leave his face, and waited until he had disappeared down the hall.

"You know," Tessa said, and Carrie turned to her. "I've been thinking about you, and Chris, and this Outdoors Club. I think it's a fabulous idea.

And I think you're overly concerned about Chris. I don't think you could arrest his personal development if you tried. He's remarkably stable for someone his age. The Universe makes use of those people, to create chaos or stability for others."

Carrie smiled. "I haven't heard you talk about the Universe and its Grand Plans for us for quite some time."

Tessa shrugged. "Some things you don't outgrow. Don't worry about Chris, Carrie. He'll be fine."

"I know." Her eyes darkened. "I know Chris can take care of himself. I'm not usually like this, Tessa. My family is the only thing that has the potential to unravel me. Even though I'm an adult with a life I've made my own..."

Tessa smiled indulgently. "Family relationships don't necessarily follow any rules." She paused. "Nor does love. You have to be careful about that one, too."

Carrie paused. "Why haven't we talked about you and Sam?"

"There's not much to say. I married Sam. We have a little girl, Kindra. We live in a beautiful house, and he gives me everything I want."

"But you're not happy."

Tessa smiled wryly. "I've told you, Carrie. Even though I've changed, women like me don't do well in relationships. But Sam understands my need for independence, and we're getting by." She paused. "Are you happy living alone?"

"I've been a loner for so long, Tessa." She paused. "I've only recently realized how much I like being single. I've never been able to control my heart. Repress it, yes. Control my actions, subordinate my passion...yes. But control my heart? Never."

"It's perfectly normal to want to be loved."

"I know. But I'm not sure that I trust myself to fall in love."

"Carrie, you worry too much."

Carrie looked up. "Only because there's another person involved in a romantic relationship. I wouldn't want to hurt that person." I

Tessa paused. "You have to work at five, don't you? Can I give you a ride?"

Carrie nodded and followed Tessa out of the classroom, turning off the lights as she did so. With a pang, Tessa realized she had never seen Carrie seem so human.

He went to the diner after the dinner rush so she wouldn't feel like he was keeping her from doing her job—from serving her snotty customers. As he walked into the restaurant he spotted Carrie—her red hair conspicuous—pressed into the corner of the wait station, trying to keep a distance between herself and the balding, pot-bellied man who was accentuating every other word with an emphatic thrust of his finger. Ralph's eyes followed the stranger until the man passed out of sight, then he shifted his attention to Carrie. He had never seen her look like she did in that moment; but when she looked up and saw him, she composed herself and smiled, so that the quiet sadness in her eyes disappeared.

"Hello, Ralph," she said, walking over to his table. "What can I get for you tonight?"

"Who was that man?"

"Corporate."

"Who?"

She turned back to him, took out her notepad and a pen. He knew she had started to memorize the orders of her customers to save paper, and he knew she did not need the pad.

"He owns the restaurant chain," she said. "He stops by the restaurant five days a week at random intervals to make sure everything is running smoothly."

"He looks like an asshole."

Carrie smiled. "I can't say anything to that right now."

His eyes searched hers. "You never used to censure yourself."

"I need this job." She saw him looking at the pad and tapped her pen against it. "When corporate is here, I have to play by the rules. All of them. That includes writing down orders. They can take this job away from me without explanation. I'm not about to give them one."

"You don't need this job," he said. "You could always teach full-time."

"Don't preach to me," she said. "What do you want?"

"From you or from the menu?" He pushed the menu away from him, not having opened it, and leaned back in his chair. "Tonight I'll settle for knowing what he said to you and why you look so sad."

She looked at him as if he were as stranger. "He caught me writing, and

236

he told me to do something more productive with my time. Like fill salt and pepper shakers. I don't know why, but for some reason that cut me to the quick." Suddenly she was angry. "I've already done all my other side work for the night, and for him to imply that filling a stupid salt and pepper shaker is more important than—"

"I suppose if corporate is here, then you can't sit down and discuss plans," he said.

She hesitated, then wrote on the pad, tore off the sheet, and handed it to him. "Here. Address. Phone. Call me."

"I thought you didn't have a phone any more."

"I've had this one for years. I discontinued it awhile ago, but now I have enough money to..." She broke off. "Do you still want iced tea to drink?"

"If I ordered a chocolate milkshake, would you have to make it?"

"Yes."

"Iced tea is fine, thank you."

She brought him back a chocolate milkshake. As she walked away, he slipped the sheet of paper into his pocket, felt it there like a shred of hope. Her number hadn't changed in the span of years that had spread them apart, only to bring them together again.

After closing the restaurant, she walked the solitary stretch of street to her apartment. The stars were not out and the air nipped at her, marked by the chill of an impending winter. Few cars passed her, and the only other sound was the gentle humming of the street lights that lined the pavement.

She arrived at the apartment building and proceeded to her room on the second floor, then paused. A young woman was waiting in front of her door, holding a green plaid suitcase that Carrie recognized.

"Carly?"

Carly turned. "Mom said you lived here. Good thing I believed her and waited. My god, Carrie, this place is a shithole."

"It works for me." Carrie removed her key from her pocket. "It's good to see you."

Carly looked down the hallway nervously "Can we go inside?"

Carrie glanced at her, then opened the door and turned on the light.

Carly followed her and quickly closed and locked the door. "Can I have some tea?"

Carrie nodded and headed towards the kitchen, where she put a saucepan of water on to boil.

"Don't you have a tea kettle?" Carly asked.

"I don't need one."

Carly paused. "You look good, Carrie."

Carrie turned and looked at her. Carly stood with her hands on her hips, the magenta on her nails contrasting the stone-washed denim of her designer jeans. She had grown taller and her body had filled out; she was five years older than she had been when Carrie had seen her last. Carrie did not blame herself for not immediately having recognized her, though Carly had not lost her fashionable sense of style, nor her cocky confidence.

"So do you," she said. "How's college?"

"It's good." Carly paused. "I'm home for a couple of days to do service work here for my Circle K group. It'll be a nice break, anyway."

"You're a junior now?" Carrie took down two mugs from the overhead cabinet. They were the only two she owned.

"Yeah."

"I was surprised when Christine told me you decided to go to St. Mary's." Carrie looked at the tea bag she had used the previous night before tossing it in the garbage and pulling a new tea packet from a box in the cabinet. "I know they have a great program for elementary education, but I'm not sure that I would have wanted to go there."

"I really don't mind going to an all women's school. There are more important things in life than guys, though I never believed it when Mom would tell me that." She took the steaming mug Carrie handed her. "I can focus my attention on learning how to be a good teacher. I don't have to worry about whether I look good or whether I'm pretty enough. And all my rivals, all my role models, are women. That's kind of empowering."

Carrie led the way to the main living area, where Carly had already dropped her bag. Carly moved the pillows on the sofa to give herself room, then picked up a shirt Carrie had left on the cushions and grimaced.

"Are all of your clothes like this?" she asked, wrinkling her nose. "Don't you buy laundry detergent anymore?"

Carrie caught the shirt as Carly tossed it to her.

"Honestly, it's not that bad. Just wrinkled." Carly rolled her eyes. "But it's the *concept*. I know you know how to do laundry because you taught me, so you're probably not doing it right for some other reason in your head." She took a sip of tea. "Have you kept up with what's going on in the family?"

Carrie paused. "Somewhat."

"I suppose you know about *Greg*."

"I've heard about him."

"I'm glad Mom's happy," Carly said. "Honestly, I am, especially because Mom really needs a break from work, sometimes, and I suppose she's lonely now that I'm gone and Chris is leaving next year. But seriously, have you seen them together? They act like they're both sixteen and falling in love for the first time. It's *disgusting*, like open PDA gross. I can't stand being in the house with them for more than five minutes."

Carrie looked at the duffel bag resting at Carly's feet. "I didn't know Greg had moved in."

"Don't worry. I'll only be here for five days."

Carrie met her eyes. "You want to stay *here?*"

"I don't know if I do or not." Carly raised her eyebrows. "Before I saw the place I was planning on asking if I could. Now I'm debating."

"You're welcome to stay," Carrie said. "I'm not around that much so you'll have quiet, and if you need anything to eat we can make a trip to the grocery store."

"Thanks," Carly said. "I don't intend to be a pain, though. It's just that old house carry memories, trap them between their four walls." Carly looked up. "And I have some things I want to talk to you about. I don't want to talk about them with my college girlfriends because I already know what they'll say, and I can't talk to Mom. She would *flip* if she knew what I was thinking about."

"We can talk whenever you'd like."

"Tonight I'll just go to bed. I'm tired." She glanced at Carrie again. "Did you just get off work now?"

Carrie nodded. Carly's eyes flicked over her simple uniform, focused on the cheap name tag pinned onto her shirt. "Mom said you were teaching."

"I am," Carrie said. "Tenth grade English, at Greensburg Salem. But I also waitress three to four nights a week, to make sure I can pay bills."

She felt Carly's eyes on her; Carly was the only person who could make her feel self-conscious. Carly's eyes flicked over Carrie once more, and then she turned away.

"You work so hard," she said quietly, and Carrie realized they had not been thinking along the same lines at all.

Carrie switched to the Sunday night shift. She used her morning off to pay a visit to Christine. The drive back to her childhood home was ingrained in her memory; she drove the twenty-four minutes without noticing the surrounding details. She got out of the Cavalier and started up the flower-lined brick driveway. She rang the doorbell and waited.

She was not surprised when no one came to the door; Christine would be at the early morning mass. She started down the steps, then turned when the door opened behind her and revealed Christine standing there in a pink bathrobe and pink fuzzy slippers.

"Carrie? How good to see you, dear!"

Carrie found herself enveloped in a hug. "You're here."

Christine laughed. "Greg has convinced me to sleep in until at least nine on Sundays, and I let him sleep till eleven. At eleven I absolutely draw the line because I told him it's important that we go to the twelve o'clock mass at Our Lady of Grace."

"Did I wake you?" The town's bells for quarter till eleven o'clock had just chimed.

"You didn't. Come into the kitchen and I'll make you some coffee." Her eyes scanned Carrie's face. "And I insist. It's no trouble at all."

Carrie followed her into the kitchen, watching as Christine bustled around.

"Carly's coming home," Christine announced.

Carrie sat down at the white kitchen table. "For five days."

Christine nodded. "She hasn't been home for that long since she left for college."

"Have you talked to her recently?"

Christine's mouth formed a line. "I'll get a phone call from her maybe once a month, and she'll pick up the phone if I call. But she's always busy, saying she can only talk for a few minutes. She called the other day, asking where you lived." She looked carefully at Carrie. "I wouldn't be surprised if Carly shows up on your doorstep for a visit."

Maybe Christine didn't know their deepest thoughts, the depths of the dilemmas they had all faced and struggled with, but she had an uncanny acumen for predicting their behavior. Carrie watched her mother turn off the coffee maker. "She already has."

"Already has?" Christine looked up. "Do you mean to say she came in last night?"

Carrie nodded. "She wants to give you and Greg some time alone."

"You mean she wants to stay with you."

"I told her she could," Carrie said.

"I knew I shouldn't have gotten her a car. Then there wouldn't be this problem. Carrie, you're kind to offer your sister a place to stay, but whether Carly likes it or not, she belongs here. Giving me time alone with Greg is an excuse. She knows Chris still lives here. And you really shouldn't expect yourself to accommodate her."

"It's nice to have someone else in the apartment." She took another sip of the coffee.

The smile hitched on Christine's face. "Oh."

Carrie put down the mug. "What?"

"I was hoping that you had found some nice man to share the precious moments of your life with, who you hadn't thought to tell me about."

"I'm not looking."

Christine paused. "You're not exactly young, Carrie."

Carrie stared at her. "I'm happy."

"Yes, I suppose you are." Christine looked down at her mug. "But love is such a beautiful thing."

"I'm not inclined to be in a relationship."

"Maybe you haven't met the right person yet." Christine paused. "But

I worry that even if you do find the right man, you won't be able to let yourself love him. You've always been close-minded about love."

"I've always known when to take risks."

Christine looked away. "Did Carly tell you she joined Circle K?"

"She did."

"And she probably told you about Greg. I know she doesn't approve."

"Does Chris?"

"Chris said he wanted me to be happy." Christine paused. "Carrie, when your father passed away…"

A door opened, then came the sound of running water. Christine looked past Carrie, briefly. "That will be Greg, getting up. We have about twenty minutes before he reenters the world, and then you can meet him. He's very particular about his morning routine, and doesn't like to be bothered until he's finished it."

"Continue."

Christine hesitated. "After your father died, I thought I would live the rest of my years as his widow. But it's amazing, how someone's annoying tendencies can grate at you over the years. With your father, it was his moods. I had to walk on eggshells around him, and I didn't realize how much energy it took to cater to his moods until I no longer had to deal with them. Maybe I feel less stressed because I'm working less and sleeping more. Or because I don't have to worry about raising you to make good decisions, now that the three of you are adults and Chris only has to finish this year." She smiled. "Now I only have to worry about you *making* the good decisions. Maybe that's why I feel so much more peaceful and relaxed. But I think a large part of what zapped my energy was dealing with your father and with Greg…"

The water turned off; a door opened in the house and closed once more. Christine listened, then turned her attention back to Carrie. "I loved your father, Carrie. But Greg never yells at me. We've never even argued. He might not be the intellectual rival of your father, nor the driven individual that your father was. But he's the most emotionally stable man I've ever met, and I underestimated the importance of that the first time around. Though I do not regret marrying your father. How could I, seeing you standing before me, knowing Chris is upstairs and that Carly is at your apartment…" Christine paused and sighed.

"You forgot Calder."

"I couldn't forget your brother. He doesn't *let* me." Christine shook her head, then became serious. "The children that come from marriage are amazing gifts, Carrie. Remember that. And despite what you say you believe about marriage, I hope that you will someday have children of your own."

They sat in silence, sipping the coffee, listening to the occasional noise that came from the bedroom adjacent to the kitchen. Carrie finished her coffee, broke the silence.

"Are you going to marry Greg?"

"I don't think so." Christine reached across the table and picked up Carrie's discarded mug, then walked over to the sink. She proceeded to wash the mugs and rinse them out. "I don't regret getting married once, but I wouldn't want to do it again."

Carrie went to stand beside her and dried the mugs as Christine handed them to her. "Why?"

Christine smiled. "It takes a lot of energy to be a good wife and mother. It was a beautiful part of my life, but I want the rest of my years here on this good earth for myself." She paused. "I have other things I want to do with my life, that I've had on the back burner because I wanted to be the best mother I could be. But now that you're grown, I want this time to be mine."

"I'm proud of you."

"You should be," Christine said. "You taught me. That's the other wonderful part of having children. They teach you things you might never learn otherwise. If you can teach your students anything half so valuable as taking hold of every opportunity." She smiled. "I always knew that you would be a wonderful teacher, Carrie. But it's almost eleven, and I have to get ready for mass. Chris gets very angry at us if we're even five minutes late."

"I won't keep you."

"I'd like you to meet Greg some other time."

Carrie hesitated. "I'd like that, too."

"You can tell Carly that I gave her my permission to stay with you, so she doesn't worry about stopping by."

"I really don't mind having her at my apartment."

"Carrie."

Carrie turned. Christine hugged her fiercely.

"It was good to see you." Christine kissed her cheek. "I love you."

Carrie returned the hug, the words reluctant on her lips. "I love you, too."

Christine released her. "Say hello to Carly for me."

"Say hello to Chris for me." She paused. "Thank you for the coffee."

"Any time. You know that." Christine smiled. "I really should go check on Greg. Close the door on your way out, please."

Carrie let herself out of the house. She wondered if Carly would be awake when she got back to her apartment, and what she could feed her for breakfast. Her cupboards were mostly bare.

She thought about stopping at the nearest grocery store and picking up a dozen donuts, but she did not know if Carly ate donuts anymore. Sunday morning donuts had been the tradition when her father had still been alive, and they had both grown up since then. Carrie passed the turn-off for the grocery store and kept driving straight. They could make a trip to the grocery store together, and Carly could pick out what she liked. She drove to the back of the apartment complex, parked, and went to her room. She knocked.

"Just a minute!" Carly's voice sounded muffled behind the door, but Carrie could hear her scrambling around. A short interval of time passed, and then the door opened and Carly stuck her head out.

"Good morning," Carrie said.

"Morning." Carly abandoned her post by the door and walked back into the room. Carrie noticed she was still in her pajamas, though it was almost noon. "Come here. I made you something."

Carrie followed Carly into the kitchen, where Carly pulled out a chair.

"Sit," she said, her back towards Carrie. "I made you breakfast, a la mode de Carly."

As Carrie sat down, Carly turned and came towards her, balancing a plate wobbling on her upturned palm. On the plate were three huge buttermilk pancakes, topped with a mound of whipped cream and sprinkled with fine cocoa powder.

"Just like I used to make them," Carly said, placing the plate in front of Carrie and sliding a fork across the table. "Wait, I forgot your orange juice. Be right back."

Carly half-skipped to the refrigerator and pulled out a glass, already filled with orange juice. "I didn't know when you would be getting back so I wanted to make sure I had everything ready for when you did get...." she broke off, stopped walking towards Carrie. "What's wrong? I thought you loved my pancakes."

Carrie's head was lowered over her plate. "I do."

"Well?" Carly set the glass down in front of her. "Maybe you're not hungry. Gosh, is it really noon? You probably already ate breakfast, and you don't want to eat pancakes for lunch."

"No, it's not that," Carrie said."I haven't eaten yet today."

"Then you should eat!" Carly said, her hands on her hips. "Oh, I bet I know. You've finally decided to go vegan, and you're looking for a way to tell me that it's a beautiful meal but that you can't eat it because I used milk..."

"The pancakes are beautiful," Carrie said. "And I did not decide to go vegan. But I wasn't expecting this, Carly. It was a very kind thing to do."

Carly stared at her. "Is that all?"

Carrie nodded.

Carly laughed. "Well, if you haven't realized it, you're being very kind in letting me stay here. It's the least I could do. I was worried when there wasn't any milk in the refrigerator that maybe you had gone vegan, but that thought crossed my mind after I had already made the pancakes."

Carrie paused. "How did you make these? I don't have any of the ingredients."

"I *know.*" Carly rolled her eyes. "Geez, what are you eating? I went through your food pantry and you have next to nothing."

"So you went shopping?"

"I kind of had to. I went this morning. I was planning on going anyway to pick up some stuff for myself."

"You went to the store in your pajamas?"

"Of *course* not." Carly looked at her disdainfully. "I woke up really early this morning for some reason, probably around five. I couldn't go back to sleep so I decided to make myself some food. Sometimes that calms me down. I figured I could pay you back for the food I used later. So I got up and tried to make something until I realized there isn't any edible food in this house. So I changed and drove out to the store and I got what I needed. Then I came back and changed and went back to sleep. I guess I didn't wake you? I was worried. The bags were rustling, and I've never been very graceful, especially in the dark. I was pretty noisy."

"You didn't wake me," Carrie said, disturbed that she had been sleeping so soundly that she had not noticed that her younger sister had slipped in and out of her apartment.

"Good," Carly said. "I didn't wake up again until around ten thirty, and then you were gone. I didn't know if you'd be freaked out if I were gone when you got back, so I decided to hang around. But that's all right because I don't go to mass anymore and I have homework to do. I'm trying to stay on top of it all even though I'm not technically responsible for any of it until I get back from our service project because—"

"Carly."

Carly looked at her expectantly. "Yes?"

"I'm glad to have you here," Carrie said. "But I don't want this apartment to become a prison cell for you. You're a woman now, and you don't need my permission to come and go as you please. Though I'd like to know where you are and how I can get in contact with you in case there's a problem. Just let me know if you need anything."

"Okay." Carly looked at her, her face angled to one side. "So where'd you go this morning?"

"I went to visit Christine."

"Mom? Really?" Carly's voice remained polite and friendly. "What did you talk about? It wasn't me, was it?"

"I told Christine you were going to stay with me."

"I bet Mom loved that one."

"She wants you to stay with me. She thinks I'll be a good influence on you."

Carly laughed.

Carrie lifted the forkful of pancake to her mouth and let the fluffy batter, saturated sticky sweet with whipped cream and maple sugar, dissolve in her mouth. "These are excellent, Carly."

"I know," Carly said. "There's more on the stove, if you want some now or later."

"There are." Carrie cut off another piece of the pancakes. "*There are* more on the stove. Not—"

"Whatever. I know."

"Grammar is important." Carrie paused. "Did you get any significant work done before I got back?"

Carly shrugged. "What else did you and Mom talk about besides me? You were gone for awhile."

"I asked about the family. We talked about Greg. Briefly."

"What about your love life? Did you talk about that?"

"We talked about my lack thereof."

Carly took the plate out from under her. "Did you want more?"

"Not right now."

Carly proceeded to the sink with the plate. "What about that one guy you met in college? Do you still keep in touch with him?"

"Who are you talking about?" she asked quietly.

"Sam," Carly said, drying the plate. "He brought you home that one time when Justine was sick. Remember?"

"I do." She looked at Carly. "I haven't talked to Sam in years."

"What happened?"

"When I moved out of the house I lived in, there was no real reason to see him."

"No reason?" Carly turned, towel in hand, and stared at her. "He really liked you, Carrie."

"I know."

"He *really* liked you. He had to in order to drive you home and put up with us there."

Carrie paused. "I didn't want to encourage Sam."

"He was such a decent guy, though," Carly said. "I really liked him. Why couldn't you have at least reciprocated a little? It could have worked out, and then I could be an aunt by now."

"I'm glad you haven't lost your sense of humor."

"Carrie."

"Carly, I didn't encourage Sam because I knew it wouldn't work out for us to be more than friends. Sam wanted a wife, not just a college girlfriend. And don't get any ideas, because Sam is married now."

Carly paused. "I can't wait to see who you end up with, Carrie. I really think that you're going to end up with someone. In fact, I know you are."

"I doubt it."

"So what, are you going to live alone?"

"Yes."

Carly put the plate in the cupboard, came back and sat at the only other chair at the table. "I really admire that you can be alone, or that at the very least you're prepared to be. I think about that a lot when whatever guy I'm with at the time wants me to give him more than I want to, followed by the 'all or nothing,' you know how that goes…" She paused and glanced at Carrie. "I'm glad I learned that from you, rather than learn it by making a mistake or having a bad experience. I've let a lot of guys leave because I wouldn't sleep with them, because I'm still going to wait for marriage, and I'm really better off for it." She paused. "Can I give you some advice now?"

"About what?" She was still trying to process the flood of Carly's words.

"About relationships. Because I've been in some and you…well, you've never been in one have you?"

"No."

Carly looked at her. "Sometimes who you fall in love with will surprise you. No one really knows what they want in another person."

"I think you'll know when you meet him."

Carly shrugged. "All I know is that I want a decent guy who'll wait for me and give me kids."

The phone rang. Carrie started to get up, but Carly motioned for her to sit, then went and picked up the phone.

"Hello," Carly said, and then her face lit up. She smirked, then silently handed Carrie the phone. Carrie put the phone to her ear in time to hear Ralph completing a sentence.

"….work for you?"

Carly was watching her expectantly.

"I'm sorry, Ralph, can you repeat what you just said? I didn't hear you." She turned her back on Carly.

"I said, do you have time to meet me tonight? We need to go over plans for the rock climbing trip to Red Valley Gorge. We also have to go over plans for some of the upcoming trips."

"I'm sorry," she said, watching warily as Carly—who had no intention of leaving her alone to complete the call in privacy—came to stand beside her. "But tonight...."

Carly snatched the phone away from her. "Tonight works," she said, dancing away from Carrie. "Yes. Sounds good. See you then."

Carrie made a last attempt to grab the phone. Carly let her have it, without resistance.

"Ralph," Carrie said hastily. "I..."

A dial tone cut off her words. Carrie walked to the phone's cradle on the wall and dropped the phone into it. She turned to Carly. "Don't ever do that again."

"I had to. Because, unlike me, you won't know when you meet the right guy." The smile didn't leave her face. "You have a date tonight."

"Do you know what you just did?"

Carly's smile faltered. "He isn't married or anything, is he?"

"No," Carrie said, trying to control her temper. "But that doesn't justify—"

"If he's not married, it's not really that big a deal, is it? Unless he's really ugly, or you hate his guts..." Carly was looking at her hopefully.

"He's not ugly, and I don't hate him."

"Perfect."

She found it difficult to retain her anger when she looked at the happiness on Carly's face. "I have to work tonight."

"You can get out of working," Carly said, confident. "There has to be someone who will take your shift. It's only one o'clock, and this is so much more important. Who is he?"

Carrie looked at the clock so she wouldn't have to look at Carly. "A teacher. We're sponsoring the Outdoors Club together."

"Well, is he old?"

She sighed, exasperated. "No. He's not old."

"So he's young and single and good-looking...and you share the same values, or at least some of them, if you're both teachers and you both like the outdoors. And someone will take your shift. So why are you so angry?"

"You're interfering with my life."

"Well, someone needs to. I mean, I know you're independent, Carrie, but geez. You need someone to make you care more about living. Your clothes are all faded or wrinkled. You don't have any food in the house...well, I guess you do now, since I got you some." Carly paused. "Do you ever stop to take a second to evaluate the quality of your life, or do you tell yourself you're happy and then keep on living the life you've made, because it only just works for you?"

Carrie moved towards the phone. "I'm going to call him back."

"No you're not."

"And cancel."

Carly put her hand on top of the phone. "You don't have his number."

Carrie removed Carly's hand from the phone and picked it up. "He just called here. I can get it."

"Carrie."

Carrie looked at Carly's face, then slowly put the phone back in the cradle. "What time did he say he wanted to meet?"

"Seven o'clock. Here."

"Here?" She turned away, but not before she had seen the explosive smile that ripped across Carly's face.

"He suggested here," Carly said. "He said he realizes how little time you have because of your work schedule, so it'd probably be best and easiest and that you'd save the most time if he met you here and he sounded like he had good intentions."

"Carly, you really have to stop speaking in run on sentences. I can only understand you half of the time." She paused. "But I guess this will be alright. We're going over plans for the club."

"*Sure* you are."

Carrie turned to her. "He doesn't know where I live."

"He sounded like he had your address."

Carrie remembered the slip of paper she had given him at the restaurant, and stared at Carly. "Seven o'clock. Here. Did the two of you agree on anything else?"

"He said to have the wine ready, and he'd bring the roses."

"Carly!"

Carly grinned. "Come on, Carrie, you know I'm not being serious. You heard our phone conversation, and it was seriously like two seconds long."

"You managed to say a lot in those two seconds."

"Shouldn't you be going? You still have to find someone to work for you, so you can keep your date tonight."

"What if I can't find someone, Carly? My shift is four hours away."

"I make the plans," Carly said. "It's up to you to make them work. I'm so glad he couldn't tell that it wasn't you speaking…or imagine what you'd be missing."

Carrie realized she was going to drive to Dee's to find someone to cover her shift for her. She took the keys Carly handed to her.

"Thank you," she said.

"Yeah." Carly seemed relieved. "I'm going to go do some homework. Do you have some place where you wouldn't mind if—"

"You can work here." Carrie took the stacks of paper off her desk and set them neatly on the floor. "And feel free to go anywhere you'd like while I'm gone."

"Thanks," Carly said, heaving her backpack onto the desk. "Just to let you know, I'm going to be dead to the world for a couple of hours."

Carrie nodded, then let herself out of the apartment and walked to the car. She did not know what she felt: anxious about the shift, confused by Carly's behavior, embarrassed about the thought of having Ralph see where she lived. But not blank.

Her sole consolation was that she would not be alone with Ralph. She still did not trust him, and Carly's presence would be a comfort. Carrie made spaghetti for dinner, noticing as they sat down that Carly ate very little and said even less, and that her eyes continually darted from her food to the clock. At half past six, she pushed her chair away from the table and carried her plate to the sink.

"Thanks for dinner, Carrie."

Carrie looked up, startled. "Are you going somewhere?"

"I'm not going to interfere with your evening."

"You won't be interfering."

Carly hesitated. "I guess I forgot to tell you that I kind of promised Mom I'd eat dinner with her and Greg and Chris. And then I'm meeting with some of the Circle K people. Our first major activity is tomorrow, and we have to work out last minute details, carpool information…stuff like that."

"How very convenient," Carrie said.

"I didn't plan this so you'd be alone with him," Carly said, glancing at her. "I'm sure he won't try anything, and if he does, don't let him. Men like a challenge, and if he likes you, he'll wait for you."

"I'm not in love with him, Carly."

"I'll be back in a couple of hours," Carly reassured her. "You can handle this. Be confident and don't worry so much."

"Drive carefully."

"Will do," Carly said, and flounced out of the apartment.

Carrie had fifteen minutes after Carly left, assuming he would be on time. She thought about doing lesson plans and rejected the idea. She had trained herself to write whenever and wherever she could; fifteen minutes was enough.

At seven o'clock sharp she heard a knock on her door. She left her writing on the table and went to the door. Ralph stood in the hallway, dressed in a white T-shirt, a navy blue windbreaker, and jeans. She stepped back, glad that Carly had left—because had she seen how handsome he looked, she would have instantly started making wedding plans.

"Hello," she said.

"Glad to see you dressed for the occasion," he said, looking her over. "You don't aim to impress, do you, Carrie? Yet somehow you leave your mark."

She looked down at herself—jeans, a white T-shirt with an evergreen tree on it. Her hair was loose and she was barefoot. She stepped aside to let him into the apartment.

He seemed amused. "And this is where you live," he said, turning to her. His nearness sent her heart racing, and he might have noticed the change in her, had the open notebook on her table not diverted his attention.

"What's this?" he asked, picking up the notebook.

"Lesson plan for tomorrow."

"This isn't a lesson plan," he said, looking at the pages of scrawled script. "Still writing novels in your non-existent spare time?"

She looked away.

"I'm glad you're still writing," he said. "And I'm glad to see you've started lying." Before she could stop him, he took her face in his hands and tilted her chin up so she was looking at him.

"You can use this desk for your notes," she said abruptly. "Spread out and make yourself at home. I have to get my notes from our previous meetings and the places I've called regarding gear and transportation—"

"Don't bother. I have that all figured out from previous years."

She looked at him levelly. "I'm not fighting the same battle with you. Do you understand?"

For a moment he stood staring down at her, then he let her go and stepped back. "Go get your plans."

She left the room, her heart racing, and wondered why there was a pressure in her chest that felt remarkably like hope—hot, burning, beautiful. But she was a professional, and she had agreed to meet him to discuss the club. She found the three-ring binder with her notes and walked back to the kitchen. She saw, dismayed, that he had not made any movement to open his folder or notebook; rather, he was looking around her apartment with interest. His eyes settled on her as she walked to the table.

"Your apartment," he said, "is not what I expected."

"You did come over to discuss plans, didn't you?"

He looked amused. "I did come over to discuss plans with you. What can I do to get you off the defensive?"

"Sit exactly where you are, and let me see your research." She stood rigidly, trying to look stern and disapproving.

He hid a smile as he opened his notes and handed them to her. "Let's have a look at the information you gathered, Miss Crenshaw."

She glanced at him. "You can call me Carrie."

He smiled. "There's a degree of formality here that I hadn't counted on. We'll go with it."

"Don't be childish."

"I'm so good at it, though," he said. "That's why I relate so well to our students."

He leaned back in the chair and stared at her. She stared back, the silence unnerving her. Suddenly, he smiled.

"If nothing else happens between us, Carrie, I'm going to wake you up. I've heard you teach with passion, and I don't doubt it...but I've never seen you look happy outside of a classroom. Granted, I've never seen you sad." He lowered his voice. "Living in neutral is no way to live. I can add some excitement to your life, if you'll let me."

"Did you not hear what I said before? If you keep talking like that, I'll drop my involvement with this club immediately."

"No need to do that. I'd miss having you around, and then you wouldn't get to see your brother." He looked through the columns she had drawn up of comparable costs, time estimations, and recommended gear.

"Don't waste your time," she said. "Your figures are better."

"Don't feel so bad." He glanced up. "I've been doing this much longer than you have. Now, I have a question for you that you'll like. Have you ever been rock climbing?"

"No."

"I should teach you some of the basics before we teach the kids. Since everything else is settled."

"So I'm just a figurehead. To save you budget money."

"What did you think you were?" he asked, pulling out a long white rope from a side pocket of the windbreaker. "I know how these programs work, and I like to do things my way. We aren't too different in that respect. That said, don't get too ruffled. I do need you." He paused, his eyes roving around the room. "Do you have a beam or anything that I...no, I see that you don't. Unless you have the kind of shower where the curtain pulls back."

"I do," she said, moving stiffly around him and leading him to the bathroom. "It's a little cramped, but——"

"Here," he said, stepping in behind her. "I brought a harness to demonstrate. Just step into it and tighten the buckles."

She took the harness from him and started to step into it; he stopped her.

"You're wearing it backwards." He paused. "Will you let me help you?"

She looked at him. He sighed. "I promise I'll maintain a professional distance."

Reluctantly, she handed him the harness.

"The loop goes in front," he said, talking to her as he tightened the straps around her waist, around her thighs. "You need to put the rope through here and tie it off so it holds, which I'll show you. But first..."

He threw the end of the rope over the rod in the shower, stepped into the bathtub and held the one end so that the rope formed a peak between them. "This is going to be attached to a rock wall, at least initially, because we're taking the kids to Lock Haven to practice before we get them out on the real thing."

He held the rope but moved towards her. The cramped space in the bathroom had already brought them close together, and she was not surprised to find she was uncomfortable.

"The rope goes through the loop and gets tied in a figure eight knot," he said. "Watch. This should hold, but just to be safe here's the follow up knot. Do you see how I did that?"

She nodded, but when he let her try she got lost, and he helped her figure out what she had done wrong. After she had successfully tied the knots three times in succession, he nodded.

"Last thing for tonight, Carrie. There are certain commands they're going to have to know: belay, on belay, climbing, and climb on. What I'm going to teach you right now. It sounds more difficult than it really is. My fifth graders can do it."

"I didn't know you taught fifth graders."

He shrugged. "Only outdoors stuff. Forget I said anything about it."

She watched him as he came to stand by her.

"You'll put your hands here. The rope will have too much slack as the person starts climbing, and you'll need to keep the tension that the climber wants. Pull up, out, down." He demonstrated. "Then you'll slide one hand, probably your left one if you're right handed, back to this point.

Let your right hand follow and repeat the same action. Let me see you demonstrate."

She repeated the gesture. He nodded, then stepped back.

"I'm going to give you some slack," he said. "You'll get the idea. Give it a shot."

She pulled on the rope as he had shown her to do; the shower curtain fell down, startling them both. The encouraging look on his face was replaced by uncertainty.

"I didn't break it, did I?"

She shook her head, then picked up the shower curtain rod and put it back in place. "This isn't going to work."

"Guess not. I shouldn't have brought the rope since I knew we'd be going over plans and comparing costs." His eyes gleamed devilishly. "But I thought that maybe we would have extra time."

The door to her apartment opened audibly. Ralph's eyes flew to the half-open bathroom door.

"Carrie?" Carly's voice rang out. "Are you here?"

"Bathroom," she said, not thinking.

She heard the clicking noise that Carly's heels made against the wooden floor of the hallway, then the bathroom door opened and Carly's face appeared.

"Hey...oh geez," Carly said. She quickly pulled the door closed. "I didn't mean to interrupt. I'll go hang out with friends or something."

Ralph laughed out loud as Carrie hastened to open the door.

"Carly, we're not..." She felt herself blushing. "Ralph was teaching me some rock-climbing skills."

Carly came to the open door, her eyebrows raised. "Hey, Mr. P."

Carrie looked at Ralph, saw the amusement in his eyes as he extended his hand.

"Carly Crenshaw," he said, smiling. "I'm sorry to not have made your acquaintance formally. Miss Koshenko raved about you."

"My chem teacher in high school," Carly said, for Carrie's enlightenment. "Really, she said something to you about me?"

He nodded. "She said marvelous things about your work in her class."

"I always liked chemistry," Carly said. "I liked doing experiments and making colors and studying spectrometry and all. But I usually blew things up, and I wasn't smart enough to take your AP class. I can't believe I didn't recognize your voice on the phone, though. I used to have the hugest crush on you." She crossed her arms in front of her chest. "I guess you can tell that I don't anymore."

"That's a shame for me," he said. "When did I talk with you on the phone?"

"Oh, this morning," Carly said. "You probably mistook me for Carrie, since she was the one who started talking."

"Really." He turned to Carrie. "I thought you sounded a bit off when I was talking to you earlier."

Carly answered for her. "She switched to the night shift and then got out of it because I had already made plans for you. But I instigated. She wasn't going to meet with you."

"You got out of work to meet with me?" he asked.

Carrie rounded on Carly. "Why would you tell him that?"

"Why shouldn't I know?" Ralph asked, his voice low.

But Carrie and Carly's eyes were locked; he fell silent and watched the unvoiced interaction with interest.

"That's why I told him," Carly said to Carrie, then turned her attention momentarily to him. "Carrie's too proud to tell you."

"Tell me what?"

"I'll leave you two alone," Carly said. "I didn't mean to interrupt, but I thought that since it's ten thirty Carrie would be alone."

Carrie's eyes widened. "Ten-thirty?"

"What time did you think it was?" Carly asked. "What, did you get lost in each other's eyes or something?"

"We must have," Ralph said. "Well, Carly, thank you for arranging for us to meet. Carrie, I didn't mean to take up so much of your time. If I can have my harness and rope back, I'll take myself off."

Carrie pulled at the knots tying her into the harness. The top knot came off easily, but as he had expected, the figure eight knot gave her trouble. He let her fumble, and she continued working away at the knot.

"Geez, Mr. P," Carly interjected. "Will you just help her with it?"

Ralph glanced at Carrie, then stepped up to her. His fingers expertly worked the knot loose as she stood rigid. He stepped back.

"I'm going to get my papers," he said. "They're still on your table and I need them. I'll pick up the harness on my way out."

Carrie nodded and he left them. When he came back, portfolio tucked under his arm, she was waiting in the hallway with the harness and a neatly coiled rope. Carly hovered like an imp in the background as Carrie handed him his gear.

"Thank you," Carrie said. "I appreciate the extra time you spent in coming here for my convenience."

"I'm willing to work around your schedule," he said. "I want you on the team, Carrie."

"That's so cute," Carly chimed in. "Now are you going to kiss her?"

"I don't think Carrie appreciates your sense of humor," Ralph said. "But I do. Goodbye, Carly. It was a pleasure to meet you. Carrie, I'll see you tomorrow."

Carrie watched as he left, then went into the kitchen to tidy up. Carly came to stand beside her, hands on her hips. Carrie felt her waiting for information, but they both remained silent.

"Are you going to tell me what happened?"

"We talked."

"It must have been an interesting talk, for the two of you to have ended up in the bathroom tied to each other." Carly looked at her, but Carrie remained quiet. "All right, then, I'm going to bed. It's been a long day, and I have to get up at seven tomorrow."

"So do I," Carrie said. "Do you want me to wake you up or do you want me to show you how to operate the alarm clock?"

Carly yawned. "Wake me up, please. I'm too tired right now to learn how to operate anything."

"Goodnight."

She paused. "Are you angry at me?"

Carrie shook her head, wondering why Carly sounded so disappointed. She poured hot water into the mug and added a tea bag. "Are you leaving tomorrow night?"

Carly sighed. "Yeah. Gotta get back to the university."

"Do you want to go out to dinner tomorrow night as a celebration of everything you've accomplished this week? Or do you have your own agenda?"

"Own agenda," Carly said. "As in homework, and then I'm having the club pick me up here." She paused. "By the way, Mr. P. is awesome. Just so you know. He'd be a lot better for you than Damien would have been."

The memories that came to her with Carly's words were unwonted and for a moment she felt drowned with regret—but she could not have acted otherwise.

She watched Carly disappear down the hall. She *had* been willing to take a chance on love...but not on those terms. Or had she simply been afraid to make a mistake, and because of that fear, ended up making an even bigger mistake?

When she had interviewed for her position at Greensburg Salem High, Tessa had stated as part of her educational philosophy that she would treat all of her students the same; meaning, she would do everything she could to challenge them and help them reach their full intellectual capacities. But Chris Crenshaw was throwing her for a loop. His papers, his assignments, his participation in class, blew away the work done by his peers. She knew how she could challenge Chris, but her approach would take her down an old road she had left increasingly behind. And if her intuition was even the slightest bit off base she could get into trouble with the school board—because what she wanted to teach Chris was outside of the curriculum.

Despite his maturity and intelligence, Chris still needed guidance and answers like any one else his age. Had he turned to the occult, like she had at his age, to find it? She knew that Chris believed in God and took his religion very seriously, and Tessa doubted he would have looked into black magic or any of the cults popularly associated with the word 'occult.' She never had. But Chris might have dappled in Tarot, meditation, focusing of chi...other occult practices which helped an individual understand human motives on a deeper level, or helped an individual learn about centering energy and focus. He had never given any indication in his writings of such seeking, but his remarks in class were a mix of conventional morality—God, ethics, sin, evil—and terms she had picked up through her studies—circulation of energy, the Universe, karma.

The honesty in Chris's writings had also surprised her, though his entries were never a call for help. She was not surprised that Chris had latched onto the profile of the Byronic hero in their class discussions. She saw how they related. Chris was civil and polite and mostly obedient—but behind that act was the same cool defiance, the same silent acknowledgment that at any moment he could flout everything and not blink an eye. In class, she had talked of the visions of the Romantics, their connection to Nature, their search for a different kind of reality, and what Chris had written in response was that everyday reality was a horrific facade, and that he occasionally got glimpses of true reality—the world underneath. The essay had sent chills through her. His words hinted that he had reached a higher level of enlightenment than she had. But she had more experience, and she could guide him around some of the snares that beginners encountered—unless he had started younger than she thought, or unless he had not started at all. Those were always possibilities, or Chris might have gained his knowledge, his intuition, and his visionary gift from outside means. By educational standards, however, there was enough in his journals that dictated she should talk to him. She did not know how to broach the subject with him, and fought the urge to talk to Carrie. Carrie and Chris were not particularly close, to her understanding—and Carrie had never approved of her occult studies.

Tessa resolved to talk directly to Chris.

Carrie was sitting in her classroom after the final bell when a gentle knock on the open door arrested her attention. She looked up and saw Miranda Baxter standing in the doorway, her books under her arm, confident and at ease. She had kept wearing flowers in her hair, but she had abandoned the coverup and dark eyeliner for the softer, natural beauty of her Latino complexion. Carrie saw her once or twice a week through belly dance practice; the other days Miranda stopped by during homeroom to say hello. The first few times Miranda had come to see her she had lingered in the doorway, unwilling to impose, until Carrie had assured her that her visits were a source of enjoyment for her as well.

"Miss Crenshaw? I hope I'm not disturbing you, but I wanted to know if maybe I could talk with you for a minute."

"Of course," Carrie said. "Please come in, Miranda."

Miranda stepped inside. "It's about our performance on Saturday." Three weeks ago, Tessa had discovered that the local library was having a national cultures day, and had asked if the girls would like to put together a short piece to present. "Tessa's been working with us really hard, but we want to practice once with you. Just because."

"Miranda, if you call Mrs. Beaumont by her first name, why can't you call me Carrie?"

"I don't know. It wouldn't feel right."

Carrie paused. "You're performing Saturday?"

Miranda nodded. When Carrie remained silent, waiting for her to continue, Miranda added, "We can't practice tonight, because Linda's mom works today and Linda has to go straight home to babysit Corey, and Tessa wants us to practice Wednesday through Thursday. We were going to get together right after school tomorrow for fifteen or twenty minutes to rehearse a couple of times, and the girls wanted me to ask you if you'd be able to come."

"Are you meeting in the classroom? Same time?"

Miranda nodded, looking relieved and more at ease. "Tessa booked us the auditorium for Friday's practice so we'll know what it's like to be up on a stage, but until then we're going to practice in 112 like we always do."

"I'll be there promptly at 3:45," Carrie said.

Miranda smiled. "Wait until you see our costumes. We sewed them ourselves. And thank you."

"You're welcome. You're going to miss your bus if you don't hurry, Miranda."

"Right." Miranda nodded. "I'll see you tomorrow."

She backed into Ralph, who had come up behind her, and instantly blushed.

"Sorry, Mr. Palmer." Miranda fled.

Ralph arched his eyebrows. "One of your tiny dancers?"

Carrie turned to him. "Does every girl in this school have a crush on you?"

He laughed. "I try my hardest not to be a subversive influence, but I can't help it. Girls are so easily charmed."

Carrie pulled the students' essays back towards her. Undaunted by her attitude, he entered the classroom and strolled up to her desk, leaning so that he hovered over her. Carrie kept her eyes carefully averted.

"Forgetting something?" he asked.

She glanced up at him, startled. "I was supposed to meet you, wasn't I, to go over plans." She started gathering the scattered essays.

"No harm done," Ralph said. "It's only quarter till. Stop and think, though, Carrie. Making plans for what?"

She paused, confused. "For tomorrow's meeting."

"Bingo. Our club meets on Tuesday, right after school."

"Oh," she said, blinking. "I told Miranda that—"

"Yes, I heard," he said. "As I was walking up to come get you, I heard, very conveniently, that exchange of words."

"I'll tell Miranda to move the meeting back," she said, her mind reeling through alternatives. "I'm sure she won't—."

"You're going to ask those girls to wait for you?"

"I can't miss our meetings. You go over so much at each meeting."

He cut her off. "Are you working on Wednesday?"

"No." She looked back at him, not understanding. He waited patiently, but she remained silent.

"Our meeting dates aren't set in stone," he said, finally. "All you have to do is ask."

She stared at him. "You would move the meeting to Wednesday? To accommodate for my meeting with my girls?"

"You know," he said. "It's not a sin to ask, Carrie. Often requests aren't even an inconvenience, and people get a kick out of knowing they're helping you out. And people always retain the right to turn you down." He cracked a smile. "That's all the pep talk and moralizing I have in me. You have to do the rest yourself."

Something in his voice startled her more than his words; she glanced at him quickly, trying to discover the cause of her reaction, but his face was smooth and unassuming—blank except for the flash of amusement in his eyes.

"Will you please move the meeting to Wednesday?" she asked, with difficulty.

"Of course," he said, promptly. "No problem at all. Now, was that so difficult?"

"Don't take that tone with me. I'm not a child."

"I know," he said, suggestively, and then his tone changed. "Was it really that difficult for you?"

"Yes," she said.

He laughed openly at her. "You always prove fascinating."

She picked up her papers, and moved to the door.

"How did asking for something make you feel?" he said from behind her, not having moved from his place near her desk.

She turned and frowned. "I don't like depending on other people. And I don't like asking for anything."

He paused. "I do things strictly because I want to, Carrie. I won't ever expect anything from you in return."

"That makes two of us." She paused. "Are we going over plans? I have essays I need to—"

"My notes are in my room."

She followed him two doors down, then put her bag and papers on the desk where he nodded. He started towards the storage space in the back of the room, then turned when he realized she was following him.

"Stay there," he said. "My kids started chemical reactions today, and I have all of their experiments in the back. Strong fumes."

She frowned at him, then went back to the desk as he disappeared into the storage area and emerged a moment later with his portfolio of notes. Her mind wandered as he started going over the agenda. He looked up once, caught her staring at him, and paused.

"What are you doing?" he asked. "You sure as hell aren't listening to me."

"I'm trying to analyze you." She noticed a hunted look entered his eyes.

"Pay attention, Carrie. This is important."

He went back to the agenda, glanced up to see her attention riveted on the storage area's door.

"Come on," he said, closing his portfolio with a snap. "You're too smart for your own damn good." He got up, went to the storage area, threw open the door. "You think I'm Bluebeard, do you? Come take in your fill."

Carrie went to stand beside him and looked into the room. On the single table in the storage closet, pans of liquid color sat neatly in rows. She turned away.

"I told you, didn't I? No secrets this time around, Carrie."

She looked at him, and he looked back at her. Her eyes measured him. "Are we finished?"

"I'll email you the agenda, since you weren't listening to any of it," he mumbled.

She smiled. "Thank you for moving the meeting. I really appreciate it, and I know my girls do as well."

"I'll see you on Wednesday. Be on time." He paused. "Look over the agenda before you come, so you know what's going on."

She nodded. He watched her leave the classroom, then moved to one of the windows and watched as she exited the building and got into her beat up Cavalier. He waited until he heard the car disappear from the faculty parking lot.

"Damn you, Carrie," he said softly, then picked up his portfolio and turned off the lights, locking the door as he left the classroom.

All the girls were there as she entered Room 112. Miranda met her at the door, greeting her cordially.

"Hi, Miss Crenshaw."

"Hello, Miranda," Carrie said. "Hello, girls. Your costumes look beautiful. I know you're eager to practice, but that will have to wait a moment. I have something for all of you."

They gathered around her as she opened the overstuffed purse she had brought and spread the contents on the desks.

"You can take what you want," Carrie said. "This is my gift to you. Good luck for what I know will be a stunning performance."

The girls exclaimed over the jeweled earrings, bracelets, and necklaces, but Miranda held back. "Won't you be coming?"

"I'm sorry. But I have other commitments for that day. Tessa will be there, though." She paused, seeing Miranda's crestfallen face.

"I forgot," Miranda said. "Chris mentioned the rock climbing trip." She reached for a bracelet and clasped it around her wrist. "These are beautiful," she said, politely. "Thank you, Miss Crenshaw. Come on, girls. Let's dance."

The girls had perfected the routine that Tessa had choreographed; they were synchronized with the rhythm and with each other. She could tell them truthfully at the end of the practice that they were well-prepared. The positive energy was high in the room as the girls left, but Miranda hung back.

"Did you need a ride home, Miranda?"

Miranda looked relieved. "If you wouldn't mind…"

"If you don't mind riding in my beat up piece of junk," Carrie said, "then it's no inconvenience."

"If you're sure."

As Carrie had expected, Miranda sat quietly in the passenger seat, looking out the window. Carrie shifted into reverse, then started forward.

"You'll have to direct me," she said.

"Turn left, then go straight for about five minutes."

Carrie glanced at her. "Miranda, we're leaving in the morning for the trip. I'm sure we'll be back in time to make it to the performance if your dance doesn't start until seven."

"I don't think Chris would like that."

"Why not?"

Miranda paused. "Chris doesn't like that I dance. He thinks it's sinful."

Carrie paused. "Do you think that dancing is sinful, Miranda?"

"No," she said. "I think it's beautiful."

"Would you consider not dancing on Saturday?"

"No. And Chris hasn't asked me to. But it'd be nice if he was there. He's never seen me dance, and I want him to." She paused. "He's seen me broken and depressed, but he's never seen me like how I am when I'm dancing. I feel so in control and confident and happy. I want him to see that I can be strong." She paused. "Turn right and…here. This one is mine."

Carrie pulled into the driveway, put the car in neutral. "I think you should talk to Chris, Miranda. He'll listen."

Miranda nodded. "Chris always listens to me, even if he doesn't like what I'm saying. Thanks for the ride and coming to practice and I'm sorry if I seem melodramatic all the time but—"

"Be confident," Carrie said.

Miranda stopped speaking, recognizing one of the phrases Carrie had emphasized in practice when the girls tried to make excuses or apologies for not being able to do something.

"Be well," she said quietly in response, getting out of the car.

Carrie waited until she was sure that Miranda could get into her house, then backed out of the driveway. She realized she would be late for her waitressing shift. The amount of times she had come to the restaurant ten or fifteen minutes late had been increasing, and she knew corporate didn't like that she didn't grovel. She did not want to lose the job, but she wondered if it mattered.

Ralph chose Carrie to demonstrate the belaying technique for the students. He set her on an intermediate course, but she had climbed almost seventy-five percent of the way before her arms started shaking and her footing became insecure. He had called her down, explained some techniques to the students, and then sent her back up. She had not been able to make it. No matter how much she willed her mind to keep tackling the wall, her body kept shaking from exertion and her stamina slackened. She fell.

The immediate pull on the rope let her know that Ralph had expected her to fall. As she rappelled down the wall she heard him explaining to the students what they should do in case they needed to fall or wanted to stop climbing, and what they should do if the climber fell unexpectedly—as she had just demonstrated.

"What Miss Crenshaw did not do," he said, "Was announce that she was going to fall. That will happen today because rock climbing engages a set of muscles you don't normally use. If your partner tells you that he or she is falling you'll have time to adjust—but you have to be prepared for the unexpected. Questions? Then pair up, and start practicing."

. As the students formed their pairs, he walked up to Carrie and told her she had done a good job. She glanced at him, angry, but stayed quiet when she saw the look on his face.

"I want you to learn with these kids," he said softly. "This isn't about getting it right the first time around. It's okay to fall. They don't have to think you know everything there is to know—that's why they have me."

She was going to respond when Judy Andrews—one of the girls who had joined the club because her boyfriend, Derrick Evans, was in it—called to her, wanting to know if she could be partners with Derrick or if he would be too heavy for her. Carrie told her she would be fine and turned to see Ralph moving among the other students, helping with knots and answering questions. She moved down the other side of the line.

"All right, Joey? Chris?"

Chris nodded at her, lowering his head over the rope, but Joey—Chris's best friend—beamed at her and asked her to check the knot Chris had finished tying. She glanced at Chris; he stepped aside. He had tied the knot wrong. She undid it and showed them the correct procedure, using the patience Ralph had used when teaching her.

The students climbed for most of the morning without incident. Ralph caught her eye to signal he was about to call for a lunch break, when suddenly Derrick Evans fell from the top of the wall and Judy panicked. Forgetting to let the rope go slack, she got the skin of her hand pinched in the belaying pulley. Before Ralph could move, Carrie was beside Judy. In that moment she caught Chris's eye; he took the rope from her so that Derrick would not crash to the floor. Carrie led Judy—sniffling—away from the group. She cleaned and bandaged the cut and kept Judy calm while Ralph led the rest of the students outside to tables covered with plates of potato chips, bread, meat, tomato and lettuce. Then Carrie went outside with Judy, and as the students hovered around the tables, she looked for Ralph. She glanced back at the students and saw that Chris was watching her; she smiled, and he turned away. Carrie continued her search and found Ralph standing under a tree around the corner of the building, smoking.

"What are you doing here?" he asked.

She was surprised by the tone of his voice. "I wanted to know where you were, in case the students would ask."

"They won't ask," he said, snubbing the cigarette on the ground. "They're eating. But one of us has to be with them at all times." He looked at her. "You know that."

She refused to be bullied by him. "The SRC crew is there supervising."

He sighed. "Carrie, do you want to know what's going to start going through their minds if you and I start disappearing at the same time? Judy and her gang are already trying to set us up."

"I didn't think—"

"Do you want them talking about us?"

"No," she said, quickly.

"Neither do I. So I suggest that you get back to—"

"I haven't been gone that long."

"Fine." He glanced at her. "Do you want to walk back holding hands?"

Her eyes flashed. He smiled, then moved back towards the students without another word. She watched him leave, anger rising in her, then started after him. She saw Ralph talking with the Student Recreation Center staff and went directly to the lunch tables. As she reached for a drink, she saw Chris come up to her.

"That was great how you handled Judy," he said, taking a diet soda from the cooler and not looking at her.

"Thank you," she said, then paused. "Chris, we should get back in time for you to see Miranda dance. If you're interested I can give you a ride over to the library."

"Thanks," he said, in a clipped voice that told her he wasn't interested. He moved off to sit with Joey. She looked up to see Ralph watching her; as soon as they made eye contact, he walked over.

"How much longer do you think we should we let them climb?" he asked. "I wanted to leave here no later than four, so we can stop somewhere for dinner on the way back."

"That should be fine," she said. "I know some of the students really want to keep climbing, but some of the students stopped climbing an hour into it and have been belaying since. I don't know whether Judy will want to keep climbing or not."

"I've noticed a general lack of enthusiasm for this," he said, surveying the students. "We should discuss with them whether they want to spend next weekend climbing, or whether they might prefer a backpacking and camping trip."

"You've already made the plans."

"I want the kids to do what they want. And what they can. Rock climbing is very physically demanding," he said. "As you may have discovered."

She smiled in response, then took the students who wanted to start climbing again back inside. At four, Ralph told them to put in their last attempts for the day, and then they drove to a restaurant where several students announced falsely that it was Ralph's birthday so the waitress would sing. Ralph took the ruse with good-natured humor and gave the free cake to the students to devour, but at odd moments Carrie caught him looking at her, frowning. Later, as she stood by the van waiting for the students to file in, she understood why.

"I bet it feels good to get waited on," he said. "Instead of waiting on other people."

"It does," she said.

He went to the other side of the van and got in. She opened her door, sat down, glanced at him, and then had her attention diverted as one of the girls in the back of the van screamed. She turned around instantly, surprised when Ralph did not seem concerned.

"Judy found a frog back here," one of the boys said. "Nasty, huge mother—"

"Derrick, watch your language," Ralph said, then paused. "And that's a toad."

"I don't care what it is," Judy whimpered, watching as Derrick made the toad dance. "Kill it."

Derrick looked at Ralph, the toad kicking frantically in his grip. "Hey, Mr. P, I read about this guy who made a hobby out of running over toads when they came out on the road to mate or—"

"Stop it." Chris's voice was chilling. He unbuckled his seatbelt and moved to where Derrick was sitting beside Judy. "Give me the toad right now."

Derrick made the toad wave at Chris, and for a moment, Carrie thought Chris was going to punch him. But Chris had made eye contact with Derrick; he put out his hand, and without a moment's hesitation, Derrick relinquished the toad. The toad, happy to be free, promptly jumped off of Chris's palm and landed on the seat, where he started thrashing as the students jerked away from him. Carrie watched her brother go pale as he bent over the seat and cupped his hands protectively around the toad.

"I'm not going to hurt you," he said, softly. "Be calm. Be still. I'm going to take you outside and put you in the grass. I *am not* going to hurt you."

Carrie got out of the van and slid open the door. Chris emerged a moment later, his cupped hands before him. He met her eyes. Then he moved away from the van to a patch of grass and crouched down. She followed him.

"Go," he said.

The toad sat in his palm, as if stunned. Chris jiggled his hands, and the toad hopped off.

Carrie paused. "Chris, everyone is waiting."

"Wait," Chris said, still crouched, staring intently at the toad. "I want to make sure he's all right."

Carrie stood and waited until the toad hopped once. Chris stood, watching as the toad disappeared. "I was worried he had gotten hurt. He twisted when he jumped off my hand, and I was afraid he might have broken his back or his legs." His face flushed crimson. "I should have known to hold him closer to the ground. What if he had gotten hurt? Then it would have been my fault and there wouldn't have been anything I could do to set it right. It wouldn't have mattered how sorry I was."

"But he's fine," Carrie said. "And you stopped your peers from hurting him. That took real courage, Chris."

"No," he said. "It's not hard to act out in front of people you don't give a shit about."

She glanced at him. "We should get back to the van."

He nodded, his face lowered, his eyes burning. He walked ahead of her and got in the van to a much sobered atmosphere.

"Hey," Joey piped up. "Is the little guy okay, Chris?"

Chris did not say anything.

"He's fine," Carrie said. "May I remind you all of the Leave No Trace ethics we've already covered?"

"That we shouldn't disturb the wildlife," Derrick said. "Mr. Palmer just gave us a speech about it."

Carrie glanced at Ralph; he must have spoken to them while she and Chris were releasing the toad.

"I'm sorry," Judy said to Chris. "It was a nasty toad, but I shouldn't have screamed."

Ralph turned his key in the ignition. "Let's get going, gang. We've got awhile to go yet."

He turned the radio on and the students started talking to one another. By the time they arrived at the school, most students seemed to have forgotten about the toad incident. Chris had not forgotten, Carrie knew; he was quiet for the entire car trip. Most of the students' parents were already at the school, waiting to pick up their children; fifteen minutes later, she was alone with Ralph and Chris.

"Do you need a ride home, Chris?" Ralph asked.

Chris looked at Carrie. She returned the look, her face as blank as she could make it.

"No," Chris said. "I'm not going home. My girlfriend is dancing in half an hour, and I want to see her."

"I'll entrust you to Miss Crenshaw, then," Ralph said.

"You don't have to call her that," Chris said, moving towards Carrie. "She is my sister. Goodbye, Mr. Palmer. Thanks for the trip."

"Delighted to have you along, Chris. Carrie..." He smiled. "Thanks for your help. I couldn't have organized everything so well without you."

"Goodbye for now," Carrie said, getting in the car and waiting for Chris to get in. She watched Ralph move to his car, then turned her attention to Chris. "I'm glad you're coming. It'll mean a lot to Miranda."

"I want you to take me home," Chris said. "I don't want to see Miranda dance."

"What?" She could not hide her disappointment in him, nor did she try. "But you just said—"

"I didn't want to say anything in front of Mr. Palmer. He would have given me a lecture," Chris said. "He thinks like you do; he thinks I should see Miranda dance."

"Why don't you want Miranda to dance?"

"Please take me home."

"Chris?"

Chris turned to her abruptly. "Do you have any idea how beautiful Miranda is?" He closed his eyes, leaned back in his seat. "When she's up there, dancing, she's going to be amazing. I know she will be because of how radiant she becomes when she just *talks* about it. If I see her dance I know I'll fall even more in love with her, and I want to be able to deal with losing her. Because it's only going to be so long before she realizes she's too good for me."

Carrie continued driving. "Miranda will be disappointed if you aren't there," she said. "And quite frankly, I'm disappointed in you right now."

"I have to make my own decisions."

"Then you should have decided to go with Ralph—with Mr. Palmer. Because by the time I drop you off at Christine's—Mom's—and turn around, I'm going to be late. And I told Miranda I'd be there."

"So did I," he said, quietly.

"What?"

"Stop," he said. "I mean, turn here. Go to the library. I told Miranda that I would watch her dance."

Carrie flicked on her left turn signal. "Dancing isn't a sin, Chris. It's a celebration of life."

He looked straight ahead. Carrie paused.

"What made you change your mind?"

"I don't want to be a jealous boyfriend," he said stonily. "I don't want Miranda to think she has to hide her passion and her beauty because I'm insecure about loving her. She told me…" he hesitated. "She told me she would stop dancing if it bothered me that much, and that was when I promised her that I would go see her dance. Because I don't want her to stop doing something she loves because of me." He closed his eyes, as if the confession had taken all of his energy to tell her. "And I gave her my word that I'd be there tonight."

Carrie parked in the library's lot. Chris followed her as she led the way to the room where the girls would be dancing.

"After you," she said, at the door.

Chris took off the baseball cap he characteristically wore. He looked at her.

"All right," he said, and took an audible breath before he entered.

272

They had arrived within moments of the performance; the applause for the previous act was just beginning to die down as they entered, and the stage was empty except for the soft lighting trained on the performing area. Carrie saw the girls in the process of going up on the stage, then spotted Tessa in the front row. She saw Miranda turn and scan the crowd, saw her eyes connect with Chris's. For a moment, she thought Miranda was going to smile, but the smile never surfaced. Miranda hurried onto the stage, the coins on her hip scarf jingling in the relative quiet of the room.

"Did you see the look on her face?" Chris asked, half to himself. "I shouldn't have come. This was a mistake."

Carrie grabbed his arm, prevented him from leaving the room. "Let's go take a seat. There's Tessa."

"I won't leave," he said, whispering so as not to disturb the other people. "But I'll stay here. I don't want to sit near Mrs. Beaumont."

Carrie glanced at him, but understood. She nodded and let him go, then made her way through the aisles. She smiled at Tessa as she sat down.

Tessa gestured at the stage and put her fingers to her lips. "Glad you could make it."

Carrie turned to the stage as an aging librarian stepped forward, squinted at a note card, and announced the group as the Golden Lotus Troupe. Then came the intoxicating rhythm, and the girls started their dance. Carrie glanced at Miranda and was relieved to see a smile on her face. Carrie understood the release and refuge Miranda felt in dancing; of all the girls in the club, Miranda had the most problematic home environment and the most pressure on her—self-induced—to do well in school and keep her life on track. The strain on the girl showed, even after she had stopped cutting herself to cope. She was not worried about Miranda's performance; her passion for the dance would carry her through.

Carrie watched, enjoying the performance because she knew the girls were having fun and dancing well. The girls came back from the performance area a moment later, flushed, and took their seats in the front row as the next act, a group of young people performing a coconut dance, took the stage. Carrie saw Miranda working her way to the back of the room, then noted a sliver of light enter the darkened room as the door opened and closed. She sat and watched a Japanese bird dance, an African story-teller, and a Native American rain dance, and then the lights came on. The librarian, looking dazed, came to the front of the room and announced that the night's scheduled festivities were over, but that the library would be open fifteen minutes later than usual to accommodate anyone who wanted to check out books on the countries represented. Carrie headed out of the room and saw Miranda standing by herself in the lobby. Miranda beelined for her and hugged her briefly.

"It was amazing," Miranda said.

"You did very well." Carrie smiled at her. The girl looked feverish, but she had felt cold. "The dance was—"

"Not that," Miranda said, an effusive smile on her face. "It was Chris. I was worried, but he...." She flushed. "I tried to talk to him about the dance right after but he wouldn't let me. He took my face in his hands and he told me I was beautiful and he kissed me. It was amazing and I'm just so happy."

"I'm going to have to yell at him for being so forward, you know." Carrie pulled a tissue from her purse and handed it to Miranda. "Where is Chris?"

"Outside, waiting for you. He said he couldn't see me anymore right now. I don't understand, but I don't think he's mad. But you probably don't want to hear any of this, since he's your brother..."

"And you're my student," Carrie said. "Go celebrate with your classmates, and be happy. You danced beautifully."

"Thank you." Miranda smiled at her and started to hand her back the tissue, damp with tears. "Oh, you probably don't want this back." She paused. "Miss Crenshaw."

"Yes, Miranda?"

"Thanks for talking to Chris. I know you must have because I swear he wasn't going to see me dance."

"Chris made the decision by himself. Miranda, I can't act as a go-between. You have to—"

"I have to talk to him myself. I know. But sometimes it's hard because he doesn't seem like he wants to talk to me. Sometimes he seems so disgusted with me, but he's mostly so sweet and..." She hesitated. "I guess it's to be expected."

"What's to be expected?"

"The mood swings, the highs and lows."

"Why?"

"I can't tell you." Miranda shifted. "Chris said I couldn't tell anyone. Excuse me, Miss Crenshaw, but I should go now."

Carrie watched, mildly concerned, as Miranda left her and entered the circle of the other girls clustered together. She caught Tessa's eye and waved, then turned and headed outside. The air was cool and calming compared with the bright, stuffy environment inside the library.

"Do you always leave the doors to your car unlocked?" Chris asked, as she opened her door and got in.

"No one would ever steal this thing," she said, starting the Cavalier. "Another reason I love it. Did you say goodbye to Miranda?"

"Yes."

"You don't want to stay any longer?"

"No."

She pulled out of her parking spot. "You're not telling me something."

"I invoke my fifth amendment rights."

She glanced at the clock. "Let's get you home. You've had a long day."

She drove him home, the music from the dance still in her head, the routine of his silence not bothering her as much as it had. She stopped in Christine's driveway, waiting, but he did not get out, and after a moment she realized he wanted to speak to her.

"What?" she prompted.

"Carrie." He paused. "This has never been about you, okay? I was angry when you left, but I don't hold any grudges, and you've been a good sister. It's about me and that's all I can say. Except that I'm sorry."

"What's wrong?" she asked with alarm, realizing he was crying. "Chris?"

He unbuckled his seatbelt and slammed the door shut behind him. Carrie restrained herself from going after him. Sometimes the best thing to do was to do nothing at all—except wait.

Carrie paused. "Miranda, is there anything you think you *should* tell me?"

"I'm not sure."

Carrie rummaged through her desk and pulled out one of the neon green pads she had been given. "Let me write you a pass. You're going to be late."

"Thank you." Miranda took the offered slip of paper uncertainly. "You're still coming to practice this Friday, aren't you?"

Carrie nodded her assent.

Miranda glanced at her. "Maybe could I catch a ride home with you? Maybe we could talk then."

"That would be fine," Carrie said.

Miranda nodded and left, and Carrie turned her attention to her first period class. She was worried, but she could not let her students see how confused she was. She was not going to stay after to do her school-related work as she usually did; she wanted to go home. But before she retreated, she would find Ralph and talk to him about why he had called her. She went to his classroom and knocked, then opened the door. She went inside.

"Hello?" She dropped her bag on one of the black lab desks and made her way to the back of the classroom. The light in the storage closet was on. He had joked about Bluebeard, but he had let her see the inside of the room. Her hand on the doorknob, she felt like she was about to do something forbidden, and she hesitated. Before she could decide what to do, the door opened and Ralph stood before her, blocking the door frame. He had on an apron, in the corner of which was a thin streak of red.

"Hi, Carrie," he said.

Her eyes went to the apron. "Is that blood?"

He laughed. "No, just a stain from a chemical reaction gone wrong. Can I help you with something?"

She took a step back. "You called and said you wanted to talk to me."

"I can't talk with you right now."

"Let me know when you can, if it's to go over plans or—"

"Tonight." His eyes bore into hers. "Let me take you out. Not to discuss plans, not to talk about teaching—"

She cut him off. "What would we talk about then?"

"We'd find something," he said. "But I don't want there to be any doubt in your mind: I'm asking you out, officially, on a date."

She stared at him. "I don't know."

"That's not very reassuring for me." He looked at her directly. "You told me you didn't want to fight the same battles. I'm not asking you to. I'm willing to go about it the old-fashioned way this time. If that's what you want."

"How much you've changed makes me uneasy." She hesitated. "What exactly did you do, that made you want to change so much?"

"I realized I loved you," he said.

She took a step back from him. "Still the charmer, I see."

He took a step towards her. "I wanted to become the kind of person you could love, Carrie."

"I don't believe you," she said. "And even if I did, that's a terrible reason to do anything. Why the hell should you care about what I—"

"It was what I wanted, too." He paused. "Sequences of unremembered nights and superficial faces didn't exactly lead to a fulfilling life."

She shook her head. "I know I'm extreme about everything, and that I hold on for far too long, but that you would still remember me after—"

He stepped up to her, took her face between his hands. "All I'm asking for is one date."

She hesitated, but she could not stop the command of her heart. "All right."

"I'll pick you up tonight at your place," he said, his eyes never leaving her face. "Sooner or later?"

"Sooner," she said. "I want to get this over with."

He laughed. "Sooner is better for me as well. Does five o'clock work for you?"

She nodded.

"Five o'clock sharp," he said, going back to the supply closet and shutting the door.

She left the school, got into her Cavalier, and drove home. She had work to do as well.

At nine o'clock, Carrie heard a knock on her door. She felt a momentary flash of anger as she got up and went to the door. Her mind had wandered since they had made the arrangement, and though she had done the work she needed to do, she had hoped—until eight o'clock—that he would pull through. It had taken her too long to give up on him, and the fact disconcerted her. She opened the door.

"Hello, Ralph," she said.

"Are you ready to go?"

"I am otherwise engaged."

He took the hand she was using to prop open the door and attempted to pull her out of the apartment. "Come on."

She withdrew her hand, turned her back on him and went into her apartment. "You're a mess, you know."

"Am I?" He looked down at his shirt and the expression on his face changed. "It's been a strange day."

"Has it?" She eyed the splotches of colors—red, orange, yellow—on the bottom of his shirt.

"Do you mind?" he asked her.

"I agree with Bernard Shaw on the account of appearances."

"What account?" He seemed amused.

"That respectability is one of the seven deadly sins." She paused. "I could care less how you look."

"Interesting," he said. "Where do you want to go?"

"We're not going out."

"I'm only four hours late. And I know you haven't been sitting here idly, waiting around for me. You've been writing or grading papers, probably glad when you thought I wasn't going to come."

She stared at him. "At least that's a consolation, to know you have so little control over my motivation."

"Control again, I see," he said. "But if you were writing, I won't stay and distract you."

She grabbed her keys and walked out of the apartment. "Let's go."

The action surprised him as much as it had surprised her. He turned off the lights to her apartment and closed the door behind him. She started down the stairs, and he hurried to keep up with her.

"Is Carly out for the night?"

"Carly left awhile ago," Carrie said. "She was doing service work for her university, but she left to go back."

"She left me a note in my mailbox at the school," he said, then paused. "I see you don't know anything about it."

She shook her head.

He took a folded scrap of paper from the pocket of his jeans and handed it to her. "She told me to make you take a chance. What made her write that?"

"I haven't the faintest idea," Carrie said. "You can't make me do anything, and Carly knows I take risks. Just not the kind that she thinks matter."

"Did she want us to go out?"

"Carly just wants me with someone. She doesn't understand that romance is not a matter of supreme importance to me."

"But it's a matter of some importance to you."

"I would hardly say so."

"Then why the modifier?"

She looked at him blankly.

"The modifier 'supreme.' If you meant that being with someone else is of no importance to you, then you would have said so."

"You're attentive," she said.

He paused. "I'm so attentive that I forgot where I parked. Wait...there."

She followed him to the midnight blue Mitsubishi and waited as he unlocked the doors. He hesitated.

"Are you going to ask why I was late?"

"I never explain myself to anyone. So I don't expect you to explain yourself to me." She paused. "You're here now."

"I feel honored that you'd hold me accountable to the same standards you hold yourself."

He paused. "I might as well tell you now that I'm not flexible with myself, either. That's not a problem, though it means that when we come together, we'll collide. And we'll both break."

She glanced at him. "Where are we going?"

"Dancing, since I know you like that."

She paused. "I'd rather not."

He stopped walking. "Then what would you like to do?"

A half moon hung in the sky, saturating the ground with silver moonlight. She glanced at him. "You're not afraid of the dark, are you?"

"No," he said. "I don't mind the dark."

"Then let's go for a walk." Impulsively, she reached for his hand, then ducked into the woods bordering the apartment complex. He followed, not having seen the path half strangled by intruding creepers. He did not wonder why she was quiet; upon entering the woods, he was instantly impressed with the stillness, the sacred serenity of the atmosphere. After some time, the woods thinned out, and she led him into a clearing.

"It's beautiful," he said, but she shook her head and put her fingers to her lips, taking his hand and leading him through the tall grass. He walked as quietly as he could, noting that she hardly made a sound. At the far end of the clearing was a tiny pond, strung with lily pads whose blossoms were just closing. Fireflies flashed, spots of blinking gold. She sat down beside an old gnarled tree.

"Do you come here often?" he asked.

She nodded. "I like coming at night better. During the day there's no guarantee I'll be alone."

"Other people know about this place?"

"There's another neighborhood beyond those woods. Sometimes children will come out here and swim. Someone tied a tire swing over the pond once, but for some reason someone else took it down. Do you like it here?"

"I do." He sat down beside her. "Why did you bring me here?"

She glanced at him. "I think it's beautiful here. And I wanted to share it with someone." She skimmed the surface of the pond with her hand. "We could go swimming, if you wanted to."

He stared at her. "I see. You're going to try to drown me."

She laughed and shook her head. He watched her, sitting in her patch of moonlight, dangling one bare foot into the scummy water of the pond. She turned to him suddenly.

"I'd love to see you paint something like this," she said.

He looked away. "I told you. I gave up painting. And I've tried to destroy most of what I've created before——"

"You haven't," she said, horrified.

"Some things aren't meant to be shared, Carrie."

"But you have so much talent."

"Painting made me crazy," he said quietly.

"That was such a long time ago," she said. "Maybe if you trusted yourself enough to try again...I'm sure that if you picked up your old paints——"

"I don't have paints. And if I did, I wouldn't let myself go anywhere near them." He paused. "Can we go back?"

She looked at him, curious. "If you want to."

He started into the woods first, having memorized the route as they walked. She hung back, walking by herself, until she realized he was waiting for her. He reached for her hand, and then they walked together until they came to the apartment complex. He looked at her for a long moment, then he dropped her hand and took a step away.

"Goodnight, Carrie. I'm sorry for being late."

"No apologies. Just do better next time."

He forced himself to take his eyes away from her. He started walking towards his car. He had a long drive, and a long night, ahead of him.

"Wait," she said.

He turned around. He said nothing.

She bit her lip. "You don't have to go home just yet, do you? Couldn't you come up for a little while?"

"Are you sure?"

She nodded. He followed her up the stairs, through the door, into her apartment. He moved closer to her as she reached inside the room to turn on the light; his hand was inches from smoothing out her hair when the lights flicked on and he saw where she had led him.

"The storage closet?" he asked, uncertain.

She had already walked inside and was stretching to reach a plastic bag on a high shelf. "I thought we could talk. And it wouldn't hurt for us to paint while we talk."

"Carrie——"

She brushed by him. "You said you didn't have paints. But I do. So there's no reason we can't—"

He grabbed her by the arm, turned her to face him. She stood absolutely still as he pulled her close, pressed his lips against her hair. He heard the bag drop from her hand and saw the tubes of acrylic paint scatter over the floor; he felt her trembling in his arms.

"What do you want, Carrie?" he said. "Do you want me to say that I adore you, that I'll always be there for you, that I'll never leave you—"

"No." Her eyes locked on his as he leaned towards her; she put a hand on his chest. "I want there to be art involved."

He looked into her moss green eyes and kept his arms around her waist. "Fine. Art can be involved. If you want it to be." He kissed her neck. "You're beautiful. You know that, don't you?"

She felt her heart racing as his lips traced a trail down her neck to her collarbones. Her hand, in his, was like ice. Slowly, he pulled her white T-shirt over her head, let it fall to the floor. His eyes lingered on her flawless skin.

She looked back at him, her eyes huge, and said nothing.

He stooped, pulling her down with him onto the floor. Sitting cross legged, his knees touching hers, he picked up a tube of acrylic paint and a tiny jet of color appeared on the plastic palette. She shivered with the first touches of paint he applied to her skin, then looked down at the image: a lone wolf, howling at the moon.

"Why?" she whispered.

He paused. "Because I don't want you to change."

She kept her eyes on him as he unclipped her bra. She felt the air on her skin, saw his eyes darken as he looked at her.

"My god, Carrie," he whispered.

"Shh," she said, taking his hands, pulling him back. "Keep painting."

She saw the torment in his eyes. His hand shook as he mixed the paint, and the first few lines he drew on her skin were wobbly. Then she saw his eyes narrow, and she knew he had ceased to see her body as a body at all. She was a canvas. The touch of his brush on her skin did not make her uneasy, as the touch of his fingers would have. Her eyes never left his face, and she realized, with every gentle stroke of the brush against her skin, that she was starting to trust him enough to want him. She didn't know how long they sat, still, silent, but eventually he looked up. She saw, in his eyes, the same vulnerability she felt. Her hand closed around his.

She dared herself to speak. "Can I try?"

"You can do anything you want," he said, handing her the palette, handing her the brush.

Her fingers were steady as she took off his clothes. She looked at him, and knew only that his nakedness was beautiful. She approached him confidently, unashamed; the paint—mostly dried on her skin—made her feel clothed. She picked up the palette. He laughed with the first touch of the brush on his skin.

"I don't know if this is going to work," he said. "I forgot that I'm ticklish."

She smiled. "I never knew that."

He looked down at his chest, at the smear of paint visible through the dark hair. "What are you painting?"

"A butterfly."

"A butterfly? Can't you paint something more manly, like a snake with fangs or—"

She shook her head, and dabbed the brush into the paint. "Do you remember the mural you painted for me, on the wall in my apartment?"

"I bet you didn't get your security deposit back."

"I did." She paused. "I painted over it. Because I was angry with you. And it won't look the same, but—"

He stopped her as she started to paint by pressing her hand against his chest and sliding his arm around her waist. He pulled her close, so that their bare bodies pressed firmly together, and then his mouth was hot against hers. She did not fight him; he was the one who pushed her away.

"No," he said.

She looked at him, looked at the streaks of paint on his body that had rubbed off from her own. "I'm all right. I'm not afraid."

He sat up. "No. This night has already been perfect."

She was quiet. "I don't understand. What did I do wrong?"

"Wrong?" He laughed. "You didn't do anything wrong. You are the single most enchanting being I have ever—" His eyes raked over her and darkened, and then he closed his eyes and paused. "Carrie, when I told you I was willing to do this the right way, I meant it. I want us to be married before we sleep together."

The smile left her face. "I don't believe in marriage."

He opened his eyes. "You don't?"

She shook her head. "I don't believe in the institution, and I don't believe in the marriage vows."

"So you won't marry me."

"I'll love you. With my whole heart, until the day I die. But I'll never marry you."

"Ironic. That presents a problem for me, because I *do* believe in marriage." He looked at her, and his dark eyes gleamed devilishly. "You won't reconsider?"

Her heart beat painfully. "I would consider a civil union contract. If I met the right person."

"Then we'll wait," he said.

She looked at him, not understanding. He handed her clothes to her. "Go take a shower. I need some time to think, and you need to get cleaned up. I'll still be here when you get back."

She took her clothes from him and found the bathroom. As the hot spray washed away the paint from her body in brown rivulets, she cried tears of gratitude, and when she stepped out of the shower, she was completely calm. She dressed quickly, then went back to the room where she had left him.

He had dressed. He stood when he saw her. She paused, then walked up to him.

"Thank you," she said.

He brushed a damp curl of her hair away from her face, then put his hand against her cheek. "Goodnight, Carrie."

She was glad that he was not ashamed, either. "I'll see you tomorrow."

He kissed her softly, and it did not occur to her until much later that it was the first time he had kissed her. Lying in her bed, thinking about him, she remembered the taste of his lips and how the kiss had felt so natural, so right, so beautiful that it had left very little impression on her at all.

Moments after the final bell rang the next day, he heard a knock at his door and looked up to find Carrie standing there.

"Come in," he said, wiping off one of the black table tops with a wet rag. "I'm just cleaning up."

"Can I help you?"

He shook his head. "But if you have some free time tonight…"

"Miss Crenshaw?"

Carrie turned quickly, and his attention followed hers. Ralph saw a young woman shifting in the doorway, her long dark hair hanging loosely to her waist, her eyes bright and nervous, her shoulders hunched because she was clasping the textbooks she held to her chest with a grip that turned her knuckles white.

"Miss Crenshaw," the girl repeated. "Miss Crenshaw, I'm sorry to interrupt your meeting with Mr. Palmer, but I couldn't wait until Friday to talk to you. I'm sorry, but I saw you come in here so I followed."

"I'm sure Mr. Palmer won't mind if we talk in his room," Carrie said.

"Of course not," he said. "I don't mind leaving."

"I'd like you to stay, Mr. Palmer," Miranda said. "Because I think you can help."

He glanced at Carrie.

"Come in, Miranda," Carrie said. "Sit down."

"Thank you." She sat and looked helplessly at Carrie. "I don't know where to begin."

Carrie pulled a chair opposite her. "Tell me why you're so upset, or what made you change your mind to talk to me sooner rather than later."

"I watched *Requiem for a Dream* last night." Miranda looked at them again, clearly terrified. "Someone told me I should watch it with Chris, so we watched it together and it scared me very badly. But he *laughed*. He *laughed* and *laughed*."

Ralph's eyes darkened. His attention shifted to Carrie, knowing she did not understand the reference.

"I know why my friend wanted us to watch the movie together," Miranda babbled. "But because Chris was laughing I know he won't stop. He won't, and I'm scared."

Carrie leaned back in her chair. "I don't understand, Miranda."

Miranda's eyes shifted to Ralph; he nodded at her.

"Best to tell her point blank," he said, quietly.

Miranda looked at Carrie. "Chris is doing drugs."

"I'm sorry," Carrie said. "I didn't hear you correctly. What did you say?"

Miranda put her hands over her eyes and began to cry. Ralph watched the alarm flash over Carrie's face as she tried to decipher Miranda's words. Then he saw her blanch, and he knew that she had finally processed what Miranda had been trying to tell her.

"No," Carrie said, stricken.

"I'm sorry. I'm sorry, Miss Crenshaw, but I know it's true because I've been there when he's…" Miranda took a deep breath. "I mean, I know everyone my age does drugs and I haven't been sheltered so I shouldn't be alarmed, but it's Chris. It's *Chris*…"

"Everyone your age does *not* do drugs, Miranda."

The sharpness in Carrie's voice made Miranda sit up straighter. She wiped away her tears with the back of her hand and sniffed. She turned to Ralph, and attempted to continue in a dignified voice.

"That's why I wanted you here, Mr. Palmer. Chris respects you, and maybe if you talked to him—"

"Blow your nose, Miranda," Carrie said, handing her a tissue. Miranda took the tissue.

"What kind of drugs is Chris doing?" Ralph asked her. Carrie looked at him, scandalized, but he ignored her.

"Mushrooms," Miranda said, her voice trembling. "Just shrooms."

"Just shrooms," Carrie repeated.

"We should talk to Chris," he said to her cautiously. "But thank you, Miranda, for bringing the situation to our attention."

Miranda sat as if stunned. "I told him I'd never tell anyone. I wanted you to be together when I told, because I only wanted to betray him once."

"You're not betraying him," Ralph said. "Any time you try to help someone who needs it, you're making the right choice."

He saw the absolute trust in Miranda's eyes as she looked at Carrie, saw how Carrie's hand on hers—the smallest touch—was giving the young woman the strength and the courage to stay calm. He understood the pyrrhic costs of Carrie's calm; she had turned a deathly shade of pale.

"What you've done took a lot of courage," she said softly. "It shows, if anything, how deeply you care about Chris."

"I don't want to hear that now," Miranda said, her eyes glistening with tears. "Right now all I want to hear is that everything is going to be okay."

"Come on, Miranda," Carrie said. "I'll give you a ride home."

"I told my mom to come pick me up today." Miranda stood shakily. "I didn't know if you'd be angry with me."

"Why would I be angry with you?"

"It's not my fault!" Miranda burst out, on the verge of tears again.

"Miranda, come here." Carrie hugged her, not letting her go as she spoke. "I'm not angry. I'm proud of you. So proud."

"I love you, Miss Crenshaw." Miranda managed a half smile, still looking badly shaken. "I really and truly do."

Carrie let her go. "You'll be all right, Miranda."

"I hope so," she said, then seemed to become aware once more of Ralph's presence in the room. She looked at him sheepishly, then turned back to Carrie. "My mom."

As soon as Miranda had gone, Carrie started pacing violently around the room. Ralph watched her warily. Suddenly she stopped, then strode across the room to him.

"You're my witness that inappropriate happened here, even though I violated some teacher's law by giving Miranda a hug. If I get sued—"

He stared at her, astonished. "Carrie, how can you be thinking about that?"

She looked about to cry. "It was a goddamn joke."

"Calm down," he said, understanding. "It could be a mistake. I'll talk to Chris."

"*I'll* talk to Chris," she said. "He's my brother."

"Whatever you think is best." He paused. "Do you really think you can handle this situation calmly?"

"Yes."

"I think I should be there," he said without pause. "Even if I'm only in the background."

She ignored him. "Did you have any idea?"

"I had my suspicions," he said.

She stopped. "And you didn't tell me?"

He dug into his coat pocket. "Don't yell at me, Carrie."

"What are you doing? You can't smoke in here."

He put the packet back into his coat. "You're not going to effectively handle the situation if you act like this around him."

"I'll control myself."

"You also don't have any experience with drugs." He looked at her. "Do you?"

"No," she said, indignant. "I should think not."

"But I do. He'll be less likely to think I'm judging him, because he knows I've been there."

"I don't see how you were justified in telling Chris that you did drugs," she said, icily. "My god, you probably got him started. Don't you know how much he idolizes you?"

"I suspect that Chris has been doing drugs long before he met me." He paused. "What I told him about my history was an attempt to make him comfortable enough to be able to come talk to me, if he—"

She turned away, frustrated and overwhelmed. "I can't have this conversation right now."

"That's fine," he said. "But I'd wait at least a day before you talk to Chris. Give yourself some time to calm down."

"I'm not going to be calm until this misconception has been cleared up," she said.

He watched her leave the school and slam the door to her Cavalier. As he heard the car screech away, he knew Chris was in deeper trouble than he knew.

Carrie pulled into the driveway in front of the Crenshaw house on Thursday evening. Her nerves and her mind would not allow delay; twenty-six hours separated the discovery and the imminent inquisition. Already her emotions were superceding her professionalism; by the time she reached the front door, she was nervous and on edge. She knocked, waited. She checked her watch—six o'clock. Chris should be in the kitchen, making himself dinner, having just arrived home from varsity track practice. She raised her hand to knock again when the door opened.

"It's not him!" Miranda called over her shoulder, before she turned shyly back to Carrie. "Hi, Miss Crenshaw. We thought you might be the pizza guy."

Carrie remained silent as Chris came to stand by Miranda. The look on his face changed from nonchalant curiosity to a distinct guardedness when he saw her.

"Hello, Carrie," he said.

"I need to talk to you." Carrie looked directly at him. "When would work best for you?"

"Now. Let's talk outside. Until our pizza comes, anyway."

Looking past him, Carrie realized that Miranda had already retreated into the house. Chris stepped onto the porch and pulled the door shut behind him.

"Miranda said she told you," he said, calmly.

"Is what she told me true?"

"Of course it's true." He smiled bitterly. "Miranda doesn't lie."

"How could you, Chris?" she exploded.

The look he gave her was not cold, but empty. "Do you have any idea how hard it is for me to get up in the morning in this body, knowing that I'm a contemptible member of the human species?"

She struggled to understand him, to give him the opportunity to explain himself.

"Why did you start?"

"When I was younger. After Dad died."

"Not when. Why."

"Why," he repeated. "I wanted to have visions. I wanted to go on a spirit quest because I was too confused, too lost, too undirected and unfocused. It's hell to live like that. I know you and Mom have told me several times to stay away from drugs, but so do other people, like community directors, schools. Leaders of society. And why does society forbid things? Why, in the past, have newspapers been censured, liberators been imprisoned, universal suffrage prohibited? Why? Because they pose a threat to society. And I hate society. I hate its doctrines of duty, responsibility, respectability; they're all false. So drugs became a gateway, a means to distance myself from society, to cleanse my perception, to teach me to rebel and to resist so I don't become an unthinking slave. Before I started anything, I thought about the knowledge I could gain, and the thought of that gain was more valuable than my unwillingness to desecrate my body with substances that would only temporarily injure me. What is a little bit of physical debilitation for priceless and lasting mental and spiritual enlightenment? These were the reasons going through my head when I decided to start using drugs."

He kept speaking, as if afraid of being interrupted. "But the drive in me—not to stray from the straight path—was so strong, so intense, that I fought for a long time, even though I felt, just as strongly, that I would have to do them to get me to the next step, to get me to where I needed to be in time to take whatever action I needed to take. It sounds vague and foolish to me as I say it to you, but it made sense to me at the time. Maybe if I had someone to talk to about it I would have acted differently, but I didn't. No, that's not true." He grimaced. "I did talk to Miranda, and she tried to talk me out of it, but I told her what I'm telling you now, which is that deep down I *knew* that they were something I had to do." He paused. "I knew because I had tried not to think about them as anything but a last resort. I prayed, I meditated, I read about the prophets and visionaries of different cultures. I learned everything I could about the subject, and then it hit me one day. Though drugs hurt you, and though they are illegal, they're natural. They're *natural*. Emerson said that artificial means only bring about artificial knowledge, and I was worried about that—that the knowledge I gained would be somewhat tainted, unpure, debased...but drugs aren't artificial."

"I think you know that's not what Emerson meant."

"That's what Mrs. Beaumont said when I brought it up in class," Chris said quietly, and it took Carrie a moment to realize that he meant Tessa—that Chris would have been exposed to *that particular essay* of Emerson's in the twelfth grade honors English curriculum. "I brought it up in discussion and that's exactly what she said. But I don't care about her class anymore, because I learned that you can get in trouble for speaking and saying what you honestly think."

She felt the conversation sliding away from the problem, but maybe

AS WE ALREADY ARE

Chris was trying to give her an important thread to follow. "She mentioned you don't participate in her class much anymore."

"I went to her class because Mr. Palmer wanted me to, and because she's a friend of yours." He glanced at her. "I went because I respect Mr. Palmer and I respect you. But then I spoke up, and I got in trouble."

"The night we went to see Miranda dance," Carrie said, still processing the previous speech he had given her. "Why didn't you want Tessa—Mrs. Beaumont—to see you? She told me she talked to you, and that you stopped coming to class."

His eyes scanned the driveway. "I wrote about my visions—because I *did* have them, after I started shrooms—and she...she held me after class one day and asked if I was studying the occult, and that she could help guide me. I don't know what all she said because I didn't want to hear that bullshit." His eyes burned with anger. "You know I believe in God and that I'm a Christian. So I decided I'm not going to waste any more of my time trying to learn from someone who believes in superstitions. Mrs. Beaumont may be your friend, but that woman is a fool." He paused. "Should we continue to discuss my drug problem, or do you want me to shut up?"

"Continue," she said, startled.

He paused. "I don't know what I was saying."

"You were talking about why you started doing drugs." She realized she sounded robotic.

"Ah. Yes." He looked up at the ceiling of the porch, then continued speaking smoothly. "I thought I'd be empowering myself. Maybe I've gained what I needed to. I don't really know. But that knowledge has come at such a price." He looked past her, and straightened. Carrie turned to follow Chris's stare, found that the new arrival was not the pizza guy. Behind her, Chris spoke, his voice a perfect study of self-control.

"I forgot to tell you," he said. "I invited Mr. Palmer over for dinner. He wants to make me one of the student guides for the trip on Saturday, and he's going to teach me and Becky—she should be here soon—what we need to know before the trip. The rest of the club members are coming in an hour."

Carrie had already recognized the midnight blue Mitsubishi; she froze as Ralph got out. She had not expected his appearance, but neither had he expected hers.

"I hope I'm not early," he said, glancing from Chris to Carrie. "Or late."

"You're right on time, Mr. Palmer," Chris said. "Thank you for coming."

Ralph turned his attention to Carrie with a look that told her he had analyzed the situation.

"There are times when adults must be adults," he said softly to her. "When young men insist on acting like little boys."

Chris looked up angrily. "I'm capable of making my own—"

"Don't shout at me, boy."

Chris paused, glowering. "I'm not shouting."

"You've been shouting at Miss Crenshaw as well, undoubtedly," he said. "If you want to be treated like a man, you need to stop acting like an indignant adolescent child."

Chris looked at Carrie uncertainly. She had not realized he had been yelling at her until she heard, because Ralph had stopped him temporarily, that Chris's voice was hoarse.

"I'm sorry, Carrie." Chris lowered his eyes. "Mr. Palmer, you're embarrassing me."

"I'm glad I am," Ralph said, coldly. "I can't say I'm proud of you right now."

Chris inhaled sharply. His hands, hanging by his sides, balled into fists. Ralph put his hand on Chris's shoulder.

"Let's talk," he said.

Chris shook off Ralph's hand. Carrie had never seen him so angry, so defiant, so close to crying in public.

"You have no room to talk," Chris cried. "You did the same thing when you had to choose—"

"Is that any justification for your behavior?" Ralph's voice dropped an octave, chilling. "My mistakes? My ignorance? My desperation? Chris, you're a goddam fool."

"I am not."

"No. You're right. You're a goddam genius, which is why I'm not going to let you fall like I did." He paused. "I want to talk to you, man-to-man. We'll be back before the pizza gets here. I just put in the order five minutes ago."

Carrie had fallen silent, watching the two of them, knowing that what she was seeing and hearing only scratched the surface of what was actually passing—unspoken—between them. No matter if she loved Chris more, no matter that he was her brother, no matter that she wanted what was best for him with all her heart; Ralph would be able to help Chris more than she could. Carrie felt a wild hope that the man standing beside her could get through to her brother. She realized Chris was looking at her.

"Go with him," she said, softly.

Chris reached into his pocket, handed Carrie some rumpled bills.

"In case the pizza comes before we get back," he said, not looking at her. "And Carrie, let's go bowling sometime."

"Okay," she said, tonelessly.

She watched their retreating figures, holding onto the anxious hope that Ralph could help Chris—in a way that she could not.

The pizza arrived long before Ralph and Chris came back. Carrie put the pizza in the oven on warm until Becky and the rest of the club members arrived, then she let them enjoy it. She looked in the direction Ralph and Chris had gone before she got into her car. Her anxiety faded as she drove; she trusted him.

Though she had only been there once, she drove to Tessa's house without difficulty, listening to the melodic tinkling of the wind chimes as she turned off the motor and got out of her car. She loved Tessa's house, yet she wished fervently that she did not have to be there. She walked resolutely to the door and knocked. After a moment the door opened and Tessa came out. Her delighted smile did not assuage Carrie's nerves.

"I need to talk to you," Carrie said quietly, in response to Tessa's enthusiastic greeting.

Tessa sobered, hearing the tone she had taken. "Did something serious happen?"

"I consider it serious."

"And it has something to do with me?"

293

"It does."

"Then you had better come inside. It looks like it's going to rain, and I can smell the moisture in the air." Tessa smiled disarmingly. "Sam took Kindra out for ice cream, so we'll be able to be alone. For awhile, at least."

The inside of the house was dimly lit, with candles burning in antique lantern-shaped holders. The circular shape of the room directly through the entry reminded Carrie of a sanctuary—low lights, open space, lavender incense scenting the air.

"I hope I'm not disturbing you."

"No, you aren't. You never do." Tessa paused, following Carrie's attention to the incense. "I was just praying for guidance."

Carrie sat down. The time had come to talk to Tessa about what was on her mind, and she wanted to address the problem immediately—but Tessa seemed troubled, confused. "About what?"

Tessa sat down beside her, close. "I started off thanking the Universe. For everything. For you, for my past friendships, for my students and my teaching, my intelligence and my health—everything. Because I think that's important. But I'm not happy. I should appreciate my husband, my daughter, my job—but instead I feel like they've distracted me from turning inward and discovering the actions I need to take. I've been on edge, feeling displaced, for about two weeks, and it makes me nervous because I have no answers and I don't know where to go." She smiled. "I thought this kind of angst would end with adolescence. College at the latest. But we never outgrow our issues, do we? We live through them, over and over, in different forms." She paused. "A good indication of that would be you and Ralph. I finally figured it out, Carrie."

Tessa had caught her off guard. "What?"

"I talked to Damien about you, once, a long time ago. And of course, you've talked to me about him," she said. "I've noticed a strong dynamic—a connection—between you, from the first time I saw you together. Your effect on him, his effect on you...both of you, to put it simply, become charged. You can see the same marked differences in individuals who have suddenly become completely aware and self-conscious." She paused. "It took seeing you and Ralph together repeatedly to make me realize who he really was. I'm ashamed of myself for being so blind; it should never have taken me so long. But I think there is something remarkable in your reaction to each other, and I no longer disapprove of the connection."

"Tessa," Carrie said, after a moment. "I came here to talk to you about—"

"There's a meditation I do," Tessa said. "Where you climb a mountain and enter a tunnel, and when you come out of the tunnel you can go right or left. The right path leads back down the mountain, back the way you've come, and the left leads further down the tunnel. And while you stand there trying to decide, there's an earthquake. The path leading back the way you've come gets blocked, and you have to move forward. You're forced. You don't have the choice." She paused. "I should get back to my meditation before the incense burns out. But before you leave, let's talk about Chris. He is what you came to talk to me about, isn't he?"

Carrie looked at her and realized she was facing her best friend—her only true friend. Carrie exhaled sharply. "You talked to Chris about the occult."

"I had to." Tessa stiffened. "Your brother has visions, Carrie."

"I know. He told me."

"They'll make him more vulnerable. He needs a guide."

"Chris believes in God," she said. "His faith is strong. His god will protect him."

"But if he's looked into the occult, that won't matter."

"He hasn't."

"Can you be sure?"

"Chris has never done so much as look at a Ouija board," Carrie said. "You scared him, Tessa, despite his belief that it's all bunk…"

"If he truly believed it was all 'bunk'," she winced, "then he wouldn't be afraid."

"You're his teacher," Carrie said. "He feels obligated to listen to you. That's the part of it that scares him."

"I won't speak to him about it again, Carrie, unless he approaches me first. I give you my solemn word." Tessa looked at her earnestly. "I don't want you to be angry with me."

"I want you to swear you won't talk to him about it again." She paused. "Unless he asks you."

"You know how seriously I take oaths."

"That's why I'm asking you to do it. This is important to me, Tessa."

"Then I swear," Tessa said, getting up. "For you."

Carrie stood. "Thank you. I'll let you get back to your meditating."

"I didn't want to make anyone angry." Tessa walked to the door, opened it for her. "And I wish I could apologize, but I can't. I thought it was the right thing to do."

"It didn't affect Chris one way or the other." Carrie forced a neutral expression onto her face. "Goodnight, Tessa."

Tessa nodded, closed the door behind her and turned to the room with its soft lights, scented air, emptiness. She remembered sitting close to Carrie, a perfect current of warmth and understanding flowing between them. She went and spread herself out on the sofa in the room. She closed her eyes and listened to the delicate music of the chimes in the background, inhaled the smoke of the incense, and retreated further within herself.

"You hold the ball like this," Chris said the next day as she stood beside him in a smoke-filled alley. Her attention diverted by the myriads of people who were ignoring her as surely as she was observing them, Carrie turned to him.

"Pay attention carefully," Chris said. "I want you to have fun, and I think you'll have more fun if you do well."

"All right, show me." She stepped up to him with exaggerated gravity, trying to dispel the awkwardness—forcing him to crack a smile.

"One. Two. Three. Four," he counted as he went through the motions: the graceful arch of the ball as he brought it behind him, the clean sweep as his arm swung forward, the quivering jolt of the ball as it hit the alley, the upward salute as he followed through. She watched the ball curve towards the gutter, then angle in at the last moment to attack the head pin. Chris turned and swaggered back towards her, a flush on his pale face. From the moment he had stepped into the alley he had been transformed.

"That's called a strike," he said. "If you get all the pins down in two tries, then it's called a spare."

"That was wonderful, Chris. How do I do that?"

"You practice," he said. "Carrie, look at the screen. See how I have an X, but I don't have any numbers yet? That's because when you get a strike or a spare, you get a bonus and you add your scores differently. I'll tell you about that later. Here, use this ball. It looks like it would work for you."

She took the ball from Chris and walked up to the lane. The pins faced her, a solid rank. She exhaled. She tried to imitate the approach she had seen him use. Step forward, let go, follow through. The ball clunked out of her hand, dribbled its way to the pins, ended its journey.

"Good," Chris said from behind her. "You got one pin."

"Not a gutter ball," she said, walking jauntily back to the computer screen. "See, I know something about bowling, after all."

He laughed. She realized she could not remember the last time she had heard him laugh.

"I know you can do better than that though," he said. "Stand at the line and bring your arm straight back this time. You get one more shot."

She stood at the line and brought her arm back like a robot. She released the ball, watched it roll into the gutter.

"It didn't work," she said, turning to find he had his hand across his forehead.

"Carrie, that's not what I meant," he said. "I meant that you should start your approach from the line."

"Let's make this a practice round," she said, taking a seat on the blue plastic chairs clustered around the terminal. "You can teach me the basics, and then I'll actually try."

"You should always try."

She ended one of the Crenshaw mottos. "Because that's how you learn, and you should always do your best."

He grinned. "No. Because if you tried on the first throw and got one pin down, I'd be afraid to see what would happen if you didn't try."

"I'd probably throw it into the next lane," she said. "Has that ever happened to you?"

"Yes," he said, looking away.

She laughed. "How did that happen? What did you do?"

"The ball got stuck on my fingers. Sometimes that happens to me." The tops of his ears were burning red.

"Were your teammates angry at you?"

"No. They laughed, because we're all in this together."

"They sound like nice people, these teammates of yours."

"They're my best friends," Chris said. "They remind me that not all humans are completely bad."

She paused as he went up to the terminal, retrieved his ball, got a split, got a spare. When he sat down she walked up to the line with confidence, her eyes on the pins, her thoughts on her brother's words. The ball left her hand automatically. She turned on her heel, walked back to him.

"Nice," he said. "Carrie, you got a strike."

She turned, let out a whoop. When she turned back, he was smiling.

"That's why I love this game," he said. "It's fun."

"You've got a good thing here," she said. "Something you love, people you know, somewhere to go." She broke off, started singing. "When times get rough..."

He slapped his forehead. "Why do you like to sing so much?"

"I just do."

"You're like the bird in 1984," he said. "Who sings even though no one is listening..."

"You're reading 1984?"

"On my own," he said. "I love it."

She let him persuade her into two more rounds, then forked over a twenty dollar bill to the owner of the place as Chris packed his ball and took off his shoes. She stood waiting until he came up to her.

"How much was it?" he asked.

"Already took care of it." She shook her head as he started to protest. "I insist. You gave me the lessons."

Once they stepped outside the alley, he headed straight towards their car. She noticed how outside of the bowling alley his shoulders had hunched again, the feverish color in his cheeks had faded, the gleam in his eyes had winked out and become hollow.

"Do you love him?" he asked quietly, getting into the car.

She started the engine, then glanced at him. "Who?"

"You know."

"I don't know."

He ignored her. "Are you going to try to find out?"

She paused. "We don't need to talk about this, Chris."

He paused. "Okay. But can I tell you something?"

She hesitated. "What?"

"You need to talk to him."

"We talk."

"Before the trip," he stressed. "And you need to listen. Really listen."

"I don't know what you're talking about."

He glanced at her, then settled back into his seat. "Just try to stay open, okay, Carrie?"

She pulled the car into the driveway of their childhood home; she turned to him. His eyes were somber—the line of his lips, grim. She nodded. He held her gaze for one more moment, then opened the car door.

"Thanks for taking me bowling." He paused, lingered. "And don't worry about me. I'm going to get my act together."

She watched him walk up to the house, his shoulders hunched. Her hands clenched around the steering wheel. She wished she could help him, but she knew he would have to find his own way.

Ten minutes before the end of her third period class she heard the announcement, riddled with crackly static, that those students participating in the Outdoor Recreation Adventure Club trip were to be dismissed. Unlike Ralph—who had one of his preparatory periods at that time—she was obligated to finish her class, and was the last one to arrive at the front entrance to the school, fifteen minutes after the initial announcement. She smiled at the club members, received enthusiastic smiles from all but two. Chris barely acknowledged her and Judy looked pale with fear—but she had expected that. What she came unprepared for was Ralph's behavior. He was quiet, surveying the club members. He acted as if he had not yet seen her, as if she were not even there. She moved beside him, took the clipboard from his hand with affected calmness.

"Is everyone here?"

"You're late," he said.

She could not read the tone of his voice. Without answering him, she turned to the assembled group of students with a genuine smile on her face. Joey and Chris were in a corner, talking quietly; Judy was listening to Derrick tell her about the goals he had made in the soccer match the night before. The other students were talking as a group; she had all of their attention before long.

"We're all here," she said. "Is everyone excited?"

Becky laughed. "You should be a second grade teacher, Miss Crenshaw. You're so enthusiastic about everything."

Carrie saw Ralph look at her suddenly, but she pretended not to be aware of him. "We're going to need permission forms if—"

"I've already collected them," Ralph said.

She looked at him. "Any more gear?"

"Let's go, gang," Ralph said to their students. She found him looking at her as the students filed past them, and she looked directly back at him. Their eyes locked, and when he didn't look away, she knew something was weighing heavily on his mind. She focused her attention on what she knew: she was leaving for the Dolly Sods Wilderness in West Virginia with Mr. Palmer and ten young men and women. She was safe; they would not return to being Ralph and Carrie until much later.

As she slid into the passenger seat of the van across from Ralph, she saw a smile creep onto his face. She turned to confront him, but found he was looking over the directions he had taped to the steering wheel. She fiddled with the radio knob until she found the station channel requested by the students.

"Are you set with your other classes?" Ralph asked, forcing her attention to him.

"I talked to the substitute in advance," she said. "I talked to my students as well. They know what to do, and I doubt they'll give her any trouble."

Ralph nodded, and they talked of inconsequential things. She wondered what he really wanted to say to her as the black asphalt continued to spread out in front of them, seemingly endless. She listened to the banter in the van, smiled as a few brave voices sang along with the radio, noted the shifting dynamic as the students began to fall asleep one by one.

"You can sleep if you want to," Ralph said, his eyes still on the road. "I know how to get there."

"I don't think I should sleep."

"I can always wake you up if I need something. You should rest, so you have energy for the trip." He paused. "I want to think, and I want to do it without you watching me."

"You are highly impertinent," she said.

"Not impertinent," he said with affected gravity. "Just observant. You like to watch people and try to figure them out. That's all I meant." He paused. "But considering what I thought you were going to say, I'll take impertinent as a compliment."

She turned from him, and without meaning to, she fell asleep. She woke an hour later, as they crossed the border of Maryland, and found that she and Ralph were the only ones awake in the van, and that he was staring at the road with a dogged, pensive look on his handsome face, his eyes following the lines of the road in front of him like a zombie's.

"Do you want me to drive?" she asked softly, so as not to startle him.

He looked at her, gave no sign that he had heard her.

"Pull over," she said.

"Why?"

"You need a nap."

He shook his head. "We're almost there. I can finish it out."

"So can I."

"I know you can, Carrie." His eyes were still on the road.

"You should call me Miss Crenshaw."

"I don't like titles."

"They're a form of respect."

"They're a way of creating distance between the teacher and the students so they obey."

"Your students call you Mr. Palmer."

"They do," he said. "But I've given them the choice of calling me Ralph." He paused. "I'm not calling you Miss Crenshaw."

She paused. "If you drift off the road—"

"I'm used to long drives. I have my tricks." He arched his eyebrows and began to sing along with the Pink Floyd song playing softly on the radio. "The lunatic is in my head…"

She suppressed a laugh. He glanced at her, then fell silent.

"Please sing." The sound of his voice, low, melodic, filled her with a deep sense of peace. The tension, the weariness, ebbed out of his face. For a moment, she felt they were alone in the van. Suddenly he broke off his soft singing.

"I packed a tent for each of us," he said. "We're all going to be sleeping in the same area, but we can decide how we want to place our tents relative to theirs—"

"When we get there," she said, wishing he had not broken the beauty of the moment.

As the students began to wake up, the van was filled by their various conversations once more. Ralph and Carrie settled into comfortable silence. They stopped only once, and that was so Carrie could move a tortoise out of the van's way. The students piled out of the van, glad for an opportunity to stretch and move around. After the backpacks had been unloaded and strapped onto the students' backs, however, Carrie caught more than one of them looking back at the van wistfully while others, like Chris, had their eyes already focused on the trail.

"Remember this will be the hardest day," Ralph encouraged. "After this your group will start eating the food, and your packs will get lighter. We're only walking three miles to get to our first campsite. Let one of us know if you're having difficulty. We're not out here for speed or distance, and you're not here to prove how tough you are. So if you find blisters popping up on your feet tonight, I want to know about them. And I want to see you helping each other, and remember the Leave No Trace Ethics—"

"All right, Mr. P," Derrick said. "We know. Can we get going?"

He paused. "We're going as one group. Look out for the person in front of you and behind you while we're on the trail, and don't wander off by yourself. I highly encourage you to spend some time by yourself on this trip, but not until we get to the campsite." He grinned at them. "I want to make sure we all survive."

"Mr. Palmer, are you serious?" Judy whimpered. "Miss Crenshaw, is he serious? Derrick said there were coyotes here."

"There are," Ralph said. "Keep your eyes open, and you'll probably see some of their scat along the way. But they won't attack you. Most animals, except the insects, will keep their distance, and the bears shouldn't come into camp as long as your groups properly dispose of your garbage and hang the rest of your food in bear bags at night."

"Bears?" Judy wailed.

Ralph shook his head. "Single file. Follow me."

Carrie's mind wandered as they walked. She tried to listen to the sounds around her, but they were drowned out by Judy's chattering, and Carrie was glad when they arrived at the campsite, a shaded area bordered by Red Creek rushing and flowing along a bed of large, craggy rock formations. When Carrie stepped into the area, the first members of the group had already started setting up camp. Carrie dropped her pack near a tree, then bandaged the blisters on Judy's feet.

"Miss Crenshaw." Becky ran towards her, gasping, laughing. "Miss Crenshaw, you have to see this."

Carrie walked with Becky, and then she stared. Chris and Derrick had changed into swimming trunks and were standing ankle deep in the rapidly running water as they stared down the gradual drop in front of them.

"Hi, Miss Crenshaw!" Derrick said, waving. "You should have seen—"

"Derrick, what are you doing?" Judy had hobbled over, and was looking at Derrick hysterically. "Derrick, you're going to get hurt."

"Nah, babe," he said, sitting down on the edge of the rock slide, rapids of white foam quickly covering him. "It's like a natural water slide. Mr. P just did it and he didn't get hurt."

Astonished, Carrie followed the gradual drop with her eyes and saw Ralph stand up, sending the water sloughing off his navy blue swim trunks.

"That's what I wanted you to see," Becky whispered to her. "Chris wanted to try it but he didn't know if it was safe, and then Mr. Palmer just took off his.... well." Becky blushed. "He just jumped right in." She turned glowing eyes out across the water. "Chris! Chris, I want to try it, but I'm afraid I'm going to slip and fall. Can you help me?"

Carrie watched Chris walk confidently across the slick stones. He offered Becky his hand. She grabbed his entire arm and leaned heavily against him as he walked with her back to the rock slide. Meanwhile, Derrick was trying to persuade a very unwilling Judy to join him. Carrie saw Becky sit down in the rapids and look with affected fear over her shoulder at Chris; he grinned, then pushed her. Carrie watched apprehensively as Becky went squealing down the drop, knowing that hospitals were not easily accessible. She turned in time to see Derrick grab Judy's arm and attempt to pull her, fully clothed, across the rocks.

"Derrick," she said, sharply, and he dropped Judy's arm just as Ralph came up to them—dripping wet, his dark hair alternately spiked and plastered against his head.

"Miss Crenshaw," he said. "Care to swim? It's perfectly safe. Maybe not perfectly, but the most you risk, really, is a banged up shin or two."

Carrie looked longingly at the water. "I think one of us should remain with the other campers."

"Mr. P," Derrick said, grinning. "I say on the count of three, I'll take Jude and you can take Miss Crenshaw."

"I hope you're not being serious, Derrick."

"I'm not joking," Derrick said. "Come on, Mr. P. You're always telling us how we should live, take part in everything instead of watching life go by…"

"Derrick." His voice was grim. "What is the number one threat to us on this trip?"

Derrick, sobered by the tone of Ralph's voice, looked at him for approval. "Dehydration?"

"That's during the day."

Beside Carrie, Judy spoke quietly. "Hypothermia."

"Right." Ralph ignored the hostile look that Derrick shot Judy. "Do you think it would be wise for Judy and Miss Crenshaw to get wet when they have a limited supply of dry clothes, night is approaching, and nights here are cold?"

"I wasn't thinking about that," Derrick said, not looking at Ralph or Carrie.

"No harm done," Ralph said. "Hazard two, these rocks are slippery.

You wouldn't want to drag someone across them. It would be too easy to fall and get hurt."

Becky had successfully climbed back up the rock slide. She gave Chris an enthusiastic hug. Ramrod straight through the hug, he smiled at Becky and flashed her a thumb's up when she pulled away. Beside her, Ralph had extracted an apology from Derrick.

"I'm going to go help some of the students set up their stoves," Carrie said. "They were complaining about being hungry."

"Send some people out for firewood," Ralph said, watching as Derrick made his way back across the rocks. "We'll have a small fire tonight and go over some objectives for the trip. I brought an excerpt from some nature writing I want to read. Do you need help with the stoves?"

"Go have fun," she said, then paused. "Though some of our campers might be joining you out there, if they end up setting themselves on fire…"

He laughed and seemed on the verge of saying something, but, fearing the look in his eyes, she turned and walked back to the campsite. He watched her walk up the embankment, then turned and found Chris watching him. Their eyes locked; a look of understanding passed between them. Then Chris smiled and turned his attention back to the water. To the delight of Becky and Derrick, he went down the rock slide on his stomach, seeming more like a part of the landscape than separate from it. Ralph watched him briefly, understanding the comfort that Chris found in nature, and then he shook the water from himself as best he could and followed the path Carrie had taken. He saw her bent over a stove, explaining its function to a group of hungry-looking young adults, when the ground beside her burst into flames. The students gave a hoot as Carrie sprang into action, stamping the fire out and then telling the group of kids—more patiently than he would have—that they had to be careful not to get lighter fluid on the ground, and to always crouch when lighting the stove so that they could jump back if something happened. Smiling, he moved off to where he had set up his tent. He knew he trusted her more than she trusted herself.

After the group had eaten and built the campfire Ralph took control, reading the passage he had planned, letting them know they had a certain amount of freedom with their time and how they used it—they were almost adults—and once again repeating that they look out for each other. Then, despite the anxious look Carrie gave him, he turned them loose for the night.

"And that's it," he said to her as the students filtered to tents, to the creek's edge, to the surrounding woods. "You keep an eye on things, but they're largely on their own. Are you going to bed?"

"Not just yet," she said. "I'm going to stay up for awhile."

"Where did you set up?" he asked her. "In case something comes up and I need to get hold of you at a moment's notice."

She hesitated. "I haven't set up. Yet."

"Carrie. Setting up camp is the first thing you do. You know that. It's dark now. How are you going to see?"

She paused. "The tent you packed for me is different than the ones you gave the students. I don't know how to set it up."

"Why didn't you ask me for help? Or you could have asked one of the kids."

She detected a hint of anger in his voice, but more than his anger, she felt his disappointment in her.

"I'll help you," he said. "Where did you leave your tent?"

She led him to the tree where she had moved the tent.

"As far away from mine as possible," he said. "Good. You'll be able to help the students on this end of camp if they need it. But you set it up just fine. Did you want me to check something?"

She looked at the tent, confused. "But I didn't set it up."

She saw him watching her, and then they both started as the tent nearest hers opened and Chris emerged.

"I set it up for you," he said, quietly. "You were taking care of Judy, and then you started helping Micah and Nathan with their stove. I didn't know if you would have time before it got dark. I didn't mean to eavesdrop but I overheard you talking."

"Thank you, Chris," Carrie said.

"This is my tent, or Joey and Don and my tent." He paused. "I don't think that was a very grammatical sentence. But I wanted to be near you, in case you needed something."

She saw Ralph looking at her, but she could not speak.

"I'm going for a walk," Chris said. "I want to see the stars. I didn't mean to disturb you."

"Maybe Joey would want to go with you," Carrie faltered, looking significantly at Ralph.

"I want to be alone." Chris smiled. "I love it here. It's so peaceful. Goodnight."

"Goodnight," Ralph said calmly. Carrie watched anxiously as her brother's lanky silhouette blended into the surrounding darkness. When Chris was gone she turned to Ralph.

"He'll be fine," Ralph assured her. "He's not going to do anything illegal. He's learning to get away from that, and he wants to stay away from others who are doing it. That's part of why he wants to be alone."

"Do you mean—"

"I let them make their own choices. I don't know how to stop them, Carrie. But don't worry about Chris. We had a long talk, and he's done. And he understands Nature too well to play games with her. He won't get lost and he won't get hurt."

She paused. "What did you say to him?"

"I let him know I wasn't judging him and that the choice was his." Ralph paused. "Besides that, I don't remember. Chris was willing to stop. Eager, even. It was like he was waiting for someone to give him the permission to stop." He paused. "We also talked about you."

"I don't see why I would have come up."

"Don't you?"

She avoided his gaze, determined not to answer him.

He glanced at her. "Chris tells me you had an interesting relationship with your father."

"We didn't get along." She paused. "What else did Chris tell you?"

"He told me how independent you were. But I already knew that." He turned from her and fixed his eyes on the sky. "But he also told me something I didn't know. He told me that once some jerk broke your heart."

She wondered how she had ended up with only him beside her.

"God, it's a beautiful night," he said, and turned. "I wish I were alone with you."

She could not speak. He smiled, laughter dancing in his dark eyes.

"You should get some rest. You'll need energy for tomorrow's hike. Wait until you see what I have planned. Sleep well, Miss Crenshaw."

She kept her eyes on the ground until she thought he would have stopped looking at her—but when she raised her eyes he was still there, his eyes alight and burning. She swallowed, the bolt his gaze sent racing through her body not entirely unwelcome.

"Goodnight, Ralph," she said.

He walked towards the fire, and she retired into the tent Chris had set up for her. The ground was hard beneath her sleeping pad, and she felt safe. With fresh air filtering in through the mesh of the tent, with the knowledge of the stars above her, the water beside her, and the woods around her, she fell asleep easily, exhausted and grateful.

She left her tent as the sun rose, unaccustomed to the stiffness in her joints and the moist chill of the early morning. She did not know what time it was, but staying at the camp was not an option; she had put on every layer of clothing she had packed and she was freezing. She headed into the woods, walking briskly to warm her shivering body. She understood now why ancient pagans had worshiped the sun; she praised its first rays of warmth, and paused in a thick copse of trees and looked around her. The early morning light gilded the leaves, the wisps of gossamer strung between the tree branches, the drops of dew beading the ground. She remained motionless, captivated, until she felt the calming stillness of the wilderness start to settle inside her, and then she hurried on. To be filled by that depth of serenity in small, episodic bursts was refreshing, but she would not want that kind of inner stability for more than a moment. Peace and stability came with their price. She would rather pay the price of chaos than that of stagnation, because stagnation meant death—and change meant growth.

As she walked back into the camp, she saw that Ralph had gotten up and was crouched near the fire pit, a handful of small sticks in his hands.

She fought a sudden urge to go back to her tent—he had not yet seen her—but she stopped herself, and walked towards him. Because she kept her eyes down she did not know when he became aware of her presence, or what kind of effect it had on him.

"Come here," he said, his voice smooth, without any trace of the grogginess of awakening. "I want to show you something."

She stepped closer to him and crouched down, trying to hide the fact that she was shivering.

"This is a good trick to use in case you get up early," he said. "And you're cold."

She watched as he pushed away the top layer of ash in the pit and covered the embers still burning from the night before with the tinder he had collected. A spurting flame soon licked at the thicker wood he added.

"Move closer if you're cold." He stood and moved away from her, his eyes locked on the flame. "I'm going to get the cub scouts up."

She withdrew from the fire, reluctantly leaving its warmth. "I'll get the girls up."

She heard him go to the nearest tent and warn the campers inside that if they refused to get up, he would start singing. She moved quickly off towards the girls' tents, and moments later heard Ralph start belting out a song, purposefully off tune. She knew the girls in the first tent were up before she called to them; she could hear them giggling.

The group gathered. Ralph gave them the choice that day between two day trips. He would not tell them what each day trip involved; he told them they had to vote blindly and go with their gut instinct. One—five hands—same for choice two. He turned to her.

"One or two," he said.

"Two," she said.

"Two it is," he said, then turned to the campers. "You don't need your packs. Bring your journals and water bottles. Everything else can stay here."

Only when they started walking did Carrie realize the symbolism of her choice. One: solitude, aloneness, self-reliance, unity. Two: companionship, dependence, duality. A dim sense of unease shot through her. She shifted the fanny pack she had brought containing the first aid kit, and for a brief moment, she felt, powerfully, as if she were carrying a child. *His* child. She forced herself to remove her hand from the bulge of the pack. The feeling passed. She continued walking. She looked up when Judy stopped in front of her and saw Ralph and the leaders waiting for the rest of the group. She became aware once more of the fresh cool air, the sun beaming down through the canopy of leaves, the vibrant green surrounding her.

"We're almost there," he said. "When we get past this next stretch, we're going to be at 3800 feet."

The figure meant nothing to her until she stepped out into the clearing and saw her reaction mirrored on the faces around her. Large craggy rocks cracked the ground and overlooked a sheer drop. The untouched landscape sprawled beyond, the morning mist coating the tiers a cerulean blue. For the first few moments no one spoke, and then on their own accord the students separated and went to various spots along the precipice's edge. Ralph stayed quietly by her side as her eyes swept over the vista, then he left her alone. She walked towards the center of the overhanging area, careful to avoid the cracks and gulleys, but could not bring herself to approach the edge. She sat down, her lower body completely supported, her palms secure on the hard, cold surface of the rock. She closed her eyes and tried to imagine that she was not 3800 feet in the air, then felt someone sit down beside her. She turned and saw Judy, her arms clenched around her legs, looking out over the vast expanse. Carrie found she was glad for the company.

"How are your feet doing, Judy?" Carrie asked, noting that the girl had taken off the stiff black boots she had bought for the trip. They were laying, battered and scuffed, on the marble face of the rock.

"They hurt," Judy said, then quickly added, "but I'm not complaining, Miss Crenshaw."

"You're a trooper."

"Can I talk to you? Or if you want the quiet, I could leave."

She paused. "What's bothering you, Judy?"

"I don't know if I should have come on this trip." Judy looked at her. "You know I signed up for this club because of Derrick. It was important for me to try the outdoors because it's important to him. But I hate bugs and I can barely walk." She paused. "I'm not good at this. Derrick's already taunting me because of the blisters on my feet, and they're not even my fault. I thought we'd spend more time together because of the trip, but he's always off exploring with other people and I rarely see him." She paused again. "That's what I'm thinking about when I look out at these hills, while other people are being swept away by the beauty. I feel so stupid."

"I know you aren't stupid," Carrie said. "And you've already succeeded on this trip. You're here, aren't you? Every time you try something new you've already succeeded. You'll finish out the trip, and you'll have memories." She paused. "And the scars to prove it."

"Are my feet going to scar?" Judy asked, horrified.

"No, Judy. As long as we take care of them. You don't have to tell Derrick about your blisters, but don't hide them from me."

"Okay." Judy relaxed. "You're right, though. I might not like everything about this trip, but at least I know that I've given this a try. And I'll appreciate everything I already have more when I get back home. Because I will get through this trip." She paused. "But Mr. Palmer said it might rain tonight, and I'm terrified of storms." She paused. "My grandad got struck by lightning in a storm, and his heart failed. He *died*. Miss Crenshaw, I don't want to be out here if it's going to storm. There's no place to take shelter."

"If it storms we'll probably go up into the trees," Carrie said, thinking of the woods that bordered the flat, open area where they had made their campsite.

"Like John Muir?" Judy asked, her eyes wide. "I don't even know if I can. I've never climbed a tree…"

Carrie turned her face away to hide the uncontrollable smile that sprang to her lips. She remembered the article Ralph had read to the campers around the fire the previous night—an excerpt of Muir's writings, in which he described the compulsion that made him go out in the midst of a powerful storm and climb to the top of a tree to get the overall effect. Ralph had advised against imitating Muir after he read the excerpt—looking directly at Derrick and Chris as he did so—but had encouraged the campers to explore with Muir's enthusiasm, and to treat their nature experience with the same aggressive and fearless attitude.

"Miss Crenshaw, you're laughing at me!"

"I chose my words poorly." Carrie turned to her solemnly. "Don't worry, Judy, no one is going to try to make you climb a tree. I meant that since we're on a campsite where the ground is mostly flat, we'll probably go up into the woods where the trees are spread out evenly. It'll be safer."

"So I shouldn't be nervous?"

"The Outdoors Club has been around for years," Carrie said. "No one has ever gotten seriously injured."

"I…I think I'm going to go sit by myself for awhile, since we're supposed to."

Carrie was sad to see her go. She must have fallen into a daze as she looked out at the vista, because when Ralph startled her out of her thoughts, the sun's light had changed drastically.

"We might get a storm tonight," he said, looking out at the horizon. "Couple of rain clouds in the distance. I'm going to take the students who want to go back to camp. You can stay longer if you'd like. Chris is staying, and he knows the way back."

She climbed to her feet. "I'd prefer to go. My thoughts aren't particularly agreeable to me right now."

"Then you should stay," he said. "Beauty like this won't give you time to think."

"I know the way back," Carrie said, realizing how Judy must feel. "You can stay. I'll take the students who want to go back."

"You're sure?"

She nodded, then took half the students back to the campsite without incident. Ralph's crew got back in time to cook and clean, and after another two hours, when the sun had sunk and an early twilight enveloped the sky, the storm struck. Carrie was at the end of camp opposite of Ralph when the first flash of lightning broke and the rain starting pouring down. She sent the students near her to their tents for rain gear.

"I'm going to go round up the stragglers in the woods," Ralph shouted, coming towards her. "Take everyone else to the hills and spread them out. Keep them calm, Carrie. I'll be up in a minute."

She watched Ralph jog towards the path leading away from the camp.

She led the students up into the hills, explaining the emergency drill as they walked. Then she separated them, keeping Judy—already pale and trembling—nearest her. She crouched down beside her.

"Are you all right?" she said softly.

"Of course she is," Ralph said, coming up from behind her with three campers trailing him. "Aren't you, Carebear?"

Judy, still looking shaken, smiled at the nickname—one Derrick had come up with for her because she required so much attention.

"I'm okay," she said.

"Derrick," Ralph said, turning to the first rain-splattered camper. "Fifteen feet to the left of Judy. Megan, to the left of him. Becky, go directly behind Miss Crenshaw and spread out. Did you all hear me?"

Becky did not move. "Where's Chris?"

Ralph turned to Carrrie. "Was Chris in the original group you brought up?"

"He went exploring," Becky said, interrupting. "I wanted to go with him because of the storm, but he said he wanted to be alone."

"Becky, please go stand behind Miss Crenshaw."

"But—"

"We're going to do a run through, gang," Ralph yelled to the crouching campers, then lowered his voice as he turned to Carrie. "I want to see if anyone else is missing, then I'll go find Chris. He has too much wilderness common sense to have gotten into trouble. Did you explain the drill to them?"

Carrie nodded, and he turned away from her quickly.

"Megan?" He paused, then said loud enough for everyone to hear, "Well, it looks like we've lost one already."

"Oh, I'm here, Mr. Palmer," Megan said loudly from Judy's left. "I didn't know we had started."

"Judy!"

Judy started, roused. "Here!"

A minute later he turned to Carrie, who had remained by his side and watched as he called the names of the campers as easily as if he had the roll sheet in front of him.

"He's the only one missing," he said. "Stay here and repeat the drill I showed you."

"Let me go," Carrie said. "When the storm picks up, they'll want you here."

"You could handle this, Carrie," he said. "But you can go if you want. Get him up here as soon as you can."

He walked over to where Becky was crouching. Carrie followed him.

"Becky," he said. "Do you know where Chris went?"

"He headed down Red Creek trail," she said, promptly starting to stand. "I'll show you."

"You're staying here," Ralph said firmly. "We need to keep you safe. Carrie can handle it. Now please stay low to the ground."

Carrie had already started down the hill; Becky's eyes followed her, but she obeyed Ralph and returned to her spot. As Carrie sloshed through the tall grass, the rain started coming down harder. She felt the impact of the drops piercing through her light rain coat. A crash of thunder broke above her head, followed by a bolt of lightning ripping the sky apart. Two minutes away from the campsite she found Chris leaning against a tree, his face uplifted to the rain and his eyes closed, the collar of his rain jacket open and the T-shirt underneath soaked through. She called to him. He opened his eyes, as if awakening from a dream, and saw her.

"Hi, Carrie," he said. "Am I in trouble?"

"No, you're not in trouble," she said. She looked at him and she wanted to leave him there. She had never seen him look so happy, so completely at peace. "But we have to—"

"We have to go back to the group." Chris nodded, peeled himself away from the tree with resignation. "I understand. But we'd be just as safe here. You know that, don't you?"

"I don't want them to worry."

"You're not worried, are you?" he asked, his solemn, peace-filled eyes probing hers. "You're not afraid, are you?"

The thunder roared, and she jumped. "It's just a storm."

"We should get to them before God gets really angry," Chris said, striding away from her down the trail with complete composure. "At least that's what it sounds like, doesn't it? God getting angry. But we know now that's not true. This..."

"Chris, I can't hear you."

He paused, let her catch up to him. "Seeing this storm lets me know that I'm not alone—in having this inside me. God must feel like this, too."

"The worst of the storm hasn't come yet," Carrie said. "We should hurry."

"I'm grateful someone else understands," Chris said, his eyes scanning the canopy of leaves above them.

"Button your collar, Chris," she reprimanded. "You want to stay as dry as possible."

"No," he said. "I want to get wet. I want to be uncomfortable. I don't like all this gear, all this food, all these precautions. They take us away from what we're supposed to be doing, which is connecting with nature. I like being cold. I like being uncomfortable. I like the rawness of the wilderness, because it's real."

"Do you know the drill, Chris?"

He glanced at her. "I know the drill."

She heard Ralph calling names, heard responses. He acknowledged them as they joined the circle, directing Chris to one spot and her to another. She looked at him incredulously, and a flash of lightning revealed the grim expression on his face.

"Go," he said. "Now."

She obeyed him. She crouched low to the ground and pulled her knees into her chest to stay warm as the rain soaked her. She had not expected the fear as a sudden realization dawned on her. No matter how competent and knowledgeable Ralph was, he could not control the elements. If lightning struck a person, or caused a tree to fracture and fall, there was nothing that either of them could do. She had not realized the fact of her mortality and helplessness as she did in that moment, nor had she ever felt closer to him. She saw him, illuminated by the flashes of lightning, standing tall in the midst of the storm. Above the thunder and roar of the rain, she heard his voice: strong, loud, clear. She hated crouching, feeling helpless and vulnerable and afraid, able to do nothing but put her head down on her knees as the rain pelted down and stung her…

"There was a time," Ralph's voice, quiet, beside her, "when you weren't afraid of storms."

She looked up, met his eyes, felt a surge of strength. He stood and started making rounds of the campers. By the flashes of the lightning she could see Judy near her, shaking, and she could hear her sobbing. She stood and went over to where Judy was rocking herself back and forth.

"Judy," she said, putting a hand on Judy's water-logged arm. "Everything is going to be fine."

"No." Judy sobbed, lunged for her. "Miss Crenshaw, someone's going to die…"

Carrie sat down beside her. "Listen to Mr. Palmer's voice, Judy, and everyone else answering. Everyone else is fine. You will be too."

"Chris!" Ralph yelled.

Judy paused in her sobbing, drew in a ragged breath. Carrie waited, on edge, straining to hear the answering call.

"Chris!"

Another flash of lightning illuminated his profile as Chris stood. The hood of his rain jacket fell back, and he stared at the thunderclouds.

"Bring it on!" Chris yelled up at the sky. "Bring it on, bastard!"

Carrie's heart jumped as Chris threw back his head and howled. She was not the only one glad for Chris's outburst. From various parts of the woods, she heard them—cheers, howls, laughs—and she smiled and let the rain pelt the hood of her faulty raincoat from her face. She stood and went over to Ralph.

"We're in the eye of the storm," he said. "It's going to be peaceful, and then it's going to start up again. But we're through the worst of it. I want you to go make sure everyone is okay, then come back here."

She did, and they conferred. Ten minutes later, he told the campers they should leave their wet clothes in the tents' vestibules, then sent them down the hills. He hung back with Carrie as they went. The rain continued to fall sporadically.

"We'll give them six minutes to get changed and comfortable, then we'll go check on them." Ralph leaned against the tree nearest them. "Carrie, I want to ask you something."

She looked at him, wishing she could see his face.

"I'm not into ceremony," he said. "So excuse the lack of charm. But if I don't say this directly, I won't be able to. I want you to marry me."

The fiercest clap of thunder, the sharpest bolt of lightning, did not send as strong a jolt through her heart as his words did. A protest rose to her lips, along with a thousand excuses and reasons why she couldn't marry him. But she could not utter them. She could not speak.

"Be serious," she said, finally.

"Be serious." He laughed. "I say I want to marry you and she says be serious."

"You did not say you wanted to marry me," she said, struggling to find words that made sense. She could not trust the instinct that she wanted to marry him. "You said you wanted me to marry you."

"How unromantic," he said. "What a way to propose. But I hardly know what I'm saying right now." He paused. "I remember what you said before, Carrie. Let me rephrase. Will you sign a civil union contract with me? We can go about it any way you want. There doesn't have to be a ceremony, or a church, or a white dress…"

"No."

"Think about it."

She shook her head.

"Why?" He stepped closer to her. "I see how you look at me. I know how you feel about me, and I know you love—"

"Marriage is slavery. *Slavery.*"

"It wouldn't be. Not if you married me." He paused. "I'm scared as hell right now, Carrie, but I'm sure about this."

She stepped away from him. "Why did you have to ask me tonight? Do you have any idea how awkward it's going to be between us for the rest of the trip? We still have three days and two nights left."

"You're better at hiding your feelings than I am," he said. "And I had to ask you tonight because the storm set something loose in me."

"It set something loose in all of us but—"

"My timing is terrible. But don't you feel that it's right?"

She looked away. "We should check on our campers. If someone catches hypothermia—"

He gripped her arms, forced her to look at him. "Carrie, answer me."

"I can't give you a simple answer to that question," she said, trying to brush by him. "Nor do I have the time to tell you all my reasons."

"Tell me some of them. Tell me one."

"One," she said, trying to look angry, trying not to let him see how his touch was affecting her and how broken she suddenly felt inside.

"You had better make it a good one. Because I can read the look in your eyes."

She made herself say the words. "I don't want to marry you."

"I can't argue with that," he said, letting her go. "But I'm not giving up on you. I'll get you the next time around."

Her heart soared at his words. He left her, started pacing back and forth in the enclosure. She raised the sleeve of her rain jacket, saw that his fingers had bruised her skin.

"What's the real reason, Carrie?" he said, turning back to her. "We don't have to have a ceremony. And you'll never be obligated to do anything you don't want to do." He stopped speaking and turned his back on her. "And we should check on them. We really should check on them."

They did not speak on the way down. She followed him down the hill but went to the left, towards the majority of the girls' tents, while he went to the right.

"Warm and dry?" she asked outside the first tent, then moved on after receiving an affirmative response. After she had made her rounds she hesitated, then went to Ralph's tent. He was standing outside, looking up at the sky, and did not notice her immediately.

"How are the boys?" she asked.

"Fine," he said, the anger gone from his voice. "The girls?"

"They're fine," she said.

"Goodnight, Carrie." He ducked into his tent.

She shivered as she listened to the tent's zipper closing him off from her, then went to her tent and closed herself in. She stripped out of her wet clothes and tossed them into the vestibule, then laid down inside her dry sleeping bag. She focused her attention on the sound of the rain gently knocking against the tent, the solidness of the earth beneath her, and her gratitude that the storm had passed over them without inflicting any injuries. But these thoughts expired, and she quietly cried herself to sleep.

The next day was the hardest for her. She slipped into the driest clothes she had and went outside to greet a morning that was cold and unforgiving. She saw Ralph tying a rope between some trees and went to him.

"Good morning, Carrie," he said when he saw her, then turned back to his work.

"What are you doing?" She was glad that their was no open hostility in his voice, and in the early morning light his proposal seemed as unreal as the storm.

"I'm hanging up a clothesline," he said. "When the kids get up they'll need it, and the sooner the sun dries their clothes, the sooner we'll be able to get moving. Did you sleep well?"

She nodded. He handed her a skein of rope.

"Here. You can help me."

She took the rope and watched his hands—strong, capable—then moved away and repeated the action, waiting for his approval. He came to stand by her, not close enough, and nodded.

"Good," he said, and paused. "I meant to tell you last night that you did a good job with the kids, but I got distracted. Go around to the other side and keep tying the knots until you run out of rope."

After the campers got up and filled the clothesline with their dripping belongings, Ralph led them along the path they had taken the day before to get to the vista, but made a different turn. They came out into an area along the edge of the woods where a waterfall, swelled from the rain, cascaded down in deafening sprays of white foam.

"If we came here yesterday," Ralph said, as the students looked on, "we could have played where that water is falling now. But there are some natural pools if you go farther down. Feel free to explore the surrounding woods if you don't want to swim."

More frequently, Carrie found she went off by herself—never far, and the campers always knew where to find her. But the more time she spent by herself, the more she found she also liked to be around the other members of the group. She went where she felt called to go—but if someone followed her there, she welcomed the company. She stayed on the outcrops of rock near the edge of the pool where some of the students were swimming, and she watched the insects dancing across the surface. She let the blank unconsciousness of nature steal over her mind until she saw someone come up beside her.

"Do you ever turn over rocks?" Chris asked her. "Sometimes you can find creatures if you do."

He reached into the stream and carefully tilted up a rock. "I don't like showing people because they'll hurt what I find. Not always intentionally, sometimes they just want to move it to show other people. But I can show you. Here, look."

She left her spot and went to where he was, and she looked at the surface of the rock he had turned over.

"That little squiggle is a planaria," he said. "We learned about them in biology. You can catch them if you put raw meat in a container and put it in a muddy area. If you cut off a part of their bodies, they can regenerate it. But I didn't do that, because planaria have simple nerve systems, and they can feel pain."

"What is that?" Carrie asked, pointing to a clump of pebbles surrounded by what looked like a green leaf.

"Probably some kind of larvae." Chris brushed the stones off. The leaf-like creature fell into his hand, uncurled and revealed itself to be a worm. Carrie grimaced, but Chris let the larva crawl across his palm.

He watched the tiny creature's progress. "They were born in a shape that earns them so much hate from everyone, and the saddest point of it all is that they aren't *ugly*. Really look at him, Carrie. See his eyes, his tiny little feet? And he's such an awesome shade of green. If people would only look they would realize how amazing this little larva is." He put the larva back onto the rock where it curled up, then put the rock back in place. He stood, then paused. "I don't want to go back."

She watched as he skipped a rock across the water's surface. "You don't miss anything from back home?"

"I miss Miranda." He paused. "Nature's a retreat, but I don't belong here. For as much as I love it here, I am a human being, and I have a duty to my fellow human beings."

"Your only duty is to yourself, Chris."

"I know you believe that. But I can't. It's too egotistical. I have to help other people for my life to have meaning." He paused. "I didn't know I would miss Miranda this much. She doesn't even think I care about her."

"Why does she think that?"

He watched the striders skimming the surface, then turned to her. "I stayed distant from Miranda because I didn't want to hurt her. I thought she understood that, but she thought it was because I had stopped liking her and I didn't want to be near her."

"Tell her when you get back."

"I will," he said. "I was waiting to make sure I really feel the way I think I do, because so often I feel blinded, unconnected from what I really think at all. But out here there's nothing to confuse me, and last night in the storm, when I stood up, it's like the rain beat away all this extraneous stuff, and all I could think about was her."

"You helped a lot of people last night by acting the way you did."

He looked at her blankly. "Were people afraid?"

"I was afraid." She skimmed her finger along the water, sending a water strider skittering. "I was afraid of dying, or of someone getting hurt."

"Maybe you were afraid because something isn't right in your life, and you need to fix it before you can face the unknown in peace."

"Maybe," she said. "Maybe I'm more out of touch with myself than I thought."

"That's why it's important to come out here," he said. "But also why it's important to talk to other people. It never hurts to get a different perspective." He paused. "You should talk to Mr. Palmer. He might have reasons that would startle you for doing what he did."

"He's always been very kind and encouraging, Chris."

"Not always."

Her heart lurched with his words. "What are you talking about?"

"He told me he was going to propose to you," Chris said, looking intently back at the water. "I hope he already has, because if not then I just spoiled the surprise."

"When did you talk to him?" Carrie said, startled, then, "Why would he tell you before he asked me?"

"Maybe he was asking for my help," Chris said. "Since you're both acting like children about this." He paused. "I suppose you rejected him. Did you *want* to?"

"I want to know when you talked to Mr. Palmer. And I want to know what else you said."

Chris shrugged.

She looked at him. "I have reasons, good reasons, for acting as I did."

"I just don't want you to wake up some day and regret that you didn't act when you had the chance." He looked directly at her. "I have two questions I want to ask you."

"Go ahead."

"How would you feel if he settled down with someone else?"

"It would only prove that I was right to stick to my guns," she said, affected.

"That was my second question," Chris said. "Do you really want to be alone, or do you simply like the image of being a lone wolf? Because if you act against what you really want, nothing good ever happens."

She took a deep breath. "Right now I'm confused. When the confusion clears up, I won't leave him hanging. But it would be unfair to promise him anything before then, Chris."

"If that's your main reservation," he said quietly, "You should talk to him. False assumptions cause people to make the biggest mistakes of their lives. And don't you want to know what I was talking about earlier?"

"You're being very cryptic."

"I don't mean to be," he said, standing. "I didn't know if I should talk to you or not, but we ended up in the same place and you seemed sad. I'm sorry if I disturbed you."

"You didn't disturb me."

He looked at her, uncertain, then started down the path. She thought about what he had said. Fifteen feet away from her, Chris emerged from the woods and went to stand pensively by the water's edge. From her vantage point, Carrie saw the other camper before Chris did; Becky crept up on him from behind and made a bird call, and when Chris turned around, she gave him about half a second to react before she pushed him into the pool, then jumped in after him. When Chris came back to the surface Becky was already laughing. Chris tackled her and forced her under the water; she re-emerged sputtering. Ralph, who had directed his attention to them by that point, made a comment—incoherent to Carrie in the distance—which set Chris and Becky laughing. Carrie, watching, could not help but smile.

The rest of the trip passed without incident. Before Carrie was completely ready to leave, they had hiked out of Dolly Sods. After reentering civilization, Carrie was surprised by how easily and readily she accepted the change. Yet she could not be at her ease, because before the end of the trip, there was something momentous she needed to do. Until it was done, she would have no peace.

They arrived back at the school late on Monday night. While the campers called their parents and waited with Ralph, Carrie drove Chris home, neither one of them saying much. She dropped him off and went back to the school to find that the five remaining students looked fit to drop. The adventurous spirit in them sated, they wanted to return to their houses and their beds, their televisions and their radios. While she waited, she glanced occasionally at Ralph. He also looked exhausted, his lean face haggard with fatigue, but there was a restless energy in his eyes. Only when the last student had left did he turn to her.

"I have to drive the van back," he said. "Will you follow in your car, and then give me a ride back here?"

She nodded, and fifteen minutes later they approached the lane to the school they had left. She hesitated in the parking lot, then put the car in neutral and pulled up on the emergency brake. "I want to talk to you."

He paused in the act of unlatching his seatbelt and looked at her. "About?"

She took a deep breath. "I want to marry you."

He sat up straighter. "You changed your mind?"

"I said I wanted to marry you. I didn't say that I would."

"Dashed be my hopes," he said, settling back into his seat. "But I'm not talking to you about this in a car in a deserted parking lot. Let's go for a walk."

She parked the car, got out shakily. He glanced at her, then instinctively took her hand.

"Neither of us have any idealizations about marriage," he said. "Which is why I think it could work, in our case."

She glanced away from him, focusing her attention on the road.

"I will not swear to obey you," she said. "I will not take you for better or worse."

"You've done your homework," he said, smiling.

"Please be serious."

"I'm serious," he said, quietly. "I apologize for interrupting."

She thought carefully about her words. "I will never belong to you. I retain my right to my own mind, body, and spirit, and my right to leave you if you ever try to make me compromise."

"I already told you I'd never make you do anything you didn't want to," he said, then paused in response to the look she gave him. "You have to leave me room for rejoinders."

"Fair enough," she said, relenting.

"Continue with the ultimatum."

"I don't want a ceremony. No cake, no flowers, no hiring a priest or a limousine. And I would feel ridiculous in a wedding dress. Like a doll. The thought makes me shudder."

"I understand," he said. "We'll get registered and sign the papers in our street clothes." He paused. "Anything so that it doesn't seem like we're actually married."

She glanced at him. "That's not what I—"

"The ceremony means nothing to me," he said.

"There's something you should know." She paused. "I'm afraid I'm going to wake up one morning and feel like I've compromised, and that I'm going to leave without giving you a moment's notification."

He considered. "Carrie, would you respect my right to do the same thing? To get out, if I felt like I was compromising myself?"

"Of course," she said.

"Then I see no problem with that condition."

"I have one final reservation."

"Let's hear it."

She turned and faced him, her eyes piercing. "I don't want you to change. I don't want this marriage to compromise you."

"Thank you," he said. Then, "You're aware, Carrie, that I will do as I please. You don't have to approve or support me, but you have to respect that I'll make my own decisions."

"Conceded."

"Conceited? Yes, I am."

"Point conceded. I meant that—"

"I know what you meant, Carrie. I was trying to lighten the mood. I feel as though we're discussing the terms of our death warrants."

She relaxed, if only slightly. "What else?"

"Have you thought about children? Because I want to be a father, at some point in my life. And I want the child to be my own."

She hesitated. "I want to have a son. But under no circumstances am I naming him Ralph. I care for you dearly, but your name is simply horrible."

He turned to her, saw a hint of amusement in her eyes before she sobered. She looked at him levelly. "If we bring a child into this world, circumstances being as they are, I will stand by that child before everything else. Before myself. Before you."

"So be it," he said. "Then there's only one other potential obstacle."

"What?" Her eyes tore into him, impatient now that she had all but committed herself.

"I need to know if you trust me," he said.

She walked a pace away from him, agitated. He watched, giving her time to decide, every moment of her indecision painful to him. Finally, she came back.

"I can't say that I trust you. But I trust you more than I've ever trusted another human being." She paused. "Will that do?"

"It will," he said, after a pause. "Now this has all been very nice and formal, but all I want to do right now is kiss you."

She put her hand against his chest to prevent him but he overpowered her, and she wrapped her arms around his neck and kissed him.

"So we're engaged," he said, grinning. "How soon would you like to be married?"

She turned her face away from him, unable to hide the blush in her cheeks, the smile that revealed how ridiculously happy she felt. "Is there a reason to wait?"

"Scandalous," he said. "But for your sake, I'll give you time to back out. How does the end of the school year sound? Summer marriages are supposed to be particularly lovely."

"April thirtieth."

"Why then?" The date was less than a month away.

"Because I can't wait any longer than that to be with you."

He looked at her, his eyes on fire, and suddenly something inside of her shrank—a distant warning sounding in her mind. The look in his eyes changed, and he scanned her face carefully.

"What, Carrie?"

"You have my promise," she said softly.

"And you have mine." He raised her hand to his lips, kissed her palm. "Goodnight, sweetheart. I'll see you tomorrow."

Carrie got into her car, haunted by the final look in his eyes. But as she drove home, she realized she did not feel the slightest doubt about what she had just done.

The end of March arrived. Carrie had not talked to him about their engagement since the night they had agreed on its terms, but she could tell by the way he looked at her, touched her, spoke to her, that he had no intention of backing down. Nor did she. The thought of their upcoming union and her certainty about it both exhilarated and terrified her.

On the first day of April, five days after the end of the camping trip, Carrie looked out her window as the yellow school buses drove away. She was filled with a sense of urgency and impatience. She wanted the thing finalized. She proceeded to his classroom in a frenzy.

The door to his room was closed; she knocked, and receiving no answer, went in.

"Ralph?" she called.

There was no response, but the door to his supply closet was ajar. She walked to the closet. She went inside, turned on the light switch, and stared.

The light dimmed; she turned. He was standing in the doorway, his face unreadable.

"It's Wednesday," he said. "We don't meet on Wednesdays."

She had gone pale. "You told me you stopped painting."

He stepped into the studio, blocking her exit. Her eyes flew over him—the apron flecked with paint, the pallette and tube of oil paint in his hand.

Suddenly she felt chillingly cold. She crossed her arms over her chest. "What else have you lied to me about?"

"I haven't lied to you."

"I asked you—"

"And I said that I had to make certain sacrifices that prevented me from living the life I wanted to lead. But I could never give up my painting. It's my curse." He smiled. "I'm surprised you're not happy to hear I've kept up with my art, Carrie."

"I can't marry you," she said. "Not if I can't trust you. And how can I trust you if you're going to bend the truth?"

He laid the palette and the paint down on a shelf beside him. He looked at her for a long time, and then he moved forward.

"You promised me," he said. The look in his eyes was wild, defiant.

She looked back at him. "Why didn't you tell me? Why are you hiding your talent again? You have all these paintings finished, the world is dying for your art, and you keep it locked up here—"

"Look at them, Carrie," he said, gesturing at the paintings. "They're depraved. Grotesque. A sane person couldn't have painted them."

He turned from her, closed his eyes and put his hand on his forehead. She stood watching him, then forced herself to move. She reached out her hand. Her fingers trembled as she touched his shoulder. He turned instantly towards her.

She paused. "I need to be able to trust you. If we're not honest with each other, then this relationship will never work."

"I've never lied to you," he said. "To the rest of the world—yes, I have lied. The rest of the world be damned. But I promised myself I would never lie to the woman I loved. And I knew, all those years ago..."

All of a sudden, she went numb. She couldn't think, she couldn't feel. She looked at him, fighting the emptiness that washed over her.

"I still want to marry you," he said. "I love you, Carrie."

"Do you want to go now?"

He stared at her. "Now?"

"You said we could be married in our street clothes."

"Carrie, do you realize what you're saying?"

"I gave you my promise," she said.

"I release you from your goddamn promise," he said. "You'd be putting your life in my hands…"

She looked at him levelly. "I've put my life in your hands every time we were in the wilderness. I trust you. I made my choice and I intend to go through with it."

A frenzied, half insane look came into his eyes, and he grabbed her hand in a grip that hurt. "Carrie, if you're in earnest, let's go now."

So they went. He signed the papers rashly, became impatient when she took her time and read every word of the documents. Yet she would not let his impatience pressure her, and when she finally signed her name below his, she did so with certainty and self-possession, her eyes following the papers as they disappeared for the records. She turned to him. With her signature his brow had cleared, his face relaxed. The light in his eyes had lost some of its intensity, but there was a leer on his lips that she did not like. She had to stop herself from flinching as he took her hand.

"How do you feel about this?" he asked.

"It was what I expected." She studied him. "Are you upset?"

"No. I'm the happiest man alive. Now that you're my wife."

She did not care for the word. As he turned to her again she saw that same look in his eyes, a look she understood but did not like.

His grip on her hand was painful. "Let's go home."

She knew what would come next and wondered if her sudden, strong feelings of revulsion were indicative that she had made a mistake after all.

As soon as they arrived at his apartment, she felt the weight of his expectation. There was no hesitation, no spontaneity, no gentle words. His naked need…and hers. She undressed, and he paused only long enough to take off his clothes. She cried out in pain when he entered her, then waited for the act to be done. Finally he collapsed onto her and felt her shuddering. He held her in his arms and felt her blood on his thighs;

he realized the comfort she took from his warmth as she curled her body against his. As she lay in his arms, as he looked at the face he had loved for so long, he realized he was more afraid than he had ever been in his life.

She woke in the middle of the night to find his arm carelessly around her waist, his breath hot on the back of her neck. She went to stand in front of his window, wanting to leave. She opened one of the slats in his blinds, looked out at the night and the full moon. She stood for a moment, the silver moonlight filtering into the room and staining her skin, and then she turned and looked at him—a dark, vague shape barely discernable in the shadows of the room. She let the blind slip back into place, stopping it from clattering against the others so she would not disturb him. She watched him as she slipped into her clothes. She was scared, but she also remembered how he had been when it was over, when she was exhausted and shaking, feeling torn open and exposed. He had kissed her gently on the forehead, he had held her in his arms until her shaking had passed. She had felt safe. She felt mildly ashamed of what they had done, and she was afraid to be there when he woke. But she went back to the bed and she crawled into his arms, and she fell asleep listening to the beating of his heart.

He woke at 5 A.M. as he always did. He had feared that she would disappear in the middle of the night but she was there, sleeping beside him. He cleaned the room quietly, then went about his morning routine—shower, paper, lesson plans, coffee. He wanted to let her sleep; he knew how tired she was and he didn't want to be there when she woke up.

"Good morning," she said, startling him. He turned, saw her standing behind him in the kitchen, wrapped in the white terry cloth robe he had left out for her.

"Glad you're awake," he said, trying not to stare at the swells of her breasts visible through the gap in the robe. "I thought you might sleep in."

She came to stand beside him. "I smelled the coffee."

"Do you want some?"

She leaned against the counter. "Since it's already made."

He handed her a mug.

"I know I bled, Ralph," she said, reluctantly. "But I didn't see—"

"I washed the sheets before you woke up."

She looked at him. "Thank you. I'm sorry you had to do that."

"*I'm* not." He paused. "How do you feel?"

She set the mug he had given her down on the kitchen counter. "I didn't like it. I think it was the expectation. I didn't like how planned out it felt."

"That was because we waited," he said, disappointed.

She paused. "I'd like to try again," she said, stepping up to him. "Without all of that."

He picked her up and put her on the counter. His mouth was hot on her skin; her body seemed to melt into his. He smothered his smile in her hair as she wrapped her arms around his neck, then carried her into their bedroom.

"Carrie," he said, two weeks later. "You're glowing."

She sat up, put her hand on the side of his face. "You're a beautiful man."

He sighed. "Most men don't like being called beautiful, Carrie. We prefer handsome, manly—"

She laughed. "I could hardly care. You're beautiful."

He turned to her, surprised. Her eyes were brilliant, her cheeks red like the blush of a newly opening rose. "I'm glad you're happy."

"Oh my god," she said suddenly. "We had to be at the school half an hour ago."

He left her scrambling in the bedroom and went back to the kitchen. He picked up his coffee, sipped it slowly. She came out five minutes later, her hair brushed, her face washed, in her waitressing uniform—the only other clothes she had stashed in her car when she had followed him home to his apartment the night before. He looked her over, amused, and turned away with a smile.

"You might want to remove your name tag," he said. "If you insist on wearing that."

She glanced down, unpinned the plate from over her left breast and looked at him. "If we leave now, and you drive about seventy miles an hours, we'll be able to make it to the school before the first bell rings."

"Carrie," he said. "It's Saturday."

"What?"

"Saturday," he repeated.

She tackled him, then. He pinned her to the ground, held her until her laughter had quieted; then, he made love to her again.

The school year slipped by, ended. She continued waitressing in the evenings, though she told him she planned on quitting as soon as she landed a full time teaching position.

She was working an evening shift, counting down the time until she could be with him again, when she looked up and saw Tessa—visibly pregnant—walking towards her.

"Hi, Carrie," Tessa said, noticing the direction of Carrie's eyes. "About four months. I know, surprise."

A little girl of about two years old—her blonde hair sticking out from her head in pigtails—bounded up and hugged Tessa around the legs, almost knocking her off balance.

"Kindra." A look of pain crossed Tessa's face. "What has Mommy told you about..."

Carrie watched them, mother and child, with the faintest hint of repugnance, then glanced up as another person joined them. She recognized him immediately.

"Carrie?" His voice was deeper, but she recognized it as well. "Can it really be you? It's good to see you again, after all this time." He paused. "Tess told me you were in the area, but I'm surprised I haven't seen you before now."

"Sam is a politician now," Tessa said, bending over to tighten the little girl's pigtails. "He's a very busy man."

"And this is your little girl." Carrie stared at the child who had started acting like an angel as soon as Sam appeared.

Sam put his hand on the child's head, between the baubles. "This is Kindra."

"She's beautiful."

"Not when she's in terrible two mode," he said. "But thank you."

She had not realized how much she missed Sam until she saw him. She saw he was looking at her carefully, and recognized the look that came into his eyes. Sam had always listened carefully to her and given her his honest, objective opinion, and she wanted that now. The little girl had disappeared, unnoticed, until she returned with her face covered with marinara sauce and an empty plate balanced in her hands.

"All done, Mommy," she announced.

"Oh, Indy." Tessa took the plate, snatched a tiny hand in her perfectly manicured one. "Excuse me, Carrie. I don't mean to be rude, but we're going to go tidy up, aren't we?"

There was a pause as Tessa marshaled the little girl to the restroom. Sam looked at Carrie as if drinking in her features; she stared back, analyzing the changes the years had brought. Dressed in business attire, with a full beard and mustache, he should have been unrecognizable, though the warm concern in his eyes was distinctly Sam.

"You look like you're doing well," she said. "How have you been?"

"Good," he answered. "All things considered."

He glanced past her as Tessa led Kindra, cleaned, back to them.

"All done." Tessa released Kindra, who instantly went to Sam and hugged his leg. "Carrie, I know you haven't seen Sam for quite some time now, and I'm sure he's dying to catch up with you. And we should talk. I know how crazy summer can be, but if you have time, please come visit us."

Sam nodded. "Tess, does she have our address?"

"Carrie knows where we live," Tessa said. "She's been over before, when you've been out campaigning. Goodness, Kindra, *behave* yourself." Tessa turned on Sam abruptly. "You're not helping. How can you let her behave like this in public?"

The little girl had been trying to pickpocket his keys from his back pocket, and Sam had been laughing silently as he foiled her attempts. With Tessa's words he became solemn and picked Kindra up. After Tessa turned back to Carrie, he slipped the keys out of his pocket and handed them to the little girl, who held them above her head for a moment in victory and then set them clinking against each another.

"Tomorrow, even," Tessa said, looking disapprovingly at Kindra and Sam, who returned her gaze blandly. "We'd love the company."

"I can't, tomorrow," Carrie said. "I have a meeting. Planning for next year's Outdoors Club."

Tessa looked at her attentively. "How is that going? Are you and Ralph getting along?"

"We got married."

Sam's eyes went wider than Tessa's. "I never thought I'd see the day—"

"Don't be ridiculous," Tessa said. "If you saw them together, you'd know it was inevitable. Congratulations, Carrie." She paused. "We should be going. It's past Kindra's bedtime, and I don't want you to get in trouble."

"It was a pleasure to see you both again."

Tessa smiled, took hold of Kindra's hand and pulled her away from Sam. "Sam, I'm going to take Kindra out to the car. Would you mind taking care of the bill? Then I expect to see you, in the next five minutes."

Sam pulled out a wallet and removed several crisp bills, his face averted. He waited until Tessa had left with Kindra, then looked up.

"Take us up on our offer," he said. "I'm gone most of the day, and I doubt that Kindra, dear little angel that she is, would be Tessa's first choice for constant company."

"I'll stop by."

"Goodnight, Carrie," he said. "I look forward to seeing you soon."

She watched him leave, her mind clearing. Sam had been the one to help her through her previous confusions; she did not wonder why she felt so close to him. But if Sam had reappeared in her life, she realized he might have to help her again…or she would have to help him.

The Wildcards. What she lived for, though with Damien, she had already been dealt the largest one of her life.

She decided to pay them a visit the next day. She walked up to the front of Tessa's fairy house, then knocked. The silence that followed seemed as unnatural as her irregularly beating heart. She knocked again, without certainty, feeling relieved that no one was there to receive her, thinking maybe she hadn't really wanted to see him again. She was turning to leave when the door opened.

"Carrie!" The enthusiasm in Tessa's voice was ridiculously exaggerated. "How good of you to come here! I'm so sorry I took so long coming to the door. The truth is that I just was lying down to take a little nap and didn't hear the bell. *Do* come in."

"I'm sorry not to have called." Carrie stared at her. "I could come back, if this is a bad time—"

"Please don't go," Tessa whispered. "Sam isn't here right now, but I'd love for you to come in and chat. I just put Indy down for her nap, so we should be able to speak in peace…"

Carrie followed her into the house.

"Would you like some tea? I'm so sorry I don't have any ready—"

"But you didn't know I was coming."

Tessa smiled. "It will only take a moment, you know. I'll just go ahead and make you some. I've just had Sam buy me some imported white tea."

"Sit down, Tessa," Carrie said firmly. "Tell me what's wrong."

Tears started slipping down her face, but Tessa brushed them away and managed a smile. "I'm sure nothing is wrong. My hormones are acting up because of the pregnancy. I got this way when I had Kindra, too…"

"Are you lying to me?"

Tessa looked at her, and Carrie noticed for the first time the dark circles under her eyes. "Do you promise you won't tell Sam?"

"Everything you say to me will remain in strictest confidence, unless you give me explicit permission to tell him," she promised

"I don't want him to know," Tessa said. "He tries so hard to make me happy. He never complains about Kindra, and it's clear he loves her, and it's clear he still loves me because he's so gentle and kind…" She sighed. "I should never have married him, Carrie. I should never have married *anyone*. I can feel the winds changing, and here I am with a husband and a child and another one on the way…" She paused. "Carrie, I'm so sorry. You just got married and I'm telling you such depressing—"

"Shut up, Tessa."

Tessa smiled. "Thank you for coming over. I've really needed to talk to someone."

Carrie broke the silence that set in. "I didn't even know, until I saw you at the restaurant last night."

334

"That's one good thing about cold spring weather," she said. "Bulky sweaters can hide a lot, not that there's that much to hide right now."

Carrie paused. "I can help out, Tessa, if you ever need—"

She shook her head. "The sad part of this is that Kindra's not even a naughty child. Sam, when he's home, does a wonderful job taking care of her. But he and I talked last night—or rather, he planned out for me where he thinks we should go from here."

"And?"

Tessa swallowed. "He suggested I take a year off teaching, so I could be with him and the kids. But I *can't* stop teaching, Carrie; it's the only thing that keeps me sane. If I don't have somewhere else to go, if I have to stay imprisoned in this house with two children…" She paused. "He didn't say anything explicitly last night, but I know he wants *more*. But it's my body that has to carry the child…I'm sorry, Carrie, I'm a mess…"

Carrie slipped an arm around her, waited while Tessa dried her eyes and composed herself. They sat for a moment in silence, and then Tessa spoke, calmly.

"I told you I was afraid this might happen."

"You did."

"And you told me not to worry. Until later. Well, it's later." Tessa pushed herself away. "I know I shouldn't ask you. I know the choice is mine. But I've been so tired lately that I can't think straight. What do you think I should do now?"

"I think you should do what you need to do."

Tessa smiled, slightly. "The funniest thing is that Sam has no idea. He thinks everything is perfect, that everything is fine. And why should he think otherwise? He's the *model* husband…" She stopped speaking abruptly and sat up straighter. "That will be Sam, getting back…"

Carrie had not heard anything, but presently a key turned in the lock, and Tessa turned to the door expectantly.

"Perfect timing, dear," she said, as Sam walked into the living room. "Sam, Carrie's here."

"So I see," he said, nodding at Carrie in acknowledgment as he went to Tessa and gently kissed her cheek. "How was your day, love? Has Kindra behaved herself?"

"She's sleeping. Sam, I was just telling Carrie how much you'd like to take her to Café Michel tonight. You'd like that, wouldn't you, dear?"

Sam frowned. "You and I were supposed to go out tonight. I called Mrs. Lamberry to take care of Kindra…"

"But you didn't know that Carrie would stop by," Tessa said. "And I absolutely insist."

"Then you should come with us," Sam said, his eyes troubled. "You deserve a break from being in the house." He paused, then looked from Tessa's unrelenting gaze to Carrie. "You wouldn't like Café Michel, Carrie."

"Nonsense," Tessa said, firmly. "She'll love it. Carrie, I'll pick out something for you to wear and then I'll take Indy to her Grandma's. Carrie, I'm sure that something I own would fit you."

"I'll wear what I have on," Carrie said, confused. "But thank you for the offer."

"Then Sam will have to dress down."

"Honey," he said. "It's Café Michel. My business associates might…" He broke off. "All right. If it will make you happy."

Tessa smiled. "Why don't you have Carrie sign her book, before you go?" She turned. "Carrie, he's followed your work. He told all our friends about your first novel. Would you be so kind to sign this copy for him, Carrie? He would be *so* happy if you would."

Carrie took the copy of her novel that Sam handed her. "Do you have a pen?"

"Right here." Tessa handed her an old-fashioned ballpoint pen. She took the book from Carrie as she finished signing it, then handed it to Sam. "There, dear."

Sam stared at Tessa. "Are you all right, honey?"

"I think I need some time to be alone tonight." She paused. "If you'll just take Carrie to Café Michel, and I'll take Kindra to her Grandma's…" She walked out of the room, came back holding a sleepy Kindra. "I'll take the van. Be back by eight."

With the click of the door she was gone.

"She means she'll be back here by eight, in case I need to get in contact with her," Sam said, distracted. "Carrie, you won't like Café Michel. It's an upscale gourmet restaurant that I absolutely loathe. I don't even know if they have any vegetarian options."

"Why does Tessa want us to go there so badly, if you dislike the restaurant so much?"

Sam shrugged. "Occasionally Tessa gets a spontaneous idea and goes with it. Her intuition is usually accurate."

"Then let's go."

"If you're sure." He glanced at her. "Let me change."

As he headed towards the back of the house she looked around the kitchen, noticing the stick figure drawings on the refrigerator and the cheerful domestic touches—flowers, a porcelain hanging reading *Home Sweet Home,* candles on the table. Sam came back in jeans and a polo shirt, a perplexed look on his face. He remained withdrawn as they drove to the restaurant, and seemed oblivious to the scandalized look the elegantly dressed hostess gave them.

"Two," he said. "Non-smoking."

The hostess reluctantly showed them to a corner of the back room, where she left them without another word. The interior of the restaurant—red table cloths, long white taper candles burning brightly on each table, golden chandeliers dazzling in the center of the ceiling—made Carrie nervous to look at the menu. She grimaced.

"They want eight dollars for a side salad, Sam," she said.

"Don't worry," he said. "I'm paying."

A waiter, dressed completely in black, moved to their table, and Sam spoke before Carrie could protest.

"Paul? Do you have any vegetarian options?"

"I am sure that Antonio could fix Mademoiselle a masterpiece," the waiter said.

"I would be fine with pasta," Carrie said.

"Very good." Paul hesitated, then took the menu from her. He turned expectantly to Sam.

"Pasta for me as well," he said. "You still don't drink, do you Carrie? Then two waters, as well."

"Very good," Paul repeated, and moved off.

Sam looked down at the linen tablecloth in front of him. "Did Tessa say what was bothering her?"

"I think you should talk to her yourself, Sam."

"I've tried." He looked tired. "She always says that everything is fine, that I'm a wonderful husband and that she has no reason to be unhappy." He looked at her. "I genuinely love Tessa, and she knows that. I don't understand why she can't be honest with me."

"What do you think the problem might be?"

He paused. "I really don't understand why she's so unhappy. I have a good job. We have a beautiful home, and a beautiful and healthy little girl and another child on the way. I give her everything she asks for. We've never argued in the four years we've been married, and I'm not aware of ever having said a harsh word to her. She tells me everything is fine, but she closes off more and more. She watches what she says to me and how she acts. And she doesn't sing anymore. She used to sing all the time, when we were first married. I don't know why that bothers me so much, but it does. It wasn't that she has a particularly beautiful voice—she doesn't—but I loved to listen to her sing, because I thought it meant she was happy..."

"When did she start to withdraw from you?"

"Around the time Kindra was born." He kept his eyes down. "I was in California when she went into labor—a month prematurely. I wasn't able to make it back in time, and she delivered our child alone. The birth went smoothly, no complications, and Kindra is a darling child. And I've cut down my work hours so I can be an active father. But none of it seems to matter. I don't think Tessa can forgive me for not being there when she needed me." He paused. "I hate to tell you this, but marriage can really strain a relationship."

She smiled. "Then I'll have quite roller coaster ride in the upcoming years."

The lull in their conversation was broken by Paul, who dropped off the side salads that accompanied their meals and disappeared.

"Tell me about him," Sam said. "About your husband."

"I wouldn't know where to begin."

"What does he do? How did you meet?"

"He teaches at the high school where I work. He's an artist in his spare time."

"The last person you fell in love with was an artist as well, wasn't he?"

"Yes."

He stared at her, then put down his fork. "Carrie."

"I love him, Sam." She paused. "He goes by Ralph Palmer now."

"He changed his name?"

"He didn't want to be haunted by his past. He's changed from since you last knew him."

"You love him enough to defend him," Sam said. "That will have to be enough for me. Here's our pasta. Looks delicious, Paul."

"Very good, sir. May I get you something else?"

Sam glanced at her; she shook her head. "No. Just the check, at your convenience."

"The meal has been paid for in full, sir."

Sam arched his eyebrows at Carrie. "How did you arrange for—"

"I didn't pay the bill, Sam."

Perplexed, he turned to Paul. "Was it my wife, Paul? Did she call in, and—"

"No, sir. That gentleman, sir, over there. With compliments to the lady, that she looks beautiful tonight." Paul paused. "His words, you understand, Mademoiselle."

"Thank you," she said.

Sam scanned the restaurant. "Did you see who he—"

She did.

"Carrie," Ralph said, coming up to them and catching her eye. "Did that genial waiter pass on the compliment that you are looking exceedingly lovely tonight?"

"I thought you were staying at your studio for awhile," she said, then realized how her words had sounded. She turned quickly. "Sam, this is my husband."

"Damien DeMatteo," Sam growled.

"Ralph, if you please." He turned to Carrie. "You should have said husband of the moment, my dear. I do believe Sam means to take you away from me."

"Have you been drinking?" Carrie asked, smelling the bourbon on his breath. "I thought you told me you stopped."

"Just a little, sweetheart." He shifted his attention to Sam. "You must excuse her lack of self-possession. I'm sure Carrie didn't expect to see me here tonight."

"Maybe you and I should talk," she started.

Ralph leaned forward, his face inches from hers. He kept his dark eyes on her, his voice low. "I trust you, Carrie. Only because you're too damn honest to be disloyal to me. I assume you're enjoying your dinner?"

Sam glanced at her, then refocused his attention on Ralph, without affinity. "I'm going to pay you for the meals."

"I can support my wife, thank you."

"Then perhaps I could buy you a drink," Sam said, his eyes locked on Ralph's. "Unless you've had too much already."

"Damned if I did. Carrie, I'll see you at home."

"I'll go with you," she said, her eyes never leaving his face—the face that, because of the alcohol, had resumed its wolfish features. There was a sharp light in his eyes, a rough gravel note in his voice. "I'll—"

"She said you had changed," Sam said. "It doesn't seem to me like you've changed at all."

He leered at Sam. "Perhaps I'm a bit drunk. I'll take my shameful self away. Goodnight, dear lady and Sir Lancelot."

"Let me drive you home," Carrie said. "Sam, we really should drive him home…."

Sam nodded. Carrie directed him to Ralph's apartment then helped Ralph out.

"I'm sorry, Sam," she said, through the window.

She felt his eyes on her as she walked Ralph to the front door. She heard Sam drive away, then turned to search his scathing stare.

"Did I embarrass you?" he asked, leaning against the wall.

"We'll talk later." She looked away from him. "You're going to have to take me to pick up my car tomorrow, from Tessa's."

He looked at her, and she looked away. He passed out in their bedroom, and Carrie fell asleep on the sofa that night.

When she woke she found him in the kitchen in his flannel and plaid robe, coffee in hand, his profile rigid and straight, she realized—in a flash—that something about him had changed.

"Good morning, sunshine," he said, not turning around.

Her heart skipped. "What time is it?"

"10:30," he said. "Relax, Carrie. We don't have anything to do today."

"But I've wasted the whole morning. And when I sleep in this late I always feel terrible."

He turned to her. "I need to talk to you."

She glanced at him as he came to sit by her. "About last night?"

"I told you I wasn't perfect," he said. "Sometimes I relapse."

"For no reason?"

"For no reason," he repeated. "Of course not for no reason." He paused. "I found something in our garbage can after I got back from the studio last night."

She looked at him.

He paused. "You're pregnant."

She took hold of his hand, suddenly uneasy. "This wasn't how I planned on telling you."

"Carrie…" he dropped her hand, stood, started pacing. "I can't be a father."

She looked at him levelly. "You said you wanted children."

"I've made so many mistakes in my life." He walked away from her. "I thought I had changed, but when I found out last night I panicked and—"

"You got drunk," she said, unbelievingly. "At Café Michel."

"I meet people there occasionally from my artistic circle." He looked at her. "Last night I didn't know where you were, and I didn't know where else to go."

Her eyes searched his. "It's not going to be the same story over again. We're so much older now. Last night was the first time you've gotten drunk, since marrying me." She paused. "That I know about, at least."

"I think I'm going to need some help," he said quietly. "Especially with the parenting…"

"That's why we're doing this together."

"I want to be a good father."

She looked into his eyes, and for the first time, she realized how afraid he was.

"You will be," she said, and kissed him.

He changed as her pregnancy progressed. He stopped smoking. He made sure she ate more healthily; he conferred with Dr. Stoddard—her obstetrician—about how much she should exercise to stay in optimal health. Yet he gave her the space she needed. And Carrie never had to worry about whether the child would be a source of tension between them. Ralph glorified in her changing body, and the very thought of fatherhood elevated his spirits. The biggest source of contention between them was over the gender of the unborn child.

She returned from shopping one night to find him pacing around their apartment.

"Carrie," he said. "I can't."

Her heart sank, and her hand went instinctively to her stomach. Her eyes fixed on him—steel.

"You can't do what," she said, softly.

He stopped pacing. "I can't keep calling the child 'it.' We have to name him or her." He crossed the room, handed her a sheet of paper. "I looked up some names. I want to know what you think."

She followed him to the couch and sat down, then glanced over the list of names. She flipped the paper and stared at the empty back.

"Where are the boys' names?"

He stared at her blankly. "I didn't look up any."

"You really want a daughter, don't you?"

He paused. "What do you think of the names?"

She put her hands over the paper. "I should tell you something."

"None of them are right," he said, and stood abruptly. "I knew it."

"They're beautiful names," Carrie said. "But there's a tradition in my family…"

"What is it?" he said. "Of course we'll follow it."

"The child's name has to begin with a C," Carrie said, then paused. "But it's really a silly tradition. I like these names. Elena is pretty, and Isadora sounds unique…"

He started pacing again, then his face cleared. He came back to her, grabbed her hand.

"Carmen," he said. "If the baby is a girl, let's name her Carmen."

Something about the name made her uneasy. "How did you think of it?"

"She was a gypsy," he said. "Independent, clever, manipulative, wildly free."

"You want our daughter to be like that?"

"I want her to be able to take care of herself," he said. "I want her to be able to stand up for herself and to be able to fight against all odds."

She looked at him, startled by his intensity.

"I can't make you understand," he said, pacing. "I have to show you. Stay here."

"Where else would I go?" she asked as he headed for the door. "Where are you going?"

He shook his head and left her. She closed the door after him. She took a shower and changed into pajamas, and was sitting at the table looking over his scribbled list of names when he came back and handed her a thin rectangular box.

She spent the next two hours and forty-five minutes cuddled on the couch with him in his dimly lit apartment, her head nestled on his shoulder and his arm loosely around her as they watched Georges Bizet's opera, *Carmen*.

"What did you think?" he asked her, immediately after the final aria.

"It was amazing," she said, still enraptured.

He put his hand on her stomach. "I mean for our child, Carrie."

"The way she died," she said. "Murdered by a crazed ex-lover."

"Think rather of how she lived," he said. "Without fear. She even faced death with defiance."

She looked into his earnest eyes and thought of Carmen's fierce independence, her blatant disregard for conventional rules, her extreme self-assertion, her fearlessness, her will to get what she wanted, her violent fight for a gypsy's freedom. "What does the name mean?"

"Song," he said. "Or less commonly, a poem. I thought you would like that, since you write and you like to sing. Our child would have to write the verses to her own song…"

They decided to name the child Carmen, if the child were a girl.

The child was due to arrive the following January. Carrie resented the possibility that she might not have the choice of teaching full time for another year, but she wanted to raise the child herself. Though she had not wanted to become a mother so soon, she was enjoying the pregnancy and the surprises it had already brought.

Every night, Ralph wanted to talk about the future: how they would budget a combined income, whether they should buy a house, what they should start looking into in terms of setting up a trust fund for Carmen.

"And we should talk about how we should raise her," he said, his hand tracing figure eights on the small of her back. "And whether or not you'd be willing to stay home full time."

"I want to teach."

He paused. "Do you really need to work? I make enough from my art and teaching to support us—the three of us—if we aren't extravagant."

"I like working." She began to understand the panic Tessa had voiced to her.

He thought in silence, one arm behind his head, the other loosely around her waist. "What about this, Carrie? If you stay at home with Carmen, you can spend most of your day writing. Those will be your only two responsibilities: being a writer and being a mother."

"And you don't think she'll interrupt my writing? Children are a lot of work. And I don't want to be alone all day in the house, if we buy one. Can we go to sleep? We don't need to figure out everything tonight."

"What if I'm a bad influence on her?" he asked. "What if I can't be a good father?"

"You'll be fine," she said, wanting to go to sleep. "I'm not letting you raise her by yourself. I'll be here."

"I've fucked up so many times," he said. "But I was the only person who had to deal with the consequences. Or you. But an innocent little child who automatically trusts me because I'm her father…"

"We'll do the best we can," she said, losing patience with him. "We can't know the future, and even should Carmen come to hate us or the choices we make for her, we'll know we had the best intentions. *We* will. Together. We're in this together now."

His only response was to pull her closer to him and keep her locked to his side. "You've given me something to live for."

His words melted her anger. She kissed him gently. "I love you."

"Really?" he asked, sarcastically.

She laughed; she couldn't help herself. "It's complicated. It's always been complicated. But it's always been there, and this time, you went about it the right way."

"I even asked you on a date."

"Yes. You did." She put her head on his chest.

"And to think I almost lost you," he continued.

She paused. "What if I lose the child? Would you still love me?"

"Don't talk about that," he said, so sharply that his words stung her.

"It happens," she said, looking up at the ceiling. "I'm being practical. You're the one who wants to think practically with your talk of college trust funds and—"

"Is something wrong with that?"

"No."

"I'm sorry," he said coolly, withdrawing his arm from around her. "When you said that, about losing our child, did you want me to say something romantic like 'I'd still have you'?"

"It would have been nice," she said, nettled.

"For as much as the thought scares the hell out of me, I really want this child." He paused. "But I would still love you, Carrie. I don't know how you could doubt that."

She relaxed. "Of course I want her to be born beautiful, healthy, and strong. But we have to acknowledge the possibility that something might go wrong."

"No, we don't." He turned to her, and in the moonlight that filtered into the room, she could see his eyes burning. "You say you want our child, but do you really? Do you really want someone who's going to impinge on your freedom?"

"What are you saying?" she said, aghast. "Are you implying I would do something to harm my baby?"

He sat up. "Would you have come up with that accusation if you hadn't already been thinking about—"

"Don't touch me." She moved away from him. "I wouldn't have even thought about it had you not accused me."

"I didn't accuse you of anything."

She stared at him. "You've never hurt me as much as you did just now. Nothing you've ever done—"

"Forget I said anything about it," he said, turning on his side and facing away from her.

"You think I would hurt my child." Her eyes were still wide with horror. "I can't forget that you'd think me capable of harming my child."

"Our child," he said. "Goodnight."

She paused, then lay back down and faced the opposite side of the room, uncontrollable tears splotching the pillow beneath her. She felt cold, and she tried to do what he had encouraged her to do—forget. But she tried to forget him, tried to forget that the man beside her was legally her husband. Tried to picture that, once again, she was by herself, alone in bed late at night....

"Carrie." The way he said her name was like a ghost shivering in the coldness of the room. "Are you awake?"

Ten minutes, maybe, had elapsed since he had last spoken to her. She let another minute drag by while she decided whether she should answer him. Then she said, "I'm not going to be able to sleep tonight."

"I'm sorry," he said.

His words hung in the oppressive air, and she shivered.

"I don't want us to argue," he said, more loudly.

She turned to him. "But I like arguing."

"We can argue about philosophy, about our expenses…but not like this," he said. "Not where one of us shuts down and refuses to talk. It's no precedent to set, when we have such a long road ahead of us."

He fell silent and she lay listening to the sound of the cicadas singing outside of his window. She put his arm around her and snuggled into him. He bowed his head so his chin rested on top of her hair, and she fell asleep. When she woke in the morning, he was gone.

She wandered around his apartment that morning, feeling lost, wondering where he had gone and why. She made coffee, she pulled out her notebook, she sat down on his sofa; then she began to write. She lost track of time; she didn't hear him enter the room, didn't know he was there until he spoke.

"Carrie."

She looked up, alarmed by the tone of his voice, and found him staring at her intensely, a look like lust in his eyes. His entire body was charged, trembling with energy; his hair was disheveled, he was only in his boxers, and his bare skin was streaked with various colors of paint.

"Come here," he said, grabbing her hand.

Her notebook fell open onto the floor. She stumbled after him, trying to keep her robe closed and belted. "Where have you been?"

"Never mind, never mind," he said, pulling her out onto the balcony that connected to the apartment, and then to a door in the wall outside. She had never noticed it, had never been on the balcony before, had not known either was there because he always had the blinds shut and she had never thought to look. He threw open the door.

"I want you to see. It's the best thing I've ever done."

She drew aside the cloth sheet that covered the entrance and stepped into a medium-sized room that smelled strongly of oil and acrylic. She paused, afraid to move.

"Where's the light? I can't see anything."

He moved into the area from behind her, reached above her head. There was the grinding of a pull chain, a single click, and then the area was flooded with light. She found herself confronted by a life-sized canvas streaked in violent colors. A little girl, head lowered, sat on a swing in the foreground, beside a tree.

"It's a masterpiece," he said. "Every line, every color, every contour..."

She turned to him, saw the half-crazed awe and happiness in his eyes as he looked at the canvas. "It's not nearly as good as some of your other ones."

"Damn the other ones. This one I *felt* inside of me. This one is real. Look at her, Carrie. She's *alive*."

Carrie looked and felt a chill run through her. The little girl's cheeks burned a blush apple red; the realistic twinkle in her eye startled Carrie as surely as if the painted eyes had blinked at her. Carrie half expected the painted swing to start moving. She shivered.

"Ah," he said, watching her face eagerly. "Now you see it."

She turned away from the painting. It was the work of his genius, she could not deny that, yet the portrait left her disturbed, uneasy, in a way that his other paintings had not. "You're a mess."

"Is that all you can say?"

Carrie turned, half-unwillingly, back to the painting. "That's not our daughter, is it?"

"No," he said. "I'm going to call it 'Orphan.' Precisely what our little Carmen will never be."

"She's beautiful," Carrie added. "But she scares me."

He paused. "Come on. The light shouldn't hit it, not until it dries, but I wanted you to see her."

Carrie followed him back into his apartment, her hand protectively on the bulge of her stomach. "I didn't even know you had a studio here."

"Of course not," he said. "It's my space. And when we move to our house, you can have your own room for writing and I'll never go into it."

"I'd like that."

"I know it," he said. "Carmen can have a room, too." He paused. "I'm glad you understand what goes into something like that. It's as if…for those hours…my mind gets possessed…"

She went to the kitchen sink, dampened a dish towel and came back to him. She started sponging the paint smears off his body. "Don't talk about it."

"Does it ever make you feel like you're going insane?"

She nodded. After long hours spent in her writing zone, she wanted nothing more than to be held, to feel the warmth of something alive and human—but she had never had anyone.

"Time to come back to me," she said, embracing him. "But I understand."

She saw he was grateful for her presence, but also afraid—because the feelings of extreme loneliness, of estrangement and coldness and alienation fed the artistic temperament. He stepped away from her before long, and she understood.

"Will you sing for me?" he asked, quietly. "I love it when you sing."

His eyes thanked her when she had finished the song, but he moved by her without saying anything. She retrieved her fallen notebook and gingerly smoothed out the wrinkled pages. Moments later she heard the shower running, and when she went to check on him fifteen minutes later, she found him sprawled on the bed, naked and fast asleep. She covered him with a quilt and went back to the living room. She wrote, and hours later when she went looking for him found that he was still fast asleep. She left the apartment and went for a walk, her body soaking up the warmth of the sun. She walked to the nearby park, sat down on a bench, folded her hands over her stomach, and watched the children jumping around on the playground as their mothers sat on the other park benches and chatted.

Of course she wanted Carmen. Of course she wanted Carmen to grow up happy, healthy, relatively normal. But with a mother like her and a father like Ralph, she wondered about the chances of that ever happening.

Two days later they had a major fight, when he insisted that Carmen be brought up with the Roman Catholic religion. She knew he had been raised with religion only to reject it later on,

and asked him why he wanted to give their child convictions neither of them believed. He said he had gotten comfort from the thought of God in his darkest times; he wanted Carmen to have the option of prayer. But Carrie did not want to raise her child with religion unless it was a decision Carmen made herself. She wanted to stress a love and appreciation for all forms of life, along with tolerance for others and loyalty—above all else—to oneself. He had lost control at that point, letting logic fly to the winds and letting his anger drive him. She hated seeing him like that, and she had walked out on him. She had taken her car and driven to the grocery store to pick up food they needed, and was still fuming inwardly at him when she turned the corner of the bread aisle and almost ran into Christine.

"Carrie," Christine said. "Carrie, you're pregnant."

She stared at her mother, startled. "The baby's due in January. Didn't I tell you?"

"You did *not* tell me." Christine paused. "So I'm going to be a grandmother."

"We're hoping for a girl. But we won't know until the baby is born."

"We?" Christine repeated.

"My husband and I," Carrie said.

"Your *husband*. How long have you been married?"

"A legitimate five months."

Christine paused. "Congratulations."

"Thank you." Carrie frowned. "I'm sorry that I didn't tell you. I've had so much going on…"

"You've always been so strongly against marriage," Christine said. "I'm so glad that you went through with it. You must have been a beautiful bride."

"There wasn't a ceremony," Carrie said. "We signed a civil union contract."

Christine smiled. "Now I can relax. That sounds more like you. I was starting to think I didn't know you as well as I thought I did, and as you'll learn, not knowing your children in one of any mother's greatest fears. I'm very happy for you, honey."

Carrie paused. "How have you been?"

"Everything is always the same for me," Christine said, then smiled. "Honey, if you need anything, you'll let me know, won't you? I've been through the process before. Four times."

"I'll let you know. But I think we'll be fine."

"If you ever need a *babysitter*," Christine insisted. "Or if you ever need a break…."

Carrie laughed. "Don't offer. I might take you up on it."

"I'm serious," Christine said. "Don't hesitate to call if you need anything. I'd like to get to know my granddaughter or grandson."

"Of course you will," Carrie said. "And you'll be a fabulous grandmother."

"Will I get to meet your husband?"

"I'm sure he'd be delighted to see you again."

"Again?"

"You met, briefly, while I was in college." Carrie saw that Christine made the connection; she also saw that Christine was not surprised.

"Did you go on a honeymoon?"

"No," Carrie said. "He wanted to take me somewhere fancy, but I wouldn't let him. Because of summer, it feels like we're on vacation anyway."

"He's a teacher?" Christine asked hopefully.

Carrie nodded.

"And everything is okay?"

"We're fine."

"I was always the peace-keeper," Christine said. "I know you didn't necessarily respect me all the time because of that, but when you have children you need to make sacrifices."

"We'll get through it. How's Chris?"

Christine smiled, uneasily. "Chris has a new friend he met on that nature trip of yours. Maybe you could tell me something about him. Derrick Evans?"

"Chris is friends with *Derrick*?" Carrie asked.

Christine nodded. "Apparently they became closer over the length of the trip. To put you in confidence, Carrie, Chris's best friend Joey has started smoking pot, and Chris wants nothing to do with that. Chris tells me Derrick doesn't drink and doesn't smoke, but based on your reaction right now there is something I should know about this boy, isn't there?"

"There's nothing wrong with Derrick." She paused. "He just doesn't seem like someone Chris would get close to. Have you talked to Chris?"

"I have, but I couldn't make heads or tails out of what he was saying." She paused. "He said Derrick is an ironic hero."

"Might he have said a Byronic Hero?"

"I don't know what that is."

"It's an English term for a certain character type," Carrie said, scanning the items in Christine's buggy, realizing she could tell exactly what food Chris would have requested. "But I would say the term applies more to Chris than it does to Derrick."

In answer to Christine's look of inquiry, she continued. "The Byronic hero describes a kind of individual created by George Gordon, Lord Byron. These men—dark, aloof, intelligent—were often alienated from and weary of the world. They had superior knowledge and insight and a contempt of everything earthly because of it. They faced whatever came their way with defiance and without fear, because they didn't care about much of anything at all. They lived above convention, morality, restraint. Sorry for sounding like a textbook." She paused. "But I wouldn't worry about Chris."

"He's changing," Christine said, quietly. "I know that comes inevitably with adolescence, but—"

"Chris will find his own way."

"He has a streak of whatever you have," Christine said. "But sometimes I worry about him. Don't look at me like that, Carrie, it's a mother's job to worry."

"It shouldn't be," Carrie said. "Especially at Chris's age, when he's capable of making his own decisions."

"I know you view family as a potential danger." Christine smiled, but the smile was bittersweet. "But family, as I hope our family is, can be a source of support and a great blessing. A mother's love should be unconditional. I hope you'll give that to your child."

Carrie returned Christine's look without answering, her hand on her stomach. Christine broke the eye contact first.

I was just picking up some necessities," Carrie said. "Then I'm going to work after I drop them off."

"I'm happy for you," Christine said, taking her hand and squeezing it. "But I won't detain you any longer."

"It was good to see you."

"Carrie." Christine paused. "Let me know when the baby is born. And then let me know again, in case you forget."

She promised, and pushed her buggy away. If she loved her family as much as she said she did, then she should want to see them more—but a large part of her still did not want to get too close.

As soon as she walked into the restaurant, she knew she would have to leave. Though the baby was not due for several months, Carrie felt ill. She went into the restroom and vomited, and when her manager gave her permission to leave for the night, she made her decision spontaneously; she quit.

On the drive home she reflected on her behavior and resolved not to tell Ralph about her decision. But she hoped he would be home, to help her forget about the night, before she realized she had left him in the middle of a fight and had not talked to him since. Her heart sank when she opened his apartment door to find the lights dim, a candle flickering on the table beside a long-stemmed red rose, and soft music playing in the background; she would have preferred to find him angry at her. She snapped on the lights.

"You ruined the ambiance," he said.

She moved into the apartment, dropped her bag on the kitchen counter. "What ambiance?"

"I was trying to be romantic. To say I was—"

"Don't say it," she said. "And you know I don't care at all for romance. It nauseates me."

"Why do you have to be so damned hard to please?" he asked, getting up and starting towards her.

"I'm not hard to please," she said. "A pack of pens would have pleased me more than all of this hullabaloo. I can never have enough pens."

She had gotten him to smile. "How was your shift?"

"I want you to help me forget about it." She went to sit close to him. "Can you do that?"

"I thought you said you didn't like romance."

"I'm not talking about romance." She put her hand on his leg. "You know why I don't like romance."

He raised his eyebrows. "I have no idea."

"It's not straight-forward." She moved her hand up his thigh. "It's calculated, created for an effect. That effect is to distract one's attention away from underlying issues, to cover up—"

He kissed her passionately, stopping her words, then put his hand over her mouth as she looked at him. "Sometimes you think too much, Carrie."

She removed his hand. "We still haven't resolved the issue from the morning."

"I'm content to let you raise Carmen however you want," he said. "As long as you promise me that you'll accept her right to choose a religion for herself once she gets older."

"Is that all you want?"

"For now, angel."

"Don't—"

"No, I won't be romantic again since it gets you so upset." He smiled. "What kind of pens do you like?"

"So much drama," she said. "Half the time I know you love me. The other half of the time, you seem like you want to kill me."

"Surely not half of the time," he said, and paused. "Neither of us wants to back down, but goddamn it, Carrie, at least I'm *trying* to negotiate." He paused. "I can't help it. Something about you brings out the worst in me."

"How very flattering," she said.

"It's not intentional." He looked away. "You asked why I was ashamed of my paintings, Carrie. Why I hide them away. Because painting, creating, has the same effect on me. It brings out this depravity. The more I paint the more control I lose, and the more I see you, the more inspired I am to paint."

"What do you want me to do? Wear a paper bag over my head?"

He started laughing. She tried to appear indifferent, but when he looked at her, she smiled.

"It won't always be like this," he said. "I'm damned if it will be. But I wish I didn't feel like it was out of my control."

"I'll try to work with you," she said.

He turned to face her, and suddenly their hands intertwined. He pulled her close to him, hugged her, let her go.

"I love you," he said. "I'd change everything about me that disappoints you if I could. I'd give up everything to make this work. But I don't know that I can. And I don't know if that's going to be good enough for you in the long run. Goodnight, Carrie."

"Where are you going?" she asked, alarmed.

"I'm going for a walk," he said.

"I'll come with you."

He shook his head. "I'll be back tomorrow morning, before you wake up. You probably won't even notice that I'm gone."

"What is that supposed to mean?" she cried, but he had already gone out and closed the door behind him.

She stared at the door he had closed in her face. She knew she spent hours writing, oblivious to the world, but he spent hours in his studio;

he should have understood. They still had their beautiful and passionate moments. But the dynamic of their relationship—hot, cold, from one extreme to the other and back in constant bursts—fatigued her, sapped her energy. And in less than three months they would be bringing a child into their world. She wondered if the child's presence would make it easier or harder for them to keep everything together.

She heard him come back two hours later. She slipped into the bedroom and stripped, then slid into bed and pulled the covers up to her chin. When he came in, she listened to the soft rustle of his clothes as he took them off, and she pretended to be asleep. She felt him standing by the bedside, looking down at her.

"Carrie," he said. "Are you awake?"

She said nothing, and a moment later she felt the covers shift as he pulled them back and lay beside her. She heard him sigh, and though he did not toss and turn—probably to keep from disturbing her—she knew he was still awake and thinking.

"Ralph," she said, after the silence had stretched on. "I've been thinking."

"So have I." He paused. "You're entitled to the first word, since I walked out and didn't give you a chance to say what you were going to say."

She did not know how she would be able to say the words on her mind, but she knew she would say them because they needed to be said.

"Do you think we made a mistake?" she asked, and the words hung in the air like a death blow.

He shifted, so that she felt his breath on the back of her neck as he put an arm around her. "Do you?"

"No. I don't. We had no illusions; we knew we would clash. We knew we would have problems."

"I'm glad that you feel that way, because I—"

"But I don't know if it would be a mistake for us to remain together." She paused, hearing his sharp intake of breath.

"I don't understand why you're so ready to give up," he said. "If you decide you want this to work, it will. I'm not asking you to compromise, but we need to communicate more." He paused. "I know we're not as happy as we could be as a couple, but do you really think we'd be happier apart?"

"No," she said, feeling a pang in her heart.

He took his arm away from her waist and lay on his back, facing the ceiling. "You know, Carrie, if you had only been an idealist's goddess or muse to me, I would have awakened by now. My image of you would have been shattered, and I would have been hollow and empty. But that hasn't happened." He paused. "I've never asked you to sacrifice for me. I've taken every possible opportunity to encourage—"

"But you begrudge me the time I take for writing." She paused. "If you won't admit it, then I'll admit I resent that you paint."

"What?"

"*I'll* admit to it. It's not a beautiful or a saintly feeling, this resentment, but I hate that you can lock yourself in a studio and not think about me for hours. I hate that you can tune into a higher vision, something more powerful and consuming than our love could ever be. I hate knowing that you need this thing—your art—more than you could ever need me, though I'll bear your children and probably end up compromising, in some way, for you or for them. I hate that you're so goddamned self-contained."

"But so are you."

"So am I," she repeated.

He paused. "You wouldn't want me to love you too much, Carrie."

"I understand that as well. And I don't *want* you to give up your painting. I would hate *you* if you gave up your painting. But how I'm feeling, all of it combined...it's too much. If you say that you don't feel the same way about me, you're a damn liar." She paused. "I love you. But that's what we're up against."

"Damn it," he said.

She moved away from him, towards the window. "We haven't yet learned how to be independent together. I don't even know if that's possible, and if it's not..." She looked over her shoulder and saw he was sitting with his shoulders hunched, his head in his hands. She went to sit beside him on the edge of the bed, letting her shoulder and thigh touch his, taking one of his hands gently. He sat up straighter and looked at her. "What do you want me to do?" he asked.

She glanced down at his hand, clasped between both of hers, resting on her stomach. "Let's wait for the baby to come."

He started to nod, then stopped and withdrew his hand from hers. "Promise me I'll get to know my child. That you'll let me. That you won't—"

"I won't keep you from her," she said. "Unless you give me reason to. No matter what happens between us."

"Promise me."

"I promise."

He looked past her, out the window.

"It's too late to go for a walk," she said.

"I wasn't thinking of going for a walk. I just went for one." He looked away. "Let's go to bed."

She moved to the other side of the bed and lay down. He lay beside her, facing the wall, but as she drifted off to sleep, it was as if he wasn't there at all.

The baby—a girl—was born two months premature. Ralph had made her go to baby preparation classes so she knew what was happening when her water broke in his apartment—but it was not Ralph who took her to the hospital. He was out, arranging for his first public display of art in five years, and she did not call him. In her panic she did not even think of calling him. There was a knock on the apartment door, and it had been Sam coming to invite her to dinner with him and Tessa. She had opened the door and fallen into his arms in a dead faint; *he* had been the one to take her to the nearest hospital. She awoke from her swoon half-delirious, in the midst of a searing contraction. The nurse by her side wiped her brow and told her to push, but as Carrie struggled she felt a reassuring pressure on her hand. She turned, saw Sam.

"The baby's coming soon," Sam said. "Hang in there, Carrie."

"Ralph." She turned to the nurse. "Ralph...I want...Damien..."

"He's coming," Sam said, ignoring the stare the nurse was giving him. "I'm staying with you until—"

"Go away." She ripped her hand out of Sam's, turned to the wall. Her body felt like it was being torn apart. Later, she only remembered when Ralph entered the room. She was fiercely glad he was there, that he had come...

"Carrie," he said, bending down close to her. "Why didn't you call me? I came as soon as I heard, but it was that bastard..."

The nurse mumbled something. Carrie wished the nurse would shut up. Ralph moved his hands, cool hands, to her shoulders in a grip that hurt. She liked the feeling of his hands on her, the pain starting up in her arms focusing her attention away from the larger wrenching pain. As he shook her, she realized he was as besides himself as she was.

"Carrie, why didn't you—"

She blacked out. She remembered regaining consciousness for a moment, to hear the nurse telling her to *push*. She could not remember if she screamed, but then there was a great empty feeling inside her and it was quiet, too quiet, and she passed out in a black wave of pain and panic and fear that the child—her baby—had been born dead.

She woke on clean sheets. The sweat had been sponged from her face; her hair had been dried and combed. She remembered what had happened and she kept her eyes closed, straining to hear the sounds she most longed to hear. But what she heard first was a low, gentle hum. Ralph. She opened her eyes. He was sitting with his head down, holding one of her hands in his.

"Where's the baby?" she said, startling him. "The baby, the baby..."

"She's fine," he said. "She's beautiful. But Carrie..."

"*Where is she?*"

"She's in the neonatal ward," he said, keeping his hand on hers. "We can go see her tomorrow."

"Is she okay?"

"She's fine," he repeated. "She has large almond eyes and her head is covered in black fuzz. You'll see her after you've regained some of your strength."

"Why can't I see her now?"

"The doctors need to keep her here for awhile so they can monitor her progress." He paused. "She's very small, Carrie. Because she's so early.

They think it's in her best interest to keep her here, for now."

"Hospitals are breeding grounds for all kinds of illness, you know that, how could you even consider—"

"You were very brave," he said, bending over and kissing the top of her forehead. "I'm sorry that I wasn't here for most of it." He paused. "They kicked me out of the birthing room because I lost control. I don't really know what…I'm sorry if I scared you or if I hurt you, and I'm sorry that you had to go through this alone, without me by your side…"

She paused, the gentleness of his kiss on her forehead calming her. "Do you think it would be best for her to stay here?"

"I don't want to take any chances. There's a risk either way, but the doctors know better than we do. I think it would be best to go with their advice." He paused. "I could stay in the waiting room outside of the nursery if it would make you feel better. I know it would make me feel better."

"It's always going to be like this," she said, awed. "Worrying about whether we're making the right choice for her, when there's no way we can possibly know—"

"Not always," he said. "Once she becomes an adolescent, we'll start worrying about the choices she makes for herself."

She smiled at him, then her smile sagged. "I want to hold her."

"You have to be patient," he said, smoothing her hair away from her face.

"I don't want to name her Carmen," she said suddenly. "Not so dramatic of a name for her if she's weak."

"You can name her whatever you want to." He paused. "But I have a suggestion."

"What?"

He looked at her. "While I was pacing around the waiting room, I found a book of baby names and I heard the name *Chloe* in my head. Chloe Crenshaw-Palmer. It's a beautiful name for a girl."

She waited.

"The name is Greek. It means blooming and verdant." His voice broke. "I was hoping that with a name like that, she would—"

"We'll name her Chloe," Carrie said.

He fixed his eyes on her, then he stooped and kissed her cheek "You're beautiful, too."

Suddenly he frowned, put his hand up against Carrie's forehead. "You're warm. Are you feeling okay?"

She nodded, realizing she liked it better when he was concerned about the child instead of treating her like one—and suddenly she felt helpless, lying in the hospital bed, broken and aching and waiting.

"Can you take me home?" she asked.

"The doctors say you should rest." He paused as she pushed herself away from him, then pulled her to him and kept her anchored by his side when she tried to stand. "You're going to accept the doctors' advice whether you like it or not, and then we're going to get you home safely. I thought we were past this power struggle. Let it go, Carrie."

She leaned into him, wearily rested her head on his shoulder. He put his arm around her, then helped her lie back. Two hours later he signed the forms he needed to sign and carried her easily to the car. By the time he drove back to the apartment, she was fast asleep.

She woke in the morning to the sound of gentle hammering. There was a dull pain in her lower body, but otherwise she was filled with peace. Her arms felt liquid in grace as she stretched them up to the ceiling; her entire body felt filled with a warm, golden light. The hammering stopped for a brief interval, and Ralph peered into the room.

"Good morning," he said, seeing her awake.

"Good morning," she said, watching as he walked into the room. "What are you doing?"

"Building a crib," he said, laying the hammer on the oak dresser. "Did I wake you?"

"I should get up anyway," she said, wincing as the pain flared in her body.

"Rest," he said. "You did a great job, yesterday. Carrie, I wanted to tell you that..."

He broke off abruptly and turned from her.

She glanced at him, curious. "Why are you upset?"

He turned. "Why am I upset? Because every time I try to tell you how I feel I end up sounding ridiculous."

"I didn't say anything."

"I know. You rarely do, Carrie." He went and sat on the edge of their bed. He took her hand. "We need to talk."

The feeling of panic that coursed through her shattered the dreamlike peace of her waking moments. "What if I don't want to?"

"We have to," he said. He let go of her hand and stood. "You said we could talk once Chloe was born."

"That's fair," she said, while he stood with his back to her. "But look at me when you're talking to me."

He smiled. "You sound like a mother already."

"Would you sit down? I feel like you're about to fly away."

He sat down on the bed, his head bowed, his brow creased, his hands in his lap.

"I can't do this," he said.

"Of course you can."

"Any time anything happens, I go crazy. You deserve someone who's more stable."

"But I chose you," she said. "I love you."

He sat with his hands clenched together. "I watched you bear my child. Carrie, you have no idea how that affected me..."

"So tell me. It'll be a bonding experience."

"Don't mock me." He paused. "This fear of failure, of not being able to measure up..."

Their eyes locked, and he frowned. "I want to know why he was the one you called and not me."

"I didn't call Sam." She paused. "Chloe came *two months early*. Haven't you realized that I was just as surprised by the timing as you were? I couldn't have called you to let you know, even if I had wanted to..."

"What are you saying? That when you went into labor Sam suddenly showed up to take you to the hospital?"

"Something like that."

"Do you expect me to believe that?"

"The truth is always the most difficult thing to believe."

"Why were you with him?"

She narrowed her eyes. "Don't insult me."

He paused. "I find it extremely convenient that Sam was there."

"So do I. Since you weren't." She paused. "Though I don't hold that against you, since you were working on your art. How did the display go?"

"It doesn't matter," he said, staring at her. "I left it as soon as I heard—from Sam—that you had gone into labor."

"I don't hold it against you that Sam was the one who helped me," she repeated. "Everything worked out. Isn't that what matters?"

The intensity in his eyes arrested her attention, and she could not look away.

"Do you know that you very rarely say you love me?" he asked her.

"Don't be ridiculous."

"Will you say it to me now? Carrie?" She looked back at him, her lips pressed together. He waited, and then he stood. "I should go back to work."

"We already set up the nursery."

"I'm changing the crib because she's so small." He picked up the hammer from the dresser. "The doctors said we might be able to bring her home soon."

Carrie turned away from the door as he passed out of the room. She closed her eyes.

"My god," she said, to the empty room. "Can't you *tell* I love you?"

A week later they brought Chloe home, Ralph driving and glancing at them every few moments while Carrie held the tiny child, bundled in a pink fuzzy blanket. Chloe Crenshaw was a beautiful little girl with her delicate features and solemn dark eyes, but she was deaf in one ear and blind in one eye. Carrie held her, dazed. Her relationship with Ralph seemed petty in comparison, and she wondered if her irrational attraction to him had been—always—about creating this tiny child, who was now her responsibility.

"Don't hold her so tightly," Ralph said, breaking into her thoughts. "You'll suffocate her."

"She would cry if I were hurting her," Carrie said, adjusting the baby's position.

"She hasn't cried yet." Ralph reached over and tucked the blanket around Chloe. "That's another thing, besides her size and early birth, that has the doctors worried."

She made a face at the child, trying to get a smile. But Chloe continued looking away, paying very little attention to her.

"Sing to her," Ralph said. "She likes that."

Carrie started to sing, and at the first notes, the child fixed her large brown eyes on Carrie. Ralph sensed that Carrie wanted to be alone with the child, and left her to take care of Chloe when they arrived at the apartment. She went to the rocking chair he had bought for her the day before and sat down. She sang and rocked the baby for an hour without getting the smallest reaction from her, until she stopped rocking, stopped singing. Then Chloe began to squirm violently.

"Hush," Carrie said, patting her on the back, staring at her helplessly, not knowing how to make her stop. "Chloe, sweetheart, baby...Ralph!"

He stopped what he was doing immediately; the next moment, he was standing in the doorway.

"Help," Carrie said. "I don't know what I did."

"Give her to me." He took the child, cradled her in his arms. "There, baby girl, calm down."

The child quieted instantly, while Carrie looked on in silent wonder.

"That's a relief. She was just upset. She wasn't having a seizure or anything." He looked up and caught the expression on her face. "What?"

"You're so calm," she said.

"Nothing to be worried about. The neonatal ward said she was out of the danger zone, that she'll be fine. Carrie, what's wrong?"

"My hormones are fucked up," she said, fiercely wiping away the tears that had sprung to her eyes. "That's all. That, and the fact that I'm glad you're here. I'm glad that I'm not a single mother, that I don't have to raise her alone. Look at her. She loves you."

He stared at her, cautious. "Why don't you let me take care of her for awhile? Take some time for yourself. Take a hot bath with some candles and music, take an hour to read."

"I'm all right."

"You need to take care of yourself," he insisted, bouncing Chloe gently on his knee. "Especially now. And no more arguments between us for at least a fortnight."

She smiled. "A fortnight?"

"That's what happens when you make me read Jane Austen so I can discuss it with you," he said. "What were you thinking? What was *I* thinking?"

She paused. "How long do I have to wait before I can go back to work?"

He frowned and stopped bouncing Chloe. "We'll talk about that later. Just relax, recuperate, get to know our daughter…"

"I intend to go back to work."

"Not now," he said, carrying Chloe to her crib.

Carrie was left with the image of the child looking gravely over Ralph's shoulder, her eyes wide and watching her silently.

She roused herself despite the pain in her body; she wanted to be up and moving around. Though they had not had any problems with Chloe, the fear of complications and illness lurked in Carrie's mind. She wanted to see Chloe again. And she was hungry. She went into the kitchen, found Ralph seated at the table with Chloe sleeping on his shoulder. A number of pamphlets were spread out in front of him.

"What are you reading?" she asked, going over to him. "Anything interesting?"

"Might interest you," he said, leaning back so she could look at the pamphlet.

She scanned the title, recoiled.

"Premature babies are at greater risks for neuroduptal and respiratory disorders," he quoted, turning his attention back to the pamphlet. "Some other complications involve blood infections, tachycardia, pneumothorax…"

She went to the refrigerator. "That information is probably for severely premature babies. The real danger zone exists for babies born at twenty-eight weeks or before…"

"Twenty-eight," he said thoughtfully. "Carrie, did you know that premature babies are twenty-eight times more likely to die within the first month of life than normal—"

"Stop it."

He looked down at the table. "I'm sorry."

"Don't ever refer to our daughter as being other than normal. We're lucky that she's as healthy as she is." She paused. "Isn't that ironic? If you would have told me during my pregnancy that I would be standing here, wishing my daughter were normal, that she *were* like everyone else, I would have called you crazy."

"Why did it happen?" he asked, rifling through the pages of a book he had open in front of him. "I know you're substance-free. Do you have anemia, cardiac disease, diabetes—"

"No," she said.

"What about during your pregnancy? Did you feel any abdominal pressure?"

"If I did I thought it was cramps."

"Why didn't you tell me?"

"It's not my fault. Don't act like I could have prevented it somehow." She glared. "Maybe it had to do with how she was conceived, because I'm pretty sure I conceived her on our wedding night, when I felt—"

"Carrie."

She paused. "If she was born from passion, do you think she would have been born that way?"

"That would be ironic," he said. "If, because we waited, she was..." He paused. "Would you have wanted another child?"

"No," she said, then realized she had not even hesitated before responding. "I love Chloe."

"So do I."

He closed the pamphlet and book in front of him. "I know you've been reading since she was born. And I bet you've come across the same information that I have. Part of which says that often, should things go badly with the child, the couple falls apart. That if things are going badly, it's important for the parents to love and support each other, until the danger has passed, or through the grieving process. We're lucky that she's as healthy as she is, because had we been tested like that, I don't know that we would have made it through."

"Give me the baby."

"She's sleeping."

"Give her to me," Carrie said. "I'm putting her in the nursery, and then I'm going to show you how strong our relationship is."

Surprise flickered into his eyes as he handed Chloe to her. Carrie carried the child to the nursery and put her in the crib. She stopped for a moment and stared at the sleeping child—the tiny face a mask of innocence and vulnerability and trust. Then she went back to the kitchen, and found Ralph putting on his jacket.

"Where are you going?" she asked.

"Out," he said. "I need to go out for awhile."

"But...what I said..."

"You need to heal," he said, violently sticking his arm into the sleeve hole in his jacket. "And if I stay I'm going to be tempted to do what I shouldn't."

She stared at him; he returned her gaze, then left. She wandered to the nursery and sat down. The little face was enough to comfort her, and as she sat there watching Chloe, she was not driven to write or seek or fight. She was content to be alone with her daughter, knowing that no matter what the future might bring, for that moment they were both all right.

The night was cold, giving him no comfort. Ralph walked along the deserted provincial streets until he came to the highway, and then he kept walking. He had gotten into exercising—the toned muscle of his body was a constant surprise to him—and when his bouts of creativity came on, he felt comfort in knowing that his diseased mind was no longer housed in a diseased body, the upshot of which was that he could, and did, let his imagination take him farther than he had previously dared. The physical strength acted as a protective shield against his deepest fear—of, ultimately, losing control of everything. He had been close, and he never wanted to be that close again.

Café Michel was a forty-five minute walk, both ways, but the walk invigorated him. He did not go out often, but when he went out he only went to the Café. He went for the atmosphere. Something about the plenitude of mirrors, the low-hanging Tiffany lamps, the varnished mahogany side paneling and the absolute paucity of art soothed his tormented soul.

While walking, he wondered if Carrie knew that Chloe's premature birth had affected him in profound ways. There had been his reaction during the birth—his complete lack of control as he had stormed into the birthing room and physically shook the woman he loved more than his art, more than his life, whilst she was in the midst of pain and a difficult labor. Then there had been his thoughts after the labor, the awareness of his own incompetence as a father. And the feelings that came when he woke up every morning and saw Carrie sleeping next to him. Every time he caught her off guard, when she didn't know he was looking, he could see—in her eyes, in the lines of her face and her posture—that she was not happy, not satisfied. He wondered if she even knew she was unhappy; she was focused on her writing, and she had never seemed to care about her own contentment.

He had anticipated the moment when he would become a father. Perhaps justly, he had not been given a clean slate; his child had been born prematurely, deaf in one ear, blind in one eye. He did not want to consider that his sperm might have been defective or damaged by his previous substance abuse. His research into the subject reassured him it was unlikely, and let him focus on how he had acted: projecting his anger and frustration onto Carrie, watching her take it all in stride. It was the same pattern on a different scale. It was enough to make him want to leave her, without even a note explaining that she would be better off without him.

Then the bright lights of Café Michel came into view. The hostess, a slender young woman in a slinky black dress, looked him over as he approached the host podium.

"I'm meeting someone," he said quietly. "She should be here soon. Could we have a booth towards the back of the restaurant? Somewhere relatively private?"

The hostess nodded, glancing at him unreservedly as she reached for two menus and sashayed away from him. He followed her, not paying attention to his surroundings as he walked, sitting down without question at the table to which she directed him.

"I hope this will be all right."

"Charming," he said. "Miss, the young woman…"

"I'll make sure she finds you," the hostess said with a wink.

Ralph did not watch her go. He did not open his menu, and he did not notice when Sylvia Christianson walked over wearing a silver sequined gown that clung to her curves, her long black hair brushed straight and loose down her back. She watched him for a moment, then sat down, an amused smile on her full lips.

"Damien, dear," she said, her voice as sultry as her darkly lined eyes. "Are you thinking again?"

Her voice, though soft, jarred him from his thoughts.

"Guilty," he said.

She smiled. "Well, we both know you're anything but innocent. You really shouldn't fight so hard against yourself. You can't change who you are."

"But doesn't it matter that I'm trying? Goddamn it, sometimes I think you women…"

"So charming tonight," she remonstrated, spreading a look of disdain across her features. "I don't know why I came. You do this every time. And don't put me in a category with that woman."

"That woman is my wife."

Sylvia cocked her head. "What happened this time, for you to call and tell me to meet you in such a hurry? You can't expect me to keep indulging you on a moment's notice. You act like you were nothing more than a spoiled child."

He did not answer. Calmly, she unrolled the silverware, shook out the linen napkin and spread it on her lap. "I wanted to congratulate you on your newest break-through, Damien."

"Don't call me that."

"I can never remember, though, what asinine name you want to be called. What is it again?"

"I don't want you to call me that, either."

"Well, what am I supposed to call you?" She pouted, pursing her lips. "You and I go back. You'll always be Damien to me." She reached across the table, caressed his arm, withdrew her hand. He had not responded to her touch; he never did. She paused."Tonight we celebrate. I've ordered us some champagne. Here it is now."

She smiled graciously as the waiter placed two long stemmed champagne glasses in front of them, then left the bottle to chill in a silver bucket of ice on the table. She raised her glass.

"To your genius," she proposed, then waited, her glass suspended in the air. When he did not move, she clinked her glass against his stationary one.

"And so life goes on," she said, with a small smile. His face was unresponsive. She looked at her champagne glass, took a sip, put the glass on the table. "For God's sake, drink it, don't stare at it. It's high quality, I promise you."

He looked at the glass in front of him, the same resolution coming into his eyes as he picked up the glass, downed it as he would have a shot.

"I fear I'm not being very good company," he said, his voice low.

"You never are," she retorted. "Not anymore. Pretend you're not married to her. Pretend—"

"Sylvia." He started to get up. "I'm wasting your time."

She put her hand on his arm, stopped him. "I'm lonely. You're not wasting my time." She waited until he sat down again, smiled. "Have you ever stopped to think if you hadn't chosen her, if you had—"

"You haven't even asked how Chloe is doing," he said, not looking at her.

"Is that what you named her? I can never seem to remember."

"When are you available next?" he asked. "I'm going to need you for about three hours, a couple of nights this week."

"Must we always be so businesslike?" She caught his chilling stare, sighed. "Tuesday and Wednesday I work late. I can clear any other night after five, if you give me a day's notice."

"Thank you," he said.

"Does it help?" she asked seriously, searching his face.

"It helps."

"Then I'm happy to oblige." She paused. "How much?"

"How much do you need?"

"Three hundred dollars would help."

"You don't need that much money."

"But I like having it."

"Monday, I'll expect you from six to nine," he said.

His expression did not change but she turned, followed his eyesight, and saw a stocky, good-looking man dressed in casual business attire striding towards them briskly. She glanced back at Ralph; he had relaxed and was browsing through the menu in front of him carelessly. He did not look up again, not even as the man stopped in front of their table and stood looking down at them. She cleared her throat.

"May I help you, sir?"

"Are you aware this man is married?"

"Damien, dear," Sylvia said. "I believe this man wants to talk to you."

Ralph looked up. "Sam. Good to see you. How are the wife and kids? The career?"

The scowl did not leave Sam's face. "Who is she?"

"I would have introduced you earlier, had you given me the chance." He remained unfazed. "Sylvia, this is Sam, a friend of my wife's. Sam, Sylvia. Come now." He paused, seeing the fierce light had not left Sam's eyes. "You must remember her."

Sylvia stared at them, resolute. "Why should he remember me?"

The two men locked eyes.

"Damien," Sylvia prompted.

"Ralph. My name is Ralph." He dropped his gaze from Sam and smiled at her. "Sylvia, Sam should remember you because he saw a portrait I had painted of you once, a long time ago." He paused. "Would you please excuse us for a moment, Sylvia?"

He was sure that Sam was watching him as they walked out of Café Michel. He leaned against the brick wall of the restaurant and lit a cigarette. A flare of anger flashed across Sam's face. "If you're cheating on Carrie…"

"It's none of your business," Ralph said, and raised an eyebrow.

"So help me God, if you give me the slightest reason to—"

He dropped the cigarette, ground it into the pavement. "Don't worry, Sam. I will take care of Carrie…"

"Carrie can take care of herself."

"Then you shouldn't be worried about her. Now I consider this conversation closed."

"I have more to say to you."

"This is not the time."

Sam's eyes narrowed. "There's not going to be a better time."

"There will be. Since you seem particularly dense tonight, let me elucidate. Your wife—my sister, let me remind you—is sitting in the restaurant waiting for you. And on this night you're spending together, without the kiddies, here I am, taking up some of that valuable time." He shook his head. "Have some common sense."

Sam looked at him. "That's a clever way of putting it, making me seem the inconsiderate one so you can go back to your liaison guilt-free, while Carrie sits at home by herself..."

"She's with our daughter." He paused. "How many children do you have, now?"

"Two."

"Carrie told me about Kindra. How old is your second?"

"Tessa just had him."

"A boy?"

Sam looked at him. "I'm going to tell Carrie about this."

"About what?"

"About seeing you here tonight, with that other woman."

"That would be bold."

"You don't think she'll believe me?"

"She'll believe you too readily," he said. "She won't leave me though, and I won't leave her. Do you hear that, Sam?" He paused, shook his head. "Stupid. You've prepared me by telling me you'll talk to her. I'm going to see her before you do. Don't you think I could construct a story as to why I was here with Sylvia tonight?"

"I could tell her you would do that, too."

Ralph frowned. "Don't play games with a master, Sam. You'll get burned."

"Don't underestimate me."

"I have much more serious things to be worried about." He took a step away from Sam, then walked back into the restaurant without another word. Sam exhaled, then followed. Ralph had already sat down at the table with Sylvia; Sam passed by without another glance at him. But the expression he had seen on Ralph's face haunted him as he sat down at the table with a smile for Tessa, who was oblivious to everything that had just happened. As much as he wanted to protect Carrie, that expression of sad confusion on Ralph's face stayed with him.

Ralph got back to the apartment much later and was not surprised to find that Carrie had turned off lights. He slipped inside quietly; she was a light sleeper, and she had not been sleeping well. Not because Chloe was keeping her up with fussing—Chloe had never even cried. But Carrie had been waking up every hour, instinctively, and going to check on her. She was always considerate of him; if Ralph had not been as restless as she was, he would not have noticed. Little things that she did for him like that—being quiet in the night when she got up, having coffee ready for him in the mornings—made it difficult for him to understand her. He didn't understand why she had to resort to subtle ways of letting him know she cared for him. He started towards their bedroom, stopped, decided he would sleep on the couch rather than risk disturbing her sleep. But he wanted to check on Chloe.

He made his way to the nursery and was surprised to find the door cracked open slightly. He paused, then slowly pushed the door open and started. Carrie was sitting near Chloe's crib, wrapped in a shawl, staring blankly at the child as if transfixed. She glanced up as he came in, but her expression did not change.

"You startled me," he said. "I thought you were a ghost."

"I'm not."

He went over to her, put his hands on her shoulders. "What are you doing up? Not waiting for me to get back…"

"Don't touch me." She turned from him, her shawl slipping off her shoulder and revealing a bare arm. "I'm tired."

He backed away from her and pulled up a chair, setting it closer to Chloe's crib than to her. He looked at the child, sleeping peacefully.

"She's beautiful," he said.

"I'm glad she's not beautiful. She's going to have to develop a strong personality if she wants to be noticed. Isn't it better that way?"

He paused. "Do you want to go on a date, sometime? Maybe if we set aside a time each week when we could—"

She stared at him. "The only reason this is working is because we don't see each other that much." She paused. "We've never had anything in common."

"That's a fucking lie."

"Don't swear around the baby."

"I'm sorry, Chloe." He leaned back in his chair. "Carrie, sometimes, you're absolutely exasperating. Things between us won't get better if you aren't willing to try."

"I'm not sure I want them to."

"What?"

"Maybe I just wanted the child," she said. "Maybe I never wanted you at all. And I'm not sure I like this, being a wife."

"Carrie."

"I told you this might happen," she said, and he saw the tears glistening behind the fierce light in her eyes. "I *told* you I might want to be alone."

"You *are* alone, don't you see that?" He felt himself losing control, but he didn't care. "You have a child that doesn't respond to you, and I wouldn't call myself a loving husband."

"Fuck you," she said, turning her face away from him.

"Don't swear around the baby."

"You're irritating me." She was no longer crying. "I wish you weren't here."

"Our life together doesn't have to be a prison sentence," he said, suddenly calm. "If we work together—"

"If you were both gone, I would still be fine. I would still be complete."

"You would be empty. You've realized that, and it scares you. Carrie, look at me. Listen to me. You want to leave because you realize you finally have something you don't want to lose, and you don't like the power that has over you. Closing yourself off from me, from Chloe, means asserting your independence, and that's why...are you even listening to me?"

"Somewhat," she said.

"I think you should get some sleep," he said. "You're tired. No, you're *exhausted*. If you got some sleep, everything wouldn't seem so bad."

Carrie stood looking down at Chloe, her back to him, her hand on the rim of the crib.

"Sam called me," she said. "Did you and Sylvia have a good time tonight?"

He stared at her, startled by the indifference in her voice. "You don't sound surprised."

"I've regressed to being a loner again," she said. "Can I hold it against you for regressing to what you were before?"

"What the hell do you mean?"

She turned to him. "How long did you think we would last? I meet up with you four years later and I don't even *recognize* you. You're respected, you're patient, compassionate, dedicated, adored by your students, admired by your peers. But I knew that who you're pretending to be now isn't who you are."

"I *have* changed," he said. "You're making the biggest mistake of your life in not realizing that, Carrie. We could be happy. I don't understand how you can be so blind."

"Watch it," she said.

Ralph looked down at their sleeping child and realized his mistake. But his emotions pushed him past caution.

"Say what you want to me." He stared at Carrie, loving and hating her. "This is the first time you've said anything to me at all."

She did not hesitate. "I always knew that someday you would show me you hadn't really changed."

"Do you know what I think, Carrie? I think you *know* I've changed. But you don't want me to have changed, because you're still in love with Damien, because he was less of a threat to your independence..."

"Is what he said true?" she cried suddenly, her mask of self-possession breaking. "Are you cheating on me?"

"Sylvia *models* for me, Carrie. That's all. Nothing has happened between us since I married you..."

"Before?"

"Yes."

She looked at him without emotion. "I fail to believe that you paint her at Café Michel."

"Damn it," he exploded. "Do you want to know the truth, Carrie? I meet with her to talk. To *talk*. She's someone who knew me from before.

Before I had a wife who despises me and a child I keep expecting to find dead every morning when I wake up. Someone who appreciates my successes and doesn't make me feel guilty for feeling happy when I know that any moment Chloe could..."

He paused, because she was looking at him with her eyes full of tears. His anger slipped away; he could barely speak.

"I'm not cheating on you, Carrie."

"I wish I could believe you," she said.

He stared at her. She stared back at him. Between them, Chloe began to cry. They both froze.

"She's crying." Carrie turned to the child. "She's *crying*."

The child's cry sounded like an exotic, exciting music. He crossed the room and picked up the wailing child, gently. "Is she hungry? Does she need changed?"

Finally, Carrie took the child from him, went to the chair, offered the child a breast and quieted her. Ralph stood watching them, too torn to speak, not knowing whether he should stay or leave. When Chloe had finished, Carrie handed the baby to him.

"You need to burp her," she said. "She never will, for me."

He took the child, patted her on the back, then wiped the child's mouth with the bottom of his shirt. Carrie put Chloe in her crib.

"Did I say she wasn't beautiful?" she asked, tucking the soft pink blanket around her. "I lied."

She looked up, saw him looking at her. She turned away. "I still don't like you very much right now."

He hesitated, then went to her. His raised her face so her lips could meet his; she trembled at his touch. The kiss lasted a moment, and then she turned her face away. He glanced at her and then left, resigning himself to the couch though he already knew he would not sleep.

When Carrie woke the next morning, she crept towards the nursery but stopped as she entered the living room. He was sprawled on the couch, fast asleep. She went over to him and gently ran her fingers through his hair, then recoiled as he woke. Her back was to him as he sat up and focused on her.

"Carrie? Is everything all right?"

She hated that they were both on edge all the time. "I'm sorry I woke you."

"Were you going to check on Chloe?" he asked.

"Yes." She paused. "Then I want to go grocery shopping."

He stared at her. "What do we need?"

"Nothing. But I want to go. I want to do something that makes me feel normal…"

He stood, stretched. "I'm coming with you. I want to go grocery shopping, too."

"Someone has to stay with Chloe."

"We'll drop her off at your mother's. She's an emergency nurse, and she's raised four children. Chloe will be fine with her."

"I don't want to unload Chloe on—"

"You know your mother won't mind. She hasn't seen Chloe since we brought her here. Call her."

Carrie was surprised when Christine reacted with uninhibited enthusiasm, and answered Ralph's inquisitive stare with a nod of her head. He left halfway through her call, then came back with Chloe cradled in his arms.

"Ready," he said.

"You forgot her blanket."

He stepped aside as she went by him and came back with the fuzzy pink blanket folded under her arm. She handed him the blanket, watching as he tucked it around her.

"You know Christine is a fabulous grandmother, to take our little darling on such short notice," he said, as the child cuddled into him.

"She knows I'm impulsive. And she's been telling me that I…that we…need to spend more time together. That it might make everything better between us."

Ralph froze. "You talk to her about us?"

"Does that make you uncomfortable?"

"I wish you would talk to me before you talk to her. It doesn't seem right that I'm your husband, and I don't know what's going on with you."

"I need you to be patient."

"I've told you before that I'm not a patient person."

Carrie put her arms out for the baby. Ralph handed Chloe, bundled up, to her. As Carrie moved the cover away and gently kissed the child on the forehead, Chloe started to squirm. Carrie's expression changed; she lost her confidence, the glow left her eyes, and she turned to Ralph and indicated that he should take the child. He stepped away from her, shook his head.

"She loves you more," she said, helplessly. "She'll behave if you take her."

"She'll calm down in a moment," he said. "Hold her close and talk to her. You're not doing anything wrong."

She turned her attention doubtfully to the child, rocked her back and forth and talked to her quietly. Chloe continued to squirm, and then she gave up and lay quietly in Carrie's arms. Carrie looked up.

"You understand her?"

"I feel..." he paused, uncomfortable. "I feel a bond with her."

"She is your child."

"But I don't know any more than you what the hell I'm doing."

Carrie winced. "I don't want her to learn bad words."

"I'll drive," Ralph offered. "She looks perfectly peaceful with you."

"Maybe we should stay here," Carrie said, rocking the child. "She's never been this good for me."

"Let's go grocery shopping, Carrie. It might be nice to get away. If only for the morning."

"But she's so beautiful when she's like this."

"We'll only go for a little while. You already called your mother."

She started towards the door reluctantly with Chloe nestled in her arms. Eventually he persuaded her to give Chloe to Christine, who assured them that taking care of Chloe for a couple of hours would be a delight. Ralph complimented Christine on how well she was looking, then guided Carrie back to the car when she started showing signs of distress at leaving Chloe. Carrie quickly pulled herself together; he kept his eyes straight ahead.

"I want to talk to you," she said finally, as he started driving along the familiar roads. "About some of what you said last night. I was emotional, and exhausted. You revealed a lot to me, and I never took the time to react. Or to let you know that I appreciated having you share your thoughts with me."

He waited for her to continue.

"I want you to be happy," she said, quietly. "Do you doubt that?"

"No," he said.

She glanced at him. "I didn't know that I made you feel guilty. That you felt you couldn't tell me about your accomplishments because I'd think it was a sign that you don't love Chloe. I've been so caught up in what I'm feeling that I haven't considered what you might be experiencing. I'm sorry that I drove you to another woman to find some comfort."

His expression changed. "I told you I'm not cheating on you."

"You'd have every reason to. I wouldn't be angry if you were. I'd just want you to tell me."

"I'm not cheating on you, Carrie." He paused. "While we're learning how to handle Chloe, we should work on us."

She hesitated. "If you need time away, tell me. I've told you to tell me. And I want you to tell me about your other life, as well. I care about your work. I care about what's important to you." She broke off, turned to face him. "When Chloe gets out of the danger zone, when she gives her first tantrum, when she has her first kiss and gets her first job, I want you to be there. I want you to witness her growing up with me." She paused. "I want to apologize for accusing you. I should know that people change. I know it can't be easy for you, being constantly reminded that I doubt you."

"It's not easy," he said, turning into the supermarket parking lot. "But I understand. And I appreciate that you've acknowledged that all of this—our relationship, staying an artist, being a father—has been difficult for me as well. No one else really has."

She sat reflectively in the passenger seat as he got out of the car. He opened her door with such an air of chivalry that she could not help but smile as she took his hand. He did not let go of her hand, and they walked across the parking lot linked.

"I feel ridiculously happy," she said, suddenly.

"Then I'm not letting go of your hand until we get back to the car."

"That will be awkward."

"It will be interesting."

She was regretful when they got back to the car and he released her hand to start unloading the bags of groceries from the cart. She watched him with growing alarm.

"Did we buy all that?" she asked, seizing a bag. "Count Chocula? Are we even going to eat this?"

"We had fun picking it out," he said, cramming the last bag into the trunk. "And we need to eat something. We can afford it. Relax."

She was pensive as he got into the car. He glanced at her.

"Out with it," he said. "What's on your mind?"

"Nothing."

"Carrie."

She bit her lip. "We can't be extravagant like this."

"Yes, we can."

"How can we afford it?" she asked, turning to him. "You aren't selling your paintings. I went to see your art gallery exhibit last night. I picked a painting and I asked one of the men how much it was—"

"Why did you do that?" he asked angrily.

"It crossed my mind that if I'm not going to work any more I need to know that you can support us, and I wanted to know how much one of your paintings would go for...."

"When did you decide you weren't going to go back to work?"

"Don't distract me. Why aren't you selling your paintings?"

"There's no reason I should," he said. "Chloe's bills are paid."

"What if she goes into remission?"

"Going into remission is a good thing, Carrie," he said. "Do you mean, in case she has future problems? We won't talk about that."

"We need to—"

"We'll talk about it if the time comes," he said.

Carrie glanced at him. "I opened what I thought was a hospital bill the other day, but it was a letter from the hospital thanking your for a very generous gift of twenty-five hundred dollars. You donated twenty-five hundred dollars to the hospital...."

"Do you dare put a price on our daughter's life?"

"I'm just saying that we have to be careful. That it might be a good idea for you to sell some—"

"I'm not selling. I've told you I'm ashamed of them." He paused as the car lurched to a stop. "Shit."

Carrie looked up, startled. "What happened?"

"Tire must have blown," he said. "Come on."

She got out of the car, closed her door, heard it lock. She made a sudden movement towards him as he closed his door. "Wait—"

"What?"

She stepped back a pace. "You locked the keys in the car."

"Shit," he said.

"We could smash the window," she suggested.

"Smash the…five minutes ago you were lecturing about wasting money, about being careful—"

"Wait a minute," she said, and left him. She went to the side of the shed and came back holding a long, pliable metal wire. "Can you use this?"

"For what?" he said.

"I know you can pick locks." She handed him the wire. "You told me about the times when you stole in college…."

"Mind you, I've put all that behind me." He went to work on the door.

She turned her back to him, stared up at the sky, heard him muttering. Then she turned.

"Ralph."

"Not now."

She looked at the skyline until, five minutes later, she heard him exclaim triumphantly. She turned and saw he had successfully opened the car door.

"Now, what did you want to tell me?" he asked, a flush in his cheeks and a glitter in his eyes.

"I have a spare key on me."

He stared at her. "You're kidding."

"No. Last time I took the car out—"

"I don't even want to know," he said, throwing the metal wire away from him. He grabbed the keys from where they were dangling in the ignition. "I'm going to get the spare out of the trunk. I'll show you how to use the jack."

She paused, recoiling inwardly from his anger. "You know, this is going to be kind of fun. It's been a long time since I've learned how to do something like this."

He glanced up at her suddenly, and the anger faded out of his eyes. "Watch," he said.

Half an hour later the offensive flat was removed, the car was ready, and she felt years younger. She looked at him as he got back into the car. "That was fun."

"I'm glad you had a good time. Shit, Carrie, it's already three o'clock. You should call your mother, make sure she's not worried that we're dead in a ditch somewhere or that we ran off together…"

"She knows we wouldn't leave without Chloe." Carrie called Christine, then turned to him. "She didn't answer."

"We'll be there soon enough. You can take a power nap if you want. I'll wake you once we get there."

"Just for a moment." Carrie reclined and fell asleep.

He did not stay true to his word; he let her sleep, and she woke as he pulled into the parking lot of their apartment complex to find him with Chloe perched in his lap, one of her tiny hands on the steering wheel. She sat up abruptly.

"I put her in her carseat while I was driving," he said, before she could speak. "I just brought her up here because she reached for the wheel when I unbuckled her."

Carrie cocked her head. "Where did she get that outfit?"

Chloe was looking at her with a dazed expression on her face, her dark hair curling under a tiny blue sailor's cap.

"Christine took her shopping," he said.

"Does she think we can't clothe our daughter?" Carrie reached across the seat, plucked Chloe off his knee.

"You know your mother likes to shop."

"You look adorable," she said to the baby, and kissed her on the forehead. "I love you."

Ralph unbuckled his seatbelt and got out of the car quickly. The car door closed behind him, and she watched as he made his way to the house's entrance. She was not troubled by his change in mood. What she had felt for him that afternoon had been brief, a flash, and it had disappeared. Watching him walk away, she found she did not care if she had made him angry.

Tessa was surprised when she looked up and saw Sam getting out of the car she had heard park in their driveway. She knew he was supposed to be at a business meeting, and he never missed a meeting. She pulled off her green vinyl gardening gloves and tipped the brim of her straw bonnet back.

"What's wrong, Sam?" she asked, standing.

"I want to talk to you."

She paused. "Don't you have a—"

"Tessa, this is more important."

She sighed. "Come inside, then you can tell me whatever you want to about Carrie."

"I never—"

"You forget that I'm psychic." She paused. "But I can't read your mind. You have to let me know what's bothering you."

He hesitated. "I need to know that she's all right."

"Only that?"

He nodded. Tessa glanced past him to where the chimes were dancing and singing in a patch of light.

"If you want to know if she's all right, you should talk to her yourself," Tessa said. "You were also one of her closest friends."

"I don't think so."

"Then you've noticed it, too."

"Noticed what?"

"That peculiar quality to her affection," she said. "Carrie never let me down, but I always got the feeling that if I disappeared she wouldn't give a damn. It's not that she doesn't care, Sam. She's never learned how to love. But I'm rambling."

"I find it a very interesting digression," he said. "Please continue."

"No, I've lost my train of thought. What were you saying?"

"I wondered if you knew anything about her life. Now."

"I know little more than you do, I suppose. Only that she married my brother, and that they have a little girl who was in critical condition for awhile but who is now considered safely past the danger zone."

"Is Carrie happy?"

"Is anyone?" Tessa paused. "I've never known Carrie not to be content."

He stared at her. "Then you think he's the right man for her?"

She took a moment to answer. "She seems to think so."

He paused. "I think he might be abusing her. I ran into him the other night and he almost started a fight with me, and I remember what he was like in college…"

"He's changed, Sam." She paused. "He works at the same school I do and has always shown impeccable character. I didn't believe it at first, but no one can wear that kind of mask for so long." Tessa glanced at him reprovingly. "Sam, you're jumping to conclusions. Do you honestly think Carrie would still be with him if she were in danger?"

"I don't know whether she would or not. She might, just to see if she could survive."

"You're forgetting that she has a child to consider, and you know as well as I do that she would never put that child in danger purposefully. Trust me, Carrie can take care of herself."

He felt deflated by the cold surety in her voice. "That's the problem, Tessa. There's going to come a time when she needs someone's help, and then do you think she's going to ask for it? Do you think she'll even know who she can go to, if no one reaches out to her now?"

"Not you," Tessa said, firmly. "Not me. I care about her as deeply as you do, Sam, but I know I can't help her. It doesn't matter how much I want to help her, or how close our friendship was. Personalities click in different ways, for different reasons, and I will not be playing that role in her life."

"I can't take such a passive stance," Sam said, getting up.

"Sam." Tessa's voice was firm. "It's not your place to interfere with something you don't understand."

He turned back to her. "Do you know something I don't?"

"Sit down."

He remained standing. Her eyes flashed at him.

"Take life as it comes," she said. "And let be what will be."

He opened his mouth, closed it. She held his gaze.

"You have a business meeting," she reminded him. "Don't forget to pick up Kindra from daycare when it's over."

He started towards the door. The encounter had left him numb. He stepped outside the house, and never had the sunshine felt so good, never had the thought of seeing his children—Kindra, Jake—filled him with so much warmth.

Carrie rarely had a chance to see Chloe alone—only during feedings, and if she woke early in the morning to see her. Otherwise the baby was with Ralph. Despite his explosion a few weeks prior about needing a place to go away from the apartment, he never seemed to tire of the baby. Carrie wondered at his resilience; he even started taking Chloe into his studio outside the house, which she found out one day when sitting at the kitchen table with a cup of coffee, her notebook open in front of her, the pen in her hand idle as she wondered where her husband and her child had disappeared for the previous four hours. Then the door leading to the patio had opened and Ralph—bare-chested due to the heat of July—had come in, carrying a paint-specked Chloe in his arms.

"Close your eyes and pretend you don't see us," he said, as soon as he saw her. "I'm going to clean her up right now."

She was too speechless to retort, and he sneaked by her. She followed them to the bathroom, where she saw Chloe sitting naked in the blue porcelain sink, her large head supported by one of Ralph's strong hands, streaks of color running off her skin as he sponged the paint away.

"Wash her hands first," Carrie said, stepping into the bathroom. "What if she puts them in her mouth? She could get sick."

"You're a good little girl, aren't you?" he said to the baby, who was looking at Carrie with her dark almond-shaped eyes. "You wouldn't do something like that, would you, precious?"

Chloe turned toward the sound of his voice, reached out a tiny red hand and grabbed the dark hair on his chest. She pulled, trying to stand up in the sink, and after a moment Carrie realized he was laughing too hard to realize the danger of the situation. She moved quickly, picking up

Chloe from under the arms just as the baby started to slip.

"Were you even watching her while you were painting?" she said, forcing Chloe's tiny hands under the water. "She could have eaten something or—"

"She was too busy painting," he said, smiling.

"What?"

"She was painting. I let her choose the—"

"You let her use her *hands*?"

He stepped around her. "There's nothing in the paint that can hurt her skin. Her hands might be discolored for a few days, but that will be the worst of it."

"It can't be good for her to be around those fumes," she said, frowning.

"We were using acrylics," he said. "They don't emit strong fumes, and I left the door open. Do you want to see what she made?"

She shied away from the anger she heard in his voice. "Let me get her clean first."

He lingered in the doorway, staring at her, but she kept her eyes on the baby. When she risked looking over her shoulder, she found he had slipped away unnoticed. She wrapped a towel around Chloe, then carried her to the bedroom. She took her time drying each little limb, enjoying the time she had alone with her daughter.

"Did you have fun with your crazy father?" she asked softly, smoothing out Chloe's soft patch of dark hair.

The baby looked at her. Carrie dressed her in rainbow shorts and a tiny white tank top that Ralph said Chloe had picked out from the store by herself. As she left the room, she caught sight of their reflections in the mirror and paused. Before that moment, she had not seen herself with the child. The result shocked her; with her darker complexion and striking eyes, Chloe did not even look like her child. Carrie stood looking down at Chloe, and realized she had never experienced such crushing doubts or been so shaken in her self-confidence. Then Chloe shifted the slightest bit in her arms, breaking the trance. Carrie hugged the child to her, watched the twin images repeat the action, and left the room. She stepped into the kitchen, and her step faltered.

"I thought you'd be in the studio," she said, composing herself.

Ralph looked up from where he was standing near the kitchen table, poised over her writing. He met Carrie's eyes, and there was an anger and frenzy in them that she had never seen before. But the emotion passed, gone before its chill had left her.

"There are my girls," he said softly, and crossed the room to where Carrie was standing and watching him. He took Chloe from her, and then, very slowly, he put his arm around Carrie and drew her close to him. The gentleness in the gesture startled her, and she stood motionless as he kissed the top of her head, then rested the top of his chin there. When he finally let go of her and stepped away, the look in his eyes scared her.

"Why are you looking at me like that?" she asked.

"Do I have to have a reason?"

"I'm sure you do."

He smiled, only slightly amused. "Always on the defense, my dear?"

She walked by him to the patio's door, then stepped into the sunlight. The door to his studio was closed, and she paused before realizing that he was not planning on coming out after her. Finally she opened the door. The air in the studio was cool and fresh, tainted only faintly by the metallic smell of the acrylics. He had set up a standing fan in the corner of the studio, and he had spread Chloe's pink blanket on the concrete floor. Carrie stooped and picked it up, shaking dust from the fuzzy fabric and folding it neatly as she stood in the center of the studio, staring at what she presumed was Chloe's creation.

He had let Chloe dip her tiny hands into the paint without consideration of color compliments or composition, then turned her loose. The vibrant streaks of color overlapped in edges of thick milky brown, but there was a certain charm in the chaos, in the clash of colors and their deformed shapes. In the center of the painting was the delicate imprint of a child's hand inside a larger one: his hand. Without thinking, she put her hand up on the painting against it, felt the paint cool and slick against her skin. She withdrew her hand quickly, and found she had not left a smudge on the painting. Only the two hands, one tiny and one large, remained within the splotchy whirlwind of colors. She shivered and backed out of the studio, closing the door behind her.

She paused outside, reveling in the sun's warmth. She would no longer ignore the tension between them. He had never shied away from her; their problems always came back to whether she was willing to work through them or whether she wanted to walk away and let go. He had left her in control. She did not give him enough credit for his efforts; he took care of the baby uncomplainingly when she didn't want to. Carrie had often emerged from the study, chilled after having been in the writing zone for so long, to find him romping around the living room with the baby, or sitting quietly on the sofa reading to her while Chloe looked around the room with her wide eyes. Seeing him interacting with their child made Carrie feel a different kind of trust in him.

She thought about what a difference that made as she stood outside on the balcony, and then she went inside. She found him in their bedroom, reading, with Chloe sprawled on her stomach near the foot of the bed. Her defenses kicked in.

"Are you watching her?" She moved quickly into the room. "What if she falls off the bed?"

He put aside what he was reading and looked up as she examined Chloe. "I'm sorry, Carrie."

She paused, instantly regretting the tone she had taken with him. "I didn't mean to sound like such a bitch."

He didn't respond. She went to their bed and sat down, putting Chloe between them. "We should talk to Dr. Stoddard about getting a hearing aid for her. I've read that could help her keep up with her peers, especially since she's only partially deaf."

"I also read a study about preemies and what factors go into determining how fast they progress," he said. "To see if there is anything we can do to help her."

"What did the study say?" She noticed that Chloe crawled towards Ralph.

He gathered Chloe into his arms. "Before two years, genetic as well as environmental factors play an equal role." He paused. "After two years, environmental factors become more important."

"Environmental factors?"

He paused. "The study used the term 'maternal efficiency' and how it was sometimes the determining factor."

She moved away from him, away from Chloe. "Are you trying to imply that I'm not a good mother? That I'm not spending enough time with her? Do you think I'm neglecting—"

"No, Carrie. Damn it, no. I wasn't trying to imply anything." He looked at her. "I wanted to ask if you thought 'maternal' was the key word. The study was done in Scotland during a time when most of the men worked, and the women raised the children. I was wondering how the results would differ in Western societies, where there are two parents to care for the child, or the child gets raised by a nanny or daycare center—"

"Why were you reading about a study done in Scotland anyway?" He always made her feel like a failure as a parent; he was always one step ahead of her.

"I wanted to know if you think a mother shares a special bond with the child, or if the father's affection can be just as valuable as the mother's."

"I don't know," she said. "But I hope that 'maternal' isn't the key word in that study, because Chloe clearly loves you more than me. Now please excuse me. I need to change her diaper."

She left the room and went to the bathroom, half hoping he would follow her. Their exchange of words had been the closest they had come to arguing in weeks, and she realized how much she missed that time when they had let their words fly rather than tip-toe around each other. She carried Chloe to the nursery, then went back to the bedroom and saw that Ralph had resumed reading. Then, she saw what he was reading.

"Ralph, please don't—"

"Your sentences always seem to start like that," he said, flipping a page. "And I'm enjoying myself. You've never let me read your work."

She looked at him. "It's not finished."

"I'll be damned if I'm going to put it down now that I've stumbled upon it." He met her eyes. "Though I understand, now, why you never wanted me to read any of it before."

"I don't ever let anyone read what I've written before I have the entirety of the first draft written out."

He closed the notebook and put it back on the night stand, away from her reach. "You said I was your Muse."

She saw what was coming. "You are."

"I read that scene," he said. "That last one. The one you must have written this morning, when Chloe and I were painting. I didn't realize how much I had hurt you. I'm sorry."

She kept her eyes on his face. "Don't think my writing is based on—"

His voice was harsh. "Don't lie and tell me it's not."

She was surprised that the tears and anger came back, that one reference to their past made the old wounds open up, that five years and two novels later, she had still not succeeded in burying the old hurt. "Why did you have to bring it up?"

"Because I want you to know that I'm sorry."

"It doesn't matter now," she said. "It would have mattered then, but it doesn't matter now."

"Do you still want me to hurt you, manipulate you, play mind games with you? Is that what it takes to make you happy? *I'm* your husband, but this...*this*," he gestured at the notebook, "is what you're writing about. This is who you're stuck on. Damien. I've tried being honest with you, Carrie, I've tried to become a man worthy of your love...and you tell me it doesn't matter to you."

She turned away from him.

"I'm not letting you off the hook that easily," he said, after a pause. "I've lost my temper and I can't take my words back, but I can apologize for them. And I do."

She turned to see him watching her cooly, with a spark of the keen insight into people—and women in particular—that she had noticed about him.

"I'm going to start waitressing again," she said.

"School starts up again for me in less than a month. We can't leave Chloe here alone."

"We can get a babysitter if there are time complications."

He stared at her. "Is that what you want?"

She nodded. He sat very still.

"We'll do what we have to." He put Chloe down in the center of the bed, then stood and walked past her. "Excuse me. I need to shave."

She stood uncertainly in the middle of their bedroom, hearing the click of the electric razor turning on, the muffled sound of the blade. She was still standing in the same position when he came back into the room. He crossed the room to his side of the closet and dried his face with the towel he had put there, because there was not enough room in the tiny bathroom.

"We should probably get her that hearing aid," he said, glancing at Chloe.

She did not like the look in his eyes. "Yes, we probably should."

When the school year started in early September, Carrie started waitressing in the evenings at a different restaurant. She had the mornings free to spend with Chloe, but despite the time she spent with the child, she could not get Chloe to give her more than a half-smile. The fear of something suddenly going wrong with the baby preyed on her mind when she was alone with Chloe, and the child's presence filled her with despair. Carrie would spend the morning trying to write, but her attention was constantly diverted by the baby, whose almost complete silence made her worry that something had happened, made her abandon the notebook and check on the child at various intervals. And when Ralph came home after teaching, often enthused to tell her about something that his students had said or done, she could not look him in the eye, could not listen to his stories without having her conscience jar her. She saw how he looked at her then, but he rarely commented.

"This would be perfect," he said one day, after he had come home and started dinner for him and Chloe, because Carrie was on her way to the restaurant. "If."

She was in their bedroom changing into her waitressing uniform, but she heard him. Though she was only in a bra and her black, knee-length skirt, she stepped into the kitchen, saw Chloe sitting on his knee. His attention was on a paper in front of him—probably a student's essay— and he had a pen in his hand that he was trying to keep away from Chloe, who was reaching for it ecstatically.

His eyes flicked over Carrie's half-naked body. "Beautiful home, beautiful wife, beautiful kid, good job."

"It would be perfect, if," she repeated.

"If this was what you wanted, too," he said. "But you're unhappy. Don't lie to me."

She crossed her arms over her chest, though he was no longer looking at her. "I haven't said anything."

He laughed. "You will, once you think about what I just said. My picture of perfection." He broke off as she continued to look at him blankly, then he smiled without emotion. "It must be absolutely repulsive to you, Carrie, this picture of domesticity. Dinner on the stove, 'Honey, I'm home'…"

"Don't."

He laughed again, a bark. His eyes narrowed, gleamed. "You once asked me how long would I last. I'm turning the question around. How long can you?"

She turned and left the kitchen, went back into their bedroom and finished getting dressed. She pulled back her hair, grabbed her keys, had to pass through the kitchen on her way to the door and found that he had once more returned his attention to the paper in front of him.

"I won't be back until late," she said, grabbing a windbreaker; September had brought a brisk chill. "Don't wait up. I know you'll take care of Chloe."

Her words had become routine, and were routinely met with his silence. She would return later to find Chloe tucked into her crib in the nursery, sleeping peacefully. Sometimes he was up, sometimes he was asleep—and that always determined which one of them would sleep in the bed, and which would sleep on the couch.

After Chloe started crawling at seven months—something that neither Carrie, Ralph, nor Dr. Stoddard had expected to happen that early—Carrie found that writing while in the apartment was impossible. Sometimes Chloe would crawl over and sit near the desk where Carrie was trying to write. Once in her sitting spot she never moved, never cried or made a motion to be picked up, but the child's presence still arrested Carrie's attention. She felt that Chloe was watching her, constantly watching her with her dark somber eyes, and though she never was when Carrie turned and looked at her, still she could not shake the chill that came with the feeling. If Chloe was not there, however, she was crawling around the apartment, curious about everything, getting stuck behind furniture, finding ways to hurt herself; Carrie needed to watch her constantly.

The long hours of the restaurant tired her, and when she got home at night she started soaking her feet and waking up the next morning tired and aching…to silence. The constant motion of waitressing exhausted her, but she thought the constant, ceaseless silence of the apartment unnerved her more. Ralph left for the school by six thirty, and when Carrie woke there was only Chloe and the silence. Sometimes she would take Chloe to the park and sometimes she would listen to music, but she could not write and she could not calm her nerves.

She hid her changing mental state from Ralph, even as she hid the fact that she had decided to quit her waitressing job. She went to a café in the evenings instead of the restaurant. There, she felt herself coming alive again, the passion she found in her writing making the return to the house at the end of the night that much harder.

So eventually she stopped facing reality altogether; she told Ralph she worked at night and she told Christine she worked in the morning, and then she dropped Chloe off at Christine's and picked her up before five, when Ralph got home. And then she would leave. Sometimes she would write in the morning, sometimes she would write at night. Her days and her nights began to blend, but she did not tell Ralph or Christine what she was doing. She did not let them know that the time they thought she was spending at work or with her daughter was really time she was spending by herself.

She rarely saw Ralph and so he had few opportunities to question her—but one night her cover was blown. She was getting ready to leave, when Ralph caught her in their bedroom. He stepped inside and he closed the door, then stood in front of her only exit. He looked at her without speaking. She sensed, from the rigid way that he held back his shoulders, from the set of his jaw and the steel in his eyes, that he had something to say to her and that he wouldn't let her leave until he had said it. These moments, when they came face to face, always made the intimacy that had existed between them once seem impossibly far away.

"Is this how you want to live, Carrie?" he asked quietly.

She smiled, unsure of how much he knew. "No greeting?"

"Is this how you want to live?" he repeated.

She crossed the room, put the bed between them. "Where's Chloe?"

"In the nursery. Answer my question."

She turned to face him. "If you want me to answer your question, then you need to define how you think I'm living."

"You know what I mean."

"You always assume that I know what you mean. I don't. Most time, I don't have the slightest idea."

His jaw clenched. "Don't you want to spend more time with Chloe? More time with me?" He paused. "Time is passing, Carrie. She's going to grow up. I'm going to grow old."

She was startled to see a hunted look in his eyes—a look of urgency and weariness. She had not noticed the silver threads that had crept into the opaque black hair near his temples. He looked thin; his eyes burned in a face that seemed wolfish in its leanness.

"Have you lost weight?" she asked.

"Thirty pounds."

"My god," she said, her eyes widening. "Are you okay?"

He turned away from her. She closed the distance between them and made him face her by gripping his shoulders; she felt how he responded to her touch.

"Damn you," he said, his eyes flashing with anger as he stepped away from her. "You always do this, Carrie. Don't distract me."

The tone of his voice raised the devil in her, the wildness in his eyes shook her to her core. Her thoughts left her and all she knew was that she wanted him. They hadn't been together a handful of times since Chloe had been born, and she missed him. He took a step towards her, then he stopped. His head jerked from side to side as if he had been slapped.

She sat down on the bed. "Ralph."

He turned away from her. "You have to work."

Her eyes baited him. "Get over here."

"Carrie." His voice broke as she started unbuttoning her blouse.

She pulled the blouse over her head, tossed it to the corner of the room, openly challenged him. "Do you want me to say I hate you? Will that get you over here any quicker?"

She was in his arms before she realized he had moved. When he kissed her, she thought he was going to suffocate her with his need. When his clothes were off, she saw how bony he had become—all sinewy muscle. And when she looked at her body as he rose above, she saw the stretch marks the birth had left on her stomach and she was shocked. Even as he went into his own world of release and oblivion, she remained shocked that he was right—that time had passed, that they were getting old.

Something else had also changed. The anger and frustration that had once escalated their passion had created a wall between them. They were apart, even as they were uniting. There was no love in what he was doing to her. The thought filled her with a vague sense of horror, but she could not bring herself to tell him to stop. She lay underneath him motionless, his every thrust a shock to her numbed system. She tuned him out, she tuned herself out. Eventually the distant humming in her ears receded and she came back, found that he was laying beside her and breathing heavily, the breath sounding raspy in his thin chest. She turned her head, slightly, and saw the tension had gone from his face. He opened his eyes and turned to her. He kissed her gently.

"Your lips are cold," he said.

"I'm cold," she said.

"Carrie." He stopped. "Are you all right, sweetheart?"

She nodded and kept her eyes on the ceiling, wondering how her face could stay so still when there was a great, gaping chasm opening inside her.

"Maybe there is hope for us," he said, touching her face.

"I'm tired," she said, and though her voice was steady she felt like crying.

"With good reason." His eyes remained locked on her face. "Damn, you had to work."

"Not tonight. I didn't have to work tonight."

He looked at her, hard, then settled back onto the pillows. "I'll let you rest. I love you, Carrie."

"Ralph."

"Yes?"

She shivered. "I hate you."

"You...what?"

She turned away from him, curled herself into a ball under the covers, let her hot tears fall on the smooth, cool pillow case. She let herself cry, uncontrollable sobbing intakes of breath. She felt the bed sag as he sat up and bent over her. She did not recoil when he put a hand on her back, when he pulled the wet strands of her sweaty hair away from her face. She let him, and he let her cry and sat very still. She did not know how long she cried into his shoulder, how long he sat there silently. She knew only that at some point a great calm came over her, filling the emptiness that had been there.

"Carrie," he said. His voice was calm in the stillness. "What do you—"

His voice broke. There was silence. Then he exhaled, a long, sibilant, empty sound. "What do you want me to do?"

She latched onto the rhythmic sound of her breathing, in and out, in out, calm, relaxed, in control. Then she spoke.

"I want you to leave," she said, the strange sense of calm pervading her senses.

He remained motionless on the side of their bed, his face marble. Not a twitch, not a single change of expression.

"I want you to leave," she repeated. "And I want you to take Chloe with you."

Very slowly, he smoothed the covers around her. He stood, and then he bent and kissed her gently on her forehead. His lips felt cool and dry against her feverish, sweat-stained skin.

"I love you," he said.

The click of the door closing let her know he had gone, and she could only turn to the wall beside the bed, suddenly flooded with cool, sweet relief.

She went to sleep at some point because she woke the next morning filled with a tight sense of anticipation lodged in her stomach. She pushed away the covers, still damp—from her tears, his semen, their sweat—and rose. The sense of calm from the night before had not left her, but she saw that her naked body trembled in the mid-morning light. She slipped into her robe and walked into the kitchen, the living room. Empty.

The nursery door was open. She went in and saw the empty crib, and the knowledge hit her like a sledge-hammer. She turned away from the

room with its rocking chair, the brand new teddy bear, the books—ABC
and 1,2,3—stacked on the dresser near the wall opposite the crib. She
closed the nursery door behind her. She let herself out of the silent
apartment and onto the balcony.

She went to his studio's door and opened it. He had left the paintings
of the children he had made before Chloe's birth, had left the ones of his
models and the ones of her. He had taken only the painting that he and
Chloe had made together. She sat down on the cold, bare floor in front of
the empty space where the painting had hung. She did not cry. She was
very cold. Her mind filled in the canvas, the tiny child's hand-print inside
the larger, adult one. Every hope of her life seemed to have hung there;
she had blinked and it had all disappeared. She sat and she stared but the
world would not go back to being right.

She knew that he had left, but sitting in the studio, shivering in the dim
morning air, she could not yet believe it, could not register that he had
taken Chloe and left. Finally she stood and left the studio, a dull ache in
her heart.

His absence opened her eyes. She began to see that she had started to
neglect herself: her well-being, her friendships, her relationships with the
other people she cared about. She realized the change when she went to
tell Christine what had happened and saw the wrinkles around the corners
of her mother's eyes and lips, saw that Chris had sprung up even taller and
that his face had taken on a long, hungry look. When she asked him how
everything was going, he answered her in the deep-throated voice of a
man. When Carrie left the house she was deeply shaken, caught off guard
by the blatant passage of time while she had been involved in her own life.
She saw Tessa in the grocery store and realized for the first time that they
hadn't spoken in almost a year. She saw that Tessa had started to age. The
next day she ran into Sam, and did not recognize him. She looked at
herself in the mirror and didn't recognize her frenzied eyes, the dark
circles under them, the tired longing in the droop of her shoulders, the
downward curve of her lips. Suddenly she realized that, for a long time,
she had been blind to the fact that she was unhappy with how her life had
been going.

She associated her initial pangs of emptiness with his absence. But she knew he was at the school, teaching, and she did not go to him. There was only what was, not what could have been, and she let the thought move her forward. She realized quickly that the presence she missed more was her daughter—that core part of herself that she had lost. She worked on re-establishing her life, on putting more energy into her writing and finding what closure she could through it. She started to substitute teach at any school other than Greensburg Salem High. She made an attempt to make regular rendez-vous with the only people who had cared about her unconditionally—Sam, Tessa, Christine—and she forced herself to keep these meetings sacred.

"Why don't you go after Chloe?" Tessa asked her. "Courts wouldn't separate you from your daughter."

And she had responded with the cold truth: that Chloe loved Ralph, and that Ralph understood the child's emotions when she did not and was better equipped to handle the finances that would come with any possible medical complications. She told Tessa another cold truth: she trusted him to take care of the baby, and she didn't trust herself to give Chloe the kind of love a baby needs.

With Tessa and Christine, she let herself be completely open. With Sam she was more cautious. Sam always seemed to have something on his mind, but he was the person who understood why she had become the person she had become—more than Ralph, more even than Tessa—and what she felt for him, and what he felt for her, Carrie came to realize was a very deep friendship.

Carmen Crenshaw was born eight and a half months after Carrie woke up and found herself in the empty apartment—a child who had resulted from his lust and repression and her pain and complete submission. Carmen weighed a whopping six and a half pounds, and she was the most beautiful baby Carrie had ever seen. Her eyes were gray-hazel-blue, her complexion a glowing caramel, and the hair on her head a deep rich brown. As Carrie lay in the hospital—Christine holding her hand after the difficult labor—she heard a deep, rich wailing as the doctor cleaned the baby off, and thought the sound the most heart-warming song she had ever heard.

With Carmen the process of motherhood was different; with Carmen, the process was right. Carrie loved the baby fiercely the first time she was put into her arms, and cried in gratitude when the child curled into her and closed her eyes, seeming to love her, too. Carrie had spent the pregnancy worried that she would miscarry or give birth prematurely like she had before, worried while in labor that the child would be born with serious congenital defects—a missing eye, an enlarged skull, a tail. But Carmen was beautiful, defying her worry and anxiety, and Carrie loved her. Carmen was a reason for her to begin the search once again for happiness and peace. Carmen was a reason to build herself back up, to reinvent herself on a more stable foundation. Carmen helped her move on.

Carrie had wondered, at one time, what could make her stay in her hometown. Now she wondered what would happen that would let her leave. Despite the support she got from Christine, Sam, and Tessa, she was in a rut, going nowhere. Despite the love surrounding her and the hope Carmen's sweet face gave her every day, Carrie felt imprisoned, trapped within the boundaries of the provincial town but unable to take the risk and start again somewhere new. Though she had taken small steps. New apartment, new novel, new school district, new focus. Steps which were not enough. What she wanted was a complete break. But maintenance problems and squabbles with the school board were not enough to drive her over the edge.

The phone call did it. The phone call came when she was approaching the end of her twenty-seventh year, when Carmen was almost one.

"Carrie." His voice, familiar and unexpected, after the standard beep. Then a long, long pause. A dense, heavy silence. A sharp intake of breath, before his voice began again, steady. "I'm calling to tell you that we're...that Chloe is fine." A pause. "She's beautiful." Another pause. "If you care...you should, but...." His voice did not waver, but there were thirty seconds worth of dead silence between those words and his final ones, which were, "maybe, someday, Carrie..."

"Maybe someday," she said quietly, staring at the phone after the heavy clicking sound and dial tone let her know he had given up. She opened her arms as Carmen toddled towards her on the kitchen floor and

398

scooped the child into a fierce hug. The final words he had spoken to her, that last night, came back to her with haunting clarity.

I love you.

But he would be fine; he had Chloe. She had Carmen, and she was happier off without him. She tickled Carmen, received a gurgling giggle. She smiled, then carried the child over to her playpen and fenced her in before returning to the phone. She called Sam and told him what she planned to do. Then she went to the playpen and looked into the child's eyes—bright blue, brimming with life.

"Upsy-daisy, kiddo," she said, picking Carmen up, then holding her in the stillness of her one-room apartment, in the silence that was sacred until Carmen squealed to be put down. Carrie put her down and looked around the apartment. The thought of leaving no longer daunted her as it had before. She would not leave immediately or rashly, as her instinct prompted her; she would settle her affairs, sell the apartment, find a place to go. But she would leave. The promise of that resolution hung in the air, invisible but palpable, along with a sense that, even in the midst of her uncertainty, everything was exactly as it should be.

PART THREE

Carmen Crenshaw looked out at the large oak tree near her window. The Maine winter had stripped the branches to skeletons, and from the vantage point in her room she could see the outline of the church with its tall steeple against the horizon. She had never been there; her mother—whom she called Carrie because she knew how much it annoyed her—never went to church. Carmen didn't go either. She didn't like the thought of an all powerful man up in the sky who had planned her life and could jerk her from point A to point B like a puppet on a string. She didn't like the thought of God, and she didn't like the thought of Judgment. She preferred to think she could do whatever she wanted.

Her eyes, blue-gray, shifted from the church to the hills beyond—hazy outlines barely visible in the approaching dusk. She had wanted the room because of the view of those hills, which promised escape and something in the distance, and because of the tree. She looked at the hills, the church, the dark skeleton arms of the trees, and then she left her room and went downstairs. The smell of spices and freshly cooked vegetables became stronger as she descended, and she peeped into the kitchen as she passed. Carrie was not there, so she went in and lifted the silver lid off the pot on the stove. Curry. Again. She scraped the curry into a bowl, then opened all the windows. She devoured the curry in her room, then went downstairs quietly. She passed the kitchen and noticed the windows had been closed. She smiled; Carrie had emerged from her lair. She continued down the hallway with its bare walls, then opened the door to Carrie's lair without knocking.

"Hiya, Mom," she said, striding into the room, noting as she did that her mother had somehow managed to stuff even more books into the bookshelves and even more papers onto the pile growing on her desk. "I thought we could chat."

For a moment Carrie sat as if she had not heard or understood. Then, without the slightest change of expression, she pushed away the papers in front of her and straightened in her chair.

"What do you want to talk about, Carmen?"

Carmen leaned against the door. "I saw you made damn curry again."

"I've told you not to swear," she said, then, "Carmen, do you know what season it is?"

"Do you think I'm stupid? It's winter."

"Then can you tell me why the windows were open?"

"Because I opened them." She shrugged. "I don't like how the curry smells. I was going to close them after it didn't smell so bad."

"Don't lie to me."

"Why do you think I'm always lying to you? I don't like curry. And you make it all the time."

"And you always eat it."

"I do not. I throw it away because it makes the whole house smell."

"Honey," Carrie said, emphasizing the word. "I find bowls encrusted with curry in your room all the time."

Carmen put her hands on her hips. "Why are you going in my room?"

Carrie looked at her. "Must you always act so childish? You're thirteen years old, Carmen."

Carmen stared at her. "If all you want to do is argue, I'm going to leave. I was trying to be nice."

"I noticed that you called me Mom." She frowned. "What do you want?"

"I don't want anything. Just to talk."

"What would you like to talk about?" she repeated.

"You look really old."

"Thank you, Carmen." Carrie sighed. "I am old. I'm glad I look my age."

Carmen paused, knowing that Carrie didn't approve of how she dressed. "What are you working on, anyway?"

"My lesson plans for tomorrow."

"Do you like teaching?"

"Yes."

"I bet your students aren't bad like me."

"You choose to be bad," Carrie said. "But you aren't bad with anyone but me. Would you care to explain that to me? The neighbors are always telling me what a beautiful girl I'm raising, and I get glowing reports from your teachers."

"Why do you read these books?" Carmen went over to a section of the bookshelves and scanned the titles.

"Because you frustrate me."

"I think you're cute," Carmen said, pulling out a book and rifling through the pages.

"Excuse me?"

"I think it's cute that you read up on problem children, like you think these books will explain me to you." Carmen tossed the book on the desk. "Wasn't Ophelia the girl who killed herself in *Macbeth*? Is *that* what you want me to do?"

"Ophelia was a character in *Hamlet*." Carrie picked up the book Carmen had tossed at her, went to the shelf, and put the book back in its place. "It's a different Ophelia, Carmen, and no, I do not want you to kill yourself."

"I bet you wish I was gone."

"Life would be easier if you were," Carrie said. "But not better. I'm glad you're here."

"Is that what those books told you to say?"

"No, Carmen. Devil child that you are, I love you."

"I bet those books didn't tell you to call me a devil child. Don't you know what that could do to my self-esteem?"

Carrie sighed. "Carmen, if you're going to act like this, I'm going back to my work. But if you can act like a mature young lady—"

"I saw the parfait you made for me in the fridge. Thanks."

Carrie stopped speaking in mid-sentence. "You're welcome."

"It was really good."

"I'm glad you liked it."

"By the way, I'm thinking about having sex with Eric Styles. That's what I really wanted to tell you." She turned on her heel to go.

"Carmen."

"What?" She turned around. "Just because I'm thirteen doesn't mean...why aren't you mad?"

"Would you like to talk about this like two adults?"

"No. I'm not really thinking about doing...that."

"You wouldn't have brought up that subject if something hadn't been on your mind."

"I could just be trying to get a reaction from you. Isn't that what your goddam books tell you?"

Carrie looked at her levelly. "Carmen, I'm going to make some hot chocolate. It's drafty in here, since you opened all the windows, so I'm going to drink the hot chocolate in the living room. You can come if you would like."

Carmen bit back a smile as she followed Carrie out of the room and into the kitchen. She watched silently as Carrie put water on the stove to boil, then measured the cocoa powder, sugar, brown sugar, and vanilla extract into two mugs; Carrie had made hot chocolate from scratch since Carmen had been a little girl. The rich smell of the cocoa filled the kitchen. Carrie handed her a mug, then went to the living room and sat down on the sofa. Carmen sat down in the chair opposite her.

"Now. What's on your mind?"

"I feel like I'm in a shrink's office," Carmen said. "Do you really have to start off this conversation with that kind of a question?"

"I'm listening." Carrie took a sip from her mug and made a slight grimace as the liquid scalded her tongue.

"I..." Carmen twisted the mug around in her hands. "God, this is so awkward. I've never *talked* to you before. I think this is a really bad idea."

"We used to talk all the time," Carrie said, then prompted. "You really like Eric Styles."

"Yeah. I do. I've been going out with him for a week."

"And he asked you to sleep with him?"

"You ask me that like you're asking about the weather," Carmen said angrily.

Carrie looked at her daughter's indignant face. "You have to tell me what's going on if you want me to be able to understand what you're—"

"I know," Carmen interrupted. "But you've already guessed it so you're not going to make me *say* it are you?"

"You've already said it," Carrie said. "So I think you can tell me again. I'm sure we're talking about the same thing."

"Eric asked me to sleep with him," Carmen said, abandoning her hot chocolate. "Like I even know how to do that. He acts like…I'm old."

"You matured early," Carrie said. "And you act older than thirteen."

"I thought you said I acted like I was two."

"Carmen."

"You tell me that all the time!"

Carrie paused. "He might think it's appropriate behavior."

"*Is* it appropriate behavior?"

"Not for someone who is thirteen. Believe me on this one, Carmen. You're too young." Carrie paused, relieved that Carmen was still listening to her. "You would be moving too fast. I should never have let you go out with him in the first place. I should have made you wait until you were sixteen."

"No, you didn't do anything wrong," Carmen said quickly. "You let me make my own choices. You're a good mom."

"I don't know about that," Carrie said. "But the thought of going out with him seemed to make you so happy. The last time I remembered seeing you that happy was when I bought you that pink dress for your first Valentine's Day dance."

"That was centuries ago. How do you even remember that?"

Carrie paused. "What do you think you should do, Carmen?"

"Maybe it is too fast. I don't even know."

"It happens when a man—"

Carmen covered her ears with her hands. "Don't say it! I know *that*."

Carrie watched until Carmen had lowered her hands from her ears. Then she opened her mouth to speak, and was instantly met by a shriek of protest from Carmen.

"If you say it, I swear I'll leave the room!"

"I was going to ask you a question."

Carmen looked at her cautiously. "What?"

"Have you talked to Eric about waiting?"

"It wouldn't do any good." Carmen paused. "He's *so* popular. I know that if I ask him to wait he'll find some girl who won't tell him no, and then he won't ever think about me again."

"You won't know unless you try."

"No, I know. If I say no, he'll drop me."

Carrie paused. "Is that really the kind of guy you want?"

"No, he's not worth it." Carmen looked down at her hands. "But I still want him. Even though I know..."

Carrie was no longer looking at Carmen, no longer looking at anything in the room. Her eyes were unfocused and dim, as if seeing something from a very great distance.

"When I tell him no..." Carmen paused. "Are you okay?"

Carrie blinked. "Yes, I'm listening. Please continue."

"I guess I don't *need* a boyfriend. You've always been alone." She hesitated. "I mean, can I ask you a question?"

"I'll answer it if I can."

She paused. "Why don't you ever talk to me about my dad? Why do you hate him so much?"

"I don't hate him," Carrie said. "Your father and I decided we'd be better off apart, so we went our separate ways. He told me he loved me before he left and then he was gone, and I have you and my students, and I'm happy."

"Don't you ever get lonely?"

A shadow passed momentarily over Carrie's face. "Romantic love doesn't seem important to me anymore, honey."

"I want to meet him," Carmen said, suddenly. "Can I?"

"You have that right," Carrie said. "I won't stop you."

"Don't you want to see him again?"

"No."

"I can't meet him on my own. I want you to be there, too."

"Honey, I don't know if your father would want to see me again."

"I thought you said you parted on good terms." She paused. "You won't know unless we try."

"If I wanted to try, I would." Carrie took another sip of hot chocolate. "Sometimes, Carmen, people leave for good reasons. There is no self-evolution in raising the same old ghosts. Your father is a part of my past, and it's better for me that way. But if you want to meet him, I'll give you his address and his phone number."

"Not right now. I have other things on my mind." Carmen paused. "You're really not lonely?"

"You shouldn't use another person to fill a gap in your life. If you never listen to me again, I want you to remember that. You should never be with someone because you think you need him. You should be with someone because you want to be."

"I know. I *know*."

"Then you're smarter than I was at your age. It took me years to learn that one, and I had to learn it the hard way."

"I changed my mind." Carmen's eyes began to gleam. "I want to meet my dad as soon as possible, and I *definitely* want you there. Don't you think you should face him?"

"No," Carrie said, standing. "No, I don't."

"Where are you going? For one of your walks?"

"You don't have to be so sarcastic. I'm going to the kitchen to wash my cup." She paused. "But now that you've mentioned it, a walk sounds like a good idea. Would you like to come with me?"

"Are you serious? There's a foot of snow outside."

"Maybe you'll have a snow day tomorrow," Carrie said. "Wouldn't that be nice?"

"It must be real nice, going for walks when you don't want to face reality."

"Really," Carrie said. "It must be *really* nice to go for walks when—"

"Can you stop being an English teacher for a second?"

"Grammar is important," Carrie said. "How you speak can influence how people view you. If you speak well, you'll also write better, and I want you to be able to write well…"

"Like you should talk about writing."

Carrie froze. "What?"

"When was the last time you wrote anything? The last book I read of yours was published *eight years* ago."

"I didn't know you read my—"

"I might have." Carmen paused. "So what's the real story? Dad and you broke up and you stopped writing and now you hate men?"

"You wouldn't understand, Carmen."

"I might. You never know unless you try."

"Remind me never to give you advice again," Carrie said, trying hard to keep her voice serene. "No, I shouldn't have said that to you."

"All you do is write the same story over and over again," Carmen continued. "Haven't you ever fallen in love with anyone besides Dad?"

"That's enough from you."

Her eyes burned insistently. "I want to know."

The cup Carrie was washing flew across the room and broke against the wall, scattering the clean kitchen tiles with ragged ceramic shards.

"That's enough," Carrie said. "I've had enough from you tonight, Carmen." She paused, exhaled. "But I enjoyed our talk. I'm glad you felt like you could come talk to me when you had something really pressing on your mind."

"If you're glad then why do you sound like a robot?"

"Go." Carrie flung her finger at the door.

Carmen tiptoed past her, exaggerating her steps as she sidestepped the visible chunks of broken mug.

"Carmen."

She turned. "What the hell do you want now?"

"I want you to bring down the dish you used for the curry, do you understand? If you leave it in your room, we're going to get ants."

"Don't go in my room!" Carmen yelled, then bolted up the stairs. She slammed her door, knowing the sound would carry, then stood looking at the door, half afraid that Carrie would come after her. She wished she could remember precisely how she had gone about making Carrie so angry. Five minutes passed, and then Carmen relaxed and went to the window. She looked out and saw only the single light of the distant church in the darkness.

She wished it were summer. Then she could climb out onto the tree's flat branch, and under the sheltering canopy of the tree's leaves, she could let her imagination carry her away from the house and away from her life—to that distant place beyond the hills. Somewhere far away—into something different and new and better.

Carrie waited until Carmen had gone to bed, then reached for her coat and the matching misshapen scarf that Carmen had made her, before the adolescent years had hit. Carrie paused as she looked at the stitches in the uneven weave, then wrapped the scarf around her graying tresses and let herself outside. She walked down the snow-clotted roads, slightly comforted by the delicate snowflakes sprinkling down. Stars fallen out of the sky, Carmen had called them, when she had been younger—much younger. Everything had changed, as if by black magic, when Carmen had turned ten and started an early puberty.

She thought about Carmen's words as she walked. She had promised herself on leaving her hometown ten years ago that she would heal, but she realized she had not, not even remotely. She thought of him often. She thought of Chloe, too.

She had gone out for coffee with him after the night he had left the phone message for her. Not for one moment of the meeting had he taken his eyes from her, but Chloe, a tiny, misshapen thing with a patch of dark hair on her head, had not seemed happy to see her. Chloe had clung to him, screaming when Carrie tried to hold her. She had left Carmen with Christine for the meeting; Carrie did not want him to know about the child, or how she had struggled with being a single mother. He had seen that she was tired, but she had not let him discern the true reason why— that Carmen, even then, was a high-spirited imp of a child. He had called her a month after their meeting and she had ignored him, and then several months after that he had shown up at her apartment: neatly dressed, cleanly shaved, completely sober. He told her he had found out from Christine where she had moved; he asked if they could talk. Carrie was glad she had left Carmen with Christine that night; he did not learn of their second child. There had been awkward silence and tentative small talk. He was fine, she was fine, Chloe was fine and with a baby-sitter for the night. Then silence. When he started crying, she realized he was as broken as she was, and then it had been deja vu, with the twist that after the night of violent passion she had been the one to pack off a child and he had awakened to an empty apartment.

She had left him in the middle of the night to pick up Carmen, and asked Christine why she had given out her address. She listened as Christine insisted that Carrie and her husband needed to talk, that the lack of closure in such a high intensity relationship was unhealthy. Carrie had left with Carmen that same night. It was the first time she had felt betrayed by her mother.

It was getting colder as she walked.

Going to Maine had been Sam's idea. When she told him about her decision to leave for good, he had told her his family owned a two-story house in Maine that they only used in the summers. She had convinced Sam to sell the house to her. He had surprised her by moving to Maine after his divorce with Tessa was finalized, and he had helped her acclimate. A new house in a new state, a new phone number, and Sam the only one who knew where she had moved. At least she had tried to start over.

Her thoughts, unwanted guests, turned to Carmen. Though Carmen despised her, Carrie was proud of her daughter; Carmen had become a sharp-witted, sarcastic, confident young woman who knew just how far she could push people, who worked hard to get what she wanted, who was self-possessed and independent—to other people. But was Carmen happy? Carrie knew the answer to that from the frequently slammed doors and reclusive behavior, from Carmen's general dissatisfaction and irritability. She had a stranger living in her house, not a daughter.

Carrie turned back into her driveway and beat the snow from her scarf and coat before she ventured inside the house. She was tired and stiff, and she wanted to sleep. Her lesson for the next day was planned, her alarm was set, and she had done enough thinking for the night. She washed the single porcelain bowl—curry encrusted—in the sink in the kitchen before she went to bed. She was too restless to sleep despite her exhaustion.

"Hey, Carrie." A pause. "Mom?"

Carrie became aware of her daughter's voice distantly, and found she had passed out in her study while working. The walk the night before had taken its toll on her; middle age was not as forgiving of restless night wanderings as was youth. She straightened and looked at Carmen, whose slight frame did not even come close to filling the doorway. Carmen had come to her study twice in the past two days; she had not come that often in the past two months.

"What, honey?" Carrie tried to hide her exhaustion, knowing that Carmen held it against her that she was a single mother who taught a bunch of seventh and eighth graders to support them.

"Your boyfriend is here." Carmen's eyes, cold blue grey, gleamed. "Do you want me to tell him you're indisposed?"

Carrie straightened. "I've told you not to call him my boyfriend. We're friends. Old friends."

Carmen snorted. "If that's what you are, then why does it matter what I call him?"

"Carmen." Carrie fell silent. She knew she could not explain how close she felt to Sam because he had helped her during her college years and her declining marriage—because he was the one she went to when Carmen had driven her past her limits. Sam had seen her cry, he had made her laugh, he had seen her weak as much as he had seen her strong. She was more comfortable with him than she had been with her mother, her husband, her own child. She realized that Carmen was staring at her with the familiar mix of detachment and impatience, and she tried to focus. With Carmen, anything except full alertness would prove fatal.

"Please tell him I'll be out in a minute," she said.

"Alright." Carmen's eyes narrowed. "He's in the living room. I'll leave you two alone."

Carrie tried, as she always tried, to maintain her composure until later, when she could discuss her frustration with Sam and ask for his advice. Despite the fact that Tessa had gained sole custody of their daughter, Kindra, Sam took good care of his son, Jacob. Though not as smart or as good-looking as Carmen, Jacob seemed far more balanced. Sam had told Carrie he never fought with his son, that Jacob felt close to him and took his advice seriously, that Jacob was dependable and never complained— unlike Carmen, who would purr at Carrie one moment and then explode

410

at her the next. Sam would visit Carrie occasionally, and they would sit and talk about the nature of existence and the parenting mistakes they had made.

Knowing Sam was there invigorated her from her soporific state; she left the study and proceeded to the living room. Despite her teasing, Carmen did not like Sam, and made herself scarce when he came to visit. Carrie stood in the doorway, waiting until he had acknowledged her presence.

"Carrie." Sam sat as upright as he could—the years had added a slight stoop to his shoulders. "You're as thin as a bird."

"And you're as gray as a ghost," she said. "How are you doing, Sam?"

Self-consciously, he smoothed back his hair—a premature, distinguished silver—and smiled as she took a seat beside him. "I've been well, all things considered. And you?"

She nodded, patted him affectionately on the leg, but remained quiet. The older she got, the more she realized that words had the most power when the fewest of them were used.

"Writing at all, Carrie?"

"Trying to," she said. The question, the answer, had become a routine procedure, like the greetings they had exchanged.

"I've been thinking," he said. "About your writing. Have you considered going back to school and getting a Masters in creative writing? It might help."

She shook her head. "I hate the school system too much to go back."

"For goodness sake, you're a schoolteacher."

"The paradox of my life," she replied. "Besides, with Carmen being—"

"Thirteen?" His eyes reproached her. "She's old enough to look after herself for the couple of hours each week you'd be in class, and if you don't trust her you could always drop her off with us. Now that I'm freelancing, I'm home all the time."

"Are you really writing for a living? That's wonderful, Sam." She paused. "Thank you for the offer, but I'm going to have to pass." She knew Carmen was in her room; she heard the bass notes of a hip hop cacophony through the ceiling. She wondered for a moment if she should attempt to save her child's eardrums, but Sam didn't seem to mind the noise. "I don't trust Carmen enough to leave her with you. You don't know what that child is capable of."

He smiled sympathetically. "More drama?"

"No more than usual." Carrie changed the subject. "The problem isn't that I can't write, Sam. The problem is that I don't like what comes out when I sit down in front of a blank page."

"You don't have to write the truth. That's why they call it fiction."

"What I write about him *is* fiction," she said. "I create lives by tweaking the real events that actually happened." She paused, then walked over to the window. "The problem with writing lies, Sam, is that I start to confound them with the truth. If I had loved him like my memories want me to believe, then I would not have left him when he came back to me. When I finally got up the courage to go—"

"I don't know if I would call it courage."

"Call it cowardice if you prefer. But I thought when I left Greensburg that I would be scared, sad…but I wasn't. I only felt relief. I felt the fullness in my heart as I drove away from it all, our things in the trunk, my baby in the backseat, my eyes on the horizon…"

"You're talking like a writer."

She shrugged, continued. "I felt like I had somehow escaped something terrible, that everything had played out exactly as it had needed to play out. I learned that the emptiness inside had been created by a lack, that leaving had filled the gap with my newly found freedom. That's all I've wanted, Sam. Freedom."

"And control."

"I don't have control." She smiled. "Nor do I have freedom. And I've devoted my life to having both."

"That's the first time I've heard you admit that."

She looked at him steadily. "Because I want freedom and independence, it makes sense that I would want power and control."

He paused. "Writing…the truth…might help you get some closure."

"The time for that has passed. I'm fine, thank you, Sam." She closed her eyes. "I feel like we've had this conversation several hundreds of times."

"I'm sorry if I'm boring you, Carrie. You just don't seem happy."

"Happiness is elusive," she said. "Contentment is much easier to attain. When I—"

"How do you wish you would have acted, ideally?"

"When?"

"From the start," he said.

"Just the same." She paused. "To say otherwise would mean that I regret the way I've lived my life, and I don't. But if I could, there's something inside of me that I would change."

"What?"

"Carmen calls it my 'inability to love.'" She paused. "Once something, or someone, is gone, I usually find I don't miss them at all. When I lose someone, I feel more complete."

"You've always been backwards."

She offered no protest. "What was different with Ralph...or Damien...or whatever you want to call him..."

"Asshole."

She blinked. "Don't call him that."

He paused. "I'm sorry. What was different about Ralph?"

"I felt the same excitement, knowing that I could leave him and live without him. But what was different about that feeling of excitement was that..." She paused. "I thought I would see him again. In the back of my mind I felt that nothing was really over."

Neither one of them moved, until she spoke again.

"Thank you, Sam."

"For what?"

"For not saying something cliche. Like I'm better off without him. Like I'm doing fine by myself." She stood and went into the kitchen.

He followed her. "You're welcome. But you are better off without him, and you are doing fine by yourself. No one's perfect, Carrie."

She took out two plates, handed one to him. "I made oatmeal raisin cookies last night."

"My favorite."

"And one of Carmen's—second only to cheesecake. They're in the gingerbread tin, if you want some."

He opened the tin, releasing the rich smell of warm raisin and crunchy oatmeal, and loaded two cookies onto his plate. "Did you have a fight with her last night?"

"Why do you think we're always fighting? Sometimes we do all right."

He looked at her. "Any time you bake you're upset about something."

She sat down at the kitchen table. "Last night I went for a walk, but I didn't want to go to bed when I got back, so I made some cookies. Hardly anything unnatural in that." She looked up and perceived his pointed stare, and sighed. "You're too perceptive, Sam. We did fight last night. I got angry and I threw a glass against the wall."

"Oh, Carrie." He paused. "These are good cookies. Thank you."

"You're welcome."

"I have something for you." He reached into his pocket and pulled out a rectangular slip of paper, which he handed to her. She looked at it briefly.

"It's the phone number for the Castle Rock Writer's Group," he said.

She looked a warning at him; he deflected the blow of her eyes by going to the table and sitting down.

"I was passing through the downtown area," he said. "Laura's Bistro closed down, and there's a new store in its place. It looked interesting so I stopped in. You should go, if you have the chance. I think you might like it. The store is called the Green Bottle."

A hint of curiosity lit her green eyes. "Why do you think I would like it?"

"They sell candles and teas. And books, hundreds of new and used books. Everything from modern fiction to books in different languages. The front of the store is a café. Homemade scones and muffins, that kind of thing." He paused. "I saw a flier up on one of the bulletin boards for this group. Apparently it's just getting started. They could probably benefit from having a creative writing teacher and a published author, and you might learn something."

"This is very kind. But I don't have time."

"You can make the time," he said. "They meet once a week, on Tuesday nights from seven to nine. You can make time. Carmen can come over if you don't want her to be alone for that two hour period."

"You're not going to go?"

"I gave up my creative writing when I became a freelancer. I don't want to write in my free time."

"Maybe you need to go more than I do."

"I picked up the flier because I was thinking of you. I went into the store because it reminded me of something you might like. This experience is meant for you."

"You can be very persistent."

He sighed. "Give it a try."

"Why do you want me to do this?"

"Because I remember how happy writing can make you." He paused. "The first time you gave me a short story you had written and asked me for feedback, I thought you were going to blow a nerve. I had never seen so much fire in your eyes."

"I didn't know I had left such an impression."

"You looked beautiful. I couldn't forget."

"That was a long time ago."

"Sometimes, it's not such a bad idea to look back. To look back and remember what you loved, what made you happy." He paused. "Sometimes the past can help you."

"Sometimes it can eat you alive." She looked at him. "If you want me to do this, Sam, I'll give it a try. To pay you back in part, for being a true and constant friend."

"You don't need to pay me back for being your friend." He stood. "I should probably go now, Carrie. I have to pick up Jacob from practice, but since you live out this way I thought I would stop by."

"Wait. Let me get some cookies for you to take home." She came back a moment later with a plate wrapped in aluminum foil for him. "I'll think about the writers group, Sam."

He nodded, then went outside and raised his hand in greeting. He watched as Carmen retreated without waving back; the heavy purple drapes lining her window fell back into place and obscured her from his view. He was aware that Carmen did not like him, but he rarely saw her and wondered why her antipathy should bother him so much.

The clock in his car showed him he had talked with Carrie for longer than he had estimated. He had just enough time to pick up Jacob from weight-lifting practice; if he was late, Jacob would be angry. Sam backed out of the driveway and headed onto the open road, breaking the speed limit by an acceptable five miles per hour.

Jake Sampson pulled over to the side of the road and eyed the girl in the front seat of his car.

"Have you thought about what I asked you last time?" he asked her.

She nodded, making the blue and silver earrings she was wearing—shaped like Indian dreamcatchers—dance and quiver as if in a delicate wind.

"Well?"

She turned her head and looked out the window. She had pulled her shiny hair back with a silver barrette clip, and the motion exposed the flawless curve of her neck. "I talked about it with my mom."

"Jesus, Carmen." He slammed his fist onto the steering wheel. "Do you have to talk to her about everything?"

"Relax," she said. "She thinks I'm considering sleeping with Eric Styles."

"And why the hell does she think that?"

"I used him to divert her attention while bringing up the same subject, because I wanted her advice." Her eyes sought his approval. "Don't worry, Jake. She doesn't know about us."

His eyes narrowed. "How can you be sure?"

"Do you think she'd let me go over to your house when your dad isn't there if she knew what was really going on?"

"I'd see you anyway." His hands clenched the steering wheel. "What makes me fucking angry is that you have to tell her every goddamn fucking thing. I mean, Jesus Christ, Carmen, how old *are* you?"

"Would you calm down?" She glanced at him from the corner of her eye as she started searching through her glittery purse. "Here, look what I brought."

He eyed the lime green packet she threw at him. "Where'd you get it?"

"One of my friends bummed it from the store where she works."

"You don't have friends."

She shrugged. "So I lifted it."

He unbuckled his seatbelt. "Are you sure?"

"Scared." Her eyes were focused on the frozen scene outside the car.

"You were scared when I taught you how to give head, too, but that worked out all right when we tried it. Didn't it, Carmen?"

"It sounds so dirty when you say it." She wasn't looking at him, and from the view of her profile he could see that she was shaking.

"Hey, babe," he said, gently. "No one's forcing you. I'll hold onto this until you're ready. Check the glove compartment. I got you a surprise."

She glanced at him, then popped open the glove compartment door and extracted a carton of cigarettes. He watched her slip a thin white cylinder between her trembling fingers.

"Thanks," she said as she rummaged through her purse again and came out with an orange Bic lighter. "You care if I smoke?"

"Why the hell should you ask me? If you want to, go ahead."

"I just wanted to ask. I know you don't smoke and you don't like it when I do. I was trying to be nice."

"If you don't stop being so nice I'm going to slap you."

"You touch me like that and I'll kill you." She paused. "Hey, Jake, how do you get these? Because you're not old enough to buy them either."

"I have to do some shit to get them for you. But you're worth it." His eyes darkened momentarily, and he looked away. "Why do you always have to ask someone before you do anything? Are you a woman or are you a kid?"

"I know what *you* are. An asshole."

"What?"

"But only to me. I know how kind you are to your dad and my mom, and all your past girlfriends rave about you."

"You talked to my exs?"

"Yeah."

"You little bitch."

She smirked. "Before I blew you, I wanted to know what I was getting into. How's that for a rhyme?"

"Come here, you little sneak," he said, taking the lighter from her.

She leaned towards him until he had lit the cigarette for her, then she

417

settled back against the passenger seat. "You know what, Jake? I wouldn't want you if you treated everyone else like you treat me."

"There must just be something special about you," he said.

"Thanks for the compliment," she said, opening the window of the car.

"What the hell are you doing, Carmen? It's cold."

"Do you want your dad to find ashes in the car? No, I didn't think so."

He sat in silence as she finished smoking the cigarette, flicked the butt away, hid the pack in her purse and rolled up the window.

"Thank you," she said. "I really appreciate that you waited for me to calm down a bit."

He nodded, glanced at the blinking numbers on the car's clock. "We've got another hour before your mom gets back from that thing of hers. What exactly is it?"

"Some creative writing thing." She looked at him, tweezed eyebrows arched, when he snorted. "Your dad was the one who got her to go."

"Funny." He paused. "Carmen?"

"What?"

"Are you ready to try it now?"

"I guess."

He took her hand in his and noticed she was shivering. "I have an extra sweatshirt in the back of the car if you're cold."

"I'm not sure how this works," she said. "But aren't you supposed to take my clothes off, and not try to encourage me to put more on?"

His laugh brought a crimson blush to her cheeks. He let one of her long curls slip like silk through his fingers. "I like you a lot, babe."

"You're a pervert, to like someone so young."

"You're only a couple of months younger than me. No big deal."

She didn't say anything. He took her hand and put it between both of his, trying to warm her. Her nails were painted the color of bruises. He raised the hand to his lips, kissed her palm. She opened her door and got out, then lay down in the back seat and trained her eyes on the ceiling. He crawled on top of her.

"Ow," she said as his weight landed on her, then giggled, the sound muffled against his chest. He propped himself over her on his fists and reached for her jeans, but she scrunched herself into the crack of the seat, indicating that she wanted him to lie down beside her. He noticed how tense she was and knew that would never amount to a good lay, so he decided to be patient for awhile and complied. She put her head on his shoulder, and he wrapped one arm around her and let his other hand rest on her breast. He could feel her heartbeat.

"Are you worried that I'll talk?" he asked, confused by her fear. "I won't. It will stay between the two of us, like everything else has." He turned his head towards her. "Or are you afraid you're doing it for the wrong reason?"

She turned to face him. "What do you think my reasons are?"

"I don't know," he said. "So you have one more thing to tell your mother?"

She put her hand over his mouth. "No. Because I like you."

He lipped her fingers, leaned in, and kissed her.

She kept her eyes closed as he pulled away. "I'm not going to tell anyone either."

He started tracing loops on her skin under her shirt. "So no one will know."

"Do you understand why that's important?"

He was getting impatient. "Why is it important, babe?"

"I want to know I'm doing it with you because I want to, and not because I want a reaction from other people. I don't like posing."

He laughed. "Carmen, you pose all the time."

"I do not pose." She pushed herself away from him.

"Yes, you do, babe." He caught her and pulled her to him, excited by her resistance. "But it's okay. It makes you interesting."

She shrieked in outrage and struggled against him, but he silenced her with kisses. He felt her relax, then felt her arms clasp tightly around his neck. Her breathing was heavy when he pulled away from her.

He moved his hand between her legs, manipulated the heat there. "Carmen, do you want to?"

"Yes!" she cried, pulling him against her, and he did not ask her again.

She hoped Jake had done a good job of tidying her up after they had finished. She had wanted to do nothing more than lie in his arms, her head nestled on his chest, and let his warmth drive the pain away. But he had been focused, knowing he needed to get her back to his house, knowing they needed to make some stops before they got there. They had detoured to a Kwik-Mart on the way back, and he had used some damp paper towels from the run-down restroom to spot-clean the car's interior. She had waited in the store, sheltering from the cold, and she had felt foolish when he had come back with the sopping pile of towels in his arms. But the cashier had not given him a second look; the cashier had been staring at her.

In the car, Jake had kept glancing at her, and it had made her uneasy. Then, on the car ride home, Carrie's eyes had kept flicking towards her. Carmen had checked her reflection as best she could using the blurry side-view mirror, but she couldn't see anything wrong with herself. She bolted out of the car as soon as Carrie pulled into the driveway; she wanted to see if her appearance had changed, if her shame was written so clearly on her face.

She raced up the stairs to her room and felt relieved when she saw the familiar tree, the colorful bed with its patchwork quilt, and the bare white walls. Beyond the comforting interior of her space, out through the black darkness screened by her window, she could see the steeple's light, burning bright and constant as always. She closed the door to her room and inhaled sharply, then walked haltingly to the vanity mirror above her dresser. She sighed in relief; she looked the same as she always had. Her lips looked a little fuller, her eyes looked a little brighter, but besides that she looked the same. Carmen jerked as a knock sounded against her door. She checked her reflection once more, then opened the door.

"What?" she demanded.

"Are you all right? You ran out of the car so quickly."

"I have a lot of homework I have to do."

Carrie paused. "You look different, Carmen."

She looked at Carrie, panic beginning to rise in her. "What?"

"You look very happy." Carrie watched her closely. "About something."

She turned away as a fierce blush burned across her cheeks. Carrie waited, then spoke.

"I had to wait for you for almost an hour. I knew I didn't have to worry because you were with Jake, but I would have appreciated a phone call from you, young lady."

"How was your writing thing?"

"Carmen, do not change the subject on me. Where were you?"

"I'm sorry!" Carmen exploded. She had made a point of never apologizing to her mother, not even when she was wrong, but now she would say anything to get Carrie to go away and leave her alone. She was torn: she wanted to think or drown her thoughts in sleep, she hadn't decided. "It won't happen again. I'm sorry."

Carrie hesitated, and Carmen saw that the apology would be enough to prevent further questions. But Carrie still looked suspicious.

"I think I'll stay home next Tuesday night," Carrie said, after a pause. "Maybe you and I could do something together."

Carmen flicked her eyes at her mother. "I said it wouldn't happen again. I don't know why you're so worried. Jake wouldn't let anything happen to me."

"I'm so glad you have someone like Jake in your life. Someone like a big brother."

"Oh god, don't call him that."

Carrie looked at her inquiringly. "You're sure you're okay?"

"I told you I'm fine! Jesus Christ, I told you it wouldn't happen again, will you please leave me alone?"

"I've told you to watch your language," Carrie said sharply. "I don't even know where you learned to speak like that."

Carmen sighed as she turned away from Carrie. "Why do you care? You're not even religious."

"Because it makes you sound...Carmen! Close that window, it's twenty-four degrees outside!"

Carmen turned from where she was standing by the half-opened window. A flurry of snow blew in, covering her bronzed arm with a fine sheet of powder.

"I want to be alone," she said.

"So you're trying to freeze me out of your room?"

"If you don't leave, I'm going to climb out the window."

"You're acting ridiculous. Come in here this instant!"

Carmen sat straddling the window ledge, one leg in her room, one leg exposed to the elements. "I'll be out the window before you can stop me."

The lines in Carrie's face tightened. She turned and left the room, closing Carmen's door loudly behind her. Carmen closed the window, the tinge of guilt she felt superceded by relief.

Suddenly she wanted to be with Jake. They hadn't talked much, not after. If she went downstairs, she would get interrogated; the easiest way for her to get out of the house unnoticed would be to crank music and put the CD on repeat, so it would sound like she was there, then slip out onto the tree branch. She had slipped out of the house like that before—but that had been during summer, and she could see a thick coat of ice slicked onto the frosted bark of the tree. Her hands found the bottom of the window and pulled up. Her eyes were on the church in the distance and the fiery fly light of the steeple. A blast of cold air from the opened window woke her, as if from a trance, and she let the window pane fall back into place. She knew she could call Jake to come pick her up, but she dismissed the idea as soon as it came into her mind. Carrie would hear a car coming or leaving the house. And to Carmen, calling Jake seemed like taking the easy way out. She would climb down the tree, and then she would walk the four miles to his house.

Her heart pounding in her chest, she put a Beach Boys CD in her player—nothing her mother would come up to claim was inappropriate. She turned the volume up loud enough to be heard, but not loud enough that their neighbors would complain. She went to the window and hesitated; then the cold air came into her room at full blast. She took another look at the tree trunk, then chucked her gloves back into her room. Even if her hands froze, she wanted her grip. She looked at the distance below leading to the white ground and shivered. Then she went under the window's opening, searching for the branch outside that would help her keep her balance.

Her hands found the branch, recognized its familiar shape down to the irregular bumps and grooves. Her hands felt burned by cold fire, and she wondered if she would leave some skin on the bark. She pulled one hand away, found her fears unwarranted, and gritted her teeth against the cold.

First one foot, then the other, until she was standing on the branch. She wanted to start down the tree, but she would do the job right. She needed to close the window. Carmen crouched to her knees for better balance, wrapped one arm around the trunk, and stretched for the window. A shudder of wind slammed into her and she recoiled, hugging the tree trunk until the gust had passed. She waited until there was no wind, then let herself free fall towards the window. Her fingers scraped the ledge, held. Her body in plank position, she looked down through the angle of her arms—a fifteen foot drop below her.

Then there was a low rumble she recognized and a blinding flash of white light. She held her body rigid as Carrie's car backed out of the garage. Carmen held her breath, the muscles in her arms crying with fatigue. The car did not stop and Carrie did not see her, and the lights of the car faded into the black background of the night. In that moment of illumination, Carmen had seen in the window's reflection how she would have to reposition her body to get back to the tree trunk. Still balanced, she raised one arm, grasped the knob attached to the bottom of the window and pulled down. She removed her hand before the glass pane could slam down onto it. Feeling a sense of accomplishment, Carmen pushed herself up and back. For a moment she flailed, then her arms wrapped around the upper branch of the tree. She clambered down; only when she reached the ground did she realize that she had left her key in her room, and Carrie would have locked the front door before she left.

Carmen stood under the tree and looked up at her window with its bright light. She could hear, faintly, the Beach Boys singing about sunny skies and good vibrations. She covered her chapped hands with the ends of her sweater's sleeves and trudged through the snow. She did not panic; if she couldn't get into her house, Jake's house was only four miles away.

Carmen had a moment of hope. Carrie never left the house that late; if she was that upset about something, she may have forgotten to lock the door. Carmen walked up to the porch and tried the knob with her numb fingers. A smile frosted on her face as the knob turned easily under her hand. She stomped the snow from her shoes, then went into the kitchen. She wondered where her mother had gone. She tried to make the cocoa that Carrie made and burned her tongue, then poured the bitter conglomeration of ingredients down the sink and reached for a packet of Swiss Miss instant cocoa.

She went up the stairs and entered her room to a blast of light and the Beach Boys singing about Kokomo. She crossed the room quickly and silenced the CD. Carrie had bought the album for her two years ago; Carmen had outgrown the Beach Boys. She didn't like songs that spoke of places she would never go, of things she would never do. The closest she would get to the heat and excitement of Pasadena or Kokomo was a fireplace in Jake's house when his father wasn't home, and the closest she would get to cruising in a T-bird was driving with Jake in the beat up Honda he had gotten for his sixteenth birthday.

Carmen felt a tug in her stomach and turned to face her reflection. She convinced herself that she could not be as sad as she felt, because there was that blush in her cheeks and that twinkle in her eyes. Only the rigid line of her mouth hinted that something inside didn't feel quite right.

She went to her window, looked down, shuddered. She locked the window, then drew the heavy purple curtain over it. She only saw the danger of a situation after the situation had passed. She could have *died*, and that was not the kind of escape she wanted.

Despite the ice-slicked asphalt road, Carrie drove fast. Her wheels spun out of control twice, but she dismissed the incidents without so much as an exhalation of breath. She was glad that the roads had gotten much worse since she had left Sam's house an hour earlier; otherwise, she would have had to chastise Jacob for taking Carmen for a drive in such inclement weather.

She had promised to talk with Sam after the meeting, but he had not been there when she picked up Carmen. She could have called him to cancel, but she liked to keep her engagements—especially with Sam, who was one of two people from her past who had kept in touch. Months after she left Sam told her that Chris had called him and asked about her, and he had given Chris her new phone number. She talked with Chris on a monthly basis, but the phone calls were always short. Though he did not speak of their calls to Christine, he updated her on family news. Calder was still a bachelor, but with his choice of whatever money could buy because of a job on Wall Street. Carly was teaching kindergarten at a local school; she still wanted children but had not married. Chris did not talk much about himself.

Life required sacrifices, and Carrie's family had become one. Her husband had become another, and Chloe yet another. All were sacrifices that life and self had demanded, and she had not fought.

The drive calmed her. Before getting out of the car, she arranged her shawl over her loose curls and slipped on her black polyester gloves. The wind chilled her, and she hurried to the front door.

"Carrie?" Sam opened the door. "I didn't think you were coming."

"I know I'm late." Her teeth started chattering and cut short her apology.

He ushered her inside and removed her shawl as she picked off her gloves. The gesture made her uncomfortable; she did not care to have him standing so close to her, and she moved away from him as soon as he had finished unwinding the fabric from around her neck.

"I can't believe you drove in this," he said, looking out the window slit in the door.

"I told you I would come."

He shook his head. "Come into the living room where it's warmer. I made a fire."

"It's beautiful," she said, as she walked into the room and saw the flames dancing in the grate.

"I didn't think you would be crazy enough to come," he said. "Or I would have waited for you to get here to start it. Fire is more your hobby than mine."

She laughed. "Days gone by, Sam."

He sat down on one of the green upholstered sofas in the room. "How was the workshop? You must have good news, to have come all this way."

She shook her head. He looked at her, disappointed.

"You didn't enjoy yourself?"

"I don't like talking about negative things."

"Why you were disappointed? You can be as positive about it as you want to be."

She smiled at him, then became serious. "We didn't work on fiction writing at all. Tonight was actually the first meeting, so we went over introductions."

"How many people were there?"

"Five? Maybe six?" She paused. "They're all college kids, Sam. They're going to write about getting drunk or getting laid…"

"That's not what you wrote about at that age. Not what I wrote about. They might surprise you, if you leave yourself open to the chance."

"I'm old, Sam. This group isn't for me."

"You like being a nonconformist," he said. "Nonconformity bypasses all rules, including barriers set up by age."

"That might be true, but I don't want to go back. Since that's the case, I don't need any other excuse."

He leaned forward. "What did you do? Look at their faces for five minutes and decide they weren't worth your time? Judging people so quickly isn't like you."

"Yes it is," she said. "I judge people all the time. But for whatever reason, no one ever thinks I do."

"Maybe because you listen so well."

"Or because I don't interrupt. Like you do."

He smiled. "What else were you going to add?"

"I'm not sure about the group."

"Then you should go back."

"I don't know that I should."

"Carrie, would you sit?"

"I'd prefer to stand." She paused. "Where were you today when Carmen was over?"

"I was here," he said, startled. "Why, was there a problem?"

"I couldn't find them until an hour after I said I was going to be here, because Jacob took Carmen out driving." She paused. "I couldn't find you, either."

"I was in the basement writing," he said. "I am a professional. That's what I do."

"That's hitting below the belt," she said.

"That's anger," he said. "Misprojected. But I apologize."

She glanced at him, her irritation fading. "What's wrong, Sam?"

He got up, then sat back down. "This isn't easy for me to say."

"What?"

"I found out why your daughter doesn't like me." He paused. "She's worried we're going to get married."

Carrie laughed. "What put that idea into your head? I'm not legally divorced, and I've stressed to her that you and I are friends."

"Your daughter hates me, Carrie, and I'm almost positive that's the reason why."

"Is this really that important to you?"

"The marriage itself isn't what Carmen would be upset about. I should have realized she would be more complex than that, but I didn't see. If we got married, then she and Jake would be like brother and sister." He paused. "I wouldn't have seen the complications with that if I hadn't gotten this." He held up a piece of paper, handed it to her. "I'm just going to let you read it."

She took the paper. Her eyes widened. She stood up.

"*What?*"

He said nothing.

"Who wrote this?" The piece of paper flapped from her fingers.

"I believe it says 'A Concerned Parent'."

She tore the paper in two, threw the torn shreds to the ground. "This is *utter bullshit*. Out of the question. She gets top-notch grades, she's involved with the community, she has good friends..."

"Jacob is upstairs in his room," Sam said quietly. "He says it's all true."

Carrie became very still. "Are you calling my daughter a whore?"

Sam picked up the pieces of paper. "How can I disbelieve what my son is telling me?"

"I can think of several reasons," she said. "Are you aware of what a beautiful young woman Carmen is? Do you know how many rumors have been started by boys with over-active hormones and imaginations?"

"Are you sure they're rumors?"

"She's *thirteen*." Carrie got up. "I hadn't even been kissed when I was thirteen. And Carmen isn't stupid. She would *never* be stupid enough to do something in a place where she could so easily get caught..."

"I didn't write the note, Carrie."

She went to the fireplace and stood looking at the dancing flames. He watched her, the usual good humor gone from his eyes.

"I'm sorry," came a voice from behind them, startling them both. "Mrs. Crenshaw, I had no idea she was so young. I swear, she told me she was fifteen…"

Sam made a motion to get up from the sofa. "I told you to stay in your room. I said I would discuss this with you later."

Jake glanced from his father to Carrie. "Mrs. Crenshaw, you have to believe me."

"Go to your room," Sam ordered.

"Let me talk." Jake recoiled from the look Sam gave him, but stood his ground. "The note isn't completely true, though. I'm the only one she's…" he stuttered to a stop.

Sam turned to his attention to Carrie. Every line of her face was a steel cable; her expression pained him.

"Jake, go to your room," he said. "Now."

Jake looked at Sam, hurt and angry, but he left the room obediently. Sam turned to Carrie, saw she had put on her coat and was holding her scarf and her gloves in a death grip. She strode out of the room without speaking, and he followed her to her car.

"I thought it was best to show you," he said. "But I wanted to talk to you."

"I'll handle Carmen." She got in the car. "You handle Jacob."

"Don't talk to Carmen now, when you're angry. Don't go and accuse—"

"I have no intention of accusing Carmen of anything." She glared at him. "Sam, let go of my door or I'll drive away with you hanging on."

"Carrie."

"Carmen's home alone. Let go of my door."

Sam stepped back. She closed the door, then put the car in reverse. She was gone a moment later, her tires fighting for grip on the slick surface of the road.

He went back into the house and headed directly to Jake's room. He had not seen Carrie that upset in a long time, and he made no attempt to disguise his anger. He kicked open Jake's door. There was a note on the bed—Jake's handwriting—but he barely recognized the sharp spikes of letters. He read, and his anger flared.

"Jake!" he yelled.

Jake was nowhere in the house. Sam went downstairs and called Carrie's phone, waiting expectantly for the answering machine to kick in. But the phone was answered after a moment's hesitation.

"Jake?" said a breathy voice. "Is that you again? I'm going to meet you right now."

"Listen to me, young lady. You stay right where you are."

A pause. "Mr. Sampson?"

"Listen to me, Carmen. I don't know what crazy stunt my son told you to do, but I want you to forget about it. Your mother is on her way home, and she wants to talk to you."

"Mr. Sampson? I'm very sorry, but I have to hang up now." A pause. "I'm sorry."

"Carmen—" He was speaking to the dial tone. He looked at the phone, then called the Crenshaw house again to find she had put the phone off the hook, so he could not leave a message.

"And the world thinks intelligence is a gift," he muttered as he headed out to his car.

He had no other way of getting in touch with Carrie, and he could not trust Jake or Carmen: two straight-laced kids, except apparently when they were together. He knew how impulsive Carrie could be, but Carmen didn't seem to have any of Carrie's moral boundaries. The thought of that scared him. He could only follow Carrie and let her know what was going on. And hope for the best.

"Carmen."

The girl jumped at the sound of her name. "Leave me alone."

Carrie did not know how long Carmen had been standing in the back alley a half mile away from the house, but she could see that Carmen had left the house ill-prepared for the cold; her body was wracked by shivering.

"Get in the car."

Carmen crossed her arms. "You shouldn't have wasted your time trying to find me. I'm not going anywhere with you."

"Why so stubborn, baby?"

"Don't call me that." Carmen shivered. "I'm not a baby."

"You're acting like one."

"You don't want to talk." Carmen was holding onto herself too tightly for the gesture to be one of defiance; she was trying to protect herself from the cold. "You want to lecture me. Jake explained the whole situation to me."

"I don't know what Jacob told you, Carmen..."

"Liar!" The fire came back into her eyes. "I bet you believe every word of it, too."

"Carmen, I'm not accusing you of anything. Let's go home and talk."

Carmen shook her head. "I'm staying here."

"In the cold?"

"I'm going to meet Jake. He's going to take me away from here."

Carmen stared at her with an expression as cold as the snow, her arms clenched resolutely around her body. Carrie leaned out the window. "You're old enough to make your own decisions, Carmen."

She did not budge.

"You know that, don't you?"

Almost imperceptibly, Carmen nodded.

"I'm going to ask you a question. Then I'll leave, if you want me to." She paused, searching Carmen's frozen face but receiving no feedback. "Baby, are you all right?"

Carmen remained standing with her arms crossed in front of her chest, but her trembling increased. After a moment, Carrie realized Carmen was crying. She opened the passenger seat's door, then waited as Carmen climbed in.

"It all happened so fast," Carmen mumbled. "I didn't even know what..."

Carrie tried to ignore the wrenching sensation in her stomach as she handed Carmen a tissue. She started to pull away from the side of the road when Carmen sat upright, a panicked look on her face.

"Jake," she said, shrinking into the cushion of the seat. "Oh my god, don't let him see me with you."

Carrie saw a gaunt figure moving towards them from the woods bordering the property. Carrie turned on her headlights and caught Jake in their beams. He froze.

Unsmiling, Carrie rolled down her window. "Jake! Come here. I want to talk to you."

He unfroze, and walked reluctantly to the car.

"Hi, Mrs. Crenshaw," he said, his eyes scanning past her. "Hey, Carmen."

Carmen's head was turned at a ninety-degree angle, her face hidden by her hair.

"Cold day to be out, Jacob." Carrie shifted to first gear. "Do you want to tell me exactly why you're here?"

He glanced once more at Carmen, then stepped away from the car only to freeze as Sam's car pulled up next to hers. Carrie heard Sam yelling, then watched as Jake got into Sam's car and Sam got out. His breath was a cloud of steam as he walked over to her car and tapped on her window.

"We should talk later," he said as she unrolled her window. "I'm going to take him home now." He paused and looked at Carmen. "I suppose you'll want to talk to…"

Carrie gave him a tired smile and nod, then rolled her window up against the cold. Carmen opened her eyes and stared blankly at the open road. Carrie drove home in silence, then opened Carmen's door for her. She went directly to the kitchen and put the tea kettle on the stove. She turned and saw Carmen lingering in the entrance, her shoulders hunched, her bleary eyes trained on Carrie's face.

"Go sit in the living room," she said.

Carmen obeyed without a word of protest. Carrie saw Carmen sit down, and kept her eyes on the unmoving silhouette painted on the wall paper. She tried to clear her mind, realizing she had no idea what to do. She filled two mugs with hot water and watched as the two green tea bags bled yellow-green swirls. She carried the tea to the living room and walked over to Carmen.

Carrie forced herself to sit down. She tried to smile at Carmen and found she could not. She put her mug of tea on the table, and noticed how badly Carmen's hands shook as she took her mug.

"When you talked to me about Eric Styles the other day," she said finally, her voice flat. "You were really talking to me about Jacob."

Carmen did not move. Carrie steeled herself, then walked to the opposite side of the room. She could see the world outside, frozen white, glittering in the light of the crescent moon. The hot tea scalded her tongue, but she was glad that the pain distracted her from saying what was on her mind.

"Are you mad?" Carmen asked, softly.

"You lied to me." Carrie turned. "I get a note, or rather, I see a note, from 'A Concerned Parent.' Saying my daughter has a reputation. For smoking. For drinking. For…" She paused and exhaled. "Carmen?"

Carmen met Carrie's eyes. "I don't drink. The rest of it is true."

The confession hit her like a shock wave. "Carmen, what were you *thinking*? Did you even consider the consequences that could come with your actions?"

"Jesus Christ," Carmen muttered under her breath.

The phrase caught Carrie's attention. She frowned. "Was it Jacob who encouraged you to start these things? Don't roll your eyes, Carmen. You are in some very deep shit, young lady."

"I didn't hurt anyone."

"You could have hurt yourself. To think that you could act so irresponsibly…"

"Will you shut up?" Carmen shrieked, standing abruptly and splattering the clean carpet with tea. "Did you even stop to think that maybe I have enough on my mind without this fucking bullshit? That maybe tonight *I want you to leave me the fuck alone?*"

She threw herself onto the sofa and cried. Carrie looked at her helplessly, then left the room and came back with a handful of tissues. She put them on the table in front of Carmen, then went over to the cedar chest in the corner of the room and opened it. She took out a blanket and went to Carmen, who had sat up and was blowing her nose sloppily into the mess of tissues. Carrie sat down beside her. She spread the blanket over them. Their shoulders touched and Carmen leaned into her, her fragile frame still shaking. Carrie slipped an arm around her, pulled her close and kissed the top of her head. She remembered that Carmen was thirteen—that her rough child was not all steel, defiance, and venom.

"I love you," she said. "We can talk when you're ready."

Carmen cried for a long time, leaving Carrie's shirt damp with tears.

"I have to ask you a question, Carmen," Carrie said, when Carmen had quieted. "Only one question for tonight."

Carmen wiped at her eyes. "What?"

"Have you been using protection?"

"Mom…I…we…" Her words failed her. "Tonight was the…we did other stuff…"

Carrie pieced together the unspoken parts of Carmen's jabbering, felt an ironic surge of relief. She pushed the blanket away.

"Get your coat, Carmen."

"Why?"

"We're going to the pharmacy. So you don't get pregnant."

Carmen paled at the word, and followed Carrie out of the house.

"What the hell were you thinking?"

"I didn't know she was thirteen. She looks older."

"I don't give a goddam how old she looks."

"You're acting like having sex is a sin."

"It is when you have it with a thirteen-year-old girl. What if she gets pregnant? What if she gave you a disease?"

"She was a virgin."

"Jesus Christ, Jake."

"Don't tell me you didn't get laid when you were my age. You're being a hypocrite. You wouldn't have a problem if it wasn't her daughter I had—"

"You want to explain your note to me?"

"I was angry."

"You were angry."

"I guess that's not a good excuse."

"You're damn right, it's not a good excuse." Sam paused. "Car privileges suspended until I can trust you again—and that's going to take a very long time. You're going to walk to Carmen's house tomorrow. Understood?"

Jake nodded sullenly.

"You're going to apologize to Carmen." He paused. "Then you're going to apologize to her mother."

"I can't."

"What?"

"I'm not apologizing when I didn't do anything wrong. Carmen is my girlfriend."

Sam paused. "I'm going to call Carrie tomorrow, and she had better confirm you were there. I don't need shit from you on this, Jake, not with everything else going on."

"Alright, Dad."

"I'm glad that's settled."

Jake was silent for a long time. "I'm going to go do homework."

"Leave your door open. I want to be able to see you."

"Door open." Jake turned and looked back. "By the way, we did use protection."

Sam remained in the kitchen after their argument, and felt as if he had been alone there all along.

At two A.M., Jake bypassed the garage to where the old Honda sat in the driveway. Worry gnawed at him the entire time he was out, but as he made his purchases, he knew he was doing the right thing, though he had broken his father's rule to do it. Maybe that was why he didn't get caught. He tried to remember the word for that and remembered that it sounded like her name, and then it came to him. Karma.

The next morning broke cold and clear, the sky a bright blue, the streets a sanitized white. He adjusted his scarf to cover his mouth and felt like a bank robber or an assassin as he trudged down the streets. Despite the cold and the pit in his stomach, he spotted the familiar house too soon. He was not looking forward to confronting the woman his father loved. Carmen, he could handle.

He walked up to the door, dusting the snow from his clothes, hair, and boots. He knocked and waited, knocked again. After a moment, the door opened.

"I'm sorry," he said, and fell silent.

The expression on Carrie's face did not change. Jake shifted, then took the small brown bag from his coat. His hand hung in the air; she did not move.

"It's a morning after pill," he explained. "We used a condom, but I wanted to make sure that she was…" He swallowed. "That I could do anything I could."

Carrie took the bag from him. "Thank you. I already put Carmen on the pill, but I'll hold onto this."

"Okay," he said. "Is Carmen around? I want to talk to her."

"I'm not so sure I want you to talk to her." Carrie paused. "I'm quite sure that she doesn't want to talk to you. We had a long talk last night."

"Oh."

"You and I are going to have a long talk as well."

"I don't want to disturb you," he said. "If Carmen doesn't want to talk, then I guess I'll be leaving."

"Do you want a ride home?" she asked, so suddenly that she startled him. He looked up and saw a hint of emotion behind the glacial glare she had fixed on him.

"I'll be all right. But I appreciate it, because I know you hate my guts right now."

"Mildly put," she said.

"Will you tell Carmen I stopped by? If you think it won't upset her."

"I'm not making any promises."

The door shut in his face. Jake turned and looked down the driveway, his breath evaporating visibly before his eyes. Without looking back, he walked out of sight of the house, then doubled back. He scanned the house's windows, paranoid that Carrie would be standing inside, watching him.

Carmen's window was covered, blocked out by what looked like a thick purple sheet. He would have to take the risk that she was in her room. He went to the oak tree he had climbed countless times before his father had sold the house to the Crenshaws. He remembered where the ridges and the grooves were that serves and hand and foot holds. He started to climb, and he did not slip once. Then he was straddling the branch in front of her window, holding onto the thin branch above his head for balance as he leaned forward and tapped once, twice. The third time he tapped out a melody on the pane, so she would not be able to mistake the noise for a branch or a creak of the house. The sheet moved away and Carmen appeared in the window. He sat back on the branch and waved. For one moment she stood as if frozen; then, she tried opening the window. He waited, watching her struggle. She stopped, then unlocked the window and pushed up. He slid into her room, none too gracefully.

"Fucking window," she said, glancing at him quickly before turning her back and walking to the center of her room.

"Why'd you lock it anyway?" he asked, following her, the heat from her room going to his head.

She sat down on her bed and watched him strip out of his jacket. "Would you close the window? I'm cold."

"Why'd you lock it?" he repeated, going over to the window and closing it, then stooping to undo his shoelaces.

"I climbed out the other night and it freaked me out. I don't like it when I do dangerous things like that."

He glanced at her. "I've climbed that tree a hundred times before. It's not dangerous at all."

"Not dangerous in winter?"

He shook his head.

"Nothing I ever do is interesting enough for you, is it?" She glared at him as he continued to unlace his boots calmly. "Don't get too comfortable. I didn't say you could stay."

"You're not mad at me."

"If you want to stay, you better apologize to me."

"Just give me a second to warm up, babe, then I'll be out of your way."

Her eyes flashed. "Jake, apologize or get the hell out of here."

He stood and shrugged. "I'm not going to apologize to you. I'm not sorry."

She stared at him, her shoulders hunched, her eyes slits of electricity. He turned from her, went back to the jacket he had taken off and searched through it for the second bag he had filled from the pharmacy.

"Your mom said you're on the pill," he said.

"Yeah."

"I wasn't thinking." He turned and saw she was fuming. He tossed the bag to her, smiled when she caught it despite his lack of warning. "Those are just in case. You know. Extra protection."

"Condoms and BC pills," she said as she opened the bag and looked inside. She tossed the bag at him. The contents spilled across the floor at his feet. "Thanks a lot, Jake. I guess that's your way of saying you want to see me."

"Hey," he said. "We'll get better at it. It was your first time and we were both impatient."

She cocked an eyebrow at him. "You must be pretty desperate to chase after a thirteen-year-old."

"Don't make me call you a bitch."

"You would have done better to buy me some cigs. Or get them from your older friends, however it is that you get them. It would've been more thoughtful, now that you know that I'm five years away from being able to buy my own instead of three."

He reached into his pocket, pulled out a slightly crumpled carton, tossed it at her. "You can have one now, if you want. The smoke won't bother me."

"Are you crazy? If my mother smelled the smoke, she'd move up my execution date."

"You're in trouble?"

"I'm on death row."

He paused. "Me, too."

She glanced at him, then moved across the room to her bookcase, pulled out a book, and stashed the cigarettes in the gap. She put the book back in its spot. He watched her every movement, graceful and smooth, while he stood before her clumsy and half-drenched with melted snow.

"So what did you do?" he said. "Did you tell your mom I raped you, then ask her to pick you up?"

"I was waiting for you." She turned to him. "I'd already been waiting for half an hour when—"

"Christ, no wonder you tell her everything. You're just a kid, after all."

"You're not such a big boy yourself, Jakey." Her eyes narrowed. "If I called my mom and she came up here, you would probably shit yourself."

"That would be just like you, to call on your mom to solve everything."

She shook her head. "It wouldn't be like me at all. Though I'm tempted to call her, just to see what would happen."

"What the fuck would you gain from that?"

Her eyes gleamed. "What would you stand to lose?"

"I've got an alibi."

"I know," she said. Her voice changed. "'Is Carmen here, Mrs. Crenshaw? I'd like to talk to her.' Fuck your alibi, Jake. I was standing in the room right next to the kitchen." She smirked. "I didn't know you could be so polite and whimpering."

"Fuck you, Carmen."

She nodded at the brown bag at his feet. "You can take that with you. You won't be using any of it on me."

He bristled and did not move.

She crossed her arms. "Pick it up now, or I'll call my mom and you'll be in a whole hell of a lot more trouble than you are now."

"Your mom knows I'm talking to you right now."

"Yeah, Jake. That's why you climbed a tree to get to my room."

He stooped, shoved the pills and packages into the bag, and stood, the thin brown paper clenched in a tight fist.

"You know what?" she said, her face pale and full of sharp lines. "You rag on me for telling my mom stuff, but you're just as bad with your dad. I bet he made you come over here. In fact, I bet he made you walk."

"You little bitch." He glared at her. "The only reason I wouldn't apologize to you was because I'm not sorry for what we did. I love you, Carmen."

There was immediate silence in the room, and then he crossed the room and slung his coat over his shoulder. She intercepted him as he headed towards the window and snapped down the lock. She faced him, blocking his exit.

"Did you mean that?"

He stepped away from her. "I always mean what I say."

She bit her lip. "But I don't. Like what I said about your dad. I didn't mean it."

He took another step away from her. "It was true enough. Can I sit on your bed?"

"Only if I can sit next to you."

He sat down. She sat next to him.

"So why are you so close to your dad?" she asked. "Why don't you want to piss him off?"

"I don't know," Jake said. "Maybe because of what happened with him and Mom. He changed a lot after the divorce. I think he misses her and Kindra. I mean, I can still see them on holidays and everything, but he doesn't ever get to see them anymore."

Her eyes lingered on his face. "You're lucky to have a dad."

"You're lucky to have a mom."

She nodded. "Too bad our parents fucked up, so we couldn't have both."

"Yeah."

She glanced at him. "I don't like that we fight."

"I don't either."

She lay down and stared up at the ceiling, her legs hanging off the edge of the bed. "My mom hates my dad, too."

"Does she?"

"Yeah."

"He was probably an asshole. Most guys are."

She propped herself up on an elbow and looked at him. "How come?"

"I'm not going to tell you how come."

"Why not?"

He looked at her, irritated. "Because guys don't talk like that. We don't just spill our guts."

"You just admitted you have emotions. How come you can't talk about them?"

"Because I can't. I know you don't have a lot of experience with guys…"

"I could get some more, if you'd like."

He glared at her. "Don't you dare."

She laughed, sat up on the bed and hugged him briefly. Feeling him stiffen, she jumped off the bed and went over to the vanity mirror. Knowing his eyes were following her, she picked up her brush and started pulling it through her waist-length hair.

"Do you ever think about your dad?" he asked.

"All the time."

"Why don't you do something about it?"

"I've tried." She laid the brush down on the dresser. "My mom really doesn't want me to see him."

"Doesn't that make you curious?"

She shrugged, turned back to the mirror. She picked up a mascara tube and started outlining her eyes. "There's not much I can do about it, is there? He lives in Pennsylvania. I'm in Maine."

"Where in Pennsylvania?"

"I'm not sure exactly. I have an address, somewhere. I pushed Mom over the edge one day, and she gave it to me so I would shut up. Safe enough, right? It's not like I have a way to get there."

"If you have an address I could drive you."

She snorted. "I'm sure Mom would love that. 'Hey, Carrie, you know that guy you forbid me to see? He and I are taking a trip to PA to see that man, you know, who you hate.' How's that sound?"

"Would you put that down? You're pretty enough without make up." He paused. "I'm being serious."

She examined her reflection in the mirror, then winked at him as she put down the tube. "There's no way."

"I have my own car. We could drive down some weekend."

"What about your dad?"

He shrugged. "He works nights. I work mornings on the weekends, to help pay bills and shit. We don't really intercept."

"He'd still know if you're gone."

"Yeah." Jake paused. "I could tell him that I needed to get away for awhile. He'd understand that. You could come up with an excuse."

"I can't disappear for a weekend without having my mom notice."

"You could," he insisted. "Haven't you noticed that you can get whatever you want?"

She smiled at him. "Just because I don't take no for an answer." She walked over to her CD player. She picked up the black case beside it and shifted through the plastic sleeves, then put the case down. "You're really serious? You'd drive me to PA if I could get it cleared with my mom?" She started pacing as he nodded. "What if there's something wrong with him?"

"What do you mean?"

"What if he's crazy? Or maybe he's dangerous." She paused. "There has to be some reason my mom doesn't want me to see him."

"You think he's a psycho?"

"I don't know. I'm just hypothesizing."

"You would say that."

"Why the fuck shouldn't I? It's not like you don't know what I mean. We learned about the scientific process in like what, third grade?"

Jake paused. "He can't be that dangerous, or Mrs. Crenshaw wouldn't have given you his address."

"I told you, she probably doesn't think there's any conceivable way that I would actually get there. And he might not even live there anymore. She hasn't seen him in like twelve years."

"Twelve years?"

"Maybe not that long. I don't know how old I was when we left."

"Do you remember him at all?"

She shook her head.

"We should check on that address before we drive down," he said. "It's like a whole day's drive, and gas is getting really expensive."

"I'll earn it from you," she promised.

He paused. "Do you have a phone number?"

"No."

"We can ask the operator. They're usually pretty good with that. All you have to do is give them the person's name."

"I don't know his name."

"How could you not know his name?"

"Crenshaw is my mother's maiden name," she explained. "I don't know what my dad's name was. I just know my mom met him through the school where she was teaching back then."

"What about a birth certificate?"

"How would that help?"

"If they were still together when you were born, his name might have been on your birth certificate. Or hyphenated, at least."

"It's a start."

"You know, Carmen, you don't really seem like you want to find him."

"I do," she said. "I just don't like going about it like this."

"Like what? We haven't done anything yet."

She paused. "Everything's going to have to be in secret."

"It's not like you have a lot of options here."

"I know. But what if we find him, and he's madly in love with my mom and wants me to give her a message? Or what if he holds me hostage because he hates my mother so much? I don't know anything about him."

"He was a teacher," Jake said. "Only certain people can become teachers. Don't you know how much shit our teachers take from us every day?"

"You should probably get going," she said. "If you're warm enough to walk back."

"You want me to leave?"

"I just don't want you to get caught here."

"You mean you want some time to be by yourself to think."

She smiled. "I'll change, you know, if you start to understand me."

"Don't worry. I'll never understand you." He put on his jacket, moved to the window, unlocked it.

"Will you be okay going down that way?"

"Easy."

"You'll call me?"

He shook his head. "What if your mom—"

"Call after three. I'll be home. She stays at the school till five."

"All right."

"Be careful going down the tree."

He paused. "Are you alright?"

"What do you mean?"

"With what happened in my car."

She put her hands on her hips. "You wouldn't want to start a discussion on our feelings, would you?"

"Carmen."

"Then don't ask." She went to the mirror, yanked the brush through her hair. "I'm not spilling my guts to you if you're going to be such an asshole about—"

He crossed the room and took the brush from her hand. She stood still as he divided her hair into two sections, then plaited the sections into braids.

"That's cool, that your hair stays like that," he said, stepping away from her as he finished. "Even though I didn't tie it with anything."

She turned to face him. "When did you learn to braid hair?"

"It's no big deal."

She touched a braid. "You just apologized to me, you know."

"How the hell do you associate braiding your hair with apologizing?"

"Because you were gentle. That shows you know you hurt me."

His eyes darkened momentarily. "You think too much."

"You talk too much. Kiss me before you go."

He kissed her. "You know something, Carmen? When I said I loved you, you didn't say it back. I'm going to hold that against you."

She smiled, but he could see he had shaken her. "I'll make it up to you somehow."

He shook his head. "Just keep it in mind, that's all."

"Don't say it again, Jake. It freaked me out."

"Thanks," he said. "I got that, though."

"Call me?"

"Yeah." He went to the window, opened it.

"Jake. If you come back, use that drum beat again on my window. Then I'll know it's you. Since it's the one you taught me."

"I'm glad to see that you recognized—"

"Will you get the hell out of here? You're letting all the cold air in."

He smiled as he turned away from her and slid onto the branch, then heard the window slam shut behind him. He was down the trunk in a matter of seconds; he looked up and saw her looking down at him. He gave her a thumbs up, saw her small wave in response. As he started walking, he hardly noticed the cold.

Carrie had paused outside the door when she heard them talking. She had listened, then left as quietly as she had come. She would not try to keep Carmen and Jake apart. She would not cause that lack of closure in her daughter's life. But she would not let Carmen go to Pennsylvania. She

443

went back to Carmen's room, heard her singing. She knocked. The singing stopped.

"What do you want?"

Carrie heard the note of panic in Carmen's voice. She cleared her throat.

"Dinner in five," she said.

"Is it curry?" A pause. "Carrie, it's not curry again, is it?"

"Curry," Carrie confirmed, then turned and walked down the stairs so she would not hear Carmen's pretended sigh of disgust.

Carmen looked at Jake, looked back at the clock. "You should leave. She could come back any minute."

"I thought you said the group met for two hours, babe."

"It does. But she might come home early if she's really disgusted with the other writers."

"Chill," he said. "I hear the sound of her car and I'm out your window, down the tree, on my way. Half a minute, tops." He raised an eyebrow at her. "You can time me if you want."

She moved away from him, recognizing the look in his eyes. "I don't like you going down the tree in winter, when there's all that ice slicked on. You could get hurt."

He laughed at her.

"Well, you could," she insisted. "And if you get hurt, if you *died*, what would I do?"

"Miss me, I guess."

"Jake."

"Come here. I have something I want to talk to you about seriously."

She glanced at the clock but went to him. She sat on his lap and twined her arms around him. He removed her arms from his neck and held them at her sides as he kissed her, then gently moved her off his lap.

"I can get the car for a weekend," he said. "Even on probation. I told my dad I wanted to get away, just for a couple days. That I would pay for my own gas and that I'd bring the car back in tip-top shape. He said I could if I behaved myself." His grin grew. "Whatever that means."

"Jake, stop." She giggled as he laid a sloppy kiss on the underside of her jaw, then pushed him away. His eyes followed her as she went to the vanity mirror.

"So what are you going to say so we can go?"

"To my mom?" She paused, brush in hand. "I haven't thought about it. I mean, she's never going to let me go by myself, and I can't tell her I'm going with you."

"I'm surprised she lets you stay home alone, after she got that letter." He paused. "I'd think she would care about you more."

"She does care." Carmen winced as the brush came in contact with a knot. "Oh, shit."

"Let me do it," he said, getting off the bed.

"I can do it," she said, but let him take the brush. He used his hand to make a line between the knot and the rest of her hair so he wouldn't pull, then worked the brush through the knot.

"It's not that she doesn't care." Carmen reached for the carton of cigarettes he had brought her, pulled one out and started to light it. "It's like—"

"She'll smell the smoke."

"Shit," she cried, looking at the cigarette in her hand. "What was I thinking? But it's a perfectly good cig. Can't waste it."

"Carmen, it's freezing."

"Put your coat on," she said, standing near the open window and exhaling smoke. "This will only take a minute. I'm done after this one. Promise."

"Jesus Christ," he muttered, shrugging into his jacket while looking at her.

"What I was saying," she said, looking at him pointedly, "was that it's got to be part of her philosophy. She probably thinks that if she gives me more freedom or whatever, then as a result I'll make better choices because I won't want to betray her trust." She paused. "And I don't want to betray her trust again. That sucked."

"Do you want me to leave?"

She nodded. "But I want you to come back."

"It's damn cold out."

"I could..." She hesitated. "I could go downstairs and make some hot cocoa. Some to warm you up now, some to take with you?"

"Sounds good. I'll come with you."

"You should stay here."

"Come on, baby," he said. "The fearful are caught as often as the bold."

"Helen Keller said that."

"Did she? I just know I heard it somewhere and liked it." He grabbed her hand. "Let's go right now. I'll make myself scarce if your mother comes home early. I don't want to get you in any more trouble."

"You mean you don't want increased supervision," she retorted. "You don't want to make it any harder on yourself to get a piece of my ass."

"Carmen."

She tightened her grip on his hand, made him flinch. "It's the truth, isn't it?"

"Since when have you cared about telling the truth?"

She shrugged, trying to decide whether she wanted to use the Swiss Miss mix or if she wanted to attempt Carrie's recipe. As she put the kettle on to boil, she grabbed the raw ingredients and started measuring them into two mugs.

"Secret recipe," she said. "I've never gotten in right. Just a warning. But it'll be worth it to see your facial expression, if it's good or if it's gross."

"You think my face is funny?"

She giggled and unscrewed the cap of the vanilla extract.

"Just a drop," he advised. "Too much will make it taste bad."

She looked at him. "Maybe that's what I've always done wrong. I figured that since it smelled so good—"

"Do you have a spoon?"

She looked at him, then opened a drawer and handed him a teaspoon. He took the bottle of extract from her. "Have you tasted the stuff?"

She shook her head.

He filled the teaspoon with the syrup-colored liquid. "Open."

She opened her mouth and he put the spoon to her lips, then laughed at her expression as she swallowed. Carmen flung the spoon into the sink.

"I knew you were mad at me," she said, scrunching up her face. "But I didn't know you would try to poison me."

"Just a drop," he cautioned.

"Just a drop," she agreed, dripping the extract into the mugs before filling them with water from the shrieking kettle. She grabbed two spoons and handed him a mug.

"Here. We can drink in my room."

He followed her up the stairs and sat down on her desk as she took a seat on her bed.

"How is it?" she asked anxiously.

"Perfect."

"You didn't even taste it."

"It's hot. That's all I care about." He took a sip to appease her. "It's good. Really good."

She took a sip of her own mix, not believing him. For once, the hot chocolate tasted as good as when her mother made it. Better, even. She crossed her legs Indian-style on the bed, then put her mug on the floor.

"What's wrong?" Jake asked. "Don't you like it?"

"We didn't make any for you to take home. You can have mine."

"You should drink it."

"I don't want it." She got up. "Let me go get a lid, so it stays warm for you."

"Carmen, relax. It's not that important."

She sat back down. "Is that your way of telling me you don't like it?"

"That's my way of telling you I'd rather talk to you than have you worried about some stupid hot chocolate." He stared at her. "You're beautiful when you smile."

Her cheeks burned crimson. "So what am I going to tell my mother, so I can run away with you?"

He laughed, went over and put his arms around her from behind. She closed her eyes, then turned to him.

"What if I told her the truth? I mean, she might take it as a joke, or she might tell me I couldn't, but we could still go anyway."

"Revealing your game plan to the enemy is never a good way to go," he said, tucking a strand of her hair behind her ear so he could see the glitter of her earrings, how the beads fell elegantly past the curve of her neck and jaw line. "I don't think your mom would go for it."

"I'll tell her I want to sleep over at a friend's house."

"I thought you were grounded."

She sighed. "I could tell her I joined the service club at the school, and we're doing a weekend project?"

"Your mom works at the school, Carmen. You'd get caught red-handed in a lie."

"Why should I even say anything?" She frowned. "Why can't we just go?"

"Look. Your mother will definitely know you're missing. I don't want the police chasing after us while we're chasing after your dad."

"I'll think of something." She moved away from him. "Does my room reek of cigarette smoke?"

He shrugged. "I can't tell. I don't think so."

"Good. I really don't need her getting on my case about that right now."

"You shouldn't smoke."

"You shouldn't criticize."

"I'm thinking about your health," he protested. "I don't want you to die of emphysema or lung cancer or something."

She laughed. "If I die of something related to smoking, it's going to be years from now, when I'm old and ugly. We'll have broken up by then anyway. You won't have thought of me in years."

"Don't say that."

"Say what?"

"You won't ever be ugly."

She glanced at him, then looked away. He went to her and kissed her, then stepped back and picked up his jacket.

"I think you can close that window after I leave," he said. "Your room should be okay."

"You're not going out the window, are you? You could use the door."

"I'm going out the window." He zipped his jacket closed. "You're way too worried about the danger element, so I'm going to show you that there's nothing to worry about."

"Please be careful."

He raised his shoulders, stuck out his chest, smiled. "I'm Superman. I can do anything."

She frowned. "You can't bring yourself back to life if you fall and break your neck."

He stepped confidently over to the window. "Knock on wood."

She knocked on her desk and he looked back at her, amused, before he slipped out the window. She went to the sill and watched him descend, sighing with relief as he landed safely in the snow drifts. Then she raced out of her room and into the street.

"Jake!" she called, hurrying after him.

He turned as she approached. "What's this?"

"Cocoa." She smiled shyly. "You left it in my room."

He pulled her into a one-armed hug, planted a kiss on top of her head. "Thanks, Carmen."

Her cheeks burned. "I didn't want you to be cold."

"Your little nose is already pink with the chill. Go home."

She looked at him defiantly. "I will. I just wanted to bring you—"

"Did you ever find out where your dad lives now?"

She blinked away the snowflakes that landed on her eyelashes. "Not yet. I found out his name though. Ralph Palmer. I used the directory and wrote down some numbers, but I'm waiting to use the phone when Mom isn't around. I was going to do it tonight when she was at that writer's thing, but then you showed up...I mean, I'm glad you showed up."

"Let me know what you find out."

"I will. See you soon?"

"Count on it. Good luck."

Shivering, she watched him trudge through the snow until he turned around.

"Go home!" he called. "It's freezing."

She waved. In her haste to get him the cocoa she had forgotten her coat. She started walking home. When she looked over her shoulder, she saw only the empty street. She raced back to the house, stomping her feet on the welcome mat before she went inside, where it took her several minutes to get warm.

"Some kid at the group gave you this?" Sam asked, looking up from the papers he was holding. "What's he like?"

Carrie shrugged. "Seventeen? Complex issues, buried anger and resentment. Tons of talent."

"Now are you glad you stuck with it?"

"Third time's a charm."

"Must be," he said. "This is good. Relevant to you, too."

She shifted her position on the sofa in his living room. "How so?"

"You don't have very healthy relationships with people. Look at your only real romantic relationship, and how that affected you. Coming from that, you can't have a very normal understanding of how romantic relationships should work."

"That's not true," she said. "Human beings begin to think hypothetically in adolescence. And I have an imagination, Sam."

"That's obvious," he said. "I meant that I'm glad you're getting exposed to other views, even if it's vicariously through stuff like this."

"I read a lot. I've been exposed, before—"

"I know that you know there are other kinds of relationships out there, but the one closest to your heart is the one influencing you the most."

"Naturally."

"Nothing wrong with that," he agreed. "Except if it limits your creativity. Look at a lot of your main male characters, if you want an example of what I mean. Dark, tragic, violent—"

"Ralph wasn't," she said, her voice quiet but firm.

"I don't want to awaken old demons."

"The demons have been faced."

He glanced at her. "Then why are you still writing about him?"

She shrugged. "I'm not writing about him. I'm using that character type because I find it fascinating. And I think a lot of my female readers can relate to being attracted to someone who isn't good for them."

Sam got up. "Do you want anything to drink?"

She followed him into the kitchen. "Do you have hot chocolate?"

"I don't think so, unless Jake bought some."

She went through the cupboards until she found what she needed. "No vanilla extract, but that's all right." She went back to him, stayed his hand. "Let me make you a cup."

He glanced at her hand on his own, and she removed it quickly. He continued to unscrew the cap from the bottle of rum. "Thanks, but I'll stick with rum and coke. I don't like drinking when the boy's around. It sets a bad example. But I'll have an occasional drink on the sly."

She stepped back. "You drink too much."

"Life isn't always beautiful, Carrie."

Frowning, she went back to the counter and mixed the raw ingredients together, smashing them down into the mug before she added the water. He watched her, sighed, screwed the top back onto the bottle and put it back in the cupboard.

"On second thought," he said. "That smells pretty damn good. Maybe I'll have a cup after all."

The smile on her face made it worth it for him. Mugs in hand, they went back to the living room and sat down.

"How's Carmen?"

She looked at him. "How's Jake?"

He looked up at the ceiling. "Do you think we did the right thing, telling them they couldn't see each other?"

"They betrayed our trust."

"Did they? We never told them they couldn't sleep together. We just assumed they wouldn't. Forbidding Jake to see Carmen just doesn't seem right to me."

"What doesn't seem right to me," she replied. "Is having a sexually active thirteen-year-old. Maybe we were a little harsh. But she's too young."

"There's no question about that," he said. "I apologize again for my son's behavior, Carrie."

"He came over last week and apologized." She omitted that he had climbed the oak tree and snuck in to see Carmen.

Sam paused. "I thought I had raised him better than that."

"He's young, Sam."

"That's no excuse," he said. "Thank god they used protection and you got her on the pill. If it's any relief to you, Jake isn't promiscuous. We talk pretty openly about what's going on in his life, and he hasn't slept with many—"

Carrie shook her head. "He could hurt her in other ways, Sam."

"I don't approve of his actions," he said, after a pause. "But I don't doubt his intentions. If he slept with Carmen, he must really care about her."

"Well, isn't that a relief."

He looked at her steadily. "There are worse young men than my son whom Carmen could have ended up with."

"I know. But a lot of the time, I worry about Carmen."

"A lot of the time I worry about Jake," he said. "But we can't live their lives for them. We can't make their choices for them."

"But it's so frustrating, watching her make these mistakes."

"I think you're underestimating Carmen. She's a better kid than you're giving her credit for. She's always very polite."

Carrie stood up. "She smokes. She's having sex. One of these days, Sam, I'm going to come home and there's going to be a syringe in the trash or—"

He went to her, put his arms firmly on her shoulders. "Calm down."

Her shoulders slumped and she turned away. She strode over to the counter and picked up her mug and she chugged.

"Are you sure I can't make you a drink?" Watching her made his throat burn.

"No alcohol." She paused. "Do I really seem that frazzled?"

"For you, yes."

She sighed and sat down. "I worry, Sam."

"Every good parent does," Sam said. "You're not alone."

"Thank you for helping me keep things in perspective."

He sat down on the sofa and took her hand, pressed it. He understood when she didn't pull away.

"I hate this," she said. "I want to be able to have a conversation with Carmen without threatening or punishing her. Or having her yell at me. I want her to tell me what's going on in her life. And she hates me."

"It's her age." He paused. "Think about you and your mother."

"That's true," she said. "But I don't know why my mother and I got closer. Maybe Carmen and I never will. And I don't want her to feel like I did during these years. So alone. And she keeps so much inside…"

"She seems like she's able to handle herself pretty well. This seems like…a bad judgment on her part."

452

"This isn't the first time she's surprised me." Carrie paused. "She's never done anything like this before—that's why the letter shocked me so much. But as she was growing up, I'd think everything was fine, and then all of a sudden I'd get a call. Saying she did something crazy." She turned to look at him, and the remnants of tears glittered on her cheeks like shards of broken glass. "She was five when I got the first call. From a police officer, saying he had found her playing in the storm drains on the west side of town, and what was I thinking, letting a child play alone in the middle of nowhere? I was thinking she was upstairs in her room, sleeping..."

She shook her head. "When she was seven I got another call from her second grade teacher, who said that during recess Carmen had climbed the flagpole and refused to come down after explaining she was hoping a cloud would come by and carry her away. The list goes on, but I'll spare you. All these outbreaks in a pattern, a pattern of her holding everything inside and then having it blow up..."

"She has her friends."

"Her friends never come over." She paused. "I think a lot of the time she says she spends with her friends is time spent with your son."

"He's not a bad kid, Carrie."

"I know he means a lot to her. Carmen told me Jake has been her first...everything." She paused. "He might have been the only bright spot in her life, and now I've tried to take that away from her."

"You've tried to protect her," he corrected. "You've tried to be a good parent."

"Trying doesn't mean anything."

"You're being extreme again," he said. "Parents make mistakes. Telling Carmen she couldn't see Jake might have been one, but there are bigger issues here. Her compulsive behavior started before she met Jake, so cut him out of the picture for a minute and answer this question for me. What's standing between you and Carmen?"

She was quiet. He found it hard to sit still as he gave her time to think.

"She wants someone to understand her," Carrie said, finally. "She wants love. She wants stability and hope." She paused. "She wants a normal family."

"Don't be so hard on yourself."

She shook her head. "I've given up, Sam. I tried to spend more time with her when she was younger, but when she turned ten and started to hate me, I couldn't...I couldn't be in the same room with her without souring her mood or provoking an argument. So I retreated to my lesson plans, and when those were done I used my writing as an excuse. Now I stay in my study, because dysfunction has become routine. I don't blame her for wanting to escape." She looked at him. "I'm venting."

"You're allowed."

She leaned back into the sofa and sighed, unaware that her shoulder was touching his. She looked at the ceiling. "I get frustrated. It's like beating my head against—"

"I'll let you vent," he interrupted. "But I won't let you rant your way into using clichés. For shame."

She looked at him, her face worn and drawn, and then she started laughing. She laughed so hard her shoulders shook, and before she had composed herself he found himself grinning as well. She laughed so seldom, but when she did it was contagious.

"What else?" he asked. "Can you think of anything else standing in the way?"

Suddenly somber, she shook her head. He paused.

"Why do you think she hates me so much, Carrie?"

"She doesn't hate you. She's a complex person."

"Freud had a theory," Sam said. "That subconsciously people love what they think they hate, and vice versa. For example, you'll love parents who beat you because subconsciously you hate them so much that you're afraid of the violence of your feelings. So rather than confront your feelings, you consciously project them the other way."

"You think Carmen loves you?" she asked doubtfully. "That would explain the animosity she feels towards me."

"I think Carmen loves what I am." He paused, searching her face. "Or am I way off base here?"

She shook her head. "I'm not following you."

"I'm a father," he said. "That's what Carmen loves about me. She wants her father."

Her eyes jerked to his face. "If that's your theory—"

"Hasn't she mentioned him to you?"

"A couple of times. She knows nothing about him, except that it hurts me when she brings him up. So she brings him up. He's never meant more to her than that."

"Maybe you should think about that again."

"I didn't forbid her to see him."

"But you've made it clear that you don't want her to see him."

"I don't stand in the way of anything she does, unless it's something that could harm her. She could look for him if she wanted to."

"Maybe she needs more than your permission. Maybe she needs your approval."

"No," she said, grabbing her mug and striding into the kitchen. He found her scrubbing the cocoa residue violently off the bottom of the mug.

"Leave it, Carrie. I'll clean it later."

"Might as well clean it while I'm here," she muttered.

He walked away and let her finish what she was doing. She followed him to the living room.

"You're angry with me," she said.

He turned to face her, so abruptly that she stepped back. "Why do you think that is?"

"I don't know."

"Because of this estrangement between you, and him, and her. Her father is a part of the picture, whether you've tried to cut him out of it or not."

"Are you defending him?"

"No. But I don't agree with you on this one."

"I didn't expect this from you, Sam," she said, hurt. "You, who know my story better than any one else—"

"I only know half the story. So do you."

"You know what—"

"I know how much it hurts," he said, turning, "to be told that you can't see your daughter. To wake up each morning wanting to say you love her, to see that she's alright, and being told by a goddamn court that your ex has sole custody..."

Carrie looked at him, stricken. "Sam…"

He turned from her, a sob hitching in his throat. She stepped back, not having known how deeply her words would affect him. The front door opened, and she could see the puffy dark blue of Jake's jacket as he stepped into the house. Before he could come into the room, Carrie stepped over to Sam.

"Sam," she said. "Sam, I'm so sorry."

He inhaled sharply. She took a step back, watching as he composed himself, then turned as Jake entered the room.

"Hi, Mrs. Crenshaw," he said cautiously. "Are you leaving?"

"It's been a long day."

"Let me get your coat."

"Thank you," she said, through her teeth. "But I'll show myself out."

Jake paused as the door closed behind her, then went into the living room where Sam was standing.

"Hey," he said.

"Hello, Jake."

"You alright?"

Sam turned, looked at his son standing hunched in the door way. "You must be freezing. There's some cocoa near the stove, if you want some."

"Thanks, but I just had some."

"I thought you said you were shoveling driveways to make some extra money for that road-trip you want to take, once you get your privileges back."

"You want some? It's still warm."

"Just said I had some, son." He paused. "I can smell it from here. Same kind." He turned around, eyeing Jake critically. "She's driving you crazy, isn't she?"

Jake jolted, though he should not have been surprised that Sam knew exactly what was going on in his life, for however little they interacted.

"Like mother, like daughter," he stammered.

"Go to your room, Jake." Sam turned around, looked out the window.

Silently, Jake started towards the stairs. His father's words glanced off him; when Sam had spoken, Jake had seen the faintest traces of a smile in his father's tired face.

Carrie shivered as she climbed out of the car and made her way through the snowdrifts to the front door. She fumbled with the keys, dropped them, slammed her hand against the wood before she stooped to pick up the keys. She got the door open and strode inside.

"Carmen!" she yelled. "Why is it so cold in here?"

She already knew the answer. She looked around the empty room, not caring that she was losing her temper.

"Carmen! Get down here!"

She heard a door upstairs open, slam shut. She ascended the stairs in a rage. Carmen looked up from where she was sitting on the bed, startled, as Carrie crashed into the room, the door slamming into the dresser close to it, toppling the pewter animal figurines Carmen had accumulated.

"Carrie!" Carmen jumped off the bed. "Look what you did!"

She hurried over to the dresser to rescue her fallen animals. Carrie grabbed her by the arms.

"Why the hell are all the windows open?"

"What the fuck!" The color drained from her face. "Let go of me!"

Carrie did not loosen her grip on Carmen's arms. "How the hell do you expect me to keep paying the bills if you keep this up? Do you know how much our heating bill was last month? Four hundred and fifty-three dollars! Four hundred and fifty-three!"

"Not just four hundred. Four hundred and *fifty-three*."

Carrie backhanded her across the face. Carmen reeled back, her hand pressed against her face in shock.

"Jesus Christ!" she screamed. "What the fuck is wrong with you!"

"Don't swear. Don't you fucking swear at me."

"Hypocrite." Carmen gritted her teeth against the tears welling in her eyes. "You're such a—"

"What the *hell* are these?" Carrie crossed the room, jerked the white carton off the desk and turned.

Carmen went a shade paler. "Cigarettes. Mom, they're just cigarettes…"

"You're too young to buy *just cigarettes*. Did Jake get these for you?"

"A long time ago."

"Was Jake here when I was gone?"

"I don't have to—"

Carrie grabbed her by the arm, dragged her into the bathroom, shoved her inside. She opened the carton, shook the cigarettes into the toilet, flushed them. She threw the empty packet at Carmen's face, where it bounced off her forehead and fell to the floor. Carmen looked at her, stunned.

"I'm tired of this bullshit, Carmen," she said. "I'm tired of your attitude, and I'm not going to tolerate it anymore. You're going to get a job so you can pay for what you just pulled downstairs, and when you're not at school or work, I'm going to know where you are at all times."

Carmen stood motionless. "I can't work and keep up my grades."

"You should have thought of that before."

"You're ruining my future."

"You're not going to have a future if you keep acting like this. What's next, Carmen? Or are you already doing drugs?"

"I would never!" Carmen shrieked. "How could you think I could be so stupid?"

"You haven't given me any reason to think otherwise."

"I can't work. When am I going to see my friends?"

"*Friends?* I've never seen your *friends*, Carmen. You've been hanging out with Jake, doing only God knows what..."

"I hate you!" Carmen screamed as she ran out of the room. A door slammed, and a second later punk rock was blaring loud enough to vibrate the floorboards. Carrie streaked out of the bathroom, placed herself in front of the door and drove her elbow into it.

"Shut that off!" she yelled.

The music cut off abruptly, but Carrie heard the sound her elbow had made when contacting the door—like a gun going off. The symbolism struck her. Just as suddenly her anger was gone, leaving her coldly empty. She stood in front of Carmen's door, shaking. The silence lengthened, and then Carmen spoke.

"Why don't you go for a fucking walk?" Her voice sounded choked. "Maybe when you come back I'll have killed myself and you won't have to worry about the fucking heating bill anymore..." Carmen laughed. "Know what the fucking suicide rates for kids are right now, Carrie? I bet that's in your magazine of the month..."

Carrie's hands clenched into fists. "Open the door, Carmen."

"So you can beat me? No way."

"I'm sorry."

The door swung open and Carmen stared at her from glinting, red-rimmed eyes. "You're not sorry. Don't apologize for something you don't regret. Isn't that one of your fucking maxims? Look, Carrie, something you said sunk in."

"Carmen." Carrie struggled to keep her voice neutral. "I'm sorry I hit you. I shouldn't have lost my temper."

"Yeah. Whatever."

"What else do you want from me?"

"Nothing. I don't want anything from you." Carmen's eyes were slits of gray ice. "It's too bad I have your fucking genes. I'd get rid of them if it were biologically possible."

"I want to be a part of your life, Carmen."

Carmen's voice was suddenly calm. "I don't want you to be a part of my life. You've made my life a living hell. I want you to leave me alone. I opened my door just so I could say that to your face. I have something else I want to say to you, too."

Carrie paused. "I'm listening."

"Good." Carmen looked directly at her. "It's a good thing I don't know where my dad is, because if I did I'd leave you forever and I wouldn't look back. And you know it, too, or you'd help me find him."

"I'm going for a walk."

"Good. Go for a fucking walk."

"Watch your language," Carrie said, turning away. "And you had better be here when I get back. And if you slam your door, you're grounded for a month."

She heard Carmen's door close softly behind her, then she heard a muffled scream. She bit her lip, then went to the front door, opened it, closed it. She retreated to the living room; she waited. Half an hour later she saw Carmen tiptoe down the stairs.

"Room," Carrie said.

Carmen jumped, then made her way back to the stairs.

"Carmen," Carrie said. "Don't climb out your window. Do you hear me?"

"You can't stop me."

"I'll have them cut down the tree," Carrie said, softly.

Carmen froze. "You wouldn't. You love trees."

"I love you more."

"Mothers who love their daughters don't hit them. You're full of bullshit."

Carrie did not move from the sofa. Within another half hour Carmen had crept down the stairs again, peeking surreptitiously around the corner to see if she was there. Carrie raised her eyebrows, received a venomous glare in return.

"Can't I even make easy Mac?"

"I'll bring it to you."

"I don't want it if you make it." Carmen sulked back upstairs.

Carrie got up and went to the fireplace. She built a fire. She went to the kitchen, put on the tea-kettle and waited until it shrieked, then poured herself a cup of tea. She went back to the living room, wrapped herself in a blanket and settled down on the sofa. She watched the flickering dance of the flames, half-wishing the flames would burn out her retinas and leave her blind so she could turn inward and attempt to quell the insanity she felt inside, threatening. Calmly, she took a sip of tea.

Her first reaction had been to go to Sam, and that was how she had known that Carmen would want to go to Jake. She understood that part of her daughter, and she would have to start from there.

Carrie took the next day off from school and went for a random drive, finding a back street that lead to a community park, past which was a small diner. Feeling nostalgic, she parked in the mostly deserted parking lot, got out, and went inside. A cowbell attached to the door handle announced her entrance, and an elderly man in a red apron looked up from where he was standing at the cash register as she walked in.

"Cold day to be out," he said, smiling at her.

She nodded. "Thirty-two, according to the radio."

"How does a nice cup of coffee sound?"

"Fabulous," she said. "Sugar, please, no cream. Is your vegetable soup vegetarian?"

"It's made of vegetables, ma'am."

She didn't trust that answer. "Just the coffee, please. And a slice of the cheesecake to go. And a paper."

"Will that be all?"

She smiled. "I'm sorry I'm such a bad customer. I'm just passing through."

The man brought her the coffee, plunked down the paper. "Four eighty-three."

She thanked him and went to a table near the back of the diner. She felt a momentary twinge of guilt that she should be teaching, but she dismissed the feeling. She was taking her third personal day in the five years she had been teaching in Maine, and Carmen would not be home until three. The time was hers to enjoy, guilt free.

She picked up the book a young person from the writer's group had recommended to her and turned a page, feeling self-conscious and silly that she was reading a book called The Art of Loving. Having read a few pages, she paused. A few pages, a few hundreds of words, and the floodgates had come crashing down.

In the beginning.... they take the intensity of the infatuation, this being crazy about each other, for proof of the intensity of their love...while it may only prove the degree of their preceding loneliness.

She closed the book and stared at it. A few pages giving her closure, making her confront the past...a part of her past. She knew she had been lonely, but had never considered that with his superficial friends, his life falling out from under him—that he might have been as lonely as she had been. The irrational attraction had resulted from the strong emotion that Fromm said was anxiety of aloneness, the desire to conquer or be conquered, vanity, love—any number of things. She hadn't denied the existence of the attraction, nor had she given into what Fromm called "fusion without integrity." She looked up, unexpected tears leaking from the corners of her eyes, and saw the elderly man watching her curiously. She smiled, then tucked the book into her purse. She would read the rest later.

She sipped the coffee and looked around the empty diner before picking up the paper. She was not sure why she had bought it—maybe to appease the old man when he realized she was only going to have a cup of coffee. She skimmed through the front page, hardly noting more than the headlines of main events. When she got to the Arts and Entertainment section she started to look more closely at the articles, occasionally circling an article she could use in her classes. The calmness that descended on her intensified her shock as she turned the page.

For several moments, she was afraid that her heart had stopped beating. At some point, she realized she had stopped breathing and drew in a long, ragged breath. Finally, she was able to center on the caption under the inserted picture.

JEAN PAUL CHRISTIANSON. Debut gallery opens December 31st.

Her heart remained painfully constricted in her chest. She thought she was hallucinating. But reading the short text that accompanied the picture of the painting confirmed her doubts.

Disciple of the late Damien DeMatteo.

No other artist would be able to capture the eerie quality in his paintings, that he had claimed resulted from his inner insanity. She was sure that he had changed his name again. Most likely for the same reason—to leave a past behind. But if "Jean Paul" was having his debut in the area on December thirty-first—two weeks away—he was close. Shakily she closed the paper, folded it in half, tucked it under her arm and slid the purse's straps over her shoulder.

"Have a good day," she told the elderly man, not pausing for his reaction, the cowbell ringing on her way out.

She tossed her purse into the back seat, then waited for her heart to begin beating normally again. She wanted to talk to Sam. Though she knew he used his mornings to write, she knew he would welcome a visit from her, that he would put aside whatever he was working on and pretend as if he hadn't been doing anything at all so she would not feel like an inconvenience. She glanced at the clock and realized he would still be sleeping.

And she wanted to finish the book. The ideas would have to whirl around and collide and somehow come to cohesion in her mind. Love moved at a fast pace and waited for no one; there was no point in delaying her reading of the book, or in thinking that in doing so she would be able to make better sense of it—if she could make sense of it at all. Erich Fromm seemed to think love was understandable; she wasn't so sure. She would finish the book and then she would visit Sam, and she would be home when Carmen got out of school.

The backhand slap had not left a bruise on Carmen's face—no discoloration, no swelling. Had she first seen Carmen in the kitchen, Carrie would have had to worry about the results of makeup and concealer, but Carmen had slept through her alarm and Carrie had needed to wake her and drive her to the school. Carmen had been quiet, but not as openly hateful as Carrie had expected; she seemed less shocked than Carrie was. Carrie didn't know how she could apologize to Carmen. She would have to start by talking to her about Jake, and go from there.

But first, she would finish the book. After parking the car she went inside and curled up on the sofa, flipping each delicate page with care, delving deeper and deeper.

Sam opened the door a minute after she rang the bell. "Hello, Carrie."

"I can leave if this is a bad time," she started.

"Would you like to come in?"

"If I'm not bothering you."

"Do you ever." He went inside, not waiting for her answer. "Don't worry. I wasn't writing."

"Were you sleeping?" she asked, noting the dim lights.

"You're not intruding." He sat down on the sofa in the living room. "What's on your mind?"

"A book I'm reading." She handed him the text. "It explains why I can't love anyone."

"You can love," he said. "Everyone is born being able to love. You need to learn how to respond to love."

When she didn't respond, he scanned the front cover. "What about this book?"

"It made me think about how I've acted in the past."

"Towards Damien."

"Towards Jean Paul Christianson."

"Who?"

She took out the newspaper, opened to the page with the painting on it, and handed it to him. "He's here."

The lines in Sam's face hardened. "The caption says disciple of—"

"I know it's him."

Sam exhaled sharply. "Remember that he's a part of your past. Through your own active choice."

"I thought about what you said," she replied. "About how he might want to see Carmen, and about how Carmen wants to see him. And this book has made me realize why it was my fault that everything fell apart."

"Why do you say that?" he asked, heavily.

She nodded at the paperback, clenched in Sam's right fist. "The book explains that true love involves responsibility and respect. Responsibility, meaning being ready to respond to another person's needs, and respect meaning the ability to see the person as he is."

"I don't see how the fault is entirely yours. We're talking about the Ralph phase of Damien now, aren't we? But even before then, you responded to his needs."

"No. I didn't."

"I doubt this book means his physical needs."

"What?"

"You were there for him when his world was falling apart," Sam said. "Do you remember that night he was drunk and you tucked him into bed?"

"How could you remember that?"

"Because you told me," he said. "You told me about countless other incidents like that, as well. I can tell you, without even reading it, that's what this book means by being ready to respond. And did you *ever* ask him to change?"

"If I had really loved him, I would have insisted that he stop hurting himself." She paused. "But I didn't."

"You didn't. Thank you for finally answering the question." He glanced at her. "What else did this book say?"

"It made me reflect on my behavior. If I had acted differently—"

"You couldn't have acted differently, Carrie. He didn't give you the option. Don't look at me like I'm telling you something you don't know. You've been telling yourself the same thing for years." He paused. "Love shouldn't make you compromise yourself. Does the book say that?"

"Give it back to me." She flipped through the pages until she came to a passage she had underlined. "Here. 'True, mature love is 'union under the condition of pursuing one's integrity, one's individuality'—"

"Rightly said."

She stood and walked across the room to the window, her back to him. "There has to be some reason he's still haunting me. And maybe now that I know what love is supposed to be…"

"You can't learn what love is from a book."

"No." She turned. "But I want to see him. I want to see Chloe. Though I'm afraid the walls might be built back up again."

"Were the walls ever down, Carrie?"

"You don't think I should see him?"

"It doesn't matter what I think. I'm more concerned about what's going to be best for you."

She paused. "You've never told me, not once, what you think about all of this."

"About what?"

"You know."

"About chasing after him? That's because I've tried to let you figure things out for yourself."

"I'd like your advice."

"You don't want my advice."

"I do," she insisted. "I know you'll tell me what you really think, and not what you think I want to hear."

"I think you've already held on for too long, Carrie. You're too good for him." He stared at her when she looked down. "I said you wouldn't want my advice."

"I appreciate your honesty," she said, "But you don't understand how complicated our—"

"I think I get it."

465

"We always seem to talk about my life, and never about yours." She hesitated. "How is your life going?"

"I'm fine. I'm always fine."

"You're so strong, Sam," she murmured.

"Don't be so hard on yourself, Carrie." He paused. "You seem sad, now, and you were so excited about this book when you came in. I feel like I've killed something with my cynicism."

"That's not the point. You *know* me. And I don't know anything about you."

"You know more than you think."

"You give and you give—"

"Carrie," he said, gently but firmly. "Friendship isn't about accounts. I know that you care about me. You've kept in touch with me over the years, and I understand what a big step that has been for you—"

"I know you know," she said, turning from the window. "You understand me. But who understands you?"

"Don't make me into a victim," he said. "I had many happy years with Tessa, I have a son who I'm mostly proud of, I have a job I love, and I have your friendship. Any of those would make me feel lucky. All of them together, and I consider myself blessed. When I say I'm fine, I mean it."

"You look tired."

His smile, meant to reassure her, hitched. "I don't like the tension in the house right now between me and Jake. Other than that, I'm fine."

"Sam—"

"*Fine*," he stressed.

"Why won't you talk to me?"

"I can't tell you everything, Carrie," he responded. "You know there are things you don't tell me."

"Not many."

"But there are some. Not because you don't trust me, but because you want to keep them to yourself. Everyone deals with things in different ways. Besides, you're hard to get a hold of."

"I'm sorry."

"I wasn't criticizing." He paused. "Carmen gets home around three, doesn't she? You'll want to be home for her, and it's already two thirty."

"Is it really?" She looked at him in disbelief. "But I got here around one."

"I enjoyed talking to you, too," he said. "Come more often, Carrie. You're always welcome. You know that."

"You know what a special person you are to me. Even though I'm not so good at showing it?"

He smiled. "Yes, we've talked about how it's hard for you to respond to love. Let me get your coat for you."

She walked with him to the front door.

"Be careful on the roads," he said.

"Thanks for making the time for me."

"You forgot your book." He started back into the house.

She put her gloved hand on his arm to stop him. "I want you to read it. Even though you seem to know what it says already."

"Maybe once I've finished, we can discuss it together," he said. "Good-bye, Carrie."

She smiled at him before disappearing through the door. He went to the living room and watched her trudge through the driveway which Jake was supposed to have shoveled before he went to school—a chore to get his full privileges back sooner. He turned from the window, went into the kitchen, and pulled out the stack of bills he had been looking at when she had come, which he had pushed hurriedly under a towel so she would not see them. Selling the old house to her at the discount he had given her had seemed like a good idea at the time, because she had needed a place to stay to get away— and she was a single mother with a teacher's salary. She had been so excited, so happy, the day she signed the mortgage, that the monetary loss had been worth it. Despite the fact that he had no idea where the money would come from, he knew that he and Jake would pull through. He didn't regret selling Carrie the house, though he had done it primarily to keep her away from *him*...

And she was going to go back to him.

Carmen walked through the door with one of the biggest smiles Carrie had ever seen on her face. Her cheeks were flushed with the bite of the cold air, and she was humming softly to herself. She spotted Carrie waiting in the living room. Her expression did not change.

"Hi, Mom."

"Do you know what time it is, Carmen?"

Carmen blinked. Her eyes flitted to the mantel, registered the clock. "It's past eleven. Wow. That went really fast."

"Where were you?"

The smile on Carmen's face froze. "Working. I got a job, like you told me to."

"You were supposed to be home eight hours ago."

"I did what you told me to do." Carmen's jaw was set, her voice tight. "What, are you mad at me now for listening to you?"

"Did you stop to think that I would be worried about you? I was about to call the police, Carmen."

"I'm surprised you didn't," Carmen mumbled. "You are a total control freak. If you're going to flip out if I come home late, why did you tell me to get a job? It's not like I can work for three hours and then come home. Were you even serious when you were talking to me last night or was it all bullshit?"

"Language."

"My god," Carmen muttered. "Are you serious?"

Carrie paused. "Where did you get hired?"

"At the corner store," she said.

"I don't want you working there."

"No, you wouldn't." Carmen's cheeks burned crimson. "You don't want me around Jake, but if I have to have a fucking job I'm going to enjoy it. That's where I got hired, and that's where I'm working."

"Carmen."

"Are you going to come pick me up at eleven every night when I get off work?" she demanded. "You're usually in bed by ten-thirty. And how are you going to drop me off at five when you don't leave the school until five? At least Jake can drive me both ways. You won't even have to be inconvenienced."

"I wasn't referring to Jake," Carrie said. "Corner stores have a bad track record for getting held up. I don't want you to be in danger."

"You think someone is going to try to shoot me?" Carmen stared at her incredulously. "That is so like you."

"Jake shouldn't be working there, either."

"So why don't you talk to Sam?" Carmen's eyes glittered. "Then both of you can try to have even more control over our lives."

"Sit down, Carmen. I want to talk to you."

She sighed. "So what else is new."

"Please sit down."

She dropped onto the sofa, letting her backpack thud to the ground. "What?"

Carrie set the plastic container of cheesecake she had bought at the diner down on the table between them.

"What is this?" Carmen asked, making no attempt to move. "A bribe?"

"A treat."

"I'm not a dog."

"I'm sorry for how I behaved towards you last night. I feel terrible."

"Thanks." Carmen stooped to pick up her backpack. "I'm not hungry."

"Carmen, please sit down."

A look of disbelief on her face, Carmen sank back onto the sofa and looked at Carrie.

"I want to talk to you about Jake."

"Here it comes," Carmen mumbled.

Carrie looked at her as neutrally as she could. "I don't approve of what you did. But I'm not going to forbid you to see Jake." She paused. "We need to come up with some kind of negotiation."

For a full minute Carmen was quiet. "You're serious."

Carrie nodded.

"Can we negotiate some other time? I have a lot of work to do and I just got home."

"You mean you want time to think of why or how I might be trying to bribe you." Carrie paused. "But if you want to talk about it later, we can. One more thing, before you go."

"What?" Carmen stood. The lines in her face were tight, her eyes wary.

"The phone bill came in today. You went over your minutes for this month."

"Sorry," Carmen said, relaxing. "I had some really good conversations and lost track of time. But you're always saying how important it is to talk to people, how you can learn so much…"

"The majority were phone numbers I didn't recognize." Carrie paused. "Who were you calling?"

"Look, I'm sorry about going over. I can pay some of the bill with the money I make at the store, okay? That's what Jake does, to help Sam out…"

"I don't expect you to pay for anything," Carrie said. "Carmen, I would advise you not to lie to me."

"I didn't say anything." Carmen paused. "But if you make me say something, I'm going to make something up."

"You were calling Ralph Palmer," Carrie said. "You called every single Ralph Palmer in twenty-five different states."

"He's my dad," Carmen said. "I want to find him. I'm not asking you to help me. Please just don't interfere."

"You must really want this, to have used 'please'."

"Mom."

"And 'Mom'."

"Carrie," Carmen said. "I—"

"You have the wrong name," Carrie interrupted her. "Try Jean Paul Christianson."

Carmen blinked. "Who?"

Without answering, Carrie went into the kitchen and came back with her purse. She pulled out the paper she had bought at the diner, smoothed out the creases, and handed the paper to Carmen.

"The man who painted that is your father," she said. "I'm sure of it."

"The paper says it was done by Jean Paul Christianson," Carmen said. "Disciple of Damien DeMatteo. Who are those people?"

She sighed. "They're all the same person."

Carmen stared at her. "My dad has three different names?"

"It's complicated, Carmen. You have to trust me on this one. If you really want to get in touch with your father, you need to find that man."

"Why didn't he pick a better name, if he was going to change it?" Carmen smoothed the pages of the paper and looked at the painting, her brow furrowing. "Can I have this?"

Carrie hesitated, then nodded. "If you want it."

Carmen folded the paper carefully, so the photo of the painting and the accompanying article faced inwards. She stood.

"He's not psycho, is he?" she asked. "I mean, he's not going to try to kidnap me or hurt me, is he?"

"No," Carrie said. "He wouldn't hurt you."

"I mean, it's just that I don't know anything about him."

"Don't chew on your hair."

Carmen removed the wet lock from her mouth and tossed it behind her shoulder. "So it's okay?"

"You can look for him if you want to. I've said I won't stop you."

Carmen hesitated. "Is it okay if Jake takes me? Since I'm too young to drive, I don't see how I'd get there…unless you want to go with me."

"You can go with Jake." Carrie looked at her levelly. "I want to be able to trust you. If you're going to go together, you'll leave in the morning and get back before dinner." She paused. "You really disappointed me, Carmen."

Carmen inhaled. "I'll be careful, okay?"

"You had better be."

Carmen hesitated. "I'd rather go with you."

Carrie looked away from her. "I don't have time."

"You don't want to," Carmen amended, slinging the backpack across her shoulder. "Just say so."

Carrie inhaled sharply as Carmen left the room, then let her breath out slowly. The thought of seeing him after all the years still unsettled her. Time should have dulled the pain, dulled the passion, dulled the bitter-sweetness…but she could not risk falling in love with him a third time. The first time she had withheld, the second time she had given in…the third time she would let go. Her eyes scanned the table for the newspaper before she realized Carmen had taken it upstairs with her. She turned off the lights, then went upstairs to her room. She had stayed up later than usual to make sure Carmen was safe, but now that her daughter had come home, she would sleep. Eventually.

Shivering outside the convenience store beside the exit of the highway, Carmen tucked her chapped hands under the cuffs of the jacket

Jake had lent her. She leaned against the cold metal of the Honda, looking listlessly around the empty parking lot as she waited for him to finish paying for gas. Her eyes trained on the slate-colored sky, the dull, deadening clouds hanging low on the horizon. She noticed that Jake paused when he came out of the store. She shrank further into the jacket to keep warm.

"Are you crazy?" he asked, walking towards her. "It's freezing out here. That's why I left the car on for you."

"I didn't want to wait in the car."

"I said I would only be a minute."

"I like to be where I can move around."

The muscles in his face tightened as he handed her a white styrofoam cup. "Here. I got you some coffee."

She sniffed. "French Vanilla."

"That's your favorite, isn't it?"

"It's your favorite."

"Shit," he said. "Your favorite is Vanilla Chai, isn't it? I knew it had vanilla in it, but I forgot..."

"This is fine. Thank you."

"Door's unlocked." He went to the other side of the car, keeping his windbreaker pulled tightly around him. "You're lucky I had an extra coat. Didn't you think you might need one?"

"I don't mind the cold," she muttered, her hands clenched into fists as she got into the car and buckled her seatbelt.

"Do you even own a coat?" He looked at her skeptically when she nodded. "I've never seen you wear one of your own."

"You aren't very observant."

"You're in a bitchy mood today."

"It's eight o'clock in the morning."

"Your idea. Not mine."

She put the coffee cup in the holder between them. "If my mother hadn't said I have to be back by mid-afternoon."

"At least she's letting you go."

"At least it's not too much of a drive." She paused. "Is it?"

"It should take us about an hour to get there, if we don't get lost."

"I'll give you gas money."

"I'd prefer something else."

Her lips curled into a smile. "Yeah, we'll see. Thanks for the coffee."

He grimaced as he started the car. "I told you to keep it running."

"Waste of energy."

"Since when have you cared?"

"It'll only take a minute to warm up," she said. "Geez, Jake."

"It's not like you couldn't have left it running."

"Come here. I'll warm you up." She linked her arm behind his head and pulled him towards her.

"Well, in that case," he said, and kissed her.

His hand crept under her jacket; she let him grope around for a moment before she pushed him away. "We should get going. This is important to me."

"Right." He straightened and started the motor.

As they drove, she snuck glances at him. Most of the time he seemed oblivious to her, his head bobbing in time with the music, his eyes focused on the road, his fingers tapping out a rhythm on the steering wheel. The rest of the time she spent looking out the window at the passing landscape, sneaking equal glances at her reflection in the rearview mirror.

"This is fun," she said.

"Glad you think so." He seemed distracted. "What do you think he'll be like?"

"My dad? I don't know."

He paused. "Do you want me to come to the door with you?"

"I want you to pull over."

"What?" He glanced at her.

She smiled at him. "I want a driving lesson."

"Right now?"

She nodded, noticing the temporary storm cloud that passed over his face. "You said you would. If I wreck your car, I'll pay for it."

"All right," he said. "There aren't many people on the road right now, anyway."

She noticed how smoothly he pulled over to the side of the road and wondered if driving was really as easy as he made it look. He put the car in neutral and got out. She hesitated for a moment, then unbuckled her seatbelt and passed him without saying anything. He gave her the keys.

"You ready, baby?" she purred, her voice low.

"I swear, Carmen," he said, his eyes not leaving her face, "if you kill us..."

She smirked at him, looked down at the wheel. "How do I start it?"

"Put it into first. Wait, first put down the clutch. The clutch is the one on...that's the accelerator!"

She eased her foot off the accelerator, laughing. "I know, I just—"

"Carmen, it's not funny. If you fuck up this car I have to pay for it, and I can't afford..."

Her eyes glittered. She tore the keys from the ignition, tossed them at him, got out of the car.

"What the hell is wrong with you?" he asked, getting out of the car.

She turned to him, eyes flaming. "What the hell is wrong with *me*? I've never driven before and I don't appreciate your attitude. What the fuck, couldn't you be more helpful and less criticizing? This should be more fun than you're making it."

"Yeah, this whole thing would be more fun if—"

"Whole thing?"

"Us," he clarified. "You and me. If you weren't so damned dramatic."

"That's how I am." She scowled at him. "If you don't like it, you can dump me. Or you can deal. It's not like you're not getting anything out of it."

"Not much," he muttered.

Her face went blank. She turned away from him and started walking. He stared after her.

"Where are you going?"

She glanced over her shoulder without slackening her pace. "There's more than one way to get to where I want to go."

He turned, went back to the car, got in. He drove up to her. She did not look at him.

"Carmen. You're being ridiculous."

She kept her eyes on the road, kept trudging forward.

"Look," he said, inhaling sharply. "I'll give you a lesson after work on Monday, okay? Right now, though, we're on a time schedule."

She stopped and looked at him. He hated that look—blank, empty—but at least he had her attention.

"I'll even let you drive us home."

She paused. "Promise."

"Sure."

She got into the car and buckled her seatbelt. "Drive."

He looked at her, not without respect. "You have anger management issues."

"Fuck you."

He glanced at the dashboard. "What do you want to listen to?"

"This is fine."

He saw she was smoothing down her hair with the aid of the rearview mirror. His eyes flicked back to the road, back to her.

"You care too much about how you look," he said.

"You care too much about criticizing me," she said. "Can't you just like me for who I am?"

"There you go, being sarcastic again."

"Criticizing," she said.

"Point taken."

She patted his leg affectionately. "You wouldn't want me if I didn't look good, Jake."

"That's not true." He paused. "I mean, if you were hideous—"

She shook her head. "Just drive."

He drove.

Carmen had planned exactly what she would say. She had visualized how Carrie would look: she would look up from the papers she was grading, her eyebrows arched. She would have a cup of tea—maybe coffee—on the right side of the table in front of her. Carmen would walk by her, not letting anything show. She would go to her room and slam her door and it would be like nothing had changed.

She hung up the coat Jake had lent her and steeled herself to enact the scene she had envisioned. She paused by the kitchen, not smelling anything—not the spicy odor of curry or the warm, cinnamon smell of the cider Carrie made every night of winter, starting with the winter solstice. She peeped into the kitchen and saw that dinner had not been started. She looked at the clock. Given everything that she and Jake had done after the visit, the time should have been later than five thirty…but dinner should have been started and Carrie should have been there. Hesitating, Carmen went to the living room, went through the adjacent door that led to the garage, registered Carrie's car therein. She retreated to the kitchen and toyed with the idea of making dinner for herself. Then, she toyed with the idea of making dinner for herself and Carrie. She smiled; making dinner for both of them would confuse Carrie. Still smiling, she put a large pot and a small pot of water on the stove to boil, then went to the fridge and the cupboard. Thirty minutes later, she drained the pasta and the broccoli she had made. She covered both pots to keep the food heated. Still no sign of Carrie.

She cleared off the kitchen table and set two places, then poured out a glass of skim milk for herself and a glass of soymilk for Carrie. She got a candle from the cupboard in the living room and placed it between the two plates. She looked at what she had created and smiled.

She used the candle in the center of the table to light a cigarette. No matter where she was in the house, Carrie would smell the smoke and come running. The smile on Carmen's face hitched as the butt burned down and she remained alone. Hastily she crossed into the kitchen, used a plate to extinguish the cigarette, tossed the butt and rinsed the plate. She went back to the living room. She wanted to find Carrie and tell her everything.

She checked the upstairs bedrooms, then walked to Carrie's study. The door was closed. Carmen paused, then knocked. The second knock also met with silence. Hesitating further, she pushed the door open.

Her mother's appearance scared her. Her graying auburn hair hung loose around her shoulders. Her face was deathly pale, seemingly bloodless. She was hunched over, her hand clawed around a pen. Carrie looked up when the door opened, and for a moment Carmen felt the fever in her mother's eyes flush over her.

"I'm sorry," she said instantly. "I didn't know you were in here."

"Carmen. You're home."

"You're…writing?"

Carrie nodded. Carmen started to back out of the room.

"Did you need something?" Carrie's eyes followed her.

"I just wanted to tell you how...how things went. And that I'm sorry I'm late."

Carrie's eyes drifted to the notebook in front of her. She did not seem to realize Carmen was demonstrating unprecedented behavior. "Can we talk later?"

"Yeah." Faced with her mother's indifference, Carmen found herself eager to appease. "Mom. I made dinner."

"Is it dinner time already?"

"It's after five. We always eat around five. I made some for you, too."

"That was nice of you," Carrie said. "I'm not hungry right now."

Carmen lingered in the doorway. "I guess I'll just leave the extra on the stove for you so it stays warm, okay?"

"It'd be a shame for the food to sit and get cold. Why don't you invite Jake over?"

"You want me to invite Jake over?"

"Only if you want to, honey."

Carmen stared at her. "Well, if that's all right...I mean, I guess I'll let you get back to your writing."

"Thank you," Carrie said. "Please close the door on your way out."

Carmen backed out of the study and closed the door behind her. She walked out to the kitchen, looked at the pots on the stove. She didn't want to see Jake again so soon. She would rather be alone. And she probably shouldn't eat the food anyway; she had used butter on the broccoli, and the sauce for the pasta wasn't fat free. Picking up her backpack, she climbed the stairs, shut herself in her room, splayed her textbooks in front of her. She tried to concentrate, ignoring the rumbling of her stomach. After two hours of unproductive studying, she picked up the adult romance she had gotten from the public library at the beginning of the week. She was distracted, but only temporarily. Her concentration wavered and her eyes glazed over the words. She glanced at the clock, saw it was eight, stood. If she didn't eat something she would never get anything done; she could wash the butter off the broccoli. She abandoned her books and made her way to the kitchen, jumping when she saw Carrie there.

"I didn't know you were here," she faltered.

Carrie had pulled her hair back into a neat bun, had regained the color in her cheeks, and apparently come back to her senses. "You made dinner for me?"

"I guess I thought it might be a way of saying thank you. For, you know, letting me visit..."

Carrie waited for her to finish, and when Carmen didn't, turned her attention to the stove. She lifted the cover off one of the pots.

"Smells good," she said. "Did you and Jake eat already?"

"No. I was waiting for you, I guess."

Carrie turned to the living room, where the candle still flickered on the table. "You did all that, too?"

Carmen nodded. Carrie raised her eyebrows.

"You aren't pregnant, are you?"

"No. God, no." Carmen shifted. "But I do have something I...I want to talk to you about."

"Are you hungry?"

Carmen nodded, and Carrie took the lids off the pots and began portioning out the food.

"I don't want that much," Carmen said.

"I want you to eat."

"I'm not going to become anorexic," Carmen said. "You can trust me to get my own food."

Carrie relinquished the serving fork to her, watched critically as Carmen pushed half of each original serving size back into the pots, and then walked with her to the dining room. They sat down.

"This is the first time we've sat down to eat together and actually talked. In a long time."

"Geez, don't get sentimental about it, okay?"

A grimace flittered over Carrie's face. "Were you smoking in here?"

"No," Carmen said.

"You know better."

"I won't do it again." Carmen picked up her fork.

Carrie looked at her. "Purely business, then. How was your day?"

Carmen hesitated. "Jake and me...I mean, Jake and I...went to see him today."

Carrie waited.

Carmen took a deep breath. "He said he's not my dad. He was really pissed off because I had lied on the phone and said we were interested in his art, and I don't think he wanted to talk to me. He said he didn't have a daughter and he...he slammed the door in my face." She bit her lip.

"What did he look like?" She didn't want to make Carmen cry, but she was curious.

"He was tall." She seemed glad for the guided question. "Really thin. He had white streaks in his hair and patches of white near his temples. His face...his face looked dead."

"Dead?"

"I don't know. Maybe 'mean' would have been better."

"I'm sorry it didn't work out, Carmen," Carrie said.

Carmen shrugged. "Whatever. Some people are mean."

"What time did you get back?"

"Just a little while ago." She paused. "Jake took me to the roller-skating rink after. I was really upset, and he wanted to make me feel better. Then he bought me ice cream and we...well, you know. We hung out for awhile."

"Why were you upset?" Carrie seemed to have become a statue—still, calm, colorless. Carmen glanced at the ceiling, flustered.

"Because...I don't know! He felt...." She paused. "He felt like my father, okay? I can't even say what that feels like since I've never had a father, but it was like something in me knew."

Carrie looked down. "He said he didn't have a daughter, and then he closed the door in your face?"

"Yeah."

"That's exactly what happened?"

Carmen nodded.

Carrie paused. "How did you start the conversation?"

"I said I was your daughter."

"Did you use my name?"

"Well, I kind of had to. And then he slammed the door in my face."

"You mentioned my name and then he slammed the door in your face?"

"Do you have to keep repeating everything I say?"

479

"I'm sure that man is your father, Carmen." She paused. "But he might not know about you."

"*What?*"

"I never told him you were born. He and I had already separated."

Carmen's eyes widened. "You never told him about me? You mean you sent me over there to make a total fool out of myself?"

"I never sent you, Carmen."

"Like it makes any difference!" she cried. "How could you?"

"It's complicated."

"Complicated!" She swept the plates off the table. "I can't believe this!"

"Calm down," Carrie said, stooping to pick up the plates Carmen had knocked over. "You're making a mess."

"I'm making a mess?" Carmen kicked the plate out of her hand, sending it flying against the wall. "You've made a mess out of my life!"

"Don't exaggerate."

"You know what? Fuck you!"

Carmen stormed out of the room, pounded up the stairs, slammed her door. She sat down at her desk and pushed her work onto the floor. She put her head down on her hands, and she could not help it. She cried.

Jake dropped his coat on the sofa, went directly to his father's study, and walked in through the open door.

"Hey," he said, then tossed him the keys to the car. "Catch."

Sam watched the keys land on the desk, then tossed them back. "You know where they go."

Jake caught the keys. "Right. Well, I just wanted to let you know I'm back. In case you need to go somewhere."

"You're late." He paused. "Car back in one piece?"

"Yeah."

"Carmen back in one piece?"

"Dad."

Sam leaned back in his chair. "How'd it go?"

"The guy was a total dick," Jake said. "That's what she said, not me. I wasn't there. I mean, I was there, but I didn't go up with her. She wanted to go alone." He caught Sam's eye. "I thought she would be safe, since I was there in the car. And I told her not to go inside the house." He paused. "I'm going to need to work some extra hours this week, so if I'm not at home I'll be at work. Just wanted you to know, so you wouldn't worry."

Sam's voice was instantly cautious. "What did you do?"

Jake shifted. "I took Carmen out afterwards to cheer her up. Because she was upset or whatever. But if I work a couple extra shifts this week we'll be okay." He paused. "That's alright, isn't it?"

"Sometimes I'm really disappointed in you. Other times, I'm damn proud." Sam paused. "Don't let your schoolwork slide."

"I don't see why it's so important."

"You don't know what you want to do yet. Best to keep your doors open."

Jake blinked. "It's just that when Carmen talks about dropping out of school, I can't ever give her any reasons why she shouldn't. It doesn't make sense, when she—"

"Does Carrie know Carmen wants to drop out?"

"Is she all you think about?"

"I think about you a lot," he said. "And whether you're turning out all right."

Jake looked at him, then looked away.

"Listen, Jake," Sam said. "You're young. You have your entire life before you, and it could be a good life. But Carmen is out of control."

"She's dealing with a lot." He thought about trying to give her a driving lesson, about how she changed moods and about how she threw tantrums—and all the other things they did together. He blinked, then turned. "You don't understand."

"Jake." Sam looked at him, hard. "Are you treating her well?"

"What are you talking about?"

"You've had girls break up with you in the past, because of—"

"I lose my temper sometimes," he said, gritting his teeth. "I'm never out of control. And I'm not going to tell you about stuff if you turn it back on me."

"Jake, listen to me. I trust you."

"Yeah."

"You're this girl's first real boyfriend."

"We're not using labels."

Sam shook his head. "I don't care if you are or not. You're setting the standard for her."

"Carmen's a tough girl. She's not—"

Sam's look cut him off. "Make sure the standard you're setting is a high one."

Jake swallowed. "I don't want to keep you from your writing."

"Remember what I said, Jake. I'm not digging you out of a hole if you bury yourself. You're old enough to be treated like an adult. When are your extra shifts this week?"

"Monday and Friday. I'll be home around eleven." He paused. "Do you want me to make dinner?"

"Order a pizza."

"What do you want on it?"

"I'll take pineapples on half. Get whatever else you want."

"Six okay?"

Sam nodded. "There should be a coupon on top of the microwave. Do you mind going?"

Jake shook his head. "No. I'll call you when I'm back."

"Be careful on the roads." He paused. "Money's in the jar. Take what you need."

"Yessir," Jake said, saluting as he left.

Money. That was what he was giving his son. Sam shook his head, looked down at the article he was editing and tried to refocus his concentration.

Somehow it would have to be enough.

"Carrie Crenshaw," Carmen said, shivering in the cold, brushing a snowflake from one of her cold-bitten cheeks. "Carrie Crenshaw is my mother."

"Little girl," the man said, standing in the doorway, frowning at her. "I told you, I don't—"

"She told me you wouldn't know about me." Carmen kept her eyes focused on the man's face, though her thoughts flew back to the car where she knew Jake was waiting impatiently. "Look, I just want a minute to explain—"

"I'm sorry," the man said, moving to shut the door.

"She said you were my father!" Carmen exploded.

The door closed in her face. Seething, Carmen kicked the door. She heard Jake start yelling at her. She ignored him and stomped through the snow to the window near the side of the house, where she could see the man peering out at her.

"You're going to have to own up!" she shouted. "You can't shut me out that easily!"

"Carmen." Jake pulled her away from the window as the man retreated. "What the hell—"

She wrenched herself out of Jake's grip. She went to the window and slammed her fist against it.

"She said you wouldn't know about me!" Carmen yelled at the top of her voice. "Listen to me!"

Jake's arms enveloped her, pinning her arms to her sides as he began to drag her back to the car. "Are you fucking crazy? If that guy calls the cops—"

"I'm not leaving until he confesses." Carmen stopped struggling in his arms and let her body go completely limp. He almost dropped her as she slipped down his body.

"Carmen...Jesus," he swore, struggling with her weight. "He's probably calling the cops right now, and we're trespassing. You're acting crazy..."

She stood abruptly and strode away from him. He paused, glancing back at the empty window before he followed her to where she was leaning against the side of his car.

"I'm not happy," he said, frowning at the smiley face she had etched into the thin layer of snow that had settled on the windshield of his car.

Her chapped hands fumbled to light a cigarette. "Yeah, but your car is. Christ, it's so cold." She gave up on the cigarette and stuffed her hands in her pockets.

He shook his head. "You're not smoking in my car."

"Your daddy gonna rag on you if I do?"

"We're not going over that again, are we?" He turned, saw her smiling sweetly at him. He frowned. "It's a nasty habit and I don't like that you do it."

"But you won't stop me." Her voice held a challenge that he didn't feel up to answering.

He turned back to his car. "Help me clear this off, will you?"

"Jesus Christ, Jake. I don't have any gloves. Do you want me to get frostbitten?"

"No," he said. "Besides, I'm done. Your door is unlocked. You can get in."

She looked at her boots, half buried in the piles of snow that had built up in the unshoveled driveway. "I told you I wasn't going anywhere. Not until he talks to me."

He looked at her imploringly. "I have to get back. I have to make up the work I missed for playing hooky with you."

"Boo hoo," she said.

"I have to work at six," he insisted. "It takes an hour to get back when the roads are clear and the roads aren't clear, so tack on another half hour. Please, Carmen. We have to leave now."

She shrugged. "You can leave if you want, Jake."

"You even think he'll talk to you?"

"If I stand here long enough."

He shook his head. "How will he even know you're out here? By the looks of this driveway, he never goes out. And it's not like he's looking out the window at you. And do you really think he'd care that you're out here, even if he knew?"

"He'd care if he found my frozen body and Carrie sued him. In fact, I bet it wouldn't even matter if she sued him. It would probably be enough if he had to see her again."

"It's not like you're giving up if you leave now, okay?"

"That's exactly what it is. That's why you used it as an example." She paused. "You just want me to get in the car."

"I just want to get home," he said. "I want to get to work on time so I don't get in trouble."

"So go."

He paused. "I'll let you start the car. That'll be lesson one."

She eyed him. "Will you let me drive?"

"You shouldn't be driving on these roads."

She held out her hand for the keys. He dropped them into her hand, wincing at the sight of her cracked, broken skin. She slipped in triumphantly, started the car without incident, and backed out of the driveway and onto the road. She caught his expression and smiled.

"I've been practicing," she said. "Don't tell my mom, okay? She'll flip."

He gawked at her. "You've been driving her car without her knowing about it?"

"Only at night, after she goes to sleep, and when people aren't on the roads. I wouldn't want to hurt anyone because I don't know what I'm doing."

The car sidled smoothly down the road. She was giving him no reason to feel nervous, but he was uncomfortable with having her behind the wheel. She turned to him, suddenly.

"Sorry, Jake," she said. "This is on purpose." She stalled the car.

"Where are you going?" he demanded as she unbuckled her seatbelt.

"Back."

"I thought we had an agreement."

She shook her head. "Nice temptation, but no."

"Then I'm going with you."

"No, you're not." Her eyes spit fire. "You're staying here. You're going to keep the car here and I'll be back within the hour. Or you can go to work and I'll bum a ride home. But you're not coming with me."

"What are you going to do?"

She shrugged. "It's all part of the plan. The plan develops as it will."

Before he could stop her, she kicked open the car door. He rolled down his window.

"What if he tries to give you trouble?"

"Mom said he wouldn't hurt me."

"I want to be there."

She shook her head. "He won't let me in if he sees you're there. Trust me, he won't let me freeze."

"You said we'd be back by five at the latest." He stared at her. "I can't leave you here."

She smiled at him. "When are you going to learn that I don't need you?"

"Fine," he said, turning away from her. "Good luck."

She stepped away from the car as he pulled away from her. She watched him go, her hands gripping the insides of the coat's sleeves. She was glad he had gone, because now she would have to succeed. Or freeze. Or hitchhike. Or call Carrie. And she didn't even know if Carrie would pick up her phone.

Tears froze on her cheeks as she trudged back to the house. She ignored them. She surveyed the empty windows, then stooped. She packed together snow in her bare hands, then assaulted the window where he had been standing before. The snowball hit the glass with a dull thud and fell away, leaving a white conglomeration of ice and snow the size of a tennis ball on the clear glass. She waited, then stooped and spent ten minutes making herself an arsenal. Her task got easier after the first few minutes, after her hands had gone numb with cold. One after another the snow missiles smacked into the window, but she did not speak until she saw his silhouette move to the window.

"I'll send my mom down here if you won't talk to me!" she shouted, and she knew he heard her because he moved away.

Angrily, she picked up the last snowball she had made and slung it against the window, where it struck the pane with such force that she heard the crack it made. The door opened. She stared at the dark, lanky figure in the doorway. He stepped out into the snow silently and closed the door behind him. She walked over to him, her hands shoved in her pockets, her shoulders slouched.

"I'm sorry about the window," she said, head lowered against the cold. "But I need to talk to you."

He did not say anything, and she glanced up. He stood before her in a pair of ratty jeans and a thin black dress shirt, wrinkled and open at the throat. His hair was disheveled and his eyes dark and tired. She stood before him with her hands tucked into Jake's jacket, her teeth chattering from the cold, her long brown hair and the hood she was wearing speckled with snow.

"Damn persistent little devil," he said, finally. "How long have you been standing out here?"

Her teeth chattered in reply. He glanced at her, shifted, said nothing. Suddenly, she straightened and glared at him.

"You could ask me inside," she said. "It's freezing."

"My house is no place for you," he said, taking a cigarette from his pocket and putting it in his mouth. "Tell your boyfriend to take you home."

"He left. He had to work." She paused. "Can I have one of those?"

He eyed her critically. "Carrie lets you smoke?"

"So you do know my mother," she said triumphantly.

"I knew a Carrie Crenshaw," he said. "But you're no daughter of mine." He paused. "Though if I did have a daughter, it wouldn't hurt for her to be so damn persistent."

"Maybe you and Carrie should talk."

"What does she need? Money? How much money does she need?"

Carmen stared at him. "*She* doesn't need anything from you. But I need you to admit you're my father."

"Look. Little girl." His eyes burned. "I don't want anything to do with Carrie Crenshaw, and I don't need pesky little kids coming around bothering me." He glanced past her. "Destroying my house—"

"I said I would pay for the window."

"Do you know how much windows cost?"

"I'll save up. I have a job."

"You have a job and you smoke." He paused. "Anything else that I should know about you?"

"I'm not coming back."

"Good," he said. "It only took...how many times have you come by? Four?"

"Five."

"You're not going to send her over here?"

"No."

"Good," he said, then, "Why aren't you coming back?"

She shrugged. "You came and talked to me. So I'll leave you alone."

He looked away. "I can't give you a ride home. I don't drive anymore."

"Whatever. I can walk." She turned from him. "I was planning on it anyway."

"That dickhead boyfriend of yours," he said, making her turn. "Call him and tell him to give you a ride. Don't let him treat you that way."

She turned. "Have a nice day, Mr. Palmer."

"Come here," he said.

She shivered, then stepped closer.

"My name is Christianson," he said. "Are we straight on that?"

Still shivering, she shook her head. He looked directly at her.

"What's your name?"

"Carmen."

He cleared his throat. "You said your name is…Carmen."

For a moment, neither one of them spoke. "Look, I gotta get going. I have a long walk home and I don't want to be on the streets when it's dark." She paused. "It might take me awhile to get that check for your window. I only make about five bucks an hour, and that's before taxes."

Her phone went off, startling them both. She turned away from him.

"Hey, babe," she said, listening. "Yeah. See you."

When she turned around, he was still there. She was surprised. And she wasn't. She looked away. "My boyfriend says he'll come back for me."

"How old are you?" he asked, after a moment.

"Thirteen." She shrugged. "You should go inside. It's cold, and you aren't dressed appropriately."

He stared at her, then turned and went into the house. The door closed behind him. She pulled Jake's jacket tightly around her and walked calmly to the end of the driveway. She watched the swirling snow flakes and let her mind go as numb as her snow-burned cheeks. Five minutes later, she saw the weather-beaten Honda coming towards her. She could see the scowl on Jake's face through the windshield. He pulled up to the curb; she did not keep him waiting.

"Got what I wanted," she announced as she opened the door.

He glowered at her. "Were you expecting me to come back?"

"You're too good of a person to have left me abandoned in this weather with a strange man."

He grumbled as he pulled away from the curb. "I'm going to be late for work again. I'll be lucky if I don't get fired." He paused. "Here. That's for you. Since your hands look like shit."

"Thanks." She took the bottle of hand lotion from him and turned so he wouldn't see her expression. "It's only four-thirty. I can help you get caught up once we get back."

"Tell me we don't need to come back, now that you've talked to him."

She hesitated. "We need to come back one more time. I broke his window."

"Carmen!"

She settled back into her seat. "He didn't seem to mind. He seemed pretty cool about it, actually. I mean, he still seems like an asshole, but maybe he has a reason. Maybe if that were resolved, he wouldn't be such a bad guy."

"Maybe you should give it up."

"Maybe you should shut up and drive."

Jake slammed on the brakes, the momentum of the sudden stop throwing her forward so that her head glanced off the dashboard. "Don't talk like that to me, Carmen."

"Jesus Christ, Jake," she muttered, putting her hand to her forehead, relieved to find she was not bleeding.

"You should be wearing your seatbelt. Then that wouldn't have happened."

She looked at him. "I don't like the way you're starting to treat me."

"If you stopped being so goddam infuriating, I wouldn't have to treat you like this." He gritted his teeth. "I'm not a bad guy. You provoke me."

"Hey, Jakey," she said. "I wasn't complaining. I was just stating an objective fact. Surely you can't take issue with that?"

She kept the expression on her face frozen so he would not be able to read her: smile lingering, eyes blank, head cocked at him, eyebrows lifted. He licked his lips, aware of how dry his mouth had suddenly become.

"I'm sorry, Carmen."

"It's alright."

"No, it's not." He shook his head. "My damn temper…"

She put her hand on his thigh, moved it towards his groin. "You're not going to lose me."

"Sometimes I wish I didn't know that." He grimaced, color rising to his cheeks. "Jesus, Carmen, you're going to make me get us into a wreck."

"Do you want me to stop?"

"No. But can you wait?"

She removed her hand and looked out the window. "Will you sing to me?"

"Sing to you?"

She turned the radio down and looked at him. "Why not?"

"I don't sing."

She started singing. His hands tightened on the steering wheel; he snuck a sidelong glance at her. Her voice was beautiful, and he wondered how something that sounded so innocent and pure could come from the person sitting across from him.

"I wish you wouldn't sing."

"I thought you liked it when I sing."

He turned the radio off. "Not today."

"Fine." She glanced at him. "Since you're on a major power trip today, I'll just sit here and be silent."

"But we're still on for tonight."

"Of course." The smile she gave him was deadly. "I'll meet you out back around midnight."

"Eleven. We close at ten, weekdays." He paused. "We'll work this out, Carmen."

She looked at him. It was a look he recognized. A look she gave him when she wanted to tell him something in that special way of hers. He sighed. "Go ahead."

"We've gotta get out of this place," she sang. "If it's the last thing we ever do…"

He found himself nodding, even as he tightened his grip on the steering wheel.

"Someday," he said. "Someday when I get my shit together…not my academic shit, but the other shit…"

She smiled and patted his knee, saying she understood.

Sam was glad of the table between them; Kindra could not see how much his hands were sweating underneath it, or how tightly clasped together they were.

"Did you have enough to eat?" he asked.

"Yeah, Dad."

"Do you want a take-home box?"

She looked askance at him, then shook her head. "That would be so tacky."

"Do you want to go shopping?"

She sighed. "You mean, do I want you to drop me off at the mall with twenty bucks and have Jake pick me up an hour later? Sure."

He slid the money across the table. She took it.

"When's Jake getting off work?"

The smile on his face felt forced. "Ten."

Disappointment flickered over her features. She could have been a pretty girl, with Tessa's genes, but the haughty arrogance constantly on her face made her ugly to him. "But Mom's picking me up at eleven. So I only get to see him for an hour?"

"You can see him as much as you like. Just not me."

"Yeah, it's kind of stupid," Kindra said. "I mean, for us to meet once every three months. It's like, a waste of time, you know."

He looked down at the remains of his burger—nothing but the pickle. The food always sat in his stomach like a rock, but he somehow managed to finish it every time. "How's your mom?"

"Why do you always ask that? She's fine."

"If I drop you off at the mall now, do you want Jake to pick you up?"

"Yeah, I guess. If he wouldn't mind."

"I'm sure he wouldn't mind," Sam said, not telling her he had limited Jake's driving privileges. "Are you finished, or do you need more time?"

"Check," Kindra said, catching the eye of their waiter as he walked by.

Within seconds the waiter returned with their bill, smiling at Kindra as he handed the bill to Sam. The look the waiter gave his daughter made Sam's heart lurch.

"You're getting so old," Sam said as he signed the bill, trying to ignore the sum. His daughter had expensive taste, and he could refuse her nothing.

"Thanks a lot, Dad."

He looked up, found her looking out the window, and realized he had violated another one of the unspoken taboos of talking to adolescent girls—though he had no idea which taboo he had broken. They drove to the mall in silence, and Sam found himself wishing away the time he had looked forward to for the previous three months.

"Be careful," he said, as he dropped her off at the main entrance to the mall.

She rolled her eyes at him. "It's not like there are snipers hiding in the mall."

"I guess I won't see you until May," he said. "Take care of yourself. Love you."

"Thanks for the money."

"Call if you need anything."

"Will do." She gave him the briefest of waves. "See you in three months."

He tried not to watch her as she walked into the mall, but he couldn't help himself. She had become too grown up for comfort, and she had become a stranger. He forced himself to drive away as the glass doors of the mall closed behind her.

"Jake," he said to his son's voicemail. "Remember to pick up your sister from the mall tonight at ten." He paused. "Love you."

He dropped the phone onto the passenger's seat. Maybe the food sat so heavily in his stomach because he wasn't used to eating at nine o'clock. He and Kindra always ate late, so he could drop her off at the mall and let her wander before Jake picked her up. He shouldn't feel guilty; the kid got twenty dollars out of it. And he got something to look forward to every once in awhile, though their interaction was always the same. Like playing a broken record and hearing the needle stop, start, screech across the black plastic in fast forward, skipping the notes, distorting the sound. But at least it was a tune he had come to recognize. There was some comfort in that. He was doing the best he could.

Jake convinced the manager to let him leave early. By ten o'clock he had picked Carmen up and taken her to the shed behind an abandoned warehouse that they had found the year before. Once the space heater he had brought with him started to warm up, so did Carmen. They made out for an hour before he started undressing her.

"Does your mom know you have these?" He squeezed a breast and slipped his hand down her side—indicating a matching purple thong and bra, each with a metallic butterfly clipped onto the center.

"No. I handwash them." She pushed him away. "Why do you always have to—"

His phone rang.

"Who the hell is calling you right now?" Her eyes narrowed as she picked up his phone and looked at the screen. "Who is Kindra?"

He crossed the room, took the phone. "Hey, sis."

The tension left Carmen's face, replaced by impatience. "Jake, can't you talk to her some other time?"

"Oh, shit. I didn't get your message…all right. I said I'm going."

Carmen looked at him as he ended the call. "Going?"

"I have to go."

"Go where?"

"It's my sister's weekend to visit. I completely forgot about her." He checked his watch. "I was supposed to have picked her up a half hour ago. Put your clothes on, Carmen."

She gaped at him, hands on her hips. "Jake, are you *serious*?"

He shrugged. "You said you wanted to meet her."

She glared at him, then went to the corner of the room where he had thrown her shirt and pants. She slipped into them silently, then turned to him. He came to her and slipped his coat around her shoulders, then stepped outside of the shed. When they reached his car, she kept walking.

He had expected an explosion from her—after a period of silence like the one she was giving him, she usually exploded. He followed her. "Why are you so pissed?"

"I don't want to meet your sister." She barely glanced at him. "I'm going home."

"Let me drive you."

"I want to walk."

"You're going to freeze."

"Fuck you, Jake," she said with perfect composure.

"Fine. If you're going to be a bitch about it."

She flipped him the finger, kept walking. He got in the car and started the engine. He drove away, keeping his eyes on the road even as his thoughts wrenched back to her. He checked the rearview mirror and he didn't see her; he called her but her phone was off.

"Fuck you, Carmen," he said, jamming his foot down on the accelerator, his heart flipping as the car started hydroplaning. After he regained control, he realized he had forgotten to breathe for the entire interval, and let his breath out in a ragged sigh. When he pulled into the mall's parking lot fifteen minutes later, he saw Kindra waiting and expected her to be angry. She was.

"Hey, sis," he said as she got in, his thoughts still with Carmen. "How's it going?"

Kindra squawked at the time. "It's eleven fifteen."

"Yeah, hey, I'm sorry. I got sidetracked." He could have been getting laid; he found that he had very little of his usual tolerance for her whining.

"Mom is going to *flip*."

"She won't care if you're with me," he said. "As long as you're not with Dad—"

"Which means she is. And she's not going to want to be alone with him. You know how much she hates him. Can't you go any faster?"

"Do you want me to wreck?" He turned his attention back to the road. "It might be good for him to have to talk to her."

"She hates him."

"She has no reason to." He paused. "Dad has his flaws. But he's never done anything to deserve her hatred. Unless there's something I don't know about."

"Oh, please. We both knew everything about them. After Dad lost his job and we moved, our house was too small not to overhear everything, and you actually cared about that stuff. Can you go any faster?"

"No," he said. "The roads are bad. But look at it this way, we're spending quality time together."

"I missed you, Jake," she said, after a pause. "I hate this divorce thing."

"Yeah. It sucks. But you know you can write, call."

"You're always at work when I call. And you don't ever answer my letters."

"I'm kind of busy," he said. "But I read them. Like you have a crush on some guy, and you're having trouble with science—"

She settled back into her seat, satisfied. "What were you doing that made you so distracted?"

"Work."

"Dad said you'd be done by ten."

"Yeah," he said, thinking of the bare floor of the shed, how they'd had to cover it with an old rug he had found in the attic so they wouldn't get splinters, of the gaps in the boards they had to stuff with rags lying around to keep the outside chill from entering the asylum they had created. He found he had a hard time remembering what Kindra had said to him. "But we…it takes us about an hour to close."

"I guess I didn't think about that. So, Jake."

"So what."

"Do you have a girlfriend yet?"

"Yeah."

She squealed. "My little brother has a girlfriend! Is she pretty?"

He felt his cheeks growing red. "Yeah, Kindra."

"What does she look like?"

"Long brown hair. Blue eyes."

"She sounds beautiful."

"She is," he said. When Kindra talked to him like that it was easy for him to forget that she was older than he was—though he knew she talked to him like that because she would always see him as her little brother.

"How old is she?"

He hesitated. "She's younger than I am."

"Well, that's normal." She paused. "What were you doing with her this late at night?"

"I didn't say I was with her."

"But you were. I can read it in your face that you were."

"I was going to give her a ride home. We work together."

"Be careful, baby boy," Kindra said softly. "Any girl who moves too fast has issues. Major ones."

He thought about Carmen. "She has some issues. But I like her."

"As long as you know what you're getting yourself into."

He raised his eyebrows at her.

"That drive was fast." She sat up straighter. "And there's Mom, waiting in the car. Well, it was good to see you for the fifteen minutes that I did."

He pulled up beside his mother's car and parked. He got out with Kindra and went to the car. Tessa looked up, and seconds later he found himself enveloped in a hug, the smell of his mother's perfume in his nostrils, the wool scarf she had around her neck scratching against his face.

"Jacob, you've grown so handsome," Tessa said as she stepped away from him.

"Yeah. Good to see you, Mom."

"How are you? Are you ready to come visit me next weekend?"

He nodded. "You're coming at five?"

She smiled. "I'll make you sloppy Joes. Those are still your favorite, aren't they?"

"I like Chicken Christie."

"Chicken Christie?"

"Dad makes it." He saw her scowl. "But I like your sloppy Joes, too."

"We'll plan on it then." She smiled at him, put a hand against his face, grimaced. "You're freezing. Doesn't your car have heat?"

"It does. But I usually have problems with the rest of the car if I turn the heat on."

"Do you want a new car?"

"I'm attached. I do all my own work on the car. My car, I mean."

"If your father won't let you get a new car…"

Jake shrugged. "Dad said I could get one if I could pay the insurance. And I can't. Not right now."

"Do you want me to give you the money?"

His cheeks burned. "No, I'm fine."

Kindra honked the horn. Tessa kept her eyes on Jake's face. "You'll tell me if you need anything."

He nodded. "Yeah."

"Kindra has a test tomorrow," Tessa explained. "That's the only reason she's so eager to get home. How are your grades, Jake? Are you thinking about colleges yet?"

"My grades are good," he said. "College is still pretty far off." He didn't add that he wanted to drop out, to work at the convenience store and shack with Carmen in any place they could find—good enough until he found out where he wanted to go.

"I'm so glad you're staying focused. You know how important grades are." She paused. "We'll talk more next weekend. It'll be a nice little vacation for you."

"Yeah. I'll see you then."

"Take care of yourself, Jacob."

"Have a safe drive home."

She smiled, got in the car. He stood, shoulders hunched against the cold, as he waited for the car to pull away. He wondered when his mother had become a stranger. When they had both become strangers. Then Tessa looked up and smiled at him and Kindra waved, and his thoughts shattered. He waved back, watched them drive away, and stood for a moment with his back turned to the house. He pulled out his cell phone and dialed Carmen's number again. He thought about hanging up on her voicemail. But when the beep sounded he found himself talking.

"Hey, babe," he said. "Just calling to make sure you're safe wherever you are. I'm not worried, by the way. I know you can take care of yourself. Have a good night, Carmen."

The message seemed lame to him. He went inside. His father was nowhere to be seen, and he wasn't going to wait around to be reprimanded for getting home so late. He cleaned the dishes in the sink, dried them, then headed to his room. He had homework to do if he was serious about staying in school. He sat down at his desk, but before midnight, the textbook had become his pillow and he was fast asleep.

Carmen saw Carrie waiting for her in the living room, reading. She delayed in hanging up her scarf and Jake's jacket and wished she had taken a change of underwear. She could tell that Jake had liked the matching purple set, but the metallic butterflies were cold against her bare skin, the lace bit into her side, and the bra was a size too small. He had liked the effect of that, but it was a choice that was killing her. She slammed the door shut, then plastered a smile onto her face.

"Hi, Carrie."

"Sit down." Carrie put aside her book. "You and I need to have a talk."

"Since we're talking about talking," she said. "Guess who I talked to today?"

"You're going to listen to me first."

"Jean Paul," she said, plopping down on the sofa. "He actually talked to me today."

"I told you I didn't want to have anything to do with him."

"He said the same thing about you." She saw the flash of emotion cross her mother's face. "I'm so glad we're one big happy family."

"Sam told me you were thinking about dropping out of school," Carrie said quietly. "Is that true?"

"You know what else, Carrie? I told him my name this time, too, and it looked like someone smacked him over the head. So maybe you were wrong, and maybe he does know about me."

"Carmen, I've started getting complaints from your teachers. Teachers who raved about you at the beginning of the school year. I want to know what's going on, young lady."

"He left me to freeze in the cold. You'll never believe how he treated me. He called me all these names and made me cry, and I thought, I really thought, that he was going to hit me." She saw the look that crossed Carrie's face suddenly, darkly. She paused for dramatic effect. "Why did you marry such an asshole?"

"Did he threaten you?" Carrie asked, her voice so low that Carmen could barely hear her.

"He said if I came back...I don't want to repeat it. It was *horrible*."

The coldness in Carrie's eyes startled her. "What did he say to you?"

"Well, it wasn't so much."

"*What did he say?*"

Carmen thought about telling Carrie it was all a mistake, that she had been lying. She was frightened by the grim seriousness in Carrie's voice. But she couldn't control her words.

"He said I was a bitch," she lied. "He said he wanted nothing to do with me, and that he never wanted to see you again. The rest I *really* don't want to tell you."

Carrie's face was marble by the time Carmen finished speaking.

"He said he never wanted to see me again," Carrie said, her voice flat. "But he thinks he can talk to you like that..."

Carmen watched her for a moment, then made a tentative step towards her. "Mom?"

Carrie turned, but did not smile. "Dinner's in the fridge. Blue Tupperware, labeled Tuesday. I would have kept it warm, but I didn't know what time you were getting home." She paused. "Carmen, I'm going out tomorrow night. I'll leave you some money on top of the refrigerator and you can get take out or pizza or save the money and eat left overs. You're on your own tomorrow night."

She stared at Carrie, at a loss. "So you trust me again?"

"No. But I've realized that you're going to live your life however you want, and then you're going to have to accept the consequences. I'll be here for you, but I'm going to let you make your own choices."

"I'm thirteen."

"Then you should act it." She paused. "If you weren't my daughter, I wouldn't like you very much."

The shock on Carmen's face was genuine, but failed to phase Carrie. She brushed by Carmen.

"Blue Tupperware," she repeated. "If you don't like it, toss it and make yourself Mac and Cheese or something."

"You aren't going to see *him* tomorrow, are you?" Carmen called after her. "Because I don't think that would be a very good idea!"

A door closed down the hall. Carmen stood in the kitchen, seething. She stripped out of the bra and flung it onto the sofa, somewhere Carrie would see it on emerging from her study. She would see how long it would take for Carrie not to care; she guessed about five minutes. She smirked and turned to look at the bra once more, and then the smile sagged. The purple plush of the cups jutting up towards the ceiling looked unnatural against the brown and beige tones of the living room. Ashamed, Carmen grabbed the bra and ran up to her room, where she was glad to be alone.

Carrie had expected a mansion or a shack—something extreme. Not the white and brown stucco house, inoffensive though without any touch of warmth or decoration. No welcome mat, no one had shoveled the driveway, and the doorbell remained silent after she forced herself to press it. All right for him…but not for Chloe. She cringed to think of what the little girl would have gone through and become, with only his guidance.

She knocked, her heart pounding. She tried to keep a look of composed anger on her face. After a moment, she steeled herself and knocked again. Her mouth was dry; intuition told her that he had heard her, and would ignore her. She remained standing silently on the porch, then reached into her purse and found an empty envelope and a pen. The cold had frozen the pen's ink; she searched again, and found a mechanical pencil. She scribbled on the back of the envelope, put it in his mailbox, and headed back to her car. She was not worried. He would be in touch.

The next time Carmen threw a snowball at his window, she coated it with water first, turning the packed snow to ice. The snowball went clean through the window, shattering the hairline crack and leaving a hole the size of a baseball in the windowpane.

"Score!" she yelled.

A minute later he opened the door and came out barefoot, a look of wrath on his face, his black hair an electric cloud behind his head. His expression changed as soon as he saw her.

"Hiya, Dad!" Carmen called.

He opened his mouth, then simply stood there. She out-waited him.

"Where's your coat?" he yelled, not budging from the door.

"Whatever!" she yelled back. "Come make a snow angel!"

He stood staring at her as she dropped down into the snow. She looked up at the sky, languidly moving her arms up and down. Finished, she stood and brushed herself off, then put her hands on her hips hands on her hips and looked down at the angel shape she had made.

"You don't mind it, do you?" she asked.

"No," he said. "It's pretty."

"Take you back to when you were a kid?"

He paused. "Why can't you ring the doorbell, like a normal person?"

"Why don't you fix it, then maybe I will." She rang, demonstrating that the doorbell didn't work.

"You could knock."

She shrugged.

"Carmen."

"What?"

He hesitated. "You're being truthful when you tell me that Carrie Crenshaw is your mother."

"Yep."

"Is it..." He stopped. "Is it possible, that..."

"You want to know if some other man could be my father?" She sighed. "No. Mom's not normal. She could have found someone else, believe me, but all she does is work. All the time." She looked at him, shrugged. "I wouldn't have cared if she was with someone else. I just want a dad. I don't care who he is."

He paused. "When you say she works, you mean that she writes."

"No. She teaches."

"She's still teaching?"

"Are you?" she asked. "You were a teacher, right?"

"I was. A long time ago."

"So what happened?" She pulled out a pack of cigarettes.

"Give me that."

She glanced at him, then handed the pack to him. "You know, if you want one you could ask nicer...hey!"

He dropped the crushed pack onto the ground and put his foot over it.

"Hey," she repeated. "That cost me. Not exactly money, but like they say time is money and it took me some time to earn that..."

"A girl your age has absolutely no reason to smoke."

"Maybe I'm stressed."

"Giving yourself lung cancer isn't a valid way to cope." He paused. "I don't care what your mother lets you do. When you're on my property, you will not smoke."

"When I'm on your property," she repeated. "Does that mean you want to see me again?"

When he didn't answer her, she paused, then reached into her pocket once more.

"Here," she said. "You might want these, too."

He took the other pack of cigarettes. "Does Carrie buy these for you?"

"Carrie? Are you serious? Jake gets them for me."

"Is he here?" His eyes scanned the space behind her. "I want to talk to him."

"No," she said kicking at the snow accumulated beside the porch.

"How did you get here?"

"I drove."

"You drove?"

"I taught myself. But don't worry, I'm a totally safe driver and it's his car, so if I wreck it's not like Carrie will have to know…" She cocked her head at him. "Can we go inside? It's freezing out here."

Before he could respond, she ducked past him and darted into the house.

"Why is it so dark in here?" she asked.

"Carmen, I don't want you in here," he started.

She flipped on the light switch by the door and gawked.

"How do you live here?" she asked, picking her way through the accumulated debris on the floor.

"I wasn't expecting company," he said.

"Gross." She picked up a rumpled sock laying on the brown leather sofa and held it away from her for effect, then turned it right side out and folded it. "Can I clean? I like cleaning."

"No," he said. "You're going to leave. This house is no place for a kid."

"I'm not a kid." She paused. "Even my room doesn't look this bad. Look at all these bottles. How much beer do you drink in a day? And this place reeks."

Before he could answer she moved through the room, went into the adjacent kitchen and surveyed the area. When he didn't join her she went back to the living room, to find him collecting the empty beer bottles in a pile against his chest.

"You should recycle those," she dictated. "Hey, let's make a deal. You stop drinking and I'll stop smoking."

"I want you to call your mother and tell her to come pick you up."

"I don't know her number," she said. "I just hit one on my phone if I need to call her, and I don't have my phone."

"There's a phone book in the kitchen."

She pouted, but he wasn't watching for her reaction; he was absorbed in picking up the bottles scattered around the room. Sighing audibly, she went into the kitchen without any intent of looking for the mentioned phone book. She noticed a single piece of paper on the table and picked it up. On the back was written a brief message and a phone number. She recognized Carrie's handwriting, and glanced up as he came into the kitchen.

"Good," he said. "You found her number. The phone is in the corner. The last time I checked, it worked."

"Who's Chloe?" Carmen asked.

His face crumpled. The reaction was so dramatic and intense that she opened her mouth to apologize, but found she could not speak. He turned from her abruptly.

"Call her," he said, almost inaudibly.

She watched his retreating form. His reaction to the simple question had paralyzed her; no emotion that had ever crossed Carrie's face had remotely resembled the hurt and chaos that had passed over his face. She stuffed the envelope into her pocket and wondered if she should leave, and as she thought she started to soak the dishes accumulated in the sink to loosen the grime caked onto them. Then she crept into the living room and searched through the hallways until she came to a closed door. She stopped when she heard the muffled sound of crying coming from within. Scared, she retreated away from the dim hallway, back to the well-lit kitchen where the scent of the liquid detergent had intermingled with the smell of mold. She searched for a sponge, found one jammed in the back of a cupboard above the sink. Grimacing, she plunged her hands into the soapy water, shuddering at the feel of the slime against her skin.

To distract herself she sang until she had washed the last dish. She turned to search for a dish towel and saw him standing in the doorway.

"You have a beautiful voice," he said, softly. "But what are you still doing here?"

"Just doing the dishes." She paused. "Are you angry with me?"

He shook his head. "I'm not angry with you. But I wish you would go home."

"I'm sorry if I offended you earlier. Honestly, I really didn't mean to."

"Snoopy little girl," he said. "Sticking your nose in other people's business."

"It's my business. I want to know my father." She stopped before she added that she wanted to understand about him and Carrie. "Are you him?"

"Maybe I am."

She pulled the envelope out of her pocket and attempted to give it to him. "You don't have to believe me, but I know this is my mom's handwriting. The note tells you I'm—"

"I know what it says. I've read that note dozens of times…" He trailed off, and paused before speaking again. "If I am your father, Carmen, I want you to stay away from me."

"But I don't want to," she said. "Shouldn't it be my choice?"

He paused. "I want to show you something."

She watched curiously as he exposed his leg to mid-shin.

"This," he said, indicating the tiny black box strapped onto his ankle. "This is a little contraption that monitors where I am at all times. If I leave my house, the button glows red, and I go to jail."

"You're under house arrest," she said. "Cool. Jake and I watched this one movie together, Disturbia, and in it there was a guy who was under house arrest, too." She paused when he remained silent. "What did you do?"

"I'm not going to discuss it with you."

"Bullshit," she said, and immediately bit her lip when he glanced at her. She hadn't been aware that profanity had become second nature to her. "I mean, what I meant to say was, why would you have showed me that thing if you weren't going to tell me why you have it?"

"I thought it would make you go away."

"Oh please," she said. "Geez, I might be thirteen, but I know people make mistakes. So what did you do?"

"DUI," he said. "Two."

"So that's why you don't ever leave the house." She looked back at him, unable to stand the silence between them. "So. Mom said you like to paint."

He looked at her sharply. "Is that so?"

"Can you show me some of your stuff?"

"Not today."

"I've always wanted to learn how to paint. Hey, you could teach me. I can even bring my own supplies, so you won't have to let me use yours."

"That won't be necessary."

"I'm glad you'll share your materials," she said, deliberately misinterpreting his words. "Because like I said, I only make about five bucks an hour, and I'm still saving up for your window."

"You see this place," he said after a pause. "You see the empty bottles, you saw the black box. You saw the kitchen. Why the hell would you want to come back?"

"Isn't it obvious? Look, you're a mess. And remember how I said I liked to clean?" She turned her face away from him until the tears were gone and she had her voice under control. "I'm coming back. If you don't want me to drive then I'll have Jake bring me. I don't care if he has to wait in the car, or if I have to walk. I'm coming back. Even if it's just to give you money for that window, or to bring you something to put over it because I guess you can't really go to the store to get it, can you?"

"Thursdays, from four to seven," he said, "I'm free to do whatever I want."

"I'd hate that," she said. "You can't even go out to see people, which is why I'll come visit you. It'll make you happier, it really will. But just don't be mean to me any more okay? Because life isn't too good right now."

He looked at her, looked away. "Don't have her bring you."

"I won't."

"Call Jake to come pick you up."

"I can't. I took his car. Just let me drive back," she coaxed. "No, you don't have to ask me to call my mom. She's at a meeting, anyway."

"Then I'll call you a taxi."

"Dad."

He paused. "I'll call you a taxi."

He got up from the sofa and went into the kitchen. She listened to him talk, then looked at him as he came back into the room.

"Here." He handed her money. "There's a tip there for the driver, too."

"This is way too much money for a cab ride," she said, her eyes wide.

"Buy yourself a coat," he said, then frowned. "No cigarettes, you hear?"

"I never buy cigarettes." She stared at him. "How is Jake supposed to get his car back if I take a taxi?"

"I'll have someone drive it back," he said. "What's his address?"

She pulled out the slip of envelope. "Do you have a pen?"

"Somewhere." He went into the kitchen and came back with a permanent marker. "Use that."

She scribbled on the clean side, handed the envelope to him.

"Can you call the person before eleven?" she said. "That's when Jake gets off work, and if the car isn't back by then his dad might notice. I mean, it's kind of complicated. Like on days we have school, Jake goes straight from school to work and doesn't take the car, but Sam lets him drive to work occasionally even though Jake lost most of his driving privileges."

He took the paper but did not look at it. "Your taxi should be here."

"Will you call the guy? I don't want Jake to get in trouble." She crossed the room to the front door, looked out the window, squinted to see the driveway. "No, it's—"

When she turned around, he had disappeared. She turned back to the window, and waited for the taxi to come.

Carmen slid out of the car. "Wait here."

"You want me to sit in the car?"

She nodded. Jake looked at her, frowning.

506

"How long is this going to take, babe?"

She shrugged. "As long as it takes."

"Why can't I come with you?"

"He doesn't like you."

"So fuck him," Jake said. "This used to be our time together, and now all I do is spend it driving you places and waiting for that asshole to—."

"Don't call him an asshole." She turned on him. "Don't worry, you'll get your fucking time later."

"What the hell has gotten into you?"

"I don't know, Jake. What the hell has gotten into me?"

"Certainly not me."

She slammed the door shut. He rolled down his window as she walked towards the front door.

"What would you do if I just left you here?" he yelled.

She flipped him her finger and kept walking. She hurried inside when the door opened, felt relief flood through her when the door closed. She didn't think Jake would hurt her, but…

"Wow," she said, shrugging out of her coat. "It looks good in here." She turned to him. "You cleaned?"

He stood by the door, keeping his distance from her. "In case you would come back."

"I told you I would. Did you clean the kitchen, too?"

She ducked in, came back smiling. "And you started to recycle. That's great. It's really great. So what did you do on your day off?"

He had not moved. "Bought groceries."

"Yeah? That sounds exciting."

He shifted. "How was your week, Carmen?"

"You mean, like school? You know."

"I don't know."

"It's not a big deal. School." She stooped and unlaced her sneakers. "Did you go to college?"

"I did."

She looked up, then placed her sneakers side by side. "Did you think it was worth it?"

"It depends on how you spend your time there," he said.

"Well, if it's anything like high school, I don't want any part of it." She stretched. "I think I'm going to drop out, after this year."

"Don't do that."

"I don't like high school. I don't want to deal with that sh—", She stopped herself. "With all the stuff, like cliques and stuck up teachers and pointless assignments."

"What would you do instead?"

She shrugged. "I guess I'd have to figure it out."

"Carrie won't let you drop out of school."

"I thought maybe I could live here, with you," Carmen said, after a pause. "If you'd let me, I'd take care of all the legal stuff."

"If you lived here I would make you go to school."

"You're *such* a teacher." She made a face, then sobered. "Why'd you quit, anyway?"

"Bratty kids," he said. "And I was made to realize that it wasn't who I was."

"Who made you realize that? Was it Carrie?"

He hesitated. "It doesn't matter."

"What a bitch," she said, with sudden anger. "You were doing great, and then—"

"Don't call your mother a bitch."

"Well, if she is then she is."

"You can find other ways to express your anger."

"All right. I'm sorry."

"Never explain," he said. "And never apologize. I believe that's one of your mother's favorite quotes, borrowed from something she read by Stephen King." He paused. "She loved to read him."

She raised her eyebrows at him. "Do you still love her?"

"No," he said. "I don't."

"You talk about her all the time, you know."

"Carmen," he said. "I wasn't lying the other day, when I said I wanted nothing more to do with her."

"Why?"

"That's between your mother and me."

"You must really hate me," she said, folding her hands in her lap.

"Since you hate her so much and you know I'm her daughter. You must really be putting forth an effort to have me in your sight."

"You don't remind me of her." He paused. "But I don't hate her. I'm indifferent."

"That's even worse." She stood up. "So, can you give me a tour of the house?"

"A tour?"

She nodded. "Show me around."

"You want to see my studio, you mean."

"I want to see everything. And make it take as long as possible. Jake needs to sit out there and cool down."

He looked at her cautiously. "You've seen the kitchen and the living room."

"Do you have a basement?" Already she envisioned a trap door, candles on stone walls, the steady drip of water from the depths.

Instead he lead her to a carpeted area whose walls, if bare, were dry.

"There aren't any windows," she said.

"Most people break in through basement windows," he said. "Granted, the house was built like this when I moved in, but I consider it an added benefit. Though there is a way to break into the house. I'll show you later."

She followed him up the stairs. "Attic next."

He shook his head. "I never go in the attic."

"Why not?"

"The family that lived here before left some of their possessions there," he said. "I'm not going through them."

"There might be some good stuff up there."

"This is an old house," he said. "The attic probably isn't safe. There might be rats."

"I like rats."

"There are definitely spiders."

"I don't like those so much."

"No," he said, a light flickering across his face. "My kids—"

"You said you didn't have kids," she reminded him.

"My students," he amended. "I asked my students one year what their biggest fears were."

"Spiders?"

He nodded. "Not insects. Specifically spiders."

"So no attic," she said, after a pause.

"Not my room, either," he said. "My room is off limits."

"You sound like Bluebeard."

He looked at her; she looked back.

"Haven't you ever heard of Bluebeard? He killed all these wives of his who weren't faithful to him and locked their bodies in a room." She stopped, shrugged. "Carrie read it to me when I was little. It was her favorite story for some reason."

"How appropriate for a child."

"It's a kid's story," she said, defensively. "You know, like a fairy tale?"

"I wasn't read fairy tales when I was a child."

"I can bring you the book she used to read to me," Carmen started. "I'll even read to you."

"I'm not a child."

"You'd be surprised what you can learn from kids' books, though. Sometimes if you can keep the kid in you alive, you can stay human. You know?"

She paused when he did not respond. "I really like all the spare rooms. They'd look great with some stuff in them. I wouldn't even be picky."

"I'll show you my studio," he said, walking away from her.

She hurried to keep up with him as he led her to another bare room. He opened a door on the right that looked like a closet.

"Cubby space," he said. "No lights. Watch your step."

"This house is insane." She crouched to half her height to avoid hitting her head off the low ceiling. "Why would you put your studio—"

She broke off as she stepped out of the corridor. They were in a room shaped like a pentagon, the domed ceiling rising high above her and every wall made of glass. Despite the cold outside, the air in the room was humid and heavy. Thin rods bordering the pentagon held dozens of hanging pots of plants with leafy vines which curled to the floor. Easels were spread around, scattered at various angles. Some of the canvases were completely blank, some had slashes of bold brush strokes. In one corner was a stack of blank canvases; in the opposite corner a small table was cluttered with tubes of paint, a palette, and a jar of water where brushes were soaking. The metallic smell of paint hung in the air.

"Wow," she said. "You'll show me how to paint like that, right?"

His eyes had taken on a far off look upon entering the studio. "Some other time."

"Why not now?"

Without further prompting, he went to the table, selected a brush, picked up the pallette and squirted new color onto it. He crossed to a blank canvas, barely waiting for her to come over to him.

"This is your basic brush stroke," he said, slashing paint across the canvas. "You can use it for a big, bold effect."

And then he stopped instructing her. He seemed to forget about her. She watched as he worked with increasing frenzy. When he finished, he turned and looked at her.

"Child's Play," he said, his voice hoarse. "You can have it, since you brought it up."

She cocked her head at the canvas. "But I don't get it."

"Step back," he said. "You will."

She took a step back. She took another step back. She crossed to the end of the room, and then she stared.

"It's a little girl," she said. "But she looks so sad."

He turned away from the canvas, offered her the brush. "You."

She came back to him, took the brush from him and saw that his hands were shaking. She saw that the crazy light had not left his eyes.

"Anywhere," he said, reading her mind. "There. Go over there."

She crossed to the easel he had indicated, one that faced the glass wall away from the entrance to the cubby hole. Just beyond the glass panes the sky had turned a dark, swollen gray; she had not been aware of how much time had passed. The untouched white of the canvas was as intimidating as the darkness of the slate sky. She swallowed, looked down at the paint brush trembling in her hand, at the smeared residues of paint he had left on the pallette. She raised the brush but could not touch the easel. She turned to him and shook her head.

"I can't do it."

"You can," he affirmed, but took the pallette and brush from her. "Maybe just some other day."

"Thanks for the painting," she said, ashamed of her defeat. "But since it's still wet, I'll pick it up next time I come."

"I don't want it. Not in the house."

She looked at the cubby hole. "How am I supposed to get out of here without getting paint all over myself? There isn't even room for me to stand."

"I forgot," he said. "You can break into the house through this room. But it's late. I'll show you some other time."

"Show me now," she said, her interest piqued.

He crossed to the glass wall closest to the cubby, pushed on a pane gently and then slid it down to reveal a three by five foot rectangular gap. "The bricks on this end of the house, below the glass wall, are uneven. You can find footholds and handholds, if you need to."

"How'd you figure that out?"

"Before I was under house arrest," he said. "I'd forget my keys and lock myself out of the house. This is the only room I really need to get into, so I added the windows, tore down the stucco on this side, and made some builders put in the brick."

"Why didn't you just hide an extra key outside your door?" she asked.

"I used to climb," he said. "I miss it."

"Can I try it? Now?" She thought of the ice-slicked tree outside her window and found the thought of climbing down the wall in the middle of the night did not intimidate her.

"No," he said.

"Please, Dad?"

"That sounds so strange," he said, softly. "But no, you cannot. You have to go home now."

In her excitement about the hidden escape route, she had forgotten that the painting she was holding was wet. She pulled a hand away, saw her fingers were streaked with red, and quickly turned, lest he should see how she had ruined the painting. As she turned, she noticed another painting hanging on the only solid wall, above the entrance to the cubby hole. She crossed the room and studied the painting. There were two handprints in the center: one small, one large.

"I like that," she said.

"So do I," he said, his voice quiet. "Carmen, your boyfriend has been honking his horn incessantly for the past half hour."

She became aware of a muffled noise that might have been a car horn, and realized she had tuned Jake out.

"All right, I'm going." She wrenched her eyes away from the painting on the wall, then looked helplessly at the cubby hole. "How do I get this thing open?"

He opened the cubby hole door, then led her back to the living room. She put on her sneakers and her coat. She walked to the door and looked back.

"Bye," she said.

He nodded at her. She opened the door, steeled herself to be yelled at by Jake. He stopped honking the horn when she emerged, but she could feel his glare from the distance.

When Carrie went into Carmen's room on her weekly mission for collecting used dishes, she saw the painting sitting on Carmen's vanity mirror, taking up precious space in the glass. The painting's presence let her know that Carmen had continued seeing him, and that he was letting her. She would not ask Carmen about the painting; she was tired of fighting with her second daughter.

The ghosts of the past had intensified their hauntings; more and more frequently, her memory would open like a window and she would glimpse an incidence of something he had done: of a dinner he had made her or of a raspberry he had blown on Chloe's stomach to make them both laugh. Memories that confused her. She realized she was steeling herself for another confrontation with him. He was no longer a matter of pride; he was a step that needed to be taken. If he was willing, they could attempt to figure out why they had been brought together in the first place and what kept bringing them together over the years. Lust factored into her attraction, but her thoughts about him had stretched on for almost twenty-years—she doubted that lust alone could be so powerful. But should they fail this time, there was no hope for them, and she would realize the situation as such. Maybe then she would finally be able to move on fully with her life.

But he had not called her about her note, in which she had written only that she needed to talk to him about Chloe. How he could have ignored to contact her befuddled her; she would attempt, this last time, to make sense of it all, and if she could not, she would let him go.

In the back of her mind, one force continued to drive her. He had been her Muse; he still was. With the discovery of his presence in the area, she had experienced a burst of creativity and vitality. She no longer cared if she offended the school board; she took risks with her classes, and she was finally getting through to her students. She was writing again. The only area of her life that hadn't changed positively was her relationship with Carmen. Carrie's eyes teared up; she realized she wanted him there, that she had always wanted him there to help her raise Carmen. She had deceived herself; Carmen had never been *hers*, she had always been *theirs*, and Carrie had wanted that. The most she had to lose was the time it would take to drive to his house and back. She had grown up; she would not let him hurt her, and she would not let herself hurt him.

Heart pounding, eyes blurring with tears, she grabbed her keys, slipped into her coat, and scribbled Carmen a quick note. She put the note on the refrigerator with a smiley face magnet that Carmen had brought home from a school assembly in middle school. She looked at the magnet—*Be like me! Drug free!*—and let the tears run down her face. Better for the reservoir to run dry before she got to his house. Had he ever seen her cry? She could not remember. She would not let him see her cry now. She went to her car and opened the car door. She loved him, so she could not let him see any form of weakness.

She sat in the car. How could it be right for her to go to him, if those were the thoughts running through her mind? Love was not about defense, about protecting the self. Love was about being open, being vulnerable. That was why she had always been against it, why being in love had never worked for her. She wanted to get out of the car; instead she turned on the ignition and heard the single beep that told her to buckle her safety belt. She slipped the belt on and thought that Sam had been right; she could love. She didn't have to make the ultimate choice; if she put herself out there, he could make the choice to turn her down. Whatever happened would happen.

She backed into her mailbox. She kept going. The mailbox, leaning grotesquely at an angle, was a sign to her to slow down, to be careful…or a sign that something crooked could still be perfectly functional.

She went with her second interpretation.

She noticed three things had changed when she pulled up to the house: the driveway had been shoveled recently, a rectangular piece of storm paper was covering an area of broken window, and the lights were on. She made her way to the front door. She was having difficulty breathing. She pushed the doorbell before she remembered it didn't work, and was greeted by a clear ring. Her heart lightened when he did not come, then she steeled herself. She had come with a purpose; she would not leave. She forced herself to focus on wishing that he would give her a chance.

She knocked again, and the door opened. She was face to face with him and she could not speak. If he was Damien he would have let her flounder; if he was Ralph he would set aside his feelings and try to help her along. Either way she would have understood him. But as she looked into the depths of his brown eyes, she realized he had reached a new level of complexity, and this time she would have to make the first move.

"I need to talk to you," she said.

He started to close the door.

"Wait!" she cried. "One minute. Give me one minute of your time. I need to talk to you about Chloe."

He said nothing, but left the door open.

"Please let me see her." She swallowed. "She's *my daughter*. You're still my husband. I know I'm not making sense and I need to slow down but I can't…"

The stricken look never left his eyes, and he remained silent.

Carrie tried to control herself. "Is she here? Can I see her? Please?"

He roused himself. "No."

"Please. Only for a moment."

"No."

"I just want to see her." Carrie felt like crying. "You can pretend I'm not here."

"Chloe's dead," he said. "She got sick, and my money couldn't help her. A pulmonary infection killed her when she was two."

She stared at him.

"I tried to tell you," he said. "You had made yourself unavailable."

"I'm sorry," she said. "Do anything you want. Scream at me, blame me…"

He shook his head. "I don't want anything more to do with you."

She stood motionless as he closed the door on her. She turned and walked away from the house. The air froze the tears that leaked out of her eyes as she got into her car. She looked into the rearview mirror as she drove away, until the white contour of the house blurred into the background of the snowflakes falling from the crying sky.

Carrie did not go straight home. She drove for an hour before she realized that she was driving aimlessly, and then she drove for another half hour. She kept the radio off, the window rolled down so the cold air could bite her. She saw his dark eyes in her mind, full of pain…

She pulled over. She let herself cry. She pulled back onto the road and kept going.

The sun had long since sunk when she pulled into the driveway of her house. The sky was swollen and no sliver of moon alleviated the consuming darkness. She walked inside the house and saw Carmen sitting in the living room. Carrie took her time taking off her scarf and coat. When she glanced up Carmen had left.

Carmen's resentment stung her, showed her that she had not gone as numb as she had thought. Carrie went into the kitchen. She would force herself to eat, to take care of herself. She measured out a spoonful of lavender tea she had bought at the Green Bottle and added hot water, then she made herself sit down and be still.

She wanted to call Christine. She realized she hadn't spoken to any of them in four years. Even the phone calls with Chris had stopped. That was how life went. Carmen did not know her grandmother, her uncles and aunts…Carly, in particular, would have been so disappointed. She wondered how they had all changed. Despite Christine's vision of keeping the family tightly together, Carrie had sensed the changing dynamic, as early as when Carmen had been born: Calder moving to Wall Street, Carly almost done with college, Chris grown up…her, invisible most of the time. The disintegration had happened in both of the Crenshaw families. The images in her mind had been real—singing songs with Justine around the piano while Jonathan played, discussing life with Chris while they set the table for dinner, pretending annoyance when Carly insisted on painting her nails an absurd shade of pink—but those memories were no longer relevant, nothing more than passing waves of nostalgia.

Carrie wondered why Christine had let family become her life's goal. Keeping a family together was impossible. Yet she was not sure the alternative was healthy. People should go their own ways.

She glanced at the clock and realized why Carmen had been sitting in the living room waiting for her; she had been gone for over five hours. Any amount of time that slipped so completely away from her left her feeling completely out of control. She left the kitchen and climbed the stairs. She heard Carmen's CD player blaring halfway down the hall. Carrie passed by, unwilling to handle another confrontation. The hour was late enough to justify going to bed, and she looked for no further motivation to leave consciousness for awhile. Her phone rang and she picked it up.

"Hello?"

"May I speak to Carrie Crenshaw?"

The lines in her face tightened. "Speaking."

"Carrie, this is Alberta Donaldson."

"Yes," she said. "I know who you are."

"Are you aware of the hour?"

"It's eleven."

"The neighborhood's quiet hours start at ten." The woman's tone had become one of civil hatred. "Walter and I are trying to sleep, and all we can hear is that racket that your daughter is blaring from her—"

"I'll talk to Carmen, Mrs. Donaldson."

"I don't want to overstep my boundaries, and the last thing I would want to do would be to judge someone." There was a blissful silence that lasted less than half a second. "But Walter and I can hear her music *quite clearly,* and I'm quite sure that children of Carmen's age should not be listening to those *sinful* words."

"I'll talk to Carmen," Carrie repeated. "Good night."

"We would like an apology for your daughter's complete lack of consideration. My ears are simply *burning.* You ought to be ashamed."

Carrie hung up the phone. She walked up the stairs, tapped on Carmen's door. The volume of the music lowered, but the door remained closed.

"Ten o'clock, Carmen," she said to the closed door. "You know the rules."

She went back downstairs, worried. She had not been happy with Carmen's behavior towards her, but she had tolerated it because, otherwise, Carmen had been the model young woman: polite, ambitious, involved with the community, and doing well with her school work. But Carmen's grades had started to slip, and she was destroying her positive reputation; just that week, the school had called Carrie three times on account of Carmen's disruptive behavior. Carmen wasn't considering dropping out of school any longer; she was trying to get herself expelled.

Carrie turned off the lights, slipped under the covers. She was not surprised that restlessness set in, or that her wish for sleep became a crazed desire to keep a nascent insanity at bay.

Sam and Jake went skiing that weekend—the boy's way of calling a truce. The drive to the mountains reaffirmed Sam's awareness of the need to sit down and talk to Jake. There was a latent tension between them though Sam had given him back his privileges, and soon Jake would be going to college…

"This was a nice idea," he said, glancing at Jake.

"Yeah," Jake said, his eyes on the road. "I needed a break, from school and stress. And you needed a break from working so hard."

"This trip was thoughtful, son." Sam paused. "Level with me."

"Everything's fine."

Sam knew Jake would tell him what was on his mind eventually. They listened to Jake's choice of music on the way up, some mix Carmen had burned for him. Sam always chose to drive and listen to his choice of music on the way back. They wouldn't leave the slopes until late; they'd still be on the roads around one o'clock, and Jake would usually be asleep by then. Sam liked the outings, but the actual time they interacted was limited to the way up, or the time when they might run into each other on the ski lifts. He knew that was why Jake loved the activity. It let them get closer, but it also gave them time to be alone—with thoughts or numbness, whichever they chose.

"Hey, Dad?"

"Yeah, Jake." They had been on the road for half an hour.

"How come…" he paused, and Sam saw him tighten his grip on the steering wheel. "How come when you love people you end up hurting them?"

"What are you talking about in particular?"

"My temper," he said. "Since you brought it up the other day. I mean, it's not natural, is it, to get so angry at Carmen all the time, is it?"

"Women are infuriating."

Jake turned to him, relieved. "The other day Carmen had me wait for her for an hour and a half, and then she gave me attitude. I swear I was so tempted to—"

"Keep your eyes on the road, Jake."

"She likes to provoke me. And I'm not always in control." He paused. "And she wouldn't even be interested in me if I wasn't mean to her."

"I doubt that."

"She told me so," he said loudly, his cheeks flushing. "She told me that if I ever loved her she would start hating me.

"Son," he said, after a moment. "Would you respect someone who treated you badly?"

He shrugged.

"How is she going to know she doesn't like being treated badly unless you show her otherwise?"

"Exactly," Jake said, pleased. "That's probably the only reason she's still with me."

"How are you going to learn," Sam said, interrupting him, "that you shouldn't let her treat you the way she's treating you, unless you see that it's not right?"

The question left Jake looking perturbed, and Sam prided himself on the profundity of his speech until he realized that Jake was confused—not that he was thinking about Sam's words.

"But I have seen other things," Jake said. "I've been with other girls. They're all the same, except that Carmen is more interesting."

"Because none of them have the integrity…" Sam stopped speaking, surprised by how angry he had become. "You kids think it's okay to use each other?"

"It doesn't hurt anyone," Jake said. "Not unless she gets pregnant."

"You'll see the scars later," Sam said. "That's all I'll say. What else did you want to talk about?"

"We read about…" Jake paused. "About domestic violence and stuff like that in guidance class. I don't want to become like that."

Sam tried to keep his voice neutral. "Are you afraid you're going to?"

"If I did lose control," he paused. "Do you think she would put up with it?"

"Jake."

"Yeah?"

Sam paused. "I have my doubts about your choice of Carmen Crenshaw as a girlfriend. She's too young. She's wild. She's a bad influence on you, and as to how steady she's going to prove as she gets older, I have my doubts about that as well. But," he added, seeing that Jake was ready to defend her. "She's also full of spunk, defiance, and vitality. If you try to intimidate or overpower her, especially through force, I think she'll drop you in a second. And she'd be entirely justified, in whatever she did."

Jake's face had taken on a pinched look. "Yeah, I guess. How's that article coming?"

"I finished it before we left the house, so I wouldn't have to worry about it on the slopes."

"Should be a good day," Jake said. "Lots of snow already, and it's still coming down."

The car stalled. They were on an incline, and as the car started sliding backwards Jake turned to him.

"Emergency brake," Sam instructed. "Now start her up."

The engine came to life, but the car loped forward unevenly. Jake turned the engine off, then pulled up on the emergency brake.

"Did we blow a tire?" he asked.

"Let's take a look."

They got out of the car.

"Hey, pops. Look at this."

Sam went to him and saw that the back left tire had gone flat.

"I'll set up the jack." Jake shuffled to the side of the car while Sam dragged out the spare. For the next half hour they worked side by side, saying little. When they finished, Jake turned to him.

"She good to go?"

Sam nodded. "You did a fine job."

"I learned from you." Jake handed him the jack.

As Sam walked to the passenger side of the car, he remembered how much he loved the boy. He wished it could always be like it had just been—working together, concentrating on the task at hand, no women, no baggage, no adult issues. Sam looked at Jake from the corner of his eye—to be young again.

"Ten miles to go," he said as Jake started up the car.

Alberta Donaldson squinted at the piece of paper clutched in her arthritic, liver-spotted hand, then moved her buggy down the supermarket aisle. She turned the corner and almost ran into a young woman standing near a half-full buggy. She recognized the brown-haired, blue-eyed girl who lived next door. She was recognized in turn.

"Good morning, Mrs. Donaldson," Carmen said.

"Carmen Crenshaw. How do ye do." Alberta knit her forehead, to show her displeasure at the encounter despite the civility of her words.

"I'm doing well," she replied.

The cardigan sweater and jeans she was wearing weren't exactly inappropriate—they covered her from throat to toe—but a girl her age should not have curves like that. Alberta didn't doubt the rumors she had heard about the Crenshaw girl and the handsome Sampson boy; there was too much color in the girl's cheeks, too much sparkle in her eyes. She saw Carmen watching her and cleared her throat loudly.

"Did your mother talk to you?" she asked sternly, realizing that the impudent girl hadn't even asked how *she* was doing.

"Carrie?"

"It's perfectly scandalous how you young people address your parents these days."

Carmen stared at her.

"And your *music*," Alberta continued, knowing that Carmen would apologize unlike her stubborn mother. The Sampson boy probably liked that about her, too—beauty *and* obedience. "How you could have the audacity to listen to those *sinful* words…" Alberta lowered her voice. She wanted to get her gossip straight, but she didn't want to be overheard doing it. "And you should *hear* the rumors being spread about you and that handsome Sampson boy."

"They aren't rumors," Carmen said.

Alberta stepped away, scandalized. "You act as if you're proud of your behavior."

"Jake and I are happy. And he's very, *very*, good to me." She looked at Alberta. "If you know what I mean, but no, I suppose you don't. Excuse me. I need to get some milk for my mother."

Alberta clawed at her arm. "You understand that *I* would never judge you…"

"Don't touch me," Carmen said, pushing by her. "And keep your big mouth shut about Jake and me, you old hag."

Carmen felt the old woman's eyes on her as she picked out a gallon of milk, but Alberta Donaldson did not bother her. She had more than she could handle, just with Jake. She altered her course to the front of the store and waited for Carrie, who always took the half of the list with all the random spices and food items Carmen wouldn't be able to find. She pretended to be absorbed in the racks of celebrity gossip magazines on display; she would not let Carrie know that she agreed that the magazines were a waste of time, since it made Carrie so angry if she looked through them.

Her thoughts wandered. The answer she had given Alberta did not satisfy Carmen. She and Jake were *not* happy. She felt tears welling in her eyes and bit the inside of her cheek until the tears subsided. Jake was using her for sex and she was using him for security, and he actually seemed to think that was okay…

"Did you have trouble finding anything?" Carrie asked from beside her.

"No." Carmen turned her head away quickly. Her voice came out steady, with exactly the right concentration of contempt. "Though it took me like five minutes to read what you wrote. Why can't you print?" She blindly grabbed one of the tabloid papers and tossed it into Carrie's buggy. "I want that."

Carrie picked out the magazine and replaced it on the rack. "You don't need to rot your mind with that trash, Carmen."

"*Absolutely* right."

They both turned.

"Carrie, I am shocked by how you let this child run around." Alberta pushed her buggy up to them. "I don't want to overstep my bounds, but I have *serious doubts* about your parenting ability." She sniffed. "Your brat had the audacity to call me an 'old hag'…"

Carmen risked a glance at her mother and noticed that Carrie was trying not to smile.

"I've tried to teach her that honesty is a cardinal virtue," Carrie said. She put an arm around Carmen, pulled her close.

Alberta stared. "You're as incorrigible as she is. You should be ashamed."

Carrie's eyes flashed. "I love her very much. And I'm proud of her."

Carmen felt tears welling in her eyes; she turned away.

"Well, I never." Alberta scowled. "I won't even be caught in the same aisle as either of you."

Carrie turned to Carmen as Alberta rolled her buggy to the adjacent aisle; Carmen kept her face hidden and thrust the tabloid at Carrie.

Carrie exhaled slowly. "If you want that magazine, Carmen, you can buy it with your own money."

"I don't have any money on me."

"Then you'll have to wait until next time to get it."

Carmen sighed loudly and pushed her buggy in front of Carrie's. She began unloading the items silently, deliberately mismatching the food articles on the conveyor belt.

"Honey," Carrie said. "Keep everything together. Cans first, bread last so it won't get smashed."

"This is how I do it."

The cashier, a woman with bright red lipstick, smiled sympathetically at Carrie. The look Carrie gave the woman made her turn her attention back to scanning the remaining food items. "Sixty-four ninety two."

"God," Carmen said. "That's like twelve hours worth of work. And we didn't even buy that much."

"Organic food costs more, Carmen." Carrie handed the woman three twenties and a ten.

Carmen eyed the money. "It's not like you can even tell the difference."

"Your body can. Carmen, do you mind pushing your buggy out of the way so we can get through?"

Carmen pushed the buggy forward, her head held high. Once out of the store, she shoved the buggy away from her and laughed as it crashed into a row of other buggies. Carrie continued through the lot to their parked car without glancing in Carmen's direction, then opened the trunk and began unloading the bags into the car.

"Carmen!" she called, finished. Carmen always took the minute it took Carrie to unload the bags as an opportunity to go wandering around the parking lot. What she could possibly gain from that wandering, Carrie had never understood. She left the buggy in the nearest rack, then went back to the car and got in. She pulled out the book she had brought with her and began to read, calmly. Two chapters later, Carmen returned to the car and tapped on the window to be let in. Carrie reached over, unlocked Carmen's door, silently marked her place and closed the book.

"Did you have a nice walk?" she asked as she started the car.

"Yes, I did," Carmen said cheerily. "I did a lot of thinking."

Carrie glanced at her; Carmen smiled at her sweetly. Carrie put the car in reverse and almost backed out into an oncoming vehicle. The angry driver honked once; Carrie waited until he had passed, then pulled the car out and headed towards the highway.

"I did a lot of thinking," Carmen repeated.

Carrie looked at her. "About what?"

"About you and Dad."

Carrie's hands tightened on the steering wheel. "Is that so?"

"You should keep going after him. That's what I did, and eventually he came around."

"Your father has a legitimate reason to be angry with me. Being persistent isn't going to make him come around."

"Yes, it will."

"Why would you think that?"

"He loves you."

Carrie looked down. "Carmen, you couldn't possibly understand—"

"He talks to me about you," Carmen insisted. "Not bad things, not good things. Just things. Like you used to read Stephen King, or...well, I can't think of anything else right now, but he does talk about you."

"Don't meddle in this. Please."

"I know about Chloe," Carmen said softly.

Carrie's reaction was sudden and violent. She pulled over to the side of the road, stopped the car.

"What did he tell you about Chloe?"

"She was your other daughter, wasn't she? And she was a retard or something."

"She was born prematurely, Carmen."

"Does that mean she was born dead?"

"She died when she was two." Carrie paused. "I wasn't there. Your father has every reason to be angry with me."

Carmen glanced at her. "Maybe you should talk to him."

"Maybe you should drop this subject."

"I'm just trying to talk to you."

"I said to *drop the subject.*"

"Fine." Carmen slouched in her seat. "If you're going to be like that, you might as well drop me off at Jake's."

"All right," Carrie said. "I could use the night off from your moods and temper tantrums. A nice quiet house to write in sounds good to me.

"That's the wrong turn," Carmen said, sitting up abruptly.

"Not to get to Sam's. Call Jake and let him know you're coming over for dinner. Tell him to ask Sam if that's all right."

"What if I don't want to go?"

"You just told me you wanted to go. So you're going. Call Jake."

She didn't want to call Jake; she didn't want to see Jake. They needed to talk, but Jake wouldn't want to *talk*. She thought of pretending to call him and then telling Carrie she had gotten an answering machine, but as she was thinking she had already pressed two. Speed dial Jake, and his voice came across the line.

"Hey, baby."

"Carrie wants to know if I can come over for dinner," she said, her voice flat.

"Dinner...and dessert?"

"I put you on speaker phone," she said, lying. "Behave yourself."

Carrie looked at her.

"Jesus Christ, Carmen, you put me on..." He caught himself. "Let me clear it with Dad. Hold on a minute, okay?"

"Okay."

Carmen ignored Carrie as she waited, hoping that somehow the line would become disconnected and she could tell Carrie that she couldn't go over. She could use the interim to switch her phone to vibrate, so that if Jake called back, Carrie wouldn't know.

"Babe? Dad says that's fine. What time can we expect you?"

"What time," Carmen repeated, thinking how much Jake sounded like a salesman completing a business transaction. "Geez, Jake, I don't know, that's a really good question."

"Seven," Carrie said.

"Seven," Carmen said into the phone. The clock read quarter till.

"Dad wants to know if Carrie wants to stay."

"Do you want to stay?" Carmen asked, her hand covering the receiver. Carrie shook her head, her eyes on the road.

"No," Carmen said.

"What?" It took her a second to realize he wasn't speaking to her. "Oh. Dad says there will be more than enough for four people."

"Mom has to work," Carmen said, without further consultation with Carrie. "She says to tell him thank you."

"Okay, I will." Jake's voice dropped. "Carmen, after dinner Dad has to work, too. So we'll be—"

"Speaker phone," she reminded him.

"You're not on speaker phone," he said, with confidence. "Look, I got my driving privileges back. We can go to the shack."

"Look how smart you are," she said. "You made a rhyme."

Without waiting for a further response from him she hung up and snapped her phone shut. She ignored the questioning look Carrie gave her.

"They'll be expecting me around seven," she said.

"Is everything alright, Carmen?" Something in her daughter's voice had triggered a warning, and Carmen's face had taken on a nasty shade.

"Yeah. Fine."

Carrie slowed down. "What's wrong?"

"Better keep up your speed," Carmen remarked, watching the houses go by. "We'll never get to Jake's in ten minutes if you go thirty-five."

"Don't you want to see Jake?"

Carmen shrugged.

"Are you depressed, Carmen? Do you need to see someone?"

"Oh my god," Carmen said. "Carrie, please don't start up with that bullshit. I'm not depressed."

Carrie looked at her; Carmen returned the look.

"I'll fuck life over before I fuck myself over." Her gray blue eyes were defiant. "You should know that."

Carrie said nothing. She did not even reprimand Carmen for her language.

Carmen sighed. "Will you pull over?"

"Do you want to talk?"

"No. I want to walk."

"We're still two miles from their house."

"I want to walk the rest of the way."

"Let me take you at least halfway there."

Carmen settled back into her seat. "Okay."

Carrie tried to delay, hoping that Carmen wouldn't see the mile marker click up, but Carmen put her hand on the door handle as soon as the numbers changed.

"Go straight to Sam's," Carrie said, stopping the car.

"Okay."

"Be careful."

Carmen started to say something, but stopped. "Okay. I will."

She knew Carrie's eyes were on her as she got out of the car, and ignored Carrie's genuine concern as best she could. After she heard her mother's old car drive off, she reached into Jake's coat pocket for her cigarettes, then remembered she had given them to her father. To Damien DeMatteo. To Ralph Palmer. To Jean Paul Christianson. To whomever he was, anyway. She wondered how she was supposed to be normal with such fucked up parents. Jake was probably what she deserved; she would put up with him, she would survive him, and someday she would be free of him.

She walked along the snowy sidewalk, her boots slicing through thick clumps of gray sludge. She would give him back his jacket and use her father's money to buy one of her own: a good coat, a stylish black wool one. As soon as she decided she wanted to be free.

When the door opened, she was glad to see Sam's face. She was always tempted to believe he was a good guy; he had never said a harsh word to her, and he always greeted her with that stupid, friendly grin, like she didn't know that somewhere inside him was the same cruelty that was in Jake.

"Hello, Carmen," Sam said, smiling broadly at her. "It's cold out there. We're going to eat inside tonight."

"I thought we were going to eat outside in the snow," she said. "Don't you think that would be lovely?"

The smile on Sam's face faltered. "I'll go get Jake and tell him dinner is ready. You can put your coat anywhere that isn't wood." He paused. "Isn't that Jake's jacket?"

She stared at him without answering.

"Come in," Sam said. "I'll go get Jake."

She tried to steady her breathing as Sam disappeared, realizing she was getting hysterical over nothing. She could handle Jake. The dread, the fear, were irrational and stupid. She laughed, though no one would hear her. She didn't have to be afraid because he had mentioned the shack. She could tell him she wasn't up for it. She had forgotten that Jake wouldn't do anything to lose her. He had pressured her before, but he had never forced her to do anything. She smoothed her hair, feeling the flecks of snow melt under her hand. Jake would like that; during their last walk together, he had said that the droplets looked like diamonds in a tiara, and then he had called her his princess...

Jake walked into the room. His expression was friendly, but she felt her happy thoughts vanish and her fear return.

"Hey," he said. "You look half frozen."

"Yeah," she said, choking on the word. "It's cold outside."

"Are you getting sick?" he asked, glancing at her.

She shook her head.

"That's good. You sounded for a minute like maybe you were. I thought maybe with the flu going around..."

He put his hand on the small of her back and guided her into the kitchen. She tried not to recoil from his touch or shiver when she saw the flickering candle on the table.

"Did you do this?"

"No," he said. "Dad did. He thought we could use some time alone to talk. And you should see what he made for dinner. He was a cook once, like when he was in college..."

As he hurried over to the pots on the stove, Carmen felt her eyes tearing up. She could smell the cinnamon scent of the candle from where she was standing. A single long-stemmed white rose stood tall in a crystal vase. Table, set for two.

"Hey, Carmen, come look."

She turned and saw him standing by the stove, the glass lid of a pot in his hand. She forced a smile onto her face and went to stand by him.

"What is it?" she asked, looking down into the pot.

"Italian wedding soup," he said, grinning. "Save your appetite, though. He made us a main meal, and dessert."

She looked at him, feeling an insane hope go through her as she remembered the phone conversation. "And dessert, too."

"Cheesecake with strawberries." He paused. "I know you don't want to ruin your figure, but I guess you could have a small piece. And I guess we shouldn't eat too much…" He lowered his voice. "If we're going to the shack."

The tiny, fluttering hope inside her died.

Jake was oblivious. He started ladling the soup into two bowls. Carmen forced herself to speak.

"This was really nice of your dad."

"Yeah."

"But he didn't know I was coming."

"Weird thing," Jake said. "See, I was going to call you and ask you over tonight. This was supposed to be a surprise."

"It is a surprise."

"Isn't that strange? I would have called you if you hadn't called me, so this would have happened either way." He glanced at her. "Are you upset about something?"

"No," she said, turning her head away from. "I just don't feel well." A single tear had slipped out of her eye and had rolled down her cheek. The traitorous thing had landed on his hand.

"You women are sentimental about everything," he said. "What, is it that time of the month for you or something?"

"I'm fine." She paused. "Can we eat? I'm hungry."

"Yeah, so am I." He handed her a bowl, not seeming to realize she had contradicted herself. "Let's eat."

She carried her bowl to the table and waited until he had sat down across from her. She made no attempt at making conversation.

"Dad took me skiing."

"Did he? That sounds nice." Carmen paused. "Can I have something to drink?"

Jake jumped up. "What do you want? We have milk, juice, water, lemonade…"

"Water is fine."

He came back and put the glass of tap water in front of her, so jittery that some of it splashed onto the table. "It was so great. Such an escape. We got a flat on this huge hill and I helped him change the tire and all the time it was freezing…"

"You must have been very brave," she said absently.

He talked until they finished the soup, then took her plate and went to the oven to get the main meal. She put the candle out when his back was turned, licking her fingers and extinguishing the flame so he wouldn't see or smell the smoke. He came back and put a plate of something in front of her. She realized he was still talking about the ski trip, and that she hadn't heard one word of what he had said, not since he began. She wished she had an appetite, but the rich smell of the food nauseated her.

"You're not eating," he said, pausing long enough in his monologue to look at her.

"I guess I'm not hungry."

"That soup probably filled you up. And we can save dessert." He paused. "Do you want to go?"

She hesitated. "Jake?"

"What, baby?"

She reached across the table, took his hand in hers. "Can we just talk tonight? Please? I don't...I really don't feel very well."

He leaned across the table and put his hand on her forehead. "You do feel kind of hot. Maybe you are getting sick."

She hoped so. "So that's okay?"

"Of course it's okay. We shouldn't go if you're not feeling well." He let go of her hand, stood up. "Help me with the dishes?"

There were a total of four dishes to wash; they were done in a minute, and then he turned to her.

"I'll drive you home," he said.

She shook her head. "I want to go out. But I want to talk."

"All right." He seemed relieved. "Let me tell Dad we're going."

"I'll do it."

"Do what?"

"I want to thank him."

"Okay." He looked at her as if she had gone crazy. "In that case I'll go warm up the car. Don't be too long about it."

"I won't be."

Relief ripped through her as he headed out of the house. She touched the white rose on the table, then headed down the hallway. Jake had showed her Sam's study once, and she remembered exactly where it was.

531

She knocked gently on the open door. "Mr. Sampson?"

He glanced up. "Carmen. What can I do for you?"

"Your study is so nice," she said, her eyes flicking over the walls. "Not dark and dusty like Carrie's..." She broke off, shifted. "I wanted to thank you for the dinner. It was really nice of you to go to all that work."

He also looked at her as if she had gone crazy. "You're welcome."

"I mean, it must really have been a hassle."

"No hassle. I like to cook."

"Well, thank you."

"You're welcome," he said, and paused. "Are you and Jake going to go out?"

"We're going to go for a drive if that's okay?"

"Have him back by ten," he joked, and actually got a smile from her.

"All right," she said. "Well, goodbye. And thank you."

"You're welcome," he said, for the third time.

As she left, he wondered why he felt sudden apprehension. Jake was under control. That had been the stipulation of the dinner: he treated Jake like an adult and helped him patch things up with Carmen, and Jake patched up his act and started watching his temper....

Jake had never betrayed him. Sam went back to his writing.

Jake came home two hours later. Sam heard him slam the door, then the sound of things breaking. He found Jake in the kitchen, his eyes burning, his cheeks bitten raw by the cold.

"What the hell are you doing?" he asked as Jake threw a pot against the wall.

"I'll clean up later. Promise." He turned away. "Thanks for dinner."

"What the hell happened?"

"Nothing."

"Where's Carmen?"

"I took her home. We had a fight but I kept my cool."

"This is keeping your cool?"

"Until now," he amended. He started pacing. "I think I'm going to break up with her. Too much drama." He inhaled, let out the air. "I'll clean up, and I'll pay for the dishes. But I had to blow off some steam."

"Jake."

"Thanks again for dinner, Dad. The food was great."

"I don't care about the food. What happened?"

"I'm calm now, I swear. But I might take some anger management classes." He paused. "The guidance office offers them for free at the school. Night, Dad."

Sam paused, wondering what he should do. "We'll talk more tomorrow, Jake."

"I'll look forward to it," he said, and left.

Sam went directly upstairs and called Carrie, though he was worried about the hour; he knew she went to bed at half past ten, and it was quarter past eleven. She picked up on the first ring.

"Carrie, it's Sam."

"Thank god," she said. "I was just going to call you."

He felt a twinge of fear. "Is Carmen home?"

"What do you mean, is she home?"

"Jake said he dropped her off."

The pause crackled with her silence. Then, "Where's my little girl, Sam?"

"Jake!" he yelled, covering the mouthpiece of the receiver. "Jake, get down here right now!" He turned back to the phone. "Can you come over, Carrie?"

"Sam, what—"

"I'm sure everything is fine," Sam said. "Can you come?"

"I'm leaving right now." She hung up on him.

Sam put the phone down. He looked up. Jake was standing in the doorway, his head lowered.

"What did you do?" Sam demanded.

"I don't know what—"

"Cut the bullshit, Jake."

Jake's face darkened. "She provoked me. It wasn't my fault."

"Sit your sorry ass down!" Sam yelled.

Jake jumped and moved into the room. Sam glared at him.

"Where is she?"

Jake shook his head.

"Answer me, damn you."

"I don't know," he said.

Carmen had forgotten how strong he was. When Jake had her under him, she hadn't been able to move—much. Enough to bring her knee into his balls, to get him off her. Then she had gone crazy. She had never known she could hate someone so much. She had hurt him. She had to hurt him, so that when she ran out of the shack to his car, she had time to start the car, to get away before he caught up with her. He would have come after her, had he been able to. She was lucky he had wanted to leave the headlights on so he could see her, because that meant the keys were waiting for her in the ignition...

She should have known he had something in mind, but she hadn't suspected. Lights on because they were going to talk. Talk, talk, talk, like she had *told* him before they went. He had agreed to talk. He had *wanted* to talk. He had wanted to impress on her how much she owed him, for the dinner...

But your dad made it.

But I helped.

She had told him she didn't want to, and he seemed to think that was code for yes, she wanted him. But he had underestimated her. She was glad she had taken his car and left him there. Why had she gone with him? She had trusted him. But Jake had gotten so weird...about everything. She didn't even remember what she had said, that had made him start to hit her...

She hated men, but somehow her dad was different. He was the first person she had thought about after starting up Jake's car, and she knew the way to his house. So she decided to go to him. She parked, got out of the car, closed the door quietly. She could knock, but she wasn't sure she wanted her dad to know she was there. He would make her call Carrie, make her go home. Jake lived too close to her home, and because of the tree he could get into her room. Carmen would figure out exactly where that left her in the morning, but she wanted the night away from everything.

She tried to silence the sob that broke from her cracked lips. The cold air burned her lungs as she started towards the west end of the house, her boots sinking into the snow. She stopped and scanned the brick wall in front of her. She could see where some of the bricks jutted out, where others caved in. She knew she could climb the wall and discover the glass panel. He only had to have shown her once.

She would just have to do it fast; the cold was cutting into her, and she didn't have a coat. No hat, no gloves. She wiped at the snot dripping from her nose with the back of her hand, wiped her hand on her jeans, and stepped up to the wall. The wall wasn't even as high as her tree; if her dad had climbed the wall before, then so could she.

She attempted to climb and slid down the wall. The bricks scratched at her chapped skin, making her hands bleed. She shook her hands until the pain went away, then attacked the wall and was at the top before she knew how. There was a significant ledge in front of the window, and she pulled herself onto it. She paused, trembling from cold, from adrenaline, from exertion…and Jake had hurt her, and that didn't helped. She felt secure enough on the ledge, but the cold was making her numb. She glanced through the glass walls into the dark studio, then forced herself to concentrate.

She hooked her fingers near the bottom of the window, pushed up. The glass pane did not budge. She tried pushing, and the panel popped open. It would have crashed inward had her full weight landed on it, but she had recoiled instead of fallen forward. For a moment she tottered on the ledge, then instinctively caught onto the inside of the pane. Reminding herself to breathe, she dropped into the studio. She turned to close the panel and saw she had left a streak of blood on the glass pane. She swiped it away with the sleeve of her shirt, her hands throbbing.

She was glad for the pain; it let her know she wasn't frostbitten. She pushed aside a curtain of vines, went to the middle of the studio, and lay down on the ground. In the stillness in the room, she felt a deep sense of security and peace.

She was starting to doze when the single light above her burst to life. She saw her father enter through the cubby hole door, dressed in a robe, looking half-crazed with sleep. He moved to the table with the tubes of paint and picked up the splattered pallette. He had not seen her.

"Hi," she said, loudly.

He turned.

"Carmen," he said, fully awake in an instant.

She tried not to cry. "Please don't make me go home."

He put down the pallette and walked over to her. He bent down and gently tilted her face up towards the light.

"Who did this to you?" he asked, his voice deadly.

She could no longer keep herself from crying. The tears rolled down her cheeks, and she bit her lip until the blood ran to keep herself from sobbing.

"Did your mother..." he started, stricken, unbelieving.

"No," she said. "Mom would never hurt me. I mean, please don't be mad, I only want to stay for one night."

"Jake." He stood, not waiting for her answer. "I'll kill him."

"I'll explain everything later, okay? I just want to stay here tonight."

"You can stay as long as you like. Not here, though." He paused. "Two of the rooms on the first floor have guest beds. Do you remember how to get there?"

She nodded, realizing he felt completely unprepared to interact with her.

"All right, then," he said. "Off you go. Lights are on."

"Thank you." She used his hand to climb shakily to her feet.

"Carmen?"

She turned, sure the questions would start—grateful, in a way.

"Does Carrie know you're here?"

She shook her head.

"You'll have to call her in the morning." He paused. "I don't want her to worry."

"Okay," she said.

"Goodnight." He crossed to the table, picked up the pallette, looked at the assortment of paints.

"Goodnight," she said.

He did not look up as she passed him. She bumped her head on the ceiling of the narrow corridor, but she would rather concentrate on the throbbing of her head than the dull ache in her heart.

She went down the stairs, too tired to realize that she was maneuvering through the house as if she had lived there her whole life. She turned into one of the guest rooms and closed the door. She fell onto the bed, fully dressed, and in moments she was fast asleep.

Carmen dreamed that her father was sitting on the bed, watching her sleep. In the dream he was her guardian angel, and while he was beside her she had nothing to fear. She couldn't see anything past the canopy of his white wings around her, protecting her. She had just enough time to realize what a funny angel he made, with his puff of black hair with its twin streaks of white at the temples and his fiercely glinting eyes...then she woke up.

She realized her crying had wakened her. Daylight cracked through the window in full force, and she sat up stiffly. Her hands and face throbbed, and she saw smears of blood on the sheets. Hastily she stripped the bed of the sheets and the pillow case and stuffed them under the bed. She checked the major rooms—excepting his bedroom and studio—and saw no sign of him. She found she was relieved; she wanted to do the laundry as inconspicuously as she could. And she found that a very small part of her was afraid to meet him again, despite her dream...

The house was quiet, and she took her time as she searched for the laundry room. She found a small rectangular area with a chipped white washer and dryer and a single laundry basket pushed to the side. She hurried back to the guest room, then ran back to the laundry room with the bloodied sheets. She started the load with the detergent she found in the laundry basket, then relaxed and headed back to the center of the house. Still no sight of him. She remembered the black box on his ankle; he had to be in the house somewhere.

She looked at the grandfather clock in one of the rooms and realized she would be in third period already, had she gone to school. There would be work to catch up on; algebra was kicking her around already, and missing a day would put her at least a week behind her classmates. Though she had no regrets: the harder the classes, the easier for her to flunk out of them. Then she could go and be with Jake...

Her thoughts stopped there. That plan had developed in the shack six months after they had started dating; as the sinking sun painted a lavender blush across the sky, he had promised to marry her, and she had given him her first attempt at a blow job. It had been the plan for so long that she had not realized, until then, that the plan no longer worked for her. She comforted herself by thinking about what else she was missing: Mr. Roney's eyes crawling across the front of her sweater, Mrs. Johnson disapproving of whatever she said, the school's bells insisting that they act like trained dogs...

And Miss Carpenter's chemistry class—where she would have been in half an hour. They had started experiments and she liked the applications, liked them almost as much as she liked the lab partner Miss Carpenter had assigned her: a tall, thin boy named Mark George, who had sandy brown hair and eyes the same blue ice as hers. They looked like brother and sister, Miss Carpenter had said. Carmen had always wanted a brother or sister, and maybe Miss Carpenter's remark was why Mark had gotten past her defenses so easily. But she suspected Mark's personality played an equal role. He was quiet and shy around her, but when he did speak his sarcastic humor made her laugh. She had laughed so hard, once, that she had dropped the beaker she was holding and it had shattered on the floor. Miss Carpenter had not even been angry, and neither had Mark; he had merely stooped and helped her pick up the shattered pieces, though the mishap meant they had to start the reaction series over, and that they had to stay after class until the experiment was finished. Mark never looked at her the way the other boys in the school did, and never talked about her like the other boys did, and that went a long way with her.

She liked Miss Carpenter, and she liked Mark George. Though she was sorry to miss the chemistry class, Carmen felt a deep relief that she had not gotten up in enough time to drive back for her classes. Unlike Carrie, she believed that everything happened for a reason, and she knew she had needed the day off. She wandered around the house listlessly. There was nothing for her to do: not even any books for her to read. She wondered how her father could live in such an empty house, especially since he spent so much of his time there.

She finally found him in the kitchen, a smear of red paint across his cheek.

"Hello," she said, with faked confidence.

He turned. "Good morning, Carmen."

He held something out to her, and she moved to take it. She turned the thin rectangular canvas over and smiled.

"It's so pretty," she said.

"You can put it in the guest room if you want, to brighten things up." He paused. "I wanted to get you real flowers…"

"But you can't go out."

"Not till January," he said.

"I like this better anyway." She looked at the painting of the velvety rose, crystallized with dew droplets. "Wow, you painted this?"

"I painted it." He was clasping his hands tightly behind his back and standing ramrod straight.

"Actual flowers would have died," she said. "This will last forever."

He paused. "Are you doing laundry?"

"Yeah." She grimaced, not having realized he would hear the clanking sound of the old washer. "I bled a little on the sheets last night. My hands, I mean. And I think maybe my face." She hesitated, then showed him her hands. He looked without commenting, and she stuffed her hands in the pockets of her jeans. "I'm sorry. I'll buy you new sheets, after I pay for your window."

"It's not important," he said. "I don't ever use those rooms."

"Thanks for not being mad." She paused. "I should probably go back to school soon."

"Let your mother know where you are before you do anything else."

"Do I have to? Can't I just stay?"

"Nothing comes that easily."

"Guess not," she said. "Alright, I'll call her."

"Now."

"All right."

He paused. "Will you come back?"

"Of course." She paused. "I don't know when I'll be able to, though. I might be grounded for awhile."

He smiled spontaneously at her. "I'm sorry that I didn't get to see you grow up."

"Talk to Carrie and you won't be," she retorted. "She'll tell you how lucky you are to have missed it. I'm a nightmare."

"Carmen."

"What?"

"Who did that to you?"

"I did." She paused. "I got into an accident."

He looked at her, hard, for a long time. "I'm going to my studio. If you need anything, I'll be there."

He moved out of the kitchen. Her stomach growled. She went to the refrigerator and looked inside to see a random assortment of things: a package of sour cream, a glass jar of pickles, some half-molding bread. She wondered why he had put bread in the refrigerator. She looked in the freezer; it was empty.

She didn't expect to see him again for awhile, so she didn't hesitate. But she would have to be careful, because she wasn't used to driving on icy streets with other cars around her. It was Friday—pay day—so she could stop by the convenience store and get her check, then go to the bank and cash it. Then she would have enough money to buy him some decent groceries.

She got in the car and was relieved to find that, after skidding once, she felt in control and comfortable with how she was handling the roads. Twenty-five minutes later she turned into the store's parking lot, and a minute after that the big, golden bell inside tinkled to announce her entrance.

"Hey, Davy." She smiled as she went to the counter. "Can I have my paycheck, please?"

He was an elderly man, stick thin and balding. He was quiet and kind and Carmen liked him.

"Good morning, Carmen," he said, pronouncing it *Cah-min*. "One minute, dear."

"Been slow today?" she asked when he came back, an envelope in hand.

"Slow day," he agreed.

"Probably because right now everyone is in school." She said it without thinking, but he only smiled. She opened the envelope, scanning the hours and the taxes and the total...the total that was hers. She had *earned* it.

"How did you do?" Davy asked.

She glanced up. The look on his face reminded her, for a moment, of the look on Carrie's face when Carmen had brought home her second quarter report card. Same question, too. Better a paycheck, than a report card. She had let her school work go, subtly. No more studying for tests, and she and Jake completed the fill-in-the blank worksheets her teachers gave her Mad-Lib style. She read seedy novels and classics alternatively in class behind her textbooks—not in Miss Carpenter's class, though—and her grades were in shreds. Her life had fallen apart beautifully. Soon she would fail out and then she would be free—except she didn't know where that left her anymore. She didn't want to see Jake again. But she had her paycheck, her first one, for twenty-seven hours.

"I done good," she said, and grinned.

Davy smiled. "That a girl."

Carmen glanced at the gas gauge as she got in the car. The needle was almost on 'E,' but she didn't want to go back into the store. Davy hadn't asked her any questions, but if she went back he might ask why she wasn't in school. Besides, she had enough gas to get to the grocery store. There was a gas station behind it; she could worry about gas then, if she needed to.

She thought about her father as she drove. Sometimes when she was around him she felt like he had no idea how to handle adolescent girls; other times she felt he understood her better than Carrie did. She knew he had experience working with teenage girls from the years he had spent teaching, but since Chloe had died he didn't have any experience with a teenage girl of his own, and he might have other doubts...

Her thoughts drifted but she stayed straight on the road, the car crawling at twenty-five miles an hour because she was afraid of the ice. She got to the four-way intersection in front of the grocery store complex safely and had time to check the other lanes before the truck blind-sided her. Her forehead smacked off the steering wheel, stunning her. She saw black, hazy spots, and then she lost consciousness.

Carrie got the call at 12:20, four hours after she had called the police and told them Carmen was missing.

"No," she said as she stood in her sunny kitchen. "NO. There must be some mistake. I'm coming."

She staggered to the front door. She got in the car and drove. The roads were slick with thick, dark ice, and she skidded several times before she forced herself to slow down. She could not believe that Carmen had been *driving* and that Carmen had gotten into an accident and that Carmen was in the intensive care unit hovering between life and death…

"Hold on, Carmen," she said. "I'm coming."

If Carmen died…but Carmen would not die. Carmen *would not* die. Carrie continued to drive, knowing that until that point in her life, nothing had ever been so important as having Carmen stay alive.

Carrie stood in front of the emergency room window. The color had long since drained from her face; dark, bruise-like circles underscored her eyes. Her nose was an inch from the glass pane as she watched the blue-clad doctors swarm around a lump under a white sheet—her little girl.

She felt a hand on her shoulder. She turned and Sam was there, his face full of concern.

"Sam," she said, falling into his arms. "Oh, Sam…"

He held her tightly to him, then gently led her away from the window. When they sat down in the waiting room, she didn't let go of his hand.

"Jake's in the car," Sam said. "He wanted to be here, but he didn't know if you'd want to see him."

"Go get him."

"I'll stay with you for awhile. He can stay there for awhile." He squeezed her hand, enveloped between his. "What did they say?"

"She's in critical condition."

"When was she admitted?"

"About an hour ago."

"She'll be all right."

"It's nice to hear you say so."

"You have to believe it," he stressed. "Your hope might help pull her through."

"Why the hell was she at the goddamned intersection!" Carrie yelled. "And there's no way a truck should be able to go eighty-five miles an hour! A truck shouldn't even be engineered to *drive* that fast..."

"Carrie."

"Why the hell was she even driving? Who the hell taught her to drive—"

"I taught her."

Sam winced at the sound of the familiar voice. Carrie tensed when she saw Jake standing there, holding his baseball hat in his hands.

"*You* did?" she asked.

"She wanted to learn." Jake's eyes never left Carrie's face, and he kept his expression blank so she wouldn't be able to tell he was lying. He would take the blame for Carmen this time. "Where is she? I need to see her."

Carrie hesitated, then pointed down the hallway. After Jake had left, Sam turned to her.

"Do you want me to tell him to leave?" he asked.

"They're in love, Sam," she said, tonelessly. "Having him here will help get her through this. And my daughter is just as bad an influence on your son as he has been on her."

"He still shouldn't have yelled at her," Sam said. "Though, thank God, that's all he did. For a moment, Carrie, I thought he might actually have—"

"That doesn't reassure me, Sam." She paused. "I don't want to talk about this right now."

He stood. "I'm going to go check on Jake."

She nodded absently. Sam went down the corridor and found Jake standing in front of the window, watching the doctors work. There was a smile on his lips that vanished when Jake turned and saw him.

"Hey," he said.

Sam must have imagined the smile; the boy's voice was heavy, his eyes glistening with tears. He looked away quickly, swallowing the lecture he had in mind.

"I did something really stupid," Jake said, his eyes still focused on the emergency room. "But she wanted to learn, and I could never tell her no. Seeing her like this..." He paused. "I've been afraid of losing her, but not like this. I never pictured losing her like this. If…*when* she gets out of this, I'm not going to say another harsh word to her. I'm never going to make her cry again. We'll never argue."

Sam remained quiet. Jake glanced at him, then returned his eyes to the figure lying on the cold examination table. "Is she going to be okay?"

Sam paused. "The doctors say her condition is stabilizing. But she's going to need some major corrective surgery. Some of the bones in her face got crushed."

Jake exhaled beside him. Sam looked at him sternly.

"Jake."

"What?"

"When Carmen gets out of here, you make her feel like the most beautiful woman in the world. Do you hear me?"

"Is it going to be that bad?" he asked, then saw the look in Sam's eyes. "Alright, Dad. I will."

"If you need money, ask me."

"I can take care of Carmen without your help," he said. "I'm not a child. You need to stop treating us like we're children."

"You are children." He paused. "If Carmen had acted more her age, this wouldn't have happened."

"This wasn't her fault. It was that stupid drunken driver's." He turned his attention back to the window. "It's disgusting seeing them swarm around her, like vultures over a corpse. I wish I could do something to help her."

"There's nothing we can do but wait." Sam put his hand gently on Jake's shoulder. "I'm sure the doctors will let us know if anything in her condition changes."

Jake let himself be guided away from the window. "Thanks for bringing me."

"Thank Carrie for letting you be here," he said. "Even if Carmen did take your car and leave you behind, you still lied to us when you said everything was fine."

"I'll thank her," Jake said as they returned to the waiting room. "Where is she?"

Sam scanned the entirety of the room. Carrie had disappeared.

Carrie drove with the windows open, despite the stinging rain. She needed the cold, the wet, to keep her awake; she was on the verge of collapse. The past three days before Carmen's accident had been a constant series of petty fights between them. She hadn't been able to sleep. She was exhausted, but she drove as fast as the snow-clogged streets would let her.

She pulled into his driveway. She got out of the car. She was soaked and disheveled as she walked up to the front door and rapped loudly. She did not wait for him to respond; she pounded on the door until she thought she was going to collapse. Her strength seemed to leave her all at once, and she leaned against the wooden posts on the porch for support. The lights in the house were on, she didn't understand why he wasn't coming...

The door opened, and he stepped into the light.

"What do you want, Carrie?" he asked.

"Carmen."

"Carmen stopped by last night," he said. "In *no* appropriate condition." He paused, and his voice held an edge that was pure hatred for her...not for her daughter. "She left early this morning. I don't know where she went. She's not my responsibility."

"Carmen—"

"You made sure of that," he said, interrupting her. "I wouldn't even have known I had another daughter if she hadn't come looking for me. I didn't even know she existed until a couple of weeks ago."

"There was an accident," Carrie said.

The color drained from his face. "When?"

"Today," she said. "Earlier this morning. Maybe when she left here. She's—."

"She's alive?"

"She's alive. The entire right side of her face is crushed."

He stepped back. "Christ."

She clutched her car keys in her hand. "I don't mind driving you to see her. She was admitted to the hospital a couple of hours ago."

"Is she conscious?"

"No."

"Then she won't know if I'm there or not."

Carrie stared at him. "Don't you want to see her?"

"I can't."

"You *can't?*"

He looked down. "I can't go."

She turned and started to her car. She thought she heard him call her name, but she did not turn around. She got into her car and started the engine. If he would have chased after the car, maybe she would have stopped. Maybe she would have run him over. She did not know what she would have done because he did not leave his house. She drove away.

The accident had happened on a Friday; he went to see her as soon as he could. The nurse in front of the hospital room looked up as he approached and listened as he explained who he was, and asked how Carmen was doing.

"She comes and goes," the nurse said. "She should be waking up from her medication soon, though, and she'll be clear for awhile."

Carmen was awake when he entered her hospital room. The entire right side of her face was covered by thick white gauze strips that wrapped around the side of her head. The left side of her face was scored by dozens of tiny scrapes and scratches under the one visible eye—a deep, icy blue hazed by the mists of medication.

"Is it Thursday already?" she asked groggily.

He sat down on the edge of her bed. "You're alive."

"Last time I checked." Her eyes glittered suddenly. "Are those for me?"

He handed her the flowers he had brought.

"They're beautiful," she said. "And you brought the painting you made me! Put it somewhere I can see it."

He put the canvas on the nightstand by her bed. "How are you?"

"I'm bored." She paused, then brightened. "I made you something. Look on my nightstand, where you just put your painting."

He picked up the piece of paper.

"They won't let me do anything, not even homework, because I only

546

have one eye available right now and they don't want me to strain it," she said. "But they'll let me draw because I said I would go insane if I had to sit here and do nothing. So I made that for you. It's stupid. Just a stupid crayon flower. Not like what you made."

"Thank you," he said, putting the drawing gently in his jacket pocket.

"I made it last week, and I saved it because I knew you wouldn't be able to come visit me until today. I told Mom that and she didn't believe me, but I said you would because…you know. She asked about you when she thought I was too doped up to remember, but I remembered."

"Your mother asked about me?"

"These really are beautiful." She held the flowers to her chest. "I can't smell them very well right now, but in a couple of days the bandages will come off and I should be better."

He hesitated, then put his hand on hers briefly to bring her back when she started to drift off.

"Carmen," he said. "I have to get back. The drive out took most of my time, and—"

She roused herself. "I understand."

"I wanted to see you. To make sure you were okay."

"Thanks." She looked at him, alert again. "Dad, before you go…do have a mirror? I know that sounds really weird, but they haven't let me see myself. I mean, I know I was in an accident, but I just want to see what I look like."

"I don't have a mirror," he said. "But I can tell you how you look. You look beautiful."

"Really? You're not just saying that because—"

He leaned over the hospital bed and kissed her on the forehead without thinking about it. "I love you," he said, standing. "Rest and feel better."

"Thanks for the flowers," she said. "Thanks for the flowers and for coming."

As he watched, she fell silent and her eye closed. He turned abruptly.

"Nurse," he said, starting towards the woman on duty.

"She's sleeping, Mr. Christianson."

He paused. "Sleeping."

The nurse nodded, turned a page of her magazine. "The doctors have her on a lot of painkillers. She'll heal faster if her body isn't constantly wracked by pain, but they make her sleepy. Nothing to worry about."

"Oh," he said, and looked back at Carmen. "How...how did it..."

"No one told you? She got hit by a drunk driver."

"Oh," he said.

"There's no need for you to stick around, now that she's out for the count." The nurse smiled at him. "She'll probably sleep for awhile now. She usually does in the afternoon."

He nodded, starting for the door.

"Those are lovely flowers you brought her."

He turned. "Take good care of my little girl."

"We always do, Mr. Christianson."

"Of course. Goodbye."

The nurse smiled at him, and he left the hospital as quickly as he could.

The day the results of the surgery were revealed, Carrie was the only one in the hospital room with Carmen. She sat on the edge of the bed and Carmen held her hand tightly as the nurse came towards them.

"They worked a miracle on you," the nurse said as she unwound the gauze from around Carmen's head. "You're lucky to be alive. But remember you've just been in a major accident. It could have been a whole lot worse."

The bandages were off. Carmen looked at Carrie, her eyes wide. Carrie squeezed her hand, smiled at her. Carmen's eyes slid from her to the nurse.

"Let me see," she said, hoarsely.

The nurse handed her a mirror.

Carmen screamed. The mirror went flying across the room, and the nurse gave Carrie a strained smile.

"I'll leave the two of you alone," she said, and left.

Carrie got up and went after the mirror. She came back, smoothed Carmen's hair away from her face and held the mirror out.

"Carmen. It's not that bad. You were just surprised."

"I don't want to look at it." She paused. "I would rather have died than look like this."

The cool calmness in her daughter's voice unnerved her. "Carmen, there's so much more to you than how you look."

"I can't ever be a professional singer looking like this. And if I don't have my dreams, what do I have?"

"I would encourage you to look inside and—"

"You can say that because you're a recluse. Looking inside is all you've ever done. But I care about what people think, and what are they going to think?" She paused, tears welling up in her eyes.

"Why would they think any differently of you?"

"Because we're teenagers! You know the number one factor that decides social acceptance in the United States is physical appearance. It's in one of those books you read." She bit her lip. "And I'm not beautiful anymore."

"Social skills," Carrie countered. "Number two. You have social skills you didn't lose in this accident."

"Will I always look like this?"

"You still have a lot of swelling," Carrie said, touching Carmen's cheek gently. "And you're going to have the sutures for awhile."

"How long?"

"Two weeks."

"So I'll look better with time." Carmen exhaled. "And I can stay here until then, where no one can see me."

"We're going home today." Carrie stood. "And you're going to school tomorrow. Get up. I'll take you to the Ice Cream Shack. My treat."

"Are you serious?" Carmen looked at her, terrified.

"I know it's freezing outside, but you always eat ice cream in the winter and—"

"I can't go out in public!" Carmen wailed. "Are you *insane*?"

Carrie frowned. "You have to make the best of this. You can't get any farther behind in school."

"Please don't make me go to school."

Carrie looked at her, trying to remain stern but not being able to. She sat down on the bed again.

"Maybe you could take a few extra days to catch up."

Carmen looked at her, relieved. "Yes, please."

"A *few* days, Carmen."

"Maybe you could homeschool me." She tried to smile. "Think of all the time we could spend bonding."

Carrie sighed. "Homeschooling is out of the question."

"Why?"

"Because you won't listen to me." Carrie paused. "But giving you a few days to get your head on straight and your spirits back up might not be a bad idea. Jake called, and I told him he could bring over your books later tonight. Maybe you can ask him to help you get caught up."

"Jake?" Carmen looked at her, horrified. "You asked Jake to come over tonight?"

"He offered to help you get caught up."

"He's not even in my grade. He doesn't know what homework I have."

"He got your books and assignments from your teachers." Carrie paused. "I thought that was a very kind thing for him to do, after you stole his car the other night and took it for a joy-ride. He seems genuinely sorry that he yelled at you."

Carmen paused. "Is that what he told you?"

"Is that what happened?"

Her blue eyes trained on Carrie without blinking. Carrie had never seen her so absolutely still. "Carmen, do you *want* to see Jake tonight?"

"Yes," Carmen said after a moment. "I'll see Jake."

"Are you…"

"I'm sure." Carmen stood, slowly. "Do I have clothes to change into, or do I have to go out wearing this thing?"

Carrie handed her a shopping bag. Carmen looked in, grimaced. "Gross," she said.

"They're your clothes, Carmen."

"And they're cute separate. But not together. Oh well, I guess no one is going to want to look at me any more anyway. Where's the bathroom?"

"You can change here."

"Turn around." She waited until Carrie turned around, then slipped out of the hospital gown and into the clothes Carrie had brought her. "Alright. I'm ready."

She started briskly towards the door. Carrie glanced around the room. "Don't you want to pack up your things?"

"I have everything I need."

Carrie crossed the room, picked up the flowers that Carmen had showed her so proudly a few days before. "We're not coming back here."

"Put them down. They'll die anyway."

Carrie looked at the canvas on the nightstand; she had recognized the style instantly. She picked up the painting. "What about this, Carmen?"

"No."

Carrie forced herself to say the words. "Your father would probably like to see you. Do you feel up for a visit?"

"I don't want to see him ever again."

Carrie started to reply, but Carmen walked out of the room and closed the door behind her. Carrie stood in the empty room staring at the door, then looked at the painting she was still holding in her hands. Her eyes drank in the midnight blue velvet of the background, the crystalline drops of dew on the crimson petals. She tilted the painting into the light and shivered at the effect: the rose looked like it was crying. She closed her eyes, then gently leaned the painting against the hospital pillow. She found Carmen waiting outside the hospital room, her hair arranged to cover the broken half of her face.

"Car's this way," Carrie said, and Carmen followed her out into the hospital's parking lot, head lowered, face covered, hands in her pockets and shoulders hunched against the cold.

Carrie stared at her. "Carmen, where's your coat?"

Carmen's teeth chattered. "I left it in the bag."

"Let's go get it."

"No. You said we weren't going back to the room."

"Isn't it Jake's jacket? Don't you think he'll want it?" Carrie handed her the keys when Carmen remained silent. "Get the car warmed up while I go back and get the coat. *Do not drive anywhere*, young lady."

Carmen took the keys. "I'm not planning on driving again anytime soon."

Carrie heard the engine start as she headed back to the hospital. She found the coat lying crumpled in the bag. She paused, then put the painting in the bag. She wanted to know the reason behind her daughter's sudden antipathy; Carmen had fought her tooth and nail for permission to keep seeing her father. She left the room, hoping that when she went out to the parking lot Carmen would still be there.

Sam pulled into the driveway and brought the car to a stop. "Call me when you're ready to come home."

"I wish you would have let me come by myself."

Sam paused. "I don't trust you with my car."

"I'd be careful."

"Sometimes you don't exercise the best judgment." Sam glanced at him. "Do you remember that speeding ticket of yours I had to pay last year?"

"I was going fifteen miles over the speed limit. On the highway. There was no one around me, and I was completely sober."

"You were lucky you were," Sam said. "Especially since you were going *forty-five* miles over the speed limit. But until your car gets out of the shop, you're going to have to put up with having me drive you around."

Jake sulked. "I'm not the one who totaled it."

"No. But you are the one who let a thirteen-year-old take it for a joy ride." Sam glanced at him. "Remember what I told you about Carmen."

"I will."

Sam returned his attention to the road. "Don't call too late."

"No later than eleven." Jake unbuckled his seatbelt. "Is that alright?"

Sam nodded.

Jake listened to the sound of wet tires on the slick road—then the silence, broken only by the sound of the rain hitting the pavement and melting the snow around him. He pulled his jacket more tightly around him but it was difficult; he had a stack of her books under his coat to protect them from the weather. He rang the doorbell and waited only a second before ringing it again. The house didn't have a porch or any kind of overhang, and he was getting soaked. He was about to start knocking when the door opened. He took a step back.

"Hey, Mrs. Crenshaw," he said. "Sorry I'm so late, but Dad was running late and since we only have the one car—"

"Did you bring her books?"

"Yeah, they're in my jacket. I brought her homework, too. I can come over tomorrow if she still needs more help, but tonight I…" He stuttered under her intense stare. "I have to leave by eleven."

Carrie looked at him, hard. "Carmen's a smart young woman."

"I know."

"She probably doesn't even need your help."

"Maybe with math," he said. "That always gives her trouble."

Carrie looked at him a moment longer, then turned away. "She's been under a lot of stress lately. If she seems tired, you're to leave immediately."

"Got it."

"Don't you dare make her feel self-conscious about her appearance," Carrie said, then turned her attention away from him. The table in the living room was covered with papers and she sat down in front of them, pen in hand. "Is that understood, Jake?"

"Yes, ma'am." He swallowed. "That's a lot of papers. How many students do you have?"

"I'm behind in grading."

"Too busy with your own writing?"

She looked at him pointedly. "I'm sure Carmen is waiting for you."

"Right. It was nice talking to you."

"Jake," she said, as he started to walk away. "Has Carmen mentioned her father to you at all recently? Is there anything I should know?"

He shook his head, aware that she was studying him closely. "The couple of times I took her there she wouldn't even let me come up to the front porch." He paused. "She made me wait in the car."

She met his eyes, then looked back down at the pile of papers in front of her. She heard him go up the stairs and say Carmen's name, and the sound of the door opening and closing. She would not worry; Carmen would have to find her own way. As hard as it was for Carrie to accept, Carmen would have to find her own way…or get lost in the woods.

"Come in," Carmen said, when he knocked.

He hesitated outside the door. "It's Jake."

"I know. Come in."

He proceeded with caution. "Hi."

Her face was distinctly turned away from him. She did not say anything.

He paused. "I...stopped by the hospital a couple of times. You were unconscious most of the time."

"Mom said I came and went."

"Yeah," he said, paused. "So I brought your homework."

She did not even thank him.

"So do you want to start with algebra, or would you rather do social studies, since you're better at—"

"I don't really want to think about school right now."

"Right." He put the books down, noticed a new black coat hanging on her closet door. "That's a really nice coat. Where did you get it?"

She followed his gaze to the black wool coat. "I bought it. A couple days after I got out of the hospital."

"It's really nice."

"See that plastic bag under it? Your coat is in there. I'm never going to wear it again."

"Thanks." He picked up the bag and paused. "So. How have you been?"

"Fine."

"Are you in a lot of pain?"

"No."

"Well, I guess that's—"

"You hit me again and I'll kill you." The expression on her face did not change. "I just wanted to say that straight out."

He hesitated. The silence dragged on.

"Can I see what you look like?" he said, finally.

"You can see what I look like from where you are."

"I meant..." He stopped himself. "You know, Carmen, that was a really stupid thing for you to have done, to take my car and then get it wrecked..."

She turned to face him, and for a moment his heart lurched. Then he realized she had brushed her long hair over the bad side of her face, that she looked no different except for a series of long, thin scratches along the left side of her complexion.

"Do you want me to pay for damages? I don't have the money right now, but even if I did I wouldn't give it to you."

"I want you to be more careful," he said. "That's all. I care about you."

She laughed, pulled her knees into her chest, put her head on her knees.

He cleared his throat. "I do."

"I believe you, Jake."

"I shouldn't have to defend myself."

"I said I believe you." She paused, frowning. "I wonder if you would still say that if you saw what I look like now."

"I would show you I would." He looked at her curiously. "If you'd let me see…"

She put her chin back on the tops of her knees. "I don't think so."

He slipped off his jacket and laid it across her dresser, invoking an instant protest from her.

"Don't put it there! You'll knock over my animals."

Ignoring the protest, leaving his jacket where he had placed it, he crossed the room to where she was sitting Indian-style on her bed. He cupped the good side of her face with his hand; she instantly became quiet and passive, her visible eye wide, alert. He gently touched the strip of hair covering her face.

"Don't," she said.

He brushed the hair away. She closed her eyes. He dropped his hand from her face, rested his hands on her shoulders.

"I love you, Carmen," he said.

She opened her eyes, stared at him. "Why are you smiling?"

He stared back at her, not letting the smile leave his face.

"Carmen!" She heard her mother call. "I'm going for a walk. Call me if you need anything!"

They both heard the front door close. Carmen kept her eyes locked on him as he crossed to the window.

"Your mother is crazy," he said. "It's freezing outside."

"So we're alone."

Her tone made him turn around. "Guess so."

"She'll be gone for an hour. I have a condom. Somewhere."

He paused. "Let's talk."

"Really, my face is okay. You won't hurt me."

"No."

She looked at him. "I thought that was why you said it."

"Said what?"

"That you love me." Her eyes were cold as she studied him. "Because you want to fuck around."

"Do you mind if I sit down?"

Her eyes narrowed. "Really, what is it? Am I too ugly to fuck and you're putting on a brave face? Or did your dad tell you to be nice to me?"

"No," he said, trying to control the anger that flared through him. "Not either of those."

"Why, then?" She crossed her arms in front of her chest. "Or are you just glad I got hurt so no one will know how much you fucked up my face *before* I got in the accident?"

He paused. "I never meant to hurt you."

"I find that hard to believe," she said, as he sat down beside her on the bed. "Are you trying to tell me that your fists found my face on your own?"

"I said I was sorry. It won't happen again."

She looked at him, her eyes slits. "So why don't you want to fuck me?"

"You're already good enough at fucking." He picked up a textbook from the stack, dropped it in front of her. "You could use some practice in algebra, though."

"Do you even understand this stuff?"

"I reviewed it last night. Your class is on chapter five." He opened the book and pushed it towards her. "Linear Equations. Are you ready to work?"

She got every problem right when he turned her loose on the homework assignment, though her attention remained fixed raptly on his face for the entirety of the lesson. He heard her mother return but she didn't seem to; he kept an eye on the clock while Carmen seemed oblivious to the time. At ten, he stood.

"I have to go. I can come back tomorrow if you want me to."

"You're leaving?"

"I have to get home." He opened his phone, placed a call.

"Jake?"

"One second, baby. Hey. Dad. Yeah." He closed his phone. "He'll be here in fifteen minutes. I want to walk part way, so I should get going." He paused. "Did you want to ask me something?"

"My face doesn't bother you." She looked at him incredulously.

"You look different." He shrugged. "But those stitches...they make you look tough. Exotic. Like you went through a tribal rite of passage. Or something."

Her eyes challenged him. "I'll wear my hair back like I did before."

"Like when you braid the strands away from your face? I like it when you do that."

"Then that's how I'll wear it," she said, looking away. "You're the only person whose opinion really matters to me. Everyone else can go to hell."

He kissed one of the strings of sutures that cut diagonally across her right eyebrow. "Still tender?"

"A little bit," she said, wishing she hadn't winced when his lips had brushed against her skin.

He did not seem to notice. He smiled at her. "I'll see you tomorrow. If you have any questions on the rest of that stuff you can call me. But don't call unless you have questions. You need to get rest, so you can come back to school."

"Goodnight, Jake." She paused. "Thanks for coming out."

"Not a problem." He gave her one final smile before he left. She was aware of his footsteps going down the stairs, then the creak of the front door opening, closing. She watched him trudge through the snow, and she heard him whistling.

Carrie woke in the middle of the night, feverish. The covers of the bed were tangled around her hot, sticky skin. She pushed them away and got up. The temperature of the room was stifling.

She heaved open her window and sighed in relief as the icy wind wrapped around her, then went to her desk. The words came and she did not stop them, even though the story was the one she had fought to keep herself from writing. After two hours of barely daring to breathe, she stopped. The pen dropped from her hand. She stood, aware for the first time that she had been shaking, that she was crying. She walked to the window, stared out.

"How can you still haunt me?" she asked, tormented eyes on the half moon. Her lips trembled. "Why does knowing you exist still seem so important..."

She heard a noise downstairs and froze. She left the room and proceeded cautiously. The kitchen light was on; she had turned it off before going to bed. Carrie crossed the hallway, peered in, then relaxed.

"Carmen. You scared me. It's late."

"Early," Carmen corrected. "I had to get up early, to finish my work."

"You have all of today to do your work. You should be asleep."

"I'd like to go back to school today," Carmen said, not looking at her. "I mean, if you'll take me. I'm not completely caught up, but I don't want to get any further behind."

"You want to go back to school so soon?"

"I think so. Jake helped convince me."

Carrie paused. "I'd be happy to take you to school."

"Leave in two hours, please," Carmen said as she closed the refrigerator door. "Why are you up, anyway, or do you usually get up this early?"

"I was thinking."

"About what?"

"About your father." She did not know what made her say the words, but she did not regret having said them. "And how much I still love him."

"Oh," Carmen said.

Carrie did not try to avoid the awkward silence which ensued. She waited for Carmen to leave.

"Why are you angry with him?" Carmen asked her, finally.

"Why are you?"

"I'm not. Anymore."

"You said you never—"

Carmen shrugged. "That was yesterday."

Carrie paused. "I suppose I'm not angry with him anymore, either."

"You should tell him that, not me."

"I doubt he would want to talk to me about it." She broke off, giving Carmen the opportunity to make an excuse and leave.

Carmen did not leave. "Why?"

Carrie looked at her. "My writing helps me in a lot of ways. Revisiting a work means revisiting a chunk of my life. Writing means reawakening the same feelings and keeping them alive. Without writing and revising, the memories would die, maybe like they should. But I wouldn't expect it to be the same for someone who doesn't write."

"What about someone who paints?"

"Carmen."

"Just talk to him."

"What if he won't talk to me?"

"He will." Her eyes widened. "Fuck! It's four-thirty—"

"Carmen—"

"I'm sorry for swearing. I'm going to my room anyway. I have way too much work to do to be standing here talking any longer." She paused. "Besides, I'm not the one you need to be talking to."

Carrie stared after her, then sat down. It was still too early for the sun to be up, and through the window she could see the stars, tiny dots that somehow shone in the overwhelming darkness of the sky. She sat and stared at the stars, transfixed. A numbness had set into her sleep-deprived mind and her thoughts to sludge. Rousing herself, she went back to her room. She shut the window, set her alarm for six-thirty, and laid on her bed. She did not hope to sleep, and was not surprised when she did not.

Carmen moved away from the cafeteria's assembly line and frantically scanned the crowded tables. He wasn't at the table where they normally sat, and she was afraid to approach his friends, who were all older than her. She steeled herself, then went over to the table.

"Hey guys," she said. "Is Jake here today?"

One of them nudged another. "Jake's bitch."

Her tray trembled. "What did you say?"

The boy looked at her. "What happened to you, scarface?"

"I'm surprised you even noticed my face," she said, her eyes flashing. "Considering you're staring at my tits. You want to look me in my good eye when you talk to me, motherfucker?"

The boy whistled, then spoke to the boy beside him. "I'm surprised Jake hasn't taught her to shut up yet."

Carmen threw her tray at him, then leaned towards him when he looked back at her, stunned. "Get up."

Jake's other friends were all looking at them now; some were trying to hide smiles.

"Get the fuck up," she said, her voice low. "I heard what you said, and I think you're the one who needs to shut up."

"Is she serious?" the offender asked the group. "Does she honestly think I'd fight a chick?"

"You can talk to me," she said, her hands balling into fists. "I'm right here. Or are you such a coward that you can talk about me, but you can't talk *to* me?"

One of them laughed at her. She inhaled sharply, then felt a hand on her shoulder. She turned.

"Hey, Carmen." Mark George smiled at her. "Hey, how's it going? I was wondering if you wanted to eat lunch with me today so we could have a chance to talk about our chemistry notes that are due tomorrow."

"Okay." She turned from the group of Jake's friends, her cheeks burning. "Assholes."

The group of Jake's friends had sobered as soon as Mark had appeared. They exchanged uneasy glances. "Hey, Carmen, we're only joking. You know you can sit here whether we want you to or not. You always do."

"Come on," she said to Mark, flipping them her middle finger as she started down the aisles of the cafeteria. She stopped so suddenly that Mark almost ran into her.

"Sorry," she said. "I don't know where you're sitting."

"Here," he said. "I'll show you."

He led her away from the cafeteria into a brightly lit classroom adjacent to the cafeteria.

"I always eat in here."

"Where exactly are we?"

"The APP room."

"APP?"

"Advanced Placement Program," he said. "Here, I'll introduce you to some of—"

She shifted. "I'm probably not allowed to be in here, Mark. I'm in honors, but I'm not in any Advanced."

"It's fine," he said. "Everyone is really nice."

"I don't see anyone."

He was heading to a door in the back of the classroom. "Yeah. The APP room is actually through here. I was only in the classroom because I was trying to get some homework done and it's quieter." He paused. His direct gaze on her face made her realize how exposed her marred skin was. "Do those guys have something against you?"

She shook her head and made no gesture to cover her face. His fixed focus didn't make her feel self-conscious. "They're my boyfriend's friends. They always treat me like that, more or less."

He looked surprised. "I didn't know you had a boyfriend."

"Yeah." She sat down. "There's a lot you don't know about me. Some of it would shock you. Can we sit here? I don't feel like making new friends right now."

"I don't mind," he said, sitting down at the desk beside hers. "I was sitting here anyway."

"Then you saw me talking to those guys. And you came over and rescued me."

"You were doing fine by yourself," he said, blushing. "I just wanted to talk chemistry with you, since you've been out for so long and we have these major notes due tomorrow..."

"Will you tell me something?" she asked.

"What?"

"Do you think I'm ugly?"

"No," he said. "We all know you were in a terrible accident, Carmen. I'm just glad you're alive."

She smiled encouragingly. "Come on. I look like Frankenstein."

"Frankenstein was the doctor, not the monster." He paused. "And even then, you'd have to be the monster's bride...but you don't look like her either."

"All these lines," she said, her eyebrows arched. "All the breaks..."

"They look..." he paused, looked down. "Never mind."

"What?"

"The lines look like the earth's fault lines," he said. He stood up. "Here, I'll show you."

He went to the back of the classroom, pulled up a website on the computer there. He clicked on an image, then turned to her.

"See?" he said.

She stood behind him and looked over his shoulder. "How did you know that?"

He turned back to the computer screen. "My dad was a geologist. My mom and I would go with him on his trips sometimes. We were in Peru when he explained to me about the fault lines. It's one of the happiest memories I have. It was just me and him, looking at a bunch of dirt and rocks, and he started explaining..." He paused. "We found out the month after that my dad had a brain tumor."

"What happened to your dad?"

"He died. Last year."

"I'm sorry," she said.

"I'm not," he said, getting up without looking at her. "He would have suffered a lot more if he had still been alive right now." He paused. "Do you have a lunch? We only have about five minutes left."

"I don't have one," she said. "I left it in the cafeteria."

"You can have the rest of mine if you want."

"It's your lunch."

"I don't mind sharing."

Keeping her eyes on him, she reached for his brown paper bag and peered into it. "There's still a whole peanut butter sandwich in here and a juice box."

"I pack double. In case I need extra." He paused. "There's a.... stray, in my neighborhood."

"A homeless guy?"

"No. A dog. He's my friend."

"I don't want to eat his food." She pushed the bag back towards him. "What's his name?"

"I call him Oreo."

"That's cute."

He paused. "I could bring something tomorrow for you."

"Thanks. But I'll probably eat with Jake tomorrow."

"Your boyfriend, right?" he asked, his cheeks crimson.

"Of a year." She paused. "What did you want to go over in chemistry?"

"I thought you might need help? Catching up, I mean."

"I caught myself up."

He looked down. "I just didn't want you to get behind. I did all the notes already and we can add your name to the top since it was a partner activity and that will take care of that. Maybe some other time I can explain the experiments to you so you understand about the reactions that took place and…"

The bell rang and she stood. "Mark."

"What?"

"We have chem next," she said. "Walk me there?"

"Sure," he said.

She smiled at him. "You're a real gentleman."

She did not have to look at him to know he was blushing, so she did not look.

Carmen successfully evaded Carrie's questions and retreated to her room. She sat in her room on her bed, listening to the steady pulse of her music as she read through Act Five of *Romeo and Juliet*. One more scene to go, and she would be completely caught up. Mainly because Jake had helped her with the math, and Mark had done all the science. Mark had insisted on getting her credit for the assignments, even though she hadn't done anything to help him. And he had not asked for anything back. She resolutely turned a page. Her phone rang. Pushing the play away from her, she answered.

"Hello?"

"Hey, babe."

She paused. "Hi."

"It's Jake."

"I know."

"Are you mad at me?"

"Why would I be?"

He paused. "I heard you went back to school today."

"Yeah, I did."

"That's great. How'd it go?"

"I was fine."

Another pause. "I wanted to be there, when you went back. In case anyone gave you problems."

"No one gave me any problems."

"I heard my friends gave you some problems."

"Oh," she said. "That."

"Yeah, that."

"No big deal. They don't matter."

"They think you're crazy."

"I don't care what they think."

He paused. "You threw your lunch at them?"

Her eyes scanned a monologue. "Yeah. I did."

"And tried to fight one of them?"

"Not my fault." She turned the page.

"That's what I love about you."

"Don't use that word."

He paused. "What are you doing right now?"

"Reading." She flipped a page. "The stupid translation takes up the whole right side of the book. Do they think we can't understand Shakespearean English or something?"

"What are you reading?"

"*Romeo and Juliet.*"

"How is it?"

"Fabulous," she said, closing the book. "But they were so stupid."

"To kill themselves over love?"

"Yeah."

"I think they were romantic."

She rolled her eyes. "You are *such* a sarcastic asshole."

He laughed. "So tell me about your day."

She didn't think he would appreciate hearing about her flirtation with Mark, so she made sure it was the first thing she told him about. "I'm caught up in science, isn't that great? My lab partner, Mark, he's so sweet…"

"Yeah," Jake said.

"He did all our work," she said, already hearing the jealousy in his voice. "Isn't that *wonderful?*"

He paused. "My friends said you ate lunch with a guy, when I wasn't there."

"Jealous?"

There was a pause. "I'll be in school tomorrow. We can eat lunch together."

"Okay."

"Carmen? How did you wear your hair today?"

"What?"

"Did you wear it over your face?"

"Yeah." She had felt fine around Mark, but she had lost her confidence because of the encounter with Jake's friends and had gone to the bathroom to rearrange her hair as soon as the lunch bell rang. She had felt slightly guilty while doing it; she remembered what Mark had said about the scars, that they looked like the earth's fault lines...

"I don't understand how you can see when you wear your hair like that. You don't have anything to be ashamed of."

"I'm not ashamed."

"Good, because you shouldn't be."

"Is something bothering you?" she asked.

"No."

"Don't you think I'm prettier when I wear my hair over my face?"

"I don't think it makes a difference."

"Then why do you care?"

He paused. "So do you need any more help?"

"No," she said, "All caught up."

"Then we should celebrate. Can I take you out tonight?"

She paused. "No. I don't think so."

There was a silence on the other line. "You're probably not even allowed to go out on school nights."

"Goodnight, Jake." She dropped the phone on her bed, tiptoed out into the hallway. She went down the stairs and checked the kitchen and living room before heading to Carrie's study. The door was closed. She knocked. Carrie opened the door immediately.

"Mom, can I go out tonight?"

Carrie looked momentarily worried. "Can't you tell Jake to meet you some other—"

"I'm not going out with Jake. I want to meet up with my chem lab partner."

"Oh." She looked relieved. "As long as you're not out past eleven. Do you need a ride somewhere?"

"No."

"Be careful, Carmen."

She went back upstairs to her room, saw that Jake had called her during her brief absence but ignored the message he had left her. She called Mark.

"Hello?" He sounded unsure as he picked up the phone.

"Hey, Mark. It's Carmen. Do you want to take me to the movies tonight?"

"Sure," he said. "Oh, Carmen, I forgot that tonight is a school night."

"Is that a problem?"

"No," he said, after a pause. "Do you want my mom to come pick you up, or—"

"I'll meet you there. Fifteen minutes?"

"Okay."

She grabbed her coat and carefully arranged her hair to cover her face, then pulled on a wool cap to keep it in place. As she walked the distance to the theater, she thought about her choice to see Mark—and how it hadn't felt like a choice, since she didn't want to see Jake. She watched her breath puff out in visible streams, but she didn't mind the cold and soon she reached the cinema. She saw Mark waiting by the ticket booth, and quickly went to meet him. She noticed that he became flustered when she smiled at him.

"Hi, Mark."

"Hello, Carmen." He paused. "You look very nice."

She realized he was only being polite. "Thank you. Do you know what you want to see?"

"I don't even know what's showing." He paused. "I don't usually go to the movies."

She tried to hide a smile. "Why don't you order your ticket first, and then I'll get mine."

He hesitated. "I thought I'd pay for your ticket."

"I want to pay for myself," she said, then added slyly, "this time."

He seemed delighted that there might be a *next* time. "If you're sure…" He walked to the ticket booth, looking confused. "One, please."

He got his ticket, stepped aside. She moved up.

"Hey, Brandon," she said. "I'm with him."

The young man stared at her, looked away.

"Five dollars," he said.

"Shoot. I forgot my money. You wouldn't mind if I just went in this once, would—"

"Five dollars."

She was conscious that he was not looking at her. "You let me in for free all the—"

"If you want to see the movie," he said. "It will be five dollars, Miss."

Her eyes flashed. "Are you serious?"

"Here. I've got you covered." Mark put down a five dollar bill on the counter. "You can pay me back later if you want."

She swatted the money away as the young man behind the counter reached for it. "I don't want to go now."

Mark looked helplessly back at the employee. "Can I get a refund, then?"

"I can do that," Brandon said, looking relieved. "If you just slide your ticket—"

"No." Carmen put her hand on Mark's arm, glared at Brandon. "He's keeping it. Come on, Mark."

Mark stared at her as she dragged him away. "I don't want to see the movie without you."

"I'll meet you inside."

"How do you—"

"Give me five minutes," she said. "I'll meet you inside."

He glanced at her. "Okay."

Mark went inside the theater. She went back to the ticket window, then tapped on the glass when Brandon ignored her.

"Brandon."

"What?" He looked up reluctantly.

She smiled. "No hard feelings, okay? I mean, it's great that you're finally doing your job."

He remained suspicious. "I still can't let you in."

"I understand." She smiled. "Like I said, it's great that you're doing your job, even if you are doing it for the wrong reasons."

He said nothing, and he did not look at her as she left. Her internal clock told her she had about three minutes left. She made sure her hair was covering the scarred part of her face. She went to the theater's other entrance and walked past the ticket booth, smiling at the ticket-taker as she walked by.

"I left my friend inside," she said, seeing the question form on his lips.

He nodded at her, confused. As soon as she passed him, the smile dropped from her face.

She found Mark waiting for her in the lobby and tapped him on the shoulder. He turned.

"Hey," she said. "Let's go."

"How did you get in?"

"Back entrance."

"But you don't have a ticket," he started.

"Do you want to say that a little louder?" she whispered. "I don't need one. I walked in here like I belonged. You can get away with anything if you do it with confidence." She paused. "Can you buy me some popcorn? I'm hungry."

He frowned. "You won't let me buy you a ticket, but you'll let me buy popcorn?"

"We can share popcorn."

"I'll be right back."

She watched the previews until he came back, heard him apologizing to the people he had to pass in order to get to her. He sat down, handed her the popcorn.

"What would you have done if your plan hadn't worked?" he whispered.

"There's a window in the back alley." She paused. "It leads to the theater's employee room. From there, take a left and climb the stairs, and you're in the lobby. That's what I did when I was younger."

"What if someone saw you?"

"Confidence," she said, tossing a handful of popcorn into her mouth.

"But—"

"Shh," she said. "Can't you see the nasty looks people are giving us for talking? The movie's starting. What did you pick anyway?"

"I thought you looked before we came in here. I just followed you."

"Looks like a horror movie. That means I'm going to end up cuddling you."

"Excuse me," the person sitting behind them said. "Are you going to be talking through the entire movie?"

Carmen turned. "We could do other things, if you'd prefer."

The woman got up and moved her seat. Carmen turned, saw Mark staring at her. She looked back at him directly.

"Here," he said. "Have some more popcorn."

She threw a kernel at him and giggled as it hit him on the forehead, then turned forward as the other people shushed them in hissing voices. She took hold of his hand halfway through the movie. He glanced over to see her watching the screen intently.

"You're really into this," he whispered, feeling how cold her hand was in his.

"Shh," she said.

The movie ended, and the lights came on. She stared enraptured at the credits as they rolled by and made him wait until the screen went blank, then she turned to him.

"That was the best movie I've ever snuck into."

"Do you sneak in often?"

"Brandon always lets me in for free, no strings attached. Until tonight. Come on." She grabbed his hand, pulled him into the theater's lobby. "Can I borrow five dollars? I promise I'll pay you back."

"Sure." He reached into his wallet and handed her a bill. "What are you—"

She took the money and headed towards the concession stand. He followed her.

"Excuse me," she said to the cashier at the popcorn stand. "I need to see a manager."

"Is there a problem?" the guy asked.

"Yes, there is. I want to see a manager."

The popcorn man exchanged a look with the soda girl. "One minute, ma'am."

"I hate it when people call me 'ma'am'," she whispered to Mark as she shook her hair in front of her face. "It makes me feel so old."

A man came out. "Someone said you wanted to speak to a manager, Miss?"

Carmen nodded and offered him the five dollars. "Here, I want to pay for a ticket."

"You can buy tickets at the front counter if you want to see a show."

"Oh, I already saw the show I wanted to see. The guy out front let me in without a ticket. I just thought you should know how sweet he is."

"The person out front?" the manager asked.

She nodded, smiling, aware that Mark had stiffened beside her. "He was so nice when I told him I didn't have any money. But my boyfriend just let me borrow some money, and I feel really bad about not paying."

"Keep your money," the manager said. "Thank you for bringing this matter to my attention."

"Really, I can keep my money? That's so kind of you. Have a wonderful night, sir." Carmen took Mark's hand and led him out of the theater, then smiled at Brandon as they passed. Mark glanced at her, but did not speak until they had walked a short distance away from the theater.

"What was that all about?" he asked, turning to her.

"I'm sorry for calling you my boyfriend, Mark. It just made explaining easier."

"Not about that."

"Wait for it," she said, her eyes on the ticket window.

Mark looked and saw the manager of the theater go to the ticket window and start gesticulating wildly.

Carmen turned and started walking. "You should probably wait here for your mom to pick you up. I walked, so I'm going to go home."

"I walked, too." He paused when she turned. "I can walk with you, part way."

"Sure." She looked over at him, saw that he was frowning. "Is something bothering you?"

He paused. "That wasn't right, Carmen, what you did at the movie theater. That guy might lose his job, and he didn't let you in for free. He was doing his job."

"He's let me in a hundred times before without a ticket," she said. "Maybe not a hundred, but you get the picture. Now, all of a sudden, he won't because I look like the monster's bride..." She paused. "He got what he deserved."

"But he was doing his job."

"Yeah. And the guy around back wasn't. But you know what, Mark? Who cares? Why not reward wrong and punish right? Why not shake things up a bit?"

He paused, thoughtful. "That's an interesting philosophy. But I'm not sure I agree with it. I think I side with Kant, that you should act only as you think everyone else should..."

"It's not like he's innocent," she said. "But here's your five bucks back."

"I don't want it."

"If you really feel that badly about it, you can give the money to the theater as a donation."

He reluctantly accepted the money from her. She paused. "Thanks for taking me out. I really liked the movie."

"I'm glad." He paused. "I should probably turn here. Will you be safe walking home by yourself?"

"I'll be fine."

"I'll see you tomorrow." He started walking away from her, then stopped and turned back. "Carmen. I...I had fun, too."

She smiled. "Bye, Mark."

She didn't get home until after eleven, but Carrie asked her no questions. Carrie was actually relieved that she had been out with someone besides Jake. On reflection, Carmen realized that so was she.

Macaroni and cheese was what the cafeteria served the next day. Carmen waited in line as a gooey mass of the yellow glop landed on her plate, then turned and scanned the crowded cafeteria. She located Jake at his usual table and went to sit by him.

"Hey," she said.

"Hey, babe. Sit down." He scooted over, making room for her.

She stood and surveyed the table. No one else at the table made eye contact with her. She sat down.

"You're wearing your hair," he said. "Like that."

"I like it better this way."

"I don't."

"I thought you said it didn't matter." She stuck her plastic fork into the oozing mess. "How was your day?" he asked.

She noticed that several of his friends had shifted, and felt Jake stiffen beside her. She looked up. She smiled.

"Hey, Carmen," Mark said.

"Hey, Mark."

"Ready for chemistry today?" Mark ignored Jake's friends and Jake's acid stare.

"Can't wait. Thanks again for doing the notes." She felt Jake slide his arm around her and glanced at him. He was looking directly at Mark, and Mark was looking directly at her. "By the way, this is Jake."

"Pleased to meet you," Mark said, in a monotone. "Carmen, I thought we could go over the notes together before class one last time, before we turn them in."

"I'm sure they're fine." She glanced from Mark to Jake and back. "I trust you."

"Okay." He seemed reluctant to leave. "I'll see you in chem."

Her eyes followed him to the APP room entrance. Beside her, Jake's friends stifled sniggers; one look at s face, however, told her he found nothing funny about the situation.

"What was that about?" he asked.

"What do you mean, what was it about?" She shrugged. "Weren't you here? We were talking about—"

"*Chemistry*," Jake said, through his teeth.

"What was with the arm thing?" she asked him. "Getting possessive, Jakey?"

"No way."

She turned away from him; his friends were pretending to be oblivious to the whispered fight. "I'm thinking about cutting my hair. Would you mind?"

"No," he said. "I wouldn't mind. I don't care one fucking way or the other."

She stabbed at her macaroni and cheese. "Just wanted to check with you."

He pushed his tray away, stood up. "I'm not hungry."

"Neither am I."

He sat back down. "Maybe I'm hungry after all."

"Don't be mad. Here, you can have my macaroni and cheese. And my fork, since you just broke that one."

He took her fork. "Thanks."

She stood. "Maybe I want to look over those chemistry notes after all."

"Carmen, sit down. I'm not mad."

She sat down.

"How short are you going to cut your hair?" he asked.

She shrugged. "Guess you'll see when I'm done."

The bell rang. He kissed her lightly on the cheek, the damaged one. He had to pull back her hair to do it. She noticed everything he did, and when they parted in the hallway, she turned and watched him go.

Carmen hoped Jake would prove her theory wrong. She hoped he would prove to her that she was paranoid. He had told her he loved her, and the words had made her melt. At first.

Carmen waited until Carrie was asleep, then she went into the bathroom. She closed the door, locked it. She pulled a razor from the cabinet of the sink, then stared at her reflection. She closed the mirror door. She had scissors to start the job. The razor would finish it.

She held a skein of her hair in one hand. She didn't care what anyone thought; the truth was more important. She cut, close to the roots, and the hair fell to the floor and laid there like limp snakes. She paused, trembling as she stared at the hair on the floor, and then she snipped again. After the third snip she started to cry quietly. Then she turned it into a game, becoming interested in the change of her appearance with each snip. Soon her hair clogged the floor around her feet, and she felt liberated. She looked grotesque.

She wet down the patchy clumps of hair that remained, then rubbed shaving cream over her head. Carefully she slid the razor over the cream, watching with fascination as her scalp was exposed in shining, naked strips. She rinsed her head and patted it dry, then collected the tendrils of her hair from the floor and the sink. She tied off the trash bag, full, and left it by the door; she would take it outside tomorrow, since Carrie was sure to wake up and question her if she heard the front door open. Carmen made sure the bathroom was spotless, then she went back to her room and curled under her covers. The pillow felt cool and soft under her shaved head. As she drifted off to sleep, Carmen thought about how she was happy with how she looked for the first time in her life.

"Good morning," Carmen said. She went to the refrigerator, opened it, peered in. "Do we have any orange juice? I don't see any in here."

Carrie stared.

"Do we have any orange juice, Carrie?" she repeated.

"Downstairs in the refrigerator," Carrie said. "On the left. By the cabbage."

"Thanks."

She went downstairs, rooted around until she found the carton. When she went back into the kitchen, Carrie was standing by the sink.

"Carmen." Her voice was neutral. "Why did you shave your head?"

"I don't know. It seemed like a good idea."

Carmen unscrewed the top of the orange juice container. "Don't you like it?"

"Well," Carrie said. "Your school doesn't have a very good heating system, and there are drafts." She paused. "We should probably buy you a hat."

"I'm not allowed to wear hats in school."

"You lose fifty percent of your heat through your head."

"I hadn't thought of that."

"We can get you a hat after school. How about that?"

"I guess." Carmen paused. "I'm going back to bed."

"You can't go to school in your pajamas."

"I wasn't planning on it." She paused. "You can stop looking at me like that."

"I wasn't expecting you to shave your head."

"Just don't schedule me for an appointment with a shrink. I'm not crazy."

Carrie paused. "I told your father he could stop by today and see you. If you wanted a visit."

"Sure," she said, then grinned. "You actually talked to him?"

"I did."

"That's unexpected. But see, not everything unexpected is bad." She breezed out of the kitchen.

Carrie picked up her mug and dumped the tea down the sink. Twenty minutes later she went upstairs and knocked on Carmen's door. When there was no response, she opened the door and found Carmen standing in front of her vanity mirror, staring at her reflection. Carrie braced herself for the imminent explosion. Instead, Carmen turned and looked at her calmly.

"I'm ready," she said.

Carrie saw, on second glance, that Carmen already had her backpack slung over her shoulder. When Carmen looked at her, Carrie detected something beneath the indignant confidence of her daughter's external appearance—a fear, an uncertainty, a desire for approval. Then the flash was gone, and there was only Carmen and her impatience.

"Let me get you one of my hats," Carrie said.

"I don't want the hat. Come on. We have to leave now or I'm going to be late."

"You won't be late. We're leaving early enough to—"

"Can we just leave? Please?"

"This will only take a minute."

"We aren't allowed to wear hats in school," Carmen insisted. "They're afraid we're going to hide weapons in them or use them as gang symbols or something."

"This is a special occasion."

"I don't want the hat. I'm not ashamed, and I don't want to hide the fact that I'm bald."

"You aren't bald," Carrie said. "You shaved your head. If you don't want to wear a hat, you might want to consider changing into something warmer. Your school is drafty, and you've already complained about how cold you get…"

Without protest, Carmen went back into her room and pulled a large navy blue hoodie over her head.

"In case I get cold," she said. "Some of our teachers let us wear the hoods up."

Carrie glanced at her as they walked out to the car. "Where did you get that hoodie, Carmen?"

She shrugged. "Jake let me borrow it. I'm going to give it back to him today."

They drove mostly in silence, but Carrie detained her when she pulled up to the school. "Call me if anyone gives you any trouble today, or if you want to come home."

Carmen unbuckled her seatbelt. "People have always given me trouble about my appearance. The only new thing will be the direction of their comments. Different side of the same animal. I can handle it."

Carrie started to respond, but Carmen had already climbed out of the car and closed the door with a bang behind her. Carrie already knew how Carmen would handle her peers' reactions: head up, shoulders back, pure self-assertion. Carrie watched until Carmen had disappeared into the double doors of the school, then she put the car in gear and drove out of the school's parking lot. She saw the lane she needed to take to get to the school where she taught and realized she could not take it. She switched lanes. Her heart pounded.

"So this is what the inside of the boy's locker room looks like," Carmen said, dropping her backpack onto one of the benches in front of the rows of bright blue lockers. His grip on her arm was hurting her, and she was trying to ignore the pain. "I've always wanted to come in here, but I was always afraid someone would catch me."

"This is too much, Carmen."

"You're the one who brought me in here," she said. "I said I was always afraid that someone would come in and—"

576

He shook her, scowling. "Why did you shave your head?"

She crossed her arms in front of her chest. "I felt like it."

She felt his anger in the marks his fingers left on her arms. The locker room was deserted that early in the morning, though other students would be arriving shortly. She went to an empty locker, opened it. "Why are these things so small? Do you think they made the lockers like this so that the seniors couldn't haze the freshmen by stuffing…"

He grabbed her shoulders and forced her to face him. "What were you thinking?"

She did not flinch. "I thought you'd like it."

"You thought I would like it? Are you insane?"

"I really don't think I am, Jake," she said, cooly. "You might be. But I was thinking that now you won't have to worry. About other guys stealing me from you—not looking like I do. I don't like you when you get jealous."

He paused. "That's really why you did it?"

"That's why you weren't upset after my accident, wasn't it?" she said. "You never liked how pretty I was, did you?" Her eyes burned at him. "You didn't like the attention I got."

"I liked that you were pretty," he said, letting her go, then caught himself. "Of course, you're still real pretty."

"The accident wasn't enough." She smiled. "But no one will want me now."

He looked at her. "I can't believe you did this for me. You have a lot of courage, Carmen."

"Are you happy now, Jake?"

He nodded. "You're amazing."

She stared at him. "I always thought you'd stop liking me if I were ugly. But now I see that it's not like that."

"Yeah." His eyes darkened as he moved closer to her.

She took a step back. "I see it's not about how I look."

"No."

She stood absolutely still. When his eyes met hers, she smiled. The smile frightened him.

"You've never wanted to love me," she said. "You've only wanted to own me."

"Don't get melodramatic, Carmen."

"I'm perfectly calm," she said.

"Then why are you acting so crazy?"

"I'm not crazy, Jake. Just tired of you."

He paused. "Are you breaking up with me?"

"I hadn't said so, but yeah, sounds like a good idea." She stepped away from him. "I'm tired of how you treat me."

His eyes flashed, and he started towards her. She picked up her backpack hurriedly and started towards the entrance of the locker room, but he caught up with her.

"You're a bitch," he said, gripping her arm. "Who's going to put up with your moods, your temper, your…" He leered. "Who's going to want you? You're a freak."

"In more ways than one," she said. "Let me go."

His grip on her tightened. She stared at him, not flinching.

"Jake," she said. "If you don't let me go, I'll scream. I'll tell everyone you're an abuser…"

He looked at her, and she looked back at him. He let her go.

"I'm not an abuser," he said, backing away from her.

"You're also no longer my boyfriend." She took a step away from him. "So stay away from me."

He took a step towards her, and she fled to the safety of the hallway. "Carmen!"

She turned and saw him standing at the entrance to the locker room, his face livid. She ducked into the first classroom on her right.

She rearranged her expression into a smile.

"Good morning, Miss Carpenter," she said.

The pause, the expression on her teacher's face, reminded her of how she looked. Carmen realized that she had forgotten about shaving her head in the past few moments.

"Good morning, Carmen," Miss Carpenter said, after a pause. "You're here early."

"I like being here before everyone else comes in. But I wanted to talk to you about what I missed when I was in the hospital."

"You seem to be caught up."

"Oh, really?" She thought about Jake prowling around the halls. "Can I just…do you mind if I stay in your room for a couple of minutes?"

"I would enjoy the company."

"I brought a book. I'll just read and let you finish your planning. I know all about that, because my mom's a teacher, too."

"What book did you bring?"

"Faust."

"That's challenging material for someone your age."

"Oh, it's a translation, because I don't know German. But I like being challenged." She paused. "You know, Miss Carpenter, it really would have been better if you had asked about my head instead of staring at it. People are so curious, but they never ask. They just pretend like things don't exist."

"I wasn't thinking about your head, Carmen. I was wondering if you would like to discuss Faust with me during homeroom sometime." Miss Carpenter smiled. "I wanted to be an English teacher once."

"Really? But you're such a great chemistry teacher, Miss Carpenter."

"You're a great student. Did Mark help you get caught up?"

"He did."

"He's a nice boy."

"I should be going," Carmen said. She had seen Jake pass by the room and continue down the hall. "I don't want to be late for homeroom. But I'd like to talk to you about Faust sometime."

The bell rang. Carmen returned Miss Carpenter's smile before drifting out into the halls. By the time she entered her homeroom, her thoughts had taken her so far away that she was not even aware of the whispering and stares directed at her.

Very few people asked Carmen directly about her appearance—but she became aware of their whispers as the day progressed. By lunchtime she had retreated into herself, hurt and confused. Several times she had reached to twirl her hair and it was not there. Several times she had a sarcastic reply ready in response to a jab at her appearance, but not the confidence to deliver the barbed remark. In shaving her head, she felt like she had become a different person.

She paused as she exited the kitchen with her tray. She had left her last class before lunch five minutes early so she could get her food without confronting a crowd of students. She crossed the cafeteria quickly, her head down, bee-lining for the classroom Mark had shown her. She could pretend she belonged there. Confidence. She set down her tray, looked at the food. Her stomach curdled. Macaroni and cheese again, and she had lost her appetite for it. The side door to the classroom opened.

She glanced up and froze. Mark stood in the doorway, a load of books in his arms. He stared at her, equally paralyzed.

"Hi, Mark," she said, finally.

"Carmen?" His eyes were wide with disbelief.

"Yeah, it's me."

He let the door to the classroom close and started towards her. "What happened to your hair?"

"I shaved my head," she said. "I wanted to."

He dropped his books onto the desk beside her. "Why?"

"I don't have to have a reason."

"But I'm sure you do."

She paused. "Maybe I wanted to see how people would react."

"I thought you didn't care about people's reactions."

"Maybe I needed to prove it to myself."

"I don't think you're telling me the truth." He paused and looked at her tray. "If you don't want to eat that we can swap lunches. I love Mac and Cheese, but my mom never buys it because of the proportion of transfats and—"

"What do you have?"

"Peanut butter and jelly. And applesauce and juice." He paused as she grabbed his brown paper bag. "Leave some for Oreo."

"How is he?"

"Mom says I might be able to adopt him."

"Awesome," she said. "Can I come over and see him if you do?"

"Yeah."

He was actually blushing. *Still?* She pushed her tray towards him. "You don't mind if I eat in here today?"

"I'd be happy for your company. And I'll vouch for you if someone comes in and asks who you are."

"Do you think anyone will?"

"No, I don't think anyone will." He paused. "So what's the reason for shaving your head?"

"My real reason?"

He nodded.

"Maybe everyone expects me to look good all the time and I'm tired of it." She hesitated. "Maybe I don't want to be beautiful any more."

"You seem to have a bit of an ego."

"Wrong answer," she said. "You're supposed to say I still look beautiful. Unless you don't think I do."

"No, I don't think you do." He paused. "But your beauty was always a distraction anyway."

She stared at him, unable to believe that he thought just like Jake. "How could you say that to me?"

"You asked," he answered. "But I don't understand why you're angry about it. I'm just saying what you said."

"What did I say?" she asked indignantly.

"You said that you don't want to be beautiful because it keeps people from valuing you for your true self. I would never want to be handsome for the same reason." He paused. "Since I've been labeled a dork, I'm free to act however I want. The only thing I have to worry about is expanding my mind, and I like it that way."

"But you are handsome," she said. "And that's *not* what I said. Don't make what I said sound so profound. You can admit that I'm shallow. I won't be offended."

"You aren't shallow."

"No?" she asked, standing up. "Why do you think I went out with Jake? It sure as hell wasn't because he treated me well."

"He is so much older than you are," he said quietly.

"Yeah. He's older than me. Which means he's more experienced than I...was." She paused. "You're a nice person, Mark, but you're a *boy*." Her words caught in her throat as he leaned in closer to her. The lack of distance between them and her reaction to him startled her.

"I bet you haven't even kissed a girl before," she whispered.

He hesitated. She grabbed him by the collar of his polo shirt.

"Do it," she said. "I dare you."

Suddenly he was kissing her, and she felt like an explosion had gone off in her head. She had never felt like that when Jake had kissed her. Somehow Mark's arms had locked around her waist, and somehow her arms were twined around his neck.

She stopped for air. "My *god* you're a good kisser."

"I'm sorry, Carmen." He let her go. "I shouldn't have done that."

"No, you shouldn't have." She paused. "How many girls have you been with?"

"None," he said, his face turning red.

"Come on, tell me. I won't be mad. Promise."

"I'm telling you the truth. Zero. I'm not ashamed of it." He stood, started pacing. "I apologize for how I treated you. I know you have a boyfriend, and I shouldn't have done that."

"I told you to kiss me." She walked over to him. "And Jake never apologizes to me. Only once, after he fucked me up pretty badly."

"I really didn't need to know that."

"I didn't mean...like that." She paused, not able to explain further. "I'm sorry I'm arguing with you."

"I like arguing," he said. "As long as you're not angry with me. Though you should be."

"I'm not angry," she said, picking up his lunch bag. "But I should go, since I'm making you uncomfortable."

"You're not making me uncomfortable. I'd like you to stay, if you—"

"No, I should go." She hesitated. "But I...I really don't want to go out there. I didn't think it would be so hard, facing people."

"You could make the experience into an experiment," he said. "Like we do in chemistry."

"What?"

"Make the experience into an experiment," he repeated. "Pretend like you're collecting data for a sociology class or something. Track the reactions of people around you, and see if you can find a pattern. Then you won't take it so personally."

"I'll try it," she said. "I'll see you in chem."

"I really like you, Carmen."

She turned and looked at him. He looked directly back at her. Not knowing what to say, she left him there and went to brave the inside of the cafeteria.

She dumped the remains of her lunch into the trash near the door of the cafeteria and stacked the blue plastic tray on top of the other ones. When she heard Jake call her name, his continued existence in her life came as a shock. She had forgotten about him.

"Carmen!"

She looked at him indifferently as he approached.

"I'm sorry," he said.

She crossed her arms in front of her chest. "If you have anything else you want to say, you had better say it now."

"I thought maybe you didn't mean what you said to me this morning." He smiled sheepishly. "Maybe we both lost our tempers a little."

"I meant what I said."

"Did I say I was sorry?"

"You could say it again."

"I'm sorry. Carmen, I lost my temper, that's all. To break up what we have over—"

"What did we have, Jake?"

He paused. "I really don't think the problem is so big that we can't fix our relationship."

"I wouldn't call what we were doing a relationship."

"You're exaggerating."

"Do you know that's what they do? They try to make you think you're being melodramatic, or that it's all your fault."

"Who?"

"Abusers."

"I'm not an abuser."

"You need help." She paused. "When we were in the locker room, today, you made me feel like a victim."

The bell rang. Students got up. She looked away. "Bye."

"I want to talk to you," he said, grabbing her arm. "Do you have time to step into the auditorium for a minute?"

"No one will be there." She looked at his hand on her arm. "I don't want to be alone with you."

He let go of her arm. "I won't hurt you. I promise."

She looked into his eyes, looked away. "Okay. Only for a minute, though."

The auditorium was adjacent to the cafeteria. Within a minute they were alone. She listened to the hum of students passing by in the hall, the noise substantial despite the closed door.

"Wait," she said, as he started to speak. "Wait until the bell rings and they're gone. I can be late to class."

"So can I." He waited until a hush fell over the auditorium and adjacent hallways. "So what were you saying?"

"I thought you wanted to talk to me."

He paused. "You said I made you feel like a victim."

She paused. "I was afraid you were going to hurt me."

"Funny. I thought *you* were going to hurt *me.*"

She smiled involuntarily and looked at the ground. She saw that his hands had clenched into fists. She looked up quickly.

"I'm sorry," he said. "Carmen, I'm so sorry. I never meant to make you feel like that. I care about you. I really do."

"You're making me uncomfortable, Jake."

He took a deep breath. "I'll get help, Carmen. I should have a long time ago, but it's never been like this before."

"Because I provoke you. I *do.*" She paused. "You'll be a lot better off without me."

"I don't want to live without you," he said. "I'll get help. I'll fix myself."

"I know you will," she said. "But I'm not going to wait around for you to do it."

"You meant what you said in the locker room? About breaking up?"

The late bell rang.

"Yes," she said. "Yes, I meant every word of it."

"Then I don't have anything left to say to you." He stepped away from her, opening the door to the auditorium so she could pass through.

"I have something left to say to you," she said.

He stood with his head hung, his arms loose by his sides. "What's that?"

"Look at me."

He looked up. She touched his face, gently.

"Good luck, Jake."

He burst out laughing. "That would have been touching. If you didn't look so bizarre."

Hurt, she turned away from him. "That's why I'm breaking up with you. Because you make me feel like shit. And I deserve more."

She strode out of the auditorium, glancing at the clock as she went. If she was any more than five minutes later than the late bell, she could get in a lot of trouble. But that was not why she hurried. If she was five minutes later than the late bell, Miss Carpenter might start to worry. And so might Mark. So she hurried.

Carmen got to the chemistry classroom five minutes after the late bell rang. She slid into her seat beside Mark and found she was not embarrassed by what had passed between them. She reached under the lab desk and took his hand. He stiffened and turned to look at her. She let go of his hand so she could open her notebook and scribble him a note, three words: *We broke up.* He looked at the note, relaxed.

Are you okay? he scribbled back to her.

She nodded, and the smile she gave him made him blush fiercely. She turned away from him. He was doing it again, making that warmth streak through her, and she had no idea how he was doing it.

What are we doing today? she wrote, knowing she would keep their first written conversation longer than she would ever keep any of her chemistry notes. The exchange and resulting feelings made her feel like she was back in the fifth grade, and she loved it.

We're studying the noble gases, he wrote. *The only relevant information you missed is…*

She reached across the desk and started writing on the lines below his. He stopped writing and let her.

Can I come over to your house after school today? To hang out? Let me know after class. Miss Carpenter is sending us evil looks.

He glanced up, saw Miss Carpenter was watching them, and deliberately took Carmen's notebook from her.

Sure, he wrote.

He waited until she had seen the word, then flipped her notebook to a clean page and handed it to her. She folded her hands over the notebook. They both looked at Miss Carpenter. She sent them a warning glance, then continued teaching as if she hadn't noticed anything at all.

Carrie stood on his porch, steeling herself. There were years between them—time during which she had grown, gained experience, made her life her own again. She had raised a daughter who was...still alive. But as she stood on his porch, she felt helpless. She waited for her evaporated confidence to return; when she had stood for five minutes staring at the door, she finally forced herself to knock.

Her hands clenched into fists and she shoved them into the pockets of her coat. She had prepared herself for him to be angry, indifferent...anything but absent. She turned to leave, but as she reached the end of the porch, she could not move onto the step below. She paused, then turned around. The door opened.

"Carrie," he said.

She fought the urge to turn and run to her car, knowing that if she didn't say it straight out she would never be able to. "You're on house arrest. For DUIs. Carmen told me." She let the words flow as they would. "When you didn't come with me to the hospital the other day, I didn't know. I'm sorry."

"You know, and you're still here? Even with the circumstances of..." He paused. "You're here to berate me, I suppose."

"I'm here to talk. If you're willing."

He looked at her, hard. "It's cold," he said, after a pause. "You'd better come in."

She stepped through the doorway into the clean, well-lit interior of the house. He went into the living room and sat down, and after a moment she followed him.

"It's good to have you here," he said.

She sat down stiffly across from him. The pounding of her heart had not subsided. His eyes lingered on her face, then he looked away. The ticking of the grandfather clock sounded loudly between them. Gripping her hands together, she cleared her throat.

"I'm…I'm sorry that I wasn't there for you, when Chloe got sick. I didn't know…"

"I know," he said.

"And I know that's my fault."

"Things were complicated." His eyes burned darkly at her. "They still are."

She looked at him. "Her death wasn't your fault. When we went in to see the doctors, after she was born, they told us to expect a relapse at any time."

"That doesn't make it any easier."

"No." She did not know what to say. "But at least you were the one there for her. She loved you."

"I loved her," he said. The clock ticked and tocked.

"About Carmen." Carrie clasped her hands in her lap, forcing herself to look at him. "I understand now why you couldn't come and I want to apologize to you, for jumping to conclusions."

"You've already apologized. And I've told you never to apologize to me for anything." He paused. "You never used to apologize."

"I was wrong this time. I was wrong to think you didn't care about Carmen."

"Fine. You can apologize to me about that." He paused. "I do care about her. It's crazy that I would get attached to some adolescent girl who comes around breaking my windows and pestering me at all hours of the day and night…"

"Carmen broke your windows?"

He studied her. "Is it true that Carmen is my daughter?"

"She's yours."

"Are you sure?"

She glanced down at her hands. "I'm positive."

"You haven't found anyone else?"

"I haven't wanted to find anyone else."

He stood, sat down beside her. "I hope you haven't been lonely."

She glanced at him. "Carmen is a constant reminder to me that sometimes solitude isn't such a bad thing."

He smiled, then sobered. "How is she?"

"She went back to school today," Carrie said. "I guess I'll hear how that went when she gets home."

He paused. "Carmen said you were teaching."

"I am."

"Why aren't you in school?"

"I took a personal day. I've saved them up over the years. Now I'm using them...to think."

He paused. "I tried to see Carmen last Thursday. I found out she was discharged."

"You should come to the house," Carrie said, feeling her cheeks burning. "Next Thursday, when you can come. I'm out most of the time, and she would like to see you."

He looked like he had something to say to her, and that he changed his mind. After the pause, he said, "I don't think Carmen wants to see me."

"Why would you think that?"

"I think she blames me. For what happened."

"That's ridiculous. She knows the accident wasn't your fault."

"I think she was on her way to buy groceries for me and..." He paused. "Girls her age are so concerned with their appearance. No wonder she hates me." He looked down at her hands. "In a way it is my fault. If she hadn't come to see me, she wouldn't have been on the road when that truck was there." He paused. "I almost got her killed, too."

Her heart lurched at his words, and she tried to redirect his thoughts. "So she came to see you that night?"

"She did."

"I wondered where she went."

"You didn't know?"

"She wasn't home, and she wasn't with Jake. Those are usually the only two places Carmen ever is." She paused. "Thank god you were here for her."

"What?"

Carrie paused. "I think she and Jake had just gotten into a fight. And she and I had argued the previous night. If she hadn't had you, I don't know where she would have gone."

"She wouldn't have—"

"Carmen's accident was not your fault," Carrie stressed.

He looked away. "I still don't think she wants to see me."

Carrie pulled a piece of paper from her purse and jotted down her address. "Come to the house. Carmen wants to see you, and I'll make sure that I'm not around."

He looked at the paper in her outstretched hand. "I wasn't going to let you in when I saw it was you."

"I'm surprised you did," she said, standing. "Thank you."

"Thank you for coming, Carrie."

She paused, her gloves clamped in her hand, and looked at him. "You're welcome." She tried to say more and couldn't, except, "Thank you for coming to see Carmen when she was in the hospital."

"I thought I'd be more angry at you," he said. "When Chloe died and you weren't available, the hatred I felt was so dark, so intense…"

Carrie's hands trembled as she put on her gloves. She said nothing, but made no move to leave.

"I've carried that hatred with me," he continued. "But now…it's gone. I can't explain why. I should hate you, but I don't. I should still feel the pain, but I've gone numb."

"Time will do that," she said. "Time has passed."

"If you have a minute," he said, and she looked up. "That picture…that picture that I made with Chloe. I still have it. In my studio. If you would like to see it."

"I had better not." She did not look at him. "I want to be home when Carmen gets home. I have to get back."

His eyes searched her face, but when she finally met his eyes, he looked away. "Then you should leave now."

"Yes." She started towards the door. "Yes, I should get back."

"Carrie."

She stood, paralyzed by the intensity of the gaze that held her in place from across the room.

"Why did you come?" he asked.

Her eyes remained locked on his. "I don't know."

Her words unfroze her. She opened the door and let the screen bang back into place. She walked quickly to her car and got in. As she started the engine, she looked up and saw him standing in the doorway, watching her. She blinked, put the car in reverse, and backed out of the driveway. The snow melting on the windshield made seeing difficult. Or maybe the tears, welling in her eyes, were what blurred her vision.

"I'm glad you came over," Mark said.

"I'm glad I could come." Carmen paused. "Can I come over again?"

"I'd like that."

"But I should get home now. I don't want my mom to worry."

"We can drive you home."

"I don't want to inconvenience your mom. I'll walk."

"No, I'll get her."

"Mark." She paused. "Your mom hasn't seen me yet."

He looked at her. "All the more reason for her to meet you. I'll go find her."

Carmen leaned against the wall, inhaled, held her breath. She and Mark had talked for two hours, and he had not even tried to kiss her. And yet, he still wanted to see her again. She couldn't understand him. She felt dizzy.

"Carmen, this is my mom."

"Hi, Mrs. George." Carmen tried to smile. "Thank you for letting me come over. You have a lovely house."

"Thank you, dear." The woman held out her hand, displaying no reaction to Carmen's appearance. She shook Carmen's hand warmly. "Can we give you a ride home?"

"I don't want to trouble you."

"I should learn where your house is, so I can pick Mark up next time you get together." She paused. "It's so good to finally meet you, Carmen. Mark has told me so much about you."

"Mom," Mark said. "Let's go. Carmen has to get home."

"He's afraid I'll embarrass him." Mrs. George smiled at her. "About the ride, dear…I insist. Mark, are you coming?"

"Of course," he said.

"I'd like to talk to you alone, Mrs. George," Carmen said, quietly. "If you don't mind."

Mrs. George looked at Mark, who shrugged, then turned her attention back to Carmen. She nodded and led the way to the garage.

"You have such beautiful eyes, Carmen," she said, once they were on the road.

"Thanks," Carmen said.

"I don't know if Mark has told you anything about me." She glanced at Carmen. "I'm guessing he hasn't. I'm a businesswoman. I like to get to the heart of matters quickly. So tell me what's on your mind."

"Mark is helping me pass chemistry." She looked at her hands. "He's been very kind to me."

"He's always loved chemistry. Never so much until this year, but—"

"Mrs. George." Carmen paused. "I don't want to say this but I have to. I just broke up with my boyfriend because…because he was getting violent…"

Mrs. George let Carmen compose herself. "Thank you for letting me know, Carmen. I can help you take the steps you need to protect yourself."

She shook her head. "I'm only telling you because he was getting jealous of Mark even though we're just friends. I wanted to warn you in case…in case he starts giving Mark trouble."

Mrs. George laughed. "I wouldn't worry about my Mark, Carmen. He has a blackbelt in three different kinds of karate. He can take care of himself. Will *you* be all right?"

Carmen relaxed. "I'll be fine. I don't think he'll do anything but I wanted to let you know, just in case. Thank you for listening to me."

"Thank you for telling me. Do I stay straight on this road?"

Carmen started to say yes, then she paused. "Do you mind if I visit my dad? He likes it when I visit him unexpectedly, and I can get a ride home from there."

Mrs. George glanced at her quickly. "I don't mind at all, Carmen."

"Then turn at this exit." She paused, feeling her heart start to pound. "Please."

Mrs. George turned. "So tell me a little more about yourself."

"I don't know what to say."

"What are your hobbies? What do you like to do in your spare time?"

She realized she had spent almost all her free time with Jake, and that she couldn't tell Mrs. George about any of that. She paused. "I like to sing. I want to be a singer."

Mrs. George smiled at her. Carmen felt the first flash of freedom she had felt in a very long time.

Carrie's eyes crawled to the clock. She had been sitting by the side of the road for twenty minutes, unable to take action. A tension headache had set in five minutes after leaving his house, and there were no painkillers in the car; she never used medication. She had waited for the headache to pass, and when it did she found she had lost her only excuse to remain by the side of the road in a state of indecision. The motivation to get home before Carmen did was gone; Carmen had called a half hour ago and asked to go to a *friend*'s house. She had given Carmen her permission, choosing to have faith that Carmen had met a good friend. She put the car in reverse, then turned and headed back in the direction she had come.

She pulled into his driveway at half past three. She had tried to compose herself on the way, tried to still her shaking and tried to stop the tears welling behind her eyes. She no longer fought her feelings, and no longer denied they were real.

She got out of her car and walked up to his house. He opened the door after her first knock.

"I was hoping you'd come back," he said.

"I don't…I don't know why…"

"Come inside, Carrie."

She followed him, but paused to yank off her shawl, her coat, her gloves and her hat. When she left the entrance, he was standing in the center of the living room.

"We need to talk," she started, but he stepped up to her and took her in his arms. His kiss cut off her words. She felt warmth flame through her body, making her feel like her heart would burst. She pulled herself away, wiped at her cheeks. "Can we talk?"

"Yes," he said, stepping away from her, sitting down. "We can talk. But I'm starting." He looked directly at her. "I still love you."

Her breath caught in her throat, and she could not speak. He did not remove his eyes from her face.

"I've always loved you," he said. "But I've never known how to show you."

"When you were Ralph—" she started.

"When I was Ralph," he repeated, his eyes sadly amused. "Yes, I suppose I have been two…three…completely different people. But let me speak, Carrie. I need to explain this to you so you understand." He paused. "Back in college, I didn't want commitment. You scared the hell out of me because you were everything I wanted…in the long run. But not at that time. Being around you reminded me that because I wasn't ready for commitment, I could be fucking up my chances with the only woman I had ever loved."

She dared speaking. "I've never stopped thinking about you."

"How could you?" He looked away. "I am your Muse."

"Not because you're my Muse. Because you're *you*." She paused. "I'm still in love with you. I've been miserable without you."

"Now you're lying," he said. "Carmen has told me that you're teaching, and that you're still writing…"

She wiped a tear away from her eye. "Could we try again?"

"Do you think it would work? Third time's a charm?" He looked at her. "There are still some of the old barriers, and now some new barriers have been set in place."

"Your house arrest."

"No. I got off that today. I was going to tell you earlier, but I didn't think it would matter. I'm a free man." He smiled at her, then the smile sagged. "Mostly a free man. I've been mostly sober these past years, but there was a period when I completely lost it. Again. That period resulted in my house arrest." He hesitated. "I'm going to need some help."

She paused. "You're not violent when you're drunk. You wouldn't hurt me. Or Carmen."

"No," he said. "But I'm quitting, nevertheless. Though you'll have to be patient with me, with the other barriers."

"What barriers?"

"I'm not a bad person. Except when I'm with you." He paused. "I never would have treated any other human being the way I treated you in college. Not even an enemy."

"Maybe you thought I could handle it."

"I'd never been in love before. Still, that's no excuse."

"I acted differently around you as well." She paused. "You made the darker side of me come out."

"That's what I mean," he said. "That's what we have to fight if we want to be together. But maybe we can't be together, even if we are meant for each other."

"I don't believe that," she said. "I think our timing was just off."

He looked at her. "Our timing?"

"In college you wanted to have fun and you were letting your talent slide, and I was focused and driven. When I met you later, married you...my dreams were sliding. And you were on top of things."

"That person wasn't who I am," he interrupted. "Do you remember telling me that?"

"You can be whoever you want to be."

There was a pause.

She looked down, continued. "Maybe now the timing is right. Maybe we're both open enough to each other, maybe we've put the past behind us."

"Come to terms with the past," he corrected. "But now Carmen is involved. If you want to try again, we both have to be committed. We have to try to make it work. Do you want that?"

His question hung in the air.

"I love you," she said.

"But do you want to be with me?"

"Yes," she said. "I know I can live alone, but I want to be with you."

He paused. "Will you be compromising yourself?"

"No."

"I don't suppose we could go through anything more," he said. "I think we've covered all the bases."

"Would you be compromising?" she asked, softly. "Don't you hate me?"

He looked directly at her. "No."

"I want you to think about my question for longer than that."

"Don't worry about the past," he said. "We can address that as it comes up." He took her hand.

She was glad he was sitting near her; his hand felt warm, comforting, strong, in her own. "I wish there hadn't been so much drama involved with this."

He paused. "You seem to attract drama. Everything happens all at once around you."

"You're the only person who has ever been able to keep up with me," she said, and paused. "Except maybe for Sam."

"Sam."

"You threw a bottle at us once." She glanced at him. "You probably don't remember him..."

"You're wrong, Carrie." His eyes burned intensely. "I thanked God for putting Sam in your path, so that you could see that not all men were like me."

She stared at him. "Are we really going to do this? Do you really think it could work?"

"It's been over twenty years." He smiled. "I think we're entitled to a happy ending."

And at that moment, Carmen walked in.

"I overheard everything," she said.

He stared at her. "Who are you?"

"Carmen. Your daughter."

He turned to Carrie. "*Your* daughter."

"Come on, Dad." Carmen stepped further into the room. "You can't disown me just because I shaved my head."

"Come here," he said. "It's good to see you."

Carmen went to him, and he kissed her on top of her bare head. She smiled, then looked at Carrie hopefully. "So you're getting back together?"

"We're going to try," she said.

Carmen looked to him for confirmation. "So I'm going to be Carmen Christianson now?"

He looked at Carrie quickly. "I'll take your name."

"You don't have to," she said softly. "Carmen, I thought you were supposed to be at a friend's house."

"I was. But I had his mom drop me off here because I wanted to apologize to Dad for not coming to see him. I tried calling you to tell you, but your phone was off." She put her hands on her hips. "So what am I going to be called now?"

"Maybe we could come up with a new name," he said. "Something that combines them all."

Carmen looked at him. "I am *not* going to be Carmen Crenshaw-DeMatteo-Palmer-Christianson."

"I thought you liked complication," he said.

"Why do we have to have a new name?" Carmen asked. "Why is a name so important? Why can't we just be who we already are?"

He looked at Carmen, at Carrie. Carmen looked at them both.

"We'll keep it simple for now," she said. "I'm Carmen. Now you, Mom."

Carrie paused. "I'm Carrie."

They both looked at him. His mouth was a tight line, and his features were taut. He looked at them.

"I don't know who I am," he said.

Carmen took his hand. "Dad."

He looked at her, glanced at Carrie. Carrie nodded at him.

"Alright," he said.

"So now that's settled, Dad," Carmen said. "I think you should come have dinner with us, though Carrie will probably make something gross like curry."

Carrie looked at his lowered face. "Please. Come home."

He looked up, met her eyes.

"Curry sounds good," he said.

Carrie held out her hand. He took it. Together, the three of them walked out to the car waiting in the driveway.

EPILOGUE

Their first fight happened two weeks after he moved in with them. Carmen wanted to go to a voice training camp in Pennsylvania in the summer and Carrie thought the camp was too expensive. They were both surprised by how quickly the situation blew out of control. Halfway through the fight, Damien raised his hand, silencing her.

"She has a job," he said. "If she wants to go to this camp, let her earn the money. If she can raise the money in time, we can decide together what weeks work best for both of us and I'll drive her there."

Carrie exhaled. "She won't like that answer."

"She doesn't have to," he said. "We're the parents."

"Then that's settled?"

"We don't have to fight," he said. "We've done enough of that. We can enjoy being happy together, guilt free."

She looked at him. "I don't need your permission to be happy."

"I think you do," he said. "I don't think anyone has ever told you that you have the right to be happy. You work yourself so hard that you never stop to wonder if you're happy or not."

She turned away from him, unexpected tears coming to her eyes. He crossed the room, wrapped her in his arms.

"Let's go away for awhile," he said. "You deserve a break."

She tried to step away from him. "I have to teach. And you have your art gallery to maintain."

"We'll go somewhere in the summer, then," he said, letting her go. "It's only a couple of months away. Where would you like to go?"

"Honestly?"

He nodded. "Honestly."

"I miss my family. Chris, Carly, Calder...my mother. I know they're all in separate states, but my family has a tradition of coming together for a week in the summer...at least they did. When we take Carmen to her camp, I'd like to visit them." She paused. "Since it's in the same state."

"We'll go."

"Thank you," she said. "I didn't think it would mean so much to me, but—"

"I liked your mother when I met her," he said. "All those years ago."

"You *charmed* her."

He laughed. "In the meantime, we're going to do at least one thing together each week as a family."

"We always eat dinner together. And we have studio time," she said, thinking of the time the three of them went into the greenhouse annex and she wrote, he painted and Carmen composed. She didn't know how their daughter could write songs without any instrument in front of her, but somehow she did.

"And you and I will do something together," he said. "Whether it's going for a walk, going out to lunch..."

"But Carmen."

"Carmen is old enough to take care of herself," he said. "And if you're worried about her being alone, then I'm sure Mark wouldn't mind taking her off our hands for awhile."

Carrie smiled, and he kissed her gently before stepping away.

"I have some painting to do."

"I have some writing to do," she said. "Then I'm going to bed. Don't be afraid to wake me up, if you come in and I'm asleep."

"Goodnight, Carrie." He paused. "I won't keep you up."

Somehow, he could always tell when she wanted to be alone. "Thank you."

He nodded and left her. She went to the room in the house that she had made into her writing room, and closed the door behind her.

Carmen glanced at Carrie as they pulled into the familiar driveway. "Isn't Dad waiting for us at the studio?"

Carrie nodded, not looking at her as she parked and pulled the keys out of the ignition. "I'll just be a moment."

"Is Grandma going to be mad if we're late?"

"Carmen, this will only take a second." Carrie turned to her. "Do you want to stay here?"

Carmen nodded.

"I'll be right back." She got out of the car, went to the front door, and knocked.

Sam opened the door and ushered her inside. "Can I get you anything, Carrie?"

She shook her head. "I just came to say goodbye, Sam. For now."

"You're leaving today?"

She nodded.

He looked down. "How long will you be gone?"

"A couple of weeks," she said.

"I'll water your plants for you," he said. "And we'll keep your lawn mowed."

"Thanks, Sam," she said, and hugged him. She hugged him for a long time. He looked at her as she stepped back.

"What was that for?"

"I don't know if I've ever told you how much you mean to me," she said. "You're a good friend."

"I know." He paused. "You've told me."

"You know I love him," she said.

He looked down. "I know that, too."

"But I love you, too," she said. "You'll always have a place in my heart that he can never fill."

"That means a lot to me," he said, quietly. "Goodbye for now, Carrie."

She squeezed his hand, started towards the door. "I'll see you when I get back, Sam."

"Carrie."

She turned. He smiled.

"Kindra sent me a letter. She wants to come up for a weekend. To see Jake...and me."

599

"That's wonderful, Sam," she said, smiling. "It seems like you've gotten closer."

"We have. I don't know how it happened."

She laughed, thinking of herself as a young woman, and of Carmen—though Mark had been a good influence on her. "Adolescent girls go through phases. You have to wait them out."

"Kindra's in college now."

"She grew up that fast?" Carrie asked, stunned.

"She's studying Spanish at the University of Maine. She was on the Dean's List last semester." Sam paused. "And she wants to start visiting more, on the weekends."

"Congratulations," Carrie said. "On all accounts."

He smiled at her. "You had better get going. You don't want to be late. Don't worry about a thing."

"Take care of yourself until I get back."

He nodded, and she headed for the door.

Carmen saw Jake head out of the side door of the house when her mother went in. He walked up to the side of the car and tapped on the glass. She rolled down her window.

"Hey," she said.

"Hey."

"Hold on a second. The air conditioning is on." She rolled up her window, got out of the car, and closed her door.

"You look good," he said.

"Thanks. So do you."

"Your hair's growing back nicely."

She nodded. "Thanks for noticing."

His eyes lingered on her face. "How have you been?"

"Happy," she said, looking directly at him. "You?"

He looked down. "Good."

She paused. "How are your anger management classes?"

"Helpful."

"Really?"

He nodded. "Yeah."

"I'm glad."

He put his hands in his pockets. "How are you and Mark doing?"

"Great."

"He's treating you well?"

"Very well."

"You deserve it."

She paused. "Have you found anyone else yet?"

"I'm not looking."

She looked down. "Jake, I—"

"I'm not hitting on you," he said, then winced at the expression. "I'm glad you and Mark are doing well together." He took a step back from her. "I should go. Some of the guys and I are going to go play pool."

She smiled at him. "Kick some ass."

He smiled. "I will. Take care of yourself, Carmen."

She heard a honk behind her. She turned and saw a car had pulled into the driveway.

"Perfect timing," she said.

"Yeah." He paused. "It was good to see you again."

"Good to see you, too, Jake."

He walked by her. She got in the car, watched the other car drive away. She honked the horn and realized the gesture had been unnecessary because Carrie had come out of the house anyway. Carrie walked to the car and got in.

"Let's go get your father," she said, and pulled out of the driveway.